新制多益

全攻略：培養**聽力**・**閱讀**實戰能力！

完全自學
NEW TOEIC

BASIC
LC+RC

附音檔
QRcode

笛藤出版

新制多益全攻略：培養聽力閱讀實戰能力!完全自學NEW TOEIC
/ 元晶瑞, NEXUS多盎研究所著. -- 初版. -- 臺北市：笛藤,
2019.10
　　面；　公分
譯自：New toeic basic LC+RC
ISBN 978-957-710-772-5(平裝)
1.多益測驗
805.1895　　　　　　　　　　　　　　　108017135

新制多益全攻略：培養聽力閱讀實戰能力!

完全自學NEW TOEIC （附音檔QRcode）

2019年11月18日　初版第1刷　定價 580 元

作者	元晶瑞、NEXUS多盎研究所
譯者	張亞薇
編輯	江品萱
封面設計	王舒玗
總編輯	賴巧凌
發行所	笛藤出版圖書有限公司
發行人	林建仲
地址	台北市中山區長安東路二段171號3樓3室
電話	(02) 2777-3682
傳真	(02) 2777-3672
總經銷	聯合發行股份有限公司
地址	新北市新店區寶橋路235巷6弄6號2樓
電話	(02)2917-8022・(02)2917-8042
製版廠	造極彩色印刷製版股份有限公司
地址	新北市中和區中山路2段340巷36號
電話	(02)2240-0333・(02)2248-3904
印刷廠	皇甫彩藝印刷股份有限公司
地址	新北市中和區中正路988巷10號
電話	(02) 3234-5871
郵撥帳戶	八方出版股份有限公司
郵撥帳號	19809050

新制多益

全攻略：培養**聽力**・**閱讀**實戰能力！

完全自學
NEW TOEIC

基礎問題到進階題，豐富的解題技巧 + 詳細的試題解析
多益滿分講師 + 頂尖多益團隊，帶你理解出題方向，突破英文難關！

元晶瑞、NEXUS多益研究所／著

BASIC
LC+RC

附音檔 QRcode

隨書附
★★★★★
超級完整解析本
自學不求人！

笛藤出版

　　「好的開始是成功的一半。」在我超過 15 年的講師生涯中，看過許許多多因為錯誤的學習方法而受苦的學生們，因此我非常強調好的開始的重要性。明明有最正確又有效率的方法，卻聽信他人推薦的實戰手冊，鑽研百思不得其解的題目而浪費時間，或反覆閱讀塞滿密密麻麻說明的厚重教科書，這樣的學生不在少數。然而盲目背誦單字或自創方法不斷反覆進行聽力題目，最後可能必須付出更大的努力和精神。

　　對於即將開始準備考多益的人來說，本書《完全自學新多益》會指引你最扎實且快速的捷徑。也許你會反問「學習真的有捷徑嗎？」然而無論何種領域，對於擁有成功學習經驗的人而言，捷徑是真實存在的，那就是將可信任的內容以經得起考驗的方法進行學習。花大錢上補習班，在不符合程度的課程上投資時間，就像讓體力普通水準的人去做奧運等級的運動，不但無法提升實力，更會造成受傷和帶來挫折感。

　　要掌握學習捷徑，首先必須要有「實際考試中出現的題目，實際考試時能給予幫助的內容」。念一些定位在初級教材卻與考試無關的基本內容只是浪費時間而已。假設有好的內容，身為初學者的我就能提升實力並且拿到高分嗎？如果忽略自身的學習能力，只是不斷反覆練習考古題的話，學到的解題技巧和題型極為有限，整體的多益成績也會停滯不前。

本書從多益新手和英語初學者的問題點切入，不但提供了在實際考試中能獲得目標分數的技巧，也包含文法、單字、逐步解題的方法，同時精準掌握新多益考試的走向，除了簡單的題目之外，也有效列出每個月定期考試中出現的基本題型，可以按照自己所訂立的目標分數和高得分方向來學習。我相信這本書會是你開拓未來人生的起點。我在此向出版此書的 NEXUS 出版社社長獻上誠摯的感謝。

元晶瑞

Dedication

To my parents
Without whom I would not be living my best life

致我親愛的父母，元永熙 & 朴來順
希望您們健健康康，未來也請與我攜手共進…

CONTENTS

FEATURES

從基礎到實戰
用一本書解決的
階段性學習法

LC
Step 1　類型分析
Step 2　聽力和聽寫的訓練
Step 3　基本掌握
Step 4　實戰練習

RC
Step 1　基礎文法類型分析
　　　　+ Practice
Step 2　基本掌握
　　　　+ 文法/詞彙/閱讀理解
Step 3　實戰練習(Part 5, 6, 7)

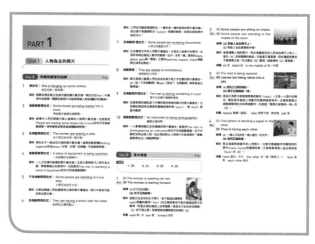

為了使第一次接觸多益考試的人們能夠輕易理解，
本書以簡潔結構和詳細說明編排而成。此外，本書
只收錄分析多益考試時必備的內容，希望在最短時
間內達成750分的目標分數。

作者Know-how
簡單詳盡的
答案與解析

不需要另外購買書籍，本書附有解析書，可以查看
答案與解析。書中有關答案的關鍵字予以標示，能
夠輕易尋找並了解答案。

可以獨自學習的
多益考試
超強資料

1　為了因應實際考試，除了收錄美式、英式、澳式發音之外，也收錄了考場版本的MP3。可以掃描QR Code或從google雲端下載音檔。

2　藉由Listening聽寫課程進行複習，提升聽力能力。可以掃描QR Code或上google雲端使用。

簡單快速的
MP3使用法

1　掃描下方QRcode或輸入https://bit.ly/2IN9ADE進入google雲端

2　選擇要聽的部分，可以自己完成聽力測驗。

（雲端連結）

新多益的關鍵資訊

從韓國時間2016年5月29日，台灣2018年3月定期考試開始，新多益考試根據目前英語的使用環境而出現異動。雖然題目總數和考試時間維持不變，但各單元的題數進行了調整，出現以前未曾有過的圖表、文字訊息、聊天對話和三重短文等新短文類型。

⊕ 新多益的考試結構

結構	Part	各Part內容	題數	時間	計分
Listening Comprehension	1	照片描述	6	45分鐘	495分
	2	一致性問答	25		
	3	簡短對話	39		
	4	說明句	30		
Reading Comprehension	5	填入短文空格	30	75分鐘	495分
	6	填入長文空格	16		
	7	單一短文	29		
		雙重短文	10		
		三重短文	15		
Total		7 Parts	200題	120分鐘	990分

⊕ 新多益的異動部分

Part 1 從10題減至6題

Part 2 從30題減至25題

Part 3 從30題增至39題，＜3人對話＞，＜5句以上對話＞，新增＜意圖、時間資訊連貫題目＞

Part 4 30題不變，新增＜掌握意圖題目＞、＜時間點資訊連貫題目＞

Part 5 從40題減至30題

Part 6 從12題增至16題，新增＜選擇適合的句子＞

Part 7 從48題增至54題，新增＜文字簡訊‧線上聊天短文＞、＜掌握意圖、插入句子題目＜三重短文＞

新多益的關鍵資訊

Part 3	掌握說話者意圖的題目	2~3題	詢問對話中說話者意圖的類型
	時間點資訊連貫題目	2~3題	掌握對話時間點資訊(圖表、表格等)之間連貫性的類型
	3人對話	對話短文1~2則	部分對話中出現3名以上說話者
	5句以上對話		對話增至5句以上的類型
Part 4	掌握說話者意圖的題目	2~3題	詢問對話中說話者意圖的類型
	時間點資訊連貫題目	2~3題	掌握對話時間點資訊(圖表、表格等)之間連貫性的類型
Part 6	選擇適合的句子	4題(每則短文1題)	・選擇適合填入短文空格的句子 ・選項皆和短文有關,需掌握前後文的一致性
Part 7	插入句子題目	2題(每則短文1題)	選擇適合插入句子的正確位置
	文字訊息線上聊天	各短文1題	2名以上說話者的文字簡訊,數名說話者參與的線上聊天
	掌握意圖題目	2題(每則短文1題)	・詢問對話中說話者意圖的類型 ・從文字簡訊、線上聊天短文中出題
	三重短文	短文3則	有關3則連貫短文理解度的題目

個人學習進度表

2周密集計畫

如果想要在沒有多益基礎下短期內快速提升能力的話，必須集中研究LC。與RC相較之下較為簡單的LC是提高分數和自信的關鍵。如果曾經研讀過一兩次多益題型，想要短期內專注練習以取得目標分數的話，可以在2周內完成。

LC

第1天 （　月　日）	第2天 （　月　日）	第3天 （　月　日）	第4天 （　月　日）
PART 1 Unit 1, 2, 3	PART 2 Unit 4, 5	PART 2 Unit 6, 7	PART 3 Unit 8, 9

第5天 （　月　日）	第6天 （　月　日）	第7天 （　月　日）	
PART 3 Unit 10, 11	PART 4 Unit 12, 13	PART 4 Unit 14, 15	

RC

第8天 （　月　日）	第9天 （　月　日）	第10天 （　月　日）	第11天 （　月　日）
PART 5 Unit 1, 2	PART 5 Unit 3, 4, 5	PART 5 Unit 6, 7, 8	PART 6 Unit 9

第12天 （　月　日）	第13天 （　月　日）	第14天 （　月　日）	
PART 7 Unit 10, 11	PART 7 Unit 12, 13	PART 7 Unit 14, 15	

從基礎開始詳細研究各階段的
4周完成計畫

一周5天共維持4周，每天同時練習LC和RC的計畫，對沒有考過多益，或想要按照階段學習以達到目標分數的人們來說，是最適合的安排。執行4周完成計畫再考多益的話，可以預期能夠獲得高分。

1周	第1天 （ 月 日）	第2天 （ 月 日）	第3天 （ 月 日）	第4天 （ 月 日）	第5天 （ 月 日）
LC	PART 1 Unit 1	PART 1 Unit 2	PART 1 Unit 3	PART 1 複習與線上 聽寫複習	PART 2 Unit 4
RC	PART 5 Unit 1	PART 5 Unit 2	PART 5 Unit 3	PART 5 Unit 4	PART 5 Unit 5
2周	第6天 （ 月 日）	第7天 （ 月 日）	第8天 （ 月 日）	第9天 （ 月 日）	第10天 （ 月 日）
LC	PART 2 Unit 5	PART 2 Unit 6	PART 2 Unit 7	PART 2 複習與線上 聽寫複習	PART 3 Unit 8
RC	PART 5 Unit 6	PART 5 Unit 7	PART 5 Unit 8	PART 5 複習	PART 6 Unit 9
3周	第11天 （ 月 日）	第12天 （ 月 日）	第13天 （ 月 日）	第14天 （ 月 日）	第15天 （ 月 日）
LC	PART 3 Unit 9	PART 3 Unit 10	PART 3 Unit 11	PART 3 複習與線上 聽寫複習	PART 4 Unit 12
RC	PART 6 Unit 10	PART 7 Unit 11	PART 7 Unit 12	PART 7 Unit 13	PART 7 Unit 13
4周	第16天 （ 月 日）	第17天 （ 月 日）	第18天 （ 月 日）	第19天 （ 月 日）	第20天 （ 月 日）
LC	PART 4 Unit 13	PART 4 Unit 14	PART 4 Unit 15	PART 4 複習與線上 聽寫複習	詞彙練習& 利用測驗 最後複習詞彙
RC	PART 7 Unit 14	PART 7 Unit 14	PART 7 Unit 15	PART 7 Unit 15	詞彙練習& 利用測驗 最後複習詞彙

PART 1

聽完音檔之後,
從四個選項中選出最符合敘述的照片。

題目數	難易度
共6題 (1至6題)	低

滿分訣竅

掌握答案類型,從(A), (B), (C), (D)逐一刪去不適合選項來解題!

❶ 正確描述照片的詞彙和時態。

❷ 刪去不正確的選項,留下一個Best Answer。

學習方法

❶ **準備** 掌握Part1的句型結構和詞彙。

❷ **實戰** 將各Unit題型分段解題,應用在實戰題目中。

教材結構

Unit 1	人物為主的照片	一人獨照、兩人以上照片
Unit 2	風景為主的照片	物品為主的照片、風景為主的照片
Unit 3	高難度 — 混合照片	答案為針對不顯眼的部分做描述、 答案為間接描述的部分

001

(A) He's leaning against a fence.
(B) He's walking up the stairs.
(C) He's standing next to a sign.
(D) He's carrying a backpack.

(A) 他正靠在圍欄邊。
(B) 他正走上樓梯。
(C) 他正站在標誌旁。
(D) 他正背著背包。

解析 這是以獨照人物為主的照片，必須熟記描述照片中人物的動作和狀態的動詞。即使有許多可以描述的動詞，四個選項當中以(C)「男生在標誌（sign）旁邊」 的描述最為恰當。

Know-how

刪去法（選出Best Answer） 解題　　(A)　　(B)　　(C)　　(D)

❶ 不要預測答案，仔細聽每個選項，從中刪去錯誤的選項。

❷ 確定是錯誤的選項打 **X**，在小錯誤的選項╱，沒發現錯誤或不確定是否正確的選項畫上底線做標示。

❸ 聽完之後刪去兩個選項，比較剩下的兩個選項之後，選擇無誤的答案。

(A) He's leaning against a fence.　　沒有依靠的動作，也沒有圍欄。
(B) He's walking up the stairs.　　沒有樓梯。
(C) He's standing next to a sign.　　對於標誌的用詞不太確定，但這是最適合的選項。
(D) He's carrying a backpack.　　沒有看到背包。

❹ 四個選項一聽完，立刻選出最適合的答案，之後接著聽下一題。不要對上一個題目耿耿於懷。

❺ 答案: (C)

Unit 1　人物為主的照片

A 一人獨照　　　🎧 002

大多是根據照片中某個人物的動作或姿勢來出題，重點是熟記可以當作主詞的單字和人物的動作或姿勢。

例題1

(A) The woman is cooking in the kitchen.
(B) The woman is wiping the counter.
(C) The woman is serving some food.
(D) The woman is washing the dishes.

(A) 女子正在廚房裡做菜。
(B) 女子正在擦拭流理台。
(C) 女子正在上菜。
(D) 女子正在洗盤子。

解析 必須練習正確聽出描述照片的動詞，並且串聯受詞。照片中的女子戴著（wearing）項鍊，正在廚房流理台附近（near the counter）做擦拭（wiping）的動作。　　　答案: (B)

🎧 003

➡ 引導正確答案的單字 Check!

❶ 在, 站, 走路：be動詞, stand, walk, stroll

❷ 坐：sit, be seated, be taken, be occupied

❸ 斜靠，靠著：lean, rest

❹ 放：put, place, lay, leave

❺ 做事, 使用, 抓：work, use, hold, grab, grasp

❻ 搬運, 載運, 卸下：carry, move, load, unload

❼ 清理, 擦拭, 清掃, 抹：clear, wipe, scrub, sweep, mop

❽ 割草坪, 拿耙子耙草：mow the lawn, rake

❾ 倒入, 攪拌, 混合, 煮：pour, stir, mix, boil

❿ 穿：wear（描述穿著的狀態）※ 注意：put on（描述穿上的動作）

B 兩人以上照片

出現兩人或兩人以上人物的照片。在區分各個人物的動作時，需要確認人物之間的相互
關係或照片背景。

例題2

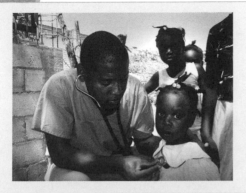

(A) A girl is being examined.
(B) A doctor is prescribing some medicine.
(C) The man is putting on a uniform.
(D) The man is holding a microphone.

(A) 女孩正在接受看診。
(B) 醫生正在開藥。
(C) 男子正在穿上制服。（動作）
(D) 男子正拿著麥克風。

解析 像醫生的男子正拿著聽診器檢查（examining）孩子。醫生（doctor, physician）可能在治療（treating）病患（patient）或者照顧（taking care of）病患。掌握兩人或複數人物之間的關係性，分辨出正確的動作。 答案: (A)

➲ 引導正確答案的單字 Check!

❶ 給： give, pass, hand (over)
❷ （彼此）說話： chat, discuss, converse
❸ 多： be full of, be filled with, be crowded
❹ 聚集： be gathered together, be grouped together
❺ 看, 凝視, 審視： stare, glance, gaze, peer, face, review
❻ 檢查, 瀏覽： examine, inspect, check, browse
❼ 握手, 互相問候： shake hands, greet each other
❽ 接受訂單, 選擇： take an order, select, choose
❾ 撿起, 放下, 放入： pick up, put down, put in, deposit
❿ 啟動, 調整, 處理： operate, adjust, handle

📝 邊聽邊寫，完美掌握的聽寫技巧　　🎧006

※ 比起文法類別，集中在動詞的「時態」和「分析」為佳。

❶ 及物動詞的現在進行式：be + -ing ➡ 正在~
He's holding a bag.　他正拿著包包。（人拿著包包的照片）

❷ 被動語態的現在進行式：be + being + p.p. ➡ (主語) 正被~
Books are being placed.　書籍正被擺放。（人擺放書的照片）

❸ 過去分詞當形容詞使用：～的
Customers are seated around the table.　客人們圍著桌子坐下。

❹ 不及物動詞的現在完成式：已經～
The train has arrived at the station.　火車已經到達車站。

❺ 不及物動詞的現在進行式：正在~
They're walking side by side.　他們正肩並肩地走著。

📝 一起來聽音檔中讀出的動詞時態，留意語調和斷句的部分，試著邊寫邊唸。　　🎧007

1.　She _____ _____ up some clothes.

2.　Some boxes _____ _____ _____ into a truck.

3.　The women _____ _____ a sofa.

4.　A piece of equipment _____ _____ _____.

5.　Some people _____ _____ at a bus stop.

6.　They _____ _____ a snack near the water.

7.　Some people _____ _____ documents.

8.　They _____ _____ at workstations.

9.　The man _____ _____ something in a pot.

10.　An instrument _____ _____ _____.

18

📝 從基本開始到精確掌握的訓練

1.

(A)   (B)

2.

(A)   (B)

3.

(A)   (B)

4.

(A)   (B)

利用刪去法選出Best Answer

1.

(A)　　(B)　　(C)　　(D)

2.

(A)　　(B)　　(C)　　(D)

3.

(A)　　(B)　　(C)　　(D)

4.

(A)　　(B)　　(C)　　(D)

5.

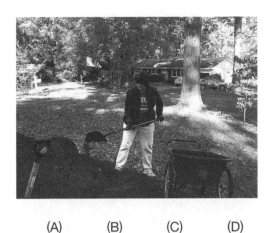

(A)   (B)   (C)   (D)

6.

(A)   (B)   (C)   (D)

答案有疑慮！

- 刪去法的訓練 -

雖然是「看完照片」選出答案的題型，
但如果只練習描述照片的正確詞彙，
在高難度題目中的出錯機率反而會增加。
作答時須試著降低答案的期待值，
選擇「最適合的答案」！

Unit 2　物品／風景為主的照片

A　物品為主的照片

🎧010

大多在照片中央出現具體的事物或物品，重點是描述作為主語出現的物品名稱和事物的謂語動詞和時態。

例題1

(A) They're working in the office.

(B) Some merchandise has been set on the floor.

(C) Chairs have been stacked up.

(D) There is a plant sitting on a desk.

(A) 他們正在辦公室工作。

(B) 一些商品已擺放在地上。

(C) 椅子已堆疊起來。

(D) 書桌上放著一個盆栽。

解析 辦公室裡出現各種器具、家具、盆栽等，把句子從頭到尾完整聽完之後，訓練自己找出錯誤之處。書桌上放置的盆栽除了sit之外，也可使用be placed來表達。　　答案：(D)

🎧011

➡引導正確答案的單字 Check!

❶ 有, 在：there is/ there are ~

❷ 放著：be placed, be left, be laid

❸ 位於：be positioned, be located

❹ 堆著, 展出：be stacked, be piled, be stocked, be arranged, be on display

❺ (擬人化) 坐著：be sitting, sit

❻ (擬人化) 站著：be standing, stand

❼ 面向：be facing

❽ 俯視：overlook

❾ 排列：line (up)

❿ 懸掛在～：hang, be suspended from

B 風景為主的照片 🎧 012

照片中央出現具體的風景，除了各地點出現的事物之外，也要熟記與其背景相關的詞彙。初學者會因為許多不熟悉的詞彙而覺得困難，但相對來說，特定詞彙已經列在選項之中，只要熟悉經常出現的詞彙表達，就能夠選出正確答案。

例題2

(A) The roof of a house is being repaired.
(B) A walkway is crowded with many people.
(C) A pathway leads to an outdoor structure.
(D) The building overlooks the parking lot.

(A) 屋頂正在維修中。
(B) 步道上擠滿人群。
(C) 步道通向戶外建築物。
(D) 建築物俯瞰著停車場。

解析 掌握能描述照片中的步道(walkway)延伸而至的建築物(structure)、建築物的所在地、樹木(trees)樣貌的詞彙，選出正確答案。各種事物／風景的表達方式有其限制，要點如下。

答案：(C) 🎧 013

● 引導正確答案的單字 Check!

❶ 有關路, 橋, 樓梯的表達方式

stairs / steps 樓梯　　extend (一直)延伸　　run / pass / go (路) 經過　　railing 欄杆
handrail 扶手　　lead to 連接　　curve 彎曲　　spiral 螺旋狀的　path / trail / road / street 路

❷ 有關水, 船, 航海的表達方式

oar 槳　　　　dock / port 港口　　row / paddle 划槳　　edge of the water 岸邊
fountain 噴泉　　be floating 漂浮　　be docked[tied off / anchored] 停靠

❸ 有關倉庫, 工地的表達方式

tool 工具　　ladder 梯子　　heavy machinery 重型機具　　wheelbarrow 單輪手推車
dirt / soil / earth 泥土　　structure 構造,建築　　container 容器, 桶子
scaffold 鷹架(施工時的安全措施)

❹ 有關街道, 交通的表達方式

traffic light 紅綠燈　　traffic sign 交通標誌　　intersection 路口　　lamp post 路燈
sidewalk 人行道　　crosswalk 斑馬線　　newsstand 報攤　　bike rack 自行車架

❺ 有關室內, 賣場的表達方式

prop up 支撐　　floor / level 地板, 樓層　　lighting fixture 照明　　fix / mount (牆壁等) 固定
sofa / couch 沙發　　stool 凳子, 托架　　products / merchandise / items / goods 商品, 產品

❻ 有關晚會, 活動的表達方式

event 活動　　track 痕跡　　gathering 聚會　　cover 遮蓋　　patio 庭院
column 柱子　　porch 門廊　　awning / shade 遮雨棚　　canopy (如屋頂般垂掛的) 罩棚

📝 邊聽邊寫，完美掌握的聽寫技巧　　　🎧 014

※ 熟記作為主語出現的各種物品／地點，以及表達這些主語的「謂語動詞」。

❶ There is/There are + 名詞 + 副詞子句(地點)

There are chairs next to the bed. (床旁邊有幾張椅子的照片)

❷ There is/There are + 名詞 + -ing + 副詞子句(地點)

There are books sitting on the table. (桌上放著幾本書的照片)

❸ 主語(事物) + have/has been + 動詞的過去分詞

Boxes have been stacked in the warehouse. (箱子堆放在倉庫裡的照片)

❹ 主語(事物) + is/are + 動詞的過去分詞

A rug is located in front of the window. (地毯位於窗戶前方的照片)

❺ 事物的擬人化(不及物動詞的現在進行式)

A carpet is lying on the floor. (地毯鋪在地板上的照片)

📝 一起來聽音檔中讀出的動詞時態，留意語調和斷句的部分，試著邊寫邊唸。　　🎧 015

1. ＿＿＿＿＿＿ ＿＿＿＿＿＿ a door beneath the staircase.

2. Some merchandise ＿＿＿＿＿ ＿＿＿＿＿ on shelves.

3. Waves ＿＿＿＿＿ ＿＿＿＿＿ against the rocks.

4. A lamp ＿＿＿＿＿ ＿＿＿＿＿ in the corner of the room.

5. Shelves ＿＿＿＿＿ ＿＿＿＿＿＿＿ with bread.

6. Computers ＿＿＿＿＿ ＿＿＿＿＿ ＿＿＿＿＿ next to each other.

7. A picture ＿＿＿＿＿ ＿＿＿＿＿ above a chair.

8. An awning ＿＿＿＿＿ a store entrance.

9. The lights ＿＿＿＿＿ ＿＿＿＿＿ ＿＿＿＿＿ on.

10. A row of windows ＿＿＿＿＿ ＿＿＿＿＿ a street.

📝 從基本開始到精確掌握的訓練

1.

　　(A)　　　　　　　(B)

2.

　　(A)　　　　　　　(B)

3.

　　(A)　　　　　　　(B)

4.

　　(A)　　　　　　　(B)

📝 利用刪去法選出Best Answer

1.

(A)　　　(B)　　　(C)　　　(D)

2.

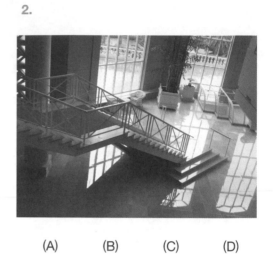

(A)　　　(B)　　　(C)　　　(D)

3.

(A)　　　(B)　　　(C)　　　(D)

4.

(A)　　　(B)　　　(C)　　　(D)

5.

(A)   (B)   (C)   (D)

6.

(A)   (B)   (C)   (D)

被動語態的現在進行式
能夠描述風景照片？？

be being p.p.作為及物動詞的被動語態現在進行
式，主要代表照片中某個人物的動作，但請記住即
使不是人物也能夠使用！

例如clothing is being displayed意思就是「衣服正
在展示中」，這類題目的出題機率雖然不高，
但當出現展示櫃的照片時，
不要忘記可能會出現這種答案！

Step 1　類型分析

A 答案為針對照片中較不顯眼部分做描述時　🎧018

高難度題型的答案是針對照片中出乎預期的部分所做的描述，最常出現的部分是地面、天花板或角落等出現的小細節，描述這些細節的選項往往是答案。遇到這種情況，與其觀察照片進行預測，更好的方法是聆聽時將選項中的主詞一一和照片比對，選出正確答案。

例題1

(A) White lines are painted on the road.
(B) Cars are moving in both directions.
(C) Pedestrians are crossing the street.
(D) Trees are being planted along the road.

(A) 道路上漆有白線。
(B) 汽車行駛於雙向道。
(C) 行人正穿越馬路。
(D) 樹木正沿著道路種植。

解析 照片中首先可以看到汽車、道路和房子，但答案是一般人容易忽略的地面上畫有白線(white lines)的斑馬線(crosswalk)。必須練習利用刪去法將錯誤的選項刪除，選出正確答案。　　　答案：(A)

🎧019

➡ 引導正確答案的單字 Check!

❶ 答案非人物的動作，而是位置、服飾、髮型、飾品等的情況

wear clothes 穿衣服　　　　　　　　have hair[a beard] 擁有頭髮[鬍鬚]
wear shoes[accessories] 穿鞋子[戴首飾]　　be at[near] the table 在桌子[桌子附近]

❷ 答案為地面、地板的情況

shadow 影子　　　　　track (地面的) 蹤跡　　be shaded[shielded] 被(影子)遮蔽
be polished 光亮，清潔　calm water 靜水　　　be reflected 反射
water on the floor 地板上的水

❸ 答案為天空，天花板的情況

clouds in the sky 天空的雲　　　　　　　smoke in the air 空氣中的煙霧
sunlight through the clouds 陽光透過雲層　lighting fixture from the ceiling 天花板的燈具
landscape 風景

❹ 答案為不顯眼的事物時

power outlet on the wall 牆上的電源插座　　gap between the desks 書桌之間的空隙
empty[be unoccupied] 空著[閒置的]　　not in use 不使　　chairs pushed 放置在桌子底下的椅子

B 答案為間接描述事物、狀況時 　　　　　　　　　　　　　🎧 020

以間接性的「其他詞彙」取代直接性的詞彙來描述具體事物、狀況，提高了難度。只要能夠掌握
使用其他詞彙來傳達相同意思的重新詮釋(paraphrasing)，就能在高難度題目中選出正確答案。

例題2

(A) They're swimming in the ocean.
(B) They're sitting around the table in the meeting room.
(C) Some people are enjoying some time together.
(D) Some people are digging the soil on the ground.

(A) 他們在海裡游泳。
(B) 他們圍坐在會議室的桌子旁。
(C) 人們一起享受時光。
(D) 人們在地上挖土。

解析 照片中的人們坐在沙子上彼此聊天，一起度過時間、享受時光(spend some time, enjoy some time together)，使用間接描述的選項為正確答案。解題技巧在於把聽到的選項和照片做比對，比先看照片進行推測更好。　　　　　　　　　　　　　　　　　　　　　　**答案：(C)**

🎧 021

● 引導正確答案的單字 Check!

※ 以間接性詞彙描述直接動作的情況

❶ eat, drink 吃，喝 → have a bite, taste, sip 嘗一口 → enjoy 享受

❷ walk 走路 → stride, stroll 大步走，漫步 → take a walk 散步
　　→ spend time outside, enjoy 消磨時間，享受時光

❸ cut 剪 → trim, chop, slice, dice, peel 修剪，剁切，削(皮) → cook, prepare food 做菜

❹ examine, check 檢查 → repair, fix, improve 修理，改進

❺ look, see 看 → face 面對 → having an interview 接受採訪

❻ point to, write on the board 指出，寫出 → teach, show 教，指引

❼ talk, speak 說話 → discuss, chat, confer, converse 討論
　　→ have a meeting[conference] 開會

❽ be seated, be sitting 坐 → attend, participate 參加
　　→ be engaged in, be involved in 參與 → be in session, be in progress (活動)進行中

📝 邊聽邊寫，完美掌握的聽寫技巧 🎧 022

※ 一同了解各式各樣描述同一照片的詞彙，以及經常出現的錯誤。

❶ Some people are sitting at the table. → Some of the seats are occupied[taken].
某些人坐在桌子前。　　　　　　　　　部分座位被佔用。

❷ Some of the seats are empty[unoccupied]. → Some seating spaces are available.
部分座位是空著的。　　　　　　　　　　　　　部分座位可供使用。

❸ There are rocks on the ground. → The place is deserted. → The landscape is dry and rocky.
地面上有石頭。　　　　　　　這個地方很冷清。　　　景觀乾燥且多岩石。

📝 一起來聽音檔中讀出的動詞時態，留意語調和斷句的部分，試著邊寫邊唸。 🎧 023

1. He's _____ _____ the counter.

2. A man _____ _____ a customer's hair.

3. She has her _____ _____ _____.

4. A street lamp _____ _____ _____.

5. Power cords _____ _____ _____ into a wall outlet.

6. Trees are _____ _____ on a building.

7. A lid _____ _____ _____ from a paint can.

8. Some bikes _____ _____.

9. Some of the spectators _____ _____ hats.

10. Sunlight _____ _____ through the clouds.

📝 從基本開始到精確掌握的訓練

1.

(A) 　　　　　(B)

2.

(A) 　　　　　(B)

3.

(A) 　　　　　(B)

4.

(A) 　　　　　(B)

📝 利用刪去法選出 Best Answer

1.

　　(A)　　　　(B)　　　　(C)　　　　(D)

2.

　　(A)　　　　(B)　　　　(C)　　　　(D)

3.

　　(A)　　　　(B)　　　　(C)　　　　(D)

4.

　　(A)　　　　(B)　　　　(C)　　　　(D)

5.

(A)   (B)   (C)   (D)

6.

(A)   (B)   (C)   (D)

什麼！
Part 1比想像中更困難？

「聽說Part 1比較簡單，爲什麼我覺得很困難？」
這是我經常收到的提問。
「是讀的量太少，不是內容困難。」
集中精神，完整複習到UNIT3的話，
Part 1要拿滿分就是囊中之物。
即使唾手可得，不認眞奔跑的話是不行的。
加速吧！

PART 2

聽完一個題目，從三個選項中選出最適合的答案。這種題型在試卷上沒有其他資訊，純粹仰賴聽力作答。

題目數	難易度
共25題 （7至31題）	中／中上

滿分訣竅

熟悉問題類型，刪去錯誤的選項來解題！

❶ 聽完疑問句型，掌握正確答案。→ **聽力訓練**

❷ 熟悉各類型的答案和錯誤選項。

❸ 刪去不正確的選項，留下一個Best Answer。

學習方法

❶ **準備** 掌握Part2的問句類型，並熟悉各類型的答案。

❷ **實戰** 將各Unit題型分段解題，應用在實戰題目中。

❸ **複習** 將問題和解答放在一組，聆聽的同時複習問題的類型和答案類型。

教材結構

Unit 4 疑問詞疑問句 I　　疑問詞who, where, when－代表一個意義的疑問詞

Unit 5 疑問詞疑問句 II　　疑問詞how, why, what/which－代表數種意義的疑問詞

Unit 6 Yes/No疑問句 I　　肯定, 否定／附加疑問句等－Yes/No疑問句的框架

Unit 7 Yes/No疑問句 II, 其他類型　　勸導／提議直述句, 選擇疑問句

例題和滿分訣竅

🎧 026

Mark your answer on your answer sheet.

(A)　　　　(B)　　　　(C)

Where would you like to put these shelves?

(A) It looks much better.

(B) They did it themselves.

(C) Let's hang them above the desk.

你想把這些架子放在哪裡？

(A) 看起來好多了。

(B) 他們自己做好了。

(C) 我們把它們掛在書桌上面吧。

解析 作為疑問詞Where的正確答案是包括地點在內的句子。聽完問題(Question)之後，必須能夠找出疑問詞類型的＜Where + put(主動詞)＞。錯誤通常出現在發音或聯想上較為熟悉的詞彙，但並不是問題的適合答案，(A), (B)適合做為How的問句回答。正確答案是包括「書桌上面」詞彙在內的(C)。

Know-how

刪去法（選出Best Answer）解題：　　Q.　~~(A)~~　~~(B)~~　(C)

❶ 仔細聽完疑問句之後，掌握（疑問詞主語+主動詞／疑問詞+助動詞+主語+主動詞）的意義。

❷ 確定是錯誤的選項打X，在不確定是否正確／沒發現錯誤的選項畫上底線做標示。

❸ 聽完之後刪去錯誤的選項，選擇最正確無誤的答案。

Where would you like to put these shelves?

(A) It looks much better.　　　　適合當作疑問詞How的答案。

(B) They did it themselves.　　　發音類似shelves/selves的錯誤。

(C) Let's hang them above the desk.　地點介係詞片語適合當作where的答案。

❹ 答案: (C)

Unit 4　疑問詞疑問句 I

 Step 1　類型分析

A　Who 疑問句　　　🎧 027

雖然是詢問「誰」的疑問詞，但答案往往不是人。包括代名詞「I」在內的各種職業／職務級別／團體名稱也有可能是答案。

例題1

Mark your answer on your answer sheet. **(A)**　　　**(B)**　　　**(C)**	Who can help me with the report? (A) Sure, put the table here. (B) I should have some time. (C) He needs a new printer.
	誰可以幫忙我寫報告？ (A) 當然可以。把桌子放這裡。 **(B) 我應該有時間。** (C) 他需要一個新的印表機。

解析 須熟記能夠作為疑問詞Who答案的各種人物／部門／公司名稱。代名詞「I」也可能是本人自願幫忙的典型答案。(A)由於疑問詞疑問句中不會出現Yes/No或Sure的回答，因此不是答案，(C)無法得知代名詞He指的是誰，也不是答案。　　　　　　　　　　　　　　　　　　　　　　答案: (B)

🎧 028

➡ 疑問詞 Who 正確表達 Check!

❶ 代名詞 I/You
　I can do it. 我做得到。　　　　　　　I have some time. 我有時間。
　It's your turn. 輪到你了。　　　　　　It'll have to be me. 應該是我。

❷ 各種人稱名詞（專有名詞）
　It's Lisa's shift. 是麗莎值班。　　　　Mr. Lopez from R&D. 是研發部門的洛佩茲。

❸ 職業／職務／身分

receptionist 接待員	accountant 會計師	mechanic 技師
plumber 水電工	director 經理	secretary 秘書

❹ 部門/公司名（包括專有名詞）

sales department 銷售部門	accounting office 會計部門	public relations 公關部
corporation 有限公司	publishing 出版社	trading company 貿易公司

❺ 人物描寫
　The man from the head office. 來自於總公司的人。　　The woman with long hair. 長髮女人。
　The man in the corner. 角落的男人。

B | Where 疑問句 🎧 029

熟記地點單字和介係詞有助於找出Where疑問句的答案。如同疑問詞Who般，各種地點/部門／
客戶／資訊來源等都可能是答案。

例題2

Mark your answer on your answer sheet. (A)　　　(B)　　　(C)	<u>Where</u> will the conference <u>be held</u>? (A) In Hamburg. (B) Next September. (C) Use a conference call. 會議將在哪裡舉行？ **(A) 在漢堡。** (B) 明年九月。 (C) 採取電話會議。

解析 地點疑問詞Where的答案可能是包括專有名詞的各種地點。即使是不太熟悉的專有名詞，如果可能作為
地點，就先保留下來之後再選擇。(B)適合做為When疑問句的答案，(C)是重複單字的典型錯誤答案。

答案: (A)

🎧 030

➡ 疑問詞 Where 正確表達 Check!

❶ 地名（包括專有名詞）

　in Dusseldorf, Germany 在德國的杜塞爾多夫　to Buenos Aires 到布宜諾斯艾利斯

❷ 物品擺放的位置

　on the desk 書桌上　　　　　　　　　next to the cabinet 在櫃子旁
　in the drawer 在抽屜裡　　　　　　　Leave it on the table. 放在桌子上。
　on the cover of the magazine 在雜誌封面上

❸ 人前往的地點

　here behind the door 在門後面　　　on the fifth floor 在5樓
　in the lobby 在大廳　　　　　　　　to the basement 往地下室
　downtown 市中心　　　　　　　　　in the Hong Kong branch 在香港分行

❹ 描述地點

　around the corner 就在附近　　　　next to the new restaurant 在新開的餐廳隔壁
　Go straight and make a left. 直走左轉。

❺ 與疑問詞Who相容的情況

　executive 管理者　　　　　　　　　representative 代表
　human resources 人資　　　　　　　shipping department 物流部門
　From my president. 來自我的董事長。　Mr. Baker should have it. 貝克先生應該有。

C When 疑問句

需熟記與詢問時間的疑問詞When搭配出現的介係詞／連接詞／副詞詞彙，試著做區分過去式／現在式／未來式的聽力練習吧。

例題3

Mark your answer on your answer sheet. **(A)** **(B)** **(C)**	<u>When will</u> the current tenants <u>vacate</u> the apartment? (A) I'll sign the lease. (B) At least two bedrooms. (C) By the end of the month. 目前的房客什麼時候會搬離公寓？ (A) 我會簽署租約。 (B) 至少有兩間臥室。 **(C) 到月底。**

解析 句中出現的主動詞多少有點難度，但選項當中表達時間的只有(C)。為了正確解開高難度的題目，也要熟悉表達時間的介係詞和助動詞。雖然其他選項出現和房產相關的詞彙，但與疑問詞When並不連貫。

答案: (C)

➡ 疑問詞 When 正確表達 Check!

❶ 各種時間表達

on Friday 在週五   at noon 在中午

yesterday 昨天   in July 在7月

❷ 過去式

ago ～之前   last 上個～

two hours ago 2小時前   last night 昨晚

❸ 未來式

in ～之後   next 下個~

in a month 一個月後   next summer 明年夏天

❹ 時間介係詞／連接詞片語

before/after 之前/之後   as soon as 一～立刻

not until 直到～   when/once 當～時, 曾經～

When the prices go down. 當價格下跌時。

Before the meeting is over. 會議結束之前。

Not until 5 o'clock tomorrow. 明天下午五點以後才行。

As soon as Mr. Kurosawa comes back. 黑澤明先生一回來。

❺ 其他表達

Check the schedule. 查看行程。   The sooner, the better. 愈快愈好。

It's already over. 已經結束了。   I lost all the paperwork. 我弄丟了所有資料。

Step 2 聆聽和聽寫的訓練

Answers_P.008

📝 邊聽邊寫，完美掌握的聽寫技巧   🎧 033

※ 解析重點集中在句型結構的時態／動詞／主語(3～4個單字)。

❶ 使用一般動詞的疑問詞疑問句 (疑問詞+ do(es)/did + 主語+主動詞)：專注聽出至少4個單字。

<u>Where</u> <u>did</u> <u>you</u> <u>leave</u> your blue folder? 你把藍色文件夾留在哪裡？

❷ 使用be動詞的疑問詞疑問句(疑問詞+be動詞+主語)：專注聽出至少4個單字。

<u>Where</u> <u>is</u> the updated <u>itinerary</u>? 更新後的日程表在哪裡？

❸ 使用俗諺／助動詞的疑問詞疑問句：聽出疑問詞，主動詞。

<u>When's</u> the safety inspector <u>due to visit</u> the factory? 安全檢查員何時參訪工廠？

📝 填空時注意與最前面的疑問詞之間的連音，並跟著讀讀看。   🎧 034

1. Q: _____ are we _____ _____ the concert?

    A: _____ _____ o'clock.

2. Q: _____'s _____ _____ the projector in the conference room?

    A: Our _____ _____ team.

3. Q: _____ is the updated sales _____?

    A: The _____ should _____ _____.

4. Q: _____'s the closest _____ _____?

    A: _____'s _____ on 11th Street.

5. Q: _____'s going to _____ at the publishers' conference this year?

    A: It _____ been _____ yet.

6. Q: _____ should we _____ on a new contract?

    A: _____ _____ we _____ the current one.

7. Q: _____ can we _____ these new product samples?

    A: In the glass case _____ _____ _____.

📝 從基本開始到精確掌握的訓練

1. Mark your answer on your answer sheet.	(A)	(B)
2. Mark your answer on your answer sheet.	(A)	(B)
3. Mark your answer on your answer sheet.	(A)	(B)
4. Mark your answer on your answer sheet.	(A)	(B)
5. Mark your answer on your answer sheet.	(A)	(B)

📝 利用刪去法選出 Best Answer

1. Mark your answer on your answer sheet.	(A)	(B)	(C)
2. Mark your answer on your answer sheet.	(A)	(B)	(C)
3. Mark your answer on your answer sheet.	(A)	(B)	(C)
4. Mark your answer on your answer sheet.	(A)	(B)	(C)
5. Mark your answer on your answer sheet.	(A)	(B)	(C)
6. Mark your answer on your answer sheet.	(A)	(B)	(C)
7. Mark your answer on your answer sheet.	(A)	(B)	(C)
8. Mark your answer on your answer sheet.	(A)	(B)	(C)
9. Mark your answer on your answer sheet.	(A)	(B)	(C)
10. Mark your answer on your answer sheet.	(A)	(B)	(C)

機率排名第1的答案是「不知道」句型→記熟之後，一旦出現這個選項就準備選擇！

能夠使用在會話中的各種「不知道」句型，無論在哪種題目中，都可能是正確答案。即使沒有聽清楚題目，選項中如果聽到「不知道」的句型，可以思考看看是否為答案。

🎧 037

① 不知道

I don't know. 我不知道。

I'm not sure. 我不確定。

I forgot. 我忘記了。

I can't remember. 我不記得了。

I wish I knew. 但願我知道(我不知道)。

I wish I could tell you. 但願我能告訴你。

I was about to ask you. 我正要問你。

② 沒說所以[還沒決定所以]不知道

No one told me. 沒有人告訴我。

I haven't heard. 我沒聽說過。

It depends on ~. 取決於[要看]～。

I haven't been told. 我沒有被告知(被動語態)。

It hasn't been decided. 尚未決定。

It hasn't been confirmed. 尚未確認。

They're still discussing. 他們還在討論。

It will be announced next month. 將在下個月公布。

They didn't tell me anything. 他們什麼都沒告訴我。

③ 非負責人所以不知道

I'm not in charge. 不是我負責。

It's not up to me. 不是我決定的。

I can't decide. 我決定不了。

④ 其他人知道

Let me find out for you. 我幫你打聽看看。

Jimmy might know about it. 吉米可能知道。

Ask Ms. Kang. 問問江小姐。

Check the itinerary. 查看行程。

I have to call. 我得打個電話。

You can check it online. 你可以上網查查看。

Blake is in charge of that. 那個由布萊克負責管理。

You'd better talk to Ms. Lee. 你最好和李小姐談談。

⑤ 沒做，沒有

I didn't go. 我沒去。

It's already over. 已經結束了。

I didn't read it yet. 我還沒讀它。

I don't have one. 我沒有。

I didn't check. 我沒有檢查。

Unit 5　疑問詞疑問句 II

A　How 疑問句　　　　　　　　　　　　　　　　　🎧038

與How一同出現的動詞、形容詞、名詞使得意思變得多元化。需熟記具備多種意義的疑問詞How在句型中的用法。

例題1

Mark your answer on your answer sheet. (A)　　(B)　　(C)	How would you like to pay for your purchase? (A) Can you gift-wrap it? (B) By check, if possible. (C) Sure, here you are.
	您想如何支付購物費用？ (A) 你能把禮物包裝起來嗎？ **(B) 可以的話用支票。** (C) 當然，給你。

解析　How和動詞結合時，主要用來詢問方法。當How作為詢問方法的疑問句時，需熟記經常出現的常識性答案。上列的問句中，典型的支付方式是信用卡和支票，(A)選項並非付款方式，而是商店(store)的聯想詞gift-wrap，(C)的錯誤在於疑問詞疑問句中無法使用Yes/No來回答。　　　　　　答案: (B)

🎧039

> ## ➡ 疑問詞 How 正確表達 Check!
>
> **❶ How ~ 一般動詞: 方法**
>
> How ~ contact (聯絡方法) → call 電話　　　e-mail 電子郵件　　　in person 親自
> How ~ register (註冊方法) → visit 拜訪　　　online 上網　　　fill out the form 填寫表格
>
> **❷ How + be動詞/become: 狀態**
>
> better 更好的　　　　　　　efficient 有效率的　　　　productive 多產的
> bad 差的　　　　　　　　　long 長的　　　　　　　　boring 無聊的
>
> **❸ How + 名詞/形容詞**
>
> How much ~ 多少(金額/量)　　　　　How many ~ 多少(個數)
> How long ~ 多長(時間/距離)　　　　How far ~ 多遠(距離)
> How soon[late] ~ 多快/慢(時間)　　　How often 多經常(頻率)
>
> **❹ How的慣用法**
>
> How did the interview go? 面試怎麼樣？
> How is the new project coming along? 新項目進展得如何？
> How do you like your new company? 你覺得你的新公司怎麼樣？

B Why 疑問句 🎧 040

疑問詞Why很難只根據疑問詞來選擇答案，必須對於表達做某個動作的原因或目的方法，以及各種原因和說明的例子加以熟悉，才能順利解題。

例題2

Mark your answer on your answer sheet.	<u>Why</u> are they <u>raising</u> the toll <u>prices</u> on Highway 15?
(A) **(B)** **(C)**	(A) To pay for road constructions costs.
	(B) It's near exit 10.
	(C) Up to 75 kilometers an hour.
	他們為什麼要調漲15號高速公路的通行費？
	(A)支付道路建設費用。
	(B)靠近10號出口。
	(C)每小時高達75公里。

解析 高速公路通行費的調漲以to不定詞的目的型態（想要～、為了～）作為回答，(A)是說明目的最典型的句子，(B)適合回答Where的疑問句，(C)是Highway的聯想誤解。關鍵是思考通行費的調漲理由。

答案：(A)

🎧 041

➲ 疑問詞 Why 正確表達 Check!

❶ 針對Why的疑問句以表達目的作為答案

to不定詞的目的 → To make it visible. 使其可見。

For+名詞 → For a meeting. 為了參加會議。

So (that) → So that everyone can be there in time. 這樣每個人都能及時到達那裡。

❷ Why + not 開始的疑問句的典型解釋

I've been busy. 我一直很忙。	I haven't had time[a chance]. 我沒有時間[機會]。
I'm not feeling well. 我不太舒服。	Something came up. 出了點事情。
It's mandatory. 這是規定的（強制性的）。	I had a previous engagement. 我有約。

❸ Why don't you/we ~: 勸導、勸說的句子(Yes/No疑問句)

Why don't you ~? 你不如～好嗎？	Why don't we ~? 我們不如～好嗎？
Why don't I ~? 我來～（好意）。	Why not ~? 何不～？

C What/Which 疑問句

帶有具廣泛意義的疑問詞what的疑問句，根據連接的詞彙不同，可能有各式各樣的答案。What/Which與名詞結合時，經常以選擇物品的標準作為解答。練習使用刪去法可以解開高難度的What疑問句。

例題3

Mark your answer on your answer sheet. (A)　　　(B)　　　(C)	What's the return policy for items purchased online? (A) He came back yesterday. (B) We offer a full refund. (C) In the inventory. 網上購買的商品的退貨政策是什麼？ (A)他昨天回來了。 **(B)我們提供全額退款。** (C)在庫存中。

解析 熟悉與題目中return policy（退貨政策）有關的詞彙refund（退款）/exchange（換貨）/store credit（抵用額度）有利於選擇答案。(A)He的特定人物並不存在，(C)是出現與購物聯想的詞彙inventory的誤答。　　　答案:(B)

043

◯ 疑問詞 What 正確表達 Check!

❶ What + 名詞型：熟記典型的標準答案類型。

What + cost[estimate / charge / fee] ~?	價格→ 與 How much的答案類似
What + color[shade] ~?	顏色/色彩→ yellow 黃色　blue 藍色　light 淺色　dark 深色
What + job[position / opening] ~?	職務/職位→ sales 銷售　accounting 會計

❷ What + 動詞型：熟記典型的標準答案類型。

What did you order for lunch?	午餐菜單→ 各式食物名稱
What's in the box?	箱子裡物品種類→ 各種事務用品/機器名稱
What's your plan for the holiday?	休假計畫→ 與各種計畫/行程有關的內容

❸ What 的慣用法和標準答案類型

What do you do (for a living)?	詢問職業時→ 各式職業/公司詞彙
What do you think of the proposal?	對於提案的意見→ 好/不好的詞彙
What made[caused] the problem?	問題的原因→ 不足之處的詞彙
What is the presentation about?	簡報的主題→ 公司業務相關的詞彙
What's going on? / What's wrong?	詢問問題出在哪裡時→ 各種問題點
What does the secretary look like?	詢問外貌時→ 描述外貌特徵的詞彙

📝 邊聽邊寫，完美掌握的聽寫技巧　🎧 044

> ※ 為了釐清疑問詞本身的意義，必須區分伴隨出現的動詞/名詞/形容詞。
>
> ❶ 疑問詞+ 動詞/be動詞: 為了了解意義，必須解析主動詞。
>
>   <u>Why</u> <u>hasn't</u> the performance <u>started</u> yet? 為什麼表演還沒開始？
>
> ❷ 疑問詞+ 形容詞/名詞: How 根據結合使用的形容詞/名詞而具有各種意義。
>
>   <u>How</u> <u>much</u> are the exercise classes at your gym? 你健身房的健身課程多少錢？
>
> ❸ 慣用法: 不同於原本規則的使用法以「默背」方法最有效。
>
>   What's the new manager like? 新經理怎麼樣？（個性描述）

📝 填空時注意與最前面的疑問詞之間的連音，並跟著讀讀看。　🎧 045

1. Q: ＿＿＿＿＿＿ ＿＿＿＿＿＿ the sales last quarter?

   A: ＿＿＿＿＿＿ than expected.

2. Q: ＿＿＿＿＿＿ ＿＿＿＿＿＿ ＿＿＿＿＿＿ buy a less expensive camera?

   A: I ＿＿＿＿＿＿ ＿＿＿＿＿＿ the design.

3. Q: ＿＿＿＿＿＿ ＿＿＿＿＿＿ ＿＿＿＿＿＿ ＿＿＿＿＿＿ for a living?

   A: I ＿＿＿＿＿＿ at a hospital.

4. Q: ＿＿＿＿＿＿ ＿＿＿＿＿＿ is yours?

   A: ＿＿＿＿＿＿ ＿＿＿＿＿＿ in the corner.

5. Q: ＿＿＿＿＿＿ ＿＿＿＿＿＿ do you ＿＿＿＿＿＿ for copying?

   A: ＿＿＿＿＿＿ cents ＿＿＿＿＿＿ page.

6. Q: ＿＿＿＿＿＿ ＿＿＿＿＿＿ you ＿＿＿＿＿＿ for the meeting?

   A: The ＿＿＿＿＿＿ was really＿＿＿＿＿＿.

7. Q: ＿＿＿＿＿＿ do you ＿＿＿＿＿＿ ＿＿＿＿＿＿ the train station?

   A: A ＿＿＿＿＿＿ is ＿＿＿＿＿＿ ＿＿＿＿＿＿there.

📝 從基本開始到精確掌握的訓練

1. Mark your answer on your answer sheet. (A) (B)

2. Mark your answer on your answer sheet. (A) (B)

3. Mark your answer on your answer sheet. (A) (B)

4. Mark your answer on your answer sheet. (A) (B)

5. Mark your answer on your answer sheet. (A) (B)

Step 4 實戰練習 🎧047 Answers_P.011

📝 利用刪去法選出Best Answer

1. Mark your answer on your answer sheet. (A) (B) (C)

2. Mark your answer on your answer sheet. (A) (B) (C)

3. Mark your answer on your answer sheet. (A) (B) (C)

4. Mark your answer on your answer sheet. (A) (B) (C)

5. Mark your answer on your answer sheet. (A) (B) (C)

6. Mark your answer on your answer sheet. (A) (B) (C)

7. Mark your answer on your answer sheet. (A) (B) (C)

8. Mark your answer on your answer sheet. (A) (B) (C)

9. Mark your answer on your answer sheet. (A) (B) (C)

10. Mark your answer on your answer sheet. (A) (B) (C)

最常出現的錯誤「發音相近」→ 凡是發音類似的詞彙可能是陷阱！

除了選擇疑問句之外，其他疑問句中出現的詞彙同樣列在選項中，或出現發音類似的詞彙時，極有可能是陷阱題，必須小心避免誤選。

🎧 048

① 直接使用相同單字或使用一語多義/衍生字時:**掌握前後文的意義。**

promote 促進；升遷	enter 進入；參加；輸入
close 關；近	order 順序；訂購
book 書；預約	rest 休息；剩下
suit 西裝；適合	leave 離開；留下
appointment 約定；任命	fair 公平的；博覽會
check 確認；支票	sign 標誌；簽名
board 董事會；搭乘	carry 搬運；處理（商品），賣
change 換；零錢	store 商店；儲藏

② 使用發音類似的詞彙時:**避免因發音相似而誤答。**

launch 著手進行(新產品) - lunch 午餐	mind 在意 - remind 提醒
disappoint 失望 - appointment 約定	expect 期待 - inspect 檢查
resign 辭職 - design 設計	contact 聯絡 - contract 合約
price 價格 - prize 獎	walk 走路 - work 工作
train 火車 - training 培訓	office 辦公室 - official 官方的
write 寫 - right 正確的	read 閱讀 - lead 領導，指引
address 致詞 - dress 衣服	pass 經過 - path 小徑
road 路，道路 - load 負載	full 充滿的 - pull 拉
fast 快速的 - past 過去的	low 低的 - row 排，行列
director 經理，主管 - directory 電話號碼簿	direct 指導 - direction 方向

③ 答案中出現錯誤的聯想詞時:**必須集中在主題，避免被聯想詞混淆。**

today → tomorrow	no → sorry
flight → gate	order → menu
medical → drug	register → seminar
party → cake	store → discount, gift
professor → university	

Unit 6　Yes/No 疑問句 I

Step 1　類型分析

A　肯定的疑問句

🎧049

按照〈助動詞＋主語＋主動詞～〉或〈be動詞＋主語～〉的順序，肯定時回答Yes，否定時回答No的類型稱為Yes/No疑問句。不同於疑問詞疑問句的是，至少必須準確聽出主動詞的意思，作答的方法屬於簡答題，需要多訓練才能夠正確回答肯定/否定。

例題1

| Mark your answer on your answer sheet.

(A)　　(B)　　(C) | Do you enjoy your job as a bank teller?
(A) I'll tell her tomorrow.
(B) A different account.
(C) I like it a lot.

你喜歡銀行出納員的工作嗎？
(A) 我明天會告訴她。
(B) 一個不同的帳戶。
(C) 我非常喜歡。 |

解析　使用主動詞enjoy詢問是否喜歡的問題，〈(Yes)＋非常喜歡〉是表達肯定的典型方式。Yes/No疑問句與其說具有難度，出錯的原因大多在於不懂表達肯定/否定的方法。(A) her是不存在的人物。(B)出現與銀行聯想的帳戶並不正確。　　　　　　　　　　　　　　　答案:(C)

🎧050

➡ Yes/No 疑問句正確表達Check!

❶ 完整句子Yes/No

Yes, + I think so. / I'd like that. / That's my goal. / No problem. / That's what I heard.
我想是的。　　　我喜歡那樣。　那是我的目標。　沒問題。　　　我是這麼聽說的。

No, + I don't think so. / I doubt it. / Not yet. / It's not necessary. / Not that I know of.
我不這麼認為。　　我對此表示懷疑。還沒。　　　不需要。　　　據我所知並非如此。

❷ Yes + 詳細內容

你會參加嗎？　→ Yes, + I'll there by nine. / I'll go with Michael. 我9前會到。/我會跟麥克一起去。
你看過報告了嗎？→ Yes, + it was impressive. / From the company Web site. 令人印象深刻。/ 從公司的網站。

❸ No + 否定的理由，提出其他對策

你會參加嗎？　→ No, + I'll be busy then. / Sorry. + Maybe next time. 那時我會很忙。/ 也許下次吧。
你看過報告了嗎？→ No, + I was in Singapore. / Tell me about it. 我人在新加坡。/ 說給我聽吧。

❹ 省略Yes/No的回答：熟記以典型的細節/理由作為答案的方式。

你會參加嗎？　→ I'll be there by nine. / I'll be busy then. 我9前會到。/那時我會很忙（沒辦法去）。
你看過報告了嗎？→ I presented it to the board. / Tell me about it. （是，）我提交給董事會。/ （不，）說給我聽吧。

B 否定疑問句／附加疑問句 🎧051

無論是肯定疑問句或否定疑問句，肯定時回答Yes，否定時回答No。例如，無論問題是「吃飽了嗎？」或「還沒吃飯嗎？」，吃飽時回答Yes，還沒吃則回答No，附加疑問句也是一樣，吃飽的話Yes，還沒吃的話No，但Yes/No後面連接的內容必須與前後文一致，才能避免選錯答案。需要掌握否定疑問句與附加疑問句的特點。

例題2

| Mark your answer on your answer sheet.

(A)　　　(B)　　　(C) | Don't you need a password to log on to the computer?
(A) We don't have a logo.
(B) Yes, but I can't remember it.
(C) He's at the computer lab.

你是否需要密碼才能登錄電腦？
(A) 我們沒有商標。
(B) 是的，但我不記得了。
(C) 他在電腦實驗室。 |

解析 在是否需要密碼的否定疑問句中的確需要〈Yes＋but～〉的答題形式，回答記不得了是正確答案。就像肯定疑問句一樣，需要熟記否定，附加疑問句加上Yes/No的回答方式，甚至當高難度題目中沒有Yes/No的答案時也要能夠猜對。(A)使用和log發音相似的logo，(C)中的He並沒有這樣的人物，因此此不是正確答案。　　　　　　　　　　　　　　　　　　　　　　　　　　　　　　　　　**答案:(B)**

🎧052

➤ 否定附加疑問句的正確表達Check!

❶ 使用助動詞/代動詞直接回應的類型

　It seems like a while since we had a vacation, doesn't it?

　➡ 解析：Yes, it does. / It sure does. 是的，沒錯。

　➡ 誤解：Yes, they would. / Sorry, I can't. （代名詞、動詞、時態等錯誤）

❷ 解釋類型(Yes, but ~)

　沒有受訓過嗎？ → Yes, but it was long time ago. 有，但那是很久以前了（得重新來過）。

　你沒有訂嗎？ → Yes, but the delivery is taking longer. 有，但交貨時間很長。

❸ 對於勸誘/勸導的正面回應(That's a good idea 類型)

　要不要外食？ → That's a good suggestion. 這是個很好的建議。

　要不要連絡承包商？ → It's worth trying. 值得一試。

❹ 對於追究/遺忘事情的正面回應(Thank you for reminding me 類型)

　不是該出發了嗎？ → Thank you for reminding me. 謝謝你提醒我。

　必須呈交報告了，不是嗎？ → Oh, I almost forgot. 我差點忘了。

C 間接疑問句以外的其他帶名詞的疑問句

使用「Do you know～」等間接迂迴地詢問時，句子既長又難以理解，但回答方法通常與Yes/No疑問句類似。對於帶有Yes/No和不帶有Yes/No的典型答案，可以再次透過間接問句來複習。

例題3

| Mark your answer on your answer sheet.

(A)　　(B)　　(C) | Can you tell me how to cancel my reservation?
(A) Sorry, we are sold out.
(B) Call the customer help desk.
(C) The flight leaves tomorrow.

你能告訴我該如何取消預定嗎？
(A) 抱歉，已經賣完了。
(B) 請致電顧客服務中心。
(C) 飛機明天起飛。 |

解析 詢問取消預定的方法時，使用「Can you tell me ~」的間接問句。正確答案是省略Yes，直接告知取消方法的(B)。(A) Sorry是No的意思，後面的內容和前文不一致，(C)出現了reservation的聯想詞彙flight，都是不正確的答案。　　　　　　　　　　　　　　　　　　　　　　　　　答案: (B)

🎧054

➡ 間接疑問句/帶有名詞疑問句的正確表達Check!

❶ 經常使用的表達

Do you know ~ 你知道～嗎？　　　　　Can you tell me ~ 你能告訴我～嗎？

Did you hear ~ 你有聽說～嗎？　　　　May l ask ~ 我可以問你～嗎？

Do you think ~ 你覺得～嗎？　　　　　疑問詞＋do you think ~ 你覺得～嗎？

❷ 使用疑問詞疑問句的間接疑問句: 正確答案經常出現省略Yes/No的情況。

Do you know where I can find a cash machine? 你知道哪裡有提款機嗎？

➡ (Yes.) There's one in the lobby. (是，) 大廳裡有一個。

➡ Sure, let me show you. 當然，我來告訴你。（Yes＋細節情況）

❸ 其他帶有名詞的疑問句

Do you think I should call the director? 你覺得我應該打電話給經理嗎？

➡ Yes. He might have a better idea. 是的，他也許有更好的點子。(Yes＋細節內容)

➡ (No.) Why don't we wait until next week? 我們何不等到下週？(No＋提議對策)

Step 2　聆聽和聽寫的訓練

Answers_P.013

📝 邊聽邊寫，完美掌握的聽寫技巧　🎧 055

※ 了解形成Yes/No疑問句的各種動詞形態，並掌握「主動詞」的意義。

❶ 助動詞+ 主語(人稱) + 主動詞: 必須解析主動詞的意義。

<u>Didn't</u> <u>we</u> just <u>call</u> the maintenance office? 我們不是剛打電話給維修辦公室嗎？

❷ Be 動詞(時態) + 主語(人稱) + 主動詞:確認 <be + -ing>，<be + p.p.> 句型。

<u>Are</u> <u>you</u> <u>moving</u> into the new office this month? 你這個月要搬進新辦公室嗎？

❸ 完成動詞(時態) + 主語(人稱) + 主動詞: 熟記完成動詞的時態和用法。

<u>Has</u> <u>Mr. Lee</u> <u>visited</u> the factory before? 李先生以前是否參觀過工廠？

PART
2

📝 填空時注意句子結構（代動詞＋主語＋主動詞），並跟著讀讀看。　🎧 056

1.　Q: ＿＿＿＿＿ ＿＿＿＿＿ ＿＿＿＿＿ on the new project?

　　A: No, I'm ＿＿＿＿＿ ＿＿＿＿＿.

2.　Q: You ＿＿＿＿＿ ＿＿＿＿＿ the proposal, have you?

　　A: No, I'll do it ＿＿＿＿＿ ＿＿＿＿＿.

3.　Q: ＿＿＿＿＿ you ＿＿＿＿＿ the training last month?

　　A: No, I ＿＿＿＿＿ ＿＿＿＿＿.

4.　Q: Do you think ＿＿＿＿＿ ＿＿＿＿＿ ＿＿＿＿＿ for the airport now?

　　A: ＿＿＿＿＿ ＿＿＿＿＿ the flight schedule first.

5.　Q: ＿＿＿＿＿'ll ＿＿＿＿＿ ＿＿＿＿＿ new employees soon, right?

　　A: Yes, we're ＿＿＿＿＿ ＿＿＿＿＿.

6.　Q: Do you know ＿＿＿＿＿ ＿＿＿＿＿ ordered the pasta dish?

　　A: The ＿＿＿＿＿ at table ＿＿＿＿＿.

7.　Q: ＿＿＿＿＿ we ＿＿＿＿＿ the conference until February?

　　A: The hotel charges a ＿＿＿＿＿ ＿＿＿＿＿.

51

Step 3　基本掌握　 057

Answers_P.013

📝 從基本開始到精確掌握的訓練

1. Mark your answer on your answer sheet.　　　　(A)　　　(B)

2. Mark your answer on your answer sheet.　　　　(A)　　　(B)

3. Mark your answer on your answer sheet.　　　　(A)　　　(B)

4. Mark your answer on your answer sheet.　　　　(A)　　　(B)

5. Mark your answer on your answer sheet.　　　　(A)　　　(B)

Step 4　實戰練習　 058

Answers_P.014

📝 利用刪去法選出Best Answer

1. Mark your answer on your answer sheet.　　　(A)　　(B)　　(C)

2. Mark your answer on your answer sheet.　　　(A)　　(B)　　(C)

3. Mark your answer on your answer sheet.　　　(A)　　(B)　　(C)

4. Mark your answer on your answer sheet.　　　(A)　　(B)　　(C)

5. Mark your answer on your answer sheet.　　　(A)　　(B)　　(C)

6. Mark your answer on your answer sheet.　　　(A)　　(B)　　(C)

7. Mark your answer on your answer sheet.　　　(A)　　(B)　　(C)

8. Mark your answer on your answer sheet.　　　(A)　　(B)　　(C)

9. Mark your answer on your answer sheet.　　　(A)　　(B)　　(C)

10. Mark your answer on your answer sheet.　　　(A)　　(B)　　(C)

1. 反問的類型 ➡ 經常是正確答案！

回答問題時通常是直述句的方式，但也有可能是以反問作為答案。尤其多益考試中經常出現以反問方式作為正確答案。

🎧 059

① 問題的反問類型

Q: When would you like to meet? 你想什麼時候見面？
A: How about Friday? 週五怎麼樣？

② 直述句的反問類型

Q: This coat needs to be repaired. 這件外套需要修理。
A: Oh, what's wrong with it? 噢，有什麼問題嗎？

③ 選擇疑問句的反問類型

Q: Would you like to go to the movies or a concert? 你想看電影還是聽演唱會？
A: How about going shopping? 購物怎麼樣？

2. Which疑問句類型 ➡ 確認選項中是否有the one字眼！

Which疑問句主要為〈which +名詞〉句型，這時名詞中含有one的the one經常是正確答案。

🎧 060

① the one 類型

Q: Which car is yours? 哪一台是你的車？
A: The one parked in the corner. 停在轉角的那輛。

② 比較級或最高級的類型

Q: Which chair needs to be repaired? 哪張椅子需要修理？
A: The smaller one. 小的那張。

③ both / either / neither 類型

Q: Which design do you like? 你喜歡哪一種款式？
A: Either one is fine. 任何一種都好。

Step 1 類型分析

A 勸導/勸誘/提議型 🎧061

出於好意提議某個物品或動作的疑問句。一般人最熟悉的是Yes/No疑問句，但其他較不熟悉的類型也經常出現在多益中，最好加以分類並熟記。

例題1

| Mark your answer on your answer sheet.

(A)　　(B)　　(C) | Would you like a copy of our newsletter?
(A) I'm feeling better.
(B) That would be nice.
(C) In the newspaper.

你想要一份我們的公司報紙嗎？
(A) 我覺得好多了。
(B) 那太好了。
(C) 在報紙上。 |

解析　〈Would you like + 名詞〉是「你想要～嗎？」帶有好意的提議（offer）疑問句類型，回答可能是〈Yes, 表示感謝+ 補充內容〉形式，〈No（拒絕）＋拒絕理由〉等典型Yes/No疑問句的答案類型。

答案:(B)

🎧062

➡ 勸導/勸誘/提議句型與正確表達Check!

❶ 勸導/勸誘的問題和回答類型

Let's ~. / How about ~? / What about ~? / Why don't we ~? 我們～吧！/我們～好嗎？

Would you ~? / Could you ~? / Will you ~? / Why don't you ~?（你）要不要～？

→ Yes 型回答：Sure, of course. 當然好。　That's a good idea[solution]. 好主意。

→ No 型回答：I don't think that's possible. 我不認為這行得通。

我們去吃飯好嗎？ → Yes, + I know a good Korean restaurant. 好，我知道一家很棒的韓國餐廳。
　　　　　　　　　Sorry/No, + I need to finish this report by this afternoon.
　　　　　　　　　抱歉，我必須在下午前完成這份報告（我會忙到下午，不行）。

❷ 好意/提議的問題和回答類型

Would you like + 名詞 ~? / Do you want + 名詞 ~（你）想要～嗎？

Should I ~? / Do you want me to ~? / Would you like me to ~? / Could I ~? 需要我～嗎？

→ Yes型回答：That would be great. 那就太好了。　Thank you. / I appreciate it. 謝謝你。

→ No型回答：No thanks. 不了，謝謝。　I can manage. / I can handle it. 我可以處理。

還需要什麼嗎？ → Yes. I'd like some water, please. 是的，請給我一些水。
　　　　　　　　It's okay. Just the check, please. 不用了。麻煩結帳。

B 直述句 🎧063

這是Part 2題目中出題頻率最高的類型。不是詢問別人而類似自言自語的形式，一開始會讓人不知如何反應，但答案仍屬於Yes/No疑問句〈Yes + 肯定〉，〈No + 否定〉的典型句型。

例題2

Mark your answer on your answer sheet. (A)　　　(B)　　　(C)	I already saw that movie. (A) The theater's nearby. (B) What did you think of it? (C) Two tickets, please. 我已經看過那部電影。 (A) 電影院在附近。 **(B) 你覺得怎麼樣？** (C) 兩張票，謝謝。

解析 只要針對直述句說話者的行為或意見給予回應即可。當他說已經看過了電影，經常會使用what/when/where/how等疑問詞來反問，(A)、(C)都是根據movie詞彙聯想出theater, tickets的典型錯誤答案。

答案:(B)

🎧064

➲ 直述句的正確表達Check!

❶ 提出問題點時: 積極想要解決的回應

I can take care of it. 我可以處理。　　　　　I'll do it right away. 我立刻去辦。

I'll get it for you. 我幫你拿。　　　　　　　Let me see what I can do. 我來看看我能做些什麼。

❷ 有關好消息/壞消息: 與說話者產生共鳴的回應

That's good news. 那真是好消息。　　　　　That's good to know. 很高興聽到這個消息。

I'm sorry to hear that. 聽到這個消息我很難過。

You'll do better next time. 你下次會表現得更好。

❸ 有關具體事實: 正面態度的回應

I'll be there. 我會去的。　　　　　　　　　I'm looking forward to it. 我很期待。

聽說推出了新的飲料。 → When will it be on the market? 什麼時候上市？

What kind of flavors are they? 有哪些口味？

❹ 提出某項意見時: 同意 → Yes + 詳細內容/ 反對→ No + 理由，其他對策

So do I. 我也是。（肯定的同意）　　　　　　Neither have I. 我也沒有。（否定的同意）

這房間不錯。 → Yes, + it's big enough to accommodate everyone.

是的，夠大足以容納每一個人（大小合適）。

Actually (No), + Room 207 might be better.

其實/不，207號比較好（其他房間比較好）。

C 選擇疑問句

兩個選項中選出一種的選擇疑問句除了典型答案之外，也要熟悉其他各種回答方式，才能在高難度題目中順利拿分。從比較簡單的簡答型開始，到高難度的回答類型都要熟記。

例題3

Mark your answer on your answer sheet. (A)　　　(B)　　　(C)	Would you like to <u>eat inside</u> or <u>out on the patio</u>? (A) I set the table. (B) We ran out of them. (C) It doesn't matter to me. 你想在裡面吃或在露台上吃？ (A) 我擺好餐桌了。 (B) 我們用完了。 **(C) 對我來說無所謂。**

解析 這是餐廳的對話，對於在室內用餐或在戶外用餐的詢問，無所謂（都可以）是選擇疑問句的典型回答。(A)使用餐廳的聯想詞彙table，(B)適合做為提出某種要求的回答。　　　　　　　　　答案: (C)

🎧066

⤷ 選擇疑問句的正確表達Check!

❶ 回答類型 1: A or B 兩者擇一

詞彙重複出現的特別情況 → I prefer A. 我選擇A。 / I would like B. 我選擇B。

換成解釋的表達 → A: Do you prefer soup or salad?
　　　　　　　　　B: I prefer Soup[Salad]. → Something light. 清淡的食物。

❷ 回答類型 2: 任何一個都好(either) / 兩個都好(both)

Either will be fine. 都可以。　　　　　　　It doesn't matter. / I don't care. 無所謂。
I have no preference. 我沒有偏好。　　　　Whichever is cheaper. 以便宜的為準。
I use both. / I like both. 兩個我都用/都喜歡。 They are about the same. 都差不多。

❸ 回答類型 3: 都不要(neither) / 沒有其他選擇(plan C)嗎？

I want something else. 我想要別的。
Neither. / I don't like either one. 我不喜歡任何一個。
Do you have plan C? / How about plan C? 沒有其他選擇(plan C)嗎？

❹ 考試中經常出現的選項

now or later 現在或以後	today or tomorrow 今天或明天
Thursday or Friday 週四或週五	inside or outside 室內或室外
deliver or pick up 送貨或提貨	you or someone else 你或別人
call or e-mail 電話或電子郵件	original or revised one 原件或修訂本
continue or take a break 繼續或休息一下	here or somewhere else 這裡或別的地方

Step 2 聆聽和聽寫的訓練

Answers_P.015

📝 邊聽邊寫，完美掌握的聽寫技巧　　　　　　　　　　　　　🎧 067

※ 正確答案的類型十分多元化，需要熟悉題目中經常出現的各種答案。

Q: The printer is not working. （指出問題點的直述句）印表機沒反應。

A: ① Let me take a look at it. 我來看看。（提出對策）

　② We are getting a new one soon. 我們很快就會有一個新的。（提出對策）

　③ Does it need more ink? 是不是墨水不夠？（細節問題反問）

　④ You'll have to plug in the power cord. 你得插上電源線。（表示沒有問題）

PART
2

📝 填空時留意句子結構（助動詞＋主語＋主動詞），並試著邊寫邊唸。　　🎧 068

1.　Q: Do you want me to ＿＿＿＿＿ ＿＿＿＿＿, or ＿＿＿＿＿ you an ＿＿＿＿＿?

　　A: I ＿＿＿＿＿ ＿＿＿＿＿.

2.　Q: ＿＿＿＿＿ ＿＿＿＿＿ ＿＿＿＿＿ me the scissors, please?

　　A: Yes, ＿＿＿＿＿ they are.

3.　Q: The photocopier is ＿＿＿＿＿ ＿＿＿＿＿ ＿＿＿＿＿.

　　A: We should ＿＿＿＿＿ ＿＿＿＿＿ ＿＿＿＿＿ right away.

4.　Q: ＿＿＿＿＿ ＿＿＿＿＿ ＿＿＿＿＿ have a coffee break?

　　A: Sure, that's a ＿＿＿＿＿ ＿＿＿＿＿.

5.　Q: Should we order ＿＿＿＿＿ ＿＿＿＿＿, or ＿＿＿＿＿ ＿＿＿＿＿?

　　A: We need ＿＿＿＿＿.

6.　Q: ＿＿＿＿＿ ＿＿＿＿＿ ＿＿＿＿＿ it to the shareholders' meeting tomorrow?

　　A: ＿＿＿＿＿ ＿＿＿＿＿ I could.

7.　Q: We can ＿＿＿＿＿ ＿＿＿＿＿ ＿＿＿＿＿ after all.

　　A: That's very ＿＿＿＿＿ ＿＿＿＿＿.

57

Answers_P.016

📝 從基本開始到精確掌握的訓練

1. Mark your answer on your answer sheet. (A) (B)

2. Mark your answer on your answer sheet. (A) (B)

3. Mark your answer on your answer sheet. (A) (B)

4. Mark your answer on your answer sheet. (A) (B)

5. Mark your answer on your answer sheet. (A) (B)

Step 4　實戰練習　🎧 070

Answers_P.016

📝 利用刪去法選出Best Answer

1. Mark your answer on your answer sheet. (A) (B) (C)

2. Mark your answer on your answer sheet. (A) (B) (C)

3. Mark your answer on your answer sheet. (A) (B) (C)

4. Mark your answer on your answer sheet. (A) (B) (C)

5. Mark your answer on your answer sheet. (A) (B) (C)

6. Mark your answer on your answer sheet. (A) (B) (C)

7. Mark your answer on your answer sheet. (A) (B) (C)

8. Mark your answer on your answer sheet. (A) (B) (C)

9. Mark your answer on your answer sheet. (A) (B) (C)

10. Mark your answer on your answer sheet. (A) (B) (C)

1. 勸導/勸說/提議疑問句的答案類型→ 默背並在出現題目時做好答題準備！

對話當中各種形式的「不知道」無論在哪一類題目中都可能是正確答案。

① 肯定的回答

Sure. 當然。	Certainly. 的確。
No problem. 沒問題。	I'd be glad to. 我很樂意。
Why not? 有何不可？ / 當然。	That would be nice. 那太好了。
That sounds like a good plan. 這聽起來是個好計畫。	That sounds great. 聽起來很不錯。

② 拒絕的回答

I wish I could. 但願我可以。	Thanks, but ~. 謝謝，可是～。
I'm afraid I can't. 我恐怕不行。	It hasn't been confirmed. 還沒有得到證實。
They're still discussing. 他們還在討論。	It depends on. 這取決於～/視情況而定。

2. 直述句的回答類型→ 注意贊成或反對的表達方式！

直述句中關於對方的意見表示同意或反對經常是正確答案，反對的情況時，間接表示比直接表達更常出現，需要特別留意。

🎧 072

① 同意的回答

Right. 對。	That's a good idea. 那是個好主意。
Exactly. 一點也沒錯。	I think so. 我也這麼想。
That's what I think. 我就是這麼想的。	

② 反對的回答

This one is better. 這個比較好。	Do you really think so? 你真的這麼認為嗎？
I'm afraid I can't. 我恐怕不行。	I noticed few problems. 我注意到幾個問題。
We should check it again. 我們應該再檢查一下。	

PART 3

聽完2～3人所進行的簡短對話，從題目卷上列出的3個選項中選擇最適合的答案。

題目數	難易度
共39題 （32至70題）	中上

滿分訣竅

將紙本出現的題型和音訊檔聽到的提示正確組合的訓練。

❶ 掌握各種題型(GQ/SQ)並且快速閱讀的訓練。⋯▶ 閱讀理解訓練
❷ 熟悉耳朵聽到的對話句型結構和發音。⋯▶ 聽力訓練
❸ 讀完3種問題之後，聆聽音檔的同時開始答題。⋯▶ 組合訓練

學習方法

❶ **準備** 掌握Part 3題型的理解方法和各種問題類型/主題句型。
❷ **實戰** 將題目加以分級，訓練解開大多數的題目。
❸ **複習** 答錯的題目透過音檔 (1) 練習重新解題 (2) 進行聽力練習，重複聆聽比較不懂的部分。區分因失誤答錯的題目和答不出來的題目。

教材結構

Unit 8	問題類型 I	General Question/Specific Question ▶ 確實理解並正確作答
Unit 9	問題類型 II	集中分析新類型 ▶ 精準掌握令人混淆的新多益題型
Unit 10	主題 I	日常生活相關主題 ▶ 懂多少聽多少！
Unit 11	主題 II	職場生涯相關主題 ▶ 完成多益高難度主題

32. Why is the woman calling?

(A) To report a defective product
(B) To inquire about an order
(C) To request a custom design
(D) To make a payment

33. Where does the man work?

34. What most likely will the man do next?

32. 女子為什麼打電話？
(B) 為了詢問訂單

33. 男子在哪裡工作？

34. 男子最有可能接下來做什麼？

W Hello. This is Emily Wilson from BNB Enterprises. I'm calling to let you know that I've received a box of office supplies from your company that I didn't order.

M Hi, Miss Wilson. Let me check that for you. Okay, I've found BNB in the database and it looks like you clicked yes on the recurring order button when you placed your order online last month. That means you want the same office supplies to be delivered to you every month.

女 你好。我是BNB企業的艾米麗·威爾遜。我打電話是想告訴你，我從貴公司收到了一箱我沒有訂購的辦公用品。

男 妳好，艾米麗。我幫妳查一下。好的，我在數據庫中找到了BNB公司，看起來您上個月在網上下單時，在「重複訂購」按鈕上點擊了「是」。這代表您希望每個月都能收到同樣的辦公用品。

解析 讀完題目之後，掌握詢問主題的General Question。女子(the woman)的問題極有可能出現在最前面的部分，聆聽音檔的同時，瀏覽一遍各個選項，選出可能性最高的答案。選項(A)的瑕疵(defective)物品在聽力中並沒有提到，也沒有(C)的客製化設計 (custom design)，更沒有談到(D)的金錢部分。這類題目尤其需要練習將主題/目的相關的題目Paraphrasing（重新詮釋）。

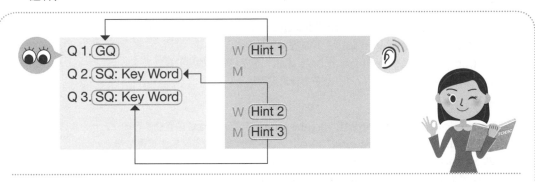

❶ 先讀完3個選項之後，在每個選項上標出Key Word，記住問題。

❷ 將問題記在腦中，眼睛看著選項，耳朵聆聽對話，從可能性最高的選項依序選擇並排列。

❸ 帶著音檔結束時，3個選項也全數瀏覽完畢的決心，配合速度解題。

❹ 答案：32 (B)

Unit 8　問題類型 I

 Step 1　類型分析

A **General Question** 綜合問題（主題/目的、地點/職業）　🎧 074

主要有三個題目，首先出現第一個題目以詢問對話的主題/目的，以及說話者的職業或談話地點。通常提示也出現在最前面的內容，訓練自己聽完第一個句子之後選擇正確答案。

例題1

(Where) most likely are (the speakers)? (A) At a conference hall (B) At an airport (C) At a luggage store (D) At a clothing store	W Hi. Can you help me? <u>My suitcase was broken</u> when I was leaving the airport yesterday, <u>so I need to buy a new one.</u> M You came to the right store. What kind of luggage are you replacing? A small carry-on, or something larger?

解析 **女** 你好，你能幫我嗎？我昨天離開機場時行李箱壞了，所以我需要買一個新的。
　　 男 妳來對商店了。妳想換什麼樣的行李箱？一個小的登機箱，還是更大一點的？
　　 Q 說話者最有可能在哪裡？
　　　(A)會議室 (B)機場 **(C)行李商店** (D)服飾店

解析 這種題型是聽完對話內容，推測談話的所在地點。最前面提到「行李箱壞了，所以需要買一個新的」的地點是商店(store)。雖然出現機場(airport)的單字，但並不是談話的所在地，並非單純憑藉聽得懂的詞彙來選擇地點，而是聽完對話之後，思考地點的可能性，再選擇答案。
答案: (C)

🎧 075

⊃ General Question 題型的正確表達Check!

❶ 詢問主題/目的的題型

What are the speakers mainly discussing? 說話者主要討論的是什麼？
What are they talking about? 他們在談論什麼？
What is the purpose of the man's call? 男子打電話的目的是什麼？
Why is the woman calling? 女子為什麼打電話？

❷ 詢問地點/職業的題型

Where does this conversation take place? 這段對話是在哪裡進行的？
Where do the speakers most likely work? 說話者最有可能在哪裡工作？
Who probably is the man? 男子可能是誰？
Who is the man talking to? 男子和誰說話？

❸ GQ重新詮釋(Paraphrasing)

How much is it? 那多少錢？ ➡ Asking for the price information 詢問價格資訊
Do you have seats for the flight to New York? 有飛往紐約的航班座位嗎？
➡ Reserving a ticket 預訂機票
Do you have enough ingredients for the chicken special? 你有足夠的配料製作特製雞肉嗎？
➡ Availability of a dinner special 晚餐特色菜的可能性

B Specific Question **女子/男子，過去/未來的時間點** 🎧076

出題機率高，一組題目中有2個以上的題目。常見的是詢問文章中具體的(Specific)部分內容，需要確認作為Key Word的女子/男子的動作、特徵、時間點、地點、方法等，掌握對話裡的Key Word就能選對答案。只要集中在具體內容就能解題，對初試者來說是有利得分的題型，必須加強練習。

例題2

When did the woman place the order? (A) In May (B) In June (C) In July (D) In August	W Hi. I ordered 20 sets of bracelets on May 15th and they didn't arrive until the end of June. This is unacceptable. M I'm sorry. We usually have a lot more orders in June and July because of the summer season. Let me check your records first.

解析 **女** 你好。我在5月15日訂了20套手鐲，直到6月底才到。這是無法接受的。
　　　男 很抱歉。由於夏季的關係，我們通常在6月和7月有更多的訂單。讓我先檢查一下您的記錄。
　　　Q 女子什麼時候訂購的？
　　　(A) 5月 (B) 6月 (C) 7月 (D) 8月

解析 即使出現好幾個時間點，必須正確聽出女子(the woman)過去(did)訂購(order)的時間點。記下問題，找出關聯部分的Specific Question，就能在聽到選項的瞬間知道哪一個是正確答案。謹記答案並非談話中最容易聽懂的部分，而是題目所要的答案。　　　　　　　答案: (A)

🎧077

➡ Specific Question 題型的正確表達Check!

❶ 指出女子/男子的題型

What does the man suggest the woman do? 男子建議女子做什麼？
What does the woman offer to do? 這位女子提供什麼服務？
What does the man mention about the company? 男子提到公司的什麼事？
Why does the woman say, "It'll be ready soon"? 為什麼女子說「很快就會準備好」？

❷ 指出具體時間點/地點/方法的題型

What did the woman do last month? 女子上個月做了什麼？
Where did the man just return from? 男子剛從哪裡回來？
What will the woman probably do next? 女子下一步可能會做什麼？
How will the man get to the conference? 男子要如何去參加會議？

❸ 出現過去/現在/未來式時態的詞彙

過去：just 剛, 不久前　　recently 最近　　already 已經 previously 先前　　last time 上次
　　　originally 原本　　used to 過去經常～　　was(were) supposed to 本來應該～
現在：currently 目前　　now 現在, 如今　　for now 目前, 暫時　　regularly 定期地
未來：will／be going to 將～　　next／now／first 下次/現在/第一次　　next month 下個月

快速讀完Part 3的3組題目，掌握GQ/SQ，並快速將重要的Key Word圈選起來。尤其要確認SQ的性別、主要動詞和時間點！

例題	
What are the speakers discussing?	GQ
What does the man plan to do?	SQ
What does the woman she will send?	SQ

1.　1) Where does the man most likely work?　_____

　　2) What does the woman want to do?　_____

　　3) What does the woman make a suggestion about?　_____

2.　1) What are the speakers discussing?　_____

　　2) According to the woman, what did the feedback show?　_____

　　3) What will happen in September?　_____

3.　1) What kind of business do the speakers work for?　_____

　　2) What did the woman forget to bring?　_____

　　3) According to the man, why is the event important?　_____

4.　1) Where does the conversation most likely take place?　_____

　　2) What does the woman say the men will do this week?　_____

　　3) What does the woman ask Fernando?　_____

5.　1) What did the man recently do?　_____

　　2) What is the man looking forward to?　_____

　　3) Why does the man say, "There's a class tomorrow night"?　_____

第1階段 先閱讀題目之後，一邊聆聽一邊解題。
第2階段 重聽一次，試著填寫空格。
第3階段 邊聽MP3，跟著逐句唸出來。

1. Where is the conversation taking place?
   (A) At a museum   (B) At a theater

   > M　Hi, I'd like a ticket to the ＿＿＿＿＿＿＿'s special Egyptian ＿＿＿＿＿＿＿
   > ＿＿＿＿＿＿＿. I've heard wonderful things about it.
   >
   > W　I'm sorry, but the exhibit is very popular and we've already sold out of tickets for
   > the morning. We still have some available for this afternoon, though.

2. Who probably is the woman?
   (A) A photo journalist   (B) A store clerk

   > M　Hi, I am calling because I ＿＿＿＿＿＿＿ a camera from ＿＿＿＿＿＿＿
   > ＿＿＿＿＿＿＿ a few days ago and there is a problem with some buttons.
   > They don't work well.
   >
   > W　Well, if you bring your camera back to the store, we'll be glad to look it over for
   > you.

3. Why is the man unable to meet today?
   (A) He's visiting a client.   (B) He's leading a training session.

   > W　I have a presentation to one of my clients tomorrow. How about meeting today
   > instead of tomorrow?
   >
   > M　Oh, I'm sorry. I'll be ＿＿＿＿＿＿＿ a ＿＿＿＿＿＿＿ ＿＿＿＿＿＿＿ most
   > of the day. I'm teaching new staff the new accounting software.

4. What does the woman offer to do?
   (A) Provide directions   (B) Change the meeting time

   > M　My appointment is in 5 minutes, and I probably won't be able to make it on time.
   >
   > W　Oh, don't worry. The meeting place is less than a 5-minute walk from here.
   > ＿＿＿＿＿ ＿＿＿＿＿＿ ＿＿＿＿＿＿＿ ＿＿＿＿＿＿＿ ＿＿＿＿＿
   > tell you how to get there?

PART
3

4-1 General Question 集中 Practice 080

1. Where most likely does the man work?
   (A) At a hotel
   (B) At a hair salon
   (C) At a dry-cleaning business
   (D) At a home improvement store

4. What is the conversation mainly about?
   (A) Organizing a training session
   (B) Preparing for a business exposition
   (C) Finding a guest speaker for a convention
   (D) Creating an employee handbook

2. What are the speakers talking about?
   (A) A refund
   (B) A store
   (C) A sale
   (D) A repair

5. What industry do the speakers most likely work in?
   (A) Food production
   (B) Machinery sales
   (C) Event planning
   (D) Textile manufacturing

3. Who most likely is the woman?
   (A) An author
   (B) An account
   (C) A librarian
   (D) A bank clerk

6. What are the speakers discussing?
   (A) A billing error
   (B) A missing document
   (C) An incomplete shipment
   (D) A damaged product

PART

3

1. What does the woman ask the man to do?
   (A) Revise a plan
   (B) Copy an invoice
   (C) Request a refund
   (D) Change a delivery date

2. What does the man suggest?
   (A) Call the maintenance department
   (B) Replacing a machine
   (C) Getting a discount
   (D) Visiting a nearby store

3. What does the woman offer to do for the man?
   (A) Add his name to a list
   (B) Give him an estimate
   (C) Waive a fee
   (D) Send a bill in the mail

4. When is the department heads' meeting?
   (A) Today
   (B) Tomorrow
   (C) In two days
   (D) next Monday

5. What does the woman say she will do at noon?
   (A) Bring an item for repair
   (B) Attend a training session
   (C) Meet with a friend
   (D) Go home for lunch

Coupon		
Buy ··············		Save
1 gallon	····	10%
2 gallons	····	15%
3 gallons	····	20%
4 gallons	····	30%
Valid in-store-only 5/20 ~ 5/26		

6. Look at the graphic. Which discount will the woman receive?
   (A) 10%
   (B) 15%
   (C) 20%
   (D) 30%

※ 利用刪去法選出 Best Answer

1. Why is the man leaving the office?
   (A) To buy some supplies
   (B) To eat lunch
   (C) To give a lecture
   (D) To go to an appointment

2. What does the woman agree to do?
   (A) Send an e-mail
   (B) Pass on a message
   (C) Find a document
   (D) Work on the weekend

3. What time will the man meet his client?
   (A) At 2 p.m.
   (B) At 3 p.m.
   (C) At 4 p.m.
   (D) At 5 p.m.

4. Where does the woman most likely work?
   (A) At a hotel
   (B) At an architectural firm
   (C) At a movie theater
   (D) At a restaurant

5. What is causing the problem?
   (A) Malfunctioning equipment
   (B) An incorrect bill
   (C) Noise from construction work
   (D) A shortage of trained staff

6. What will the woman probably do next?
   (A) Speak to her manager
   (B) Call the construction company
   (C) Offer a reduced price
   (D) Check for an available room

7. Why did the man call the woman?
   (A) To ask for directions
   (B) To order some cake
   (C) To reject an offer
   (D) To say he will be late

8. What does the woman recommend?
   (A) Revise the event schedule
   (B) Taking public transportation
   (C) Arranging for a delivery
   (D) Requesting a refund

9. What does the man say he will do?
   (A) Confirm the business hours
   (B) Ask a coworker to help
   (C) Submit the registration form
   (D) Pay for the purchase

10. What type of event are the speakers discussing?
    (A) A company party
    (B) A business conference
    (C) A birthday party
    (D) A music festival

11. What does the woman ask the man to do?
    (A) Reserve a banquet hall
    (B) Hire some new staff
    (C) Transport some equipment
    (D) Perform with a band

12. What does the man say he has to do on Saturday afternoon?
    (A) Speak at a conference
    (B) Work an additional shift
    (C) Meet with supervisors
    (D) Attend a sporting event

13. Who most likely is the man?

    (A) A restaurant chef

    (B) An architect

    (C) A financial advisor

    (D) A real estate agent

14. What is the woman considering doing?

    (A) Moving into a new location

    (B) Expanding her business

    (C) Opening a bank account

    (D) Constructing a new house

15. What does the woman ask the man to do?

    (A) Prepare a report

    (B) Pay for the consultation

    (C) Create a design

    (D) Sign a contract

16. Why is the woman calling the man?

    (A) To report an equipment problem

    (B) To confirm a schedule

    (C) To ask about the product price

    (D) To request personal information

17. What does the woman mean when she says, "I'm interviewing someone here in five minutes"?

    (A) She needs the man's help immediately.

    (B) She does not want to be disturbed.

    (C) She is late for the meeting.

    (D) She needs more people to help her.

18. What does the woman say is unusual about the interview?

    (A) It will be recorded.

    (B) It will be held on a weekend.

    (C) I will be conducted face-to-face.

    (D) It will last for five hours.

Unit 9　問題類型II

 Step 1　類型分析

A　各種對話類型（3人對話，2人對話）　🎧083

Part 3的題型大部分是男女輪流對話，總共進行4次。而新式題型則是3人對話（2女、1男/1女、2男）的形態。 3人談話和2人談話總共可進行7~9次，隨著次數增加，句子也愈長，重點不是談話而是「題目」，GQ出現在第一句，SQ出現在Key Word前後句。

例題1

What does the woman ask Bob to do?

(A) Set up a conference call with clients
(B) Review a budget proposal
(C) Share information at a meeting
(D) Contact another department

M1　We need to do something to increase our sales of the new sports footwear.
W　The results from the market research are pretty promising. <u>Bob, would you be willing to present the data at the next sales strategy meeting?</u>
M2　Sure, I could do that.

解析　**男1** 我們需要做些什麼來增加新運動鞋的銷售量。
　　　女 市場調查的結果是很有希望的。鮑勃，你願意在下一次銷售策略會議上介紹這些數據嗎？
　　　男2 當然，我可以。
　　　Q 女子要求鮑勃做什麼？
　　　(A) 與客戶建立電話會議　(B) 審核預算提案　**(C) 在會議上分享資訊**　(D) 連繫其他部門

解析　即使有3人談話，也要先確認題目，等聽到女子(the woman)對Bob提出要求(ask Bob to do)的部分時，從中聽出對Bob提到的具體內容。對話中的data(數據) 被重新詮釋成為選項中的information(資訊)，information代表獲得各方資訊的詞彙，必須記熟。　　答案: (C)

🎧084

➡ 3人談話的題型Check!

❶ 題目出現複數的性別/姓名

What are the men asked to do? 男子們被要求做什麼？
➡ 聽清楚男子被要求的事情，以及女子是否提出要求或指示。

What are Abram and Rebecca concerned about? 亞伯蘭和麗貝卡擔心的是什麼？
➡ 提到2人擔心的部分，代表3人中有2人面臨同樣的處境。最後2人一起行動/決定的可能性很高。從這些人當中只要聽到其中1人擔心的內容，就可以準備答題。

❷ 從音檔最起初的部分得知有3人談話

2人談話：Questions 32~34 refer to the following conversation.
3人談話：Questions 32~34 refer to the following conversation <u>with three speakers</u>.

❸ 然而最重要的部分仍然是GQ/SQ。

解開客觀的問題題型時，最重要的是在解題時保持專注力。與其理解所有內容，更應該專注在每個題型和敘述，以求得正確答案。

70

B 有關表格/時間資料的題目

Part 3題目的後半部會出現2～3種有關表格/時間資料的題型，為了掌握題目內容，必須瀏覽一遍圖表。對初試者來說，比起冗長又難以了解的閱讀理解題型，這種題目更容易一目瞭然抓到重點，反而有利。首先分析表格之後，根據音檔的內容來解題。

例題2

Schedule	
Dance	Time
Jazz Dance	2 P.M.
Latin Dance	3 P.M.
Hip-hop	4 P.M.
Ballet	5 P.M.

Look at the graphic. What class does the man want to attend?

(A) Jazz　　　　(B) Latin
(C) Hip-hop　　(D) Ballet

W Welcome to Passion Dance Studio. Can I help you?

M Yes, I'm here for Judy's dance class at four o'clock. Is there a locker room so that I can leave my bags and personal belongings?

W Sure, you can check in with your ID and get your locker keys.

(解析) 女 歡迎來到熱情舞蹈工作室。我可以幫您什麼嗎？
男 好的，我是來參加4點茉蒂的舞蹈課的。請問有更衣室可以讓我放包包和個人物品嗎？
女 當然，您可以提供您的身份證辦理登記並領取儲物櫃鑰匙。
Q 請看這張表格，男子要上什麼課？
(A) 爵士舞 (B) 拉丁舞 **(C) 流行舞** (D) 芭蕾舞

(解析) 和往常一樣先讀完題目，男子所參加的課程透過音訊檔和表格來確認。最後(1)先記下題目,(2)從表格中選擇有關的資訊,(3)再次從選項中選擇答案，按照這樣的步驟進行，相對來說更容易選出正確答案。　　　　　　　　　　　　　　　　　　　答案: (C)

➡ 表格/時間資料的題型 Check!

❶ 表格/目錄形式（價格/型號/日程等）

Oak Street Building Directory

Office	Location
Green Construction	Suite 103
PST Systems	Suite 105
Law office of Joseph	Suite 212
Kim Dental Clinic	Suite 202

❷ 各種圖表形式（圓餅圖/矩形圖等）

Votes for New Cafeteria Food

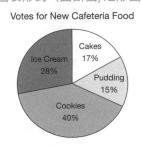

❸ 地圖/路線圖（配置圖/平面圖）

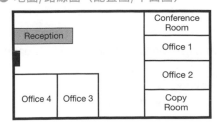

❹ 折價券/廣告單（票券/折扣券/收據等）

C 詢問說話者意圖的題型

找出引號中的句子在前後文的意義，這種找出說話者意圖的題目和選項敘述最長，只憑談話的一部分內容來選擇答案，屬於閱讀理解型/推論題型。每屆考試的出題頻率約2~3題，必須快速瀏覽完文章之後，一邊解析一邊掌握整體的內容，雖然棘手但可以試著多練習。

例題3

What does the woman mean when she says, "I really can't say"?

(A) She is not allowed to reveal some facts.
(B) She cannot make a commitment yet.
(C) She needs to wait at the office.
(D) She should correct some errors first.

M Would you like to consider joining our team for our new contract with Ocean Booking? They're looking for an advertising agency.

W It sounds exciting. But I really can't say. I still have to finish some works for McNeal Corporation. I can ask my manager, though.

(解析) **男** 您願意考慮加入我們的團隊以獲得與海洋預定公司簽訂的新合同？他們正在尋找一家廣告代理人。

女 聽起來令人興奮。但我沒辦法說。我仍要為麥克尼爾公司完成一些工作。不過，我可以問問我的主管。

Q 女子說「我沒辦法說」是什麼意思？
(A) 她不被允許透露一些事實。 **(B) 她還不能做出承諾。**
(C) 她需要在辦公室等待。 (D) 她得先改正一些錯誤。

(解析) 面對同一個團隊中為了新顧客而尋找幫手的男子提議，女子「我沒辦法說」指的是手上還有其他工作尚未完成，要理解成拒絕的意思。這種題型是一旦掌握關鍵句子，就能輕鬆解題，因此需要反覆不斷練習。

答案: (B)

● 詢問說話者意圖的題型Check!

❶ 詢問說話者意圖的題型

Why does the woman say, "I've met with Jeannie Kang before"?
為什麼女子說：「我以前見過珍妮・康？」
➡ To reassure the man 為了使男子安心

[男子不知道珍妮・康是怎樣的人，女子說自己見過，要他不需擔心的意思。]

What does the woman imply when she says, "I don't know"?
女子說：「我不知道」時暗示些什麼？
➡ She cannot fulfill the man's request. 她不能履行男子的要求。

[對於男子提出增加休假時間的要求，女子回答「我不清楚。」，間接表達拒絕的意思。]

❷ 詢問說話者前後文意思的題型

What does the man mean when he says, "I only get paid once a month"?
男子說：「我一個月只領一次工資。」的意思是什麼？
➡ He doesn't have money for a purchase. 他沒有錢買東西。

[女子炫耀自己買的東西，男子表示自己只領一次薪水，意思是買不起那樣的東西。]

What does the man imply when he says, "I have to finish the layout for tomorrow's paper"?
男子說：「我必須為明天的報紙完成排版。」暗示了什麼？
➡ He is concerned about a deadline. 他擔心截止期限。

[說出對方要做的事情，同時表示自己必須做完的具體工作，要求加快進度。]

第1階段 先閱讀題目之後，一邊聆聽一邊解題。

第2階段 重聽一次，試著填寫空格。

第3階段 邊聽MP3，跟著逐句唸出來。

1. Who most likely are Samantha and Nathan?

(A) Apartment managers (B) Potential home buyers

> M1 Welcome, Samantha and Nathan. I'm glad you decided to come take a
> _____ _____ the _____.
>
> W We really liked the _____, but we have some concerns.
>
> M2 We're worried about the cost of major renovation like the roof of the house.

2. What does Frank advise the woman to do?

(A) Send a confirmation letter (B) Come to the Beijing Branch

> M1 Frank, is there anything else Jennie needs to know?
>
> M2 Just one more thing; _____ _____ _____ _____
> e-mails to clients confirming anything you discuss over the phone. They want all
> communication to be in writing.
>
> W Got it, Frank. Thanks. I'm sure you'll do well at the Beijing Branch, too.

3. What does the woman mean when she says, "two hours wasn't enough"?

(A) She really enjoyed the performance. (B) She was late for the show.

> M I heard you went to the new musical at the Circle Theater. It was for two hours,
> right?
>
> W Yes, but two hours wasn't enough. I think I'm _____ _____ next
> weekend. Would you like to come with me?

4. Why does the man say, "That's a big increase from last year"?

(A) To deny a requested budget change (B) To indicate that some news is good

> W The company director _____ _____ marketing department's
> _____ by $300,000.
>
> M That's a big increase from last year. Do you know how that money will be used?
> We could definitely use some new office equipment.

3-1 時間資料題目的集中 Practice

Length of Contract	Price per Month
3 months	$50
6 months	$40
1 year	$30
2 years	$20

1. Look at the graphic. How much has the woman agreed to pay per month?
   (A) $50
   (B) $40
   (C) $30
   (D) $20

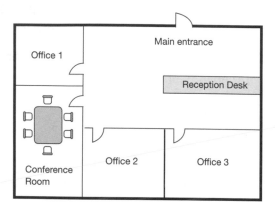

3. Look at the graphic. Which room will the man most likely go to?
   (A) Office 1
   (B) Office 2
   (C) Office 3
   (D) Conference room

How Do We Find Employees?

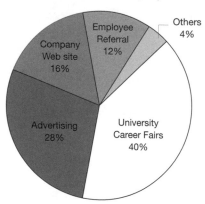

2. Look at the graphic. Which method does the man suggest using?
   (A) University career fairs
   (B) Advertising
   (C) Company Web site
   (D) Employee referrals

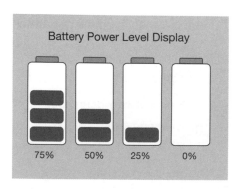

4. Look at the graphic. According to the woman, how many bars will be displayed when the battery should be replaced?
   (A) Three bars
   (B) Two bars
   (C) One bar
   (D) Zero bars

1. Why does the woman say, "These shoes look great"?
   (A) To convince her friend to buy shoes
   (B) To show interest in making a purchase
   (C) To compliment her coworker
   (D) To ask for gift wrapping

3. What does the man imply when he says, "but that was quite a while ago"?
   (A) A deadline is approaching.
   (B) New staff must be trained.
   (C) A procedure has been improved.
   (D) A decision should be reconsidered.

PART
3

2. Why does the man say, "I'm waiting for the department budget proposal"?
   (A) To request a document from the woman
   (B) To ask for a deadline extension
   (C) To inform the woman about a scheduling change
   (D) To explain why he cannot make a decision at the moment

4. What does the woman imply when she says, "That would require significant revisions to our pricing strategy"?
   (A) She doubts a change will be implemented.
   (B) She thinks the suppliers should be replaced.
   (C) She believes some data are incorrect.
   (D) She needs more time to make a decision.

※ 利用刪去法選出 Best Answer

1. Why does the woman want to save money?
   (A) To take classes
   (B) To purchase a car
   (C) To start her business.
   (D) To move into a new apartment

2. What does the man recommend?
   (A) Applying for a loan
   (B) Talking to a financial planner
   (C) Using an online program.
   (D) Working extra hours

3. What is the woman concerned about?
   (A) The quality of a program
   (B) The cost of a program
   (C) The security of a Web site
   (D) The terms of a contract

4. Who most likely is the woman?
   (A) A telephone operator
   (B) A post office clerk
   (C) An office receptionist
   (D) A sales representative

5. Why is the man visiting the office?
   (A) To attend a meeting
   (B) To apply for a job
   (C) To repair some equipment
   (D) To make a delivery

6. What does the woman imply when she says, "Ms. Dunmore is in a meeting with clients right now"?
   (A) Ms. Dunmore has an important document.
   (B) Ms. Dunmore is not available.
   (C) A meeting room cannot be used.
   (D) The meeting is taking longer than usual.

7. Where do the interviewers most likely work?
   (A) At a factory
   (B) At an electronics store
   (C) At a TV station
   (D) At a movie theater

8. What requirement do the speakers discuss?
   (A) Wearing safety gear
   (B) Owning proper equipment
   (C) Having management experience
   (D) Having a flexible schedule

9. What does the man agree to do next?
   (A) Show a video
   (B) Provide references
   (C) Tour a facility
   (D) Sign an employment contract

10. What are the speakers mainly talking about?
    (A) Presenting at a conference
    (B) Creating product brochures
    (C) Updating a company Web site
    (D) Ordering some stationery

11. What problem does the woman notice?
    (A) A deadline has been missed.
    (B) An identification badge is not working.
    (C) A phone number is missing.
    (D) A name is spelled incorrectly.

12. Why does the woman say, "It's easy to miss"?
    (A) To express her understanding
    (B) To clarify the job description
    (C) To explain a procedure
    (D) To warn about the delay

Tea Type	Time in Hot Water
Green	2 minutes
Peppermint	3 minutes
Black	4 minutes
Herbal	6 minutes

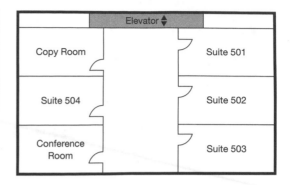

13. Why does the man want to try a new tea?

(A) It has better flavor.

(B) It is getting popular these days.

(C) It is the only kind sold in this store.

(D) It has health benefits.

14. What will the man receive with his purchase?

(A) An extra tea sample

(B) A free tea pot

(C) A gift certificate

(D) A parking validation

15. Look at the graphic. How long should the man leave the tea in hot water?

(A) 2 minutes

(B) 3 minutes

(C) 4 minutes

(D) 6 minutes

16. What does the man ask the woman to do?

(A) Use a different entrance

(B) Wear an ID badge

(C) Turn off her cell phone

(D) Come back at a later time

17. What does the woman request?

(A) A signature for a delivery

(B) A different appointment time

(C) Directions to an office

(D) Advice about parking

18. Look at the graphic. Which office does the woman need to visit?

(A) Suite 501

(B) Suite 502

(C) Suite 503

(D) Suite 504

Unit 10　主題 I 日常生活

 Step 1　類型分析

A 購物/大眾交通/便利設施的使用 🎧092

Part 3最重要的部分是正確分析題目並選擇答案。但當集中在分析題目,而聆聽短文的專注能力下降的話,也無法正確作答。熟記Unit 10, 11中各種主題經常出現的描述方式,並對各式題型多加練習吧。

例題1

What kind of business is the man calling?	M Hi, this is David Kim. I was a patient at your medical clinic but I recently moved. I requested that my records be sent to my new doctor here, but he hasn't received them yet.
(A) A post office (B) A doctor's office (C) A copy center (D) A delivery service	W Mr. Kim, yes. I see the request in your file, but because it's not signed, we haven't been able to transfer your records.

解析 男 你好,我是大衛·金。我是你們診所的病人,但我最近搬家了。我要求把我的病歷寄給我的新醫生,但是他還沒有收到。

女 好的,金先生。我在你的檔案裡看到了請求,但因為沒有簽名,我們還沒能轉移你的記錄。

Q 男子致電到什麼單位?
(A)郵局 **(B)醫生辦公室** (C)影印店 (D)送貨服務

解析 詢問男子致電到什麼機構的General Question,提示在前面的部分,由於第一句出現patient(病患),medical clinic(醫療診所)的單字,可以得知男子打電話到醫院,也能夠推測出女子是接待員(receptionist)。熟記考試中經常出現的狀況/描述,就能專注於各式題型並且選出正確答案。　　答案:(B)

🎧093

➡ 經常出現的日常生活相關詞彙 1 Check!

❶ 商店/購物

buy/purchase 購買	cash 現金	credit card 信用卡	ship/deliver 運送	carry 運輸
stock/inventory 庫存	receipt 收據	exchange 換貨	refund 退款	return 退貨
cash register 收銀台	survey 調查	cashier 收銀員	free/complimentary 免費	

❷ 餐廳

patio/outside 露臺/室外	recipe 食譜	chef/cook 廚師	ingredient 材料	diner 用餐者
server/waiter 服務生	caterer 宴會承辦人	today's special/lunch special 今日特餐/商業午餐		

❸ 醫院

pharmacist 藥師	prescribe medicine 開藥	regular checkup 定期檢查

❹ 銀行/金融機構

teller 銀行職員	deposit 存款	withdraw 提款	open an account 開戶

B 旅行/休閒生活 🎧094

為了掌握多益的題型，必須了解一般大眾的日常生活。除了購物/大眾交通/便利設施之外，也需要加入特別的旅行、有興趣的運動或看電影等背景知識一起練習。試著多進行結合背景知識並快速瀏覽題目的訓練吧。

例題2

What did the man hear on the news?

(A) A new café will be opening soon.

(B) A job is available at the news station.

(C) A business is under new management.

(D) A concert will be held at the theater.

M Charlotte, did you hear tonight's news report? There's going to be a special concert at Lehmann Theater to raise money for renovations.

W Yes, I heard about that. In fact, I'm volunteering to help out during the concert. I'm going to sell refreshments.

解析 **男** 夏洛特，妳聽到今晚的新聞報導了嗎？萊曼劇院將有一場特別的音樂會，為整修籌集資金。
女 是的，我聽說了。事實上，我自願在音樂會上幫忙。我打算賣點心。
Q 男子在新聞中聽到了什麼？
(A) 一家新咖啡館即將開業。　　(B) 新聞台有一份新工作。
(C) 一項業務由新的經營團隊管理。　　**(D) 音樂會即將在劇院舉行。**

解析 男子聽到的內容很可能就是他要描述的話。因此聽到男子第一句話說即將有一場特別的音樂會時，就要知道直接選擇正確選項。　　答案：(D)

🎧095

➲ 經常出現的日常生活相關詞彙 2 Check!

❶ 旅行相關(飯店/航空公司)

travel agency 旅行社	airline 航空公司	itinerary 旅程	postpone/delay 延後
destination 目的地	stopover 中停/過境	sightseeing 觀光	departure/arrival 出發/抵達
flight attendant 空服員	reserve/book 預訂	aisle seat 靠走道座位	window seat 靠窗座位
single 單人房	double 雙人房	suite 套房	accommodation 住房

❷ 電影院/博物館

theater 劇院	cinema 電影院	performance 表演	play 戲劇
show/showing 演出	sculpture 雕塑	box office 售票處	museum 博物館
exhibit 展示	wing 側廳	art 藝術品	craft 工藝品
potter 陶藝家	permanent exhibit 永久展覽		

❸ 慈善活動

charity event 慈善活動	benefit 有益於, 好處	proceeds 收入	public facility 公共設施
volunteer 志願者	help/aid 幫忙	support 支援	local resident 當地居民
community 社區	contribution/donation 捐獻/捐款	local business owner 本地企業主	

❹ 房地產

real estate 房地產	apartment 公寓	rent 租賃/租金	lease 租約
utility 公共設施	landlord 房東	tenant 承租人	manager 管理人
neighborhood 街坊/鄰里	spacious 寬敞的	furnished 配有家具的	

第1階段　先閱讀題目之後，一邊聆聽MP3一邊解題。
第2階段　重聽一次，試著填寫空格。
第3階段　邊聽MP3，跟著逐句唸出來。

1. Who most likely is the man?

(A) An auto mechanic　　　　　　　(B) A computer technician

> W　Hi, I'm calling to get some _____ _____ my _____. If I use it for more than an hour, the body of the machine gets really hot.
>
> M　Hmm.. sounds like you have a problem with your battery. Is it plugged in all the time?

2. What are the speakers discussing?

(A) A doctor's prescription　　　　　(B) A product price

> W　Hi, my doctor _____ a _____ for some medicine to _____ _____ about an hour ago, and I was hoping the order might be ready for me to pick up.
>
> M　I'll just check on that for you. Can I have your name please?

3. According to the man, what service is available?

(A) Free installation　　　　　　　(B) Home delivery

> W　I'd like to _____ these pots and pans, but I came here by bus so I won't be able to carry them home.
>
> M　That's no problem. _____ _____ _____ them to your house free of charge if you want.

4. What does the woman want to do?

(A) Return to the warehouse　　　　(B) Exchange of a product

> M　There's a setting that allows you to save power. That way, your battery can last longer.
>
> W　Yes, I know the power saving setting. But it still isn't long enough. I'd like to _____ this phone, and _____ a _____ _____ with a longer battery hour.

📝 從基本開始到精確掌握的訓練

1. What is the conversation mainly about?
   (A) A defective product
   (B) An expired warranty

2. What does the man ask the woman to give?
   (A) A manual
   (B) A sales receipt

3. What does the man suggest the woman do?
   (A) Get a refund
   (B) Speak to a technician

4. Who most likely is the man?
   (A) A tenant
   (B) A realtor

5. What does the woman say she likes about the apartment?
   (A) The rental fee
   (B) The location

6. What will the woman do on Monday?
   (A) Pick up some keys
   (B) Move to a new home

7. What does the woman want to do?
   (A) Buy some tickets
   (B) Open a bank account

8. Why does the man say he cannot help the woman?
   (A) The tickets are sold out.
   (B) He can accept only cash.

9. What does the man suggest the woman do?
   (A) Purchase the tickets beforehand
   (B) Keep the receipt with her

10. What did the woman recently do?
    (A) Taught a writing class
    (B) Cancelled the enrollment in a class

11. What caused the delay?
    (A) A computer system malfunctioned.
    (B) A form was not completed.

12. What does the man suggest?
    (A) Registering for another class
    (B) Checking the Web site for its status

PART
3

※ 利用刪去法選出 Best Answer

1. Who most likely is the man?
   (A) A train conductor
   (B) A hotel employee
   (C) A taxi driver
   (D) A travel agent

2. Where does the woman want to go?
   (A) To a restaurant
   (B) To a conference center
   (C) To a train station
   (D) To a science museum

3. What does the man tell the woman?
   (A) The fare has recently increased.
   (B) The drive will take longer than expected.
   (C) A flight schedule has changed.
   (D) The business will close early.

4. What did the man have a problem doing?
   (A) Using a Web site
   (B) Reserving transportation
   (C) Finding a conference room
   (D) Contacting a client

5. How will the man get to the hotel?
   (A) By subway
   (B) By bus
   (C) On foot
   (D) By car

6. What hotel amenity does the man ask about?
   (A) City tours
   (B) Dining options
   (C) The fitness center
   (D) Internet access

7. Why is the woman calling?
   (A) To discuss a delivery
   (B) To ask about a warranty
   (C) To report a problem
   (D) To cancel an appointment

8. When will the delivery be made?
   (A) This morning
   (B) This afternoon
   (C) Tomorrow morning
   (D) Tomorrow afternoon

9. What is an additional fee for?
   (A) Delivering merchandise
   (B) Assembling furniture
   (C) Using an express service
   (D) Removing an old appliance

10. What problem is the man reporting?
    (A) Some paint is peeling off.
    (B) He lost the keys to his apartment.
    (C) A sink is not working well.
    (D) A light is broken.

11. What does the woman instruct the man to do?
    (A) Stop by the office
    (B) Pay a fee
    (C) Take a picture
    (D) Submit a request online

12. What is mentioned about the building supervisor?
    (A) He needs to order some parts.
    (B) He was just hired by the management.
    (C) He knows about the building rules.
    (D) He also lives in apartment complex.

13. Where is the conversation taking place?
    (A) At a restaurant
    (B) At an airport
    (C) At a bus station
    (D) At a travel agency

14. According to the woman, what will the men receive?
    (A) A parking pass
    (B) A travel guidebook
    (C) A seating upgrade
    (D) A discount voucher

15. What will the men most likely do next?
    (A) Visit Mexico to meet the family
    (B) Change the hotel reservation
    (C) Eat at a nearby restaurant
    (D) Return to their original flight

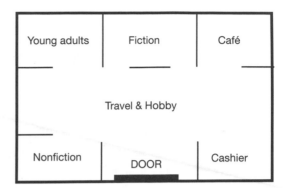

16. Who most likely is the man?
    (A) A restaurant server
    (B) A sales clerk
    (C) An author
    (D) A delivery person

17. What does the woman say she heard about the book?
    (A) It will provide opportunities for discussion.
    (B) It is the first book in the series.
    (C) It is difficult to understand for young people.
    (D) It has been a best-seller for months.

18. Look at the graphic. In which section is the book that the woman is looking for?
    (A) Young adults
    (B) Fiction
    (C) Nonfiction
    (D) Travel & Hobby

Step 1　類型分析

A 各種企業協議　🎧099

多益的宗旨是以英語消除職場生活方面的難題。對職場生活不了解的應試者來說,在透過多益熟悉公司和職場生涯的知識,並選擇正確答案時需要獲得幫助。尤其必須熟記公司為了開拓事業而與各家企業簽訂契約,彼此獲得協助的相關詞彙。

例題1

(Why) is the woman (calling)? (A) To follow up on a project (B) To negotiate a price (C) To inquire about a banquet room (D) To change a reservation date	W　Hello, I'm planning a company dinner for the Capital Motor Vehicles. Are there any large banquet rooms available at your hotel on March 5th? M　Let me check it for you. But first, could you give me a rough estimate of how many people will be attending? I want to make sure the room is big enough.

解析　女　你好,我正在為Capital Motor Vehicles籌劃公司晚宴,3月5日酒店是否有大型宴會廳可供使用呢?
　　　　男　我幫您查一下。但首先,您能大概估計一下將有多少人出席嗎?我想確保房間是夠大的。
　　　　Q　女子為什麼打電話?
　　　　　　(A) 對項目採取後續行動　　(B) 議價
　　　　　　(C) 詢問宴會廳的情況　　(D) 更改預訂日期

解析　汽車公司的職員為了舉辦公司活動而預約宴會廳。單純站在一般消費者的立場來看,前往飯店不只因為旅行,也有與各種企業聯絡討論合作的內容,需要了解這些常識。　　　　答案: (C)

🎧100

➡ 引導正確答案的職場生活相關詞彙Check!

❶ 協議/交易

contract 契約	terms/conditions 條件	presentation 發表	demonstration 彩排
acquire 收購	merge 合併	negotiate 協商	win the bid 獲得競標

❷ 顧客/承包企業

client 顧客	supplier 供應商	service agent 代理商	competitor 競爭者
quote 估算	appraisal 估價/評估	cost estimate 成本估算	

❸ 生產商

facility 設施	machinery 機械	assembly line 組裝線	raw material 原料
workforce 勞動力	shift 輪值	manufacture 製造	safety inspection 安全檢查

❹ 管理/販售

cost/expense 成本/費用	management 管理者	performance 成果/執行
evaluation/review 評估	sales 銷售	profit/income/revenue 利潤/收入
attract customers 招攬顧客		

公司內部各個部門之間經常需要業務合作。例如，汽車公司擁有銷售部、會計部和廣告部，也有負責維修影印機的事務管理部，另外停車管理部、清潔部門等，也都可能出現在談話中。只要根據音訊檔中給予的提示，讀完題目之後選擇答案即可。

例題2

What are the speakers discussing?

(A) Sales promotion of a product
(B) Reservation for an overseas trip
(C) Directions to a meeting room
(D) Reimbursement of expenses

W Hi, this is Melanie from sales. I submitted the expense report for my trip last week. Can you tell me when I can be reimbursed for that?

M Hi, Melanie. Actually, your report is missing a receipt for your hotel stay. We need to have all the receipts to process the payment.

PART
3

解析 女 你好，我是銷售部的梅蘭妮。上週我提交了旅行費用報告。你能告訴我什麼時候可以報銷嗎？
男 妳好，梅蘭妮。實際上，妳的報告缺少一張飯店住宿的收據。我們需要所有的收據來處理付款。

Q 說話者在討論什麼？
(A) 產品促銷　　　　(B) 預訂海外旅行
(C) 前往會議室的路線　**(D) 費用報銷**

解析 為了報銷(reimbursement)銷售部的出差費用，必須將附有收據(receipt)的報告交給會計部(accounting)獲得批准(approval)。必須熟悉各個企業和部門的業務知識再試著解題。　　　答案:(D)
🎧102

➡ 經常出現的職場生活相關詞彙Check!

❶ 部門相關業務

department / division 部門	branch / location 分店/位置	regional office 區域辦事處
sales 銷售	financial statement 財務報表	quality control 品質管理
public relations 公關	review 審查	technical support 技術支援
accountant 會計師	accounting 會計	auditor 會計稽核員
reimbursement 報銷(費用)	publicity 宣傳	release date 上市日期
marketing 行銷	research and development 研發	survey results 調查結果
maintenance / facility 維護/設施	below standard 低於標準	cleaning crew 清潔人員
advertisement team 廣告團隊	new product development team 新產品開發團隊	

❷ 文件相關業務

report / document 報告/文件	material 資料	proposal 提案	summary 簡介
correct/revise 修改	draft 草案	figures 數據	
final version 最終方案	deadline 期限	extension 延期	
contract / agreement 合約/協議	proofread / edit 校對/編輯		
review/go over 審查	submit / hand in 提交		

❸ 辦公設備/用品相關業務

envelope 信封	printer 印表機	office supplies / stationery 辦公用品
letterhead (印有公司名稱的)信紙	office equipment 辦公設備	
photocopier / copy machine 影印機	projector 投影機	be broken 故障
not working 失靈	replace 更換	

Step 2 眼睛和耳朵完美搭配 Practice 🎧 103   Answers_P.042

第1階段　先閱讀題目之後，一邊聆聽MP3一邊解題。
第2階段　重聽一次，試著填寫空格。
第3階段　邊聽MP3，跟著逐句唸出來。

1. What are the speakers discussing?
   (A) A staff orientation　　　　　　(B) A building project

   > M　Good morning, Ms. Taylor. Here's the _____ _____ from Ocean Building Company for the staff cafeteria we are planning _____ _____.
   >
   > W　Well, building a brand-new cafeteria requires extensive work, but it is higher than we originally thought.

2. Who most likely is the woman?
   (A) A magazine reporter　　　　　　(B) A restaurant owner

   > W　Thank you, Chef Carlos for meeting with me. _____ _____ wants to _____ an _____ about your unique cooking project. Could you tell us more about it?
   >
   > M　Yes, I was inspired by the paintings in the museum and came up with this new series of dishes.

3. What is the woman concerned about?
   (A) Submitting late work　　　　　　(B) Finding some documents

   > M　Ms. Hong, I need to be at home early for an urgent family matter. Do you mind if I work from home?
   >
   > W　Not at all, but what's the _____ of the budget you've been working on? The _____ for the project is coming up quite soon. I'm worried about _____ our work _____.

4. What does the woman suggest?
   (A) Offering product discounts　　　　(B) Starting an online advertising campaign

   > M　To start the meeting, I'd like to talk about the recent drop in sales for our vitamin products.
   >
   > W　What we really should do is to _____ _____ on social media _____ _____.

86

📝 從基本開始到精確掌握的訓練

1. Why is the woman calling?
   (A) To request some information
   (B) To welcome the man to the company

2. What does the man ask about?
   (A) An identification badge
   (B) An orientation schedule

3. What does the man say he is doing?
   (A) Filling out some forms
   (B) Signing an employment contract

4. What event did the man miss?
   (A) A marketing presentation
   (B) A board meeting

5. Why did the man miss the event?
   (A) He was on a business trip.
   (B) He thought it was on a different day.

6. What does the woman suggest the man do?
   (A) Watch a video online
   (B) Attend a different presentation

7. What are the speakers mainly discussing?
   (A) An article that the woman will write
   (B) The career of a well-known actor

8. Where does this conversation probably take place?
   (A) At a theater
   (B) At a newspaper company

9. What will the woman probably do next?
   (A) Exchange her ticket
   (B) Call for an interview

10. According to the man, what special offer is available for new customers?
    (A) A product discount
    (B) Next-day delivery

11. What is the purpose of the sign?
    (A) To indicate a location
    (B) To announce a renovation

12. What does the man suggest doing?
    (A) Collecting client suggestions
    (B) Using waterproof material

Answers_P.045

※ 利用刪去法選出 Best Answer

1. Why is the woman visiting the place?
   (A) To make a reservation
   (B) To attend a seminar
   (C) To buy some coffee
   (D) To cancel a membership

2. When will the event begin?
   (A) At 8 o'clock
   (B) At 9 o'clock
   (C) At 10 o'clock
   (D) At 11 o'clock

3. What is the woman looking for?
   (A) A machine to make a copy
   (B) A location to meet clients
   (C) A restaurant for a party
   (D) A place to get a beverage

4. What product are the speakers discussing?
   (A) Sunglasses
   (B) Hiking boots
   (C) Headphones
   (D) Blue jeans

5. According to the man, what are the customers worried about?
   (A) Durability
   (B) Price
   (C) Ease of use
   (D) Style

6. What does the woman suggest?
   (A) Testing a competitor's product
   (B) Conducting a customer survey
   (C) Delaying a product launch
   (D) Talking to an expert

7. What problem does the woman report?
   (A) Business is unusually slow.
   (B) Some of the customers complained.
   (C) There are not enough employees.
   (D) The price of some ingredients has increased.

8. What does the man suggest?
   (A) Offering outdoor dining
   (B) Moving to another neighborhood
   (C) Lowering some prices
   (D) Catering corporate events

9. What does the woman ask the man to do?
   (A) Hire a new chef
   (B) Prepare some food samples
   (C) Get ready for an inspection
   (D) Organize a training

10. What did the man do in China?
    (A) Bought some property
    (B) Visited some suppliers
    (C) Attended a professional conference
    (D) Trained some personnel

11. What problem does the man mention?
    (A) Some items are expensive.
    (B) Some clients are not satisfied.
    (C) Some products had low quality
    (D) A contract has to be renegotiated.

12. What does the woman suggest?
    (A) Renting storage space
    (B) Advertising on the Internet
    (C) Reimbursing for a purchase
    (D) Ordering a small sample

13. What does the man offer to do?
    (A) Purchase tickets
    (B) Make a reservation
    (C) Check a calendar
    (D) Call a colleague

14. What is Pablo needed for?
    (A) Translating a document
    (B) Contacting an agency
    (C) Repairing some equipment
    (D) Preparing a trip overseas

15. Why does the man say, "Maria lived in Spain for about seven years"?
    (A) To recommend Maria for a promotion
    (B) To suggest that Maria help with a task
    (C) To correct some mistakes
    (D) To warn about some dangers

Melbourne Technology Conference Fees		
Day 1 Only	Member	$70
	Non-member	$80
Day 2 Only	Member	$95
	Non-member	$105
Both Days	Member	$150
	Non-member	$170

16. What problem does the woman mention?
    (A) A Web site is not working.
    (B) A bill is incorrect.
    (C) Some staff members are unavailable.
    (D) Some schedules have not been updated.

17. Look at the graphic. How much will the woman most likely pay?
    (A) $70
    (B) $80
    (C) $95
    (D) $105

18. What does the man ask the woman to provide?
    (A) A registration form
    (B) A meal preference
    (C) A company name
    (D) An identification number

PART
3

PART

聽完一人獨白形式的短文後，針對試題上
列出的3個問題一一選出適合的答案。

題目數	難易度
共30題 (71至100題)	中／中上

滿分訣竅

將紙本出現的題型和音檔聽到的提示正確組合的訓練。

❶ 掌握各個題型(GQ/SQ)並快速瀏覽。⋯▶ 閱讀理解訓練
❷ 熟記耳朵聽到的各種談話(討論結果)主題和句子。⋯▶ 聽力訓練
❸ 讀完3個題目，一邊聽音檔，同時解題。⋯▶ 組合訓練

學習方法

❶ 準備 掌握Part4的短文結構和描述。
❷ 實戰 將題目加以分級，訓練解開大多數的題目。
❸ 複習 答錯的題目透過音檔 (1)練習重新解題(2)進行聽力練習，重複聆聽比
　　　 較不懂的部分。(3)若特定主題較弱，針對該主題練習讀完短文後加
　　　 以解析。

教材結構

Unit 12 主題 I 　公共介紹
Unit 13 主題II 　錄音訊息
Unit 14 主題III 　新聞/廣播
Unit 15 主題IV 　公司生活

🎧 106

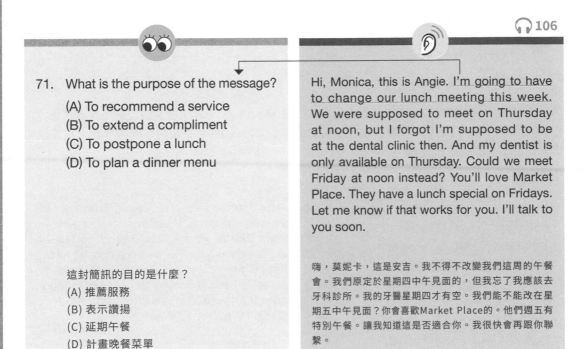

71. What is the purpose of the message?

(A) To recommend a service
(B) To extend a compliment
(C) To postpone a lunch
(D) To plan a dinner menu

這封簡訊的目的是什麼？
(A) 推薦服務
(B) 表示讚揚
(C) 延期午餐
(D) 計畫晚餐菜單

Hi, Monica, this is Angie. I'm going to have to change our lunch meeting this week. We were supposed to meet on Thursday at noon, but I forgot I'm supposed to be at the dental clinic then. And my dentist is only available on Thursday. Could we meet Friday at noon instead? You'll love Market Place. They have a lunch special on Fridays. Let me know if that works for you. I'll talk to you soon.

嗨，莫妮卡，這是安吉。我不得不改變我們這周的午餐會。我們原定於星期四中午見面的，但我忘了我應該去牙科診所。我的牙醫星期四才有空。我們能不能改在星期五中午見面？你會喜歡Market Place的。他們週五有特別午餐。讓我知道這是否適合你。我很快會再跟你聯繫。

解析 事先瀏覽題目，能夠預測音檔即將出現的訊息。音檔的目的主要會出現在第一句自我介紹的句子之後。在一開始的自我介紹之後，聽到必須更改午餐約定的部份時，立刻寫下postpone(延期)，並選擇重新詮釋(paraphrasing)的選項(C)。只要熟記Part 4的音檔以「自我介紹+來意+詳細內容+聯繫請求」的形式出現，就能有助於選擇答案。

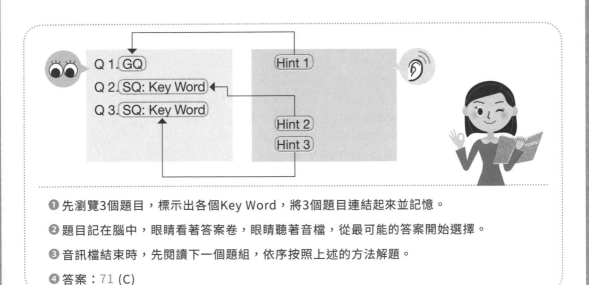

❶ 先瀏覽3個題目，標示出各個Key Word，將3個題目連結起來並記憶。

❷ 題目記在腦中，眼睛看著答案卷，眼睛聽著音檔，從最可能的答案開始選擇。

❸ 音訊檔結束時，先閱讀下一個題組，依序按照上述的方法解題。

❹ 答案：71 (C)

Step 1 類型分析

A **場內介紹**(交通/賣場) 🎧107

場內介紹是由一人透過麥克風向多數人傳達的談話(short talk)形式，主要典型的短文內容是「公告」+對聽者的「指示」。訓練方法是從開始的部分掌握GQ的地點和說話者的提示，在請求和指示部分了解詳細的SQ內容。

例題1

What is the reason for the delayed departure?

(A) Some passengers are late.
(B) There is stormy weather.
(C) Some baggage still needs to be loaded.
(D) The traffic has been really bad.

Attention passengers. This is your captain Jeremy speaking. Welcome to Alta Airlines flight 380 to Rome. Our departure will be slightly delayed while we take care of all the passengers' baggage. This is a full flight, so it's taking a little longer to get your luggage onto the plane. But we should be ready to take off in about 15 minutes.

〔解析〕 乘客注意。這是你們的機長傑若米。歡迎來到阿爾塔航空380航班飛往羅馬。在處理所有乘客的行李時，我們的出發時間會稍有延遲。這是一班客滿的飛機，所以把各位的行李搬上飛機要多花一點時間。但是我們大概15分鐘後就可以起飛了。

Q 延遲起飛的原因是什麼？
(A)有些乘客遲到了。(B)暴風雨天氣。**(C)有些行李還需要裝載**。(D)交通非常糟糕。

〔解析〕 Part 4是一旦出現主題，接下來的內容具有連貫性的題型。學習分析各個地點/主題的題目和短文，便能夠提高答題準確率。可以推測意思是在客滿的班機上裝載行李比預計多花了一點時間，因此約晚15分鐘出發。 答案: (C)
🎧108

引導正確答案的題目與描述 Check!

❶ 經常出現的題型

Who is the talk intended for? 談話以誰為對象？
➡ Travelers 旅客[詢問聆聽對象是誰的GQ提示出現在短文的開始部分]

Who can park on the second floor? 誰能在2樓停車？
➡ Visitors to the building 大樓訪客 [Key Word是second floor]

What are the passengers asked to do? 要求乘客做什麼？
➡ Take out their tickets 拿出他們的票[對聽者的要求出現在短文的後半部]

❷ 經常出現的交通相關詞彙

arrival 抵達	departure 起飛	boarding 登機	boarding pass 登機證
captain/pilot 機長	flight attendant 空服員	check-in bags 托運行李	carry-on bags 登機行李

❸ 經常出現的延遲/取消原因

inclement weather 天氣惡劣	mechanical problem 機械故障
connecting flight 轉機航班	runway management 跑道管理

B 參觀/介紹 🎧109

具有典型的Part 4結構，通常團體領隊(guide)在自我介紹和地點介紹，並說明參觀處之後，接著依次說明參加者的注意事項。

例題2

How long is the tour expected to last?

(A) 30 minutes
(B) 60 minutes
(C) 90 minutes
(D) 120 minutes

Welcome to the Sakamoto Art Museum. My name is Becky. Our tour today will last about 1 hour, and it will focus on the museum's collection from ancient Greece. There is also a gift shop in the lobby where you can get books on today's exhibits if you want to learn more about them after the tour. Now let's get started. Let's look first at the large piece of pottery that stands in the center of the room.

PART 4

解析 歡迎來到坂本美術館，我叫貝琪。我們今天的參觀將持續1小時左右，重點會放在古希臘博物館的收藏品。大廳也有一個禮品店，如果您想在參觀結束後了解更多相關訊息，可以在這裡購買與今天展品有關的書籍。現在我們就開始吧。首先我們看一下位於房間中央的大型陶器。

Q 參觀預計持續多久？
(A) 30分鐘 **(B)60分鐘** (C)90分鐘 (D)120分鐘

解析 從短文開始可以得知這是博物館導覽人員進行介紹的內容。一般來說，有關參觀的介紹中，把前面提到的時間one hour(1小時)改成60 minutes(60分鐘)就是答案。先說明整體的行程和注意事項之後再開始參觀，需要多加練習並熟記流程。　　　　　　　　　　　　　　　　　　　　　　答案: (B)

🎧110

➡️ **和參觀有關的題目和描述Check!**

❶ 經常出現的題型

Who probably are the listeners? 誰可能是聽眾？
➡ Theater patrons 劇院觀眾[詢問說話者/聽者是誰的GQ提示出現在短文的開始部分]

What will be provided for listeners? 將提供什麼給聽眾？
➡ Local maps 當地地圖 [聆聽說話者提供(give)和聽者獲得(receive)的部分]

Where are the listeners supposed to go at 2 o'clock? 聽眾應該在2點去哪裡？
➡ To the information center 到服務台[指定時間內到某處集合的內容出現在後半部]

❷ 經常出現的觀光相關詞彙

historic site 歷史遺跡	fortress 堡壘	river cruise 遊船	hiking trail 健行步道
exhibit 展示會	excursion 遠足	wing 側廳	admission 入場費
sightseeing 觀光	collection 收集作品	painting 畫作	souvenir 紀念品
sculpture 雕刻	modernism 現代主義	impressionism 印象派	pottery 陶器
photography 攝影	museum 博物館	gallery 畫廊	landmark 標誌物/里程碑
main attractions 旅遊熱點/觀光景點			

❸ 其他敘述

complimentary/free 免費的	safety gear 安全裝置	prevent accident 防止意外
be prohibited 禁止	be allowed to 允許～	refrain from 避免～
be required to 必須～	be sure to 務必～	don't forget to 記得～

第1階段　先閱讀題目之後，一邊聆聽MP3一邊解題。
第2階段　重聽一次，試著填寫空格。
第3階段　邊聽MP3，跟著逐句唸出來。

1. Where is the announcement being made?

   (A) In a grocery store   (B) In a cooking school

> Attention Hillman's _____ _____. While you're in the store today, be sure to check out our newly expanded bakery _____ located right next to the dairy products. Our bakers have been busy creating new cakes and bread for you.

2. What was the cause of the delay?

   (A) There was bad weather in the area.   (B) An airplane needed more fuel.

> Attention passengers of flight 1820 to Casablanca. We apologize for the delay while the aircraft _____ _____ _____ but we are now ready to begin boarding. It's going to a full flight.

3. Who probably is the speaker?

   (A) A professional singer   (B) A theater manager

> Good evening and welcome to the Berkley _____. Tonight's _____ _____ will last for approximately 2 hours. There will be a 15-minute intermission during which you can enjoy drinks and refreshments available in the lobby.

4. What will the company offer at a discounted price?

   (A) A sightseeing tour   (B) The evening meal

> There was some mix-up in our schedules and we will be staying at a different hotel. The new hotel is as pleasant as the one we reserved before. We're very sorry for the inconvenience. To _____ _____ _____ the confusion, there will be a special discount on _____'s _____ buffet.

📝 從基本開始到精確掌握的訓練

1. Who is speaking?
    (A) A photographer
    (B) A tour guide

2. Where is the announcement being made?
    (A) At a photography studio
    (B) At a historic building

3. According to the speaker, what is prohibited?
    (A) Taking flash photographs
    (B) Using mobile phones

4. What is causing a delay?
    (A) An engine problem
    (B) A flat tire

5. According to the speaker, at what time is the bus expected to depart?
    (A) At 1 P.M.
    (B) At 3 P.M.

6. What does the speaker ask the listeners to do?
    (A) Return on time
    (B) Find their tickets

7. For whom is this announcement intended?
    (A) Airplane passengers
    (B) Air traffic controllers

8. What are the listeners asked to do?
    (A) Turn off electronic devices
    (B) Prepare for landing

9. When can the listeners leave their seats?
    (A) After the captain gets off the plane
    (B) When they safely land on the ground

10. Who probably is the speaker?
    (A) A weather forecaster
    (B) A travel agency employee

11. What will be provided for listeners?
    (A) Light snacks
    (B) Drinking water

12. What time are the listeners leaving?
    (A) 10:00 A.M.
    (B) 10:30 A.M.

PART
4

※ 利用刪去法選出 Best Answer

1. Where most likely are the listeners?
   (A) In an airplane
   (B) On a train
   (C) On a bus
   (D) In a waiting room

2. What is the cause of the delay?
   (A) Some workers are loading the luggage.
   (B) There is a stormy weather.
   (C) A vehicle has to be refueled.
   (D) Some passengers have not yet arrived.

3. What does the speaker say he expects will happen?
   (A) Weather conditions will get worse.
   (B) A flight will arrive on time.
   (C) Some seats will be available.
   (D) Some food will be provided.

4. What is the main purpose of the talk?
   (A) To introduce a new employee
   (B) To describe a nature tour
   (C) To give an award
   (D) To promote a product

5. What are the listeners invited to do during the tour?
   (A) Take a break in the middle
   (B) Come to a dinner party
   (C) Take pictures
   (D) Bring some food

6. What does the speaker suggest?
   (A) Walking carefully
   (B) Putting on safety glasses
   (C) Asking questions
   (D) Waiting in line

7. What is being announced?
   (A) The closing of a store
   (B) The opening of a new business
   (C) Special prices on some items
   (D) Trading price for a certain product

8. What are listeners invited to do?
   (A) Close the register
   (B) Pay for the purchase
   (C) Shop at the new store
   (D) Come back the next day

9. What do green sings identify?
   (A) The clothing department
   (B) The emergency exit
   (C) The direction to the manager's office
   (D) The open registers

10. Where is the tour most likely taking place?
    (A) At a fashion show
    (B) At a fabric factory
    (C) At a trade fair
    (D) At an outdoor market

11. What does the speaker say has changed about the tour?
    (A) The duration
    (B) The distance
    (C) The starting location
    (D) The tour leader

12. What does the speaker offer the listeners?
    (A) A special discount
    (B) A longer tour
    (C) Free samples
    (D) Discussion time

13. Where is the announcement being made?

  (A) At a museum

  (B) At a university

  (C) At a department store

  (D) At a restaurant

14. What are the listeners waiting to attend?

  (A) A lecture

  (B) A documentary film

  (C) A special exhibition

  (D) A musical concert

15. What does the speaker imply when he says, "there will be another showing at 2 o'clock"?

  (A) He wants to get a deadline extension.

  (B) A renovation will be completed.

  (C) The listeners should return at a later time.

  (D) The listeners should make a reservation.

Oceanfront Island Ferry	
Departures	Arrivals
9:30 A.M.	10:00 A.M.
10:30 A.M.	11:00 A.M.
6:30 P.M.	7:00 P.M.
8:00 P.M.	8:30 P.M.

16. What has caused the cancellation?

  (A) Mechanical problems

  (B) Security issues

  (C) Bad weather

  (D) A lack of passengers

17. Look at the graphic. What time will the ferry leave?

  (A) 9:30 A.M.

  (B) 10:30 A.M.

  (C) 6:00 P.M.

  (D) 8:00 P.M.

18. What does the speaker say listeners may want to do?

  (A) Travel the next day

  (B) Visit the souvenir shops

  (C) Take a picture of the scenery

  (D) Wear warm clothing

PART
4

Unit 13　主題II － 錄音訊息

 Step 1　類型分析

A 個人錄音　🎧114

電話訊息是致電者以〈自我介紹+來意+請求連絡〉的形式，在對方的語音信箱(voice mail)或答錄機(answering machine)中留言。由於是對方不在時或沒有影像的語音訊息，在一開始會先自我介紹。須確認GQ/SQ的題型，從重點內容選擇正確答案。

例題1

(Who) probably is (the speaker)? (A) A receptionist (B) A doctor (C) A patient (D) A ticket agent	This message is for Hillary Garner. Ms. Garner, I'm Peter calling from Dr. Thorne's office to confirm your appointment. Your annual physical check-up has been scheduled for 10:30 a.m. on Monday, July 10th. Please come 10 minutes early to fill out a health questionnaire before meeting with the doctor.

[解析] 這個訊息是給希拉里加納的。加納女士，我是彼得，我從索恩博士的辦公室打電話來確認您的預約。您的年度健檢時間定於7月10日星期一上午10點30分。在與醫生會面之前，請提前10分鐘到達以填寫健康問卷。

Q　說話者可能是誰？
(A) 接待人員 (B)醫生 (C)病患 (D)售票員

[解析] 醫院幫醫生接聽電話並處理預約的人稱為接待人員(receptionist)，須注意並非打電話的地點在醫院，就一律選擇醫生作為答案。　　　　　　　　　　　　　　　　　答案: (A)
🎧115

➡ **引導正確答案的題目與描述Check!**

❶ 經常出現的題型

Where is the speaker calling? 說話者在哪裡打電話？
➡ Shipping department 配送部門 [確認「從哪裡/到哪裡」之後，找出致電者的部門的GQ]

What is the purpose of the call? 電話的目的是什麼？
➡ To request more information 要求更多資訊 [出現自我介紹和目的]

What will happen on August 20th? 8月20日會發生什麼事？
➡ Opening a store 商店開幕[聆聽特定日期的SQ]

❷ 經常出現的目的

I'm calling to 我打來是想～　 This message is for 這條訊息是給～
to change[update] 為了變更　to order 為了訂購
to reserve[arrange / schedule / plan] 為了預約/安排/計畫

❸ 不在時的敘述

not available[unable] to take your call 無法接聽電話　contact the assistant / colleague 聯絡助理/同事　call a different number 撥打另一個電話號碼　leave a message 留言

B 企業錄音 🎧116

當企業營業時間結束或正在通話中,會播放錄音檔。相較於以職員為對象,以客人為主的情況更多,因此語氣較為鄭重,以固定模式介紹企業名/位置/營業時間/電話號碼等特定事項。這種題型一開始的內容可能比較瑣碎,只要多加練習,就能夠很快選出答案。

例題2

Why can't they answer the phone?

(A) Their business hours are over.
(B) Too many people have called.
(C) They closed early today.
(D) The phones are being fixed at the moment.

You have reached the Beacon Maintenance and Warranty Service Department. We're sorry, but all of our operators are busy taking calls from other customers. Please hold and yours will be taken as soon as possible. Thank you for your patience.

解析 歡迎致電燈塔保養和維修服務部門。很抱歉,我們所有的接線員都在忙著接聽其他客戶的電話。請稍等,我們將盡快接聽您的電話。感謝您的耐心等待。

Q 為什麼他們無法接聽電話?
(A) 營業時間已結束。　**(B)太多人打電話進來。**
(C)今天提早關門。　　(D)目前電話維修中。

解析 錄音的播放原因/目的也與GQ有關聯,因此很可能出現在短文的開始部分。介紹企業名稱之後,說明目前線上人員均在忙線中而無法接聽的(B)是最適合的選項。其他選項都不在錄音的內容中。　　　答案: (B)

🎧117

🡒 引導正確答案的題目與描述 Check!

❶ 經常出現的題型

Who is this message intended for? 訊息是留給誰的?
➡ Bank customers 銀行顧客[詢問對象是誰的GQ答案在短文的開始部分]

Why are the callers listening to this message? 為什麼致電者聽到這項訊息?
➡ It's a national holiday. 是國定假日。[在介紹企業之後出現播放訊息的原因]

What is the listener asked to provide? 聽者被要求提供什麼?
➡ Reference number 參考號碼(訂單/預約編號)[企業的確認/提問時需要詢問號碼的SQ]

❷ 經常出現的企業錄音相關描述

operator 接線員　　automated service 自動化服務　　star key 米字鍵(*)
sharp key 井字鍵(#)　weekdays 週間　　weekend 周末　　holiday 假日
service agent[representative] 服務人員
business hours / hours of operation 營業時間/辦公時間
stay on the line / hold 等候　　　　The line is busy. 忙線中。
press 1 請按1　　　　　　　　hang up and call again later 掛掉重打
You have reached ~. 歡迎致電~。　Thank you for calling ~. 感謝致電~。

❸ 經常請求的內容

return a call 回電　　　　　make a decision[choice] 選擇
compensate / make up for 補償　　give[provide] more information 提供更多資訊

第1階段　先閱讀題目之後，一邊聆聽MP3一邊解題。
第2階段　重聽一次，試著填寫空格。
第3階段　邊聽MP3，跟著逐句唸出來。

1. What business is the speaker calling?

   (A) A doctor's office   (B) A transportation service

   > Hello, I'm calling about a problem I had with _____ _____ _____.
   > I ride the 6 o'clock bus home from work. Yesterday evening, I waited for the bus for
   > over an hour before giving up and taking a taxi home.

2. What problem does the speaker report?

   (A) A printer is not working properly.   (B) A finance report is not ready in time.

   > Hi, this message is for the technology department. This is Gena Williams from
   > finance. I'm calling because _____ _____ has _____ again and
   > this is the third time this problem happened this week.

3. What is wrong with the number that was dialed?

   (A) Nobody is at home right now.   (B) It is the wrong number.

   > I'm sorry. The number you have dialed is _____ _____ _____ any
   > more. Please check the number and call again later.

4. What number should you press for the arrival schedule?

   (A) Number 1   (B) Number 2

   > You have reached Delta Airlines Automated Information Service. At any time during
   > this message, press 0 to be connected to one of our service agents. For departure
   > schedules, press 1. For _____ _____, press 2.

📝 從基本開始到精確掌握的訓練

1. Where does the speaker work?
   (A) Marketing
   (B) Advertising

2. Why has the meeting been rescheduled?
   (A) Some materials were not prepared.
   (B) A conference room was not available.

3. What does the speaker ask the listener to do?
   (A) Reserve a flight
   (B) Contact him

4. Who are the intended listeners for this message?
   (A) Telephone operators
   (B) Store customers

5. What should listeners do in order to speak with a representative?
   (A) Press one
   (B) Push the star button

6. If listeners want to find the nearest store, what should they do?
   (A) Go online
   (B) Visit the store

7. Where does the speaker work?
   (A) At a hotel
   (B) At an electronics store

8. What is the phone call about?
   (A) A defective product
   (B) A forgotten item

9. What information does the speaker need?
   (A) A mailing address
   (B) A description of an object

10. Where is Patrick Darrel?
    (A) He is at a conference.
    (B) He is on another line.

11. When will Mr. Darrel receive the message left on the machine?
    (A) Before he goes to work every morning
    (B) At the end of each day

12. What are listeners asked to do if they need immediate help?
    (A) Hang up and call again later
    (B) Talk to Mr. Darrel's secretary

PART 4

101

※ 利用刪去法選出 Best Answer

1. Why is the speaker calling?
   (A) To explain a problem with an order
   (B) To apologize for a defective item
   (C) To change a delivery address
   (D) To announce a price increase

2. What does the speaker recommend?
   (A) Using an express service
   (B) Requesting a partial refund
   (C) Switching to a similar product
   (D) Calling a different supplier

3. What is the listener asked to do?
   (A) Return an item
   (B) Call the speaker
   (C) Check a Web site
   (D) Fax a receipt

4. What type of business recorded the message?
   (A) A hotel
   (B) A pharmacy
   (C) A public library
   (D) A department store

5. What does the business guarantee?
   (A) All payment options are accepted.
   (B) All calls will be answered in the order received.
   (C) Medicines are double-checked for safety.
   (D) Orders will be filled within a day.

6. Why are the listeners instructed to press 3?
   (A) To speak with a pharmacist
   (B) To cancel the order
   (C) To confirm a reservation
   (D) To find out the business hours

7. Who most likely is the speaker?
   (A) An architect
   (B) A financial advisor
   (C) A real estate agent
   (D) A maintenance worker

8. What does the speaker say is a problem?
   (A) An office is far away from downtown.
   (B) Some staffs have not been trained.
   (C) A deadline cannot be extended.
   (D) The rent is higher than expected.

9. What does the speaker ask the listener to do?
   (A) Return the call promptly
   (B) Review a document carefully
   (C) Recalculate the cost
   (D) Submit a deposit

10. What is the message mainly about?
    (A) Scheduling a safety inspection
    (B) Ordering out-of-stock items
    (C) Arranging a tour of a building
    (D) Reserving a meeting place

11. What is the listener asked to do?
    (A) To provide an alternative date
    (B) To confirm a renovation schedule
    (C) To give the names of participants
    (D) To submit the payment beforehand

12. According to the speaker, what should the listener be aware of?
    (A) An increase in admission fees
    (B) A restriction on group sizes
    (C) Rules about taking photographs
    (D) Ongoing facility maintenance

13. Where most likely is the speaker?

(A) At a post office

(B) At an airport

(C) In a taxi

(D) On a train

14. What does the speaker imply, when she says, "Can you believe it"?

(A) She was annoyed.

(B) She was excited.

(C) She was confused.

(D) She was embarrassed.

15. What does the speaker ask the listener to do?

(A) Open the window

(B) Check the security system

(C) Meet with a colleague

(D) Pick up a package

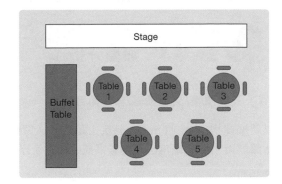

16. What is the speaker calling about?

(A) A retirement party

(B) A musical performance

(C) A wedding banquet

(D) An awards banquet

17. Look at the graphic. Which table does the speaker refer to?

(A) Table 1

(B) Table 2

(C) Table 3

(D) Table 4

18. Why does the man want to arrive early?

(A) To change into a uniform

(B) To prepare a speech

(C) To talk with other guests

(D) To visit backstage

Step 1　類型分析

A　天氣預報/交通預報/談話節目　🎧121

以新聞廣播(broadcast)為特定主題的方式只會出現用於播放的固定詞彙或題目，因此只要根據新聞類型，熟記經常出現的答案描述和重新詮釋的方式，就能輕鬆解題。

例題1

Who probably is the speaker? (A) A weather forecaster (B) A police officer (C) A commuter (D) A bank clerk	And now a special weather update from UPNX. The weather service just revised the snow predictions for Saddleton County. Now, we're expecting 7 inches of snow starting around 3 in the afternoon, continuing throughout the night. The snow will stop around 7 tomorrow morning. We'll keep you informed every 30 minutes.

(解析) 現在有一個特殊的天氣更新來自UPNX。氣象服務站剛修改了薩德爾頓縣的降雪預測。現在，我們預計將有7英寸的降雪，從下午3點左右開始，一直持續到整個晚上。雪將在明天早上7點左右停止。我們會每30分鐘通知您一次。

Q　說話者可能是誰？
(A) 天氣預報員　(B)警察　(C)通勤者　(D)銀行職員

(解析) 詢問職業的GQ從出現廣播的名稱，並告知天氣現象的第一句內容可以得知，說話者是氣象播報員。
答案: (A)

🎧122

➡ 引導正確答案的題目與描述 Check!

❶ 經常出現的題型

Who probably is the speaker? 說話者可能是誰？
➡ A show host 節目主持人[GQ出現在前面介紹節目和邀請來賓的部分]

What will the listeners probably hear next? 聽眾接下來可能會聽到什麼？
➡ An advertisement 廣告 [未來預測的問題可以從最後一句話得到提示]

❷ 廣播相關詞彙

stay tuned 繼續收聽　we'll be right back 我們馬上回來　live 實況轉播

❸ 交通相關詞彙

commuter 通勤者　　driver 司機　　accident 事故　　detour 繞道
roadwork/construction 修路工程/鋪設　different road/alternate route/alternative 替代路線

❹ 天氣相關詞彙

temperature 溫度　cold/chilly 冷的　hot/scorching 熱的　sunny/clear 晴朗的　overcast 陰沉的
foggy/misty 霧濛濛的 shower/rain 雨　snow/blizzard 雪　　chance/possibility 可能性

❺ 談話節目相關詞彙

program 節目　　　host 主持人　　guest 來賓　　interview 訪問

廣播和新聞中容易混淆的主題(Topic)，例如與地方團體(local community)有關的新聞和各種企業的商業新聞，即使出題率不高，也會出現社會層面(social section)的相關內容。高難度的Part 4主題經常以類似Part 7的短文來出題，必須有效率地進行練習。

例題2

What is the radio broadcast mainly about? (A) A nomination of a new mayor (B) The construction of a road way (C) A renovation of a bridge (D) The expansion of a train line	Welcome back! This is Yumi Thompson and you're listening to news at six. In local news, authorities have finalized plans for the construction of a new highway that will bypass Pleasantville City. Work on the highway is expected to begin in spring and take approximately two years to complete.

解析 歡迎回來！我是友美‧湯普森，您現在收聽的是6點鐘的新聞。地方新聞，當局已經決定興建一條繞過普萊森維爾市的新高速公路的計劃。這條公路的工程預計在春天開始，大約需要兩年時間才能完成。

Q 廣播的主要內容是什麼？
(A) 新市長的任命　**(B)道路建設**　(C)橋樑的翻新　(D)火車線路的擴建

解析 地方新聞中最常出現的是區域建設工程(construction project)相關的內容，此外還有刺激地方經濟、休閒活動等新聞內容。記熟基本詞彙，根據題型選擇最適合的答案，同時增加背景知識和解題的正確性。

答案: (B)

🎧124

➡ 引導正確答案的的題目與描述 Check!

❶ 經常出現的題型

What is the main topic of the news report? 新聞報導的主題是什麼？
➡ The merger of two companies 兩家公司的合併 [商業新聞的主題出現在前面部分]

What will be the weather like on Friday? 星期五的天氣怎麼樣？
➡ Rainy then clear 雨過天晴[SQ的Key Word是有關週五的天氣內容]

What did the council do yesterday? 議會昨天做了什麼？
➡ Approved the budget 核准了預算[專注在特定時間的SQ]

❷ 地方新聞相關詞彙

resident 居民	community 社區	committee 委員會　city council 市議會	mayor 市長
budget 預算	official 官方/官員	proposal 提案	approve 核准
plan 計畫	public hearing 公聽會	tourism 旅遊業	local economy 地方經濟
local 地方的	local event 當地活動	construction 建設工程	boost/increase 促進/增加

❸ 商業新聞相關詞彙

CEO/president/company head 總裁/公司負責人　　interview 會談
overseas expansion 海外擴展　　merger/joining of two companies 合併
acquisition/buy/purchase/take over 收購/接管
market share 市佔率　　new product 市佔率　　new branch[location] 新分公司[位置]
details 細節　　open/close 開業/停業　　employ/hire 雇用
contract/agreement 合約/協議　　condition/terms 條件

第1階段　先閱讀題目之後，一邊聆聽MP3一邊解題。
第2階段　重聽一次，試著填寫空格。
第3階段　邊聽MP3，跟著逐句唸出來。

1. Who probably is the speaker?

   (A) An air traffic controller　　　　　(B) A radio announcer

   > Now let's check on the ＿＿＿＿＿ ＿＿＿＿＿. The evening rush hour is starting
   > with ＿＿＿＿＿ on major roads. Since tomorrow is the first day of the rather long
   > holiday weekend, I'm afraid the situation will get worse. Allow extra time to get to
   > your destination.

2. Where is the speaker?

   (A) At a car dealership　　　　　(B) At a parking garage

   > Welcome to Business News on Channel 7. This is Tara Jenson, reporting to you
   > ＿＿＿＿＿ from Martin's ＿＿＿＿＿ ＿＿＿＿＿ right here in our city. Now, I'm
   > going to speak with the owner of Martin's Car Dealership.

3. What does Bradford Industries make?

   (A) Cleaning products　　　　　(B) Gardening supplies

   > Welcome to WNY radio's weekly small business report. Our first story is about
   > recent development in Bradford Industries, the country's leading ＿＿＿＿＿ of
   > ＿＿＿＿＿ ＿＿＿＿＿.

4. What are the listeners advised to do?

   (A) Take the subway　　　　　(B) Use a different road

   > The traffic is already slow on Washington Bridge. There has been an accident on
   > Highway 95 near the exit to the International Airport. To avoid this, I ＿＿＿＿＿
   > you take an ＿＿＿＿＿ ＿＿＿＿＿ such as Route 9 or local roads.

📝 從基本開始到精確掌握的訓練

1. What is the radio broadcast mainly about?
   (A) Traffic conditions
   (B) Local weather

2. What does the speaker recommend the listeners do this afternoon?
   (A) Use sun protection
   (B) Purchase new jackets

3. What will the listeners hear next?
   (A) Some movie review
   (B) Some commercials

4. What is the main topic of the broadcast?
   (A) The traffic update
   (B) A new city project

5. According to the speaker, what will begin today?
   (A) Highway maintenance
   (B) A sports tournament

6. What does the speaker suggest that listeners do?
   (A) Wait for discounted tickets
   (B) Take public transportation

7. Where does the speaker work?
   (A) At a radio station
   (B) At a movie theater

8. Who is Jacky Chang?
   (A) A movie star
   (B) A city official

9. What will Jacky Chang do at 3 o'clock in the afternoon?
   (A) Meet with Dianne Watson
   (B) Depart for the airport

10. Who is the speaker?
    (A) A climate specialist
    (B) A radio broadcaster

11. What does the speaker mention as a way of dealing with summer heat?
    (A) Taking a shower
    (B) Drinking water

12. What will the listeners probably hear next?
    (A) An advertisement
    (B) An interview

PART
4

※ 利用刪去法選出 Best Answer

1. Who is Amy Shore?
    (A) An author
    (B) An actor
    (C) A history teacher
    (D) A singer

2. According to the speaker, what will Amy Shore do this evening?
    (A) Talk about her life
    (B) Discuss current events
    (C) Offer professional training
    (D) Review a book

3. What are the listeners invited to do?
    (A) Request a song
    (B) Submit questions
    (C) Buy some tickets
    (D) Visit the station in person

4. Who is this report intended for?
    (A) Newspaper readers
    (B) Road crews
    (C) Police officers
    (D) Commuters

5. What caused the delay?
    (A) A damaged pipe
    (B) Heavy rain
    (C) A stalled truck
    (D) Weekend traffic

6. What does the speaker recommend?
    (A) Leaving early
    (B) Traveling by bus
    (C) Taking a different road
    (D) Listening for news updates

7. What is Ms. Blumberg's area of expertise?
    (A) Personal finance
    (B) Career guidance
    (C) Event coordination
    (D) Company management

8. What are the listeners encouraged to do?
    (A) Call in with their opinions
    (B) Update their résumés
    (C) Reduce the cost of living
    (D) Attend a professional workshop

9. What does the speaker say will happen next month?
    (A) A class will be offered.
    (B) A discount promotion will take place.
    (C) An interview will be conducted.
    (D) A book will become available.

10. Who is Tim Bauman?
    (A) A software designer
    (B) A financial counselor
    (C) A company president
    (D) A photo journalist

11. According to the speaker, why have the vacuum cleaners of Horseman Appliances been popular?
    (A) They're reliable.
    (B) They come in different colors.
    (C) They are inexpensive.
    (D) They're light.

12. What will Tim Bauman discuss at a press conference?
    (A) Plans for a company merger
    (B) Solutions to a technological problem
    (C) Changes in management staff
    (D) Increases in manufacturing cost

13. What is the main topic of the news report?

(A) The renovation of a tourist resort

(B) An airline merger with Central Railway

(C) Construction of a new railway line

(D) A new president for the hotel association

14. What does the speaker imply when he says, "This is what we've been waiting for"?

(A) He thinks it is taking too long.

(B) He is happy about the news.

(C) He is tired of working long hours.

(D) He is sorry for the inconvenience.

15. Who is Jamal Townsend?

(A) A ranger of a park

(B) A construction manager

(C) A member of an organization

(D) A famous travel writer

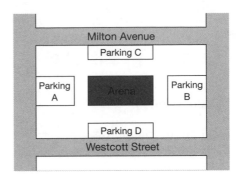

16. Why is the baseball game rescheduled?

(A) The weather has been bad.

(B) Some players got sick before the game.

(C) Not enough tickets have been sold.

(D) The stadium is being repaired.

17. According to the speaker, why might a listener watch a game on television?

(A) If a snowstorm gets worse.

(B) If tickets have been sold out.

(C) If there is no available parking.

(D) If he or she cannot find time to watch it in person

18. Look at the graphic. Which parking area will be closed?

(A) Parking A

(B) Parking B

(C) Parking C

(D) Parking D

Unit 15 主題IV — 公司生活

 Step 1 類型分析

A 活動/人物介紹 🎧128

所有的介紹(introduction)都在短文一開始說明主題和目的，基本上以介紹人物或活動的好處為內容，之後再說明詳細的日程或變動事項，並且請求聽眾(listeners)配合。從經常出現的活動和主題開始熟記吧。

例題1

Who is the workshop intended for?

(A) Clothing designers
(B) Health trainers
(C) Store customers
(D) Sales representatives

Welcome to the second session in Duffy's Furniture sales training program. Our focus in this session is on communicating effectively with our customers. Today, you're going to learn some strategies to express yourself effectively as well as to be a good listener. We'll begin the workshop with a small group discussion.

[解析] 歡迎來到達菲家具銷售培訓項目的第二節課。在這次會議中，我們的重點是與客戶進行有效的溝通。今天，你將學習一些策略，以有效地表達自己，並成為一個好的傾聽者。我們將以小組討論開始講習會。

Q 研習班的對象是誰？
(A) 服裝設計師　(B)健身教練　(C)商店顧客　**(D)銷售人員**

[解析] 以職員為對象的課程(class, course)可能以訓練(training)、研討會(seminar)、演講(lecture)等各式各樣的詞彙來作描述。從第一句聽到談話目的是為了家具店職員的銷售培訓，可以得知對象是銷售人員(sales representatives)。

答案: (D)
🎧129

➡ 引導正確答案的題目與描述 Check!

❶ 經常出現的題型

How often does this event take place? 這個活動多常舉行？
➡ Once a month 一個月一次 [活動頻率在短文的第一句介紹中出現。]

Why was the keynote speaker's speech rescheduled? 為什麼主講人的演講改期？
➡ Her plane was delayed. 她的飛機誤點了。[活動的變更事項在短文前半部出現。]

What will Ms. Emerson do next month? 愛默生女士下個月會做什麼？
➡ Visit other branches 巡視其他分行[第3人稱的未來計畫在後半部分出現提示。]

❷ 公司介紹相關詞彙

function/event 活動　　　organization/group 組織/團體　　　support 支援
organize/coordinate 組織/協調　　material 資料　　sign up/register 註冊
name tag 名牌　　delay/postpone 延期

❸ 人物介紹相關詞彙

banquet 宴會　　new employee 新員工　　retire 退休　　awards ceremony 頒獎典禮
transfer 調職　　questionnaire 調查表　　lecturer 演講者　　instructor/trainer 講師

Part 4是多益最常出現的題型。公司管理階層的說話者(speaker)向職員發表公司業績、公司政策等各種業務和部門之間的交流等,都是常見的內容。尤其Part 4和Part 7的主題經常只是換個形式來出題,需要扎實的複習以獲得有效學習。

例題2

What are the listeners asked to do? (A) Order new computers (B) Finish the work as soon as possible (C) Organize their personal files (D) Contact the moving company	Now, before we end, I'd like to briefly discuss our department's upcoming move to the Paterson Building. The company will take care of packing the computers, office furniture and files. But I'd like everyone to spend the day organizing your files and getting rid of unnecessary documents.

PART
4

解析 現在,在我們結束之前,我想簡短討論一下我們部門即將搬遷到帕特森大樓。電腦、辦公家具和文件的包裝工作將由公司負責。但我希望大家花一天的時間整理你的文件並且處理掉不必要的文件。

Q 聽者被要求做什麼?
(A) 訂購新電腦　　(B)盡快完成工作　　**(C)整理他們的個人文件**　　(D)聯絡搬家公司

解析 這是一場以搬家(moving)為主題的職員會議,大型設備和家具由公司負責搬運,並要求聽眾(listeners)整理文件,從中可以得知正確答案。補充說明,職員會議的後半也經常出現要求員工提供資料、提出意見或提交報告等內容。　　　　　　　　　　　　　　　　　　　　　　　答案:(C)

🎧131

● 引導正確答案的題目與描述 Check!

❶ 經常出現的題型

Where does this announcement probably take place? 此公告可能發生在什麼地方?
➡ A construction company 建築公司[GQ的公司/部門類別在一開始出現提示]

What caused an increase in sales? 是什麼引起銷售額的增加?
➡ New clothing line 新的服裝系列 [業績增加/下跌的典型主題在前半出現提示]

What are the listeners asked to do? 聽者被要求做什麼?
➡ Come up with a solution 想出一個解決方案[請求聽者的內容在後半出現提示]

❷ 業務/部門相關詞彙

sales 銷售	cost/expense 成本	income/profit 收入/利潤	opinion/feedback 意見
revenue 銷售收入	performance 績效	proceeds 收益	lucrative/profitable 盈利的
deadline 期限	extend 延長期限	push back 延後	printout/materials 印出/資料

❸ 其他相關詞彙

policy 政策	regulation/rule 規定	dress code 服裝規定	parking policy 停車規定
equipment 設備	public relations 公關	procedure/process 程序	
stationery 文具	office supplies 辦公用品	public image 公眾形象	
volunteer 志願者	car pool 共乘車	regular inspection 定期檢查	
employee handbook 員工手冊		office maintenance 辦公室維修	

Step 2　眼睛和耳朵完美搭配 Practice 🎧 132　Answers_P.068

第1階段　先閱讀題目之後，一邊聆聽MP3一邊解題。
第2階段　重聽一次，試著填寫空格。
第3階段　邊聽MP3，跟著逐句唸出來。

1. How often is this convention held?
   (A) Once a month　　　　　　　　　(B) Once a year

   Welcome to the _____ Water Conservation _____. All representatives attending today's program should go to the main entrance to receive their name tags and schedules. Please do not go to the reception area inside.

2. What is the main purpose of this announcement?
   (A) To announce a schedule change　　(B) To announce a maintenance job

   In today's staff meeting, first I would like to remind you that we are going to _____ _____ _____ in all offices over the next two weeks. The maintenance supervisor has asked everyone to let him know when you want the work done in your office.

3. Who are the instructions intended for?
   (A) Employees in a factory　　　　　(B) Managers in a store

   Every morning, as soon as you get in here, you should check the printed schedule to see which division you will be working in on the _____ _____. After that, you can get your _____ goggles and a hard hat for yourself.

4. What are the participants asked to do?
   (A) Complete the registration form　　(B) Send in their résumés

   Welcome to the 10th Annual Job Fair for the New York Asian Community. I know you want to talk to your potential employers or prospective coworkers. But first, I'd like you to _____ _____ all the _____ in your registration packet.

112

📝 從基本開始到精確掌握的訓練

1. How often does this event take place?
   (A) Once a month
   (B) Once a year

2. How long is the speaker's presentation?
   (A) One hour
   (B) Two hours

3. What should the listeners do if they have questions?
   (A) Stop the speaker and ask
   (B) Ask the speaker during lunch break

4. What is the announcement mainly about?
   (A) Opening a new location
   (B) Preparing for a sales event

5. What type of product does the store sell?
   (A) Clothing
   (B) Home furnishings

6. What does the speaker ask for help with?
   (A) Placing an advertisement in the paper
   (B) Hanging up a sign

7. What is the speaker discussing?
   (A) A party for a retiring employee
   (B) A schedule change for the event

8. What is Mr. Hardy's current position?
   (A) A sales associate
   (B) A general manager

9. What are the listeners asked to do?
   (A) Buy a gift for Mr. Hardy
   (B) Sign their names on a card

10. Why are the workers asked to put in extra hours?
    (A) Sales volume has increased.
    (B) Staff size has decreased.

11. Where is this announcement being heard?
    (A) In a production plant
    (B) In a sales seminar

12. What are the benefits of working overtime?
    (A) Employees can sell more products.
    (B) Employees can earn more money.

PART
4

※ 利用刪去法選出 Best Answer

1. What is mainly being discussed?
   (A) Office renovation
   (B) Directions to a site
   (C) Assembly of equipment
   (D) Seminar preparation

2. What should the listeners do tomorrow?
   (A) Arrange some meetings
   (B) Begin interviews
   (C) Pack their things
   (D) Move some furniture

3. What will the listeners receive later today?
   (A) Extra pay
   (B) A phone number
   (C) A new job offer
   (D) An e-mail notification

4. Why is the announcement being made?
   (A) To thank the attendees
   (B) To give directions
   (C) To cancel a reservation
   (D) To report a schedule change

5. What is the subject of Dr. Cullen's talk?
   (A) Marketing techniques
   (B) Design ideas
   (C) Accounting regulations
   (D) Organization skills

6. When will Dr. Cullen give his talk?
   (A) This morning
   (B) This afternoon
   (C) Tomorrow morning
   (D) Tomorrow afternoon

7. What is the purpose of the announcement?
   (A) To introduce a new employee
   (B) To describe a new printer
   (C) To report an upcoming project
   (D) To warn about the danger of deforestation

8. What benefit does the speaker mention?
   (A) Reduced harm to the environment
   (B) Increased output capacity
   (C) Greater publicity for the company
   (D) Fewer maintenance problems

9. According to the speaker, why have two training sessions been scheduled?
   (A) To lower the operating costs
   (B) To accommodate employees on all shifts
   (C) To switch to a larger room
   (D) To hire qualified trainers

10. What is the main topic of the talk?
    (A) Providing managers with training
    (B) Giving new employees more time off
    (C) Making work schedules more flexible
    (D) Boosting sales with new campaigns

11. According to the speaker, why is a change being made?
    (A) To retain current employees
    (B) To improve employee communication
    (C) To introduce better safety procedures
    (D) To follow government regulations

12. What are the listeners reminded to do?
    (A) Update the client contact information
    (B) Consult with a professional counselor
    (C) Inform their employees of company policies
    (D) Change passwords regularly

13. Who most likely are the listeners?

(A) Bankers

(B) Lawyers

(C) Drivers

(D) Entrepreneurs

14. What does the speaker mean when he says, "another conference is scheduled to begin here at 3 o'clock"?

(A) He wants to start the session now.

(B) He needs to go somewhere now.

(C) The fee was overcharged.

(D) The room needs to be reorganized.

15. What will the speaker distribute to the listeners?

(A) A sign-up sheet

(B) Training materials

(C) Employment contracts

(D) Parking passes

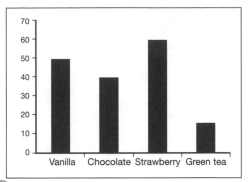

16. Look at the graphic. Which ice cream flavor will be discounted this week?

(A) Vanilla

(B) Chocolate

(C) Strawberry

(D) Green tea

17. Why does the speaker thank Bruce?

(A) He developed a new ice cream flavor.

(B) He talked with many customers in person.

(C) He proposed a sales promotion.

(D) He worked overtime for a week.

18. What does the speaker remind the listeners to do?

(A) Sign up for a task

(B) Count customers' votes

(C) Notify the winner by phone

(D) Make some suggestions

PART 5&6

		題目數	難易度
PART 5	選擇適當的詞彙或文法 填入句子空格的題型	共30題 (101至130題)	中／中下
PART 6	在較長的文章中選擇4個適合的文法、 詞彙或句子,填入空格的題型	共16題 (131至146題)	中

満分訣竅

熟記基本文法類型和詞彙,高效率解開各種題型問題。

❶ 了解文法題目的選項和空格前後的語意,尋找正確答案。

❷ 詞彙/閱讀理解型題目從前面部分開始讀起,選擇內容適當的答案。

❸ Part5, 6共46個題目訓練在15〜16分鐘內解題完成。

學習方法

❶ **準備**:掌握英語的基本詞類和句子結構。

❷ **實戰**:將各Unit文法類型和題型分段解題,應用在實戰題目中。

101. After the ------- upgrades have been implemented, the production process should run more efficiently.

(A) suggest
(B) suggested
(C) suggesting
(D) suggests

選擇詞類填入空白處是RC部分最基本的題型。主要高出題機率的詞彙和詞類變化以何種形式填入空格,需要多多練習。

這樣解題!

┌──── 名詞
▼
101. After the ------- upgrades have been implemented, the production process should run more efficiently.

(A) suggest ········▶ 動詞原型
(B) suggested ········▶ 過去分詞(包括被動語態的意義)
(C) suggesting ········▶ 現在分詞(包括主動語態的意義)
(D) suggests ········▶ 動詞的第三人稱單數形態

→ 在執行了建議的升級之後,生產過程應該能夠更有效地運行。

讀完題目,瀏覽一遍填空處和(A), (B), (C), (D)選項之後,確認是何種題型。

❶ 讀完選項,確認是測驗詞類的文法題目

❷ 了解空白處前後的語意,掌握答案的形態,能夠修飾名詞的選項只有(B), (C)兩個。

❸ 從可能的文法形態中,選擇內容上較符合的答案。名詞前面適合填入形容詞或可以充當形容詞的分詞。過去分詞具有被動語態的意義,現在分詞具有主動語態的意義,因此正確答案是(B)。

❹ 選出答案之後,熟記「implement(執行) + suggested upgrades(建議升級)」的用法。

❺ 答案: (B)

Questions 131-134 refer to the following e-mail.

From: Byung Chang Lee, Officer of Professional Development
To: All employees
Subject: New Lecture Series
Date: Monday, March 6th

Dear colleagues:

The first of our Do It On Your Own lecture series is being held on March 15. This _____ 131. lecture will be led by David Peterman, founder of the successful start-up company, Sysco Systems. Mr. Peterman _____ 132. what established technology companies can learn from start-up companies. Mr. Peterman's talk is the one of the three lectures that address start-ups and entrepreneurship. _____ 133..

As you know, Mr. Peterman is a great leader in the industry, so we hope all staff will be present. Nevertheless, you must seek _____ 134. your manager before attending.

Thank you

Byung Chang Lee

131. (A) daily
     (B) rescheduled
     (C) upcoming
     (D) final

132. (A) discussed
     (B) will discuss
     (C) has discussed
     (D) had discussed

133. (A) Many large technology companies are privately owned.
     (B) The lecture series is gaining popularity.
     (C) Mr. Peterman was born and raised here in the city of Melbourne.
     (D) Schedules and topics for the rest of the lectures will be emailed to you soon.

134. (A) approving
     (B) the approval of
     (C) who approves
     (D) having approved

This ------ lecture will be led by David Peterman, ~ 選擇正確詞彙
    131.

(A) daily   ⟶ 每天的：接下來的3場講座並不是每天舉行。
(B) rescheduled   ⟶ 改期：因為是第一次介紹，所以日程不會變更。
(C) upcoming   ⟶ 即將到來的：初次介紹的講座，適合填入即將發表的講座。
(D) final   ⟶ 最後：由於是第一場講座，與前後文不一致。

新多益

Mr. Peterman's talk is the one of the three lectures that address start-ups
and entrepreneurship. ------ 選擇正確句子
    133.

(A) Many large technology companies are privately owned.
(B) The lecture series is gaining popularity.
(C) Mr. Lee was born and raised here in the city of Melbourne.
(D) Schedules and topics for the rest of the lectures will be emailed to you
    soon.

  ⟶ 由於這是一封介紹講座的郵件，在介紹完之後，說明這是3場講座中的其中一場，
因此接下來可能會簡單介紹其他講座的內容。

首先瀏覽一遍需填入空白處的4個選項。

❶ 了解這是閱讀理解短文的類型(郵件、信件等主題)之後，開始閱讀內容。

❷ Part 5的文法類題目在解題時需確認空白處前後的語意，語彙類題目需考慮前文開始的
內容來解題。當文法上正確的選項超過2個以上時，選擇與前後文一致的答案。

❸ 新類型「選擇句子」必須選擇與前文讀到的部分連結起來最自然的句子。將新類型題目
做記號之後，閱讀時以填補一個合乎邏輯的「漏洞」方向來思考。

❹ Part 6, 7屬於閱讀理解型短文，以各種主題(Topic)反覆出題。

❺ 答案：131 (C)　132 (B)　133 (D)　134 (B)

Unit 1　名詞與代名詞

名詞用於描述具有名稱的所有人事物。名詞在句子中可以是主語、賓語和補語。名詞包括「蘋果/老師/命運」等具體的可數名詞和抽象的不可數名詞。代名詞是為了避免重複前面提過的名詞而使用的替代名詞。

 Step 1　基礎文法

Point 1　名詞的形態

1) 構成名詞的代表性詞尾

-ment	development 開發	-ness	blindness 盲目
-ity	possibility 可能性	-ency	consistency 一致性
-ance	performance 表演	-ure	lecture 演講
-th	death 死亡	-sis	analysis 分析
-ist	artist 藝術家	-ant	applicant 求職者
-er/or	instructor 講師	-ee	employee 僱員

2) 容易混淆的名詞詞尾

-tive	representative 代表	objective 目標
-al	approval 同意	professional 專家
-ing	marketing 行銷	ticketing 票務

Practice

Answers _ p. 075

1. Mr. Thompson's ------- of the stock market has been very accurate so far.
   (A) analyze　　　　　　　(B) analysis

2. Our department has been working hard to get ------- for this project.
   (A) approval　　　　　　(B) applicable

1) 名詞的作用

主語	**Admission** will begin starting next Monday. 將從下周一開始入學。
動詞的賓語	The teacher will check the **attendance** once the class starts. 課程一旦開始，老師會點名。
介係詞的賓語	You're eligible for **promotion** in two years. 你有資格在兩年後升職。
補語	Customer satisfaction is our first **priority**. 顧客滿意是我們的第一要務。

2) 名詞的位置

冠詞後	There was an **increase** in price. 價格上漲了。
所有格後	We need to reduce our **costs** in manufacturing. 我們需要降低生產成本。
形容詞後	Mr. Johnson made a good **suggestion** during the meeting. 強生先生在會議上提出了一個很好的建議。
介係詞後	The product is still under **warranty**. 產品仍在保固期內。

PART
5
6

Answers _ p. 075

Practice

3. The ------- of thunderstorms will be high this afternoon.

   (A) possible   (B) possibility

4. Mr. Yamada is a famous ------- who has won numerous awards in the industry.

   (A) architect   (B) architecturally

Point 3 名詞的種類

1) 可數名詞 vs. 不可數名詞

可數名詞具有具體形體而可以數算。單數時加上a/an，複數時加上-s/-es。不可數名詞為專有名詞或不具形體的物質/抽象名詞，不加a/an，只用單數形式出現。定冠詞the的用法可以像所有格一樣來使用。

	原型	單數	複數	定冠詞+N	所有格+N
可數	advisor 顧問	an advisor	advisors	the advisor(s)	my advisor(s)
不可數	advice 勸告	advice	-	the advice	my advice

★ 常見的不可數名詞

furniture 家具	equipment 設備	machinery 機械	luggage/baggage 行李/提包
information 資訊	evidence 證據	traffic 交通	merchandise 商品

2) 複合名詞

名詞前面主要出現冠形詞或形容詞，但也有＜名詞+名詞＞的固定形態。

marketing survey 市場調查	customer satisfaction 顧客滿意度	job description 職務說明
retail sales 職務說明	expiration date 到期日/有效日	safety regulations 安全法規
training session 培訓課程	production schedule 生產計畫	sales figures 銷售數字
application form 申請表	travel arrangements 旅行安排	confirmation number 確認單號

3) 可數名詞 vs. 不可數名詞前的限定詞

主要出現冠詞(a, an)、所有代名詞(my, his)、數量形容詞(many, much)等限定名詞的限定詞。

單數可數	複數可數	不可數名詞	可數複數／不可數名詞
a(n), each , every	both, many, all, (a) few, various[a variety of], a number of,	(a) little, much, less	all, some, most, any, plenty of, lots of

Practice

Answers _ p. 075

5. Applicants must have at least three years of experience in ------- sales.
   (A) retailed　　(B) retail

6. If the machine stops for ------- reason, you can contact us.
   (A) any　　(B) a few

Point 4 人稱代名詞

像「他/她/那個」一樣，泛指人或事物的代名詞會根據數量/性別/格式而有不同形態。

格式 人稱			主格	所有格(～的)	受格	所有代名詞 (～的人事物)	反身代名詞 (～自己)
第1 人稱	單數		I	my	me	mine	myself
	複數		we	our	us	ours	ourselves
第2 人稱	單數		you	your	you	yours	yourself
	複數						yourselves
第3 人稱	單數	男	he	his	him	his	himself
		女	she	her	her	hers	herself
		事物	it	its	it	-	itself
	複數		they	their	them	theirs	themselves

🔍 人稱代名詞的位置和作用

主格 (動詞前)	**We** will finish the project on time. 我們將按時完成項目。
受格 (動詞後或介係詞後)	I will call **him** right after the meeting. 會議結束後我馬上打電話給他。 The package was sent to **me** directly. 包裹直接寄給了我。
所有格 (名詞前)	The manager met all of **his** staff members. 經理見過了他所有的工作人員。
所有代名詞 (=所有格+名詞)	Your report is much longer than **mine**. (mine = my report) 你的報告比我的長得多。（我的=我的報告）

Answers _ p. 075

Practice

7. When you sign the contract, you have to review ------- carefully.

(A) them   (B) it

8. Our customers can access ------- information through our Web site 24 hours a day.

(A) their   (B) theirs

PART

5/6

123

Q 指示代名詞：是指這個(this)、那個(that)等表示特定人事物的代名詞。

	指示代名詞	指示形容詞
單數	this 這個　that 那個	this/that＋單數名詞：這／那～
複數	these 這些　those 那些	these/those＋複數名詞：這些／那些～

These products are imported from Spain, and **those** in the back are from France.
這些產品從西班牙進口，後面的產品來自法國。

1) that/those of＋名詞：取代前面出現的名詞

Our new product is more popular than **that of** our competitors. (= new product of)
我們的新產品比競爭對手更受歡迎。

The sales have risen 10%, compared with **those of** last year. (= sales of)
與去年相比，銷售額增長了10%。

2) those who：是指「做~的人們」

Those who are interested in this program should contact Ms. Wong by the end of the day.
對這個計畫感興趣的人應於今天結束前與翁小姐聯繫。

Q 反身代名詞

1) 反身用法：使用於賓語和主語的情況，此時不可省略。
Mr. Thomson calls **himself** a handy man. 湯姆森先生自稱是個手巧的人。

2) 強調用法：使用於強調主語或賓語，此時可以省略。
I did the most of the research (**myself**). 我親自做了大部分的研究。

3) 慣用用法：結合介係詞使用以表達慣用語意。(e.g.) by oneself 靠自己、for oneself 獨力
He fixed the copier **by himself**. 他自己修理了影印機。

Practice

Answers _ p. 075

9.　Mr. Pennington wrote the budget report all by -------.

　　(A) him　　　　　　　　　　(B) himself

10.　------- who exercise regularly also tend to eat balanced diets.

　　(A) Ours　　　　　　　　　　(B) Those

Step 2　基本掌握

Answers _ p. 075

注意文法／結構／詞彙，練習選擇正確答案。

1. ------- wrote this letter.
   (A) He
   (B) Him

2. We value ------- opinion.
   (A) you
   (B) your

3. Some people talk to ------- when they're alone.
   (A) itself
   (B) themselves

4. The room is filled with much -------.
   (A) furniture
   (B) furnitures

5. Employees requested an ------- of the deadline.
   (A) extended
   (B) extension

6. He expressed ------- for the donation through e-mail.
   (A) appreciate
   (B) appreciation

7. The company decided to move ------- head office to Asia.
   (A) its
   (B) it

8. We need to solve a few ------- before we launch the new product.
   (A) problem
   (B) problems

9. We will give you ------- refund.
   (A) a full
   (B) full

10. Everyone was invited to Larry's ------- party on Friday night.
    (A) retire
    (B) retirement

11. If you want to talk to an -------, please press 1 now.
    (A) operator
    (B) operation

12. The project is under the ------- of Mr. Baker.
    (A) supervisor
    (B) supervision

13. Have you met the ------- and discussed the design of the new building?
    (A) architecture
    (B) architect

14. The ------- in this area has been fierce.
    (A) competition
    (B) compete

PART 5/6

125

🕐 試著在限時4分30秒之內盡可能答對。

1. You have to make the ------- online if you want the discounted price.

(A) reserve
(B) reservation
(C) reserving
(D) reserved

2. The managers hope that ------- will make progress on the new system.

(A) them
(B) theirs
(C) their
(D) they

3. We offer a ------- of services to our customers with different needs.

(A) vary
(B) various
(C) variety
(D) varied

4. The airline is considered to be one of the best in terms of customer -------.

(A) satisfaction
(B) satisfactory
(C) satisfy
(D) satisfying

5. The editor invited the famous architect to write about ------- favorite hotels.

(A) he
(B) him
(C) his
(D) himself

6. Mr. White updated the company's Web site by ------- because the other programmer had a problem with her password.

(A) he
(B) himself
(C) him
(D) his

7. A number of ------- will take place.

(A) change
(B) changing
(C) changes
(D) changed

8. Every ------- in the budget committee agreed to disclose the information.

(A) employee
(B) employers
(C) employees
(D) employment

9. People who exercise regularly tend to live healthier and longer than ------- who don't.

(A) they
(B) that
(C) these
(D) those

10. You need the manager's ------- to get into the restricted area.

(A) approve
(B) approved
(C) approves
(D) approval

試著在限時1分30秒之內盡可能答對。

Questions 11-14 refer to the following letter.

Hi, Marianne,

This is David. I hope you're enjoying your new job. Everyone here at Framingham Company ------- you a lot. I'm sure you will do fine at the new company, too.
       11.

By the way, my family and I are planning a vacation in Florida. -------. Would you be
                                                                 12.
willing to make some ------- about travel destinations in the area? This will be the first
                       13.
time for us to visit the southern part of the country and we're very much excited about it.

In particular, I am hoping for your ------- on beaches in the area.
                                    14.

Thank you for your help.

PART

5

6

11. (A) miss
    (B) misses
    (C) missing
    (D) to miss

12. (A) Florida has the largest population
       in the US.
    (B) I want to get a new job at your
       company.
    (C) I know you used to live there
       before.
    (D) Please visit us sometime soon.

13. (A) recommend
    (B) recommended
    (C) recommendations
    (D) recommends

14. (A) regret
    (B) opinion
    (C) payment
    (D) job

Unit 2 形容詞與副詞

形容詞用來具體描述特性、樣子和狀態,並說明名詞。如同cold weather(寒冷天氣)、low prices(低價)等,通常放在名詞前面以修飾名詞。副詞用來強調動詞或形容詞的語意,或者修飾整體句子。

 Step 1   基礎文法

Point 1 形容詞的形態

1) 構成形容詞的代表性詞尾

-al	original	原本的	-ful	useful	有用的
-able	comfortable	舒服的	-ive	active	活躍的
-ous	famous	有名的	-ic	artistic	藝術的
-ant	important	重要的	-ent	different	不同的
-ar	similar	類似的	-ary	primary	基本的

2) 形容詞的種類

一般形容詞	beautiful, apparent	描述人事物的特性、樣子和狀態。
數量形容詞	one, each, every (a) few, several, many (a) little, less, much	描述數或量 (區分可數/不可數名詞來使用)
不定形容詞	all, some, most, other	描述不確定的數量或範圍 (可數/不可數名詞都可使用)

Answers _ p. 077

Practice

1. Dr. Keller gave a very ------- presentation at the seminar.
   (A) information   (B) informative

2. ------- customers complain about the restaurant's slow service.
   (A) Many   (B) Much

Point 2 形容詞的作用和位置

1) 名詞前面修飾名詞

限定詞和名詞的中間	冠詞(a, an, the)	It was a **beautiful** day. 那是美好的一天。
	所有格 (my, your, his/ her, our, their)	Our **excellent** reputation needs to be continued. 我們的良好聲譽需要繼續保持。
	指示形容詞 (this, that, these, those)	We gathered to celebrate this **important** event. 我們聚集在一起慶祝這重要的活動。
	數量形容詞 (few, little, many, much)	Many **notable** economists were invited to the party. 許多著名的經濟學家受邀參加了聚會。
副詞和名詞的中間		It was a very **informative** presentation. 這是一場非常有幫助的演講。
＜形容詞+ 名詞＞前面		I bought a **blue** wooden table. 我買了一張藍色的木桌。
沒有限定詞的 名詞前面		The company offers **excellent** prices. 該公司提供非常優惠的價格。

PART 5/6

2) 補語的作用

主格補語	Flat tires are **preventable**. 輪胎漏氣是可以預防的。 The new product became **popular** after the TV advertisement. 這個新產品在電視廣告之後變得流行起來。
受格補語	The management considered the new system **effective**. 管理層認為新制度是有效的。

Answers _ p. 077

Practice

3. Mr. Miyagi has waited for an ------- moment to speak with the manager.
   (A) extensively   (B) extensive

4. After the renovation, the old building has become -------.
   (A) spacious   (B) spaces

副詞的形態

1)構成副詞的詞尾

主要具有＜形容詞＋ly＞的形態。

形容詞	詞尾	副詞
sudden 突然的	+ ly	suddenly 突然地
careful 小心的		carefully 小心地
easy 容易的	y → 改成 i + ly	easily 輕易地

注意 –ly結束的詞尾並非一律是副詞，也有〈名詞＋ly〉表示形容詞的情況。

friend(名詞)+ly → friendly 友善的(形容詞)　　cost(名詞)+ly → costly 貴的(形容詞)

2)副詞的種類

時間	still 仍然	once 曾經	soon 馬上	now 現在
頻率	always 經常	usually 通常	sometimes 有時	regularly 定期地
程度	very 非常	quite 相當	extremely 極為	considerably 非常地
否定	hardly/seldom/barely 幾乎不～ (※否定副詞已經具有否定意義，不和not一起使用。) Ms. Nelson **rarely** visits the main office. 尼爾森女士很少訪問總部。		rarely 很少	never 絕對不～

3)容易混淆的形容詞和副詞

high 高的(形)	high 高高地(副)	highly 非常(副)
late 晚的(形)	late 很晚地(副)	lately 最近(副)
hard 困難的、硬的(形)	hard 認真地(副)	hardly 幾乎不~(副)
most 最、非常(副)	mostly 主要、大部分(副)	daily 每天的(形)、天天(副)

Practice

Answers _ p. 077

5. Papers were piled -------.
   (A) high　　　　　　　　　　(B) highly

6. Kevin tried ------- to get the position he wanted.
   (A) hard　　　　　　　　　　(B) hardly

副詞的作用和位置

1) 副詞修飾動詞的情況

加在一般動詞前面、be動詞和助動詞後面。完整句子中會放在句子的最後面。

一般動詞前面 (主語和動詞之間)	I **usually** <u>have</u> lunch at the company cafeteria. 我通常在公司的自助餐廳吃午飯。
助動詞後面 (助動詞和動詞原型之間)	The downtown store <u>will</u> **shortly** <u>open</u>. 市中心的商店很快就要開幕。
be動詞後面 (be動詞和-ing / p.p.之間)	We <u>are</u> **currently** <u>seeking</u> a new employee. 我們目前正在招聘一名新員工(進行式句子) Flights to Alaska will <u>be</u> **temporarily** <u>suspended</u>. 飛往阿拉斯加的航班將暫停。(被動語態句子)
have和p.p.之間	Mr. Baker <u>has</u> **already** <u>contacted</u> the main office. 貝克先生已經聯絡了總公司。(完成式句子)
完整句子後面	<u>We finished the project</u> **successfully**. 我們成功地完成了這個項目。

2) 副詞修飾動詞以外的情況時，加在修飾對象前面

形容詞前面	Winning the new contract is **extremely** <u>important</u>. 贏得新合約是非常重要的。
其他副詞前面	The manager didn't like her proposal **very** <u>much</u>. 經理不太喜歡她的建議。
句子最前面	**Fortunately**, <u>we were able to make it on time</u>. 幸運的是，我們按時抵達了。

Practice

Answers _ p. 077

7. Ms. Fernandez is ------- traveling in South America.

    (A) present (B) presently

8. Every new employee should read their handbooks ------- before they come to work.

    (A) careful (B) carefully

Point 5 形容詞的比較級和最高級

1) 形態

		原級	比較級 + than	the + 最高級
1音節	- er - est	long tall	longer taller	longest tallest
2音節以上 -ly 單字	more most	important quickly	more important more quickly	most important most quickly
	不規則	good/well bad many/much little	better worse more less	best worst most least

2) 比較級/最高級的位置和作用

	形容詞(be動詞後面)	副詞(一般動詞後面)
比較級	She is **heavier than** Jenny. 她比珍妮重。	She runs **faster than** Jenny. 她跑得比珍妮快。
最高級	She is **the tallest** girl in our class. 她是我們班上最高的女孩。	She runs **fastest** of my classmates. 她是我同學中跑得最快的。

3) 經常出題的比較級句子

as 原級(形、副) as 像～、和～一樣	The test results were not **as bad as** I thought. 考試結果並沒有我想像的那麼糟。
the + 比較級 + of the two 兩者中比較～的	This one is **the more qualified** of the two applicants. 在兩名應徵者中,這個人更有資格。
the + 比較級,the + 比較級 愈～的話,就愈～	**The more** you study, **the better** you feel about the test. 你讀得愈多,對考試愈有信心。

Practice

9. My score is as good ------- yours.

   (A) as   (B) than

10. The food quality of this restaurant is much ------- than it used to be.

    (A) better   (B) the best

📝 注意文法/結構/詞彙，練習選擇正確答案。

1. The board made a ------- decision about the employee policy.
   (A) final
   (B) finalist

2. This agency was ------- recommended by other employees.
   (A) high
   (B) highly

3. We are ------- behind schedule.
   (A) current
   (B) currently

4. Kayser is the ------- restaurant in the city.
   (A) best
   (B) better

5. Let's do our best to finish the report not too -------.
   (A) late
   (B) lately

6. If you want to get ------- information, please contact our office.
   (A) additionally
   (B) additional

7. The company tries to remain -------.
   (A) competitively
   (B) competitive

8. This new car is ------- faster than the one before.
   (A) much
   (B) very

9. The project was finished as ------- as we hoped.
   (A) successfully
   (B) successful

10. The orchestra's performance was really -------.
    (A) impressive
    (B) impressively

11. You have to make a ------- revision of your résumé before you apply.
    (A) carefully
    (B) careful

12. The new product has achieved a ------- success in the market.
    (A) remarkable
    (B) remark

13. We should be more ------- on ourselves to get the best results.
    (A) reliance
    (B) reliant

14. He's the ------- employee on our team.
    (A) most experienced
    (B) experienced

PART
5
/
6

133

⏱ 試著在限時4分30秒之內盡可能答對。

1. We should come up with an ------- way to increase profits.

   (A) effect
   (B) effective
   (C) effectively
   (D) effectiveness

2. *Financial Times* is the most ------- source of information in the industry.

   (A) rely
   (B) reliability
   (C) reliably
   (D) reliable

3. Of the two employees, Ms. Donnell is the ------- qualified to finish the job.

   (A) well
   (B) most
   (C) better
   (D) best

4. This new way of communication is ------- popular with the younger generation.

   (A) increase
   (B) increasing
   (C) increased
   (D) increasingly

5. All visitors should be ------- of others by speaking quietly in the museum.

   (A) consider
   (B) consideration
   (C) considerate
   (D) considerable

6. Toru Inc. will keep its customers' ------- information secure.

   (A) person
   (B) personality
   (C) personalize
   (D) personal

7. I am afraid the scores are not as ------- as we expected.

   (A) good
   (B) worse
   (C) better
   (D) the best

8. The new version of the publishing software is ------- better than the one before.

   (A) even
   (B) very
   (C) so
   (D) many

9. The more motivated the employees are, ------- productivity gets.

   (A) the highest
   (B) higher
   (C) the higher
   (D) highly

10. -------, I have to inform you that we will be closing this facility by the end of the month.

   (A) Regret
   (B) Regrettable
   (C) Regretful
   (D) Regrettably

⏰ 試著在限時1分30秒之內盡可能答對。

Questions 11-14 refer to the following e-mail.

To whom it may concern,

Our organization will host a conference with an -------- attendance of 1,000 individuals
on May 2nd. Your company was recommended by one of our clients, Design Pro. They
have used your services frequently and are happy about the results. --------.
　　　　　　　　　　　　　　　　　　　　　　　　　　　　　　　　　12.

However, I do have some concerns about whether your facility can accommodate our
needs. We are -------- worried about the size of the main conference room. Could you
please let me know the exact -------- of the main conference room and what other
rooms you have available?

Thank you for your time and attention.

Kimura Anderson

Minn's Marketing

---

11. (A) estimated
　　(B) estimate
　　(C) estimation
　　(D) estimating

12. (A) We will not be charging you extra.
　　(B) Could you give us some form of
　　　　discounts if it's possible?
　　(C) I'm impressed by your company's
　　　　excellent reputation.
　　(D) I will send in my deposit tomorrow.

13. (A) especial
　　(B) especially
　　(C) more especial
　　(D) most especial

14. (A) number
　　(B) time
　　(C) location
　　(D) capacity

Unit 3　動詞I－形態、主語與動詞的一致性

表達主語的動作或狀態的詞稱作動詞。動詞從原型細分成各式各樣的形態。

 Step 1　基礎文法

Point 1　動詞的形態

1) 構成動詞的字首、詞尾

-en	length 長度 → lengthen 延長	-ify	simple 單純的 → simplify 簡化
en-	large 大的 → enlarge 擴大	-ize	real 實際的 → realize 實現

2) 動詞的種類

動詞原型	助動詞後面 (can, could, will, would, must, may, might, should)	You <u>must</u> **arrive** at least one hour before the departure time. 你必須在起飛前至少一個小時到達。
	命令句	Please **repeat** after me. 請跟著我重複一遍。
動詞-ing (現在分詞)	be動詞 + -ing (進行式)	I <u>am</u> **writing** the letter. 我正在寫信。
動詞 -ed (過去分詞)	be動詞 + -ed (被動語態)	The memo <u>is</u> **posted** on the board. 備忘錄張貼在公告欄上。
	have / has / had 後面 (完成時態)	She <u>has</u> **come** to the party alone. 她一個人來參加聚會。
第3人稱單數現在式	一般動詞 + -(e)s	The manager **expects** higher profits this quarter. 經理期望本季能有更高的利潤。

Practice

Answers _ p. 079

1. The new safety policy should ------- effect as of next Monday.
   (A) to take　　　　　　　　(B) take

2. Copies of the report will be ------- during the meeting.
   (A) distributed　　　　　　(B) distribute

Point 2 動詞的位置

1) 動詞的位置

主語後面	Holiday Hotel **offers** a complimentary breakfast. 假日酒店提供免費早餐。
命令句時，加在句子的 開始、接在please後面	Please **finish** this report soon. 請儘快完成這份報告。
助動詞後面	Those who want to attend the seminar should **reply** to this e-mail. 想參加研討會的人請回覆這封電子郵件。

2) 代表性的不規則動詞

現在	過去	過去分詞	現在	過去	過去分詞
am, is/are	was/were	been	go	went	gone
become	became	become	have	had	had
begin	began	begun	hold	held	held
bring	brought	brought	keep	kept	kept
buy	bought	bought	know	knew	known
choose	chose	chosen	leave	left	left
come	came	come	make	made	made
deal	dealt	dealt	mean	meant	meant
do	did	done	speak	spoke	spoken
draw	drew	drawn	spend	spent	spent
drive	drove	driven	send	sent	sent
fall	fell	fallen	take	took	taken
find	found	found	tell	told	told
give	gave	given	think	thought	thought

Practice

Answers _ p. 079

3. Please ------- out the registration form in your packet before you go in.
   (A) fill   (B) filling

4. The problems at the factory have been ------- with promptly right after the incident.
   (A) dealing   (B) dealt

Point 3 主語和動詞的一致性

動詞須依主語的單複數做變化,並有一致性。

1) 單數・複數形動詞

根據主語的數量/格式而有不同形態。

第3人稱單數-(e)s	She **works** in the payroll division. 她在薪資部門工作。
複數 → 動詞原型	Many people **stand** in the hallway. 許多人站在走廊上。
過去式 → 過去時態	The manager **was** late for the meeting. 經理開會遲到了。

2) 從＜主語+修飾語+動詞＞結構中分辨主語

當主語後面加上長串的修飾語時,有時很難分辨真正的主語。由於修飾語不會對動詞造成影響,找到真正的主語之後,必須讓主語和動詞有一致性。

▶修飾語的種類

介係詞片語	The **employees** [in the office] **are** working hard to meet the deadline. (辦公室裡的)員工正在努力工作,以趕在最後期限前完成任務。
同位語	**Mr. Anderson,** [one of the most famous presenters in sales], **is** coming to visit us. 安德森先生(銷售界最著名的演講者之一)要來拜訪我們。
關係代名詞	The **training** [which is offered for new employees] **focuses** on company policy. (為新員工提供的)培訓著重於公司政策。
分詞片語	The **questionnaire** [provided with other materials] **needs** to be filled out. (與其他資料一起提供的)調查表需要填寫完成。

Practice

Answers _ p. 079

5. Employees in the sales department ------- the seminar every month.

   (A) attend   (B) attends

6. A customer who orders through our new Web site ------- 20% discounts.

   (A) receive   (B) receives

138

Point 4 須注意＜主語+動詞＞結構

1) to不定詞和動名詞是單數處理

to不定詞主語	To update the security system **is** necessary at the moment. 目前有必要更新保安系統。
動名詞主語	Getting some customer feedback **is** really important in marketing. 在市場營銷中，獲得一些顧客反饋是非常重要的。

2) 主格關係子句的先行詞與動詞的一致性

主格關係代名詞who / which / that後面的動詞須與關係代名詞前面的先行詞數一致。

單數先行詞	We want to hire **an employee** who **has** sales experience. 我們想聘僱一位有銷售經驗的員工。
複數先行詞	We need to send **employees** who **have** sales experience. 我們需要派遣有銷售經驗的員工。

3) 需要使用動詞原型的情況

insist、demand之類的意見/命令/請求動詞後的that子句使用＜should+動詞原型＞，有時省略should，只留下動詞原型。

主語	ask/insist/demand/require/ recommend/request/suggest/propose	that + 主語 + (should) + 動詞原型

I **insisted that** Mr. Choo (should) **go** to this year's marketing conference.
我認為周先生應該去參加今年的市場營銷會議。

＜It is ~ that ~＞中that子句不可省略，當表達重要事件時，也可能省略should，後接動詞原型。

It is	necessary/important/ essential/vital/imperative	that + (should) + 動詞原型

It is necessary that the report (should) **be** submitted by next week.
必須在下週之前提交報告。

Answers _ p. 079

Practice

7. Applicants who ------- to apply for the position should send in their résumés.
    (A) wishes   (B) wish

8. The safety rules require that everyone ------- a hard hat and a pair of goggles.
    (A) wear   (B) wears

1) 數量的主語動詞一致性: 單數名詞使用單數形容詞，複數名詞使用複數形容詞。

使用單數的數量		使用複數的數量	
a(n)/one/each/every/ this/that/a little/little/much	+ 單數名詞	a few/few both/many/several/ a couple of/a variety of/various	+複數名詞
everything/anything/nothing	+ 單數名詞	a number of + 複數名詞(許多的~)	使用複數
the number of + 複數名詞(~的數)	使用單數		

<u>Much interest</u> **was generated** due to the event. 這次活動引起了很多人的興趣。

<u>Several factors</u> **were considered** before making a decision. 在做出決定之前考慮了幾個因素。

描述部分/整體時of後面的名詞數量保持一致性		
all/some/most/ half/part/a lot/lots/plenty	of + the	不可數名詞(單數名詞) + 單數動詞
		複數可數名詞 + 複數動詞

<u>A lot of</u> **students were** present at the conference. 很多學生都出席了研討會。

<u>All of</u> **the information** necessary to assemble the equipment **is** in your manual.
組裝設備所需的所有資訊都在您的說明書中。

2) 使用連接詞連接的主語動詞一致性

使用複數	A and B A和B	
保持與B的 主動詞一致性	A or B A或B either A or B A或B not only A but also B 不只A，B也 B as well as A A以及B都	not A but B 不是A而是B neither A nor B 不是A也不是B

Ms. Kim and her trainer <u>meet</u> every week. 金小姐和她的教練每個星期見面。

Either he **or I** <u>have</u> to submit a budget report. 他或我必須提交預算報告。

Practice

Answers _ p. 079

9. Both the sales representative and the department manager ------- present at the meeting.

   (A) was   (B) were

10. The number of sales employees ------- grown rapidly for the last two years.

   (A) has   (B) have

Step 2　基本掌握

Answers _ p. 079

📝 注意文法/結構/詞彙，練習選擇正確答案。

1. Please ------- the project on time.
   (A) finishing
   (B) finish

2. Demands for the new product ------- rising fast.
   (A) is
   (B) are

3. The other department heads ------- on the subject.
   (A) agree
   (B) agrees

4. The secretary has ------- all the preparation.
   (A) finish
   (B) finished

5. There ------- plenty of time left before the workshop starts.
   (A) is
   (B) are

6. Brad ------- in the personnel department.
   (A) work
   (B) works

7. Sammie ------- the material for the presentation.
   (A) wrote
   (B) write

8. I am ------- in the advertising field.
   (A) interest
   (B) interested

9. Everyone ------- come on time for the meeting.
   (A) have to
   (B) has to

10. Books about computer technology ------- in the back aisle.
    (A) is
    (B) are

11. Can you ------- the merchandise by tomorrow?
    (A) ship
    (B) shipping

12. ------- to Gate 5 at least 15 minutes before the departure time.
    (A) Go
    (B) Going

13. Mr. Sakata will ------- the employee workshop.
    (A) lead
    (B) leading

14. The hotel can ------- more guests.
    (A) accompany
    (B) accommodate

PART
5/
6

🕐 試著在限時4分30秒之內盡可能答對。

1. We must ------- our best to keep a friendly relationship with our suppliers.

   (A) done
   (B) did
   (C) to do
   (D) do

2. Lucy ------- a new flavor for her dessert line last year.

   (A) create
   (B) creating
   (C) creates
   (D) created

3. Mr. Sato ------- the best sales person in his department.

   (A) will
   (B) be
   (C) is
   (D) are

4. Answering questions ------- the responsibility of a secretary.

   (A) is
   (B) are
   (C) be
   (D) will

5. The technicians recommend that every user ------- their password once a year.

   (A) change
   (B) changes
   (C) changed
   (D) changing

6. Your document ------- some errors that need to be fixed right away.

   (A) is
   (B) has
   (C) have
   (D) are

7. Many buildings around the city library ------- built 200 years ago.

   (A) is
   (B) are
   (C) was
   (D) were

8. Seasonal variations ------- an effect on the sales of certain products.

   (A) has
   (B) have
   (C) having
   (D) to have

9. The key to success in online sales ------- to offer goods at affordable prices.

   (A) is
   (B) are
   (C) be
   (D) being

10. Guests who ------- to eat vegetarian dishes should let us know beforehand.

   (A) prefer
   (B) prefers
   (C) preferring
   (D) to prefer

⏰ 試著在限時1分30秒之內盡可能答對。

Questions 11-14 refer to the following notice.

Attention all second-floor kitchen users

To help keep our kitchen area pleasant and clean, please be considerate when using the refrigerator and all other kitchen appliances. Please ------- any spoiled food and
11.
wipe up any spills immediately. -------.
12.

These basic ------- will prevent unpleasant smells. Also, please do not throw away the
13.
box of baking soda that will be ------- on the top shelf of the refrigerator. This will help
14.
keep the refrigerator odor free.

Thank you for your cooperation.

---

11. (A) discarded
    (B) discarding
    (C) discard
    (D) discards

新多益
12. (A) The fish will be served with cold vegetables.
    (B) Keep the surface of the kitchen counter clean after each use.
    (C) You can get a special discount when you buy more than one appliance.
    (D) Tonight's dinner specials are listed on the menu.

13. (A) measures
    (B) skills
    (C) filters
    (D) elements

14. (A) place
    (B) placing
    (C) placed
    (D) places

Unit 4 動詞2－語態和時態

主語為動詞的行為主體稱作主動語態，主語為動詞的對象稱作被動語態。

 Step 1　基礎文法

Point 1 主動語態和被動語態

1) 被動語態的形式

主動語態 (做)	He recommended this restaurant. 他推薦這家餐廳。 主語　　動詞　　　　　　受格
被動語態 (被/受到)	→ This restaurant was recommended by him. 這家餐廳受到他的推薦。 　　主語　　be動詞+過去分詞(p.p.) by +受格

※ 主動語態句中的受格在被動語態中成為主詞，主動語態句中的主詞通常換成
　〈by+受格〉形式或省略。

2) 主動語態和被動語態的區分

須考慮主語和動詞的關係，及物動詞後面有受格時是主動語態，沒有受格時是被動語態。

主動語態	**The marketing department** will **announce** a new plan. 行銷部即將公佈一項新計劃。 → 行銷部是公佈計畫的主體。
被動語態	**A new plan** will **be announced** by the marketing department. 行銷部即將公佈一項新計劃。(一項新計畫將由行銷部公佈。) → 新計劃是被公佈的對象
不可作為被動 語態的動詞 (不及物動詞)	The accident **happened** yesterday. 事故發生在昨天。 → 不及物動詞 happen, place, exist, appear, function 等無法改為被動語態。

Practice

Answers _ p. 081

1. The contract should ------- by both parties.
   (A) sign　　　　　　　　　　(B) be signed

2. Many travelers ------- this area to view the famous landmarks.
   (A) visited　　　　　　　　　(B) were visited

1) 使用by以外的介係詞的被動語態相關表達

be satisfied with 滿足於～	be crowded with 擠滿了～	be disappointed at 對～失望
be pleased with 對～感到開心	be based on 根據～	be committed to 致力於～
be interested in 對～有興趣	be concerned about 關心～	be devoted to 貢獻給～
be worried about 擔心～	be engaged in 從事～	be involved in 參與～
be surprised at 對～驚訝	be shocked at 對～感到震驚	

Our organization **is committed to** science education for children.
我們的組織是致力於兒童科學教育。

2) 給予形式(主語+動詞+間接受詞+直接受詞)的被動語態

給予形式包含2個受詞，因此有2個被動語態。

給予形式動詞: send 寄　give 給　offer 提供　show 出示　award 授予(獎項)

主動語態	The company **gave** <u>some employees</u> <u>prizes</u>. 公司給了一些員工獎勵。 　　　　　　　　間接受詞　　　直接受詞
被動語態 1 (間接受詞主語)	<u>Some employees</u> **were given** <u>prizes</u> by the company. (be+p.p.+直接受詞) 一些員工獲得了公司的獎勵。
被動語態2 (直接受詞主語)	<u>Prizes</u> **were given to** <u>some employees</u> by the company. (be+p.p.+to+直接受詞) 公司給了一些員工獎勵。(獎項由公司發給了一些員工。)

3) 期望、命令形式(主語+動詞+受詞+受詞補語)的被動語態

使用受詞補語to不定詞的動詞，在被動語態後加上to不定詞的問題是出題方式之一。

期望、命令形式動詞: advise 建議　encourage 鼓勵　expect 期待　request 要求　permit 允許

主動語態	He **asked** <u>me</u> to send a report. 他要求我把報告寄過去。
被動語態	<u>I</u> **was asked** to send a report. 我被要求寄一份報告。

Answers _ p. 081

Practice

3. Our hotel guests ------- free shuttle bus service to the airport.

   (A) have given　　　　　　　　(B) are given

4. Employees are encouraged ------- in technical training sessions.

   (A) to participate　　　　　　　(B) participated

主語與動詞一致性

英語基本時態的簡單式、進行式、完成式的用法須和主語一致(獨立子句和從屬子句的時態關係)。

1) 現在式(動詞 + -s/es)：常態的事實或反覆的動作。

> usually 通常   often 常常   every day 每天   always 總是   these days 最近

We <u>often</u> **talk** to our suppliers about the shipment.
我們經常與供貨商討論裝運事宜。

We <u>usually</u> **use** an on-line payroll system to report our work hours.
我們通常使用線上工資管理系統來報告我們的工作時間。

2) 過去式(動詞 + -d/ed不規則動詞)：過去已經結束的動作或狀態。

> yesterday 昨天   ago 之前~   last week/time 上週／上次   in + 年度

I **sent** the application <u>two weeks ago</u>. 我兩周前寄了申請表。

<u>Last week</u>, we **accepted** the CEO's proposal. 上周我接受了執行長的提議。

3) 未來式(will[be going to] + 動詞原型)：未來的預測或意圖。

> tomorrow 明天   next week/time 下周/下次   soon/shortly 很快/不久   by/until + 時間 到~

The board of directors **will visit** the factory <u>tomorrow</u>. 董事會明天將參觀工廠。

She **is going to show up** at the conference <u>next week</u>. 她將在下週的會議上露面。

4) 例外：條件/時間連接詞帶出的副詞子句，即使是未來語意也須使用現在式。

> when 如果~、當~   as soon as 一~就   after ~之後   before ~之前
> if 如果~的話   unless 除非~否則不   once 一旦~就

If it **rains** tomorrow, we will stay inside. 如果明天下雨，我們就待在室內。

When we **get** the permit from the government, we will start the construction.
當我們獲得政府許可時，我們將開始施工。

Answers _ p. 081

Practice

5. Our service representatives usually ------- 2 to 3 business days to fix your computer.
    (A) take   (B) took

6. The board of directors ------- next Friday to discuss a new marketing strategy.
    (A) will gather   (B) gathered

1) 現在進行式(am/are/is + -ing)：目前正在發生的事情。

We **are** <u>currently</u> **looking for** a temporary assistant.
我們目前正在尋找臨時助理。

Mr. Hoffman **is interviewing** some of the applicants <u>at the moment</u>.
霍夫曼先生目前正在面試一些應徵者。

2) 過去進行式(was/were + -ing)：過去特定時間內發生的事情。

When I <u>saw</u> Ann in the park yesterday, she **was playing** tennis.
昨天我在公園裡看到安，那時她正在打網球。

The employees **were working** at the warehouse when the manager <u>visited</u> the office.
當經理訪問辦公室時，員工們正在倉庫工作。

3) 未來進行式(will be + -ing)：未來特定時間內將發生的事或計畫好的未來。

The actors **will be performing** at the opening ceremony <u>when you come</u>.
當你來的時候，演員們將在開幕式上表演。

He **will be leading** a training session <u>at this time tomorrow</u>.
明天這個時候他將指導一個培訓班。

PART
5
/
6

Answers _ p. 081

Practice

7. I ------- talking to one of our clients when Michael came to visit me.

   (A) am   (B) was

8. We ------- currently undergoing a lot of changes, and we hope you can help us with the process.

   (A) are   (B) will be

Point 5 完成式

現在、過去、未來式表達的是「時間點」，而完成式表達的是兩個時間點之間的期間。

過去完成 ← 過去完成式 → 過去 ← 現在完成式 → 現在 ← 未來完成式 → 未來

1) 現在完成式(have/has + p.p.): 過去開始的事情持續到現在或造成影響時

> **since + 過去時間點** ～以來　　**for + 時間長度** ～期間　　**over the last + 時間長度** 在過去的～

We **have worked** at this company <u>for the last 10 years</u>.
我們在這家公司工作了10年。

The economy **has grown** fast <u>since the end of the 1990s</u>.
自1990年代末以來，經濟迅速增長。

2) 過去完成式(had + p.p.): 早在過去特定的時間點之前發生的事情

> **<副詞子句連接詞+過去、子句+過去完成式>** (過去) 發生～時，已經～

When we **signed** the contract, the press **had** already **known** about the deal.
當我們簽署合約時，媒體已經知道了這筆交易。

Before he **joined** our company, Mr. Anderson **had worked** in the advertising industry for years.
在加入我們公司之前，安德森先生已經在廣告業工作多年了。

3) 未來完成式(will have + p.p.): 現在或過去開始的動作將在未來某個特定的時間點完成時

> **by next + 時間** 到下個～時　　**next + 時間** 下個~時　　**by the end of + 時間** 到~末/底

I **will have finished** the whole report <u>by next Monday</u>.
到下週一我將完成整個報告。

<u>By the time the CEO visits</u> the office next month, we **will have finished** the renovation.
當執行長下個月訪問辦公室時，我們已經完成了整修工作。

Answers _ p. 081

Practice

9. Mr. Tanaka ------- for the company for the last seven years.

   (A) has worked　　　　　　　　(B) worked

10. Mr. Gordon is a famous chef whose dishes ------- received numerous awards.

    (A) has　　　　　　　　　　　(B) have

📝 注意文法/結構/詞彙，練習選擇正確答案。

1. The store is too ------- with customers during the holiday season.
   (A) crowding
   (B) crowded

2. I will ------- your place next time I come here.
   (A) visit
   (B) be visited

3. Mr. Garner ------- our company three years ago.
   (A) will join
   (B) joined

4. Ms. Robertson consistently ------- the head office every month.
   (A) visits
   (B) will visit

5. As soon as he ------- my letter, he will respond to me.
   (A) gets
   (B) will get

6. I ------- a walk in the park yesterday.
   (A) take
   (B) took

7. The farewell party ------- place next Monday.
   (A) will take
   (B) took

8. I was asked ------- Mr. Parker.
   (A) email
   (B) to email

9. She told me yesterday that she ------- in Korea last year.
   (A) has worked
   (B) had worked

10. The new project ------- by Mr. Wright, the new director.
    (A) had led
    (B) was led

11. The price of the product was too high for us to -------.
    (A) accept
    (B) acceptable

12. We need the department supervisor's -------.
    (A) signature
    (B) signed

13. The next special ------- is scheduled to open on May 1st.
    (A) exhibits
    (B) exhibition

14. The company is ------- to a safe environment for the next generation.
    (A) committed
    (B) committing

PART
5
6

⏱ 試著在限時4分30秒之內盡可能答對。

1. Our store usually ------- at 7 o'clock in the morning.

   (A) open
   (B) opens
   (C) opened
   (D) is opening

2. This picture was ------- by a famous designer.

   (A) take
   (B) taken
   (C) taking
   (D) takes

3. The company sales ------- sharply in the last quarter.

   (A) fall
   (B) falls
   (C) fell
   (D) falling

4. All payments can ------- by credit card if the amount is over $200.

   (A) make
   (B) makes
   (C) be make
   (D) be made

5. ------- 2010, the company has focused on women's apparel.

   (A) Before
   (B) Since
   (C) Last
   (D) When

6. When the Accounting Convention ------- held, Julie Parker will be present.

   (A) is
   (B) was
   (C) will be
   (D) had been

7. The additional equipment is ------- to increase employee productivity.

   (A) expecting
   (B) expectation
   (C) expected
   (D) expects

8. The apartment is conveniently ------- close to a subway station.

   (A) location
   (B) locating
   (C) locates
   (D) located

9. Maxter Motors ------- a new model last month.

   (A) introduced
   (B) introduces
   (C) will introduce
   (D) are introduced

10. A substantial increase in sales ------- two months ago due to online advertising.

    (A) will happen
    (B) will be happened
    (C) was happened
    (D) happened

⏱ 試著在限時1分30秒之內盡可能答對。

Questions 11-14　refer to the following article.

What's Happening in Our Town?

Newbury, September 1 – Until September 19, the Newbury Art Museum -------- 30
[11.]
works by Andrew Shihan. Mr. Shihan is a well-known artist residing in our
neighborhood and he was kind enough to offer this special -------- to see his recent
[12.]
works. Mr. Shihan visited small villages in Europe for the last six months. --------.
[13.]
Tickets to this special exhibition are available for $5 in addition to the regular
admission. The museum is open from 11 A.M. to 5 P.M. Monday through Saturday and
-------- on Sundays.
[14.]

---

11. (A) exhibit
    (B) exhibited
    (C) is exhibited
    (D) will be exhibiting

12. (A) price
    (B) help
    (C) opportunity
    (D) color

13. (A) He made a reservation through a
        travel agency.
    (B) His latest paintings were inspired
        by those experiences.
    (C) Europe's economy is bouncing
        back from a recession.
    (D) We have wanted to invite him for a
        long time.

14. (A) closes
    (B) will close
    (C) was closed
    (D) has closed

Unit 5　動狀詞

句子中除了動詞以外，具有動詞作用的其他詞類就是動狀詞。「相當於動詞」意義的動狀詞是to不定詞、動名詞、現在分詞和過去分詞的統稱。

 Step 1　基礎文法

Point 1　動狀詞的動詞特性

1) 像動詞般具有受詞。

The medication has been used to treat viruses. 這種藥物已被用於治療病毒。
　　　　　　　　　　　　　to 不定詞+名詞

2) 像動詞般加上補語。

I hate being late. 我討厭遲到。
　　　動名詞+形容詞

3) 像動詞般加上助詞修飾。

After carefully reviewing the contract, please sign it. 仔細審閱合約後，請簽字。
　　　副詞+動名詞

4) 像動詞般具有主動語態和被動語態

	主動語態	被動語態
to不定詞	**to + 動詞原型**	**to + be + p.p.**
	I am pleased **to announce** the award winner. 我很高興地宣布獲獎者。	I want **to be left** alone. 我想獨處。
動名詞	**動詞 + -ing**	**being + p.p.**
	She hates **submitting** reports late. 她討厭遲交報告。	She hates **being told** what to do. 她討厭別人告訴她要做什麼。

Answers _ p. 083

Practice

1. The store will be closed early ------- the new sign at the front of the building.
   (A) will install　　　　　　　　(B) to install

2. We recommend ------- the information online to obtain basic data.
   (A) use　　　　　　　　(B) using

to不定詞

以〈to + 動詞原型〉形態使用，在句子中具有名詞、形容詞、副詞的作用。

1) to不定詞的名詞作用

放在句子的主語、受詞、補語位置，意思是「做~的事情」。

主語	**To know** oneself is not easy. 了解自己並不容易。		
受詞	加上to不定詞 作為受詞的動詞	want 想要 expect 期望 try 試圖	hope 希望 ask 要求 plan 企劃	need 需要 refuse 拒絕 decide/choose 決定
	I hope **to see** you again soon. 我希望很快能再見到你。		
補語	主格補語	Our goal is **to increase** profits. 我們的目標是增加利潤。
	受格補語	The management wants the employees **to submit** their vacation requests. 管理部門希望員工們提交休假申請書。

2) to不定詞的形容詞作用

加在名詞後面修飾名詞，意思是「必須~、要做~」。

修飾名詞	We have a deadline **to meet**. 我們必須配合截止日期。
經常修飾的名詞	ability 能力　effort 努力　opportunity 機會　way 方法　time 時間

3) to不定詞的副詞作用(修飾動詞/形容詞)

具有副詞的作用，表達目的時意思是「為了~」。

修飾動詞	You'll need to study harder **to pass** the exam. 你需要更加努力念書才能通過考試。
	表示目的的to不定詞可以換成 **in order to, so as to** 使用。 You'll need to study harder **(in order) to pass** the exam. = You'll need to study harder **so as to pass** the exam.
加上to不定詞的 形容詞	be able to 能夠~　　be happy to 樂意~　　be pleased to 很高興能~ be likely to 像是要~　be sure to 務必~　　be ready to 準備要~

Practice

Answers _ p. 083

3.　The manufacturer refused ------- the defective products.

　　(A) replacing　　　　　　　　(B) to replace

4.　All employees are able ------- conference rooms by filling out a form.

　　(A) reserve　　　　　　　　　(B) to reserve

以＜動詞+ -ing＞形態像名詞一般作為主語、受詞、補語，意思是「做~事情」。

1) 動名詞的作用

主語	**Watching** movies is my hobby. 看電影是我的興趣。		
動詞/ 介係詞 的受詞	We need to consider **hiring** more staff. 我們需要考慮僱用更多員工。 We look forward to **seeing** you. 我們期待與您見面。		
	加上動名詞作為 受詞的動詞	mind 在意 suggest 提議 finish 結束	consider 考慮 avoid 避免 enjoy 享受	recommend 推薦 discontinue 中斷 postpone/delay 延期
補語	My hobby is **playing** the piano. 我的興趣是彈鋼琴。		

2) 加上動名詞的習慣用法

go -ing 去~	be dedicated to -ing 專注於~	be committed to -ing 致力於~
object to -ing 反對	look forward to -ing 期待	be devoted to -ing 致力於~
feel like -ing 想要~	contribute to -ing 對~有貢獻	be used to -ing 習於~
be busy -ing 忙於~	cannot help -ing 不得不~	be accustomed to -ing 習於~
spend time in -ing 花時間~	have difficulty[a problem/trouble] (in) -ing 做~有困難	

3) 意義上的主語

使用不定詞＜for / of +(代)名詞＞，動名詞使用所有格人稱代名詞。當句子的主語和to不定詞或動名詞在意義上的主語不一致時，用來單獨表示。

to 不定詞	My suggestion was <u>for you</u> **to start** over. / It is nice <u>of you</u> **to say** so. 我的建議是你重新開始。　　　　　　　　　　你這麼說真是太好了。
代名詞	I suggested <u>her</u> **presenting** the project. 我建議她介紹這個方案。

Answers _ p. 083

Practice

5. ------- a new product to a market requires extensive planning and research.

    (A) Launch　　　　　　　　　　(B) Launching

6. He was angry about ------- being late to work.

    (A) my　　　　　　　　　　　(B) for me

分成現在分詞(動詞+ -ing)和過去分詞(動詞+ -ed / p.p.)，具有動詞的性質，同時也有修飾名詞的形容詞作用。現在分詞具有主動語態之意，過去分詞具有被動語態之意。

1) 分詞的作用和位置

名詞前 (單獨修飾)	The hotel is going to renovate its **existing** facilities next year. (現在分詞-主動) 飯店將在對現有設施進行整修。 This is a **reserved** seat. (過去分詞-被動) 這是預訂的座位。
名詞後 (加上其他修飾句)	I have a document **containing** important details. 我有一份包含重要細節的文件。
主格補語	He became **exhausted** after hours of driving. 開了幾個小時的車，他累壞了。 <加上主格補語的動詞> be 是~ become 變成 look 看起來 sound 聽起來 feel 感覺
受格補語	I **found** the book **interesting**. 我發現這本書很有趣。 <加上受格補語的動詞> make 製作 keep 維持 find/think 發現/認為 consider 考慮

2) 表達情緒的動詞分詞

當動詞用以表達情緒時，感知情緒時使用過去分詞，引發情緒的原因時使用現在分詞。大部分的情況中，過去分詞用在人的方面，現在分詞用在事物方面。

感知情緒時	I am very **excited** about tomorrow's presentation. 我對明天的演講感到非常興奮。
引發情緒時	The test results were very **disappointing** to me. 測試結果對我來說非常令人失望。
各種情緒動詞	interest 令人興奮 surprise 令人驚訝 excite 刺激 delight 令人開心 disappoint 使人失望 please 令人高興 satisfy 使人滿意 surprise 令人驚訝

Practice

Answers _ p. 083

7. The sales data ------- in this report cannot be accurate based on my calculation.

    (A) showing   (B) shown

8. The manager was not ------- with the results of his sales representatives.

    (A) satisfying   (B) satisfied

分詞構句是將連接詞帶來的副詞子句加以改變而成。

	①可以省略連接詞　②連接詞子句和獨立子句的主語相同時則省略 ③以分詞代替(為了明確表達意思，也會留下連接詞)
形成分詞子句 主動 -ing 被動 -ed / p.p.	**When you book** a ticket online, you have to use a credit card. 在線上預訂機票時，必須使用信用卡。 → **(When) Booking** a ticket online, you have to use a credit card. 　可以省略連接詞、主語you，由於後面加上受詞a ticket表示主動-ing。 **While he was embarrassed**, he was able to finish the speech. 雖然他不知所措，但他完成了演講。 → **(While) Embarrassed**, he was able to finish the speech. 　主語he省略，因為he感受到不知所措的情緒而使用過去分詞。

Point 6 容易混淆的動狀詞用法

1) **動名詞** vs. **名詞**：動名詞後面可以加上受詞，但名詞無法。

動名詞	**Reserving** the table in advance is necessary. 提前預訂餐桌是必要的。
名詞	You have to make the **reservation** in advance. 您必須提前預訂。

2) **介係詞 to** vs. **to不定詞**：to不定詞的後面加上動詞原型，介係詞to的後面加上動名詞。

to不定詞	The company wants **to reduce** business costs. 該公司希望降低業務成本。
介係詞 to	Our company is committed **to providing** good customer service. 我們公司致力於為客戶提供優質的服務。

3) **動名詞+名詞** vs. **分詞+名詞**：動名詞後面的名詞具有受詞作用，分詞後面的名詞是分詞修飾的對象。

動名詞+ N	My hobby is **playing** the piano. 我的興趣是彈鋼琴。
分詞 + N	We should contact the **participating** company. 我們應該聯絡參與的公司。
常考的 分詞	rising cost 增加的成本　　remaining work 剩下的工作　　leading company 一流企業 experienced workers 有經驗的員工　　an updated manual 更新的手冊

Practice

Answers _ p. 083

9.　------- by his speech, the audience gave him a long ovation.

(A) Impressed
(B) Impressing

10. This manual contains information on ------- a password.

(A) creation
(B) creating

📝 注意文法/結構/詞彙，練習選擇正確答案。

1. ------- foreign languages is not easy.
   (A) Learn
   (B) Learning

2. Let's continue ------- this matter tomorrow.
   (A) discussed
   (B) to discuss

3. There is no need ------- to worry.
   (A) for you
   (B) in you

4. The company is dedicated to ------- nonprofit organizations.
   (A) help
   (B) helping

5. This special offer is good for a ------- time only.
   (A) limited
   (B) limiting

6. We have decided ------- one of the local charities.
   (A) supporting
   (B) to support

7. Please return the ------- form within two weeks.
   (A) attached
   (B) attaching

8. I am ------- to announce an award winner.
   (A) pleased
   (B) pleasing

9. ------- a healthy life, you need to socialize with other people.
   (A) Having
   (B) To have

10. I prefer to ------- the morning shift.
    (A) take
    (B) taking

11. We have received résumés from many ------- applicants.
    (A) qualify
    (B) qualified

12. I wish ------- English more.
    (A) studying
    (B) to study

13. The company conducted a survey ------- customers' needs.
    (A) to identify
    (B) identify

14. While ------- New York, you should watch a musical there.
    (A) visiting
    (B) visit

PART
5
6

157

⏰ 試著在限時4分30秒之內盡可能答對。

1. Do you enjoy ------- by yourself when you have free time?
   (A) travel
   (B) to travel
   (C) traveling
   (D) to traveling

2. We decided to ------- our products in European countries.
   (A) distribute
   (B) distribution
   (C) distributing
   (D) distributed

3. Customers are likely to favorably ------- to our new product line.
   (A) respond
   (B) responds
   (C) responding
   (D) be responded

4. PAE Resort is considering ------- the company's Web site before the next season.
   (A) update
   (B) updated
   (C) to update
   (D) updating

5. ------- its 50th anniversary, the Modern Ballet Theater will introduce a new piece by Monique Steinbeck.
   (A) In celebration
   (B) To celebrate
   (C) Celebrates
   (D) Celebration

6. We prepared for ------- production costs.
   (A) rise
   (B) risen
   (C) rising
   (D) rose

7. Have you reviewed the ------- version of the building design?
   (A) revise
   (B) revising
   (C) revised
   (D) to revise

8. The whole experience was very ------- to all the workshop participants.
   (A) satisfying
   (B) satisfied
   (C) satisfaction
   (D) satisfies

9. The goal of today's meeting is ------- much-needed help to small business owners in the area.
   (A) provide
   (B) provided
   (C) provisions
   (D) to provide

10. When ------- a package, you have to make sure that the box is securely taped.
    (A) send
    (B) sending
    (C) sent
    (D) being sent

⏰ 試著在限時1分30秒之內盡可能答對。

Questions 11-14　refer to the following letter.

Dear Mr. Guwata,

Congratulations on your new home. Birmingham Power & Electronic is ------- to
$\overline{11.}$
transfer service from your current residence to your new location on Mason Road.
However, for security purposes, your authorizing the transfer is necessary for us -------
$\overline{12.}$
our job.

To guarantee that your need for electricity is met starting the first day of your -------,
$\overline{13.}$
please sign and fax the enclosed form to 215–555–3453 at your earliest convenience.

-------.
$\overline{14.}$

Sincerely,

Rosanne Walters
Customer Service

**PART
5
/
6**

11.　(A) definite
　　　(B) possible
　　　(C) unable
　　　(D) ready

12.　(A) do
　　　(B) to do
　　　(C) does
　　　(D) doing

13.　(A) occupy
　　　(B) occupant
　　　(C) occupancy
　　　(D) occupied

14.　(A) We will send you the confirmation
　　　　e-mail as soon as we get the
　　　　authorization from you.
　　　(B) Your new place will be ready when
　　　　you move in.
　　　(C) The post office will send your
　　　　letters and packages to your new
　　　　address.
　　　(D) The questionnaire you have filled
　　　　out will help us serve you better in
　　　　the future.

Unit 6　介係詞與連接詞

介係詞後面加上名詞(子句)，連接詞後面加上〈主語+動詞〉。必須練習區分介係詞和連接詞。

 Step 1　基礎文法

Point 1　介係詞的位置和作用

1) 介係詞的位置

介係詞加在具名詞功能的(代)名詞、動名詞、名詞子句前面。這時介係詞後面具名詞功能的詞稱為介係詞的受詞，＜介係詞+介係詞受詞＞稱作介係詞片語。

名詞前	The budget report should be completed **before** the deadline. 預算報告應在截止日期前完成。
代名詞前	The travel agency will make the hotel reservations **for** us. 旅行社將為我們預訂飯店。
動名詞前	We should stay indoors **instead of** taking a walk in this weather. 在這種天氣下，我們應該留在室內，而不是散步。
名詞子句前	Could you take these documents **to** where the board meeting is being held? 你能把這些文件帶到董事會開會的地方嗎？

2) 介係詞(片語)的作用

介係詞片語在句子中具有修飾名詞的形容詞，以及修飾動詞的副詞作用。

形容詞片語	The desk **by the door** needs to be moved. (修飾 the desk) 門旁邊的桌子需要移動。
副詞子句	I've been waiting **for two hours**. (修飾 have been waiting) 我已經等了兩個小時了。

Answers _ p. 085

Practice

1. Payment made to your account ------- our business hours is not shown.
   (A) after　　　　　　　　　　(B) on

2. The updated safety manual includes guidelines ------- the entire factory.
   (A) and　　　　　　　　　　(B) for

時間與地點介係詞

1) 能夠同時表達時間、地點的介係詞

		時間		地點	
in	月/年	**in** 2017 在2017年 **in** July 在7月	大空間內	**in** Seoul 在首爾	
	季節/時機	**in** summer 在夏天 **in** the morning 在早上	特定空間、範圍內	**in** the meeting room 在會議室裡	
	～(時間)後	**in** three days 3天後			
at	相對來說較短的時區、時間點	**at** 2 o'clock 2點時 **at** noon 中午時 **at** the end of the year 年底時	相對來說較小的範圍	**at** the park 在公園	
			公司名、特定地點	**at** Kent Shipping Company 在肯特快遞公司	
on	特定日期	**on** May 28th 在5月28日	接觸的表面	**on** the top shelf 在架子上	
	星期、周末	**on** Monday 在周一 **on** weekend 在周末	在～上面	**on** the second floor 在2樓	

2) 表達時間點的介係詞

by 到～(finish/complete/submit)	**Finish** the report **by** tomorrow. 明天完成報告。
until 到～(last, wait, stay)	The store is open **until** 9 p.m. 商店營業至晚上9點。
before/prior to ～之前	**before** Monday 周一前
after ～之後	**after** 5 p.m. 下午5點以後
since 從～以後(現在完成式)	Sales have increased **since** last quarter. 自上個分季以來銷售額有所增長。

3) 表達期間的介係詞

for ～期間(+數字)	**for** a week 一周
during ～期間(+特定事件)	**during** the meeting 會議期間
within 在～之內	**within** a week 一周之內
throughout 整個～	**throughout** the next three weeks 在接下來的3周內

Answers _ p. 085

Practice

3. We watched the game ------- three hours last night.
   (A) for   (B) during

4. Mr. Wilson told his team to read the report ------- Thursday afternoon.
   (A) until   (B) by

Point 3 方向和位置

1) 方向介係詞

to 對～人、往～方向	for 朝向～	through 經過～
from 從～	into 進入～	across 橫越～
out of 在～之外	along 沿著	

This train is leaving **for** New York in five minutes. 這班火車5分鐘後開往紐約。

2) 位置介係詞

above / over ～之上	below / under ～之下	beside / next to / by ～旁邊
behind ～後面	around ～周圍	near ～附近

Mr. Benedict will show you **around** the facility. 本尼迪克特先生會帶你參觀設施。

Point 4 介係詞的習慣用法

1) 名詞+介係詞

demand **for** ～的需求	application **for** 申請～	reaction **to** ～的反應
problem **with** ～的問題	interest **in** 對～有興趣	dedication **to** 致力於～
increase **in** ～的增加	decrease **in** ～的減少	effect [influence] **on** 對～影響

2) 形容詞+介係詞

be famous **for** 以～聞名	be eligible **for** 有資格獲得～	be responsible **for** 對～負責
be entitled **to** 有權利～	be subject **to** 容易受到～	be familiar **with** 對～熟悉
be equipped **with** 配有～	be aware **of** 意識到～	be capable **of** 有能力～
be involved **in** 參與～	be absent **from** ～缺席	be different **from** 不同於～

Answers _ p. 085

Practice

5. If you have questions ------- any of our products, please contact our office.
   (A) against   (B) about

6. Temporary workers are entitled ------- paid leave.
   (A) from   (B) to

3) 動詞+介係詞

look **for** 尋找～	apply **for** 申請～	deal **with** 處理～
account **for** 說明～的原因	consist **of** 包括～	react **to** 對～做出反應
respond **to** 回覆～	talk **about** 談論～	depend **on** 取決於～

4) 動詞+A+介係詞+B

notify [inform] A **of** B　向A通報B	prohibit [prevent] A **from** -ing　防止/禁止A做～

Point 5　連接詞

像and(以及)、but(可是)一樣連接單字和單字、片語和片語、子句和子句的詞稱為連接詞。

1) 對等連接詞: 對等連接相同詞類的連接詞，形成平行結構。

and 以及(順接)	or 或者(選擇)	but 可是(轉折)
so 所以(結果)	for 因為(原因)	yet 然而(轉折)

He <u>was born in New York</u> **and** <u>has lived there for over 30 years</u>.
他出生在紐約，在那裡生活了多30年。

2) 相關連接詞

both A and B A和B都	either A or <u>B</u> A或B	not only A but also <u>B</u>
not A but <u>B</u> 不是A而是B	neither A nor <u>B</u> 既不是A也不是B	(= <u>B</u> as well as A) 不只A，B也

Both <u>the buyer</u> **and** <u>the seller</u> **have** to read the contract carefully. (both A and B + 複數動詞)
賣方和買方都必須仔細閱讀合約。

The paper is **not only** <u>recyclable</u> **but also** <u>reusable</u>.
紙張不僅可以回收利用，也可以重複使用。

3) 主語動詞一致性: 使用對等連接詞and連接的主語為複數動詞，＜A or B＞形態使用or連接的部分須和B一致。相關連接詞也是一樣，使用both連接的主語為複數動詞，＜either A or B＞、＜neither A nor B＞須和B一致。

Answers _ p. 085

Practice

7.　Most of the team members trust and ------- on the new director.

　　(A) depend　　　　　　　　　(B) dependent

8.　Neither shareholders nor management ------- the incident to be public.

　　(A) want　　　　　　　　　　(B) wants

副詞子句連接詞

1) 副詞子句的位置和作用: 加在獨立子句前面或後面以修飾整體獨立子句。

主語+動詞 連接詞+主語+動詞	連接詞+主語+動詞， 主語+動詞
獨立子句　　　　副詞子句	副詞子句　　　　獨立子句

You should lock the door **when** you leave the office at night.
晚上離開辦公室時，你應該鎖門。

Although the employees worked really hard, they couldn't meet the deadline.
雖然員工們非常努力工作，但他們還是趕不上最後期限。

2) 副詞子句連接詞的種類

時間	when/as ～時、～的話 until 到～ while 當～(但另一方面～)	before 之前 since 從～以來	after 之後 as soon as 一～就
讓步	although/though/even though 即使～也　　even if 即使是～也		
理由	because/since/as/now that 因為～		
條件	if 如果～　　　　once 一旦～　　　　unless 除非～		
目的	so that/in order that 以便～、為了～		

Even though the review was favorable, the play didn't attract many people.
即使評論很好，但這齣戲並沒有吸引很多人。

Unless written permission is given, we will not release personal information.
除非獲得書面許可，否則我們不會發佈個人資料。

Point 7 介係詞 vs. 連接詞

區分意思相同的介係詞和連接詞是出題類型，須記熟＜連接詞+子句＞，＜介係詞+名詞(片語)＞的用法。

介係詞+ 名詞(片語)	The price dropped **because of** the bad weather. 由於惡劣的天氣，價格下跌。
連接詞 + 句子	The price dropped **because** the weather was bad. 由於天氣惡劣，價格下跌。

Practice

Answers _ p. 085

9. Ms. Sirleaf was hired ------- she was the most qualified candidate.

   (A) because　　　　　　　　　(B) unless

10. I brought up the subject ------- our discussions.

   (A) while　　　　　　　　　　(B) during

Step 2　基本掌握

注意文法/結構/詞彙，練習選擇正確答案。

1. I usually go to work either by bus ------- subway.
   (A) and
   (B) or

2. We accept ------- checks nor credit cards.
   (A) either
   (B) neither

3. ------- you need my help, I'd be glad to help you.
   (A) If
   (B) Unless

4. ------- you visit my office, please call my secretary first.
   (A) During
   (B) When

5. ------- the rain, the plane got delayed.
   (A) Because of
   (B) Because

6. You will have to wait and ------- what happens.
   (A) saw
   (B) see

7. Can we stay at this office ------- the next week?
   (A) until
   (B) by

8. Inflation is having a bad effect ------- the economy.
   (A) in
   (B) on

9. Mr. Patterson has been working here ------- 2016.
   (A) since
   (B) for

10. ------- he did a good job, he was not satisfied.
    (A) Because
    (B) Although

11. I'd like to close my bank account ------- I move to another city.
    (A) before
    (B) that

詞彙問題

12. The terms of this contract are definitely ------- to us.
    (A) favorable
    (B) favorite

13. I believe that this new type of cleaning service could be a ------- business.
    (A) refundable
    (B) profitable

14. All ------- are required to register online.
    (A) participants
    (B) participation

PART 5/6

165

⏰ 試著在限時4分30秒之內盡可能答對。

1. Our new office is located ------- the top floor of the building.
   (A) by
   (B) around
   (C) within
   (D) on

2. We canceled the order ------- we couldn't get the funding.
   (A) although
   (B) in spite of
   (C) because
   (D) unless

3. If Creative Design doesn't deliver your merchandise ------- Friday, we will give you a discount.
   (A) in
   (B) at
   (C) to
   (D) by

4. We need to ------- and aggressively protect the environment.
   (A) passion
   (B) passionate
   (C) passionately
   (D) passionless

5. The recent bad weather accounts ------- the increase in tea prices.
   (A) for
   (B) in
   (C) over
   (D) of

6. Two candidates applied for the position ------- only one candidate will be interviewed.
   (A) so
   (B) but
   (C) and
   (D) or

7. Rori's restaurant accepts ------- checks nor credit cards, so customers must pay in cash.
   (A) either
   (B) neither
   (C) both
   (D) with

8. The company is famous ------- its dedication to customer service.
   (A) of
   (B) on
   (C) for
   (D) with

9. ------- the performance, do not use your cell phones and other electronic devices.
   (A) During
   (B) While
   (C) When
   (D) Whereas

10. The reception will begin ------- 6:30 and continue until 9 o'clock.
    (A) on
    (B) in
    (C) at
    (D) until

⏰ 試著在限時1分30秒之內盡可能答對。

Questions 11-14 refer to the following letter.

Bennington Apartment Complex

Dear resident,

Thank you ----11.---- your decision to rent an apartment at Bennington Apartment Complex. ----12.----. Our building is located in the heart of Philadelphia, and you will be living ----13.---- walking distance of some of the finest restaurants and historical landmarks. In addition, I'd like to remind you that as a resident you'll be responsible for arranging the activation of electricity and telephone service by your move-in date.

We look forward to ----14.---- you. Thank you.

Best wishes,

William Truman

Maintenance coordinator

---

11. (A) on
    (B) from
    (C) into
    (D) for

新多益

12. (A) Please call me at any time if you have questions or concerns.
    (B) This letter confirms that your rental contract has been received and signed.
    (C) We can set up a meeting so that you can look around the facility in person.
    (D) The rent is $2,000 a month, and you can send me a check directly.

13. (A) onto
    (B) within
    (C) beside
    (D) among

14. (A) serving
    (B) serve
    (C) serves
    (D) be served

Unit 7 關係詞和名詞子句

關係詞大致可分為關係代名詞和關係副詞，名詞子句在句子中具有名詞的作用。

 Step 1 基礎文法

Point 1 關係子句的形態和結構

「我想買的車子」中修飾名詞的形容詞子句稱為關係子句。關係詞如同連結兩個子句的連接詞一樣，同時作為前面出現過的名詞/副詞(片語)的代名詞/副詞角色。

1) 關係代名詞+ (主語) + 動詞

關係代名詞 (帶動不完全的子句)	Employees [**who** sign up for the training] should tell their supervisors. 　　　關係代名詞(who) + 動詞(sign up) [報名參加培訓的]員工應該告訴他們的主管。

2) 關係副詞 + 主語+ 動詞

關係副詞 (帶動完全的子句)	We will meet at the information desk [**where** they hand out the name tags]. 　　　關係副詞(where) + 主語(they) + 動詞(hand out) + 受詞(the name tags) 我們將在[他們分發姓名標籤的]服務台見面。

3) 形成關係子句的方法

將兩個句子共同所指的名詞改成關係詞，把兩個句子合併為包括關係子句在內的一個句子。

關係代名詞	① I have **a class**. + ② **The class** starts in five minutes. → I have **a class which** starts in five minutes. 我還有一堂五分鐘後開始的課。
關係副詞 (=介係詞+關係代名詞)	① This is **a room** + ② Leo sleeps **in the room**. → This is **a room where** Leo sleeps. 這是李奧睡覺的房間。 → This is **a room which** Leo sleeps **in**. → This is **a room in which** Leo sleeps.

Answers _ p. 087

Practice

1. I have a friend ------- works in the government.

   (A) who　　　　　　　　　(B) where

2. The office ------- the meeting is being held is on the third floor.

   (A) which　　　　　　　　(B) where

關係代名詞

1) 關係代名詞格式

與代名詞一樣，關係代名詞也有格式。先掌握關係代名詞要代替的先行詞是人還是事物，再檢查關係代名詞帶動的子句所缺少的內容。

先行詞	主格	受格	所有格
人	who	whom/who	whose
事物/動物	which	which	whose
人/事物/動物	that	that	-

2) 關係子句帶動的子句放在以修飾子句修飾的名詞(先行詞)後面。

主格	I know someone **who[that]** was born in South Africa. 先行詞(人)+主格關係代名詞+動詞 我認識一個出生在南非的人。
受格	This is the watch **which[that]** I bought from the department store. 先行詞(事物)+受格關係代名詞+及物動詞 這是我從百貨公司買的手錶。
所有格	I work at a firm **whose** office is close to my house. 先行詞(事物)+所有格關係代名詞+名詞 我在一家辦公室離我家很近的公司工作。

3) 關係代名詞which的用法

介係詞或逗點(,)後面只能使用which，不能使用that。

介係詞 + which	We should create a system **on which** we can depend. 我們應該建立一個我們可以依靠的系統。 (x) on that
逗點(,)which	Ms. Taylor won the first prize, **which** made her and her family surprised. 泰勒女士獲得了頭獎，這使她和她的家人感到驚訝。 (x) ,that

PART
5
/
6

Answers _ p. 087

Practice

3. The applicant ------- we decided to select will be announced soon.

   (A) whom　　　　　　　　(B) whose

4. The computer software ------- we purchased is very helpful.

   (A) whom　　　　　　　　(B) that

Point 3 關係副詞

如同關係代名詞，具有連接兩個句子的連接詞作用，修飾前面出現的先行詞。不同於後面加上不完整子句的關係代名詞，關係副詞後面加上＜主語+動詞＞的完整子句。

1) 關係副詞的種類

根據先行詞的種類，使用適合的關係副詞。

先行詞的種類	關係副詞	例句
地點 (place)	**where**	This is <u>the hotel</u> **where** the trade fair was held. 這是舉辦貿易博覽會的飯店。
時間 (time)	**when**	A public holiday is <u>a day</u> **when** all the shops close. 法定節日是所有商店關門的日子。
理由 (the reason)	**why**	This is <u>the reason</u> **why** I chose this job. 這就是我選擇這份工作的原因。
方法 (the way)	**how**	This is **how** I solve problems. = This is <u>the way</u> I solve problems. 這就是我解決問題的方法。 ~~the way how(X)~~

2) 關係代名詞和關係副詞

由於關係代名詞自行成為主語或受詞，帶動不完整的子句，但關係副詞具有副詞的作用，帶動完整的子句。

關係代名詞+ 不完整的子句	We offer presents for customers **who** <u>shop here regularly.</u> 　　　　　　　　　　　　　　　　　[關係代名詞主格＋動詞] 我們為經常在這裡購物的顧客提供禮物。
關係副詞+ 完整的子句	I remember the day **when** <u>we first met</u>. 　　　　　　　　　　[關係副詞＋主語＋動詞] 我記得我們初次見面的那一天。

Answers _ p. 087

Practice

5. This restaurant is the place ------- my family members have dinner regularly.

   (A) when (B) where

6. The manager explained the reason ------- we have to move to another location.

   (A) how (B) why

Point 4 名詞子句

句子中具有名詞作用的子句稱作名詞子句。名詞子句在句中主要作為主語、受詞和補語。名詞子句的形態是＜名詞子句 連接詞+主語+動詞＞。

1) 名詞子句的形態

帶動名詞子句的連接詞可以根據意思來區分。

名詞子句 連接詞	意思		
that if/whether	that 稱為～ if/whether 是否～		
疑問詞	who 誰做～ what 是什麼做/做什麼	when 何時做～ how 如何做～	where 在哪裡做～ why 為什麼做～

2) 名詞子句的作用和位置

主格 (動詞前)	**That the two airlines will merge** is certain. 可以肯定的是，兩家航空公司將合併。
受格 (及物動詞後)	Please let us know **whether you will attend the seminar**. 請告知我們您是否參加研討會。
介係詞的受格 (介係詞後)	We should think about **where we should take the visitors for lunch**. 我們應該考慮帶客人去哪裡吃午飯。
補語 (be動詞後)	The freshness of the food is **what makes the restaurant so popular**. 食物的新鮮度使餐廳如此受歡迎。

Answers _ p. 087

Practice

7. ------- the event will be held is not decided yet.

    (A) Where   (B) It

8. The supervisor asked ------- Ms. Patel was working on.

    (A) what   (B) about

容易混淆的名詞子句連接詞和關係代名詞

1) 名詞子句連接詞 that vs. if / whether

that (既定事實)	The management has decided **that** <u>they will sell the Chicago branch.</u> 管理層已決定將出售芝加哥分行。
if/whether (不確定的事)	The board of directors will decide **whether** <u>they should reduce the budget.</u> 董事會將決定是否應該減少預算。

2) that vs. what

關係代名詞 that	I met <u>a woman</u> **that** is a teacher. [先行詞○+關係代名詞+ 不完整句子] 我遇見了一位女老師。
名詞子句連接詞 that	We realized **that** there are some problems. [先行詞X+完整句子] 我們意識到有一些問題。
名詞子句連接詞 what	I cannot understand **what** she is saying. [先行詞X+不完整句子] 我無法理解她在說什麼。

3) who / which vs. when / where

關係代名詞 who/which	I saw <u>a woman</u> **who** <u>lives in my neighborhood.</u> 我看到一個住在我家附近的女人。[先行詞○+關係代名詞+不完整句子]
關係副詞 when/where/how/why	I need <u>a place</u> **where** <u>I can be alone.</u> 我需要一個可以獨處的地方。[先行詞○+關係副詞+完整句子]
疑問代名詞 who/which (名詞子句連接詞)	We don't know **who** <u>might be hired for the position.</u> 我們不知道那個職位誰會被錄用。[先行詞X+不完整句子]
疑問副詞 when/where/how/why (名詞子句連接詞)	This letter explains **why** <u>the construction is delayed.</u> 這封信解釋了施工延誤的原因。[先行詞X+完整句子]

Practice

Answers _ p. 087

9. The department director announced ------- Chris Lee got promoted.

   (A) that　　　　　　　　　　(B) whether

10. Some of the employees forgot ------- the meeting starts.

   (A) which　　　　　　　　　　(B) when

📝 注意文法/結構/詞彙，練習選擇正確答案。

1. I have a friend ------- collects tea spoons.
   (A) whom
   (B) who

2. This is the watch ------- I purchased 10 years ago.
   (A) which
   (B) whom

3. This is the town ------- I was born.
   (A) when
   (B) where

4. He was talking to a person ------- I've never seen.
   (A) that
   (B) which

5. This is the day ------- I met him for the first time.
   (A) why
   (B) when

6. This is a problem ------- I could never understand.
   (A) whose
   (B) which

7. New employees ------- wish to participate in the workshop must contact me.
   (A) who
   (B) which

8. Singapore is a city ------- has many years of history.
   (A) where
   (B) that

9. Please let my secretary know ------- you prefer to be notified by e-mail.
   (A) that
   (B) whether

10. Customers ------- purchase goods will receive their orders within three days.
    (A) who
    (B) whom

詞彙問題

11. We have to ------- our spending to stay competitive in the market.
    (A) limit
    (B) limited

12. The downtown location is ------- to major highways and subway stations.
    (A) close
    (B) closure

13. All executives including former ------- will show up at the opening ceremony.
    (A) preside
    (B) presidents

14. Many of the ------- should be eliminated to save the environment.
    (A) atmosphere
    (B) pollutants

PART
5
/
6

🕐 試著在限時4分30秒之內盡可能答對。

1. KG Bottles hired three new accountants
------- recently graduated.
   (A) which
   (B) what
   (C) who
   (D) them

2. A woman ------- I met at the party lives
next door to us.
   (A) where
   (B) that
   (C) whose
   (D) which

3. Good Neighbors is a non-profit
organization ------- mission is to help
poor children in Asia.
   (A) who
   (B) which
   (C) what
   (D) whose

4. Mr. Parker must decide ------- he will
submit the budget report.
   (A) whether
   (B) which
   (C) who
   (D) whom

5. ------- Jane particularly like about the
product is its design.
   (A) That
   (B) What
   (C) Where
   (D) Why

6. The project ------- has been proposed
by Ms. Hollaway will be accepted by
the management.
   (A) who
   (B) whose
   (C) what
   (D) which

7. The survey showed ------- customers
found the magazine appealing.
   (A) that
   (B) what
   (C) who
   (D) whose

8. Ms. Vinson will return from the United
States, ------- she received a degree
from a university.
   (A) where
   (B) while
   (C) what
   (D) whom

9. Mr. Wang, ------- is responsible for
airplane safety, should be able to
present the report to the board.
   (A) whose
   (B) whom
   (C) who
   (D) whoever

10. Please note ------- our company name
was changed.
   (A) who
   (B) whose
   (C) which
   (D) that

試著在限時1分30秒之內盡可能答對。

Questions 11-14 refer to the following notice.

Recycling Used Ink Cartridges

High Print Company is committed to preserving the environment. We urge our customers ------- their used ink cartridges, which can help save the earth. -------. All
11.   12.
you have to do is take the used cartridges to any office supply store ------- sells High
13.
Print products and drop them in the recycling bins. Then the store will return them to us for processing. Each time you recycle, you are entitled to a discount on your next cartridge purchase.

For more ------- on the discount program, please visit our Web site, www.highprint.com.
14.

---

11. (A) recycle
    (B) to recycle
    (C) recycling
    (D) recycled

新多益
12. (A) Recycling ink cartridges is easy.
    (B) To apply, contact our office at 555-1212.
    (C) If you buy more than two boxes of paper, you'll get a 15% discount today.
    (D) They were made from environmentally-friendly materials.

13. (A) who
    (B) whom
    (C) that
    (D) what

14. (A) views
    (B) matters
    (C) issues
    (D) details

PART
5
/
6

Unit 8　假設語氣・特殊語法

假設語氣是指與過去或現在情況相反的假設，意思是「要是~的話(如果早～的話)」。

 Step 1　基礎文法

Point 1 假設語氣的種類和形態

1) 假設語氣過去式: 與目前情況相反的假設

> If + 主語 + 動詞過去式～，主語 + would/could/might + 動詞原型　要是～的話，應該就～

If I **knew** his address, I **would write** to him.
如果我知道他的地址，我會寫信給他。(不知道他的地址。)

If I **were** you, I **wouldn't worry** about it.
如果我是你，我不會擔心。(假設語氣過去式的if子句be動詞通常使用were)

2) 假設語氣過去完成式: 與過去發生過的情況相反的假設

> If + 主語 + had p.p. ～，主語 + would / could / might + have + p.p.　要是~的話，應該早就~

If I **had studied** harder, I **would have passed** the exam.
如果我更努力學習，我就會通過考試了。(沒能通過考試。)

3) 假設語氣未來式: 對未來發生可能性極低之事的假設

> If + 主語 + should + 動詞原型～，主語 + will / can / may + 動詞原型
> (雖然不可能會那樣)萬一~的話，應該就會~

If I **should win** a lottery, I **will buy** you a new car.
萬一我贏得樂透，我會給你買一輛新車。

Answers _ p. 089

Practice

1. If I ------- some money with me now, I could pay for my tuition.
   (A) have
   (B) had

2. If you ------- on time for work this morning, you would have attended the meeting.
   (A) are
   (B) had been

Point 2 混合條件句

if子句和獨立子句的時態是不同的假設語氣。將假設語氣過去式和假設語氣過去完成式混合，表達「過去的事對目前的事產生影響」時使用。主要在獨立子句加上now, today等暗示目前的時間。

> **If + 主語 + had p.p. ~, 主語 + would / could / might + 動詞原型**

If you **had planned** the project earlier, it **would be** successful now.
如果你之前早一點計劃該項目，那麼它現在就會成功。

Point 3 假設語氣倒裝句

句子的主語和動詞的位置倒置稱為倒裝句。假設語氣中省略If，If子句的were, should, had加在主語前面。

1) 假設語氣倒裝句的類型

假設語氣過去式 (Were +主語～)	**Were I you**, I would start my own business. (= **If I were you**, I would start my own business.) 　如果我是你，我會開始自己的事業。
假設語氣過去完成式 (Had +主語+ p.p.～)	**Had I been rich**, I could have bought that car. (= **If I had been rich**, I could have bought that car.) 　如果我有錢，我本來可以買那輛車。
假設語氣未來式 (Should+主語+ 動詞原型～)	**Should he come** late again, he will lose his job. (= **If he should come** late again, he will lose his job.) 　如果他再次遲到，他將失去工作。

2) 假設語氣的慣用表達

if not (就算不是～，也～)	The rescue team saved hundreds, **if not** thousands of lives. 救援隊就算不是救了數千人，也救了數百人。
if so (如果是)	Is the store is open today, and **if so**, what are your business hours? 商店今天開門嗎？如果是，你們的營業時間是幾點？

Answers _ p. 089

Practice

3. If its proposal ------- more detailed, Dillan Construction might now be our partner for the city project.

(A) had been　　　　　　(B) has been

4. ------- your address be changed, please contact us.

(A) Had　　　　　　(B) Should

其他語法的倒裝句

1) 補語倒裝句: 將想要強調的內容移至句子最前面時，主語和動詞倒置。

補語倒裝句	**Enclosed** is a résumé that you have requested. (= A résumé that you have requested is **enclosed**.) 隨信附上您要求的簡歷。 **Attached** is a summary of our recent customer surveys. 附件是我們最近的客戶調查記錄。

2) 否定詞倒裝句: never, little, seldom, hardly, rarely等否定副詞出現在句首時，主語和動詞倒置。

一般動詞語法	**Never** <u>have we</u> received such good feedback. 我們從來沒有收到過如此好的反饋。
be動詞語法	**Seldom** <u>is Ms. Nagano</u> late for staff meetings. 長野女士參加員工會議幾乎不遲到。

3) Only 語法倒裝句: Only帶動的片語或子句出現在句首時，主語和動詞倒置。

Only + 副詞	**Only** <u>once has Ms. Choi</u> traveled abroad for business. 崔女士只去過一次商務旅行。
Only + 副詞 片語/子句	**Only** <u>if</u> you purchase the tickets at least two weeks in advance <u>can you</u> get a discount. 您唯有至少提前兩週購買門票才能獲得折扣。

4) So/Neither/Nor 語法倒裝句

so, neither, nor 承接前面子句的內容，具有「～也是/～也不是」的意思。

肯定 (so)	Mr. Brown attended the employee meeting, and **so did** his colleagues. 布朗先生參加了員工會議，他的同事們也參加了。
否定 (neither/nor)	Mr. Brown did not attend the employee meeting, **nor did** his colleagues. 布朗先生沒有參加員工會議，他的同事們也沒有參加。

Practice

Answers _ p. 089

5. ------- is the list of clients that you requested.

   (A) Inclusion   (B) Included

6. ------- had I seen such beautiful scenery.

   (A) Ever   (B) Never

📝 注意文法/結構/詞彙，練習選擇正確答案。

1. If we ------- in a big city, our life would be much easier.
   (A) live
   (B) lived

2. If she hadn't helped me, I ------- in trouble.
   (A) would have been
   (B) have been

3. If he ------- honest, we wouldn't be talking about him.
   (A) was
   (B) were

4. If I ------- some money with me now, I would lend you some.
   (A) have
   (B) had

5. Should you have any questions, please ------- me on my cell phone.
   (A) call
   (B) called

6. If I found money in the street, I ------- it to the police station.
   (A) take
   (B) would take

7. ------- had the meeting begun when someone asked a question.
   (A) Very
   (B) Hardly

8. If we had had more money, we ------- better equipment for the laboratory.
   (A) could have bought
   (B) bought

9. My knowledge of marketing is excellent, ------- is my ability to communicate with people.
   (A) as
   (B) in fact

10. If he ------- the contract, he would have received a bonus.
    (A) win
    (B) had won

詞彙問題

11. It will be difficult to finish the project without the help of many foreign -------.
    (A) investors
    (B) investment

12. Once you arrive at the airport, you will need to ------- all your luggage.
    (A) complain
    (B) collect

13. You can request a special ------- service.
    (A) delivery
    (B) deliver

14 We have nothing to ------- about on the construction.
    (A) lose
    (B) worry

PART
5
6

⏰ 試著在限時4分30秒之內盡可能答對。

1. If we ------- the seminar indoors, we wouldn't be worried about the weather.
   (A) holds
   (B) holding
   (C) held
   (D) hold

2. If she had received the e-mail, Ms. Jenkins ------- the report to other colleagues.
   (A) forwarded
   (B) could forward
   (C) could have been forwarded
   (D) could have forwarded

3. If this schedule ------- convenient for you, please visit the HR department.
   (A) would not
   (B) should not be
   (C) has not been
   (D) would not have been

4. ------- we rich, we could renovate our building.
   (A) Had
   (B) Should
   (C) Were
   (D) Would

5. ------- to this e-mail is our company's annual report.
   (A) Attaching
   (B) Attaches
   (C) Attach
   (D) Attached

6. Only via e-mail ------- Kellogg Construction send an estimate.
   (A) does
   (B) were
   (C) has
   (D) is

7. If we had had more time, we ------- the report more thoroughly.
   (A) finish
   (B) will finish
   (C) would finish
   (D) would have finished

8. Had the company earned higher profits, we ------- more on the production.
   (A) would be invested
   (B) would have invested
   (C) will invest
   (D) invest

9. ------- you experience any difficulties while using our product, feel free to call us.
   (A) Provide
   (B) Could
   (C) Should
   (D) Even if

10. ------- did he visit the Louvre Museum when he was in Paris.
    (A) Had
    (B) Hard
    (C) Could
    (D) Never

⏰ 試著在限時1分30秒之內盡可能答對。

Questions 11-14 refer to the following letter.

Dear valued customers:

As a preferred customer, we would like to give you a special offer on some of our hottest products. The booklet we've sent you includes discount coupons for ------- of 11. our current products. To be ------- for this offer, just present the coupon with your Maxi 12. Mart membership cards. -------. 13.

------- you have any questions on this offer, please visit the nearest Maxi Mart outlet or 14. contact our membership office at 555–2843. Thank you.

---

11. (A) many
    (B) little
    (C) its
    (D) much

12. (A) apply
    (B) tentative
    (C) responsible
    (D) eligible

13. (A) Your old membership can also be renewed on the spot.
    (B) Our store is located at 553 Main Street.
    (C) Our sales have increased 20% and profits 12% during the first quarter.
    (D) Maxi is one of the oldest supermarket chains in northern area.

14. (A) Had
    (B) Should
    (C) Unless
    (D) Because

Part 6涵蓋了Part 5的文法題目和Part 7的閱讀理解型題目。即使乍看之下是單純的文法題目，在閱讀內容的同時，從最前面以閱讀理解型的解題方式解開4個題目，是最快也最有效率的方法。

 Step 1　類型分析

Point 1　選出符合文法題目和前後文的語彙題型

Part 6不同於瀏覽空格前後，選擇正確答案的Part5題型，或是選擇適合前後文的詞彙題型，Part 6的文法題目和詞彙題目必須考慮前後句子的一致性。

Questions 1-2 refer to the following memo.

At AMCO Corporation, we take employee ------- seriously. When severe weather
is expected, we closely monitor the situation. If conditions are expected to
become hazardous, an office closure will be announced. Employees will get their
regular pay for any hours they were scheduled to work during a closure. When the
company reopens, they must return ------- for their next scheduled shift.

1.

2.

在AMCO公司，我們認真對待員工安全。當預計天氣惡劣時，我們會密切監察情況。如果預計情況會變得危險，將宣布辦公室關閉。員工在關閉期間將按照他們工作所用的時間獲得正常工資。當公司重新開業時，他們必須回到下一個預定班次工作。

1. (A) safety　　　安全　　　　　　　2. (A) the work　工作
　 (B) satisfaction　滿意　　　　　　　　　 (B) to work　　上班

解析 1. 選擇適合前後文的詞彙

與從一個句子中選擇正確詞彙的Part5不同，除了員工安全(employee safety)之外，從單句來看，員工滿意度 (employee satisfaction)在意思上也可行。但由於後面出現顧慮員工安全而關閉辦公室的內容，可以知道(A)並非答案。如果從開始讀到空格處，發現無法選出答案時，先讀到最後，再回頭重新解題是很好的解決方法。　　　　　　　　答案: (A)

2. 文法問題

return作為及物動詞，意思是「(特定物品) 退貨、歸還」，結合介係詞to表示「回到某個場合」。前面出現關閉公司(closure)的內容，當公司再度開業時，「回到工作」的內容符合前後文的一致性，因此答案是(B)。　　　　　　　　答案: (B)

選擇適合前後文的時態/詞彙/連接詞的題目

Part 6中根據時間順序理解鋪陳和文意是很重要的。出題方式是從既定的題目中找出過去式/現在式/未來式的時間點，或選擇段落和段落之間適合的連接詞。需練習正確掌握從短文開始到空格前後的內容，選擇正確答案。

Questions 3-4 refer to the following memo.

This year's <u>annual company picnic</u> ----3.---- <u>held</u> on Friday, April 5th. <u>We hope that all employees will come and enjoy some free time together</u>. All offices will be closed in the afternoon so that all of the employees can participate. Employees will be paid for the time spent at the event (up to four hours). <u>Employees may also choose to go home at noon instead of attending</u>. ----4.----, those who do so must charge four hours to vacation time.

今年的公司野餐將於4月5日星期五舉行。我們希望所有員工都能一起享受一些空閒時光。所有辦公室將在下午關閉，以便所有員工都能參與。員工將按參加活動所花費的時間獲得報酬（最多四個小時）。員工也可以選擇在中午回家而不是參加。但是在那種情況下，要申請4小時的休假時間。

3. (A) was　　　已舉行
   (B) will be　　將舉行

4. (A) However　　但是
   (B) Therefore　　因此

解析 3. 選擇適合前後文的時態
從既定句子中的時態來看，(A)、(B)在文法上都可行。但後面接續的內容出現將舉行活動，鼓勵大家參加，因此答案是未來式的(B)。選項中只留下文法上可行的答案，繼續往下閱讀內容的同時，從確定的時間點中選出答案是最有效率的方法。　　　　　　　　答案: (B)

4. 選擇適合前後文的連接詞
這是確認前後文的內容之後，選出適合連接詞的題型。因為形式和Part 5類似，只看選項的話，很容易選擇與前後文不一致的選項。需要從前面開始閱讀，正確掌握前後文語意。內容出現鼓勵員工參加野餐，或是不參加活動的話也可以回家。空格前後提到提早下班的四小時需作為休假使用，銜接到略帶轉折的語意，因此適合「可是/不過」等轉折連接詞。Therefore是表達原因帶來的結果或合理內容的連接詞。　　　　　　　　答案: (A)

選擇適合句子的題目 新多益

選擇適合句子的題目是Part 6的新題型，需先對短文內容有全盤性了解，屬於高難度題型，而相較於安插句子的題型，Part 7比較簡單。先瀏覽一遍4個題目，從中確認第幾題是選擇句子的題目，接著在閱讀短文的同時進行解題，找出內容走向是否有空缺，選出正確答案。

🔍 掌握短文中空格出現的位置。

空格出現在短文前半部時，往往是找出主題/目的的句子。空格出現在短文中間或後半部時，可能代表前面內容的闡述說明、原因、強調或結果。最好先確認選擇句子的題目在短文中的位置。

Questions 131-134 refer to the following notice. 新多益

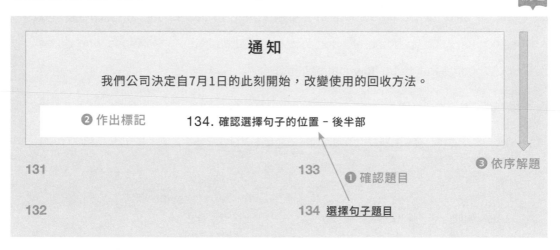

① 先瀏覽一遍題目，從中確認第幾題是選擇句子的題目。

② 在文章中圈出該題目的號碼，掌握句子需安插在短文的位置。

③ 為了能夠一次解開Part 6選擇句子的題目，從前面開始確認短文的走向，根據空格前後的一致性和詞彙，從4個選項中選出最適合的答案。

🔍 從既定句子的標題/連接詞/代名詞等獲得提示。

① 出現前言、標題、職位等時，能夠獲得提示。

② 確認連接詞前後的連貫是否自然。

③ 確認代名詞所指的意思。

選擇適合句子的題型中，如果文章前面出現介紹主題或內容的人物時，從這部分開始著手，並從前面部分開始解題。當已經預測好即將出現空格，如果有連接詞時，從中判斷短文的走向，有代名詞時，確認代表的意思，是一種不錯的策略。

Question 1 refers to the following advertisement.

Mademoiselle Clothing Shop has a job opening in your region.

Job Description: Customer Service Representative

Our customer service representatives are required to respond to all types of customer inquiries. The average day may involve answering 80 to 100 calls from customers who are seeking answers. A key function of the position is identifying and managing priority issues that require immediate attention. To ensure excellent customer service, timely resolution of the problems is of utmost importance. ----1----. Hence, the ideal candidate will be adaptable, flexible, and able to work in a dynamic environment.

Mademoiselle 服飾店在您所在地區徵求員工

職位描述：客戶服務代表

我們的客戶服務代表必須回應所有類型客戶的諮詢。平均一天可能會接80到100通尋求答案的客戶電話。該職位的關鍵作用是確定和安排需要立即關注的優先問題。為確保優質的客戶服務，及時解決問題至關重要。你不會在這份工作中連續做同樣的事情。因此理想的應徵者是適應性強、靈活，並且能在動態環境中工作。

(A) A list of our store managers is on our Web site.
   我們商店的經理列表在我們的網頁上。

(B) No two days are ever the same on this job.
   你不會在這份工作中連續做同樣的事情。

解析 從短文標題可以知道文章的目的是徵人廣告，就能從選項中刪除可能性較低的一兩個答案。從 Hence(因此)順接連接詞後面的「適應性強的應徵者」內容來看，意思是職場生活瞬息萬變，所以正確答案為(B)。　　　　　　　　　　　　　　　　　　　　　答案: (B)

PART
5
6

📝 選擇符合前後文的句子。

Question 1　refers to the following letter.

--------. We went over your résumé and were pretty impressed by your experience. Your
1.
expertise in on-line marketing makes you a highly suitable candidate for the position of
marketing director at our company. I would like to invite you to meet with a few of our
executives next week, so please call me at 555-3849 to set up a specific date and
time.

1.　(A) I'll be in the city next week, so I should be available for an interview in person.
　　(B) We're sorry to inform you that the opening has already been filled.
　　(C) I am writing to update you on the status of your job application.
　　(D) Enclosed is the document you have previously requested.

Question 2　refers to the following e-mail.

Hello, Ms. Martinez:

We are sending this e-mail to confirm your subscription to Blue Ocean Music Service.
You signed up for Passion Package, which costs $6.99 per month and includes 50
hours of music playback each month. --------.
2.
If you should wish to terminate your service, please visit our Web site and navigate to
your account setting. Once there, click the "Close Account" button.

2.　(A) Unfortunately, we're unable to process your payment at this time.
　　(B) This package also includes a subscription to our weekly newsletter.
　　(C) You can either pay by personal check or charge to your credit card account.
　　(D) We'd like to offer you a great chance to enjoy your favorite music at reasonable
　　　　prices.

⏰ 試著在限時4分30秒之內盡可能答對。

Questions 1-4 refer to the following letter.

Michael Woo

Farm Fresh Supplies

#305, 180 Garosu-gil

Seoul, Korea

Dear Mr. Woo,

We are writing to let you know about a temporary ---1.--- in our order fulfillment service on June 2. We will begin moving all of our equipment and inventory to a new warehouse in Kyoto. ---2.---. The move will take 3-4 days, ---3.--- which time we will be unable to ship overseas orders. ---4.--- any delays, please place your next order by May 20. If you have any questions, please do not hesitate to contact me.

Sincerely,

Janice Young

Customer Service Director

---

1. (A) extension
    (B) improvement
    (C) disruption
    (D) solution

2. (A) These will be available at a special price for a limited time.
    (B) You can track the status of your order online.
    (C) Warehouse facilities have become an important industry in the region.
    (D) This will prevent us from keeping a large inventory in stock.

3. (A) during
    (B) due to
    (C) rather than
    (D) may as well

4. (A) Avoids
    (B) Avoided
    (C) To avoid
    (D) Having avoided

Questions 5-8 refer to the following information.

Quality is Our Main Concern
Tata Electronics Ltd.

Congratulations on the purchase of your Tata Electronics Ltd. vacuum cleaner. It will serve you -----5.----- under the most challenging circumstances. Our 50 years of experience in the industry has taught that vacuum cleaners are not always used in ideal conditions. To meet our company's strict -----6.----- requirements, all our electronics undergo a series of rigorous tests.

Every device is exposed to heat, cold, and dust, as well as hours of repeated drops from one-meter heights. During our quality inspections, our vacuum cleaners are randomly chosen and -----7.----- these same tests by quality control technicians. -----8.-----.

That is why, at Tata Electronics, we say "quality is our main concern."

---

5. (A) faithfully
    (B) needlessly
    (C) conditionally
    (D) deeply

6. (A) pricing
    (B) educational
    (C) reliability
    (D) application

7. (A) handed in
    (B) made up
    (C) turned down
    (D) put through

8. (A) From those results, we always try to cut costs.
    (B) Even one device failing one test will stop production and we will look into the problem.
    (C) Through this process, items are shipped quickly to our clients.
    (D) Extra vacuum cleaners can be purchased with special VIP discounts.

Questions 9-12 refer to the following article.

Simmons International to buy Chiang Technology

Hong Kong, **March 10** – Simmons International announced Monday that ---9.--- would buy Chiang Technology in a deal valued at $700 million.

A spokesperson for Simmons said that the company expects to double its profits by the end of next year. It will accomplish this by making full use of Chiang's widespread distribution channels in most of the Asian markets. ---10.---.

Financial experts believe the Chiang acquisition will make Simmons the market leader in the industry of computers and electronics. "They will be well ahead of their ---11.---," said top analyst Robert Ing of Financial Times.

Simmons plans to maintain Chiang's current workforce, and all of Chiang's 250 branches around the world. ---12.---, Simmons will evaluate whether additional staff are needed.

---

9. (A) it
    (B) he
    (C) those
    (D) someone

10. (A) Offers from other firms were rejected.
    (B) Chiang has recently added 20 locations in China alone.
    (C) Another company will be acquired next year.
    (D) The employees will also be happy about the transaction.

11. (A) critics
    (B) suppliers
    (C) investors
    (D) competitors

12. (A) After all
    (B) After that time
    (C) As you have requested
    (D) As a matter of fact

PART

5
/
6

PART 7

PART 7　讀完一個或多個短文，
選出最適合的答案。
是新多益中最進階化的題型。

題目數	難易度
共54題 (147至200題)	高

滿分訣竅

瀏覽一遍題目，從文章中快速找到提示。

❶ 讀完題目並區分類型之後，從文章中標示出要尋找的內容。

❷ GQ類型主要出現在前面，SQ類型則需確認核心句子。

❸ 正確答案可能是直述，但也可能用其他方式重新詮釋。

學習方法

❶ **準備**：熟記Part 7中經常出現的題型和答案類型，以及Part 7常出現的各種主題詞彙和表達。

❷ **實戰**：正確理解大多數的題目，並從短文中尋找提示。

❸ **複習**：複習各題型的正確答案，並熟記重新詮釋的表達句型和各主題短文，迅速理解文章。

Questions 147-148 refer to the following letter.

Melisa Novak
Chicago Mills Bank
1200 Main Street
Chicago, IL 32491

Dear Ms. Novak,

I'm a manager at Chicago Mills Bank. We have an opening for a bilingual customer service representative at our call center in the main office. We have retained your information from last year's applicant data. We're interested in learning whether you still want to work with us. If so, please contact us at 312-555-3546 and set up an interview time by May 4th.

We look forward to hearing from you.

147 What is the purpose of this letter?
   (A) To apply for a job
   (B) To complain about a mistake
   (C) To confirm a reservation
   (D) To offer a job

148 What should Ms. Novak do if she wants to get this job?
   (A) Call the office and make an appointment
   (B) Send her reply with her résumé
   (C) Meet with a manager
   (D) Reorder the items

這樣解題！

首先讀完每個題目後，標示出Key Word，同時閱讀短文和題目，選擇正確答案。
❶ 讀完題目，確認GQ/SQ之後，標示出Key Word。

❷ 根據題目/短文主題預測正確答案的位置，同時解題。
   147. What is the purpose of this letter? → GQ: 出現在自我介紹後
   148. What should Ms. Novak do if she wants to get this job? → SQ: 請求/拜託的內容出現在最後

❸ 既定位置的正確答案經常以其他說法重新詮釋。
   147. We're interested in learning whether you still want to work with us.
      → (D) To offer a job
   148. Please contact us at 312-555-3546 and set up an interview time.
      → (A) Call the office and make an appointment.
❹ 答案: 147 (D)   148 (A)

 **Step 1 類型分析**

Point 1 一般性問題(General Question)

詢問短文的整體目的或原因，或詢問內容的背景。包括文章的作者或讀者是誰(Who)，為什麼寫這篇文章(Why)，主題是什麼(What)，作者在哪裡(Where)等。

🔍 **GQ 題型**

What is the main **topic** of this memo? 這份備忘錄的主要內容是什麼？
What does this article mainly **discuss**? 本文主要討論什麼？
What is the **purpose** of this letter? 這封信的目的是什麼？

🔍 **GQ 的例題與解題策略**

Question 1 refers to the following memo.

Dear Employees,

Now that summer is coming, we must think of creative ways to keep sales strong in the summer season. For the first time ever, we are holding an ice coffee flavor contest. Those employees who come up with original ideas for new energizing ice coffee flavors will have a chance to go on a trip to Hawaii.

親愛的員工們，

夏天即將到來，我們必須想出一種創新的方式來維持我們夏季的銷量。我們有史以來第一次舉辦冰咖啡風味比賽。那些為充滿活力的新款冰咖啡口味提出創意的員工將有機會去夏威夷旅行。

例題1 What is the purpose of this memo?　　　這份備忘錄的目的是什麼？

　(A) To announce a competition　　　　　宣布比賽
　(B) To publicize company profits　　　　宣傳公司利潤
　(C) To invite staff to a company outing　邀請員工參加公司郊遊
　(D) To provide information on new products　提供有關新產品的資訊

❶ 確認詢問目的的GQ。　　　❷ 找出文章前面出現的GQ提示。

❸ 確認題目有關目的/理由/地點/職業部分的位置，從既定的答案中選擇最接近的內容。不是含有特定詞彙的答案，而是選擇與整體內容接近的答案。

解析 備忘錄的第一句話點出目前狀態/問題點等，在文章最前面表明為了提高銷售額，將舉行新飲料比賽(competition)，是典型的目的題型。雖然GQ在前半部出現，與其為了解題而停留在中間部分，最好讀到最後解開SQ之後，再回頭針對GQ解題會更有效率。　　　答案: (A)

這是詢問特定時間點、人物、地點、行為等資訊的題型，需先掌握題目的Key Word，再從文章中找出相關的資訊。尤其關鍵是了解各題目、各主題的詳細資訊出現在什麼位置。過去的詳細資訊主要出現在短文的前面，對未來的行動給予指示或請求的內容出現在短文後面。

🔍 SQ 題型

1) 各疑問詞的詳細資訊題目

Where should the application form be sent? 申請表應該寄到哪裡？
When will the change take effect? 變更事項何時生效？
How can Mr. Bolton get a refund? 博爾頓先生如何獲得退款？
What are employees advised to do? 建議員工做什麼？

2) 選擇同義詞的題目

In the **e-mail**, the word **"attend" in paragraph 1, line 2** is closest in meaning to？
在電子郵件中，與第1段第2行中的「出席」一詞含義最接近的是什麼？

🔍 SQ 的例題與解題策略

Question 2 refers to the following notice.

Thank you for all of your hard work this quarter. Sales have risen substantially, and the management is delighted with the superior performance of our division. This, in turn, has led to some great news for our department. Because of our considerable profit this quarter, we will be able to upgrade our equipment including computers and new photocopiers. However, in order for all the computers and software to be installed efficiently, you will have to take Friday afternoon off. Everything will be ready for your use on Monday morning.

感謝您本季度的辛勤工作。銷售額大幅增加，管理層對我們部門的卓越表現感到高興。這對我們的部門帶來了一些好消息。由於本季度我們的利潤可觀，我們將能夠升級我們的設備，包括電腦和新的影印機。但是，為了有效地安裝所有電腦和軟體，您必須在周五下午休息。一切都將準備好以供周一早上使用。

例題2 What will happen next Monday? 下週一會發生什麼事？
(A) Some figures will be announced. 將公佈一些數字。
(B) Some furniture will be delivered. 將配送一些家具。
(C) Employees will resume work as usual. 員工們將照常恢復工作。
(D) Some construction work will take place. 將進行一些施工。

❶ 確認 SQ 的 Key Word　　❷ 找出文章的各種資訊中與 Key Word 連貫的內容。

❸ 從既定選項中選擇文章提到的直述答案，或以其他方式重新詮釋(paraphrasing)的選項。

解析 注意Key Word是next Monday，選出文章中相關的內容之後，設備、軟體的設置訂在周五，但從「周一時為了讓員工能夠使用，一切都會準備好」的內容可以得知，員工們周一會恢復工作，因此答案是(C)

答案: (C)

True/Not true 題目

True/Not true 題目必須正確了解短文前半部出現的線索以用於解題,是比較棘手的題型。必須找出題目的Key Word,將選項中既定的內容和短文中的線索進行比對,因此需要留意時間。

🔍 True/Not true 的題型

1) 必須讀完全部短文才能解題的題目

What is true about Zaha Tech? 什麼是有關扎哈科技的正確描述?
What is mentioned/indicated/stated in the letter? 信中提到/指出/陳述了什麼?
What is NOT true about Betsy's Apparel? 什麼是有關貝琪服飾的不正確描述?

2) 詢問特定詳細事項的題目

What is true about the holiday package? 什麼是有關假期套餐的正確描述?
What advantage is NOT mentioned in the advertisement? 廣告中沒有提到的優勢是什麼?

🔍 True/Not true 例題與題目的解題策略

Question 3 refers to the following notice.　　→(B)　　→(C)　　→(A)

Submissions will be judged on their appeal to a broad range of customers, as well as convenient availability of ingredients and low cost of production. Entry forms are available at the information desk and online. The deadline for submissions is the last day of the month. If you have any questions, please call Ms. Benton at extension 8237.

提交的商品將根據是否方便獲得材料、低生產成本以及吸引廣泛的消費者來判斷。報名表可以在詢問櫃檯和線上獲取。提交截止日期是本月的最後一天。如果您有任何疑問,請致電本頓女士,電話分機8237。

例題 3 What is NOT mentioned as an aspect of a good product?　　作為一個好商品,沒有提到的部分是什麼?

(A) Being inexpensive to make　　製作成本低廉
(B) Having components that are easy to obtain　　擁有易於獲得的零件
(C) Being liked by a wide range of people　　很多人喜歡
(D) Having an attractive appearance　　具吸引力的外觀

❶ 確認題目是NOT mentioned的類型。

❷ 找出提到條件/特點的部分,逐項劃掉。

❸ 刪除選項中錯誤的部分,從留下的答案中選擇一項。只要找到列出資訊的部分,就能輕易刪除不正確的選項。

解析 大部分的應試者最害怕的Not true題型,只要找出條件/特點列出的部分,相對來說就能容易選出正確答案。反而True題型才是需將短文和選項同時加以比對的棘手類型。平時必須累積閱讀短文之後記住內容的能力,才能順利解開長篇短文和選項的閱讀理解題目。　　答案: (D)

Point 4 推論題目

將短文中出現的資訊作為根據，推論出答案的題型。即使找到題目的 Key Word 和短文中的線索，仍需掌握內容中隱藏的意思，因此必須憑藉背景知識，了解選項中重新詮釋的語意。這種題型屬於從雙重、三重短文中參考幾個短文的統合型題目，經常出現在考試中。

🔍 推論題型

What is suggested/implied about Ms. Willows? 有關威洛斯女士的建議/暗示是什麼？
What can be inferred about the workshop? 關於研討會可以推斷出什麼？
What will probably **happen** next month? 下個月會發生什麼事？

🔍 推論問題的例題與解題策略

Question 4 refers to the following online chat discussion.

Sam Metcalfe [11:20 A.M.]	Ms. Stewart, your latest book is an unpredictable adventure story about two boys looking for a family treasure. How did you come up with the idea for the story?
Liza Stewart [11:21 A.M.]	I remember wanting something exciting to happen to me when I was a child. I hoped to be involved in a mystery, but that never happened to me. So I made it happen in this story.
Sam Metcalfe [11:23 A.M.]	What do your readers say about your books and their illustrated pictures?
Liza Stewart [11:24 A.M.]	I often get letters from readers who tell me the books help them feel brave when they're in tricky situations. They say they learn from the characters. That's very important to me.

山姆麥特卡爾菲：斯圖爾特女士，您最近的一本書是關於兩個男孩尋找家庭財富的不可預知的冒險故事。您是怎麼想出這個故事的？
麗莎斯圖爾特：　我記得小時候很希望發生一些令我興奮的事。我希望能夠參與一個神祕事物，但這從未發生在我身上。所以我在這個故事中實現了它。
山姆麥特卡爾菲：您的讀者對您的書及其中插圖有何看法？
麗莎斯圖爾特：　我經常收到讀者的來信，他們告訴我這些書在他們處於棘手的情況時幫助他們衍生勇氣。他們說他們從角色中學習。這對我來說非常重要。

例題4 What can be inferred about the book? 　　關於這本書可以推論出什麼？

(A) It helps readers have courage. 　　可以幫助讀者具備勇氣。
(B) It is based on real experiences. 　　這是基於真實的經歷。
(C) It is the writer's first publication. 　　這是作者的第一本出版著作。
(D) There are no pictures included. 　　裡面沒有圖片。

❶ 確認推論題目的類型和 Key Word　　❷ 比對文章的提示和選項，同時刪除錯誤的部分。

❸ 找出題目有關目的/理由/地點/職業部分的位置，從既定的答案中選擇最接近的內容。不是含有特定詞彙的答案，而是選擇與整體內容相同的答案。

解析 涉及型/推論型題目最有效率的解題方式是將 Key Word 的相關部分和選項進行比對，刪除錯誤的部分，正確答案往往是全新詮釋的選項。(B)書根據真實故事寫成，與短文內容不一致，因此並非答案。短文中提到書收錄的插圖，所以(D)也非答案。短文最後麗莎斯圖爾特說讀者們寄給她的信中提到，他們拜書所賜而能在棘手的狀況中鼓起勇氣面對，因此答案是(A)。　　答案: (A)

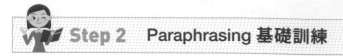
📝 請選出適合改寫底線部分的答案。

1. I met my favorite musician <u>in person</u> after the concert.
   (A) in reality
   (B) in a dream

2. He wanted to <u>determine</u> what the customers think.
   (A) tell
   (B) know

3. Customers of Bermuda Travel Agency receive <u>significant</u> hotel discounts.
   (A) great
   (B) large

4. This will help you <u>retain</u> your customers.
   (A) hold
   (B) understand

5. Unfortunately, the store went <u>bankrupt</u> last year.
   (A) very popular
   (B) out of money

6. The book explains how businesses can <u>execute</u> their strategies effectively.
   (A) carry out
   (B) make

7. You can buy all kinds of flowers at the <u>plant nursery</u>.
   (A) place for growing
   (B) place for healing

8. This voucher can be <u>redeemed</u> only by the end of this December.
   (A) restored
   (B) used

9. <u>The voucher entitles you to a boating excursion.</u>
   (A) The coupon allows a boat ride.
   (B) The flyer permits entry to a cruise ship.

10. <u>All protective clothing goes in the bins to be washed later.</u>
    (A) All protective clothing must be thrown away.
    (B) All protective clothing must be stored properly.

⏰ 試著在限時4分30秒之內盡可能答對。

Question 1 refers to the following form.

Brennan's Grocery Store Customer Survey

Dear Ms. Richards:

We appreciate your shopping at Brennan's Grocery Store. To ensure a quality experience for all customers, please answer a few questions about your recent shopping experiences.

1. How would you describe the staff at Brennan's Grocery Store? (Check all that apply.)
   ☐ Attentive   ☐ Knowledgeable   ■ Friendly   ☐ None of the above

2. How often do you leave the store without an item you need?
   ☐ Every time   ☐ Sometimes   ■ Rarely   ☐ Never

---

1. Why was the survey conducted?
   (A) To compare prices with other stores
   (B) To find out if employees are stealing
   (C) To determine the quality of food
   (D) To learn how customers are treated

Question 2 refers to the following article.

PART
7

Airport Construction Continues

Frankfurt, July 2 — A major expansion project is underway at Frankfurt International Airport. The project is estimated to cost $2.9 billion; a new terminal is scheduled to open in approximately one year.

The new terminal, however, will sit on a confined piece of land, which presents significant challenges to increasing the number of takeoffs and landings. If the airport keeps its current number of runways, the capacity to handle air traffic could reach its maximum within three years.

2. In paragraph 2, line 4, the word "handle" is closest in meaning to
   (A) touch
   (B) examine
   (C) manage
   (D) release

Question 3 refers to the following advertisement.

Central Montana Legal Aid Services

Connecting skilled lawyers with residents on very tight budgets.

Services include:

- A free, 20-minute initial consultation
- Advice in the areas of family, immigration, tax, and employment law
- Legal representation at low rates for the unemployed

◆ Note: We do not aid those with criminal cases.

Visit our Web site for a complete list of legal counseling sessions and locations. Clients should arrive early to complete paperwork. You'll also find instructions online to help you prepare for your legal advisory meeting. If you are unable to attend scheduled sessions, you may submit questions online, and a lawyer will respond in writing.

3. What is stated about Central Montana Legal Aid Services?

(A) They guarantee representation for all applicants.
(B) They only answer legal questions in person.
(C) They provide services for low-income groups.
(D) They can assist those charged with robbery.

試著在限時6分鐘(每題1分鐘)內盡可能答對。

Questions 1-3 refer to the following e-mail.

To	ann.longton@mail.com
From	services@zboutique.com
Date	April 22, 2017
Subject	Customer Appreciation Offer

Dear Ms. Longton:

Our records show that you recently returned a product you bought when you visited the Z Boutique in North Dallas. The form you completed said the product did not meet your quality standards.

At Z Boutique, we deliver only the finest quality clothing and accessories. We want to ensure that you continue shopping at Z Boutique in the future. To show our appreciation for your business, we are offering a $40 credit at one of our five stores. To use your credit, give the cashier the coupon code: "Customer Care."

Thank you for your business.

Z Boutique

PART
7

1. What is the main purpose of the e-mail?
    (A) To advertise an upcoming sale
    (B) To explain the boutique's policy
    (C) To hold on to a customer
    (D) To announce a new product line

2. What is suggested about Ms. Longton?
    (A) She was disappointed at the boutique's product.
    (B) The boutique overcharged her.
    (C) She bought the wrong size.
    (D) She discouraged other shoppers.

3. What is offered in the e-mail?
    (A) A refund
    (B) A recommendation
    (C) A replacement item
    (D) A gift certificate

THE HAPPY GARDENER

1421 Pine Bluff Road
Oklahoma City, Oklahoma 22312
(412) 555-9633

45466 Jefferson Road
Calvin, Oklahoma 22331
(422) 555-9935

If you're ready to start your own vegetable garden, do it the right way! Our plant nurseries and knowledgeable staff can provide you with all the materials and answers you need to successfully grow your own food.

Shoppers will find:

- A wide selection of books detailing gardening methods and native plants
- Local, naturally developed soils—nothing is chemically treated
- Gardening classes for all skill and experience levels (not available at the Pine Bluff store)
- All varieties of native plants and the information needed to keep them healthy

Stop by either of our locations, and allow our plant experts to answer your questions. We'll help you keep your garden growing!

- Hours of Operation -
Monday: 11 A.M. – 4 P.M.
Tuesday – Friday: 9 A.M. – 7 P.M.
Saturday: 9 A.M. – 9 P.M.
Sunday: 12 P.M. – 6 P.M.

4. What is suggested about The Happy
   Gardener?

   (A) Fruits and vegetables are sold as food.
   (B) Employees are experienced gardeners.
   (C) Imported plants are available for
       purchase.
   (D) Chemical fertilizers are on sale this
       week.

5. What is NOT provided by The Happy
   Gardener?

   (A) Training courses
   (B) Home service
   (C) Healthy planting soil
   (D) Gardening advice

6. What is available only at the Jefferson
   Road location?

   (A) Gardening guides
   (B) Native plants
   (C) Skilled advice
   (D) Training courses

Step 1 類型分析

新多益中新增了簡訊/網路聊天短文,是以掌握引號(" ")中引用句前後文的意圖/意義作為題型,必須了解短文中引用句的位置和引用句前後的一致性。與選擇同義詞的題目一樣,並非從句子表面上的意思來選擇,而需考慮前後文意義的一致性選擇正確答案。

Point 1 掌握說話者意圖的題目

🔍 掌握說話者意圖的題目

At 3:05 P.M., what does Mr. Hwang most likely mean when he writes, "That's what I thought"?
下午3點5分,黃先生表示:「我也這麼認為。」最可能是什麼意思?

🔍 掌握說話者意圖的例題與解題策略

Question 1 refers to the following text message chain.

Susan Bellaire [1:51 P.M.]	It's my first time participating in a training session online. I keep getting the message "Access Denied."
Paul Shephard [1:52 P.M.]	Let me check it for you, Ms. Bellaire.
Susan Bellaire [1:53 P.M.]	Maybe there's an issue with the access code that comes with the invitation for online training.
Paul Shephard [1:54 P.M.]	Here we go. I gave you the meeting code instead of the access code. Try 992745. It should work now.

蘇珊貝萊爾 [1:51] 這是我第一次參加線上培訓課程。我一直收到「拒絕訪問」的訊息。
保羅謝波德 [1:52] 貝萊爾女士,我來幫您檢查一下。
蘇珊貝萊爾 [1:53] 也許線上培訓邀請附上的訪問代碼有問題。
保羅謝波德 [1:54] 好了。我提供您會議代碼而不是訪問代碼。請試試992745,現在應該可以了。

例題1 At 1:54 P.M., what does Mr. Shepard most likely mean when he writes, "Here we go"?

下午1點54分,保羅謝波德先生表示:「好了。」的意思是什麼?

(A) He is about to start the training session.　他即將開始訓練課程。
(B) He has found out what the problem was.　他發現了問題所在。
(C) He's surprised by Ms. Bellaire's request.　他對貝萊爾女士的要求感到驚訝。
(D) He would like to invite her to another meeting.　他想邀請她參加另一場會議。

❶ 從短文中找到訊息傳送的時間和引用句。　❷ 從短文開始讀到引用句,同時解整體意思。

❸ 從既定的選項中找出與說話者前後意思一致的答案。

解析 Here we go是找到問題時使用的句子。引用句接下來提到了提供會議代碼,因此可得知Here we go是指找到了無法登入的原因。

答案: (B)

尋找插入句位置的題目

從[1]，[2]，[3]，[4]的位置中選擇與既定短文句子語意最適合的選項。首先讀完插入句之後，進行短文分析時，必須能夠發現語意中斷或能自然連接插入句的部分。尤其重點是檢查連接詞或特定詞彙之間是否有空格，因為從連接詞可以推測語意走向。特定詞彙重複出現的話，也是理解前後文的關鍵。

🔍 尋找插入句位置的題型

In which of the positions marked [1], [2], [3], and [4] does the following sentence best belong?
"A $10 registration fee is required to begin using our service from now on"

標記為[1]，[2]，[3]和[4]的哪個位置最符合以下句子？「從現在開始使用我們的服務需要10美元的註冊費」

🔍 尋找插入句的例題與解題策略

Question 2 refers to the following notice.

Based on the expense report from last quarter, it is clear that we need to reduce our costs for office supplies. – [1] –. One where we can cut spending is in printing and copying documents. – [2] –. While multicolor documents are more attractive and attention-grabbing than black-and-white ones, color ink cartridges are very expensive. – [3] –. Please reserve the use of the color for only those cases where visual appeal is a relevant factor. – [4] –.

根據上一季度的費用報告，我們顯然需要降低辦公用品的成本。- [1] -。我們可以削減開支的一個部分是文件印刷和影印。- [2] -。雖然多色比黑白文件更具吸引力和引人注目，但彩色墨盒非常昂貴。- [3] -。請僅在視覺吸引力是相關因素的情況下才使用。- [4] -。

PART
7

例題2 In which of the positions marked [1], [2], [3], and [4] does the following sentence best belong?
"Publicity flyers intended for clients are one obvious example in printing documents."

標記為[1]，[2]，[3]和[4]的哪個位置最符合以下句子？「為客戶提供的宣傳單是文件印刷的一個明顯例子。」

(A) [1]   [1]
(B) [2]   [2]
(C) [3]   [3]
(D) [4]   [4]

❶ 先掃描問題並確認哪一題是插入句題目。 ❷ 確認短文中[1]、[2]、[3]、[4]的位置。

❸ 從頭讀一遍短文，掌握短文的主旨、因果關係，便可試著插入句子。

解析 插入句題目是愈勤加練習就愈上手的題型。從短文結構、連接詞和特定詞彙獲得短文走向的提示，找到既定句子的正確位置。[2]前面出現能夠降低成本的其中一個部分是文件印刷，插入句的宣傳單是印刷/影印的例子之一，因此適合放在(B)。　　　　　　　　　　答案: (B)

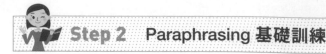

📝 請選出適合改寫底線部分的答案。

1. They <u>sampled</u> the small cups of ice cream at the store.
   (A) speak
   (B) taste

2. Kids love the park's <u>whimsical</u> statues.
   (A) amusing
   (B) sad

3. Human resources is always trying to <u>recruit</u> promising new members.
   (A) fire
   (B) hire

4. The performance showed the true <u>essence</u> of the music.
   (A) nature
   (B) look

5. Hardworking and <u>reliable</u> is how everyone describes the new employee.
   (A) experienced
   (B) trustworthy

6. All students and faculty are <u>cordially</u> invited to attend.
   (A) automatically
   (B) politely

7. There are many <u>fancy</u> boutiques on this street.
   (A) luxury
   (B) lucrative

8. This workshop teaches you how to <u>revitalize</u> your business.
   (A) fail
   (B) energize

9. <u>The illustrations bring the story to life for readers.</u>
   (A) The pictures make the book better.
   (B) The artwork is not necessary.

10. <u>The lawyer gave him representation in court.</u>
    (A) The lawyer helped the man.
    (B) The lawyer did not know the man.

⏰ 試著在限時3分鐘內盡可能答對。

Question 1 refers to the following text massage chain.

Bernadette Lang　　　　　　　　　　　　**11:32 A.M.**

I just got a call from the house 2350 Ridgeway Street. The tenants would like to move out by the end of February, but their lease doesn't expire until the end of June.

Tim Sullivan　　　　　　　　　　　　　**11:38 A.M.**

Well, tenants who leave before the lease expires must pay a fine. However, maybe the owner will waive it. Would you like to call the owner and see if he'll make an exception?

Bernadette Lang　　　　　　　　　　　　**11:40 A.M.**

It's worth a try. After all, we've got several people waiting for rental properties in the area.

Tim Sullivan　　　　　　　　　　　　　**11:45 A.M.**

Yes, and the Ridgeway Street house is an especially nice one. I'm sure it won't be difficult to find a new tenant. Let me know what you find out.

[　　　　　　　　　　　　　　　　] Send

PART
7

新多益

1. At 11:40 A.M., what does Ms. Lang most likely mean when she writes, "It's worth a try"?

   (A) She wants to persuade the tenants to stay.
   (B) She thinks the rental property needs upgrades.
   (C) She's willing to contact the property owner.
   (D) She agrees the rent should be lowered to attract potential tenants.

Question 2 refers to the following article.

Alstyle Reveals Expo plans

Cape Town, June 22 – Retail giant Alstyle Apparel revealed today that it will not be presenting its new line of clothing at this year's Cape Town Fashion Expo in November. - [1] -.

The Cape Town Expo is typically seen as one of the most significant events of the year for the clothing industry, where the biggest retailers in the nation elaborate presentations to show off their upcoming collections. However, in recent years attendance by the general public has significantly decreased. - [2] -.

In a press conference at company headquarters, Alstyle President Donatella Luciano announced that the decision to forgo presenting does not mean that the retailer will be absent from the Expo. - [3] -. "Although there will be no public presentations, we are planning to host small business-oriented meetings with distributers and retail partners," said the company spokesperson. - [4] -.

2. In which of the positions marked [1], [2], [3], and [4] does the following sentence best belong?

"Alstyle's announcement thus came as no surprise to industry insiders."

(A) [1]
(B) [2]
(C) [3]
(D) [4]

⏰ 試著在限時7分鐘(每題1分鐘)內盡可能答對。

Questions 1-3 refer to the following e-mail.

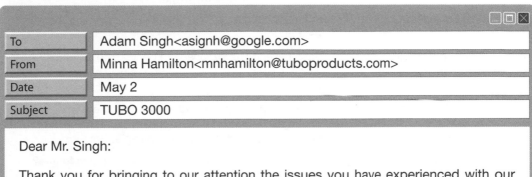

To	Adam Singh<asignh@google.com>
From	Minna Hamilton<mnhamilton@tuboproducts.com>
Date	May 2
Subject	TUBO 3000

Dear Mr. Singh:

Thank you for bringing to our attention the issues you have experienced with our TUBO 3000. We are taking steps to address your concerns immediately. - [1] -. Since the date you purchased your unit, the TUBO 3000 has been redesigned and upgraded. We have shipped one of these units to your address. I'm confident that the new version will resolve any problems you had before. - [2] -.

If it does not, please contact our office at 1-800-555-1323 for a full refund of your purchase price. Additionally we have just transferred all production to a larger building and are refining our manufacturing procedures. - [3] -.

Please let me know if there is anything else I can do. - [4] -. On behalf of TUBO Electronics, I apologize for the inconvenience this issue has caused. I hope to serve you again soon.

Sincerely,

Minna Hamilton, Customer Service Manager
TUBO Electronics Inc.

1. What is the purpose of the e-mail?

   (A) To provide details about a delivery
   (B) To respond to a customer complaint
   (C) To explain new refund policy
   (D) To advertise a new product line

2. What is NOT offered as a solution to the problem?

   (A) Repairing the purchased item
   (B) Refunding the purchase price
   (C) Offering a replacement product
   (D) Improving the manufacturing operation

3. In which of the positions marked [1], [2], [3], and [4] does the following sentence best belong?

   "Our quality control manager will visit to ensure that nothing is being overlooked."

   (A) [1]
   (B) [2]
   (C) [3]
   (D) [4]

Questions 4-7 refer to the following online chat discussion.

Kenneth Costar [9:40 A.M.]	Hi, everyone. I just got into the conference room, and I'm having some trouble with the projector. It keeps shutting off. Does anybody know why?
Beth Leski [9:41 A.M.]	That happened to me last time, too. Try pushing the red reset button.
Ji-Young Park [9:41 A.M.]	Wasn't everything supposed to be set by 9:30 for us? I hope everything is ready before the new hires start arriving.
Kenneth Costar [9:43 A.M.]	Anne Kumar was supposed to do it, but there was another meeting and it ran late. She couldn't wait, so she asked me to set up once the room is available.
Kenneth Costar [9:44 A.M.]	No, it doesn't work. Beth, can you come down for me?
Beth Leski [9:45 A.M.]	On my way.
Ji-Young Park [9:48 A.M.]	Are you guys all set downstairs?
Kenneth Costar [9:50 A.M.]	Yes, everything is ready for the presentations. I've also made hard copies of the presentations and all the forms that the new hires will need to fill out.
Ji-Young Park [9:54 A.M.]	Great. I will be there at noon to take everyone to lunch and then to the security office to pick up their ID badges. I will bring them back by 1:30 for the afternoon schedule.

Send

4. What is Mr. Costar preparing to do?

   (A) Train new employees
   (B) Copy some documents
   (C) Purchase new appliances
   (D) Meet with Ms. Park

5. Why was the conference room not set up by 9:30 A.M.?

   (A) Because the projector has been misplaced.
   (B) Because a meeting did not end on time.
   (C) Because Ms. Park was not at work.
   (D) Because new employees arrived late.

6. At 9:45 A.M., what does Ms. Leski most likely mean when she writes, "On my way"?

   (A) She's going to contact the maintenance department.
   (B) She is traveling to work.
   (C) She will finish revising some documents.
   (D) She is coming to help Mr. Costar.

7. What will happen at noon?

   (A) Employees will listen to the presentation.
   (B) Employees will return from their lunch.
   (C) Ms. Park will go to the conference room.
   (D) Mr. Costar will complete some forms.

PART

7

Unit 12 短文類型1

Step 1 類型分析

Point 1 郵件/信件

出題機率高的短文種類之一，根據寄件者的身分而泛及各種主題，因此在多重短文中也經常出現，需熟記固定模式的短文結構，以及各種業務書信主題和詳細內容。解題時先閱讀題目，掌握Key Word之後，了解郵件/信件前後的收件者、寄件者和短文前面的文章目的。

🔍 郵件/信件的內容結構

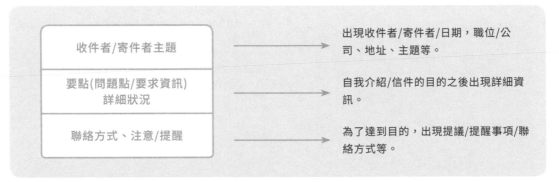

工作業務內容最常出現在信件/郵件短文中。信件/郵件中除了各種工作內容之外，對職場生活的社交活動意見也以書面形式傳遞，因此成為一種固定模式。一開始先練習掌握信件/郵件的結構，找出主題、詳細事項，之後再熟記經常出現的主題(問題點/解決方法)，以解開難度較高的題目。

🔍 郵件/信件的內容類型

1. 傳給顧客/廠商的訊息：購買商品和服務相關內容
2. 廠商之間的互傳訊息：廠商之間的合約或活動相關內容
3. 公司內部業務協助：因公司內部活動和政策異動而請求業務協助的內容
4. 廣告性內容：特定商品/活動/服務相關的廣告內容

🔍 郵件/信件的題目類型

1) General Questions

What is the main purpose of this letter? 這封信的主要目的是什麼？
Who most likely wrote this letter? 誰最有可能寫這封信？
Where is Mr. Norris currently employed? 諾里斯先生目前在哪裡工作？

2) Specific Questions

What is Ms. Naomi asked to do? 娜奧米女士要求做什麼？
What is included with this letter? 這封信附有什麼？
What is stated about the furniture Ms. Park ordered? 有關朴女士訂購家具方面提到了什麼？

Question 1 refers to the following memo.

From: Rhonda Wong
To: All employees
Date: April 23rd
Subject: Parking Changes

Dear colleagues,

<u>Please be advised that the Drew-Tech Corporation parking lot will be unavailable from June 10th through June 18th as it undergoes improvements.</u>

Employees are encouraged to use public transportation and may talk with their supervisors about the possibility of telecommuting from home. Please note that any expenses incurred while using alternative parking lots will be reimbursed.

Also, two additional parking spaces will be available once the work is has been finished. Please contact me at extension 442 if you would like to enter the lottery for these spaces.

Rhonda Wong,
Facility supervisor

寄件者
收件者
日期
主旨

目的

詳細事項

指示/提醒

寄件者

寄件者：王朗達
收件者：全體員工
日期：4月23日
主旨：停車異動

親愛的同事們，

請注意，德魯科技公司停車場將於6月10日至6月18日期間無法使用，因為將進行改良工程。

鼓勵員工使用公共交通工具，並可以與主管討論在家遠程辦公的可能性。請注意，使用其他停車場時產生的任何費用將予以補償。

此外，一旦工作完成，將有兩個額外的停車位。如果您想參加車位抽籤，請通過分機442與我聯絡。

王朗達
設施管理人

PART
7

例題1 What is the purpose of this memo?　　這份通知的目的是什麼？

(A) To advertise discount rates　　宣傳折扣率
(B) To attract volunteers for a company event　　吸引志願者參加公司活動
(C) To introduce a new supervisor　　介紹新的主管
(D) To announce a maintenance project　　宣布維修項目

解析 通常表達主題/目的在文章的最前面出現，找到因為施工關係而關閉停車場的主題之後，既定選項中的(D)是短文內容的改寫，是最適合的答案。　　答案：(D)

這是新多益新增的題型，職場同事之間為了迅速處理業務而使用簡訊或線上聊天傳遞訊息的內容。短文特點是省略主語，並出現許多口語表達方式。由於出現訊息傳送時間和名稱，很容易找到想知道的資訊位置。

🔍 文字簡訊/線上聊天結構

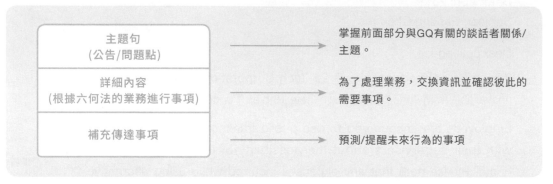

多益Part 7的文字簡訊/線上聊天並非朋友之間的私人對話，與信件/郵件一樣，大多是針對職場工作的內容。特點是簡短並時常轉換句子，因此在理解文章語意上可能會不熟悉，但是對初次接觸多益考試的人來說，反而是閱讀理解力不足也能提高答對機率的有利題型。

🔍 文字簡訊/線上聊天的內容類型

① 有關顧客和廠商：顧客和服務中心職員之間的簡單對話句

② 公司內部業務協助：有關工地或外勤員工和辦公室員工之間的業務對話

組長和部下員工之間分享業務處理狀況的內容

➡ 請勿因為是多數人之間交換的訊息而感到不知所措。一開始由組長級人物提出主題，之後帶動整體對話。最好事先讀完題目，確認詢問的是什麼人、什麼時間的訊息之後再閱讀短文。

🔍 文字簡訊/線上聊天的題目類型

1) General Questions / 推論題目

What are the writers discussing? 他們在討論什麼？

What kind of business do the writers most likely work at? 他們最有可能從事什麼樣的業務？

Where most likely is Mr. Shin when he writes to Ms. Larson?
申先生寫信給拉森女士時最有可能在什麼地方？

2) Specific Questions

At 11:09 A.M., what does Erica mean when she writes, "don't worry about it"?
上午11:09，艾瑞卡寫「不要擔心」時的意思是什麼？

What information does Mr. Keaton provide? 基頓先生提供了哪些資訊？

What will Ms. Sanders most likely do next? 桑德斯女士接下來最有可能做什麼？

Question 2 refers to the following text message chain.

新多益

Pamela Lee [4:02 P.M.]

You left in such a rush. Did you manage to catch your train?

問候語

Min-Soo Park [4:02 P.M.]

Actually no, but there's another one in 10 minutes.

Pamela Lee [4:05 P.M.]

Good for you. Were you able to send the final invoice to Mr. Emerson before you left the office?

主題

Min-Soo Park [4:06 P.M.]

Yes, but I had to send it by express mail. The fax machine wasn't working.

詳細事項

Pamela Lee [4:09 P.M.]

That's okay. He won't need it until later this week anyway. He'll get it by tomorrow.

指示提醒

Min-Soo Park [4:10 P.M.]

That's a relief.

帕梅拉李 [4:02 P.M.]
你匆匆離開了。你有沒有趕上火車？

朴民修 [4:02 P.M.]
其實沒有，但在10分鐘內還有另一班。

帕梅拉李 [4:05 P.M.]
那就好。你在離開辦公室之前是否有將最終發票寄給艾默生先生？

朴民修 [4:06 P.M.]
是的，但我不得不寄快遞。傳真機無法正常啟動。

帕梅拉李 [4:09 P.M.]
沒關係。這星期結束之前他才需要它。他明天會收到的。

朴民修[4:10 P.M.]
真是鬆了一口氣。

PART

7

例題2 At 4:10 P.M., what does Mr. Park most likely mean when he writes, "That's a relief"?

下午4點10分，朴先生表示「真是鬆了一口氣」時最有可能是什麼意思？

(A) He managed to send a fax.

他設法發了傳真。

(B) A delivery will arrive in time.

快遞將及時到達。

(C) Express option is better than regular service.

選擇快遞比普通寄件更好。

(D) An invoice needs to be revised.

發票需要修改。

解析 讀完題目之後，標示Key Word時，記下誰說過什麼話。由於傳真機故障而將文件以快遞方式寄出，明天將會到達的句子後面接上「真是鬆了一口氣」，意思是能夠及時抵達。不要只看invoice就選擇答案，必須了解引用句前後文的語意。 　　答案: (B)

📝 請選出適合改寫底線部分的答案。

1. Books and toys <u>littered</u> the floor.
   (A) messed up
   (B) arranged on

2. We provide <u>competitive</u> hourly wages.
   (A) good
   (B) aggressive

3. This is to answer your letter of <u>inquiry</u>.
   (A) request
   (B) questions

4. Customers are <u>valued</u> by the store owners.
   (A) hated
   (B) respected

5. Team B will <u>oversee</u> the renovation plan for the building.
   (A) overlook
   (B) help with

6. Chemical <u>fertilizers</u> are also on sale here.
   (A) nourishment
   (B) fuel

7. Company executives seem optimistic about future <u>expansion</u>.
   (A) profit
   (B) growth

8. One must get <u>accustomed to</u> a foreign environment.
   (A) familiar with
   (B) trained in

9. <u>The Web site has new things added all the time.</u>
   (A) The Web site tries to list the latest information.
   (B) The Web site seeks to present all the previous data.

10. <u>After next week, we can resume work as usual.</u>
    (A) We can't look for other work until next week.
    (B) We can't continue with our work until next week.

🕐 試著在限時3分鐘內盡可能答對。

Questions 1-2 refer to the following letter.

Global Travel Agency

31 Tulane Street

New York, NY

March 23

Dear Mr. Lopez,

We have received your request for the following publications.

- *Walking Tours in Paris and Rome*

- *Michelin Guides to Asia*

Your order confirmation number is M3483. As always, all maps and city guides are specially priced for our travel customers. You should receive your publications in three to five business days.

Please remember that customers of Global Travel Agency also receive a significant discount on air travel, cruises, hotels and car rentals. If you are planning a trip, please call one of our agents at 212-555-5432 and ask about this month's special offers.

Thank you for the opportunity to serve you.

Sylvia Sullivan

Senior Manager

Global Travel Agency

PART

7

1. What is the purpose of this letter?
   (A) To request information
   (B) To confirm an order
   (C) To advertise a hotel
   (D) To reschedule a shipping date

2. What is NOT mentioned in the letter?
   (A) Foreign currency exchange
   (B) Travel publications
   (C) Discounts on rental cars
   (D) Contact number

⏱ 試著在限時7分鐘(每題1分鐘)內盡可能答對。

Questions 1-3 refer to the following e-mail.

To	customerservice@furnitureplus.com
From	nwilliams443@mail.com
Date	November 27
Subject	My Recent Purchase

Dear Customer Services Manager,

Last month, I ordered living room furniture from Furniture Plus. My order included a sofa, a chair, a coffee table, and an entertainment center. I spent a total of $1,800. While shopping in the store, the clerks were friendly, and quick to respond.

However, I was disappointed in how the delivery department handled the order. I was told the furniture would arrive on November 1, but it didn't arrive until two weeks later. When I called to request some information about the delivery, I had to wait on the phone for more than 30 minutes. When I did speak to the person in charge, I realized the shipment was delayed without any notice.

Once the furniture arrived, I was disappointed again, because half the pieces were damaged. The sofa's cushion was torn, the coffee table was scratched, and the entertainment center shelf fell down.

I am expecting a full refund and a letter of apology from the store owner. Otherwise, I will encourage everyone I know to shop elsewhere.

Respectfully,

Nathan Williams

1. Why did Mr. Williams send the e-mail?
   (A) To make changes to his order
   (B) To complain about service
   (C) To report a missing purchase
   (D) To request product information

2. What is indicated about the furniture Mr. Williams received?
   (A) It was in very poor condition.
   (B) It cost less than he expected.
   (C) All the pieces were included.
   (D) It belonged to someone else.

3. What is Mr. Williams requesting from Furniture Plus?
   (A) A second couch for free
   (B) Furniture repair at no cost
   (C) A discount on his next purchase
   (D) Money and a written response

Questions 4-7 refer to the following online chat discussion.

Clare Hann [10:53 A.M.]		Good morning, team. Any news on our Oakland Park bid?
David Bowman [10:54 A.M.]		I talked to one of their managers on Friday. He said to expect a decision by Monday but we haven't heard anything yet.
Clare Hann [10:55 A.M.]		The problem is that if we don't order supplies by tomorrow, we won't get them in time to meet the deadline for the project.
Maria Mendoza [10:56 A.M.]		I've already placed the order. I did it yesterday.
Clare Hann [10:56 A.M.]		That could be a problem if we don't get the contract. We'll have to pay for the stuff we won't be able to use. How much time do we have to cancel without incurring a fee?
David Bowman [10:58 A.M.]		I figured since they chose us last time they'd probably go with us this again. Let me check.
Maria Mendoza [11:01 A.M.]		No need. I just got a call from Oakland. They said it was close, but the CEO decided to go with The Rusenski Brothers this time.
Clare Hann [11:02 A.M.]		That's disappointing. But let's not let this get us down. We'll have better luck next time.

Send

4. What are the writers discussing?

(A) A bid offer
(B) A new position
(C) A price discount
(D) A revised timeline

5. At 10:58 A.M. what does Mr. Bowman most likely mean when he writes, "Let me check"?

(A) He will ask about a deadline.
(B) He will reschedule a delivery.
(C) He will confirm an appointment.
(D) He will calculate the cost of a project.

6. What decision was Oakland Park due to make?

(A) How much penalty they have to pay
(B) Where to return their products to
(C) Who will work for their project
(D) When the final contract be ready

7. What will Mr. Bowman most likely do next?

(A) Go to a meeting
(B) Cancel an order
(C) Create a work schedule
(D) Call Oakland for reconsideration

Unit 13　短文類型2

 Step 1　類型分析

如果熟悉Part 7的短文類型，就能更快速有效率地解題。尤其如果一次將各種模式的題型記熟，下次出現類似的考題時，就能很快找到需要的資訊。

Point 1 格式

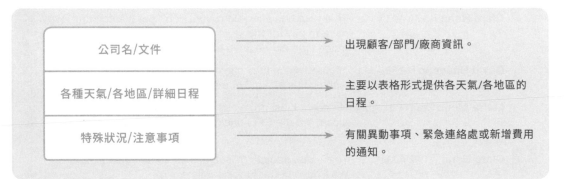

狀況或表格/格式形態的短文除了以單獨文章出現之外，也經常出現複合短文。端讀短文的句數少，相對來說可以在短時間內解題。格式最前面的主題和最後的新增資訊(注意事項)經常是正確答案的提示，是必須要確認的部分。與其逐字逐句解析短文的資訊，不如先讀完題目，了解表格/格式的特點，再尋找需要的資訊。

🔍 **各種格式類型**

❶ 發票(invoice), 訂單(order slip), 收據(receipt)：購買物品的相關格式。

❷ 優惠券(coupon), 禮券(voucher)：折價券或免費使用券通常有使用期限。

❸ 行程/時間表(itinerary, schedule, time table)：有關旅行/出差/工作日期和各場所的資訊。

❹ 問卷調查(survey, questionnaire)：有關特定商品或廠商的意見。

❺ 績效考核(performance review)：有關特定員工/部門的評估。

➡ 必須能夠根據表格/格式的種類，了解最基本的GQ, SQ(誰/在哪裡/為什麼)內容。有關SQ的事項透過讀完題目之後，尋找相關內容的方式來解題。

🔍 **格式的題目類型**

1) General Questions

What is this coupon for? 這張優惠券是什麼？
Who is Mr. Bellaire? 貝萊爾先生是誰？
What is the purpose of this form? 這個表格的目的是什麼？

2) Specific Questions / 推論問題

When was the order sent? 訂單何時發送？
What restriction is placed on this voucher? 這張優惠券有什麼限制？
What is NOT included in the itinerary? 行程中沒有包含什麼內容？

Question 1 refers to the following invoice.

Jack & Hills Office Supply

http://www.Jacknhills.com
sales@Jacknhills.com

Date: October 17, 2017

Invoice #: TP12409

Bill to:
Korex Inc.
393 West Road
North Fork, UT 84003

Ship to:
Korex Inc.
393 West Road
North Fork, UT 84003

Product Number	Items	Unit Price	Qty	Total Amount
P120	Printing Papers	40.00	30	1,200.00
P520	Toners	89.00	5	445.00
Invoice Total				1,645.00

<u>Orders over $1,000 qualify for free shipping.</u> Please call us at 555-3758 if you have any questions on our bills. Please keep this for future reference.

傑克&希爾辦公用品店
http://www.Jacknhills.com
sales@Jacknhills.com

日期: 2017年10月17日
發票號碼 #: TP12409

付款人:
柯瑞斯公司
西路393號
北福克，猶他州84003

收貨人:
柯瑞斯公司
西路393號
北福克，猶他州84003

商品號碼	商品	單價	數量	總額
P120	影印紙	40美元	30	1,200美元
P520	碳粉	89美元	5	445美元
發票總額				1,645美元

超過1,000美元的訂單可享受免運費。如果您對我們的賬單有任何疑問，請致電555-3758。請保留此收據以備將來參考。

寄件者
格式種類
參考資訊

詳細事項

參考事項
指示提醒

例題1 What is true about Korex Inc?

(A) It has recently moved to a new location
(B) It has requested a discount.
(C) It is eligible for free delivery.
(D) It orders regularly from this company.

有關柯瑞斯公司什麼是正確的？

最近搬到了新的地方。
要求折扣。
享有免運費。
定期從這家公司訂購。

解析 格式題型的解題重點是快速找出主要資訊。True/Not true題目須將短文出現的資訊和選項進行比對。訂購總額為1,645美元，根據最後的參考事項，超過1,000美元可享有免運費，因此正確答案是(C)。以發票的情況來說，經常出現與金額相關的題目。　　　　　　答案: (C)

廣告文是宣傳各種產品和服務的內容。尤其與日常生活有關的物品或服務,即使不具備專業知識也能夠解題,但徵人廣告或廠商之間宣傳服務的內容,如果具備多益背景知識會更有利。只要重複練習短文的類型,就能快速有效率地解題。

廣告文的短文結構

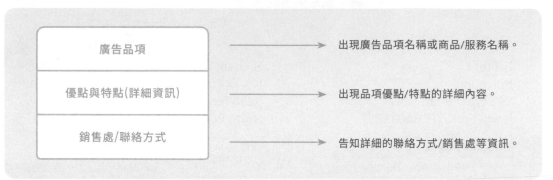

出題方式根據廣告文中介紹的物品或服務而有不同形態,但基本上短文前半部會介紹主題。同時以消費者為對象所推出的物品為了引起注意,經常以反問句或感嘆句開場。徵人廣告通常以職位名稱和列出資格條件的形式出現。

廣告文的類型

❶ 產品廣告: 說明電子產品、寢具類等各式物品的優點,以及鼓勵購買的內容。

❷ 服務/廠商廣告:宣傳房屋仲介、專人清潔等各種服務並鼓勵合作簽約的內容。

❸ 徵人廣告:各家公司說明特定職位(position)所必備的資格條件,鼓勵應徵的內容。熟記多益經常出現的職位/工作背景知識有利於解題。

➡ 先讀完題目,掌握Key Word之後,記下廣告文前面宣傳的品項,再確認短文中段提到的品項優點/廠商優點/職位的條件等,和選項進行比對,選出正確答案。短文後半部通常出現注意事項和聯絡方式。

廣告文的題目類型

1) General Questions

What is being advertised? 廣告的是什麼?

What position is being advertised? 廣告什麼職位?

For whom is the advertisement most likely intended? 誰最有可能是廣告的對象?

2) Specific Questions / 推論題目

What is the main advantage of the product? 產品的主要優勢是什麼?

What is NOT required for the position? 這個職位不需具備什麼條件?

How should interested people register? 感興趣的人應該如何報名?

🔍 廣告文的例題與解題策略

Question 2 refers to the following advertisement.

Online Personal Training

Have you ever wanted to have your own Expert Personal Trainer right at your finger tips? You need not to look any further.

廣告對象

Our Online Personal Training program makes it easy for you to receive our quality, professional fitness expertise at the touch of a button.

↳ (D)

主要優點

This program is perfect if:

→ (A)
- You want a budget-friendly way to get fit.
- You have an unpredictable schedule. → (C)
- You travel frequently.

詳細事項

Visit us at www.onlinetrainers.com for details about our services and fees, or call 1-800-555-7922 for individual consultations.

指示提醒

線上個人培訓

您有沒有想過擁有觸手可及的個人專屬私人教練？您不需要再找了。

我們的線上個人培訓計劃讓您只需按一下按鈕，即可輕鬆獲得我們優質、專業的健身專業知識。

這是一項完美計畫，只要：

- 您需要一種經濟實惠的方式來獲得健康。
- 您的行程經常變動。
- 您經常出差。

有關我們的服務和費用的詳細資訊，請參訪我們的網站www.onlinetrainers.com，或致電1-800-555-7922進行個人諮詢。

例題2 What is NOT stated as an advantage of the program?

什麼是這項計劃沒有提到的優點？

(A) Affordable prices　　　　　　　負擔得起的價格
(B) Free dietary supplements　　　免費膳食補充品
(C) Convenient schedules　　　　　方便的行程
(D) Time with professional experts　與專家共度時光

解析 廣告文的部分內容是說明產品的優點(advantages, merits)。由於條列式列出優點，經常作為True/Not true的考題。廣告內容是針對考量預算、行程忙碌的人們設計的運動課程，沒有提到飲食，因此答案是(B)。

答案: (B)

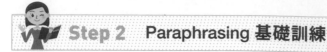

✎ 請選出適合改寫底線部分的答案。

1. Children and teenagers are the biggest <u>targeted</u> market.

   (A) expanded
   (B) aimed for

2. This is to help <u>ensure</u> a quality experience for all customers.

   (A) make certain
   (B) guarantee against

3. The singer was <u>accompanied by</u> her band.

   (A) disappeared
   (B) together with

4. I have some <u>retail</u> experience working at Gordon's.

   (A) manufacturing
   (B) vending

5. The seminar has <u>lively</u> and informative workshops.

   (A) exciting
   (B) true

6. She purchased a <u>faulty</u> product from the store.

   (A) innovative
   (B) defective

7. Please come and <u>acknowledge</u> his achievements and contributions.

   (A) recognize
   (B) distinguish

8. Mr. Brooks will <u>retire</u> next month after many years here.

   (A) promote
   (B) step down

9. <u>The offer is valid for refunds or exchanges.</u>

   (A) The offer can be used for refunds or exchanges.
   (B) The offer cannot be used for refunds or exchanges.

10. <u>She happily greeted me at the door when I visited.</u>

    (A) She said "Hi" to me right away.
    (B) She stopped me from entering.

⏰ 試著在限時3分鐘內盡可能答對。

Questions 1-2 refer to the following voucher.

VOUCHER

Big Splash Water Adventures

Issue date: January 1, 2017

This voucher entitles the bearer to a boating excursion for two with Big Splash Water Adventures.

- The voucher can be exchanged for cash only during the following times: March 1~April 30 and August 20~October 1.
- The voucher is valid only for some excursions. These include whale-watching, snorkeling, and scuba diving tours, but not shark-watching, sailing, or water-skiing adventures.
- The holder of this voucher and his/her guest must be 18 years of age or older.

Please mention the voucher when you request your reservation.

For more information about this offer, please call the Mexico Tourist Office at 52-34-555-2100.

Expiration date: August 31, 2017

PART
7

1. What can the voucher be used for?
   (A) A shark-seeing tour
   (B) A flight to Mexico
   (C) A boating activity
   (D) A free lunch for two

2. What is true about Big Splash Water Adventures?
   (A) It offers trips to monuments.
   (B) It gives vouchers for a full year.
   (C) It runs business only in the summer.
   (D) It provides a variety of tours.

⏰ 試著在限時7分鐘(每題1分鐘)內盡可能答對。

Questions 1-3 refer to the following advertisement.

Get It Together

helping you stay organized and brighten up your home!

When life gets crazy busy, our homes get messy. We don't have time to throw out the old and organize the new. Laundry piles up. Books and toys litter the floor.

But Get It Together is here to help! We organize all rooms — closets, kitchens, offices, even garages. We'll visit your home to understand your needs. Then we'll bring you shelves and containers to fit the rooms in your home. We'll take care of the clutter and get you all cleaned up.

For our Grand Opening, we will visit the first 5 customers' homes for free. Remember, only the first 5 customers will get this free service. So call soon to make an appointment: 555-2255.

---

1. For whom is the advertisement most likely intended?
   (A) Busy working parents
   (B) People with small budgets
   (C) Students living in a dorm
   (D) Children under 15

2. What is stated about Get It Together?
   (A) It has numerous employees.
   (B) The business is several years old.
   (C) Certain spaces can't be serviced.
   (D) Free service opportunities are limited.

3. Why is the business offering free visits?
   (A) To fill its schedule
   (B) To celebrate its opening
   (C) To reward its clients
   (D) To help staff members

Questions 4-7 refer to the following form.

MANILA CORP.

19 Arizona Avenue
Downtown Manila

INVOICE

Order Date: July 2nd
Order Number: 39488
Shipping Date: July 10th

CLIENT BILLING AND SHIPPING ADDRESS

Billing Name: Eastern Bank

Street: 214 Roxas Boulevard

City: Green Meadow

Country: Canada

Ship to: Daniel Adams

Customer ID: 8892

PRODUCT PURCHASED

Item No.	Item Description	Quantity	Unit Price	Total Price
13553	Writing Desk	1	$180	$180
13890	Desk Chairs	2	$130	$260
25530	Desk Lamp	1	$80	$80

Sub Total: $520

Shipping: $100

Total Amount: $620

Thank you for your business.

Sender Signature: *John Lee*

---

4. What is the purpose of this document?

   (A) To report a missing item
   (B) To bill for items sold
   (C) To change the delivery address
   (D) To return a damaged item

5. Who is going to pay for the merchandise?

   (A) Manila Corp.
   (B) John Lee
   (C) Arizona Corp.
   (D) Eastern Bank

6. How much does the customer have to pay for shipping?

   (A) $80
   (B) $100
   (C) $260
   (D) $620

7. What is NOT stated in this document?

   (A) A discounted price
   (B) An amount due
   (C) A delivery date
   (D) A shipping address

Unit 14　短文類型3

Point 1　報導

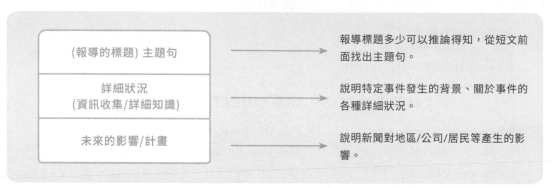

(報導的標題) 主題句	報導標題多少可以推論得知，從短文前面找出主題句。
詳細狀況 (資訊收集/詳細知識)	說明特定事件發生的背景、關於事件的各種詳細狀況。
未來的影響/計畫	說明新聞對地區/公司/居民等產生的影響。

報導所介紹的範圍廣，沒有可預測的短文結構，以連貫性的長句組成，因此是Part 7中需要高度閱讀理解力的題型。必須了解短文最前面出現的標題，投入充分的時間練習分析文章。

🔍 **報導的短文結構**

報導所使用的詞彙或句型結構和其他類型相比，比較生硬而正式，因此閱讀時難以掌握詞彙或結構上的提示。必須先了解各種報導中標題的內容，解題之後再次回顧內容。

🔍 **報導內容的類型**

❶ 商業新聞：有關公司介紹或收購/合併/新商品等的報導，與整體經濟相關的報導

❷ 社會新聞：各種事件/事故和有關天氣/健康/運動等內容

❸ 地區新聞：各種地區活動/人物介紹和設施公告內容

❹ 以趣味為主的評論：介紹特定商品評論/餐廳評論/服務評論的內容

➡ 先了解短文前半部的主題句，藉此掌握整體方向，解題時將客觀提到的背景知識和詳細事項與題目進行比對，熟記經常出現的標題和短文結構。

🔍 **報導的題目類型**

1) General Questions

What is the main idea[topic] of the article? 本文的主要觀點[主題]是什麼？

What is the press release announcing? 這篇新聞稿宣布了什麼？

Why was this article written? 這篇報導寫成的目的是什麼？

2) Specific Questions / 推論題目

Which of the following is true about Birmingham Motors? 關於伯明翰機車公司，以下哪項是正確的？

When was the first edition of the book released? 這本書初版發行的日子是什麼時候？

According to the article, what will happen in the next year? 根據這篇文章，明年將會發生什麼事？

Question 1 refers to the following article.

The Boston Globe

Business briefs

Boston, October 9— Shelby Yang, president of Max Footwear, announced yesterday that <u>the company plans to add stores</u> in Baltimore, New York, Philadelphia, and Washington DC within a year. Ms. Yang acknowledged that an earlier attempt at expansion had not been successful because the company moved too quickly. Now that Max Footwear, whose headquarters are located in Boston, has clear marketing strategies as well as the necessary financial resources, Ms. Yang claimed the expansion will be easier this time.

Max Footwear started in 1999, targeting mainly children and teenagers, and has added an adults' shoes section over the years. The company executives mostly seem optimistic about the future expansion. This year, Max Footwear expects record sales at its four stores, all located in the Boston area, due to successful advertising campaigns started recently.

主旨

主題句

詳細事項

未來計畫
和期許

波士頓環球報
商務簡報

波士頓，10月9日- 馬克斯製鞋企業總裁謝爾比楊昨天宣布，該公司計劃一年內在巴爾的摩、紐約、費城和華盛頓特區增加門市。楊女士承認，由於公司操之過急，之前的擴張嘗試並沒有成功。現在，總部位於波士頓的馬克斯製鞋擁有明確的營銷策略和必要的財務資源，楊女士聲稱此次擴張將更加容易。

馬克斯製鞋成立於1999年，主要客層是兒童和青少年，多年來增加了成人鞋款。公司高層主管們大多對未來的擴張抱持樂觀態度。今年，馬克斯製鞋希望藉由最近推出的廣告活動的成功，在其位於波士頓地區的四家商店實現創紀錄的銷售額。

例題1 What is suggested about Max Footwear?

(A) It's currently selling only to young people.
(B) It recently closed some of its stores.
(C) It will start selling at other locations.
(D) It moved its main office to Philadelphia.

關於馬克思製鞋可以知道什麼？

目前只銷售給年輕人。
最近關閉一些門市。
即將開始在其他地方銷售。
總公司遷到了費城。

解析 必須在比對推論題目既定選項的同時，確認是否屬實。短文中增加門市(add stores)的內容在選項中改寫為selling at other locations，因此正確答案是(C)。　　　　答案: (C)

報導是以大眾為對象，提供各種內容的資訊，相反的，公告/通知是將官方的內容告知給特定團體的多數人。尤其管理者或經營者為了團體中的人們，以有效率的結構交換並提供資訊，因此必須掌握要點，形態上較為簡單。

🔍 公告/通知的短文結構

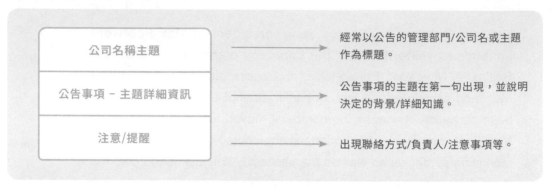

Part 7的公告/通知是有效且正式地傳達內容的短文類型。大部分在最前面出現標題或公司名，事先預告通知的內容。但由於是正式內容，詞彙或表達可能較為生硬，需要以考試經常出現的各個主題來熟記詞彙/表達方式，能更快速掌握短文結構，提升閱讀理解能力。

🔍 文字簡訊/線上聊天的內容類型

❶ 公司內部公告/通知：公告公司的政策異動、業務上決定的事項內容

❷ 以顧客為對象的公告：告知顧客商品/服務的相關事項

❸ 地區團體的公告：告知居民特定活動/工程等決定事項

❹ 特定團體會員的公告：會員的活動和促進團體的內容

➡ 先讀完題目，掌握Key Word，了解短文最前面的主題之後，將題目的選項和短文進行比對來解題。

🔍 公告/通知的題目類型

1) General Questions

What is the main purpose of the notice? 通知的主要目的是什麼？

Where would the notice most likely appear? 通知最有可能出現在哪裡？

Who probably is sending this memorandum? 誰最有可能會發送這份通知？

2) Specific Questions / 推論題目

What are the customers[employees] asked to do? 客戶[員工]被要求做什麼？

What change will take place next month? 下個月會發生什麼改變？

What should employees do when they have any questions? 員工有任何疑問時應該怎麼做？

🔍 公告/通知的例題與解題策略

Question 2 refers to the following notice.

< Great Outdoors Club >
Summer Schedule

Hiking at the Ozark Mountains – July 8 at 8:00 A.M.
Kayaking at DeGray Lake – July 10 at 10:00 A.M.
Cycling classes – Wednesdays at 5:00 P.M.
Rock climbing classes – Thursdays at 4:00 P.M.

Registration is now open for all programs and classes. Please sign up at the front desk. <u>Additional programs are in the process of being finalized and will be made public on May 30th.</u> Those who are willing to provide rides to fellow members who lack transportation are kindly requested to stop by at the front desk and talk to our supporting staff.

公司 — 主旨 — 詳細資訊 — 注意，提醒

< 葛瑞特戶外俱樂部>
夏季時間表

奧索卡山脈徒步旅行 – 7月8日上午8點
德格雷湖划獨木舟 – 7月10日上午10點
自行車課程 - 每週三下午5:00
攀岩課程 - 每週四下午4:00

現在所有課程和課程都開放報名。請在櫃台報名。其他新增課程正在做最後確定，將於5月30日公布。那些願意提供缺乏交通工具的會員們搭便車的人請到前台來告訴我們的工作人員。

例題2 According to the notice, what will happen on May 30th?

根據通知，5月30日會發生什麼事？

(A) Registration for programs will close.
(B) More information will become available.
(C) New instructors will be hired.
(D) The hiking classes will begin.

課程報名將截止。
將提供更多資訊。
將僱用新的講師。
徒步旅行課程將開始。

解析 這是以健身房會員們為對象的公告，是詢問特定時間點的典型SQ。需先讀完Key Word，從文章中尋找相關的內容。5月30日將決定並公布新課程，因此正確答案是(B)。短文中的be made public在選項中改寫為become available。　　　　　答案: (B)

PART

7

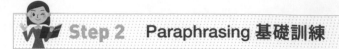

📝 請選出適合改寫底線部分的答案。

1. He asked for <u>a reduction</u> in work hours.
   (A) less
   (B) more

2. The company improved its <u>fiscal</u> situation.
   (A) strategic
   (B) financial

3. The salesman was <u>attentive</u> to what the client had to say.
   (A) carefully listening
   (B) thoughtful

4. She would like to discuss the <u>fundraiser</u> with you.
   (A) investor
   (B) charity event

5. With natural soils, nothing is chemically <u>treated</u>.
   (A) dealt with
   (B) cared for

6. Teens can face <u>tricky</u> situations at home or school.
   (A) large
   (B) difficult

7. The items were rung up <u>accurately</u> by the cashier.
   (A) precisely
   (B) carefully

8. Companies try to <u>motivate</u> their workers to perform optimally.
   (A) force
   (B) stimulate

9. <u>Casual attire is requested for attendees of this event.</u>
   (A) People should dress formally for this event.
   (B) People can dress in comfortable clothes for this event.

10. <u>Our merchandise is in high demand.</u>
    (A) Many want our products.
    (B) We have plenty of products.

試著在限時3分鐘內盡可能答對。

Questions 1-2 refer to the following information.

Jonnason & Holly, Ltd.

Dear customers,

We try to keep our catalog as up-to-date as possible by listing the latest product and prices. However, since our merchandise is generally in high demand, some items in this catalog may be no longer available at the time you browse through it. In addition, price fluctuations on the world market may require us to adjust our prices.

We therefore suggest that you visit our Web site, www.jsholly.org, where our merchandise and prices are constantly updated. At Jonnason & Holly, we strive to meet all gardening needs of our customers. We would appreciate any recommendations you may have on our future products. Your feedback will allow us to expand our product range.

Thank you for your continued patronage!

PART

7

1. What is suggested about the catalog?
   (A) It does not explain the return policy.
   (B) It has many subscribers.
   (C) It is offered for free to customers.
   (D) It may not list the current prices.

2. What are the customers asked to send?
   (A) Suggestions for new products
   (B) Change-of-address forms
   (C) Pictures of their gardens
   (D) Discount coupons for future purchases

⏰ 試著在限時7分鐘(每題1分鐘)內盡可能答對。

Questions 1-3 refer to the following article.

Art in the Park Sale, A Great Success

New York, June 19 – Paramount Square Park, which is known for its whimsical statues, was the site of Mercury Alliance's 3rd annual Art in the Park Sale last Saturday. Among the items for sale were paintings, photographs, and crafts created by the Mercury Alliance artists. After Friday's rain and thunder, Saturday's clear sunny weather brought hundreds of residents and tourists to the park. Many of them enjoyed viewing the artwork on display as they ate ice cream and sampled other treats sold by local cafés and restaurants.

Mercury Alliance faced bankruptcy five years ago, but it has turned its fiscal situation around under the directorship of Rachel Harrison. The Art in the Park Sale is one of Harrison's profit-making ideas. Another one is the Artists' Ball, which will be held downtown Sunday at Riverside Hotel.

---

1. What does the article mainly discuss?
   (A) An outdoor event
   (B) The opening of a new park
   (C) An upcoming musical show
   (D) A new program director

2. What was offered for sale by Mercury Alliance?
   (A) Statues
   (B) Umbrellas
   (C) Ice creams
   (D) Crafted items

3. What has Rachel Harrison done for Mercury Alliance?
   (A) She has recruited new members.
   (B) She has helped it establish a new foundation.
   (C) She has improved its financial standing.
   (D) She has provided art classes to residents.

Questions 4-7 refer to the following notice.

Safety Regulations

All employees are required to observe the following regulations while in this laboratory.

- Protective clothing (lab coats, gloves, masks, and goggles) must be worn at all times.

- Before leaving the lab, remove protective clothing in the changing room and put it in the bins marked "Protective Clothing."

- Plates, tubes, and other containers should be cleaned before storing them in the cabinet or in the refrigerators.

- To avoid spills, all containers must be transported on carts with protective racks or baskets. Make sure that lids are securely closed to prevent leaking.

These regulations are for your safety. Employees failing to follow the above precautions will be issued a written warning from their supervisor.

---

4. What is the purpose of the notice?
   (A) To respond to an employee complaint
   (B) To announce a new dress code
   (C) To inform employees of safety rules
   (D) To explain the use of new equipment

5. Where should employees put the protective clothing they have used?
   (A) On clothing rack
   (B) In designated bins
   (C) In storage cabinets
   (D) At their workstations

6. What should employees do before storing laboratory containers?
   (A) Label the surface
   (B) Divide them by their sizes
   (C) Discard the old ones
   (D) Wash them properly

7. According to the notice, what would be the penalty for not following the rules?
   (A) A written notice will be given by the manager.
   (B) Another will be hired for the position.
   (C) Entry to the lab will be limited.
   (D) Pay will be reduced.

Unit 15 多重短文

Step 1 類型分析

Point 1 雙重短文

根據兩則短文,解開五個題目的類型。包括2組共10個問題,也有必須參考兩則短文的內容才能選擇答案的連貫題型。根據第一則短文掌握主題,找出與第二則短文的連貫性來解題。

🔍 雙重短文的結構

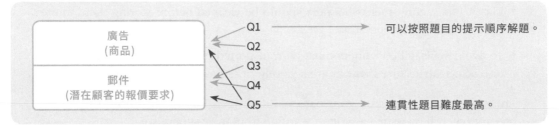

題目中詢問的資訊該如何在短文中有效率且快速地找到,在雙重短文中也至關重要。先讀完題目,找到Key Word之後,從含有Key Word的短文中尋找正確答案的線索。接著必須從短文其他的部分找出和既定選項一致的其他資訊。例如,當廣告中介紹了產品型號和價格,從郵件中找出消費者想要的型號,再次回到廣告內容找出相關的價格,並選擇正確答案。

🔍 雙重短文的類型

❶ 郵件+郵件:處理商品/報價/資訊的要求/抱怨等業務方面的回答

❷ 廣告/通知+郵件/格式:有關廣告/通知中出現的報名/疑問/要求的內容

❸ 格式+格式:在介紹/募集格式中填入回答的內容

➡ 一開始接觸多重短文時,可能會因為太多資訊而感到慌張,但不要忘記整體來說是組合各種短文來完成一個故事,需練習尋找整體性主題,並找出各個題目所需的資訊。前面提到的各種短文類型熟悉之後,也能更有效率地找到多重短文中的資訊。

Question 1 refers to the following announcement and form.

Tools for Business

標題

Is your company looking to expand, train employees to be leaders, or develop new products? Look no further!

Redman Business Solutions delivers a series of informative workshops relating to key business processes. Register online at redmanbusiness.com.

主題

1. *Leadership and Motivation* recommends resources and tactics to help you attract and retain outstanding customers.

Wednesday, May 12th, 10 A.M. ~ noon   Cost: £95

2. *Product Development* includes a detailed case study and specific action steps to help you revitalize and speed up your process for creating new products.

Wednesday, May 19th, 10 A.M. ~ noon   Cost: £135.

詳細事項

ONLINE REGISTRATION FORM

標題
(連貫性)

Name: Jennifer Tang

Address: 29 Brenton Road, Leeds, West Yorkshire

Phone No.: 555-3804

E-mail: jent@vtfinance.com

Workshop Number: 2

Date: May 12th

Comments: Several of the managers of my company are also interested in attending your workshop. Do you offer reduced rates for groups?

詳細事項
(連貫性)

PART
7

商業工具

貴公司是否希望擴展，培訓員工成為領導者或開發新產品？別再看了！瑞德曼業務解決方案提供一系列與關鍵業務流程資訊相關內容豐富的研討會。請上redmanbusiness. com網站註冊。

1. 〈領導力和動機〉提供資源和策略，以幫助您吸引和留住優秀的客戶。5月12日星期三，上午10點～中午，費用：95英鎊。

2. 〈產品開發〉包括詳細的案例研究和具體的行動步驟，以幫助您重整和加快創建新產品的過程。5月19日星期三，上午10點～中午，費用：135英鎊。

線上註冊格式

姓名：詹妮弗唐

地址：西約克郡 利茲市 布倫頓路29號

電話號碼：555-3804

電子郵件：jent@vtfinance.com

研討會編號：2

日期：5月12日

備註：我公司的幾位經理也有興趣參加您的研討會。請問是否為團體提供優惠價格？

例題1 What is the fee for the workshop Ms. Tang plans to attend?

唐女士計劃參加的研討會費用是多少？

(A) £95　　　　　　　　　　　95英鎊

(B) £110　　　　　　　　　　110英鎊

(C) £120　　　　　　　　　　120英鎊

(D) £135　　　　　　　　　　135英鎊

解析 這種題型在解題時必須掌握2則短文的整體性，當了解每則短文共約2個主題時，就能預測出題目。例題是以廣告和報名格式組成的雙重短文，最常考的題目是與第一則短文提到的各種選擇具連貫性的資訊，第一則短文介紹了2場研討會，第二則短文表示報名者選擇第2場。再次回到第一則短文，找到第2場研討會費用是135英鎊之後，就可以選擇答案。

答案: (D)

Point 2 三重短文 新多益

新多益新增的題型，根據3則短文解開5個題目的類型。共有3組15個題目，即使覺得雙重短文已經頗有難度，也不需要擔心三重短文該如何著手。三重短文的其中一則是有關另兩則短文的額外說明，因此只要視為雙重短文的形態即可。

三重短文的結構

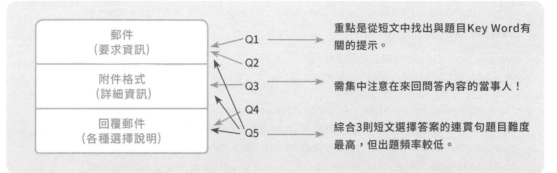

三重短文的形式經常加上雙重短文中表格/圖表的視覺資料。乍看之下，三重短文的資訊很多，但許多應試者反而認為從表格/圖表中尋找資訊較為容易。加上和既有的雙重短文一樣，大多是綜合2則短文來解題，統整3則短文內容出題的機率不高，因此與其另外練習連貫3則短文的題目，不如先讀完題目之後，進行尋找資訊的基本訓練，能更快解題。

三重短文的類型

❶ 郵件+格式+郵件：尋求解答的郵件中含有詳細資訊的回覆郵件

❷ 格式+格式+信件/郵件：透過郵件詢問的內容，並附有發票/收據的格式

❸ 廣告/公告+格式+郵件/報導：各種活動/公告中附上參加表格寄出的郵件，或與公告活動有關的報導

➡ 先找出第一則短文的主題，接著區分第二則短文是提供額外資訊，還是提供第一則短文的回應內容，之後再找出第二、三則短文和第一則短文的連貫性。

PART
7

Question 2 refers to the following flyer, list, and letter.

LOOK, Jazz Fans
Ozgul Band will be performing LIVE

Ozgul Band lead by Maya Ozgul will make you experience the true essence of Southern Jazz.

Venue: Town Record Music Store

Dates: Friday, August 10th and Saturday, August 11th

To purchase tickets in advance, send a personal check or money order to the Town Record Store by Wednesday, August 8th. You can also pay by credit card if you visit the store before August 8th. Any remaining tickets will be sold on a first-come, first-served basis in the evening of the performance. Cash will be the only acceptable form of payment on these evenings.

For further information, call 615-555-2748 or e-mail Ryan Muller at rmuller@townmusic.com.

Price List

Dates	Adults	Children under 12
August 10th	$40	$20
August 11th	$50	$25

Refunds will only be available at least two weeks before the performance. Please keep your receipt for reference.

Ryan Muller Town Record Store
1204 Wainwright Square
St Paul, MN 55112

August 2nd

Dear Mr. Muller,

I was delighted to learn that Ozgul Band will be performing at your store. I've always wanted to see them play in person and now this performance will give me the first chance to do just that. <u>I would like to purchase two tickets for adults to the first concert.</u> I am enclosing a money order to cover the cost. I plan to pick up my tickets on Monday, August 6th at the store.

Thanks,
John Anderson

看，爵士球迷

厄茲居爾樂團的現場表演

由馬雅厄茲居爾所帶領的厄茲居爾樂團將讓您體驗南方爵士樂的真諦。

地點：城鎮唱片音樂

日期：8月10日星期五、8月11日星期六

要提前購買門票，請在8月8日星期三之前將個人支票或匯票寄至城鎮唱片音樂行。如果您在8月8日之前前往音樂行，也可以使用信用卡付款。任何剩餘的門票將在演出的晚上以先到先得的方式出售，屆時現金將是唯一可接受的付款方式。

欲了解更多資訊，請致電615-555-2748或發送電子郵件至rmuller @ townmusic.com給瑞恩穆勒。

價格表

日期	成人	12歲以下兒童
8月10日	40美元	20美元
8月11日	50美元	25美元

退款只能在演出前至少兩週申請。請保留您的收據以供參考。

瑞恩穆勒城鎮唱片
1204溫賴特廣場
聖保羅，明尼蘇達州55112

8月2日

親愛的穆勒先生，

我很高興得知厄茲居爾樂團將在您的唱片行演出。我一直希望能現場欣賞他們的演出，現在這場表演讓我第一次有機會這麼做。我想在第一場音樂會上購買兩張成人票。我附上匯票以支付費用。我會在8月6日星期一在唱片行取票。

謝謝。

約翰安德森

例題2 What amount does Mr. Anderson enclose with his e-mail?　　　　安德森先生在電子郵件中附上多少錢？

(A) $40.00　　　　40美元
(B) $50.00　　　　50美元
(C) $80.00　　　　80美元
(D) $100.00　　　　100美元

解析 此例題是結合<①廣告+②價目表>的方式，讀完③郵件之後，根據表演日期/人數計算出正確價格的連貫性題目。由於表演持續兩天，第一天表演的成人門票是40美元，兩名成人的費用40X2=80，因此答案是(C)。　　　　答案: (C)

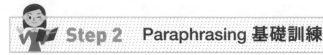

📝 請選出適合改寫底線部分的答案。

1. The company has <u>released</u> plans for a new branch to be located in Springfield.

   (A) objected
   (B) made public

2. First, <u>remove</u> all parts from the box.

   (A) assemble
   (B) set aside

3. I'm writing <u>on behalf of</u> my manager at Academic Research Incorporated.

   (A) instead of
   (B) in response to

4. The article contained a couple of <u>factual errors</u>.

   (A) typos
   (B) wrong information

5. Super Electronics is the <u>sole</u> sponsor of the sporting event.

   (A) only
   (B) enthusiastic

6. The items are currently <u>out of stock</u>.

   (A) unavailable
   (B) missing

7. The gallery has announced an <u>upcoming</u> exhibition of the works of Charles Ramirez.

   (A) approaching
   (B) successful

8. Let me <u>extend</u> my sincere apologies for the negative experience.

   (A) offer
   (B) accept

9. <u>Only qualified applicants will be asked to fill out an application form.</u>

   (A) Only qualified applicants will be invited to apply.
   (B) Only a few applicants will apply.

10. <u>This is a mandatory event for all the members.</u>

    (A) All the members are absent from the event.
    (B) All the members must participate in the event.

⏰ 試著在限時7分鐘內盡可能答對。

Questions 1-5 refer to the following advertisement and e-mail.

Emerson's Department Store

We have immediate openings for part-time entry level positions.

Housewares Department: Work at the register in the housewares department. Assist customers with purchases, returns, and exchanges. Must be available on Fridays, Saturdays, and Sundays. 15-20 hours per week.

Shoe Department: Work at the register in the shoe department. Assist customers with purchases, returns, and exchanges. Must be available on Mondays, Wednesdays, and Fridays during regular business hours. Up to 25 hours per week.

Display Assistant: Assist our designer with the setup and takedown of store displays. Help arrange floor merchandise. Must be available on Saturday and Sunday evenings. 12 hours per week.

We offer competitive hourly wages and will train all employees. To schedule an interview, please e-mail your contact information to the branch manager, Mike Anderson at manderson@emerson.com or call 612-555-2855, extension 8367.

PART
7

To:	Mike Anderson <manderson@emerson.com>
From:	Rebecca Newman <rebecca80@aol.com>
Date:	August 10th
Subject:	Job opening

Dear Mr. Anderson,

I am currently a student at Emory College and am looking for a part-time job on Saturdays and Sundays. I would like to work between 10 and 20 hours per week. I worked at Pro Athletes' Store for the past two summers, so I have some retail experience. I am hardworking and reliable and open to learning new things.

I would appreciate the opportunity to talk with you about any suitable position you may have open at Emerson's. Thank you.

Sincerely,

Rebecca Newman

1. What is the purpose of the advertisement?

   (A) To offer part-time positions
   (B) To publicize the department store
   (C) To announce the annual sales
   (D) To respond to a letter of inquiry

2. In the advertisement, the word "immediate" in paragraph 1, line 1, is closest in meaning to

   (A) direct
   (B) near
   (C) current
   (D) personal

3. What is the purpose of the e-mail?

   (A) To ask for Mr. Anderson's contact information
   (B) To inquire about the job opening
   (C) To recommend a colleague for a job
   (D) To request a reduction in working hours

4. What position suits Ms. Newman's schedule?

   (A) Branch manager
   (B) Housewares salesperson
   (C) Shoe department employee
   (D) Display assistant

5. What is NOT indicated about Ms. Newman?

   (A) She is available on Saturdays and Sundays.
   (B) She is a student.
   (C) She is currently working at a store.
   (D) She is looking for a part-time position.

⏰ 試著在限時5分鐘(每題1分鐘)內盡可能答對。

Questions 1-5 refer to the following Web page, e-mail, and survey.

新多益

| Home | Conference | Sessions | Registration | Membership |

Join us for the 10th Annual Public Accounting Conference in New York from October 8-10.

The International Public Accountants (IPA) Conference provides industry professionals with the best opportunity to discover the latest trends and changes in the area of accounting. This year's conference takes place in Manhattan, New York, and the keynote speaker is Dr. Adriana Nelson, the president of IPA. Dr. Nelson will discuss the changes in international tax laws. Other featured speakers include industry experts Ji-Seon Park, Bradley Young, Michael Yamaguchi, and Michelle Palmer. Information about the all sessions and their presenters can be found at the Sessions tab.

The conference will be held at Parkline Hotel. A limited number of rooms are available at a reduced rate for IPA members. Just provide your membership number when you reserve for your accommodations.

Registration starts on August 1. Prices increase on September 1, and some sessions will fill quickly, so don't wait. You can register online at the Registration tab.

PART

7

To: Michael Yamaguchi <myamaguchi@nieman.org>
From: Stella Hanson <Hanson85@ipa.com>
Date: October 14
Subject: Information

Dear Michael,

It was my pleasure meeting you. I appreciate that you took time to travel here to New York, and I want to thank you for your participation in the IPA conference. Your session on Accounting Practices in Asia was fascinating to me. I believe those who attended the session now truly appreciate the level of efforts that goes into dealing with international corporations and governments. I've attached the survey we received from the conference attendee Elain Chandra. Her response was typical of the complimentary comments about your session.

Sincerely,

Stella Hanson

Director, IPA Programs Committee

International Public Accountants Conference Attendee Survey

	Very Satisfied	Rather Satisfied	Rather disappointed	Very Disappointed
Registration Process			V	
Contents	V			
Venue	V			
Food & Beverages	V			

Additional Comments:

Signing in did not go smoothly. Even though I had registered a long time before the deadline, my conference package was misplaced. I had to wait for an hour to find my materials and missed the keynote address I very much wanted to hear. The presentation itself was wonderful. I especially enjoyed the session given by an accountant on Accounting Practices in Asia. It was fascinating, and I learned a lot.

Elain Chandra

1. What is indicated about the conference?
   (A) Some attendees might have received a discount on their hotel stay.
   (B) It was only open to residents in New York.
   (C) It is held in the same location every year.
   (D) All attendees had to register by August 1st.

2. What is the purpose of the e-mail?
   (A) To propose a topic for future conferences
   (B) To arrange a tour plan to New York
   (C) To ask about the conference surveys
   (D) To provide feedback on a presentation

3. In the e-mail, the word "level" in paragraph 1, line 4, is closest in meaning to
   (A) layer
   (B) amount
   (C) position
   (D) condition

4. What is suggested about Ms. Chandra?
   (A) She attended last year's event.
   (B) She thought some of the sessions were too long.
   (C) She was pleased with the registration process.
   (D) She didn't attend Dr. Nelson's presentation.

5. Which speaker did Ms. Chandra particularly like?
   (A) Ms. Park
   (B) Mr. Young
   (C) Mr. Yamaguchi
   (D) Ms. Palmer

新制多益

全攻略：培養聽力・閱讀實戰能力！

完全自學 NEW TOEIC

BASIC LC+RC

元晶瑞・NEXUS多益研究所／著

解答與解析

笛藤出版

新制多益

全攻略：培養聽力・閱讀實戰能力！

完全自學

NEW TOEIC

BASIC LC+RC

元晶瑞、NEXUS多益研究所／著

解答與解析

雷藤出版

PART 1

Unit 1 人物為主的照片

P18

Step 2 聆聽和聽寫的訓練

1 現在式：She is hanging up some clothes.
她正在掛一些衣服。
解析　服飾店店員正在掛衣服的圖片最多，需要記熟服飾的圖片中最多表達人物各種動作的動詞。現在式在Part 1中最常作為答案。

2 被動語態現在式：Some boxes are being loaded into a truck.
有些箱子被裝在貨車裡。
解析　倉庫中人們正在將箱子裝上貨車的圖片最適合。People are loading some boxes into a truck的句子改為被動語態。須多練習並熟悉造兩種動詞時態。

3 及物動詞現在式：The women are sharing a sofa.
女子們正在共用一張沙發。
解析　兩名女子一起坐在沙發上賞照片最適合。這是把容易懂的together改成share（分享、共享）的詞彙，作為間接表達。

4 被動語態現在式：A piece of equipment is being operated.
一台設備正在被操作。
解析　一名女子正在操作設備的照片最適合。尤其以事物取代人物作為主語，表達機械正在使用中，也就是把a piece of equipment的句子改為被動語態。

5 不及物動詞現在式：Some people are standing at a bus stop.
人們正站在巴士站。
解析　公車站牌處人們站著等待公車的照片最適合，照片中很有可能沒有出現公車。

6 及物動詞現在式：They are having a snack near the water.
他們在水邊吃點心。

7 及物動詞現在式：Some people are reviewing documents.
人們正在審查文件。
解析　人在河邊或碼頭附近、一邊休息一邊吃東西的照片最合適。如游泳或貼等內須多是意不足選擇頭和水（water）有關的聯想，必容的句子。

8 被動語態：They are seated at workstations.
他們正坐在工作站。
解析　正在審視文件的人們照片最適合。人們正在審查文件。須多多記熟描述人動作的動詞。此外，含有「審查」之意的examine, inspect, check等動詞也須多加熟記。

9 及物動詞現在式：The man is stirring something in a pot.
男子正在鍋子裡攪拌東西。
解析　在廚房裡用湯匙或勺子攪拌鍋子裡的食物或實驗室裡的照片最適合。尤其需記熟使用在廚房或食物的動詞，如pour（倒）、boil（煮）等基本動詞

10 被動語態現在式：An instrument is being photographed.
儀器正被拍照。
解析　一人拿著相機對準正在拍攝的照片最適合。這是把The man is photographing an instrument的句子改成被動語態。句子中雖然沒有出現人物，但必須記熟以人物照片作為答案的「被動語態現在式」的動詞時態。

Step 3 基本掌握

P19

正解

| 1.(B) | 2.(A) | 3.(B) | 4.(B) |

1 英(W) (A) The woman is washing her hair.
(B) The woman is leaning forward.
解釋 (A) 女子正在洗頭髮
(B) 女子正向前傾
正解 (B) 女子正向前傾
解析　這是正在洗手的女子照片，但不能因此選擇有wash的選項，而是必須仔細描述人物的照片。Part 1正確答案並不是有錯誤。因為女子並沒有沉頭髮，選項(A)並不正確。答案塔身體稍微的前傾的(B)
詞彙 wash 刷、洗　lean 靠　forward 往前

2 美(M) (A) Some people are sitting on chairs.
(B) Some people are standing in the middle of the room.
解釋 (A) 有些人坐在椅子上。
(B) 有些人站在房間的中間。
解析　這是複數人物照片，有在海邊游泳的人和坐在椅子上的人。首先，(A)沒有箱頭的敘述。不是房間之後，可能是游泳或(B)選項，就能得知(A)是答案。

3 英(W) (A) The road is being repaved.
(B) Leaves are being raked into a pile.
解釋 (A) 道路正在重新編起
(B) 葉子正被耙成一堆
解析　男孩正用耙子將葉集耙成一堆（rake）。尤其一人照片的情況，熟記愈多描述人物動作的動詞會有利，正確答案是以被動語態現在式來表達動作，也就是「落葉正被掃成一堆」的(B)。
詞彙 repave 重新鋪（道路）　rake 用耙子掃、掃成堆　pile 堆

4 美(M) (A) One person is handing a paper to the other.
(B) They're facing each other.
解釋 (A) 一個人正在向另一個人遞交一份文件。
(B) 他們正面對面
解析　是互相面對面握手的人物照片，注意勿根據握手所聯想到的單字shake hands而選擇答案。正確答案是兩人彼此面對面(face)的(B)。
詞彙 hand 遞交、交付　the other 另一個（兩者之一）　face 面對　each other 彼此

正解

1.(C)　2.(B)　3.(A)　4.(D)　5.(A)
6.(C)

1 美W

(A) Some people are waiting in line to board the plane.
(B) Some people are walking in the park.
(C) **Some customers are shopping indoors.**
(D) A sales person is putting a shirt in a bag.

解釋
(A) 有些人正在排隊等候登機。
(B) 有些人正在公園散步。
(C) **有些客人正在室內購物。**
(D) 銷售人員正在將一件襯衫放入包中。

解析 由商店裡排隊等待結帳的人們可以得知「在室內購物」的景象。根據圖片所聯想的特定單字很容易選擇錯誤答案,務必謹記。

詞彙 wait in line 排隊等待　indoors 室內　sales person 銷售人員

2 澳M

(A) The dishes are being washed.
(B) **The floor is being scrubbed.**
(C) The lawn is being mowed.
(D) The glass door is being opened.

解釋
(A) 盤子正被清洗。
(B) **地板正被刷淨。**
(C) 草坪正被修剪。
(D) 玻璃門正被打開。

解析 這是描繪飯店的場景中,職員用吸塵器打掃地面的照片。雖然在用了較不熟悉的單字scrub,但也許是正確選項,因此要把(B)保留。接著刪去其他錯誤的選項,再回頭選擇正確答案。(A)沒有出現盤子。(C)沒有草坪,也沒有割草機。(D)如果是正確答案,應該會出現有人開門,但是沒有人開門的畫面。

詞彙 wash(用水)洗淨　floor 地板　scrub 擦淨、擦洗　lawn 草坪　mow 割　glass 玻璃　open 打開

老師的 REAL SOLUTION
Part 1中為了拿滿分,需要降低對答案的期望值。答案往往在不是最能描述圖片的選項,而是錯誤部分最少的。像第4題的(B)一樣,不能認為是舉行派對而直接選擇,等到全部聽完選項之後再選擇答案。

3 美W

(A) **A man is grasping a broomstick.**
(B) A man is cleaning the window.
(C) A man is exiting a doorway.
(D) Some trees are being planted.

解釋
(A) **男子正握著掃帚。**
(B) 男子正在打掃窗戶。
(C) 男子正走出門口。
(D) 再種樹。

解析 這是在庭院打掃的男子照片,正確答案是握著掃帚帚柄的(A)。抓握(grab, grasp)的動詞和用掃帚掃(sweep)的動詞皆是正確答案,安全起見提是必須要再次複習。(B)即使(A)是正確答案。(C)沒有走出門外。(D)有樹木,但被動語態現在式做為答案時,照片中應需要出現種樹的人物。

詞彙 grasp 握著　broomstick 掃帚　clean 打掃　doorway 出入口、門口　plant 種植、花草植物　exit 出去、出口

4 澳M

(A) They're ordering some food.
(B) They're having a celebration.
(C) They're purchasing some goods.
(D) **They are gathered around the table.**

解釋
(A) 他們正在點一些食物。
(B) 他們正在開慶祝的派對。
(C) 他們正在購買一些商品。
(D) **他們正聚集在桌子周圍。**

解析 這是人們在咖啡廳圍坐在小桌子,享用飲料和茶點的照片。正確答案是有客人在點餐合的(D)。(A)沒有看到服務生在客人在點餐台的畫面。(B)是正在慶祝的聚會並不明確。(C)購買物品需要結帳看見到店員。

詞彙 order 點菜、訂單　celebration 慶祝活動、慶祝　goods 商品　gather 聚集　purchase 購買　around 在~周圍

5 美W

(A) **A woman is working with a shovel.**
(B) A woman is resting under a tree.
(C) A woman is putting on a jacket.
(D) A woman is cutting the grass.

解釋
(A) **女子正在用鏟子。**
(B) 女子正在樹下休息。
(C) 女子正穿上夾克。
(D) 女子正在割草。

解析 這是用鏟子挖土 (dirt, soil) 的女子照片,正確答案是使用兼具動詞/名詞的shovel的(A)。必須熟悉與其名詞有關的詞彙才能選出答案。shovel(鏟子、用鏟子挖),rake(耙子、用耙子耙),mop(拖把、用拖把拖)是動詞,broom(掃帚)是名詞,sweep(打掃、掃)是動詞。(B)沒有休息的動作。(C)沒有穿上夾克的動作。(D)沒有割草的動作。

詞彙 shovel 鏟子、鏟　rest 休息、靠　put on 穿上　cut 剪　grass 草

6 澳M

(A) One of the women is posting a sign.
(B) Some workers are installing a carpet.
(C) **A piece of equipment is being examined.**
(D) A machine is being moved across the room.

解釋
(A) 其中一位女子正在張貼一個標誌。
(B) 一些工人正在裝設地毯。
(C) **一部裝備正被檢查。**
(D) 一部機器正被搬運穿過房間。

解析 一個人正彎腰查看影印機內部,另一人則看著那人。正確答案是被動語態現在式的 is being examined (正在檢查)的(C)。需要熟記各種具有「看」語意的動作。(A)沒有人把標誌貼上佈告欄。(B)工人把鋪設地毯,但是不是裝設地毯的動作,容易犯下錯誤。(D)有機器但並沒有搬運的動作。

詞彙 post 貼上、公布　sign 標誌、標示　install 裝設　carpet 地毯　a piece of 一件(數算單位)　equipment 設備、機械　move 搬運　across 穿越~　examine 檢驗

Step 2 將錯擺寫的訓練　P24

1 There <u>is</u> a door beneath the staircase. 樓梯下面有一扇門。
解析 適合2圖建築物的外牆。在樓梯下方1樓出現的門的照片。尤其可能以各種物品、背景作為答案的照片。年輕主語並並述頭部會聽出是個句子。

2 Some merchandise is arranged on shelves.
解析 這是機器擺放的照片中最常作為答案的敘述。尤其須謹慎擺放在貨架上。一些商品被擺放在貨架上。（arrange,display,set）、堆放、放置（stack,pile,stock）的動詞在描述相同照片時，都可以使用。

3 Waves are crashing against the rocks. 海浪打在岩石上。
解析 適合海浪的海浪撞擊岩石的照片。需熟記有關的海浪（wave,surf）拍打或水波平靜（calm）的敘述。

4 A lamp is standing in the corner of the room.
解析 適合辦公室或房間角落沒有人物的照片。將物體擬作人什之後，較短的動詞語態常完成做為答案。數短的物品使用sit。房間角落中有一盞長形的室內燈最適合做為答案。
一盞燈立在房間的角落。

5 Shelves have been stocked with bread. 貨架上擺滿了麵包。
解析 適合麵包店的貨架上陳列麵包的照片。尤其被動語態完成態是在描述風景時最常使用的文法。必須熟悉並理解是「庫存」存「貨架」之意，是經常使用的名詞。stock是「庫動詞使用」描述陳列好的物品。存（have been）、描述陳列好的物品。

6 Computers are set up next to each other. 電腦並排擺放。
解析 適合書桌上整齊並排有電腦的照片。與事物有關的照片，較短的動詞語態。(have been + p.p.) 相同，一般被動時態的 (be + p.p.) 也常使用。

7 A picture is positioned above a chair. 圖片位於椅子上方。
解析 適合客廳或房間裡的沙發或床上方掛有圖片的照片。使用了出現率高的詞彙hang（掛物品）。務必熟記，這種動詞也會使用在描述將物品掛在牆壁常使用。（be positioned, be located（位於）也經時。），描述將物品掛在牆壁時。

8 An awning shades a store entrance. 遮陽板在店面的入口。
解析 適合遮陽板在窗戶上投影出陰影的照片，使用了出現率高的awning（遮陽板）多益中有時會出現特別詞彙，與其記住所有的物品單字，更好的做法是從選項中刪除比較熟悉但錯記誤的選項、縮小答案範圍。

---

9 The lights have been turned on. 燈已經打開。
解析 適合客廳或餐廳天花板上裝置的燈光已經打開。其他各種事物的背景都可能作為主語。但風景照片中不只是燈，其他各種事物或背景都可能作為主語。即便從頭到尾聽出屋聽完整選項再看不清楚，也必須聽完各選項的主語，再對照照片選出正確答案。

10 A row of windows is facing a street. 一排窗戶正對著一條街。
解析 適合傳統街邊林立的物品，這時主語須為A row數數使用。適合描述尺寸相似的物品，可能以窗戶或建築外牆數窗戶前面出現道路時，可能以窗戶或面對街道的方式來描述，尤其必須熟記a row of, a line of, a stack of, a pile of 等將多數物品加以統稱的表達詞彙。
詞彙 row 划船、列

Step 3 基本掌握　P25

正解 1.(A)　2.(B)　3.(A)　4.(B)

1 (英W) (A) They're rowing a boat.
(B) They're swimming in the river.
解析 必須熟記與水有關的基本詞彙，應用在風景照片中，例如划船以「航行、漂浮 (sailing, floating)」、「停靠、綁定 (be docked, be tied up)」、「划船」J、「划」、「槳、paddle」J的詞彙描述。由於沒有出現游泳的人，因此 (B) 是錯誤選項。
詞彙 row 划船、列

2 (美M) (A) He's opening the door.
(B) **The door has been left open.**
解析 leave在LC/RC出題機率最高的動詞之一，對於「①離開 ②留下、放置 ③保留～狀態」的語意必須熟記。因為沒有開門的人，必須選擇門已經打開的描述。
詞彙 open 打開、開啟的　leave 保留～狀態

3 (英W) (A) **Merchandise has been displayed on shelves.**
(B) Some products are packed for delivery.
詞彙 merchandise 商品、物品　display 陳列　shelf 貨架

Step 4 實戰練習　P26

正解 1.(B)　2.(D)　3.(C)　4.(B)　5.(D)

1 (美W) (A) Some cars have stopped at an intersection.
(B) **Some vehicles have been lifted.**
(C) Some workers are opening the hood of a car.
(D) Some tires have been removed from the vehicle.
解析 在汽車維修廠中車輛被舉起的狀態使用完成態被動語態 (have been lifted) 描述。remove與其事理解為「刪除」，更需要熟記。
(B) 有些車輛被舉起。
(C) 有些工人正在打開引擎蓋。
(D) 有些輪胎已從車輛中移除。
(A) 照片並無十字路口之意。
(C) 照片中工人並沒有打開引擎蓋。
(D) 輪胎沒有移除。
詞彙 intersection 十字路口　vehicle 車輛、汽車　remove 移除、拆　tire 輪胎　hood 汽車引擎蓋　open 打開

4 (美M) (A) The street is being cleaned.
(B) **Columns line a walkway.**
解析 (A) 街邊正在清理。
(B) 柱子沿著道排列。
樹木、長椅、柱子等複數物品排成一列時，可以用「有人行道排列 (column)」這時有名詞。即使不知街道 (column) 這詞專有名詞，也可以判斷有人正在打掃街道，因此刪去使用被動語態現在式的 (A)，就能選出答案是 (B)。
詞彙 clean 清理　column 柱子　line 沿著～排　walkway 步道、走道

2 (美M)

(A) They're walking up the steps.
(B) They're planting trees in pots.
(C) The floor is being mopped.
(D) **The stairs lead to the next level.**

解析
(A) 他們正在走上台階。
(B) 他們正在盆裡種樹。
(C) 地板正在拖。
(D) 樓梯通向下一個樓層。

樓梯或通道使用常現在式以通向（lead to）來描述的典型句。須描述被動語態現在式以通向某個人物或某個動作進行動作的照片。

(A) 沒有正在走路的人。
(B) 出現花盆但沒有種植的人們（They）。
(C) 沒有出現拖地板。
(D) 樓梯通向～ level 樓層、樓梯

詞彙　walk 走路　steps 樓梯　plant 種植　pot 花盆、銅子　floor 地板　lead to 通向～

3 (美M)

(A) The maid is cleaning the room.
(B) The bed is missing two cushions.
(C) **There are lamps on both sides of the bed.**
(D) The pictures are being hung on the wall.

解析
(A) 清潔人員正在打掃房間。
(B) 床上缺少兩個靠枕。
(C) 床的兩邊都有燈。
(D) 照片正被掛在牆上。

(A) 必須熟記房間中可見的床（bed）、窗戶（window）、照片（picture）、燈（lamp）、枕頭（pillow）等物品的描述方式。
(B) 床上缺少兩個靠枕。
(C) 答案是床有2個靠枕。床的上方稱為ahead、床的下方稱為foot，旁邊稱為side。正確
(D) 使用被動語態現在式（are being hung）必須出現正在掛照片的人。

詞彙　maid 清潔人員　clean 打掃、乾淨的　miss 缺少　lamp 燈　side 旁邊　hang 掛

> **元老師的 REAL SOLUTION**
> 必須能夠用各種方式描述同一張照片，才能在高難度題目中拿分。"lamps on both sides of the bed" 可以使用單數型態的either，替換成 "a lamp on either sides of the bed"，最後兩邊都有，意思等於每一邊都有燈。

4 (美W)

(A) Crops are being harvested.
(B) **Crops are lined up in rows.**
(C) A field of grass is being mowed.
(D) Trees are piled up near the sign.

解析
(A) 農作物正在收割。
(B) 一片草地正在修剪。
(C) 樹木堆疊在標誌附近。
(D) 農作物排成數列。

當描述多數的物品或以人物、經常使用及物動詞，這樣以被動語態就列（in rows）、排隊）的農作物。必須當作同時熟記「一列（in a row）」或「數列（in rows）」的詞彙。

(A) 「收割（harvest）」之意的被動語態現在式（are being harvested）
(C) 「草地修剪」之意的被動語態現在式（is being mowed）
(D) 出現標誌但旁邊沒有群眾的樹木。

詞彙　crops 農作物　harvest 收割　line up 排列　in rows 數列　pile 堆積　near 附近

5 (美M)

(A) Some cyclists are riding past the river.
(B) Some scaffolding has been erected against the stone bridge.
(C) Some pedestrians are walking across the street.
(D) **Some bicycles have been parked along a railing.**

解析
(D) Some bicycles have been parked along a railing.

腳踏車已經停放好的狀態用完成式被動語態（have been parked）來描述。完成式被動語態經常使用在事物/風景照片中，需要多加路線。橋梁之後了解照片之後預期會聯想到railing、欄杆、樓梯扶手稱為rail，必須熟記。

(A) 沒有出現騎自行車的人正在渡河。
(B) 雖然建築工程中使用的scaffold/scaffolding難以理解，即使不知道相關的意思，但還是避免因為難懂而不懂的單字，因此可以刪除此選項，但要根據自己可以理解的範圍內判斷錯誤的部分，留下可能比較難的選項，最後留見選項較難懂合的答案。
(C) 照片中沒有人物，因此刪去此一選項。

詞彙　cyclist 騎自行車的人　ride 騎乘　past 經過　scaffolding（施工地點）腳架、骨架　erect 豎立　against 支撐～、倚　pedestrian 徒步者、行人　across 穿越　park 停放、停車　railing 欄杆

6 (美W)

(A) **Buildings are located along the water.**
(B) A bridge extends across the canal.
(C) Waves are crashing against the dock.
(D) The river winds around a park.

解析
(A) Buildings are located along the water.

適合以被動語態描述著水邊的建築物。（A）是正確答案。除了描述建築物的位置之外，描述建築物的位置時可以使用be located、be positioned
(B) 沒有橋樑。
(C) 沒有海浪。
(D) 用動詞wind（蜿蜒、圍繞）可以用來表達河流蜿蜒的樣子，但照片中並沒有出現。

詞彙　be located 位於～　extend 延伸、擴展　canal 運河　wind 蜿蜒、圍繞　dock 碼頭　crash 撞擊

Unit 3　高難度－混合照片

> **Step 2**　聽聽和聽寫的訓練　P30

1 He's standing near the counter.
解析 人物照片中也會出現才是以主語的動作作為焦點的練手題目。答案是人物站在櫃台附近的描述。
他站在櫃檯附近。

2 A man is trimming a customer's hair.
解析 適合理髮師或美髮師正在剪髮的照片。看完照片之後預期會聯想到cut的動詞。答案是有cut的哈併。除此可以使用「修剪」而選擇合有cut的句型。
男子正在修剪顧客的頭髮。

3 She has her hair pulled back.
解析 這是描述照片中女子將頭髮綁起的句子，曾經出現在考古題的題目中。尤其必須熟記<have + 身體的部位 + p.p.的><文法句型。除此用頭巾覆蓋（cover）或頭巾覆蓋（bracelet）等飾品也曾經作為題目的正確答案，需多加熟練從照片中找出細微之處。
她的頭髮往後梳起。

4. A street lamp is being repaired. 路燈正在修理中。
解析：適合在路邊架上梯子、爬上電線桿修理燈的人物照片。拿著 (hold) 各種工具或處理 (handle) 的動作可以用修理中 (is being repaired) 來描述，須謹記出現機械類或手持工具等照片可能是使用「修理」的表達方式。

5. Power cords have been plugged into a wall outlet. 電源線已插入牆上插座。
解析：類似餐廳桌子上有各種食物、餐具、建築等，必須注意在高難題目中，不容易察覺的部分可能是正確答案。描述照片中可能難以察覺的部分可能是正確答案。

6. Trees are casting shadows on a building. 樹木在建築物上投射陰影。
解析：郊外風景照片中有各種樹木、長椅、建築等，必須從照片中確認是否有陰影。正確答案並不是最能觀察到陰影的部分，但選項中提到陰影時，務必記得答案可能是有陰影的事實。

7. A lid has been removed from a paint can. 蓋子已從油漆桶移除。
解析：油漆行等商店的部照片會出現各種物品，但從照片背景陳列的物品中，描述某一個已打開蓋子的油漆桶，務必記得答案可能是描述類似照片中極微小的部分。

8. Some bikes are unattended. 有些自行車是無人看管的。
解析：以事物作為主語的句子中，自行車已停放或是直立時可以使用 be parked、be located，這是前面同學判斷的部分。如果用某個有自行車的地方，可以使用 be unattended（補充一點，attend 有「參加」、「看管」、「看顧」之意。）

9. Some of the spectators are wearing hats. 一些觀眾戴著帽子。
解析：適合多數的觀眾中，有幾名觀眾戴帽子的照片。須了解高難度題型中，模糊描述並以間接方式描述內容，都可能是正確答案。

10. Sunlight is streaming through the clouds. 陽光透過雲層照射。
解析：這是透過照片中需要高度專注力才能看見天空或地面的答案。這是使用具有「射出、流瀉」意思的動作用照片照射下來的陽光，即使出現不懂的詞彙，只要先刪除具有錯誤線索部分的選項，就能縮小答案範圍。

正解
1. (B)　2. (A)　3. (A)　4. (B)

(美M) 1. (A) A worker is fixing a vehicle.
(B) A worker is wearing a safety vest.
解析：(A)一名工人正在修理一輛車。
(B)一名工人穿著安全背心。
這是看重複正在操作 (operating) 機械車的工人照片，答案是穿著背心的細膩描述句。注意不能光以動作作為選擇答案的標準。
詞彙 fix 修理　vehicle 車輛；汽車　wear 穿　safety vest 安全背心

(英W) 2. (A) They're attending a meeting.
(B) They're entering a conference room.

解析：(A)他們正在參加一個會議。
(B)他們正在進入會議室。
會議室情景中有各種物品或人們，而答案是「正在參加會議 (attend)」的句子。避免只憑聯想到conference room就選擇 (B)，另外也要熟記具有「參與 (participate)」、「參與 (be involved in, be engaged in)」之意的詞彙。
詞彙 attend 參加　enter 入場、進入　conference 會議

3. (A) The table is covered with a cloth.
(B) The table is being decorated with some flowers.

解析：(A)桌子上蓋著一塊布。
(B)桌子正在用花裝飾中。
桌上有各種物品和鮮花裝飾，而布覆蓋著桌子的句子是正確答案。描述橋上有flower arrangement，但因沒有正在裝飾的人，使用被動語態現在式的選項在風景照片中並不合適，這一點要留意。
詞彙 be covered with 被～覆蓋　cloth 布　decorate 裝飾

4. (A) A group of people are meeting around the table.
(B) People are seated in individual booths.

解析：(A)一群人圍著桌子開會。
(B)人們坐在個人的隔間裡。
辦公室中各個人們坐在個人的空間裡稱為cubicle。雖然使用了辦公室裡典型的詞彙，但人們個別坐著的敘述意外成為了答案。
詞彙 a group of 一群　be seated 就坐　individual 個人的、各自的　booth 隔間、亭

正解
1. (A)　2. (D)　3. (C)　4. (D)　5. (C)
6. (B)

(美W) 1. (A) Some bags have been placed on the floor.
(B) Some men are waiting for their bags to come out.
(C) Some papers have been spread out on the carpet.
(D) The men are working in their offices.
解析：(A)一些包包放在地板上。
(B)有些男子在等他們的包包出來。
(C)一些文件分散在地毯上。
(D)這些人正在他們的辦公室工作。
這是在售票機 (ticket machine) 前面各自做自己事情的人們照片 (A)，但答案是包包放在地上 (A)，意即不是描述項中選擇手人的主體動作，而且不須從錯誤的照片描述項中選擇答案。背景並非在行李認領處 (baggage claim)，也沒有看到等待行李的場景。
詞彙 place 放置　carpet 地毯　work 工作、做事　wait for 等待～　come out 出來　spread 分散

2 澳M
(A) The back of the chair is touching the wall.
(B) Books have been piled on the floor.
(C) The pictures are being framed.
(D) There are knobs on the desk drawers.

解析
(A) 椅背靠在牆上。
(B) 書籍堆積在地板上。
(C) 照片正被裝入相框。
(D) 桌子抽屜上有把手。

風景照片中房裡有各種物品，正確答案是描述不明顯的抽屜把。如果原本就知道這把 (knob) 的詞彙就沒問題，但即使不知道，只要先刪除其他錯選項，就能知道。(D) 是最好的答案。當照片在相框中，也沒有看到人物的照片時，便選擇現在式被動語態的選項才是最典型的錯誤。
(A) 椅子沒有靠近牆壁。
(B) 看不見地板，也沒有堆積的書。
(C) 照片在相框內，但沒有看到正在進行某個動作的照片。動詞語態表現式適合某正在進行某個動作的照片，尤其須謹記被

詞彙 back 後面、後方　touch 碰觸　pile 堆積　frame 框架、相框　knob 把手、旋把　drawer 抽屜

3 美M
(A) Some workers are stacking lumber.
(B) They're standing in line for a sporting event.
(C) Some construction work is being carried out.
(D) A wheelbarrow has been left next to a tree.

解析
(A) 一些工人正在堆放木材。
(B) 他們正在排隊參加體育賽事。
(C) 一些施工作業正在進行中。
(D) 一台手推車放在樹的旁邊。

照片想地面上正在進行挖壕溝 (trench) 的工程，以客觀描述作業正在進行 (is being carried out) 的 (C) 是正確答案。
(A) 並沒有木材，而「土」需要使用dirt, soil, earth來表達。
(B) 排隊的景象雖然可能符合照片，但不是排隊等著進入體育場。
(D) 施工現場經常出現的器具手推車 (wheelbarrow) 並沒有出現在照片內。

詞彙 stack 堆放　lumber 木材、木頭　stand in line 排隊　sporting event 體育賽事、比賽　construction work 施工作業　carry out 進行　wheelbarrow 手推車　next to ～旁邊

4 美W
(A) People are standing at the edge of the water.
(B) Some boats are docked at a pier.
(C) The buildings overlook the parking lot.
(D) The houses are reflected on the water.

解析
(A) 人們正站在水邊。
(B) 有些船隻停靠在碼頭。
(C) 建築俯視停車場。
(D) 房子反射映照在水面上。

描述水邊的房子照射在平靜的水面上，屬於高難度題目，尤其是be reflected (反射) 除了鏡子之外，也會使用在水、玻璃、電腦畫面等各種地方映照出的影像，是高難度的詞彙。與看照片預測答案，更好的方式是，與其看照片做對照，確認是否正確。
(A) 沒有人站在水邊。
(B) 沒有人站在碼頭。
(C) 可以說建築俯視，但沒有出現船隻。

詞彙 edge of the water 水邊　dock 碼頭　pier 碼頭、船隻靠岸碼頭　overlook 俯視　parking lot 停車場　reflect 反射

5 澳M
(A) One woman is putting notices on the board.
(B) One woman is taking a note while the other is talking.
(C) One woman is offering assistance to the other.
(D) The women are drinking from the same glass.

解析
(A) 一名女子正在布告欄上貼公告。
(B) 一名女子正在另一名女子說話時做筆記。
(C) 一名女子正向另一名女子提供協助。
(D) 女子們正在喝同一杯水。

像博覽會 (expo) 一樣的場合中，貌似主辦者的女子正在對另一名女子進行說明，可以使用指出的point to或或的明語意的explain，但正確答案是以客觀性在進行描述的「提供協助 (offer assistance)」。這種高難度答案往往是抽象性或客觀性的描述。因此，為了選出正確答案，最保險的作法是刪除其他不正確的選項。
(A) 沒有出現貼公告的動作。
(B) 沒有寫字的動作。
(D) 一名女子端著玻璃杯，但無法得知是否兩人共飲。

詞彙 put 放置　notice 公告、通知　board 布告欄、黑板　note 抄寫、筆記　offer 提供　assistance 協助　glass 玻璃杯、玻璃　take a note

6 美W
(A) A man is checking into a hotel.
(B) The counter has been cleared of objects.
(C) A man is putting on his name tag.
(D) They're greeting each other at the entrance.

解析
(A) 一名男子正看起來像經理的人正將手扶在檯面上。
(B) 櫃台的物品已被清除。
(C) 一個男人正在掛上名牌。
(D) 他們在入口處互相問候。

飯店櫃台一位看起來像經理的人正將手扶在檯面上，通常含1人照片會針對人物的動作來出題，但這裡使用完成式被動語態最來描述櫃檯 (詞間處) 上被清理物淨 (has been cleared) 的情境才是正確答案。如果只看到hotel的詞彙就容易出錯，必須特別注意。
(A) 男子是經理。
(C) 已經掛上名牌時會使用動詞wear，而put on是正在掛上的動作。
(D) They所指的人是誰無從得知，而greet (問候) 經常用在招呼相迎接手的動作。

詞彙 check in 入住飯店　counter 檯台　clear 清除　object 物品、put on 掛上、穿上 (動作)　name tag 姓名牌　greet 問候　entrance 入口

元老師的 REAL SOLUTION
許多英文能力好的學生經常在分析照片時出錯。到底counter, desk, table, podium, stand差別在哪裡？我們不是答案是「一樣」，可以一律視為擁有平坦桌面的家具類，而選擇哪個詞呢？不是在寫作文，而是客觀挑出錯誤的部分，須避免執著於名詞的「整體性」，而發生誤答的情況。

Unit 4　疑問詞疑問句 I

Step 2　聆聽和聽寫的訓練　P39

1
Q: When are we leaving for the concert?
A: Around one o'clock.
Q: 我們什麼時候去參加音樂會?
A: 1點左右。
解析　詢問時間屬於When的典型問答題型。

2
Q: Who's setting up the projector in the conference room?
A: Our technical support team.
A: 我們的技術支援團隊。
解析　公司或商務等對話中出現Who的問題句時,須謹記答案可能不是人名,而是部門或政策。

3
Q: Where is the updated sales report?
A: The manager should have it.
Q: 修改過的銷售報告在哪裡?
A: 應該在經理那邊。
解析　Where疑問句中的回答和Who的問題句一樣,通常是人名作為答案。須記得物品的位置會以某個特定人物來當作答案。

4
Q: Where's the closest dry cleaner's?
A: There's one on 11th Street.
Q: 最近的乾洗店在哪裡?
A: 11街有一間。
解析　Where疑問句的答案使用了不定代名詞one來當作持特定對象,藉此說明乾洗店所在的位置。詢問最近的乾洗店是指明位置的題型。

5
Q: Who's going to speak at the publishers' conference this year?
A: It hasn't been decided yet.
Q: 今年的出版商大會由誰負責發言?
A: 還沒有決定。
解析　針對所有疑問詞問句不一定有明確答案。雖然以Who詢問,但答案可以是不知道或尚未決定。當選項出現不確定的答案時,可以先放在選項的第一順位。

6
Q: When should we start on a new contract?
A: Not until we finish the current one.
Q: 我們什麼時候開始簽訂新合約?
A: 我們目前完成的之後。
解析　疑問詞When出題架構要最高是表達時間點的介係詞或連接詞。not until (直到~之後再~) 之外,也要熟記as soon as~、when/once~等連接詞。

7
Q: Where can we display these new product samples?
A: In the glass case by the register.
Q: 我們可以在哪裡展示這些新產品的樣品?
A: 在結帳台旁邊的玻璃箱。
解析　造些世至商店職員們的對話,關於商品陳列位置與結帳台旁的玻璃箱(作為回答)。雖然是有些不熟悉的詞彙,但需理解所謂的地點的意思。隨著題目的難度提高,在選項中先保留可能是答案的部分,一旦刪除錯誤的選項,即使沒有完全聽懂,仍然可以選出跟適合的答案。

Step 3　基本掌握　P40

正解
1.(B)　2.(A)　3.(B)　4.(A)　5.(A)

1
美M (A) Who's in charge of this afternoon's meeting?
英W (A) Cash or charge?
(B) Mr. Robertson is.
誰負責今天下午的會議?
(A) 現金還是信用卡?
(B) 是羅伯遜先生。
解析　使用疑問詞Who的問句以事有名詞 (B) 作為答案最適合。
詞彙　in charge of 負責 ~ charge 信用卡支付

2
美M Where is the town library?
英W (A) On Schmitz Street.
(B) From 9 to 5.
鎮圖書館在哪裡?
(A) 在史密茲大街。
(B) 從9點到5點。
解析　以Where詢問的題目答案是 (A)。即使出現Schmitz這種不熟悉的專有名詞,但只要出現專有名詞先子以保留,待刪除後經常是正確答案。
詞彙　library 圖書館

3
美M When was the order cancelled?
英W (A) By air mail.
(B) Last night.
訂單什麼時候取消的?
(A) 航空郵遞的方式。
(B) 昨天晚上。
解析　針對以時間點為When的疑問詞問句,最適合當作詢問運送方法的How疑問詞問句的答案。
詞彙　order 訂單　cancel 取消

4
美W Who wrote this budget analysis?
英M (A) The accounting department.
(B) No, I am not a writer.
誰寫了這份預算分析?
(A) 會計部門。
(B) 不,我不是作家。

5

解析　使用Who詢問時，答案除了人名之外也可能是部門，(B) 的 writer 是用了與以 wrote 音相似的陷阱題。

詞彙　budget 預算　analysis 分析　accounting department 會計部門

英(M)　Where did you see the job advertisement?
美(W)
(A) On the company Web site.
(B) A marketing position.
(C) Not much longer.

正解　(A)

解析　使用疑問詞Where詢問資訊來源的題目。尤其是地點，也可能是詢問人或資訊出處。(B) 適合回答Who的問題，雖然內容是聽完題目後容易聯想到的內容，但並非正確答案。

詞彙　advertisement 廣告　position 職位

你在哪裡看到徵人廣告？
(A) 在公司網站上。
(B) 銷售職位。
(C) 很久。

Step 4　實戰練習　P40

正解
| 1.(B) | 2.(C) | 3.(A) | 4.(B) | 5.(A) |
| 6.(C) | 7.(A) | 8.(C) | 9.(B) | 10.(C) |

1

美(W)　Where can I get the application form?
美(M)
(A) By July 2nd.
(B) On the third floor.
(C) Not much longer.

正解　(B)

解析　詢問地點，有時會以建築樓層來回答。除了房號之外，房間位置，也是典型的地點名詞。(A) 適合作為詢問時間點When的回答，(C) 也是適合When或How long表達時間點的疑問詞。

詞彙　application form 申請表　floor 樓層

我在哪裡可以拿到申請表？
(A) 到7月2日。
(B) 在3樓。
(C) 句型錯誤。

REAL SOLUTION
元老師的

疑問詞疑問句最大的特點是出現在最前面的部分，具有最重要的意義。發音容易產生混淆的只有Where。必須認清這個音，尤其英式發音在講很快的情況下，可能一次發出「ㄨㄟㄦ」的音。Where的美式發音容易和When混淆，避免和When混淆，不發「ㄜ」的音，類似「ㄨㄟ」，而美式發音在講很快的情況下，可能一次發出「ㄨㄟㄦ」的音。

2

澳(M)　When do you start your job at the bank?
美(W)
(A) In Customer Service.
(B) Please restart your computer.
(C) On March 21st.

正解　(C)

解析　詢問時間點When的疑問詞答案是出現特定日期的 (C)。尤其需記熟1日 (first)、2日 (second) 的序數日期。(A) 適合作為疑問句Who或Where的答案，(B) restart是使用與題目start相似的陷阱。

詞彙　customer service 顧客服務中心　restart 重新開始

你什麼時候開始在銀行工作？
(A) 在客戶服務部門。
(B) 請重新啟動電腦。
(C) On March 21st.

3

美(M)　Who can open the office library?
澳(M)
(A) I have the key.
(B) I report to Mr. Hendrix.
(C) Five new books.

正解　(A)

解析　針對誰有鑰匙的問題答案是 (A)，意思是我可以（I can do that）。注意避免因為題目出現到人名並選擇連結到Who疑問句的答案，但與開門並沒有連貫性 (B)。可以聯想到圖書館時容易聯想的典型錯誤。

詞彙　open 打開、開啟的　library 圖書館　report 報告、報告書

誰可以打開辦公室圖書館？
(A) 我有鑰匙。
(B) 我向亨德里克斯先生匯報。
(C) 5本新書。

4

美(M)　When did you send the report to the main office in Hong Kong?
澳(M)
(A) The headquarters is in Seoul.
(B) About two hours ago.
(C) The game will start soon.

正解　(B)

解析　詢問過去時間點的題目經常以「~ ago」、「last ~」作為回答。最適合的表達過去時間點的 (B) 是答案。(A) 適合Where疑問句，則是針對未來時間點的回答。

詞彙　main office 總公司　report 報告　headquarters 總部

你是什麼時候將報告發送到香港總部的？
(A) 總部設在首爾。
(B) 大約2小時前。
(C) 比賽即將開始。

5

美(M)　Where are the instructions for the new copier?
美(W)
(A) They are in the box.
(B) It's ten cents a copy.
(C) No, I haven't read them yet.

正解　(A)

解析　針對Where疑問句最適合的答案是新影印機的說明書在哪裡？數事物instructions（說明書）時容易以they一律視為人的意思，但這裡they作為複數物的回答，而疑問詞疑問句不會出現Yes/No回答，因此 (C) 並非答案。

詞彙　instructions 說明、指南　copier 影印機

新影印機的說明書在哪裡？
(A) 在盒子裡。
(B) 一張影印10美分。
(C) 不，我還沒讀過。

6

澳(M)　Who is the keynote speaker for the conference going to be?
美(W)
(A) I went out last year.
(B) Yes, I think they did.
(C) I'm not sure who it is.

正解　(C)

解析　Who疑問句的答案使用適合的「不知道」類型的「I'm not sure」。以「不知道」類型為答案的題目在每個月份中都會出現，必須熟記。類似為答案的是 (A) 適合回答表達時間When的疑問句，(B) 的Yes/No不過作為疑問句疑問句的答案。

詞彙　keynote speaker 主講人、主要發言人　conference 會議　be going to 將~、預定~

誰將成為會議的主要發言人？
(A) 我去年去的。
(B) 是的，我認為他們做了。
(C) 我不確定是誰。

7

澳(M)　When are we going to the theater?
美(W)
(A) We'll leave right after the dinner.
(B) The performance was great.
(C) It was $200.

正解　(A)

解析　詢問時間點的題目經常以 When 的答案。晚餐後 (after) 出發的 (A) 是正確答案。(B) 適合回答How的疑問句，(C) 則是針對How much「注意避免聽到題目中theater就選擇聯想到的詞彙。

詞彙　theater 電影院　leave 離開、出發　performance 表演

我們什麼時候去電影院？
(A) 我們將在晚餐後出發。
(B) 表演很棒。
(C) 200美元。

8 (美M)

Who's the new public relations manager?
(A) On the seventh floor.
(B) A pool of five candidates.
(C) Someone from the New York branch.

誰是新的公關經理？
(A) 在7樓。
(B) 5名候選人。
(C) 來自紐約分公司的人。

解析 針對詢問是誰的疑問句，答案往往不是人名或職位等級。(A) 適合疑問詞Where的回答，(B) 指的不是特定人物，只有「候選人」的單字似乎可能是答案，但當題目難度升高，就愈需避免只憑疑問詞來作答，而需要和前後的動詞連貫之後，從語意內容上選擇合乎一致性的答案。

詞彙 public relations 公關／公關部門　floor 樓、地板　pool 聚集處、人力　candidate 候選人、應徵者　branch 分公司

9 (美W)

When was the sculpture gallery added to the Gibson Museum?
(A) A substantial amount of money.
(B) Four or five years ago.
(C) A local artist.

雕塑畫廊什麼時候新增到吉布森博物館？
(A) 大筆的金錢。
(B) 4、5年前。
(C) 當地藝術家。

解析 針對When疑問句使用ago的 (B) 是正確答案。雖然題目有點長，疑問詞疑問句的中最重要的是找出疑問詞和主要動詞。(C) 的內容沒有相關點，並非答案。(C) 出現與題目中sculpture容易聯想的詞彙artist，但缺乏時間點相關的內容。

詞彙 sculpture 雕塑　gallery 畫廊、美術館　add 增加　museum 博物館　substantial 大量的　amount 數量　local 當地的　artist 畫家

10 (澳M)

Where's the lecture being held?
(A) Next week works for me.
(B) A well-known economist.
(C) Oh, I didn't think you could make it.

講座在哪裡舉行？
(A) 下周我可以。
(B) 一位著名的經濟學家。
(C) 哦，我沒想到你會來。

解析 使用疑問詞的題型中，難度高的題型是不直接針對疑問詞提供答案，卻可以自然形成對話。說「我沒想到你會來」的 (向抵達活動現場之後與主講人說「我沒想到你會來」) 是正確答案。雖不是Where疑問句的典型答案，但從現有的選項使用刪去法也便能夠找出答案。

(A) 適合When疑問句，(B) 適合Who疑問句。

詞彙 lecture 講課、講座　be held 舉行　work 運轉、有效　well-known 知名的　economist 經濟學家　make it 可以去、可以來

Unit 5　疑問詞疑問句 II

Step 2　聽懂和聽寫的訓練

1
Q: How were the sales last quarter?
A: Better than expected.
Q: 上個季度的銷售情況如何？
A: 比預期的更好。
解析 疑問詞How與be動詞連接時，是詢問狀態的問題。先記熟好的各種表達方式，答題時更有幫助。答案也可能是回「比上次增加了10%) 的高難度詳細描述。

2
Q: Why didn't you buy a less expensive camera?
A: I didn't like the design.
Q: 你為什麼不買便宜一點的相機？
A: 我不喜歡它的設計。
解析 疑問詞Why不僅是單件事的疑問，必須掌握提問後內容才能選出正確答案。為什麼口的答案，疑問詞Why不一定要選以Because開始的選項，聽到結束之後，選擇最適合的選項是Part 2的滿分訣竅。

3
Q: What do you do for a living?
A: I work at a hospital.
Q: 你以什麼工作為生？
A: 我在醫院工作。
解析 What do you do (for a living)？意思是詢問職業，答案可能使用表達職業的名詞，但以「在～工作」的方式來描述職場也可能作為回答。

4
Q: Which car is yours?
A: The one in the corner.
Q: 哪輛車是你的？
A: 角落的那輛。
解析 使用which (哪一個) 從選項中選一的疑問句，須謹記最常使用的回答類型是「The one ～ (～的那個)」。

5
Q: Why were you late for the meeting?
A: The traffic was really bad.
Q: 你為什麼會遲到？
A: 交通實在是糟糕了。
解析 使用Why詢問遲到原因的問句，可以以各種藉口的例句來回答。尤其針對答案中在找出原因時，交通壅塞來回答經常出現的答案，必須熟記。

6
Q: How much do you charge for copying?
A: 20 cents per page.
Q: 影印怎麼收費？
A: 一張20美分。
解析 疑問詞How根據連接的形容詞／名詞等而具有各種意義。How much是詢問間不可數名詞的數量，這裡與動詞charge (收費) 結合使用，是典型的詢問價格的疑問句。

7
Q: How do you get to the train station?
A: A friend is driving me there.
Q: 你怎麼去火車站？
A: 朋友開車送我。
解析 疑問詞How結合一般動詞 (get to) 用以詢問前往某個特定地點的方法。不只是問句，典型的答案中經常使用的public transportation (大眾交通) 和give a ride/lift (送～一程搭便車) 的用法也必須記熟。

正解

1. (B)　2. (B)　3. (A)　4. (B)　5. (A)

1

(英M) What size do you wear?

(美W) (A) I don't know the size of the apartment.
(B) 9, but I'm not sure.

你穿幾號？

(A) 我不知道這間公寓的大小。
(B) 9號，但我不確定。

解析 必須聽到之後能夠預測尺寸的答案。正確答案是9號，即使不確定也要知道 (A) 是重複題目size的陷阱，因此錯。(B) 適合。

詞彙 wear 穿

2

(英W) How long have you lived in this neighborhood?

(美W) (A) Last year.
(B) For three years.

你在這附近住了多久？

(A) 去年。
(B) 3年。

解析 How long和問距離相比，更常用來詢問時間，針對詢問How long多久的問句，(B) 使用的是〈for + 時間長度〉典型的since也可以使用since來回答，(A) 適合How long疑問而不是時間長度的問句，也就是疑問詞When的答案。

詞彙 live 居住　neighborhood 附近　for〜期間

3

(英M) Why did you come so early this morning?

(美W) (A) To finish the report.
(B) Sure, I can do that.

你為什麼這麼早來？

(A) 為了完成報告。
(B) 當然，我可以做到。

解析 詢問理由的Why疑問句中，經常以表達目的的to不定詞 (為了〜)〈作為答案〉針對高難度的Why疑問句必須掌握各種理由。(B) 使用的是表達目的的to不定詞，其中第一步是了解表達目的的to不定詞。

詞彙 early 提早　report 報告、告書

4

(英W) How often should we hold the meeting?

(美M) (A) For two weeks.
(B) At least twice a month.

我們應該多久舉行一次會議？

(A) 為期兩星期。
(B) 一個月至少兩次。

解析 結合有關How的句子根據語意可能有完全不同的意義，從一開始必須學習有關How的各種意義。針對詢問頻率的疑問句How often的答案有once, twice, every 〜等，也是最常出現的答案。(A) 適合詢問時間長度的疑問詞How long問句。

詞彙 hold 舉開　for〜期間　at least 至少

5

(英M) Which photocopier would you like to see?

(美W) (A) The one with simple features.
(B) I would like some coffee, please.

您希望看哪一台影印機呢？

(A) 具有簡單功能的那台。
(B) 我想要一些咖啡。

解析 在這種選項中與一的形式的答案 (具有〜〜的)，針對詢問物品的Which疑問句，答案往往是就明白己想要的類型。「the one」形式的答案 (B) 使用類似copy發音的coffee作為陷阱，與其選擇聽起來相似的選項，需要精益求精透過充分練習熟悉合的答案類型。

正解

1. (B)　2. (B)　3. (C)　4. (B)　5. (A)
6. (C)　7. (C)　8. (A)　9. (B)　10. (B)

1

(澳M) Why was the plane delayed?

(美W) (A) I'd like to make a reservation.
(B) The weather has been bad.
(C) At an international terminal.

飛機為什麼延誤？

(A) 我想預約。
(B) 天氣惡劣。
(C) 在國際航廈。

解析 詢問飛機誤點原因的Why疑問句，最典型的答案是天氣惡劣。除此之外，飛機機械故障 (mechanical problem) 或中轉航班 (connecting flight) 的問題也可能作為答案。(A) 是容易聯想到旅行的reservation錯誤引導，(C) 適合詢問地點的Where疑問句問句。

詞彙 be delayed 延誤　make a reservation 預約的　international 國際的　terminal 前廈

2

(美W) Which key do I use to open this cabinet?

(美M) (A) I think you're right.
(B) Try this one.
(C) I'd rather have tea.

我要用哪支鑰匙打開這個櫃子？

(A) 我覺得你是對的。
(B) 試試這把。
(C) 我寧願喝茶。

解析 選擇疑問詞Which疑問句是使用「this one 〜」來描述的句子。不在座位上的原因以 (C) 作為答案，只選擇聽得懂的最後會知道這個答案。

詞彙 cabinet 箱子、櫃子　I'd rather 我寧願〜

3

(美M) Why aren't they at their desks?

(美W) (A) On Tuesday.
(B) Of course not.
(C) They went to lunch.

他們為什麼不在他們的辦公桌旁？

(A) 在星期二。
(B) 當然不是。
(C) 他們去吃午飯。

解析 針對疑問的Why的問有各種回答方式，注意語意久以正確答案。(A) 是詢問時間點的疑問句，(B) 是Yes/No的另一種說法，不能當目的，因此不可能是最合理型由/回答。(C) 適合詢問「They went to lunch 去吃飯。

詞彙 at one's desk 在桌子旁　of course 當然　go to lunch 去吃午飯

4

(澳W) How late is the museum open?

(美M) (A) I haven't gone there lately.
(B) Until 5 p.m.
(C) For seven days a week.

博物館開放到多晚？

(A) 我最近沒去過那裡。
(B) 到下午5點。
(C) 一周七天。

解析 「How late, How early」是「多晚/多早」的意思，可以看作與When疑問詞一樣，針對營業時間的問句以 (B) 到5點為正確答案。使用與lately發音相似的lately作為陷阱。(A) 使用與When疑問詞只是聽疑問詞，須根據調整經常以最棘手的子來掌握答案的類型。題。How late不僅純只是疑問詞，須根據調整適合作為陷阱。(C) 適合詢問時間長度的How long問句。

5 （澳M）（美W）

What's the membership fee at the fitness club on Oak Street?
(A) Thirty euros a month.
(B) They were highly recommended.
(C) The shop is on Brookline Avenue.

樣樹街健身俱樂部的會員費是多少？

解析 題目雖然使用What，但詢問的是會員費，等同How much 詢問金額的內容中不只美元（dollar），也會出現以歐元（euro）和日圓（yen）。針對高難度的題型，先留下可能以金錢作為答案的選項，刪去錯誤的部分，就能選出答案。(B) 適合作為問題選擇理由的Why疑問句回答，(C) 適合作為Where疑問句的答案。

詞彙 membership fee 會員費 fitness club 健身俱樂部 euro 歐元 highly 高度地 recommend 推薦 avenue 街、路

6 （澳M）（美W）

How do I enter your contest?
(A) No, I didn't have time.
(B) The winner receives a free trip to Hawaii.
(C) The instructions are on our Web site.

我如何參加比賽？

(A) 不，我沒有時間。
(B) 獲勝者將獲得前往夏威夷的免費旅行。
(C) 說明在我們的網站上。

解析 —使用「How～一般動詞」的形式詢問參加的方法，典型的回答之一是網頁或線上申請的方法。但 (C) 轉換成在網頁上參加方法的回應，屬於「不知道」的題型。(A) 的Yes/No 無法使用方法詢問的疑問句，(B) 適合回答獲得獎金/獎品的 prize（獎品）的題目。(B) 使用了容易與contest聯想的winner作為陷阱。

詞彙 enter 參加、加入 contest 競賽、比賽 winner 優勝者 free 免費的 instruction 說明

7 （美M）（美W）

What will they be serving at the reception?
(A) What an excellent speech!
(B) Yes, their services are great.
(C) Some light refreshments.

他們會在歡會上提供什麼？

(A) 多麼精彩的演講。
(B) 是的，他們的服務很棒。
(C) 一些輕食點心。

解析 題目是關於活動中提供什麼食物。答案可能是食物名稱，但出現

refreshments（點心）的 (C) 是正確答案。同樣的道理，飲料（beverage/drinks）名稱也可能是答案。(A) 使用了似乎與活動有關的speech，但與食物沒有關聯，因此並非答案。須謹記 (B) 的Yes/No無法作為疑問句的回答。

詞彙 reception 歡迎會、派對 speech 演講 light 輕的 refreshments 點心、零食

8 （美W）（澳M）

How can I contact technical support?
(A) There's a special number you can call.
(B) Yes, she'll contact the customer later.
(C) From 8 A.M. to 7 P.M.

我該如何連絡技術支援部門？

(A) 你可以撥打一個特定號碼。
(B) 是的，她稍後會聯絡客戶。
(C) 從上午8點到下午7點。

解析 以「How～contact」形式詢問連絡方式的問題，提供號碼號碼的 (A) 是正確答案。類似的回答還有上網填寫申請表的 (on line request form)。(B) 的Yes/No無法作為疑問句回答，(C) 的時間可以回答，適合作為詢問時間長短的How long疑問句或營業時間的疑問句。

詞彙 contact 連絡 technical support 技術支援 special 特別的 number 號碼、電話號碼 customer 客戶 later 晚一點

9 （美W）（澳M）

Why did the store stop carrying Trident products?
(A) On the corner of Main Street and Bedminster Road.
(B) They weren't selling well.
(C) They're really not that heavy.

為什麼那家店停止販售Trident公司的產品？

(A) 在主街和貝德明斯特路的轉角處。
(B) 它們賣得不好。
(C) 它們真的沒那麼重。

解析 詢問特定商店停止販賣Trident的原因，尤其當出現商業用語時，會更容易選擇答案。雖作Trident的公司產品銷售不佳，因此題目意思是才能夠了解意思的棘手疑問詞。另外，動詞carry除了搬運物品之外，還具有「交易」意義，必須加以熟記。(C) 以carry詞彙具有的「搬運」意思作為陷阱。

詞彙 carry (商品) 交易 corner 轉角處、角落 sell 賣 well ～得好 heavy 重的

10 （美W）（美M）

What was Mr. Tanaka's group asked to work on this month?
(A) Sure, I'll ask him to do it.

(B) The report on alternative energy.
(C) Earlier this month.

田中先生的小組這個月被要求做什麼工作？

(A) 當然，我會請他這樣做。
(B) 關於替代能源的報告。
(C) 在這個月初。

解析 詢問公司裡進行什麼工作的題目。各種業務描述都可能是答案，而完成報告書 (report) 的 (B) 是正確答案。除此之外，包含客戶 (client)、名字的特定計畫 (project)、合約 (contract) 等也可能作為回答。(A) 的Yes/No無法作為疑問句的回答，因此並非答案，(C) 適合回答詢問時間的When疑問句。

詞彙 group 團體、小組 work on 進行～的工作 report 報告書 alternative 替代的、其他的 energy 能源、能量 earlier 更早

REAL SOLUTION

多益考試的前半部針對公司的工作職責 (job, responsibility) 出題機率相當高，尤其有關客戶的合約 (contract)、合約 (contract)、簡報 (presentation) 和報告 (report) 的主題相當常見。尤其必須會感到生疏、整個單元的難度愈高，具備愈多背知況，因此可能會感到生疏、整個單元的難度愈高，具備愈多背景知識就越有利。

Step 2　聆聽和聽篇的訓練

1
Q: Are you working on the new project?
A: No, I'm too busy.
Q: 你在進行新項目嗎?
A: 不，我太忙了。
解析：這是Yes/No疑問句的最典型回答。以<No + 原因>的方式形成形式，為之後難度較高的題型做準備。

2
Q: You haven't read the proposal, have you?
A: No, I'll do it this weekend.
Q: 你還沒看過這個提案，有了嗎?
A: 不，我這個週末會做的。
解析：Yes/No的典型回答中以<No + 其他方案>來說明現在無法進行的事情而時能夠完成。

3
Q: Didn't you receive the training last month?
A: No, I wasn't there.
Q: 你上個月沒接受培訓嗎?
A: 不，我不在那裡。
解析：否定疑問句和肯定疑問句形式相同，也就是說，有肯定時的Yes，否定時的No即可。針對為沒有參加培訓的問題，以<No（沒接受、沒能接受）+ 原因（不在那裡）>的典型方式來回答。

4
Q: Do you think we should leave for the airport now?
A: Let's check the flight schedule first.
Q: 你認為我們現在應該去機場嗎?
A: 我們先來確認航班時刻表。
解析：詢問是否現在就該出發的疑問句，使用了Do you think的疑問句。回答方式通常與Yes/No疑問句一樣。「不太清楚所以問看看」類型中出題的機率很高，必須熟悉這類的回答方式。回答方式通常通與Yes/No疑問句的雙重看看更長。回答方式（Let me find out/Let me check）」的答案從「不知道」

5
Q: You'll be recruiting new employees soon, right?
A: Yes, we're planning to.
Q: 你很快就會招聘新員工，對吧?
A: 是的，我們正打算如此。
解析：附加疑問句也是有肯定時說Yes，否定時說No。對於招聘新員工的問題以我們正計畫那件事做（We're planning to）來回答，意思是有計畫。除此之外，「That's my plan（那是我的計劃）」、「That's my goal（那是我的目標）」等也可作為回答。

6
Q: Do you know which customer ordered the pasta dish?
A: The woman at table three.
Q: 你知道哪位顧客點了麵食嗎?
A: 3桌的女士。
解析：在疑問詞疑問句前面加上Do you know形成間接疑問句的情況。經常不需Yes/No，直接使用一般的疑問句回答類型。正確答案是省略的「3號桌的女士」。此外，須記疑問詞Which不只使用在事物，也能夠以<which + 名詞>形式特別指示某人。

7
Q: Couldn't we postpone the conference until February?
A: The hotel charges a cancellation fee.
Q: 我們不能把會議延到2月份嗎?
A: 那家飯店會收取消費用。
解析：高難度的Yes/No疑問句答案有<Yes + 原因>，必須能夠確認肯定/否定語意。「不能取消嗎?」的否定疑問句中以「No（不）+ 原因（因為有違約金）」作為回答，對於高難度的題目在答題上會更有利，必須多加熟記詞彙和句型結構。

Step 3　基本掌握

正解
1. (A)　2. (B)　3. (A)　4. (B)　5. (A)

1 (美M)
Are you ready to meet now?
(A) I think so.
(B) I'm already full, thank you.
你準備好現在見面嗎?
(A) 我想是的。
(B) 我已經飽了，謝謝。
解析：對於準備好了嗎（Are you ready～）的問題，(A) 是正確答案「I think so」的問題會更多。注意避免選內容相似的選項。聽到ready to準備好～之後，再選擇正確答案。
詞彙 ready to 準備好～　already 已經　full 裝滿的

2 (英W)
Don't you want to take the subway?
(A) Yes, the bus stop is very close.
(B) Yes, that would be faster.
你不想搭地鐵嗎?
(A) 是的，巴士站牌很近。
(B) 是的，那會比較快。
解析：作為典型的Yes/No疑問句答案有<Yes + 闡述說明>、<No + 其他方法>。詢問是否想搭地鐵的問題，以「想搭」來做肯定的回答。除此之外，也可能出現<No + 提議其他交通工具>的回答。
詞彙 bus stop 巴士站牌

3 (英W)
It's sunny outside, isn't it?
(A) Yes, the clouds are gone.
(B) Saturday or Sunday.
外面陽光明媚，不是嗎?
(A) 是的，雲已經消失了。
(B) 週六或週日。
解析：表達天氣相通常以it作為主語。使用附加疑問句的形式詢問問句，以<Yes + 闡述說明>的方式描述這裡無雲氣象的晴朗天氣。(B) 週六或週日是與天氣無關氣象預報狀況的星期句。(B) 使用了容易混淆的星期名稱，但缺乏與氣象有關的內容。
詞彙 sunny 風和日麗的　outside 外面、戶外的

4.
Can you tell me what software we use?

美W (A) We didn't pay for it.

英W (B) I don't know its name.

(A) 使用間接疑問句的形式詢問軟體名稱。答案是「不知道」類型的(B)。以「不知道」類型作為答案的情況，無論疑問句形式是什麼，做為答案的機率都很高，一定要多加熟悉。

你能告訴我我們是用什麼軟體購買？

詞彙 pay for 支付~費用

5.
英W Do you want to order now?

美W (A) No, I need a few more minutes.

美W (B) Can I have the check, please?

(A) 不，我還需要幾分鐘。

(B) 能給我帳單嗎？

您想現在訂購嗎？

解析 這是餐廳服務生和客人之間詢問要點什麼餐點的對話。針對服務生貼心的詢問要點什麼餐點的對話，是以<No + 原因>形式作為答案的(A)。而(B)是在點餐完之後要結帳時才會使用的表達，因此並不合適。

詞彙 order 訂購、點 a few 幾個、少數 check 帳單

Step 4　實戰練習

P52

正解

1. (B)	2. (A)	3. (B)	4. (A)	5. (B)
6. (A)	7. (C)	8. (A)	9. (B)	10. (C)

1.
The president will be back tomorrow, won't he?

美W (A) I didn't get the present.

正解 (B) I'm not sure.

(C) No, at the front desk.

(A) 我沒有收到禮物。

(B) 我不確定。

(C) 不，在服務台。

董事長明天會回來，不是嗎？

解析 詢問董事長（第3人稱）是否會回來的附加疑問句，正確答案是典型的「不知道」類型，'I'm not sure' 即是。簡單，但須避免直接選答；持續進行刪去法的過程，才能安心應手。(A) 使用發音類似的present作為陷阱，但present類似的present是難度較高的詞彙，不適合作為答案。(C) 使用front/back的聯想詞彙。

詞彙 president 董事長 be back 回來 present 禮物

2.
Didn't you visit the factory before?

澳W (A) Yes, about a year ago.

(B) No, the facts are pretty clear.

(C) Sure, I'd love to.

(A) 是的，大約一年前。

(B) 不，事實非常清楚。

(C) 當然，我很樂意。

你以前沒參觀過工廠嗎？

解析 這是詢問過去是否做過某件事的否定疑問句，正確答案是以<Yes + 時間>形式說明的(A)。假設以No來回答時，可能出現「這是第一次」的內容。(B) 使用了與factory發音類似的fact，刪去法的缺點之一是並非單純判斷內容正確或錯誤，而是思考這個選項內容適合何種題目，答案有幫助。(C) 適合前面提問時的回答。

詞彙 visit 參觀 factory 工廠 fact 事實 pretty 非常 clear 清楚的

3.
Did you find the replacement parts for the printer?

美W (A) Under $50.

(B) They're being installed now.

(C) 25 pages a minute.

(A) 不到50美元。

(B) 它們正在安裝。

(C) 每分鐘25頁。

您找到了印表機的更換零件嗎？

解析 您找到了印表機的更換零件嗎？對於詢問是否找到某件物品的問題，答案是從<Yes / 闡述說明>的形式中省略Yes，直接說明正在安裝零件，但只要刪除錯誤選項即可找出答案。(A) 適合前面的內容就會著著選擇答案，需注意避免聽到和印表機相關的內容就急著選擇答案。(C) 使用了容易與影印機或印表機聯想的page。以「How fast~」開頭詢問速度的疑問句。

詞彙 find 找到 replacement 替換 part 零件 printer 印表機 page 頁

4.
Mr. Reed is the owner of this store, isn't he?

澳W (A) Yes, I'd like to buy something.

美W (B) Put it in the storage space.

(C) Yes, I believe he is.

(A) 是的，我想買點東西。

(B) 把它放在儲藏室。

(C) 是的，我想他是。

Mr. Reed 是這家店的老闆，不是嗎？

解析 詢問里德先生（第3人稱）是否為老闆的附加疑問句，正確答案回答「我想他是(I believe he is)」的(C)。雖然出現not字眼，但並非否定語意，意思是「要~才會~」。(B) 使用travel的意思是「我想他至~」，是錯誤的選項，而(C) 重複題型travel。

句子並聽懂題目，試著避過聽過場理解。(A) 使用了與trade(貿易)及store前的詞彙聯想的buy，是典型的陷阱。(B) 使用了與store發音類似的storage，也是錯誤選項。

詞彙 owner 老闆 store 商店、儲藏 storage 保管、儲存 space 空間 believe 相信

5.
Do you know where I should send these boxes?

美W (A) Don't forget the postage.

(B) To the address on this line.

(C) For the marketing meeting.

(A) 不要忘記郵資。

(B) 寄到這一行上的地址。

(C) 行銷會議上要用。

你知道我應該把這些箱子寄到哪裡嗎？

解析 這是加上Do you know的間接疑問句，主要詢問地點。正確答案是省略Yes，直接說明地點的(B)。使用send的想想postage時問接表達，(A) 使用了與send相關的郵寄postage(郵資)，(C) 適合作為詢問目的疑問詞Why的回答。

哪裡~。正確答案是加上Do you know的間接疑問句，主要是詢問地點的~，而以「是一行的地址(address on this line)」間接表達~。

詞彙 send 寄送 box 箱子 postage 郵資 address 地址

6.
Aren't you traveling to China at the end of this month?

美W (A) No, not until next November.

(B) Two window seats, please.

(C) The travel agency.

(A) 不，明年11月才去。

(B) 請給我兩個靠窗的座位。

(C) 旅行社。

你不是這個月底要前往中國嗎？

解析 針對對這個月日去旅行的否定疑問句，以<No + 其他方案>的典型方式回答否定語次，而最常出現的題型，尤其是「not until ~」在內容並不正確。

針對這個月日去旅行的否定疑問句，以<No+其他方案>的典型~。練習。尤其是「not until ~」的典型方式是最常出現的題型，一定要多加練習。(B) 使用travel的聯想詞彙飛機座位、是錯誤的選項，而(C) 重複題型travel。

詞彙 end 底、結束 not until 直到~才 window seat 靠窗座位 travel agency 旅行社

7. 澳M／美W

Is it going to take much longer to see the doctor?
(A) I plan to watch that show today.
(B) About 25 kilometers.
(C) **Sorry, it's been a very busy day.**

要等很久才能看醫生嗎?
(A) 我打算今天看這個節目。
(B) 大約25公里。
(C) **對不起,今天是非常忙碌的一天。**

解析 這是在醫院櫃台前可以聽到的對話。面對是否還要等很久時間的問題,表達想到的原因可以獲得對話。隨著難度提高,對話方式也有可能作為答案,便用難語選出答案。須持續練習時除詢問show外,但內容與電視節目或表述無關。(A) 使用了see的想到show,但內容與電視節目或表述無關。(B) 是提出時間問題,卻以距離來回答的典型錯誤。注意避免聽到about這個字就匆匆選擇答案。

詞彙 take 花 (時間) longer 更久、更久的時間 busy 忙碌的

---

8. 美W／美M

Do you know who'll be teaching the environmental science course?
(A) **A professor from London.**
(B) The lab equipment is brand new.
(C) It's close by.

你知道誰將教導科學課程嗎?
(A) **來自倫敦的一位教授。**
(B) 實驗室設備是全新的。
(C) 它就在附近。

解析 在Who疑問句的前面使用的「Do you know」的間接疑問句,針對詢問誰來教授特定課程的問題,以間接方式說明人物的 (A) 是正確答案。(B) 是使用science關聯詞彙equipment的錯誤選項,(C) 適合作為詢問地點的疑問句Where回答。

詞彙 environmental 環境的 science 科學 course 課程 professor 教授 lab 實驗室 equipment 設備、機械 brand new 全新的 close 近的

---

9. 美M／美W

You can reschedule the event, can't you?
(A) Don't forget to sign up.
(B) **The invitations have already been sent out.**
(C) I attended that meeting.

你可以重新安排活動,不是嗎?
(A) 不要忘記報名。
(B) **已經寄出了邀請函。**
(C) 我參加了那次會議。

解析 以附加疑問句的形式詢問是否可以變更行程的問題,屬於高難度題型。需記在省略了以肯定否定回答問題的<Yes＋關述說明>、<No＋關述說明>情況下,能夠了解是否已肯定回答問題的<Yes＋關述說明>。答案省略了肯定或否定回答,而以說明已經發出邀請函而無法變更行程的 (B) 是正確答案。(A) 是使用event聯想詞彙sign up的錯誤選項,(C) 將event換成另一種說法meeting,但使用不正確的過去時態。

詞彙 reschedule 重新安排、更改 event 活動 forget 忘記 sign up 報名 invitation 邀請函 already 已經 send out 寄出 attend 參加

---

10. 美M／澳W

Aren't you going to work out at the fitness center tonight?
(A) Did it fit in your locker?
(B) You should be able to walk there.
(C) **I won't have time today.**

你今晚不去健身中心運動嗎?
(A) 它裝得進你的儲物櫃嗎?
(B) 你應該能走路到那裡。
(C) **我今天沒時間。**

解析 針對詢問今晚是否去運動的否定疑問句,以<No＋原因>形式而省略No來回答。必須能夠在只聽到原因,就理解內容是否定而回答。尤其最常出現的回答原因是沒時間或忙碌而不做某件事情。(A) 使用fitness的發音相似的walk,是錯誤選項。(B) 使用與work發音類似的work out運動、fitness center 健身中心、be able to 可以~

> **元老師的 REAL SOLUTION**
>
> 愈是高難度的題目就愈需要背景知識,尤其舉辦活動的公司① 連絡飯店場地② 接待各個公司團體的參加人員③ 製作活動目錄和邀請卡④ 邀請演講嘉賓(guest speaker)⑤ 發放姓名卡和資料,只要掌握活動進行過程,答題時就會更有利。

Unit 7 Yes／No 疑問句 II,其他類型

P57

Step 2 聆聽和聽寫的訓練

1.
Q: Do you want me to call you, or send you an e-mail?
A: I prefer e-mail.

解析 在連絡某人時從2種方式中選擇一種的情況。Part 2中,當一模一樣或類似的單字出現在選項內,是正確答案的機率很低,但在選擇疑問句中,題目出現過的詞彙有可能出現作為正確答案。

2.
Q: Can you hand me the scissors, please?
A: Yes, here they are.

解析 (向對方做出某個請求」) 是動作的請求,尤其是主動的詞具有 hand「給」、傳遞 (＝ give, pass)」的意思,屬於經常出現在選項的詞彙,必須記住。Here you are (＝ Here it is)「在這裡」也經常作為對方物品時,也經常出現的回答。scissors以複數形式來使用 Here they are。

3.
Q: The photocopier is not working again.
A: We should call the maintenance right away.

解析 必須練習在平述句問題中的快速作答技巧。由於經常出現職場生活相關的題目,預測「正確的職員行為」是答題上的技巧。出現問題時帶著關心積極處理的態度,當辦公設備修的人經常作為正確答案。不帶著關心積極處理的態度,直接查看或致電維修的人經常作為正確答案。

4.
Q: Why don't we have a coffee break?
A: Sure, that's a great idea.

解析 以「Why don't we ~?」開始的句子代表勸誘的語意。答案是對於喝杯咖啡、休息一下的好主意。把握度微弱時,會運用<Yes＋附加說明>的形式,說明同意,和雖喝咖啡的內容。

5

Q: Should we order paper cups, or plastic ones?

A: We need both.

英W Q: 我們應該訂購紙杯還是塑膠杯？

美M A: 兩種都要。

解析 選擇疑問句的核心內容主要在後面出現，必須聽完之後提運內容。紙杯和塑膠杯的選擇中，兩者 (either)「兩者都要 (both)」、「兩者皆非 (neither)」等表達方式的詞彙可能是正確答案。熱這「都可以 (either)」、「兩個都要 (both)」、「兩者皆非 (neither)」就能快速選出答案。

6

Q: Can you make it to the shareholders' meeting tomorrow?

A: I wish I could.

英W Q: 您明天能參加股東大會嗎？

美M A: 我希望我可以。

解析 針對詢問明天是否參加的問題，雖然沒辦法去「但可以用我希望我可以 I wish I could 的方式來回答」。

7

Q: We can meet the deadline after all.

A: That's very good news.

Q: 我們終究可以在截止日期前完成。

A: 這真是個好消息。

解析 必須訓練在聽句時，能快速聽到正確答案。對話往往在職場中經常聽到的內容，對於「可以提早截止日」、「很高興」等做出回應。難度稍微增高時，可以針對截止日的詳細內容進行反問。

詞彙 take ~ off 休息、休假 bring 帶來

Step 3 基本掌握 P58

正解 1. (A) 2. (A) 3. (B) 4. (B) 5. (A)

1

Why don't you take tomorrow off, John?

美M (A) Thanks, I will.

英W (B) I can bring it in with me.

(A) 謝謝，我會的。

(B) 我可以把它帶來。

解析 對於為何不休息的提議，表示感謝並說明會那麼做的 (A) 是正確答案。由於沒有可以使用來代表那物品的，因此 (B) 是錯誤選項。

詞彙 either 兩者之一、都可以

5

It's really hot in here.

美W (A) I'll open the window.

英W (B) Let's meet there instead.

(A) 我來開窗戶。

(B) 我們去那裡見面吧。

解析 對於太熱的處理方式通常是開窗戶或開冷氣，對於先熟記考古題中出現的答案，是最安全的作答方法。(B) 使用here的相反詞there作為聯想，是典型的錯誤選項。

詞彙 hot 熱的、辣的 instead 代替

2

The air conditioner in my apartment is broken.

英W (A) OK, we'll call a repair person.

(B) I don't like their conditions.

解析 我公寓的冷氣壞了。

(A) 好的，我們打電話給維修人員。

(B) 我不喜歡他們的條件。

解析 內容是因某個問題導致冷氣故障，正確答案是要叫維修人員的 (A)。(B) 使用類似conditioner的condition的單字，是典型的錯誤選項。

詞彙 air conditioner 冷氣 repairperson 維修人員 condition 條件

3

Would you like a ride to work tomorrow?

美M (A) He doesn't work here anymore.

(B) I'd appreciate it.

英W Q: 明天你想搭便車去上班嗎？

(A) 他沒有在這裡工作了。

(B) 我很感激。

解析 以選擇疑問句詢問週一或週二中哪個時段理想。正確答案是 <Would you like + 名詞/~?> 是向對方表達善意的句型。對於提供善意時，最適常的回應表達感謝。而表達拒絕、經常使用「I can manage」、「I can handle ~」等來表達，是典型的錯誤選項，也沒有出現第3人稱的He人物。

詞彙 ride 搭乘 work 工作、運作 appreciate 感謝

4

Would you like to meet on Monday or Tuesday?

英W (A) That's a good idea.

美M (B) Either will be fine.

(A) 那是個好主意。

(B) 都可以。

解析 以選擇疑問句詢問週一或週二中哪個時段理想。正確答案是不論哪個時段都可以的 (B)。注意避免選擇題目前為止經常作為答案的 (B)。選擇疑問句是要求從兩者中擇一的提議，因此 (A) 不能作為答案。

詞彙 either 兩者之一、都可以

Step 4 實戰練習 P58

正解 1. (A) 2. (B) 3. (B) 4. (C) 5. (C)

6. (B) 7. (C) 8. (A) 9. (B) 10. (A)

1

Would you mind turning down the volume?

美W (A) Of course not.

澳M (B) Yes, I turned down the offer.

(C) Keep it in mind.

你介意調低音量嗎？

(A) 當然不會 (不介意)。

(B) 是的，我拒絕了這個提議。

(C) 謹記在心。

解析 針對表示詢問是否同意的平述句，最典型的回答是「of course not」的否定方式來回答，也就是同意之意。因為正確答案是 (A)「像一樣回答Yes的話是「拒絕」意思是「of course not」的否定方式來回答是同意之意。後面正確答案是 (A)「像一樣回答Yes的話是「拒絕」。另外，turn down 是「降低、記住」(C) 重複使用mind的詞彙 (聲音等)、拒絕 offer 提議 keep in mind

詞彙 turn down 調低 (音量等)、拒絕 offer 提議 keep in mind 謹記、記住

2

I thought the workshop was really helpful.

美M (A) That could work.

澳M (B) Yes, I learned a lot.

(C) It's new, not used.

我認為研討會非常有幫助。

(A) 那應該可行。

(B) 是的，我學到了很多東西。

(C) 這是新的，沒有用過。

解析 針對表示討論相當有幫助的平述句，最典型的回答是同意也可能出現如So did I (我也是) 的回答。如果再仔細聆聽的話，就會成為高難度的回答。(A) 適合當對方提出哪個有幫助的話。(C) 出現經常使用的new/used詞彙，但與原文內容完全無關。

詞彙 workshop 研討會、課程 helpful 有幫助的 work 成功、進行 learn 學習 used 用過的

3

Is the chairperson arriving this week or next?

美W (A) Next person in line.

英W (B) I believe it's this week.

(C) The flight will be on time.

主席是本週還是下週抵達？

(A) 排隊的下一位。

(B) 我想是本週。

(C) 航班會準時抵達。

4.

美W (A) Why don't you apply for the position?

澳M (B) We should visit there next month.

美M (C) Yes, he really deserves it.

Mr. Ottawa will be promoted this month.

解析 以選擇疑問句把握本週或或下週，適合的答案是兩者之一的 (B)。選擇疑問句的答案有可能是問的中出現的選項，但必須謹記兩者也可能作為誤導性的答案。(A) 使用與問句中 chairperson 主席，但發音類似 person 作為陷阱。

詞彙 chairperson 主席　arrive 抵達　in time 排隊的　flight 航班　on time 準時　believe 想、相信

5.

澳M Would you like to buy this one?

美W (A) I'd like some more water, please.

澳M (B) No, he can't do it now.

美M (C) It depends on the price.

您想買這個嗎？

解析 「不知道」類型「It depends on的出題機率較小，但有時「不知道」類型的選項出現兩種以上，這時高難度的題目中，有時「不知道」類型出現。(A) 以No回答時、後面應該出現不購買的原因或選擇其他物品的內容，以及無法作為購買的原因或選擇。

詞彙 promote 升職　apply for 申請～　deserve 有資格～

6.

美M Do you prefer to work in a team, or are you more comfortable working independently?

美M (A) It's quite comfortable.

澳M (B) I'm okay with either.

(C) I'll walk to work.

您更喜歡在團隊中工作，還是更適合獨立工作？

解析 針對詢問是否關買的問題，回答必須看價格再決定，答案屬於「不知道」類型，回答必須看價格再決定。(B) 以No回答時，後面應該出現不購買的原因或選擇其他物品的內容，以及無法作為購買的原因或選擇。

詞彙 last 最後、上次　rainy season 兩季

7.

美M Thank you for contributing to our museum's fundraising program.

澳M (A) Our most loyal supporters.

美W (B) On a television program.

(C) I'm glad to be of help.

解析 面對對方表示感謝時，You're welcome (不客氣) 是其中一種基本回應。當對方感謝自己做出貢獻時，以祝樂意做回應的 (C) 是正確答案。(A) 使用contribute衍生詞彙supporter 是錯誤選項。(B) 重複提到program作為誤導。

詞彙 contribute 出力、貢獻　fundraising 籌款　program作為　loyal 忠誠的　supporter 支持者　help 幫忙

8.

澳M Could you help me find my sunglasses?

美W (A) Where did you have them last?

(B) A few more drinking glasses.

(C) The rainy season begins next month.

你能夠幫我找到我的太陽眼鏡嗎？

解析 針對請求的典型回答可能是<I'd love[happy] to + 詳細內容>。但由高難度題目中會出現像 <I'd love[happy] to> 一樣省略Yes/No，直接回應的方式。如果子回答(A) 是否為答案，需要多練習你怎麼知道的方式。(B) 是重複使用glasses詞彙的錯誤選項。(C) 適合作為詢問時間的When疑問句答案，內容沒有提到物品的位置。

9.

澳M Did someone report the broken window, or should I call maintenance?

美W (A) No, it won't close any more.

(B) I just sent them an e-mail.

(C) On the second floor.

解析 高難度的選擇疑問句經常是比較的答案較難樹，使用改寫的詞彙作為答案。問題的關鍵是呈報與否，因此回答已經用e郵件呈報的 (B) 是正確答案。使用電子郵件或線上申報或傳閱問題是經常面對高難度的題目，須謹記在不是十分確定的情況下，要選擇錯誤最少的選項。

詞彙 report 報告、呈報　maintenance 維修　close 關閉

10.

美W Our train will be an hour late.

(A) I hope the client can push back the meeting.

(B) We really enjoyed the training.

(C) Track seven or nine.

我們的火車將晚一個小時。

解析 在陳述的句中，對於壞消息或情況積極處理，改善者的內容經常是正確答案。當聽到火車將延誤的句子時，必須延後與客戶會議的詳細項是正確答案。使用 train的聯想詞彙 track作為誤選，要謹記在最常喜歡這種訓練。train的聯想詞彙 track (跑道) 作為誤導。

詞彙 late 晚　client 顧客、客人　push back 往接延　enjoy 享受　track 跑道、軌道

Unit 8 問題類型 I

Step 2 閱讀題目 Practice　P64

1
1) (Where does (the man) most likely work?
SQ: 男子最有可能在哪裡工作?
2) What does (the man) want to do?
SQ: 女子想做什麼?
3) What does (the woman) make (a suggestion) about?
SQ: 女子提出了什麼建議?

2
1) What are the speakers (discussing)?
GQ: 談話者在討論什麼?
2) According to (the woman), what did (the feedback) (show)?
SQ: 根據這位女子,反饋顯示出什麼?
3) What will happen in (September)?
SQ: 九月會發生什麼?

3
1) What kind of business do the speakers work for?
GQ: 說話者從事什麼行業?
2) What did (the woman) forget to bring?
SQ: 女子忘了帶什麼?
3) According to (the man), why is (the event) (important)?
SQ: 根據男子,為什麼這個活動很重要?

4
1) Where does (the conversation) most likely (take place)?
GQ: 談話最有可能發生在哪裡?
2) What does (the woman) say (the men) will do this week?
SQ: 女子說男子們這個星期會做什麼?
3) What does (the woman) ask Fernando?
SQ: 女子問費爾南多什麼?

5
1) What did (the man) (recently) do?
SQ: 男子最近做了什麼?
2) What is (the man) (looking) forward to?
SQ: 男子期待什麼?
3) Why does (the man) say, "There's a class tomorrow night"?
SQ: 男子為什麼說,「明天晚上有課」?

Step 3 眼睛和耳朵完美搭配 Practice　P65

正解
| 1. (A) | 2. (B) | 3. (B) | 4. (A) |

Question 1 refers to the following conversation. 澳M 美W

M Hi, I'd like a ticket to the museum's special Egyptian art exhibit. I've heard wonderful things about it.

W I'm sorry, but the exhibit is very popular and we've already sold out of tickets for the morning. We still have some available for this afternoon, though.

男 你好,我想要一張博物館的特別埃及藝術展覽門票。我聽說展覽很棒。

女 對不起,這個展覽非常受歡迎,我們已經售完了早上的門票。不過,我們今天下午還有一些門票。

1 Where is the conversation taking place?
(A) At a museum
(B) At a theater
談話發生在哪裡?
(A) 在博物館
(B) 在電影院

Question 2 refers to the following conversation. 美M 美W

M Hi, I am calling because I bought a camera from your store a few days ago and there is a problem with some buttons. They don't work well.

W Well, if you bring your camera back to the store, we'll be glad to look it over for you.

男 你好,我打電話是因為我幾天前從你的商店古買了一台相機,而有些按鈕有問題,它們操作不起來不順。

女 好的,若您將相機帶回店內,我們很樂意幫你檢查。

2 Who probably is the woman?
(A) A photo journalist
(B) A store clerk
女子可能是誰?
(A) 攝影記者
(B) 店員

Question 3 refers to the following conversation. 美W 澳M

W I have a presentation to one of my clients tomorrow. How about meeting today instead of tomorrow?

M Oh, I'm sorry. I'll be running a training session most of the day. I'm teaching new staff the new accounting software.

女 我明天要為我的一位客戶做簡報。可以約今天見面而不是明天嗎?

男 喔,對不起。我今天大部分的時間要進行培訓課程。我正在教新進員工新的會計軟體。

3 Why is the man unable to meet today?
(A) He's visiting a client.
(B) He's leading a training session.
為什麼男子今天無法見面?
(A) 他正在拜訪一位客戶。
(B) 他正在主持一個培訓課程。

4 What does the woman offer to do?
(A) Provide directions
(B) Change the meeting time
女子提供什麼服務?
(A) 提供方向指引
(B) 變更會面時間

Question 4 refers to the following conversation. 美M 美W

M My appointment is in 5 minutes, and I probably won't be able to make it on time.

W Oh, don't worry. The meeting place is less than a 5-minute walk from here. Do you want me to tell you how to get there?

男 我的約會5分鐘後就要開始,我可能無法及時趕上。

女 喔,別擔心。約定地點距離這裡走不到5分鐘步行路程。需要我告訴你如何到達那裡嗎?

正確
1. (B)　2. (D)　3. (C)　4. (B)　5. (A)
6. (C)

Question 1 refers to the following conversation. 美M 美W

M ❶ Hi, welcome to Jeremy's Salon. Do you have an appointment with us?

W No, I don't. I was hoping one of the stylists might be free. ❶ I just need my hair trimmed.

男：你好，歡迎來到傑若米的髮廊。您和我們約好了嗎？

女：不，我沒有來到這裡做的髮廊。您和我們有時間—位造型師有時間，我只需要修剪一下頭髮。

詞彙　appointment 約定　stylist 美容師、造型師　free 有時間的　trim 修剪　hair salon 髮廊　dry-cleaning 乾洗　home improvement 居家裝修

1 Where most likely does the man work?
(A) At a hotel
(B) At a hair salon
(C) At a dry-cleaning business
(D) At a home improvement store

男子最有可能在哪裡工作？
(A) 飯店
(B) 髮廊
(C) 乾洗店
(D) 居家修繕店

解析　這是詢問男子工作地點的GQ，提示出現在前半段。先讀完問題之後瀏覽選項，並將聽到的對話，提出答案提示。從聽到的salon和hair的內容，但最好在第一個出現的提示中，以答案角度度（聽到第一句就出現高解題迷準備選擇 (B)，雖然後面出現頭度，選擇正確答案。

Question 2 refers to the following conversation. 美W 澳M

W I bought these sunglasses from your shop last month. Yesterday, one of the lenses came out of the frames. ❷ Can you fix them here?

M I'm sorry but the person who does the repairs is at lunch right now. You can leave them if you want, I'll make sure he fixes them as soon as possible.

女：我上個月從你們店裡買了這些太陽眼鏡。昨天，其中一個鏡片從鏡框中脫落了。你能在這裡修復它們嗎？

男：對不起，進行維修的人現在正在吃午飯。如果您願意，可以把眼鏡留在這裡。我會確保他盡快修理它們。

詞彙　lens 鏡片　frame 框、鏡架　as soon as possible 盡快　refund 退款　repair 修理、修復

2 What are the speakers talking about?
(A) A refund
(B) A store
(C) A sale
(D) A repair

說話者在談論什麼？
(A) 退款
(B) 商店
(C) 特價
(D) 修理

解析　對於詢問主題的GQ，經常需要從前半重新經這樣的詞彙中找出提示。聽到第一句描述新買的太陽眼鏡，鏡片脫落需要維修的狀況，尤其這種情況中，主題可能是「維修」，也可能是「太陽眼鏡」、「新買的商品」等作為主題。與其暗自思考什麼是主題，更好的做法是從既有的選項中，選擇最適合的部分。

Question 3 refers to the following conversation. 美M 美W

M Good morning. ❸ I wonder if the library carries a book I'm looking for. It's called Financial Forecast. The author is Angela Swanson.

W I know we have the book but our database shows that all our copies are out on loan right now. If you like, I can have the book sent from another library.

男：早安。我想知道圖書館是否有一本我正在尋找的書。它叫做財務預測。作者是安琪拉·斯旺森。

女：我知道我們有這本書，但我們的資料庫顯示我們所有的影本現在都是借出的狀態。如果您願意，我可以從另一個圖書館送來這本書。

詞彙　wonder 想知道　carry 銷售、持有　be called 叫做～　library 圖書館的、館政的　forecast 預古、預測　copy 複印、影本　loan 借出　author 作者、著者　accountant 會計師　librarian 圖書管理員　clerk 職員、店員

3 Who most likely is the woman?
(A) An author
(B) An accountant
(C) A librarian
(D) A bank clerk

女子可能是誰？
(A) 作家
(B) 會計師
(C) 圖書館管理員
(D) 銀行職員

解析　詢問關於女子職業的GQ可以從前半找出提示。需要從男子的第一句話中思考女子的職業。男子在圖書館詢問是否有自己正在尋找的書，可以得知女子是圖書館員，因此答案是 (C)。避免一聽到financial就認為是銀行職員或會計師，尤其GQ並非選擇對話中重複出現的內容，必須考慮適合談話情況的地點或職業。

Question 4 refers to the following conversation. (美W) (澳M)

W I'm glad you're here. ❹ We need to plan our strategy for next month's business exposition. So, what should we focus on first?

M Well, our advertising agency has a booth at the exposition just for two days. We really need to make a strong impression.

女 我很高興你在這裡。我們需要為下個月的商業博覽會制定策略。那麼，我們應該先關注什麼呢？

男 好的，我們的廣告代理商在博覽會上有一個展位，僅僅兩天。我們真的需要留下深刻的印象。

4. What is the conversation mainly about?
(A) Organizing a training session
(B) Preparing for a business exposition
(C) Finding a guest speaker for a convention
(D) Creating an employee handbook

就話主要是關於什麼事？
(A) 計畫培訓課程
(B) 準備商業博覽會
(C) 為博覽會尋找演講嘉賓
(D) 創建員工手冊

詞彙 strategy 策略　exposition 展示會、博覽會　focus on 關注　agency 代理商、代理公司　booth 展示攤位　impression 印象　organize 組織、組編　training session 培訓課程　prepare 準備　convention 博覽會　create 製作、創造　handbook 手冊、指引

解析 詢問對話主題的GQ提示在前半部都會出現。聽到要從business exposition (preparing for) 的答案，避免只憑聽得懂的詞彙來選擇答案。

Question 5 refers to the following conversation. (美M) (美W)

M Cathy, ❺ I've just come from the mixing room and we seem to be having trouble with the chocolate again. The consistency is too rough to be made into smooth texture for our candies.

W Oh, no. I've noticed yesterday that the chocolate didn't seem quite right as it usually is. I wasn't sure what was causing the problem though.

男 凱西，我剛剛從攪拌室裡過來。我們似乎又遇到了巧克力問題。稠度太粗糖，不能使我們的糖果做成光滑質地。

女 不好了。我昨天注意到巧克力似乎不太正常，不同以往。但我不確定是什麼導致了這個問題。

5. What industry do the speakers most likely work in?
(A) Food production
(B) Machinery sales
(C) Event planning
(D) Textile manufacturing

說話者最有可能從事什麼行業？
(A) 食物製造業
(B) 機器販售
(C) 活動策劃
(D) 紡織製造

詞彙 consistency 一致性、稠度　rough 粗糖　smooth 光滑的、柔和的　texture 質地、質感　notice 注意到、看到　quite 相當、非常　be sure 確定　cause 導致　industry 行業、產業　production 生產　machinery 機器　textile 紡織　manufacturing 製造

解析 詢問談話者工作行業的GQ提示主要出現在前半部。高難度的題目往往是關於日常生活中較不易接觸的商業狀況。廣泛涉繼生產/販售/管理/財務等各種主題的詞彙和狀況是因應高難度題目的方法。從第一句因為巧克力出現問題而無法維持精果品質的內容中，可以知道這是生產精果的工廠中出現的對話，也因此行業別是食物的製造業。

Question 6 refers to the following conversation. (澳M) (美W)

M Hi, I am calling about the shipment I got yesterday. ❻ I ordered two boxes of printing papers, but only one of them arrived.

W I am sorry, sir. Let me check your account information. Can I have your name first?

男 你好，我打電話來是有關於我昨天收到的貨。我訂了兩盒印刷紙，但只有收到一盒。

女 對不起，先生。我來查看您的帳戶資訊。請問您尊姓大名？

6. What are the speakers discussing?
(A) A billing error
(B) A missing document
(C) An incomplete shipment
(D) A damaged product

說話者在討論什麼？
(A) 結算錯誤
(B) 遺失的文件
(C) 貨品不完整
(D) 產品損壞

詞彙 shipment 貨品、裝運　printing paper 印刷紙　account 帳戶　bill 帳單、開帳單給～　missing 遺失的、缺少的　incomplete 不完整的　damaged 損壞的

解析 對於談話的主題的GQ，必須從前半部給予的提示中，找出重新詮釋的詞彙。聽到訂購兩盒產品，只收到一盒時，可以得知是關於貨品不完整 (incomplete shipment) 的談話內容。當題目難度高，詞彙愈形重要，為了能夠選出各種意思相近的詞彙，需要多加熟記。

正答　1.(D)　2.(B)　3.(A)　4.(B)　5.(C)　6.(C)

Question 1 refers to the following conversation. 美M 美W

M Ms. Nelson, the print shop called this morning. They noticed one of the names was spelled wrong in our new manual and it would take another two days to correct it.

W That's not going to work. I want to hand out the manuals on Monday morning. ❶ Could you please call the shop and ask them to deliver our order at least one day earlier?

男 納爾遜女士，今天早上印刷廠打電話來。他們注意到我們新手冊中的一個名稱拼錯誤，需要多花兩天才能修正。

女 那不行，我想在星期一早上發放手冊。可以請你致電印刷廠並且要求他們至少提早一天交貨嗎？

1
What does the woman ask the man to do?
(A) Revise a plan
(B) Copy an invoice
(C) Request a refund
(D) Change a delivery date

解析　SQ是詢問女子對男子拜託、要求的事項。這時女子所說的內容會有提示。手冊印刷需要多花兩天才能完成，女子在電話中要求提早一天，聽到這個部分就能夠選出答案 (D)。須謹記以「Could you ～？/ Would you ～？/ Will you ～？」等開始的句子在拜託或請求時使用。

詞彙　print shop 印刷廠　notice 注意、看到　spell 拼寫　manual 手冊、小冊子　take 花費（時間）　correct 修正　work 成功　hand out 發放　at least 至少　earlier 提早　revise 修改、修正　copy 影印、複本　invoice 發票、單據　request 要求　refund 退款　delivery 交貨

Question 2 refers to the following conversation. 美M 澳W

W Michael, the photocopier keeps jamming and I don't know what's wrong with it. This is the third time it has happened this week.

M Well, that machine is pretty old and we've already had it repaired so many times. ❷ Maybe it's time for us to get a new one.

女 麥克，影印機一直在卡紙，我不知道它有什麼問題。這個星期已經發生第三次了。

男 好吧，那台機器已經很老了，我們已經修了好多次。也許是時候讓我們換一台新的了。

2
What does the man suggest?
(A) Calling the maintenance department
(B) Replacing a machine
(C) Getting a discount
(D) Visiting a nearby store

男子建議什麼？
(A) 致電維修部門
(B) 更換機器
(C) 取得折扣
(D) 參觀附近的商店

解析　SQ是詢問男子提議的內容，因此必須集中在男子說話的部分。影印機不斷出現故障，男子最後說已經到了該換新機器的時候，必須從選項中選擇有replace（取代）的 (B)。意思是提議更換機器。聽到get a new one時，必須從選項中選擇有replace（取代）的 (B)。

詞彙　photocopier 影印機　jam 堵塞；干擾　suggest 建議　maintenance 維修（部門）　replace 取代　discount 折扣　nearby 附近的

Question 3 refers to the following conversation. 美M 美W

M My refrigerator is still in good condition. But I am interested in getting information on new appliances.

W Well, ❸ if you'd like me to do, I could put your name on our e-mail list. That way you'll be informed right away about any future promotions from our store.

男 我的冰箱狀態還很好，但是有興趣獲得有關新家電的訊息。

女 好的，如果您願意，我可以把您的名字列入我們的電子郵件清單中，這樣一來，您將立即獲知我們商店未來的所有促銷活動。

3
What does the woman offer to do for the man?
(A) Add his name to a list
(B) Give him an estimate
(C) Waive a fee
(D) Send a bill by mail

女子提議為男子做什麼？
(A) 將他的名字添加到清單中
(B) 提供估價
(C) 免收費用
(D) 通過郵件發送賬單

解析　題目中的offer具有出於善意的「幫忙～」之意。聽到女性銷售員說如果願意可以幫忙列入電子郵件清單時，必須選擇有add（添加）的 (A)。

詞彙　condition 狀態　appliance 電器用品　put 記入、放置　inform 通知、告知　promotion 促銷　offer 提供、提議　list 清單、列入目錄　add 加上、加進　estimate 估價　waive 免除、放棄

Question 4 refers to the following conversation. 美M 澳W

W Arnold, there's something wrong with the printer. We need to hurry to get those budget proposals printed for ❹ tomorrow's department heads' meeting.

M Don't worry, I'll make sure everything is ready by today.

女 阿諾德，印表機有問題，我們需要趕快為明天的部門主管會議印出這些預算提案。

男 別擔心，今天我會會確保一切準備就緒。

4
When is the department heads' meeting?
(A) Today
(B) Tomorrow
(C) In two days
(D) Next Monday

部門主管會議何時舉行？
(A) 今天
(B) 明天
(C) 兩天內
(D) 下周一

解析　SQ是從各種時間問中區分出正確的會議時間，尤其需注意避免只憑聽得懂的部分，或最後出現的內容來選擇答案。女子提到必須為明天的部門主管會議準備明天的部門主管會議，因此可以得知會議將在明天（Tomorrow）舉行。

詞彙　hurry 趕快　budget 預算　proposal 提案、提案書　department 部門　head 部門主管　in ～之後

Question 5 refers to the following conversation. (美M) (美W)

M Well, Ms. Sanford, we only have an opening at 11:30, or you could come back at 2:00 in the afternoon.

W Hmm. ⑤ I'm meeting a friend at noon for lunch and I don't want to be late for that. I guess I'll come back at 2 o'clock.

男 嗯，桑福德女士，我們只在11:30有個空位，或者您可以在下午2:00回來。

女 嗯，我要在中午和朋友見面吃午餐，我不想遲到。我想我會在2點過來。

5 What does the woman say she will do at noon?

(A) Bring an item for repair
(B) Attend a training session
(C) **Meet with a friend**
(D) Go home for lunch

這位女子說她將在中午做什麼？

(A) 帶一件物品來維修
(B) 參加培訓課程
(C) 與朋友見面
(D) 回家吃午餐

詞彙 opening 空位　come back 回來　item 物件、物品　repair 修理　attend 參加　training session 培訓課程

解析 SQ是詢問女子中午要做的事情，避免選擇含有易懂詞彙lunch 的選項，難度雖高，就愈容易混聽懂的部分來選擇，必須能夠選擇一過選項。聽到女子中午要和朋友見面吃午餐。犯錯。與其開上眼睛集中聆聽內容，更好的做法是閉眼睛先瀏覽一過選項，選出正確機率最高的答案。(C)。

Question 6 refers to the following conversation and coupon. (美M) (澳W)

Coupon	
Buy	Save
1 gallon	10%
2 gallons	15%
3 gallons	20%
4 gallons	30%
Valid in-store-only 5/20 ~ 5/26	

W I'd like to purchase Sparrow Paint for my kitchen remodeling. Do you carry that?

M Absolutely, and luckily for you, we're having a sale on that paint all week. Here's a coupon.

W Oh, great! My kitchen is rather small. I'll probably only need 3 gallons. So, ⑥ 3 gallons of Powder Blue, please.

優惠券	
購買	保存
1加侖	10%
2加侖	15%
3加侖	20%
4加侖	30%
優惠券使用5/20~5/26	

女 我想為我的廚房整修購買麻雀油漆。你有銷售這款嗎？

男 當然有，而且幸運的是，我們整週都在促銷這款油漆。這是優惠券。

女 喔，太棒了。我的廚房比較小。我可能只需要3加侖。所以，請給我3加侖的藍色油漆。

詞彙 purchase 購買　remodeling 改裝、整修　carry 提供、銷售　gallon 加侖、液體單位　valid 有效的　absolutely 當然、絕對地　rather 比較

6 Look at the graphic. Which discount will the woman receive?

(A) 10%
(B) 15%
(C) **20%**
(D) 30%

請看圖表。女子會獲得哪項折扣？

(A) 10%
(B) 15%
(C) **20%**
(D) 30%

解析 SQ是包含新類型的圖表/時刻表資料。先分析題目和已知的圖表附到，正確掌握題目所詢問的內容。聽到廚房專用油漆需要3加侖時，必須能夠選擇出20%的折扣優惠。

Step 5　實戰練習

正解

1. (D)	2. (B)	3. (C)	4. (A)	5. (C)
6. (D)	7. (D)	8. (C)	9. (B)	10. (A)
11. (C)	12. (D)	13. (C)	14. (B)	15. (A)
16. (A)	17. (B)	18. (C)		

Questions 1-3 refer to the following conversation. (美M) (美W)

M I'm leaving the office for about 2 hours. ❶ I have a doctor's appointment, but one of my clients might call about the meeting this afternoon. ❷ Could you give him the message for me?

W Sure, of course. What would you like me to tell him if he calls?

M ❸ Just tell him that I can meet him at 4 o'clock. That should give me enough time to get back.

W Okay, just let me know earlier if there are any changes in your schedule.

男 我要離開辦公室大約2個小時，我和醫生有預約，但是的一位客戶可能會為了關於今天下午致電。你能幫我留言給他嗎？

女 當然，沒問題。如果他的他打電話來，你希望我告訴他什麼？

男 告訴他我可以在4點和他見面。這應該能讓我有足夠的時間回來。

女 好的，如果您的日程安排有任何變化，請提早告訴我。

詞彙 client 客戶　supplies 用品、耗材　lecture 演講

1 Why is the man leaving the office?

(A) To buy some supplies
(B) To eat lunch
(C) To give a lecture

2

(D) To go to an appointment

男子為什麼要離開辦公室？
(A) 買一些用品
(B) 吃午餐
(C) 進行演講
(D) 去赴約

解析 男子的第一句話提到和醫生有約，因此 (D) 是正確答案。眼睛先瀏覽一遍三個題目，在聽力開始時，把注意力放在第一個題目上。

What does the woman agree to do?
(A) Send an e-mail
(B) Pass on a message
(C) Find a document
(D) Work on the weekend

女子同意做什麼事？
(A) 發送電子郵件
(B) 轉達留言
(C) 尋找文件
(D) 周末工作

解析 女子同意做的事情可以從男子敘述的內容中找到，因此需要集中注意力在男子的敘述部分。男子要求女子留言給客戶，女子回答 Sure，因此可以得知女子同意幫忙傳話。選項中的 pass 是 give 的相似詞。

3

What time will the man meet his client?
(A) At 2 p.m.
(B) At 3 p.m.
(C) At 4 p.m.
(D) At 5 p.m.

男子幾點會和他的客戶見面？
(A) 下午2點
(B) 下午3點
(C) 下午4點
(D) 下午5點

解析 SQ是從各個時間點中掌握正確的時間，從4點見面的留言中可以得知 (C) 是正確答案。

Questions 4~6 refer to the following conversation. 澳M 美W

M Hello, ❹ I'm staying in Room 506 and I was woken up this morning by loud hammering sounds outside. I'm on my vacation and was really hoping to be able to relax in my room and I can't do that right now.

W I'm very sorry, Mr. Williams. ❺ There's construction going on in the building next to the hotel until Friday. We already spoke to them about it early this morning.

M Well, I think I'd prefer to switch to a room on a different side of the hotel if you can.

W Certainly, sir. ❻ Let me check if we have any other rooms available for you.

男 你好，我住在506號房，今天早上我被外面傳來的鎚擊聲吵醒了。我正在度假，真的希望能夠在我的房間裡放鬆，而現在我無法實現。

女 威廉斯先生，我真的很抱歉。飯店旁邊的建築工地一直到週五。今天早上我們已經和他們談過這件事了。

男 好吧，如果可以的話，我比較想要換到飯店另一側的房間。

女 當然，先生。讓我查看一下我們是否還有其他房間可以提供給您。

詞彙 hammer 槌子、用槌子敲擊 construction 施工 go on 持續、繼續 prefer 比較喜歡 switch 更換 side 邊、側 available 可利用的、可使用的 architectural 建築的、設計的 malfunctioning 故障的 equipment 設備、器材 incorrect 不正確的、錯誤的 bill 帳單、付款單 shortage 短缺 trained 受過訓練的、熟練的 staff 員工 manager 經理、主管 offer 提供 reduced 減少的

4

Where does the woman most likely work?
(A) At a hotel
(B) At an architectural firm
(C) At a movie theater
(D) At a restaurant

女子最有可能在哪裡工作？
(A) 飯店
(B) 建築公司
(C) 電影院
(D) 餐廳

解析 SQ是詢問女子工作地點，主要提示出現在前半部。第一句男子說自己住在506號房，可以隱約得知是在飯店。當然後面也有出現提示，但從第一句的提示中就能夠選出正確答案。

5

What is causing the problem?
(A) Malfunctioning equipment
(B) An incorrect bill
(C) Noise from construction work
(D) A shortage of trained staff

是什麼導致了這個問題？
(A) 設備故障
(B) 不正確的帳單
(C) 施工噪音
(D) 缺乏訓練有素的員工

解析 詢問問題的問題點也是GQ的主要題型。根據男子的話，飯店隔壁在施工，因此 (C) 是正確答案。

6

What will the woman probably do next?
(A) Speak to her manager
(B) Call the construction company
(C) Offer a reduced price
(D) Check for an available room

女子接下來可能做什麼？
(A) 和她的經理談談
(B) 打電話給建築公司
(C) 提供降價
(D) 查看可用的房間

解析 SQ是詢問女子接下來採取的行動，須謹記造種預測未來行為的問題，提示主要出現在後半部。女子最後就會查看是否有房間，可以得知正確答案是 (D)。

M: Sherlyn, this is Henry. ⑦ I'm going to be about 30 minutes late picking you up for the company banquet. I just heard a traffic report and Oak Street is closed for repaving. So, I'm going to have to take a detour to your house.

W: Thanks for letting me know. Remember! We have to pick up the cake on our way. ⑧ We should contact the bakery right now and see if they can deliver the cake to the banquet hall.

M: Actually, ⑨ Min-Hee from the sales department lives near the bakery. I'll call her to see if she can pick it up for us.

W: That's a relief. We can make it in time for everything then.

詞彙　pick up 接送、抬起　banquet 宴會、派對　traffic report 交通報導　repave (重新)鋪設道路　detour 繞道　contact 連絡、(傳達)　banquet hall 宴會廳　relief 安心　deliver 配送　reject 拒絕　offer 提議　recommend 推薦　revise 修改　public transportation 大眾運輸　request 要求　refund 退款　confirm 確認　business hours 營業時間　submit 提交　registration 登記　form 表格　purchase 購買(物)、購員

7

Why did the man call the woman?
(A) To ask for directions
(B) To order some cake
(C) To reject an offer
(D) To say he will be late

男子為什麼打電話給女子？
(A) 問路
(B) 訂購蛋糕
(C) 拒絕提議
(D) 說他會遲到

解析　詢問男子打電話的目的，必須專注在男子說的話。一開始因為交通問題而晚30分鐘左右到，因此可以得知答案是 (D)。

8

What does the woman recommend?
(A) Revising the event schedule
(B) Taking a public transportation
(C) Arranging for a delivery
(D) Requesting a refund

女子提議什麼？
(A) 修改活動行程
(B) 乘坐大眾交通工具
(C) 安排配送
(D) 要求退款

解析　詢問女子提議的內容，必須專注在女子說的話。女子因為提到而提議致電給麵包店要求配送，因此可以得知答案是 (C)。動詞 arrange 具有「排列」的意思之外，也經常作為「安排」(行程或計畫)」使用。

9

What does the man say he will do?
(A) Confirm the business hours
(B) Ask a coworker to help
(C) Submit the registration form
(D) Pay for the purchase

男子說他會做什麼？
(A) 確認營業時間
(B) 請同事幫忙
(C) 提交登記表
(D) 支付購買費用

解析　詢問男子會做什麼事情，必須專注在男子說的話。對話的最後，男子說他會打電話給住在麵包店附近名叫明熙的同事，請她幫忙拿蛋糕，因此必須從選項中選擇與相關的內容，選項中最適合的是請同事幫忙的 (B)。須註記多益考試中，經常以名字稱呼公司裡的同事，而補叫上司時，加上Mr.、Ms等敬稱。

M: Hi, Lisa. ⑩ I heard you wanted to talk to me about the annual staff party. How is the planning coming along?

W: Well, we decided not to have a live band this year. We're renting some audio equipment to play music with. ⑪ Could you pick up the equipment at the banquet hall this afternoon and bring it to the party?

M: I wish I could help you with that. But ⑫ my son has an important soccer game on Saturday afternoon and I promised to be there. So I won't be available before the party.

W: Okay, then. I'll have to find someone else to help me with the preparation.

詞彙　annual 年度的　come along 進行　rent 租借　audio 音響的　pick up 載、抬起　available 有時間的、有空檔的　preparation 準備　conference 會議　reserve 預約　banquet 宴會　派送　staff 員工　transport 運送　perform 表演　additional 額外的　shift 輪值、換班　supervisor 主管　sporting event 體育活動、運動賽事

10

What type of event are the speakers discussing?
(A) A company party
(B) A business conference
(C) A birthday party
(D) A music festival

說話者在討論什麼類型的活動？
(A) 公司派對
(B) 商務會議
(C) 生日派對
(D) 音樂節

解析　GQ是詢問談話的整體主題，最主要的提示出現在開始的部分。第一句話詢問員工派對的進行情況，因此可以得知答案是 (A)。

11 What does the woman ask the man to do?
(A) Reserve a banquet hall
(B) Hire some new staff
(C) Transport some equipment
(D) Perform with a band

女子要求男子做什麼？
(A) 預訂宴會廳
(B) 僱用一些新員工
(C) 搬運一些設備
(D) 和樂團一起表演

解析：題目是詢問女子要求男子做的內容，因此必須專注在女子說的話。女子詢問男子是否能把設備帶到宴會廳，因此答案是搬運 (transport) 設備的 (C)。尤其在拜託別人時，經常使用 <Could you~>? 或 <Would you~>?，必須記熟。

12 What does the man say he has to do on Saturday afternoon?
(A) Speak at a conference
(B) Work an additional shift
(C) Meet with supervisors
(D) Attend a sporting event

男子說星期六下午要做什麼？
(A) 在會議上發言
(B) 加班
(C) 與主管會面
(D) 參加體育賽事

解析：男子星期六下午要做的事情很可能隨著 Key Word 裡的男子的足球比賽，聽到這個部分的時，應該這個部分的 (D)。隨著難度愈高，將短文詞彙改寫成另一種方式作為答案的情況也愈來愈常見。男子提到星期六下午要做的事情可能是 sporting event 的 game 換成另一種 soccer game。

Questions 13-15 refer to the following conversation. 美M 美W

M It's good to see you, Ms. Parker. Before [13] we start going over your restaurant's finances for this quarter, you mentioned over the phone that you're thinking about expanding your business.

W Yes, I have customers lining up to come into the restaurant, so I'd like to rent some space next to our place. That way, [14] I could expand the dining area and accommodate more people.

M Well, increasing your restaurant seating capacity doesn't always mean more profit. You'll need to hire more staff and there will be an increase in rent and maintenance too.

W That is the reason I need your consultation. [15] Would it be possible for you to create a cost analysis report so that I can get a better idea of whether this expansion would be profitable?

M Of course, Ms. Parker. Let's just go over some details together.

男：很高興見到您，帕克小姐。在我們開始檢查您的餐廳下季財務狀況之前，電話中您曾提過考慮要拓展事業。

女：是的，我們餐廳門庭若市，所以想在旁邊租些空間來增設用餐區容納更多顧客。

男：增加餐廳座位並不一定能帶來更多利潤，您必須雇用更多人力，租金和維修費用也可能增加。

女：這就是我需要您諮詢的原因。您可能做份成本分析表來幫我對於擴張計畫是否有利，有個更好的想法嗎？

男：沒問題，帕克小姐。我們一起從這些細節開始吧。

詞彙：go over 檢視、審視 mention 提及 customer 顧客 line up 排隊 dining area 用餐空間 accommodate 容納、採納 seating capacity 座位數 profit 利潤 hire 雇用 maintenance 維修 consultation 諮詢 cost 費用 analysis 分析 profitable 可獲利的 details 細節 chef 廚師 architect 建築師 real estate 房地產 financial 財務的 advisor 顧問 expand 擴展、擴張 consider 考慮 location 位置、地點 account 帳戶、帳目 construct 建築、建造 contract 合約、契約

13 Who most likely is the man?
(A) A restaurant chef
(B) An architect
(C) A financial advisor
(D) A real estate agent

男子最有可能是誰？
(A) 餐廳廚師
(B) 建築師
(C) 財務顧問
(D) 房地產經紀人

解析：題目是詢問男子是誰，提示在前半部出現。第一句身為餐廳老闆的 GQ 是指提到財務方面的內容，由此可知客業應該是了解財務方面這種工作，更重要的是能夠在最短時間內客觀地的 (C)。比地將4個選項中選出最適合的答案。

14 What is the woman considering doing?
(A) Moving into a new location
(B) Expanding her business
(C) Opening a bank account
(D) Constructing a new house

女子考慮做什麼？
(A) 搬到新的地點
(B) 擴展她的事業
(C) 開設銀行帳戶
(D) 建造新房子

解析：詢問女子考慮什麼。男子在第一句話中提到可能來自於女子的話，也可能是男子要參加擴展事業，而女子也說想要擴展座位數以容納更多客人，因此答案是 (B)。

15 What does the woman ask the man to do?
(A) Prepare a report
(B) Pay for the consultation
(C) Create a design
(D) Sign a contract

女子要求男子做什麼？
(A) 準備一份報告
(B) 支付諮詢的費用
(C) 創造設計
(D) 簽訂合約

解析：題目是詢問女子要求男子的事情，因此必須專注在女子說的話。女子最後詢問是否能提供成本分析報表，因此答案是 (A) Prepare a report。尤其在商業相關主題中，為了更容易解題，必須多熟記各種企業和部門，以及公司內部使用的報告書會議相關詞彙。

Unit 9 眼睛和耳朵完美搭配 問題類型 II

Step 2 眼睛和耳朵完美搭配 Practice

1. (B)　2. (A)　3. (A)　4. (B)

1

Question 1 refers to the following conversation with three speakers. 美M 澳W 澳M

M1 Welcome, Samantha and Nathan. I'm glad you decided to come take a look at the house.

W We really liked the property, but we have some concerns.

M2 We're worried about the cost of major renovation like the roof of the house.

Who most likely are Samantha and Nathan?
(A) Apartment managers
(B) **Potential home buyers**

誰最有可能是薩曼莎和納森？
(A) 公寓經理
(B) **潛在的購屋者**

2

Question 2 refers to the following conversation with three speakers. 美M 澳W 澳M

M1 Frank, is there anything else I need to know?
M2 Just one more thing; Make sure you send e-mails to clients confirming anything you discuss over the phone. They want all communication to be in writing.
W Got it, Frank. Thanks. I'm sure you'll do well at the Beijing Branch, too.

What does Frank advise the woman to do?
(A) **Send a confirmation letter**
(B) Come to the Beijing Branch

法蘭克建議女人做什麼？
(A) **寄一封確認信**
(B) 來北京分公司

16

W Hi, Daniel. It's Amanda from Human Recourses. ⑯ I just wanted to let you know that the computer in meeting room 2B is not working.

M Oh, I'm sorry. I can come right away and take a look at it.

W ⑰ Right now? ⑰ I don't need the computer for that.

M Oh, OK. In that case, I'll come up when you've finished. Is there any other way I can help you with your interviews?

W Thanks, but this time, ⑰ I'm interviewing someone who lives in the area so ⑱ I won't be needing video conference equipment. It'll be nice to talk to someone in person for a change.

Questions 16-18 refer to the following conversation. 美W 澳M

詞彙	
human resources 人事部門	work 運作
right away 立刻	take
a look 查看	in that case 這樣的話
area 地區	change 改變
confirm 確認	schedule 行程
report 報告、報告書	request 要求
personal 個人	immediately 即刻、立刻
disturb 打擾	unusual 異常的、少見的
be held 舉行、導辦	conduct 進行
face-to-face 面對面、當面	

Why is the woman calling the man?
(A) **To report an equipment problem**
(B) To confirm a schedule
(C) To ask about the product price
(D) To request personal information

女子為什麼打電話給男子？
(A) **告知設備問題**
(B) 確認行程
(C) 詢問產品價格
(D) 要求提供個人資訊

解析 女子打電話的原因很可能來自於女子說的話。女子第一句話提到會議室的電腦無法使用，由此可知答案是 (A)。

17

What does the woman mean when she says, "I'm interviewing someone here in five minutes"?
(A) 她立刻需要有人來幫忙。
(B) **她不想被打擾。**
(C) 她很開心會遲到了。
(D) 她需要更多的人來幫她。

She needs the man's help immediately.
(B) **She does not want to be disturbed.**
(C) She is late for the meeting.
(D) She needs more people to help her.

女子說「我五分鐘後要在這裡面試新人」是什麼意思？

解析 看似維修部門人員的男子說要立刻幫忙維修，而女子回答5分鐘後有面試。既然用不到電腦，因此可以稍後處理的內容，表示現在不必要維修，意思是不希望面試受到打擾，新頻型考題新增了推測說話者意圖的題型，是Part 3中難度最高的題型。必須掌握對話中句中的含意，再從選項中選出最高的答案，對初階考生來說，可以把說話者意圖題目自放在最後面來解題，也是不錯的策略。

18

REAL SOLUTION 元老師的

What does the woman say is unusual about the interview?
(A) It will be recorded.
(B) It will be held on a weekend.
(C) I will be conducted face-to-face.
(D) It will last for five hours.

(A) 會被錄音。
(B) 會在周末進行。
(C) **會面對面進行。**
(D) 會持續5小時。

女子說哪裡不尋常？

解析 女子特別指出的部分從女子的話中可以得到的提示。女子最後提到改變一下 (for a change) 造次面試不需透過視訊設備，而是直接談話 (talk to someone in person) 的方式，可以得知答案是直接 (face-to-face) 面試的 (C)。

經常有學生問我「新頻型考題會很難嗎？」無論哪一種考試，那需要熟悉出題類型，訓練自己在有限時間內的解題。新頻型考題也是包括比較簡單的題型 (相較資料型) 和較困難的題型 (推測說話者意圖)，和其他類型一樣，只要仔細看過每一次就沒什麼好擔心的。

男1 法蘭克，還有什麼我需要知道的嗎？

男2 還有一件事，務必向客戶發送電子郵件，確認你們透過電話討論的內容。他們希望所有的溝通都有書面紀錄。

女 知道了，法蘭克。謝謝。我相信你也會在北京分公司做得很好。

3

M I heard you went to the new musical at the Circle Theater. It was for two hours, right?

W Yes, but two hours wasn't enough. I think I'm going again next weekend. Would you like to come with me?

Question 3 refers to the following conversation. 美M 美W

What does the woman mean when she says, "two hours wasn't enough"?

(A) She was late for the show.
(B) She really enjoyed the performance.

當女子說：「兩小時根本不夠」時，她的意思是什麼？

(A) 她表示遲到了。
(B) 她表達這場演出很棒。

男 聽說妳去演藝劇院看了一場兩個小時的新音樂劇，是嗎？

女 是啊，但兩小時根本不夠。我打算下週末再去一次，你想一起來嗎？

4

M The company director increased our marketing department's budget by $300,000.

W That's a big increase from last year. Do you know how that money will be used? We could definitely use some new office equipment.

Question 4 refers to the following conversation. 美W 澳M

Why does the man say, "That's a big increase from last year?"

(A) To deny a requested budget change
(B) To indicate that some news is good

男子為什麼說：「這比去年大幅增加了許多」？

(A) 拒絕變更預算的要求
(B) 表示某個好消息

男 公司主管增加了我們行銷部三十萬的預算。

女 這比去年大幅增加了許多。你知道這筆款項會如何運用嗎？我們絕對能買些新的辦公室設備。

正解

1. (C)　　2. (B)　　3. (A)　　4. (C)

1

Look at the graphic. How much has the woman agreed to pay per month?

(A) $50
(B) $40
(C) $30
(D) $20

Question 1 refers to the following conversation and chart. 澳M

M We offer the best prices in this area. As you can see in this chart, the longer your contract is, the lower the monthly cost becomes. But there'll be some extra fee, if you can cancel the contract before it ends.

W Well, I'm going to transfer overseas in about a year, so I don't want the two-year plan. But I do want the lowest price possible. ① I guess the one-year plan would be the best.

Length of Contract	Price per Month
3 months	$50
6 months	$40
1 year	$30
2 years	$20

合約期限	每月價格
3個月	50美元
6個月	40美元
1年	30美元
2年	20美元

男 我們在這區提供最好的價格，如表格所見，合約簽得越久，月費就越低。但是在合約終止前取消的話，會收取額外費用。

女 我大概一年後會被調職到國外，所以不需要兩年方案，但是越便宜越好，我想一年方案最佳。

請看表格，女方每月同意支付多少錢？
(A) 50美元
(B) 40美元
(C) 30美元
(D) 20美元

解析 表格/視學資料相關題目的題型最常考的順序是 (1) 先閱讀題目 (2) 瀏覽圖表。聽到女子說一年方案最佳，就能選擇一年方案元價格。

(3) 其中哪些部分會從對話中出現，能夠幫助解題

2

M Good point. ② We could put more resources into our second most effective recruiting method. Actually, more than a quarter of our employees are recruited that way.

W In the past, we've been mostly recruiting new employees from university career fairs, but I'd like to do something different this time. It's just cost too much to travel to different universities.

Question 2 refers to the following conversation and pie chart. 美W

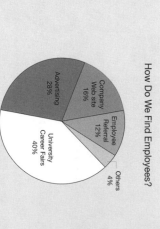

How Do We Find Employees?

- University Career Fairs 40%
- Advertising 28%
- Company Web site 16%
- Employee Referral 12%
- Others 4%

詞彙　offer 提供　chart 表格、圖表　extra 額外的　transfer 調職、遷移

length 時間長度、距離長度　contract 合約、契約　per 每～

我們如何找到員工?

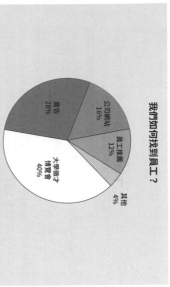

- 大學徵才博覽會 40%
- 廣告 28%
- 公司網站 16%
- 員工推薦 12%
- 其他 4%

女 在過去,我們大多是從大學徵才博覽會招募新員工,但這次我試試別的方式。前往不同的大學花費太多。

男 好點子。我們超過四分之一的員工都是透過這種方式招聘的。

女 實際上,我們最多是從大學徵才博覽會招募新員工,但這次我試試別的方法。前往不同的大學花費太多。

Question 3 refers to the following conversation and map. 美M

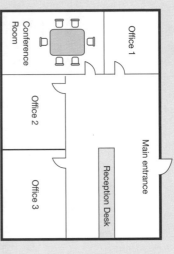

- Office 1
- Conference Room
- Main entrance
- Office 2
- Office 3
- Reception Desk

M Good morning. I'm here to deliver some furniture to Paula Jenkins. I have a desk and a chair. Where do you want me to put them?

W Oh, yes. You can put them right in her office. ③ It's the first door by the entrance next to the conference room.

3 Look at the graphic. Which room will the man most likely go to?

(A) **Office 1**
(B) Office 2
(C) Office 3
(D) Conference room

請看圖型,這個男人最有可能去哪個房間?

(A) 辦公室 1
(B) 辦公室 2
(C) 辦公室 3
(D) 會議室

解析 地圖(圖形)形式的題目,要精測對話會出現什麼內容,是比較棘手的題型。首先讀完題目,從選項中雖然房號和圖形結構,平面圖中除了 office 之外,還有 Main Entrance, Reception Desk, Conference Room。女子說放在入口處旁的第一道門的房間,就在會議室旁,而靠近會議室共有兩個辦公室,離入口最近的房間是 Office 1。一開始先看地圖的話,可能會不清楚重點是什麼,但利用所有單字和地圖做比對的方法,就能找到答案。

Question 4 refers to the following conversation and chart. 美W

Battery Power Level Display

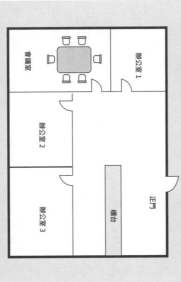

75%   50%   25%   0%

W As a lab technician, you need to monitor the battery closely; always check the display screen. If the power is too low, we won't know the exact temperature of the equipment.

M When do I change the battery?

W ④ Replace the batteries when the power reaches 25%. We don't want to replace them any earlier than we have to, nor can we wait until they run out.

---

2 Look at the graphic. Which method does the man suggest using?

(A) University career fairs
(B) **Advertising**
(C) Company Web site
(D) Employee referrals

請看圖形,男子建議使用哪種方法?

(A) 大學徵才博覽會
(B) **廣告**
(C) 公司網頁
(D) 員工推薦

男子所說的並非過去最常使用的職業博覽會 (career fair),而是所占比例居次的廣告 (Advertising)。從圖表來看,第2種最有效的方式是所占比例居次的廣告,圖表題目不像數學一樣有複雜的數值和計算,因此相對來說比較容易選擇答案。

電池電量等級顯示

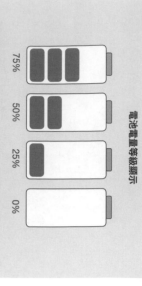

75%　50%　25%　0%

女 身為實驗室技術員，要仔細監控電池情形，一定要檢查顯示螢幕；假使電力過低，便無法得知儀器運作的溫度。
男 電池何時需要更換？
女 電池電力到25%時需更換，不可在不必要時提早或是等到電力耗盡時才進行更換。

詞彙 monitor 監控、監視　temperature 溫度　equipment 器材、設備　replace 更換　reach 到達、拿取　run out 用完、耗盡　exact 準確的

4. Look at the graphic. According to the woman, how many bars will be displayed when the battery should be replaced?
(A) Three bars
(B) Two bars
(C) One bar
(D) Zero bars

請看圖形。根據女子的說法，當更換電池時會顯示多少電量條？
(A) 3條
(B) 2條
(C) 1條
(D) 零條

解析 先瀏覽題目和選項，同時將電量到的內容和75%, 50%, 25%, 0% 做比對。聽到電量到了25%時必須更換，可以得知25%的電量會顯示1條。

Step 3 | 3-2 | 基本掌握（說話者意圖題目的集中 Practice）P75

正解
1. (B)　　2. (A)　　3. (D)　　4. (A)

Question 1 refers to the following conversation. (澳M)(美W)

M May I help you with anything, ma'am?
W Yes, ❶ I want to know how much this pair will cost. These shoes look great. But I can't find the price tag.

男 您需要些什麼嗎？女士？
女 是的，我想知道這雙要多少錢，這雙看起來不錯，但我找不到價格標籤。

詞彙 cost 花（費用）　price tag 價格標籤　convince 說服　make a purchase 購買　compliment 讚美　coworker 同事　gift wrapping 禮品包裝

1. Why does the woman say, "These shoes look great"?
(A) To convince her friend to buy shoes
(B) To show interest in making a purchase
(C) To compliment her coworker
(D) To ask for gift wrapping

女子為什麼說「這雙鞋看起來很棒」？
(A) 說服她的朋友買鞋
(B) 表示有興趣購買
(C) 讚美她的同事
(D) 要求禮品包裝

解析 詢問說話者意圖的題型選項通常比較線長，必須集中於聽取的內容（題目）才是比較線手的題型，需要多進行眼睛（眼睛瀏覽的同時選出選合的答案）的練習。且朵（聽力）搭配。看到某雙鞋子而前問價格，這句話的語意是女子有意購買。（眼睛指出的部分之外，也需要理解前後內容才能解題。如果能夠了解這是鞋店中客人和店員對話的內容，解題相對來說就會更容易一些。）

Question 2 refers to the following conversation. (美M)(美W)

M Hi, Fatima, sorry to interrupt, but I've got a management meeting tomorrow about the next quarter's expenses and ❷ I'm waiting for the department budget proposal. Do you want me to print out a copy for you or send it electronically?
W Oh, ❷ I've just finished it. Do you want me to print it out or send it electronically?

男 妳好，法蒂瑪，抱歉打擾，我明天要開管理會議，有關於下個季度的支出費用，但我還在等部門預算提案。你要我印出紙本給你，還是寄電子郵件給你呢？
女 喔，我剛剛完成，你要我印出紙本給你，還是寄電子郵件給你呢？

詞彙 interrupt 打擾　management 管理　quarter 季度　expense 花費　department 部門　budget 預算　proposal 提案、提議　print out 印出　electronically 電子方式、透過電腦　request 要求　document 文件　ask for 要求　deadline 期限　extension 延期　inform 通知　make a decision 決定　at the moment 此刻、目前

2. Why does the man say, "I'm waiting for the department budget proposal"?
(A) To request a document from the woman
(B) To ask for a deadline extension
(C) To inform the woman about a scheduling change
(D) To explain why he cannot make a decision at the moment

為什麼男子說「我還在等部門預算提案」？
(A) 向女子索取文件
(B) 要求延長期限
(C) 通知女子有關排程變更
(D) 解釋為什麼他不能做出決定

解析 當男子說自己正在等待會議文件時，女子回答剛剛已經完成，從這裡可以得知男子會議文件的相關詞彙而提案是(B)，或者即使沒有提到決定的內容，卻選擇含有explain的(D)。

Question 3 refers to the following conversation. 澳M 美W

M I think we should hire a professional painting company to come in for the paint job of apartment B5. We should do that before we show it to potential tenants.

W We considered that before, but we thought it would be too expensive.

M Yes, but that was quite a while ago. ❸ We manage more apartments now and we don't have time to do it ourselves.

男 我想我們應該要僱用專業的油漆公司來粉刷B5公寓，而且要在承租房客看到之前做這件事。

女 我們之前考慮過了，但覺得太貴。

男 是沒錯，但那也好一陣子了，我們現在管理更多間的公寓，而且也沒時間自己粉刷。

3 What does the man imply when he says, "but that was quite a while ago"?

(A) A deadline is approaching.
(B) New staff must be trained.
(C) A procedure has been improved.
(D) **A decision should be reconsidered.**

詞彙 hire 僱用 professional 專業的 potential 潛在的、可能的 tenant 房客 consider 考慮 expensive 昂貴的 manage 管理 deadline 期限 procedure 程序 improve 改善、增進 decision 決定 reconsider 重新考慮

解析 當男子說「但那也好一陣子了」時，意思是什麼？

(A) 截止日期快到了。
(B) 新員工必須受培訓。
(C) 程序已獲得改善。
(D) 應該重新考慮決定。

高難度意圖題型，聽力中必須理解的部分很多，題目的詞彙經常較難，造成此題難度較高。這是公寓管理者之間的對話，對於男子的提議，女子說已經考慮過（considered）了，但男子回答那是很久以前的事，因此題目中所引用的男子的話，意思是「重新考慮看看」，所以正確答案是 (D)。

Question 4 refers to the following conversation. 美M 美W

M The survey results showed that customers like the quality of our products, but thought the product prices are too high. Do you think we can decrease the product prices about 10 to 15 percent by the end of this quarter?

W That would require significant revisions to our pricing strategy! We need to redo the cost and profitability analysis from the first. ❹ We simply cannot take every suggestion customers make.

男 調查結果顯示客戶很滿意我們產品的品質，但認為價格太高。你認為本季結束前，產品價格能夠降低10%到15%嗎？

女 這樣我們的訂價策略需要大幅的修訂，必須先重做成本及獲利分析，我們無法採納顧客的每一項建議。

4 What does the woman imply when she says, "That would require significant revisions to our pricing strategy"?

(A) She doubts a change will be implemented.
(B) She thinks the suppliers should be replaced.
(C) She believes some data are incorrect.
(D) **She needs more time to make a decision.**

詞彙 survey 問卷調查 quality 品質 decrease 減少、降低 quarter 季 require 需要 significant 重大的、重要的 revision 修正、修訂 price 定價、價格 strategy 策略 redo 重做 profitability 獲利性 analysis 分析 simply 簡單地、只是 suggestion 建議 doubt 懷疑 implement 執行、實行 supplier 供應商 replace 更換 incorrect 錯誤的、不正確的 make a decision 決定

解析 當女子說「這樣我們的訂價策略需要大幅的修訂」時，暗指什麼？

(A) 她懷疑會實行改變。
(B) 她認為應該更換供應商。
(C) 她認為有些數據不正確。
(D) 她需要更多時間來做出決定。

難度愈高，愈需要具備公司與職場相關的常識。根據調查結果，儘管需要大幅降低公司的價格，而訊息是否能降低售價時，回答是「將需要大幅修改公司的價格策略」，意思是認為有難度，因此答案是「doubt（懷疑）是，這樣可能很低（時使用的動詞），這樣快速解析選項中的長句，必須具備足夠的閱讀理解能力。

Step 4 實戰練習

正解

1. (B)	2. (C)	3. (B)	4. (C)	5. (D)
6. (B)	7. (C)	8. (D)	9. (A)	10. (C)
11. (B)	12. (A)	13. (D)	14. (B)	15. (A)
16. (B)	17. (C)	18. (C)		

Questions 1-3 refer to the following conversation. 澳M 美W

M Hi, Amanda! How are you?

W Hello, Mark. I'm fine. I've been meaning to talk to you. ❶ I'm saving to buy a new car and I heard you just got one.

M Yeah, I'm really excited. It's always hard for me to save up for big purchases, but ❷ this time I tried an online budgeting program.

W Did it help you a lot?

M Sure it did. ❷ I used the one called easybudget.com. If you try to save, you should check it out too.

W ❸ How much does it cost? I'm not sure about spending money to save money, you know.

M Well, you get a month free. If you like then it's only going to cost you $30 for the whole year.

W That's not bad. I'll have a look at it. Thanks, Mark.

男 嗨，亞曼達！妳好嗎？

女 哈囉，馬克。我很好，我正想跟你說，我在存錢買新車，聽說你才剛買一台。

男 是喔，我超興奮的。對我來說存錢買高價品就是很困難，但這次我試了一個線上編預算程式。

女 幫助你很大嗎？

男 當然。我用了一個叫做easybudget.com的程式。如果你想存錢，應該也去試試看。

女 要花多少錢？你知道的，我不太確定要花錢去存錢。

男 這個嘛，你可以免費試用一個月，如果你喜歡，一整年只花你30美元。

女 還不錯，我會去看看的。謝謝，馬克。

詞彙 mean 想要、打算 excited 興奮的 budget 編預算、預算 check out 核對、檢查 spend 花費 whole 全部的 purchase 購買、購買品 recommend 推薦 apply for 申請 loan 借貸 financial planner 財務規劃師 work extra hours 加班 be concerned about 關心～、擔心～ quality 品質 security 安全 terms 條款 contract 合約

1 Why does the woman want to save money?
(A) To take classes
(B) To purchase a car
(C) To start her business.
(D) To move into a new apartment

解析　女子存錢的原因很可能來自於她即將說的話。女子第一句話表示自己正在存錢購買新車,因此可以得知答案是 (B)。

2 What does the man recommend?
(A) Applying for a loan
(B) Talking to a financial planner
(C) Using an online program
(D) Working extra hours

解析　男子推薦的事情應該來自於男子即將說的話。男子表示自己使用線上程式,提議對方也使用看看。因此可以得知答案是 (C)。注意避免誤選也許該加班的 (D)。如果不是此於常識或邏輯的問題,必須根據對話內容來選擇答案。

3 What is the woman concerned about?
(A) The quality of a program
(B) The cost of a program
(C) The security of a Web site
(D) The term of a contract

解析　女子擔心的事情很可能來自於她即將說的話。聽到男子的推薦之後,女子說不確定是否應該花錢,從這部分可以得知她對於線上程式的費用有些擔心,因此答案是 (B)。

Questions 4-6 refer to the following conversation. 美W 美M

W ④ Welcome to Dunmore Technology. How may I help you?

M ⑤ I'm with Quick-pro Express Shipping and I have a package for Ms. Paula Dunmore. Is she available to sign this form?

W I can sign it for her if that's all right with you.

M Sorry, this package must be signed for by Ms. Dunmore herself.

W Well, Ms. Dunmore is in a meeting with clients right now.

M Okay, I'll stop by later then.

詞彙　shipping 運輸　package 包裹　sign 簽名、標誌　stop by 順道拜訪、路過　operator 接線員　receptionist 接待員　representative 代表、代理人　apply for 申請　equipment 設備　delivery 運送

4 Who most likely is the woman?
(A) A telephone operator
(B) A post office clerk
(C) An office receptionist
(D) A sales representative

解析　GQ是詢問女子是誰,主要在聽男子的前面部分會出現職業提示,需要在聽第一句話之後,就能夠選擇答案。第一句話女子在公司接待來訪者 (visitor),可以得知是專門接聽電話的接待員 (receptionist)。整體來說,雖然出現送貨的內容,但女子和運輸主題沒有特別關係,而是在櫃檯工作的職員。

5 Why is the man visiting the office?
(A) To attend a meeting
(B) To apply for a job
(C) To repair some equipment
(D) To make a delivery

為什麼男子來訪公室？
(A) 參加會議
(B) 申請職位
(C) 修理一些設備
(D) 送貨

解析　男子來訪公司的原因很有可能來自於他即將說的話,帶來一個包裹,從這部分可以得知答案是 (D)。

6 What does the woman imply when she says, "Ms. Dunmore is in a meeting with clients right now"?
(A) Ms. Dunmore has an important document.
(B) Ms. Dunmore is not available.
(C) A meeting room cannot be used.
(D) The meeting is taking longer than usual.

解析　就話者意圖題型必須理解引用句內的意思。「目前正在開會中」的意思,也就是現在很忙無法收貨,因此正確答案是 (B)。注意避免因為 meeting 詞彙而誤選 (C) 或 (D)。

W1 Thanks for interviewing on short notice, Mr. Shin. I'm Vicky Mendoza, Head of Human Resources at Channel 5.

W2 And I'm Michelle Lawrence. ❼ I produce the weekday sports program.

M Nice to meet you both.

W2 We've looked at your résumé, and you seem to be well qualified for the camera operator position. But ❽ we're curious about your availability since our film crews often go out on assignments with little warning.

M I understand that the job requires that I should be available on short notice. That's no problem.

W1 Great. So, ❾ why don't we have a look at some of your works? You said you brought a video. Can you show us?

M ❾ Sure, the file is right here on my laptop.

7 Where do the interviewers most likely work?
(A) At a factory
(B) At an electronics store
(C) At a TV station
(D) At a movie theater

8 What requirement do the speakers discuss?
(A) Wearing safety gear
(B) Owning proper equipment
(C) Having management experience
(D) Having a flexible schedule

9 What does the man agree to do next?
(A) Show a video
(B) Provide references
(C) Tour a facility
(D) Sign an employment contract

詞彙 on short notice 突然地　human resources 人事、人力資源部　produce 製作　résumé 履歷表　qualified 有資格的　operator 操作者、電話接線員　position 位置、職位　curious 好奇的　availability 可用度、可能性　work 工作事情、作品　assignment 任務、工作　warning 警告　crew 人員、職員　interviewer 面試官　electronics 電子設備　station 電視台　safety gear 安全裝置　own 擁有　proper 適當的　management 管理　experience 經驗　flexible 靈活的、彈性的　reference 能力證明、參考　tour 觀摩　facility 設施　sign 簽名

解析 GQ是詢問面談官工作的地點，提示出現在前半部。題目中出現複數人稱 (interviewers)，提示可以推測是3人對話。但不需要因為GQ是3人，對話感到慌張，因為GQ來自於前半部，但不需於題目中的特定部分。女子的第一句介紹自己是前五頻道人力資源部的主任，而第二名女子負責製作節目，從這部分可以得知面試官是在電視台工作。

解析 就話者們提到的要求是什麼？第二名女子詢問是否能夠在不事先通知的情況下臨時出外景，因此答案是 (D)。面試情況中經常出現的詞彙之一是 requirements/qualifications (要求/資格)。

解析 男子同意做的事情，從正面回應其中一名女子的問題中可以推測出來。女子詢問是否有作品集，男子立即回應「當然 (Sure.)」，因此正確答案是 (A)。

M Diana, ⑪ I'm ready to add the changes to the employee directory on our company Web site. Could you check it over for mistakes before I upload them?

W Hmm. It looks okay so far. But... oh, wait. There's a problem here. ⑪ You've misspelled the name of the president. Actually, his name should only have one L at the end.

M Oh, I can't believe I didn't see that earlier. Thank you for catching it. It would have been disastrous.

W It's easy to miss. The important thing is that we have the correct information for visitors to our Web site.

10 What are the speakers mainly talking about?
(A) Presenting at a conference
(B) Creating product brochures
(C) Updating a company Web site
(D) Ordering some stationery

詞彙 directory 目錄、通訊錄　misspell 拼錯　at the end 最後　disastrous 災難性的、慘重的　visitor 訪客　present 發表　brochure 指引小冊　update 更新　stationery 文具　notice 注意到　identification badge 識別證　spell 拼寫　incorrectly 不正確地　express 表示　understanding 理解　clarify 澄清、闡明　job description 職位描述　warm 警告

解析 GQ是詢問主題，主要提示出現在前半部。男子第一句話打算上傳公司職員的通訊錄，請求同事幫忙檢查，從這部分可以得知談話內容是有關於更新網站資訊，因此答案是 (C)。

11 What problem does the woman notice?
(A) A deadline has been missed.
(B) An identification badge is not working.
(C) A phone number is missing.
(D) A name is spelled incorrectly.

女子注意到了什麼問題?
(A) 截止日期已過。
(B) 識別證沒有啟動。
(C) 漏填電話號碼。
(D) 名字拼寫錯誤。

解析 女子注意到部分有可能來自於女子即將說的話。女子指出董事長的名字拼寫錯誤,因此答案是 (D)。

12 Why does the woman say, "It's easy to miss"?
(A) To express her understanding
(B) To clarify the job description
(C) To explain a procedure
(D) To warn about the delay

女子為什麼說「這很容易忽略」?
(A) 表達她的理解
(B) 闡明職位描述
(C) 解釋程序
(D) 警告延遲

解析 詢問說話者意圖的題目,男子說「我真不敢相信」必須掌握引用句前後的語意。男子說「我真不敢相信」是指難免會犯錯的意思,這用句前後呼應「這很容易忽略」是指自己的錯誤的意思,以示安慰。選項當中最適合的是能夠理解男子的 (A)。

Questions 13-15 refer to the following conversation and chart.
(澳M)(美W)

M Hi, I've never been to your store before. Can you recommend something for me?
W Sure, what kind of tea do you usually drink?
M I've only had black tea. But I've read an article about the health benefits of green tea, and I'd like to try some.
W Green tea is healthy. We have several kinds, but I'd recommend a simple one to begin with. We're actually having a promotion on our basic green tea. If you buy some, you'll get a free ceramic teapot.
M That's great. I'd like to buy some. Is it prepared the same way as black tea?
W It doesn't have to stay as long in hot water. Here's a guide for you. This will help you.

Tea Type	Time in Hot Water
Green	2 minutes
Peppermint	3 minutes
Black	4 minutes
Herbal	6 minutes

男 妳好,我從來沒來過這家店。可以幫我推薦嗎?
女 當然好,您平常喝什麼樣的茶呢?
男 我只喝紅茶,但是我看了綠茶對身體有益的相關報導,所以想試試看。
女 綠茶很健康。我們有很多種類。我想先從簡單的開始推薦。事實上我們的基本款綠茶有促銷活動。購買綠茶贈送免費的陶瓷茶壺。
男 太棒了。那麼我想買些綠茶。沖泡方法跟紅茶一樣嗎?
女 不用在熱水裡浸泡太久。這個說明給您,會有幫助的。

茶的種類	熱水浸泡時間
綠茶	2分
薄荷茶	3分
紅茶	4分
草藥茶	6分

13 Why does the man want to try a new tea?
(A) It has better flavor.
(B) It is getting popular these days.
(C) It is the only kind sold in this store.
(D) It has health benefits.

男子為什麼想嘗試新茶?
(A) 味道更好。
(B) 最近愈來愈受歡迎。
(C) 它是這家店唯一出售的種類。
(D) 對健康有益。

解析 男子嘗試新茶的原因很有可能來自於他即將說的話。男子第二句提到自己讀到綠茶對身體有益的報導,因此想要嘗試看看,由此可知正確答案是 (D)。

14 What will the man receive with his purchase?
(A) An extra tea sample
(B) A free tea pot
(C) A gift certificate
(D) A parking validation

男子購買時會得到什麼?
(A) 額外的茶試用包
(B) 免費的茶壺
(C) 禮券
(D) 停車許可

解析 男子會得到的物品很可能來自於女子即將說的話。女子提到有綠茶促銷活動,購買綠茶可以得到陶瓷茶壺,因此正確答案是 (B)。

15 Look at the graphic. How long should the man leave the tea in hot water?
(A) 2 minutes
(B) 3 minutes
(C) 4 minutes
(D) 6 minutes

請看表格。男子應該將綠茶放在熱水中多久?
(A) 2分鐘
(B) 3分鐘
(C) 4分鐘
(D) 5分鐘

解析 表格/時間點的資料題型會在一開始就出現圖表,但只需在女子相關題目時才參考。選項中出現和時間有關的內容,可以發現提到茶的種類,對話中提到紅茶和綠茶,而男子想喝的是綠茶,因此必須從表格中找出綠茶的浸泡時間,因此正確答案是 (A)。

詞彙 recommend 推薦　article 報導　benefit 好處、利益　healthy 健康的　ceramic 陶瓷的　flavor 味道、香氣　popular 受歡迎的　these days 最近　extra 額外的　gift certificate 禮券　validation 批准、許可

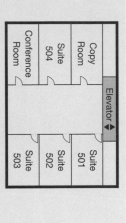

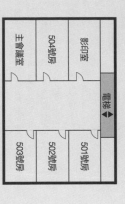

W Hi, there. I'm here to see Mr. Campbell in the IT department for an important meeting.

M OK, please fill in the sign-in sheet and ⑯ I'll give you a visitor's ID badge, which you should wear while on the premises.

W Sure. Also, ⑰ would you mind directing me to Mr. Campbell's office? I forgot to ask where his office is when I scheduled the meeting.

M He's on the 5th floor. ⑱ Go straight following the corridor after you get off the elevator and you should see the sign for his office. It's right across from the main conference room. You should have no trouble finding it.

16 What does the man ask the woman to do?
(A) Use a different entrance
(B) Wear an ID badge
(C) Turn off her cell phone
(D) Come back at a later time

解析 男子要求女子做什麼？男子第一句話提到會提供防客識別證，並要求在大樓內時都要配戴。因此正確答案是 (B)。

17 What does the woman request?
(A) A signature for a delivery
(B) A different appointment time
(C) Directions to an office
(D) Advice about parking

解析 詢問女子要求的事項也是由女子提出。女子第二句就提到當時在安排會議時，沒有問及貝爾先生的辦公室位置，請求提供前往的方法。因此正確答案是 (C)。

18 Look at the graphic. Which office does the woman need to visit?
(A) Suite 501
(B) Suite 502
(C) Suite 503
(D) Suite 504

解析 表格/圖片相關題型在看題目時，也需要同時瀏覽一遍圖表，以預測會出現什麼樣的問題。題目是詢問女子應該前往的會議室，先確認平面圖中elevator, copy room, conference

W 您好，我和資訊科技部門的次貝爾先生有一場重要會議。

M 請填寫這份的訪客登記表，這是您的來賓證，並請您在大樓內時隨身攜帶。

W 當然，可以麻煩你告訴我次貝爾先生的辦公室在哪裡嗎？之前安排會議時我忘記問他。

M 他在五樓，出電梯後沿著走廊直走，就會看到他辦公室的牌子，就在主會議室對面，很容易可以找到。

詞彙 sign-in sheet 登記表　premises 場地、樓內　direct 指導、指路
　　　schedule 行程　straight 直接、直行　corridor 走道、走廊　get
　　　off 下來　sign 標誌、標示　copy room 影印室　suite 房間、套房

元老師的
REAL SOLUTION

圖表/視覺資料的題型是只要「正確掌握題目」，就能頓時豁然開朗。並非因為圖表出現在一開始，就一定和三個題目都有關聯。先讀完一遍題目之後，以「Look at the graphic」為開端的題目才需要參考圖表資料。

① 讀完題目，掌握Key Word。
② 尋找各選項中的相關資訊並在圖表中，預想需填入何種資訊才能解題，將聽時最後會聽到的4個選項中其中一個內容。
③ 與音檔內容一致的選項就是答案。

entrance 出入口　at a later time 晚一點　request 要求　signature 簽名　delivery 送貨　appointment 約定　directions 指示、方向　advice 建議

room 等位置之後，再聆聽內容。玖目貝爾先生的辦公室是從電梯出來之後，往前直走在主會議室的對面，因此答案是 (C) 503 號房。

Step 2 眼鏡和耳朵完美搭配 Practice P80

正解
1. (B)   2. (A)   3. (B)   4. (B)

1
Who most likely is the man?
(A) An auto mechanic   (B) A computer technician

男子最有可能是誰？
(A) 汽車修理人員   (B) 電腦技術員

Question 1 refers to the following conversation. 美W 澳M

W Hi, I'm calling to get some assistance with my laptop. If I use it for more than an hour, the body of the machine gets really hot.

M Hmm... Sounds like you have a problem with your battery. Is it plugged in all the time?

女 嗨，我打電話來是因為我的筆電需要協助。如果使用超過一小時，主機會變得很燙。

男 嗯⋯聽起來是電池有問題，筆電的插頭是一直插著嗎？

2
What are the speakers discussing?
(A) A doctor's prescription   (B) A product price
說話者在討論什麼？
(A) 醫生的處方   (B) 產品的價格

Question 2 refers to the following conversation. 美W 美M

W Hi, my doctor sent a prescription for some medicine to this pharmacy about an hour ago, and I was hoping the order might be ready for me to pick up.

M I'll just check on that for you. Can I have your name please?

女 你好，我的醫生大約一小時前幫我開了處方藥到這間藥局，我想說應該準備好讓我可以領藥了。

男 我幫妳看看，請問大名是？

3
According to the man, what service is available?
(A) Free installation   (B) Home delivery

根據男子的說法，有哪些服務？
(A) 免費安裝   (B) 送貨到府

Question 3 refers to the following conversation. 美W 美M

W I'd like to buy these pots and pans, but I came here by bus so I won't be able to carry them home.

M That's no problem. We can ship them to your house free of charge if you want.

女 我想買這些鍋具，但搭公車來沒辦法全部帶回家。

男 這不成問題，我們可以免運費送貨到府。

4
What does the woman want to do?
(A) Return to the warehouse
(B) Exchange of a product

女子想做什麼？
(A) 返回倉庫
(B) 交換產品

Question 4 refers to the following conversation. 美M 美W

M There's a setting that allows you to save power. That way, your battery can last longer.

W Yes, I know the power saving setting. But it still isn't long enough. I'd like to return this phone, and get a different model with a longer battery hour.

男 這個設定能讓你節省電力，這樣一來，電池續航力會比較持久。

女 是的，我知道這個省電設定，但時間不夠長。我想退這支手機，然後換電池續航力較高的不同機型。

Step 3 基本掌握 P81

正解
1. (A)   2. (B)   3. (B)   4. (B)   5. (B)
6. (A)   7. (A)   8. (B)   9. (A)   10. (B)
11. (A)   12. (B)

Questions 1-3 refer to the following conversation. 美W 美M

W Hello, ❶ I bought a mobile phone from this store recently, but I am having a problem with it. When I receive or make a call, the screen goes blank. It doesn't show anything.

M I'm sorry to hear that, ma'am. If you bought the phone within the past six months, the cost of any necessary repairs or replacements will be covered by your warranty. ❷ Do you have your sales receipt with you?

W Yes, I have the receipt right here.

M Okay, great. Then, ❸ why don't you speak to one of our technicians at the service counter in the back of the store? They'll be happy to help you.

女 你好，我最近在這家店買了手機，但是有個問題。我撥打或接電話時，螢幕一片空白，什麼都沒有。

男 很抱歉，女士。如果您是在近六個月內購買，任何必要的修理費用或更換均涵蓋於保固範圍內。請問有帶銷售收據嗎？

女 有的，收據在此。

男 好，那就請您到商店後方的服務台，詢問任一位技術人員，他們會樂意協助您。

1
What is the conversation mainly about?
(A) A defective product
(B) An expired warranty
該對話主要是關於什麼？
(A) 有缺陷的產品
(B) 過保證期

解析 GQ是詢問主題，大多是將前半部的提示加以重新詮釋。從女子的第一句話可以得知購買近期買的手機有問題，因此答案是defective 有缺陷的、expired 過期的。並非主題，而是有關a refund 進取退款。

詞彙 recently 最近   blank 空白   replacement 替換   cover 包含、掩蓋   technician 技術人員   get 取得
warranty 保證書   sales receipt 銷售收據   defective 有缺陷的、不良的   expired 過期的   manual 說明書

2

What does the man ask the woman to give?

(A) A manual
(B) A sales receipt

男子要求女子提供什麼？

(A) 說明書
(B) 購買收據

解析 男子向女子要求的東西來自於男子的話。男子第一句話詢問女子是否有收據，因此正確答案是 (B)。

3

What does the man suggest the woman do?

(A) Get a refund
(B) Speak to a technician

男子建議女子做什麼？

(A) 獲取退款
(B) 與技術人員交談

解析 男子提議的部分也來自於男子的話。男子最後告訴女子前往服務台詢問技術人員，因此正確答案是 (B)。如果商品有瑕疵，通常認為要申請退款，但必須根據提及的內容和情境來選擇答案。

Questions 4-6 refer to the following conversation. 澳M 美W

M Hi, Ms. Yoshida. Thank you for stopping by the apartment. I can probably walk to work if I want.

W Well, I'm glad you have something you like. As you know, the current residents are moving out on Sunday afternoon. **⑥** You're welcome to pick up the keys anytime on Monday.

M Great. I'll leave work a little earlier that day so I can get the keys. And I'll start moving in on Tuesday morning.

M Hi, Ms. Yoshida. Thank you for stopping by the apartment. **④** Here is your copy of the rental contract for your new apartment. You can move in next Tuesday.

W OK, thanks. I think this apartment is perfect for me. **⑤** It's much closer to the bank I work at than my old apartment. I can probably walk to work if I want.

男好，吉田小姐。謝謝妳願意過來我們辦公室。這是新公寓租約的影本。妳下週二就可以搬進去。

女好的，謝謝。這間公寓很完美，跟我舊公寓相比，去銀行上班比較近。我很想要的話，可能還可以走路上班。

男我知道妳喜歡。妳知道的，目前的住戶週日下午會搬走，周一隨時歡迎妳來拿鑰匙。

女太好了。我那天會提早下班來拿鑰匙，星期二早上開始搬進去。

4

Who most likely is the man?

(A) A tenant
(B) A realtor

男子最有可能是誰？

(A) 房客
(B) 房屋仲介

解析 GQ是詢問男子的職業和身分，答案的提示在前半部出現。第一句話男子給女子簽約書，談到關於搬家事宜，由此可知男子是房屋仲介，而女子是新搬來的房客。

5

What does the woman say she likes about the apartment?

(A) The rental fee
(B) The location

女子喜歡這間公寓的什麼？

(A) 租金
(B) 位置

解析 女子說喜歡這間公寓的原因是離公司近，走路也可以到，因此答案是 (B)。

6

What will the woman do on Monday?

(A) Pick up some keys
(B) Move to a new home

女子星期一要做什麼？

(A) 領鑰匙
(B) 搬到新家

解析 重點是選出女子在星期一安排好的事情。主題雖然是搬家，但男子的第二段話是請對方星期一來領鑰匙，因此答案是 (A)。

Questions 7-9 refer to the following conversation. 美W 美M

W Hello, **⑦** I am calling to buy tickets for City Symphony's concert on Saturday. Could I buy them over the phone with a credit card?

M I'm sorry, but we don't sell tickets over the phone because **⑧** we only accept cash payments. But if you want to use your credit card, you can use the theater's official Web site.

W Oh, really? Do you know the Web site address?

M It's www.citysymphony.com. But don't forget. **⑨** You need to buy your tickets at least two days in advance if you want to use the system.

女哈囉，我打來是想買城市交響樂團週六的門票。我可以用電話刷信用卡買票嗎？

男很抱歉，電話無法售票，因為我們只收現金，但如果您要使用信用卡的話，可以利用劇院的官方網站。

女真的嗎？你能告訴我網址嗎？

男 www.citysymphony.com。別忘了，若要利用這個系統，請至少提前兩天訂票。

7

What does the woman want to do?

(A) Buy some tickets
(B) Open a bank account

女子想要做什麼？

(A) 買一些門票
(B) 開設銀行帳戶

解析 女子想做的事情很有可能來自女子剛說的話。女子在第一句話提到打電話來想買音樂會門票，因此答案是 (A)。

8

Why does the man say he cannot help the woman?

(A) The tickets are sold out.
(B) He can accept only cash.

男子為什麼說無法幫助女子？

(A) 門票已售罄。
(B) 他只接受現金。

解析 男子無法幫助女子的原因很可能來自於男子剛說的話。女子在第一句話提到無法幫助女子。女子的理想要用信用卡購票，男子回答只收現金，因此答案是 (B)。

詞彙

stop by 順道經過　rental contract 租約　current 目前的　resident 住戶　pick up 拿，領　tenant 房客　realtor 房屋仲介　rental fee 租金　location 位置

cash payment 現金支付　official 官方的　at least 至少　in advance 提前　bank account 銀行帳號　sold out 售罄　buy accept 接受　suggest 提議　beforehand 事前，事先　receipt 收據

9 What does the man suggest the woman do?
(A) Purchase the tickets beforehand
(B) Keep the receipt with her

男子建議女子做什麼？
(A) 事先購買門票
(B) 隨身攜帶收據

解析 男子建議女子做的事情很有可能從音檔中由男子說出。男子說在網上購票時，必須提前購買，因此正確答案是 (A)。對話中的 buy your tickets at least two days in advance 是指在選項中被重新詮釋為 purchase the tickets beforehand。

---

10 What did the woman recently do?
(A) Taught a writing class
(B) Cancelled the enrollment in a class

女子最近做了什麼？
(A) 教授了一堂寫作課
(B) 取消了課堂上的報名

解析 女子最近做的事情很有可能來自於女子前半部說的話。一開始女子就說最近取消了課程，因此答案是 (B)。題目難度為意譯，選項中必須持續進行詞彙的練習。

---

11 What caused the delay?
(A) A computer system malfunctioned.
(B) A form was not completed.

是什麼造成了延誤？
(A) 電腦系統出現故障。
(B) 表格沒有完成。

解析 delay（延誤）是造成問題的Key Word，仔細聆聽對話者說出電腦系統出現問題，因此正確答案是 (A)。退款延誤的原因是最近電腦系統出現問題的 malfunction（故障）的 (A)。

---

12 What does the man suggest?
(A) Registering for another class
(B) Checking the Web site for its status

男子提議什麼？
(A) 報名另一堂課
(B) 從網路檢查狀態

解析 男子提議的事情來自男子說的話。男子最後提到可以在網站上追蹤退款狀態，男子最後提到可以在網站上追蹤退款狀態，因此答案是 (B)。多益中出現三個題目的題型，最後一題往往是最簡單的，因此先掌握3個題目的內容，將可以答對的部分盡量全部拿分。

Questions 10-12 refer to the following conversation. 美M 澳M

W Hi, ⑩ I recently withdrew from a writing course at the Middleton Community Center due to a scheduling conflict. I was told I would get a refund for my registration fees within a week. But it's been two weeks and I still haven't received it.

M I apologize for the delay. ⑪ We had some problems with our computer system recently and several refunds weren't processed on time. Can I have your name, please?

W My name is Lana Anderson. Do you know when I might receive the refund?

M Let me check. The records show that your refund was processed today and should arrive by the end of the week. ⑫ You can track the status of your refund online at www.middletoncc.co.org.

女 你好，因為衝突的關係，最近我退了米德頓社區中心的寫作課程。款項一星期內可以退還，但過了兩星期我還是沒有收到。

男 很抱歉取消了！最近電腦系統有問題，有幾筆退款無法準時處理，請問大名是？

女 我叫拉娜安德森，請問什麼時候能收到退款呢？

男 我看看，紀錄顯示您的退款今天已經處理了，應該會在這星期前入帳，你可以在www.middletoncc.co.org線上追蹤退款情形。

詞彙 withdraw 取消、退出　conflict 衝突、糾紛　refund 退款　registration fee 報名費　apologize 道歉　delay 延誤、延遲　process 處理　track 追蹤　status 狀態　enrollment 報名　cause 引起　malfunction 失常、故障　form 表格　complete 完成　register 註冊

Step 4 實戰練習

正解

1. (C)	2. (B)	3. (B)	4. (A)	5. (D)
6. (D)	7. (A)	8. (B)	9. (D)	10. (C)
11. (B)	12. (C)	13. (B)	14. (D)	15. (C)
16. (B)	17. (A)	18. (B)		

Questions 1-3 refer to the following conversation. 澳M 美W

M Good morning, ma'am. ❶ Where would you like to go?

W Good morning. ❶ ❷ Could you drive me to the McDowell Conference Center downtown? It's near the Harborpoint Mansion on Kensington Avenue. I believe it's not that far from here.

M McDowell Conference Center? No, it's not that far, but since it's rush hour, the traffic will be bad. ❸ I'm afraid it will probably take an extra 15 to 20 minutes to drive there.

W That's okay. My meeting doesn't start until 9. I should have plenty of time.

男 早安，女士，您要到哪裡呢？

女 早，麻煩載我到市中心的麥道爾會議中心，就在肯辛頓大道上的海港角大廈附近，我想不會太遠才是。

男 麥道爾會議中心？不，不會太遠，但因為是尖峰時間會塞車，我們可能需要額外花15到20分鐘。

女 沒關係，我9點才開會，時間很充裕。

---

1 Who most likely is the man?
(A) A train conductor
(B) A hotel employee
(C) A taxi driver
(D) A travel agent

男子最有可能是誰？
(A) 火車列車長
(B) 飯店員工
(C) 計程車司機
(D) 旅行社員工

詞彙 not ～ until 直到～才～　conductor 列車長　travel agent 旅行社員工　fare 費用　recently 最近　increase 增加　take 花（時間）　flight 飛行、航班

2

解析 GQ是詢問某人的職業或身分。在前半部出現直接的提示。女子回答了自己的目的地，因此男子第一句話詢問要去哪裡。女子回答了自己的目的地，因此男子最可能的職業是 (C) 計程車司機。

Where does the woman want to go?
(A) To a restaurant
(B) To a conference center
(C) To a train station
(D) To a science museum

女子想去哪裡？
(A) 餐廳
(B) 會議中心
(C) 火車站
(D) 科學館

解析 女子想去的地點最有可能來自女子說的話。女子第一句話針對方歡她到要道威爾會議中心。因此如果沒有先讀完3個題目，便難以作答。1和第2題提示很接近，因此答案是 (B)。這個題型的第答。

3

What does the man tell the woman?
(A) The fare has recently increased.
(B) The drive will take longer than she expected.
(C) A flight schedule has changed.
(D) The business will close early.

男子告訴女子什麼？
(A) 最近費用漲價了。
(B) 開車時間將比預期的更久。
(C) 航班時刻表已更改。
(D) 營業時間將提前結束。

解析 男子告訴女子的事情100%的機率來自於男子說的話。但這個問題具體的Key Word，因此必須先瀏覽一遍選項，同時仔細聆聽內容。男子說正逢交通尖峰時刻，需要多花15～20分鐘，因此答案是 (B)。

Questions 4-6 refer to the following conversation. (美M)(美W)

M Good morning. ❹ I had trouble using the online reservation system on your Web site, so I'm calling to confirm my reservation at your hotel. My name is Jason Beck.

W Sure, let me check, Mr. Beck. Yes, I see you're arriving on November 2nd and checking out on November 8th. Would you like to use our free shuttle bus service from the airport to our hotel?

M No, thanks. ❺ I'm renting a car at the airport. But ❻ I want to make sure that I'll be able to connect to the Internet in my room.

W Of course, sir. The entire hotel has a wireless Internet network.

男 早安，我沒辦法使用你們網站的線上預約系統，所以打來想確認我的訂房。我叫傑森貝克。

女 沒問題，貝克先生，好的，您入住日期是11月2日，11月8日退房。您要利用我們從機場到飯店的免費接駁巴士嗎？

男 不了，謝謝。我會在機場租車。我想確認一下房間是否有網路連線。

女 當然，先生。整棟飯店備有無線網路系統。

詞彙
confirm 確認   connect to 進上～   reserve 預約
conference room 會議室   contact 連絡   transportation 交通運輸
amenity 設施   tour 參觀   access 使用、進入   client 客戶

4

What did the man have a problem doing?
(A) Using a Web site
(B) Reserving transportation
(C) Finding a conference room
(D) Contacting a client

男子遇到了什麼問題？
(A) 使用網站
(B) 預約交通接駁
(C) 尋找會議室
(D) 連絡客戶

解析 男子遇到的問題很可能來自於男子說的話。男子第一句話提到無法利用線上預約的系統，因此答案是 (A)。

5

How will the man get to the hotel?
(A) By subway
(B) By bus
(C) On foot
(D) By car

男子如何前往飯店？
(A) 乘坐地鐵
(B) 乘坐巴士
(C) 走路
(D) 坐車

解析 男子前往飯店的方法很有可能來自於男子說的話，但也可能是女子提出。因此必須集中注意力聆聽，找出男子前往的方法。女子詢問是否需要接駁車，男子回答會自行租車，因此答案是 (D)。

6

What hotel amenity does the man ask about?
(A) City tours
(B) Dining options
(C) The fitness center
(D) Internet access

男子詢問飯店的什麼設施？
(A) 市區觀光
(B) 餐飲選擇
(C) 健身中心
(D) 網路使用

解析 男子詢問的內容有100%的機率來自於男子說的話。男子最後詢問到飯店是否可以使用網路，因此答案是 (D)。對話中的connect除了選項中被重新詮釋為access。access除了有進入大樓等各種意義，也有進入大樓等各種意義，必須熟記。

Questions 7-9 refer to the following conversation. 美W 澳M

W　Hi, this is Sandra Stern calling. **7** You are supposed to deliver my new refrigerator today, and I'd like to find out what time I can expect it.

M　Yes, Ms. Stern. I can see your name on our delivery schedule. **8** Our people should be at your house between 2 and 4 this afternoon.

W　Thank you. And one more thing! **9** Can you take away my old refrigerator?

M　Of course. I'll instruct the delivery people about it. There is an additional cost of $20 for that service, though. You can pay when you sign for the delivery.

7

Why is the woman calling?
(A) To discuss a delivery
(B) To ask about a warranty
(C) To report a problem
(D) To cancel an appointment

女子為什麼打電話？

(A) 討論送貨
(B) 詢問保固期
(C) 報修問題
(D) 取消預約

解析　目的和主題一樣，是詢問電話好好今天會送貨，通常在前半就出現。女子第一句話提到約好今天會送貨，並詢問送達時間，因此答案是 (A)。

8

When will the delivery be made?
(A) This morning
(B) This afternoon
(C) Tomorrow morning
(D) Tomorrow afternoon

什麼時候送達？

(A) 今天早上
(B) 今天下午
(C) 明天早上
(D) 明天下午

解析　這是典型的SQ，必須選出正確的時間點。女子詢問今天的送貨時間，男子回答下午2點到4點之間，因此答案是 (B)。

9

What is an additional fee for?
(A) Delivering merchandise
(B) Assembling furniture
(C) Using an express service
(D) Removing an old appliance

什麼是額外費用？

(A) 運送物品
(B) 組裝家具
(C) 使用快遞服務
(D) 清除舊設備

解析　SQ是詢問額外費用（additional fee）的原因。女子詢問是否可幫忙清運舊冰箱，男子回答需加收20美元，因此正確答案是 (D)。題目的 additional fee是 Key Word，如果能夠從對話中找到題目的 Key Word，就能更輕易地選擇答案。

詞彙

be supposed to 應該要～　refrigerator 冰箱　expect 預計　take away 撤走　instruct 指示　additional 額外的　cost 經費、費用　sign 簽名、標誌標示　warranty (品質) 保證書　fee 費用　merchandise 物品　assemble 組裝　remove 清除　appliance 設備

Questions 10-12 refer to the following conversation. 美M 美W

M　Hi, this is Dennis in apartment 5A. **10** The sink in my kitchen is not draining properly and I'd like to have it repaired. What must I do?

W　Well, **11** you'll need to submit a work order that lists the changes you want to be made to your apartment. You can do this on the building's Web site.

M　Okay, great. By the way, is this something I can do myself?

W　Actually, **12** it's better if Mr. Hoffman, the building supervisor, does it. The building has strict regulations about what kind of cleaning supplies can be used to prevent corrosion to pipes and he knows which have been approved.

10

What problem is the man reporting?
(A) Some paint is peeling off.
(B) He lost the keys to his apartment.
(C) A sink is not working well.
(D) A light is broken.

男子呈報什麼問題？

(A) 有些油漆剝落了。
(B) 他弄丟了他公寓的鑰匙。
(C) 水槽無法正常運作。
(D) 燈壞了。

解析　男子呈報的問題很有可能來自於男子就的話。從對話的第一句話可以得知男子是公寓的房客 (tenant)。男子提到廚房水槽無法正常排水，因此答案是 (C)（not draining properly在選項中改寫成not working）。sink除了是廚房流理台之外，也可以是排水的水槽或洗臉台等。

詞彙

sink 水槽、流理台 (排水設施)　drain 排水　properly 正常地、適當地　submit 提出　list 列出清單　supervisor 管理者、主管　strict 嚴格的　regulations 規定　supplies 用品　prevent 遏止　corrosion 腐蝕、侵蝕　approve 同意、認可　report 報告、申告　peel 剝落　work order be broken 故障　instruct 指示　stop by 順道　request 申請　hire 僱用　management 管理者　complex 建築物

11 What does the woman instruct the man to do?

(A) Stop by the office
(B) Pay a fee
(C) Take a picture
(D) **Submit a request online**

女子指示男子做什麼？

(A) 順道去辦公室
(B) 付費
(C) 拍照
(D) **線上提交申請書**

解析 女子提示男子的事情100%的機率來自於女子說的話。女子要求男子在線上填寫工作通知單，因此答案是 (D)。「work除了是「工作」的動詞之外，也具有「事情」、「作業」等各種意思。

12 What is mentioned about the building supervisor?

(A) He needs to order some parts.
(B) He was just hired by the management.
(C) **He knows about the building rules.**
(D) He also lives in the same apartment complex.

提到關於大樓主管的部分是什麼？

(A) 他需要訂購一些零件。
(B) 他不久前被管理層僱用。
(C) **他了解大樓規定。**
(D) 他也住在公寓大樓。

解析 題目是詢問短文中提到 (be mentioned about/be said/be stated) 的部分。女子最後一段話提到大樓主管霍夫曼先生，他知道有關大樓使用上的規定，因此正確答案是 (C)。對話中有regulations在選項中被重新詮釋為rules。須謹記同義詞認識愈多，在高難度題目中就愈有利。

Questions 13-15 refer to the following conversation with three speakers. 〔美M〕〔美W〕〔澳M〕

M1　Excuse me, **⑬ my friend and I heard your announcement over the airport loudspeakers. You are looking for passengers who are willing to volunteer to take a later flight to Chicago?**

W　Yes, this flight is overbooked. So, if you don't mind departing at 8:00 o'clock tonight, **⑭ I can give you vouchers for $250 off for any future flights from our airline.**

M1　Well, since we're not doing anything important tonight except for checking into our hotel, I wouldn't mind getting the discount coupon. Jin Hyung, what do you think?

M2　That's fine with me. **⑮ We can just grab something for dinner at the airport while we wait.**

W　I recommend a Mexican restaurant in Concourse C. The food's pretty good and the price is reasonable. You both will like the place.

男1　不好意思，我和我朋友聽到機場廣播說，你們在找自願搭下一班往芝加哥的旅客？

女　是的，本班班機超額定位了，因此您不介意今晚8點出發的話，我可以給您我們航空公司往後任何班機折扣250美元的優惠票券。

男1　嗯，我們今晚除了要辦理飯店入住以外，也沒其他重要事情要做，我很樂意收到折價券。振亨，你認為呢？

男2　我可以，候機的同時我們可以在機場隨便吃。

女　我推薦C大廳的墨西哥餐廳，食物好吃價格也合理，兩位會喜歡的。

13 Where is the conversation taking place?

(A) At a restaurant
(B) **At an airport**
(C) At a bus station
(D) At a travel agency

談話發生的地點在哪裡？

解析 GQ是詢問談話發生的地點，主要答案是先讀完題目之後，預測答案出現在廣播或廣播的前半部。最重要的是提示談話地點是機場。第一句話提示到機場的廣播會顧意搭機的旅客，因此可以推測談話地點是機場。

14 According to the woman, what will the men receive?

(A) A parking pass
(B) A travel guidebook
(C) A seating upgrade
(D) **A discount voucher**

根據女子的說法，男子會得到什麼？

(A) 停車證
(B) 旅行指南
(C) 席位升等
(D) **折扣券**

解析 以「根據女子的說法」開始的句子，100%機率晚餐來自於女子說的話。貌似機場員工的女子說願意晚睡話可以得到折扣券，因此答案是 (D)。對話中的off在選項中被重新詮釋為discount。

（解答接右方）

詞彙　announcement 公告、通知　loudspeaker 擴音器　passenger 乘客　be willing to 願意～　volunteer 自願　overbook 超額預訂　depart 出發　off 折扣、扣除　grab 抓、吃一點　concourse 中央廣場、大廳、車站大廳　voucher 憑證、優惠票券　recommend 推薦　reasonable 合理的、低廉的　travel agency 旅行社　parking pass 停車證、停車許可證　upgrade 升級　original 原本的

〔元老師的〕
REAL SOLUTION

Part 3 會出三人對話的題型。像14和15題出現複數的男子 (men) 所詢問的內容，即屬於3人對話。但是各個題目有可能都是針對同一人來詢問，因此無須擔心存恐懼。先練習讀完題目，在將聽到對話的同時進行了解題。最重要的就是從短文中找到針對同一人來詢問的句子。貌似簡單，但因為題目是從題目得知複數的男子（可以從題目得知是3人對話的題型。因為3人對話的內容，即屬於3人對話的題型。3人對話的內容。無須3人對話。

What will the men most likely do next?
(A) Visit Mexico to meet the family
(B) Change the hotel reservation
(C) Eat at a nearby restaurant
(D) Return to their original flight

男子接下來最有可能做什麼？
(A) 前往墨西哥見家人
(B) 更改飯店預訂
(C) 在附近的餐廳用餐
(D) 返回原來的航班

解析 預測男子接下來的行為常會出現在最後出現提示，當男子說要在機場用餐，女子便推薦C大廳西哥餐廳，因此答案是 (C)。 澳M

Questions 16-18 refer to the following conversation and map. 美W

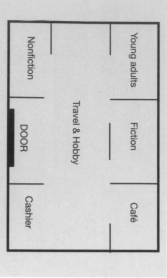

| Young adults | Fiction | Café |
| Nonfiction | Travel & Hobby | DOOR | Cashier |

M ⑯ Hi, welcome to Harpo's Bookshop. Are you looking for something in particular?
W Yes, I need a book called *Falling Stars* by Beatrice Pearson. My neighbors and I are starting a book club next week. ⑰ People say it's a good one for generating a lot of questions and comments.
M That is true. It's not very popular but it is one of my favorites too. ⑱ You can find it on the back wall of the store next to the café. The books there are arranged by author. Can I help you with anything else?
W No thanks, but I think I'll browse for a while before I make a decision.
M Sure, just call me if you need anything.

| 年輕人 | 小說 | 咖啡店 |
| 非小說類 | 旅行&愛好 | 門 | 結帳台 |

男 ⑯ 妳好，歡迎光臨哈波書店，有特別想要找什麼書嗎？
女 我想找碧翠絲皮爾森的「流星」(Falling Stars)，我和鄰居下週要開讀書會。⑰ 大家說這本書很適合提問及發表討論。
男 沒錯，這本書不是很普及，但是我的最愛之一。⑱ 那裡的書籍按照作者姓名編排，你可以在店內後方那面牆的咖啡區旁邊找到它。還有什麼可以幫妳的嗎？
女 沒有了，謝謝！我想決定前再瀏覽一下。
男 好的，有需要再告訴我。

詞彙 particular 特別的 generate 發生、產生 comment 評話、評論 popular 受歡迎的 arrange 排列 browse 瀏覽、翻閱 adult 年輕人 fiction 小說 nonfiction 非小說 cashier 結帳台 young adult server 服務生 provide 提供 opportunity 機會 discussion 討論 best-seller 暢銷書

16
Who most likely is the man?
(A) A restaurant server
(B) A sales clerk
(C) An author
(D) A delivery person

男子最有可能是誰？
(A) 餐廳服務生
(B) 販售人員
(C) 作家
(D) 送貨員

解析 GQ是詢問男子的身分，提示主要來自於音檔的前半部內容。第一句中男子對來到書店的客人表示歡迎，並詢問要找什麼書，由此可知男子是書店職員，因此答案是 (B)。

17
What does the woman say she heard about the book?
(A) It will provide opportunities for discussion.
(B) It is the first book in the series.
(C) It is difficult to understand for young people.
(D) It has been a best-seller for months.

女子說她聽說關於這本書的什麼？
(A) 它提供討論的機會
(B) 這是該系列的第一本書
(C) 年輕人很難理解
(D) 幾個月來它一直是暢銷書

解析 女子說自己開始加入讀書會，要找能夠提問和引起話題的書 (Falling Stars)，能夠問和引發對話的機會可提供討論的機會，因此答案是 (A)。對同義前有更多認識有助於解開難度較高的題目。

18
Look at the graphic. In which section is the book that the woman is looking for?
(A) Young adults
(B) Fiction
(C) Nonfiction
(D) Travel & Hobby

請看圖示。女子要找的書出現在哪個區域？
(A) 年輕人
(B) 小說
(C) 非小說
(D) 旅行&愛好

解析 表格/視覺資料的題型必須先看完題目，尤其有關地圖的圖示必須找出在對話當中出現的敘述。題目是詢問女子要找的書在哪面牆的圖示中，須找從平面圖當中出現的敘述。圖中可以看到door(門)，cashier (結帳台)，café (咖啡廳)，nonfiction (非小說區)，fiction (小說區)。因為想找女子找的書要在後方那面牆的咖啡區旁邊，由此可知在Fiction區域，尤其女子找的書在後方那面牆的咖啡區旁邊，使用前、後，旁邊等表示位置的詞彙。

Step 2 眼睛和耳朵完美搭配 Practice   P86

1

1. (B)	2. (A)	3. (A)	4. (B)

What are the speakers discussing?
(A) A staff orientation   (B) A building project

說話者在討論什麼？
(A) 員工訓練   (B) 建築工程

Question 1 refers to the following conversation. 美M 美W

M Good morning, Ms. Taylor. Here's the cost estimate from Ocean Building Company for the staff cafeteria we are planning to build.

W Well, building a brand-new cafeteria requires extensive work, but it is higher than we originally thought.

男 早安，泰勒小姐。這是大洋建設打算興建的員工餐廳的成本估價單。

女 蓋一間全新的員工餐廳的確需要大規模施工，但這超出我們原來的估算太多了。

2

Who most likely is the woman?
(A) A magazine reporter   (B) A restaurant owner

女子最有可能是誰？
(A) 雜誌記者   (B) 餐廳老闆

Question 2 refers to the following conversation. 美M 澳W

W Thank you, Chef Carlos for meeting with me. My magazine wants to publish an article about your unique cooking project. Could you tell us more about it?

M Yes, I was inspired by the paintings in the museum and came up with this new series of dishes.

女 卡洛斯主廚，謝謝您接受採訪。我的雜誌想要刊登關於您獨特的烹飪企劃案的報導，可以多告訴我們一些詳情嗎？

男 好的，我的靈感來自於博物館裡的畫作，因而想出一系列的創新菜色。

3

What is the woman concerned about?
(A) Submitting late work
(B) Finding some documents

女子擔心什麼事？
(A) 延遲繳交工作   (B) 尋找一些文件

Question 3 refers to the following conversation. 美M 美W

M Ms. Hong, I need to be at home early for an urgent family matter. Do you mind if I work from home?

W Not at all, but what's the status of the budget you've been working on? The deadline for the project is coming up quite soon. I'm worried about sending our work late.

男 洪小姐，我今天家裡有急事必須早點回家。妳介不介意我在家工作？

女 一點也不會，但你目前預算進度到哪裡了？這份專案的截止期限快到了，我擔心我們會延誤工作。

4

What does the woman suggest?
(A) Offering product discounts
(B) Starting an online advertising campaign

女子提議什麼？
(A) 提供產品折扣   (B) 展開線上廣告活動

Question 4 refers to the following conversation. 美M 美W

M To start the meeting, I'd like to talk about the recent drop in sales for our vitamin products.

W What we really should be doing is to start advertising on social media Web sites.

男 會議開始前，我想先討論維他命產品最近銷售下滑一事。

女 我們真正應該要做的事是開始在社群媒體網站打廣告。

Step 3 基本掌握   P87

1. (B)	2. (A)	3. (A)	4. (A)	5. (B)
6. (A)	7. (A)	8. (B)	9. (B)	10. (B)
11. (B)	12. (B)			

Questions 1-3 refer to the following conversation. 美W 美M

W Tim, this is Melanie from Human Resources. ① I just wanted to call and say welcome to the company. We're so happy that you have joined us.

M Thanks, I'm enjoying my first day here. ② The only thing is that I haven't received my employee identification badge yet. Where should I go to get it?

W You just have to go down to the security office on the east side of the building, and they should be able to help you out.

M Great, thanks. ③ I'm completing some payroll forms now. As soon as I'm done with it, I'll go down to the security office.

女 提姆，我是人力資源部的梅蘭妮。我打來是想歡迎你來到公司，我們很高興你的加入。

男 謝謝。第一天上班我很開心。唯一一件事情是我還沒拿到員工識別證，我應該去哪裡領取？

女 只要往大樓東側的警衛室走去，他們會協助你的。

男 太好了，謝謝。我正在寫繳薪資員表。我一寫完就去警衛室。

詞彙 human resources 人事部門   security office 保全室、警衛室   payroll 工資表   identification badge 身分識別證   request 要求   fill out 填寫   form 表格   sign 簽名、標記、標示   employment contract 勞動契約

1

Why is the woman calling?
(A) To request some information
(B) **To welcome the man to the company**

女子為什麼打電話？
(A) 要求一些資訊
(B) **歡迎男子來到公司**

解析　女子打電話的原因很有可能來自於女子說的話。女子是人事部門人員，表示歡迎新員工的加入，因此答案是 (B)。務必謹記各種部門名稱和基本的業務常識，有助於選擇答案。

2

What does the man ask about?
(A) **An identification badge**
(B) An orientation schedule

男子詢問什麼事情？
(A) **身分識別證**
(B) 教育訓練日程

解析　男子詢問的事情100%的機率來自男子說的話。男子候完之後表示自己還沒領到員工識別證，並詢問何時可以領取，因此正確答案是 (A)。

3

What does the man say he is doing?
(A) **Filling out some forms**
(B) Signing an employment contract

男子說他正在做什麼？
(A) **填寫一些表格**
(B) 簽訂勞動契約

解析　男子說自己正在填寫的事情也是100%的機率來自男子說的話。男子提到自己正在填寫工員表，因此答案是 (A)。complete在選項中被重新經釋為fill out。透過逐漸提高答案的熟悉度，同義詞作為正確答案的機率也很高，因此，必須勤加背誦熟記單字。

Questions 4-6 refer to the following conversation. 美W 澳M

W ❹ Were you there at the marketing presentation this morning? I looked for you in the audience but didn't see you anywhere.

M Oh, was that today? I'm sorry. ❺ I thought it was next week. I must have gotten the dates mixed up.

W Well, don't worry. ❻ The entire presentation was filmed and the video's going to be posted on our internal company Web site. If you want, you can just go online and watch it.

M Thank you. I'll definitely do that.

4

What event did the man miss?
(A) **A marketing presentation**
(B) A board meeting

男子錯過了什麼活動？
(A) **行銷簡報**
(B) 理事會議

解析　男子錯過的活動從女子的第一句話可以得知。女子說沒有在行銷簡報會上見到男子，因此正確答案是 (A)。高難度的題目可能是否定對方所說的內容，但最重要的是，從頭到尾仔細聆聽對話的內容。

5

Why did the man miss the event?
(A) He was on a business trip.
(B) **He thought it was on a different day.**

男子為什麼錯過了活動？
(A) 他正在出差
(B) **他以為是別的日期**

解析　男子無法參加的原因很有可能來自於男子說的話。男子以為活動是下週舉行，搞成了日期，因此答案是 (B)。難度愈高，愈經常以同義詞作為答案，必須多進行訓練以提高分析和問題理解能力，幫助在快速瀏覽一遍題目之後作答。

6

What does the woman suggest the man do?
(A) **Watch a video online**
(B) Attend a different presentation

女子建議男子做什麼？
(A) **線上觀看影片**
(B) 參加另一場簡報會

解析　女子提議的事情有機率來自於女子說的話。女子告訴男子，整場簡報會已錄製成影片，會上傳到公司的網站，因此正確答案是 (A)。

詞彙　presentation 簡報、發表　audience 觀眾　mix up 搞混　entire 整個的　film 錄影　post 公布　definitely 一定、確定地　board 理事會

Questions 7-9 refer to the following conversation. 美M 美W

M Hi, Anna. I have an assignment for you. ❼❽ I want you to write an article on the new play that is showing at the Magnum Theater this week. The last play review you wrote had a good response from our readers.

W Thank you. I was planning to see it anyway. But most of the shows are sold out.

M I've already reserved a ticket for you. And this time, maybe you can arrange an interview with the director of the play, Philip Hwang. I'm sure our readers want to know how he feels about the play's success.

W Okay, ❾ I'll make some calls right away to see if I can schedule an interview with him.

M 嗨，安娜，我有個任務要給妳，我要妳針對這週在Magnum Theater上映的新戲寫一篇文章。上篇妳所寫的戲劇評論獲得讀者很好的迴響。

W 謝謝，我已好打算要去看，可是大部分的票都賣光了。

M 我已經預約一張票給妳，這次也許妳可以安排時間訪談導演利讀者，我確信讀者想要知道他對作品大受歡迎的感想。

W 好，我立刻打幾通電話確認排訪約的時間。

7

What are the speakers mainly discussing?
(A) **An article that the woman will write**
(B) The career of a well-known actor

說話者主要在討論什麼？
(A) **女子將要寫的文章**
(B) 一個著名演員的職業生涯

詞彙　assignment 任務　article 文章　play 戲劇　review 評論、評述　response 反應　sold out 售罄　reserve 預約　arrange 安排、計畫　director 導演　career 經歷、職業生涯　well-known 知名的　newspaper company 報社　exchange 交換

8

解析 詢問對話主題的題目，最主要的提示示現在音檔的前半部。第一句話男子提到任務是撰寫文章，由此可知談論的內容主要是女子寫的報導，因此答案是 (A)。

Where does this conversation probably take place?
(A) At a theater
(B) At a newspaper company
談話地點有可能發生在哪裡？

解析 一次包含2個GQ的題目中，提示示現會同時出現在第一句。從第一句話可以知道兩人在媒體界工作，從選項來看，最適合的答案是 (B) 報社。雖然對話的主題是劇院，但撰寫報導的地方是報社。
答案是 (B) 報社。

(A) 劇院
(B) 報社

9

What will the woman probably do next?
(A) Exchange her ticket
(B) Call for an interview
女子接下來可能會做什麼？

解析 詢問接下來要做的事情，提示示通常出現在後半部。男子向女子提議採訪演講，女子回答會立刻打電話約定採訪行程。因此答案是 (B)。
(A) 更換她的票
(B) 打電話要求採訪
讓採訪要求採訪演講，女子回答會立刻打電話約定採訪行程。因此答案是
(B)。

Questions 10-12 refer to the following conversation. 美W 澳M

W Hello, a friend told me that your sign shop is having a special promotion for the first-time customers. Could you tell me more about it please?

M Certainly. Here's what we're offering. ⑩ New customers could receive their first sign order the next day after they place it.

W Really? That's good to know. I need my sign as soon as possible.

M What kind of sign are you interested in?

W Well, I own a hair salon downtown and recently opened up a branch on Central Avenue. There are many shops in the area and ⑪ I want a sign that will direct people to my new place.

M Of course. I think one of the large exterior banners will be great to help people find your store. ⑫ Given the rainy weather we have here, you might like one made out of waterproof material.

女 你好，朋友跟我說，你們的廣告招牌公司對於首次購買的客戶有特別的促銷活動。可以告訴我更多細節嗎？
男 沒問題。我們提供新客戶下單後就能收到招牌。
女 真的嗎？真是好消息。我需要能盡快安裝招牌。
男 妳想要怎樣的招牌呢？
女 我在市區開了間美容院，最近在中央大道開分店，那個區域有許多店家，所以我想要一個能夠引導人群到我找到妳的店面的招牌。
男 這種經常下雨，妳也許會喜歡用防水的材質。

詞彙 sign shop 招牌公司 promotion 促銷 downtown 市區 direct 指引、指示 exterior 外部的 banner 橫幅標誌 waterproof 防水的 material 材料、材質 offer 提供、提議 available 可供使用的、準備就緒的 customer 客人 purpose 目的 indicate 指出 renovation 改造、整修 suggestion 提議

10

According to the man, what special offer is available for new customers?
(A) A product discount
(B) Next-day delivery
根據男子的介紹，新客戶有什麼特別優惠？
(A) 產品折扣
(B) 隔天到貨
解析 題目是根據男子 (According to the man) 的說法，因此需注在男子說的話。第一句話提到屬於招牌公司 (sign shop)，可以預知會出現其他公司名稱。男子提到第一次訂購招牌的新客戶會提供隔日到貨的服務，因此答案是 (B)。

11

What is the purpose of the sign?
(A) To indicate a location
(B) To announce a renovation
招牌的目的是什麼？
(A) 標示位置
(B) 宣布整修
解析 先記下 sign 具有「標誌」的意思，接著尋找女子製作招牌的目的。女子表示自己開了分店，因此可知答案是 (A)。女子在對話中故重要製作招牌，要製作招牌，由此可知答案是 (A)。女子在對話中的 direct people to my new place在選項中故重新詮釋為indicate a location。

12

What does the man suggest doing?
(A) Collecting client suggestions
(B) Using waterproof material
男子提議做什麼？
(A) 收集客戶建議
(B) 使用防水材質
解析 男子提議的事情的100%機率來自於男子的話。經常下雨的關係，防水材質賣較佳，因此正確答案是 (B)。

正解：

1. (B)	2. (C)	3. (B)	4. (C)	5. (A)
6. (D)	7. (A)	8. (C)	9. (A)	10. (B)
11. (A)	12. (D)	13. (D)	14. (A)	15. (B)
16. (A)	17. (C)	18. (D)		

Questions 1-3 refer to the following conversation. 美W 澳M

W Excuse me. ❶ I am here to attend the Information Technology seminar. ❷ Your seminar won't begin until 10 and now it's only 9 o'clock. As you can see, I'm still preparing the room.

W I know. I got here early to find the seminar location. ❸ Do you know where I can get a cup of coffee while I am waiting?

M Sure, there's a café on the first floor of this building. I'm sure it's open.

女 不好意思。我來參加資訊科技的討論。

男 好的，您來得好早。研討會10點開始，現在才9點。如您所見，我還在布置會議室。

女 我知道，我提早來是想先找到研討會的會議位置。等候期間哪裡可以喝杯咖啡呢？

男 大樓一樓有咖啡廳，我確定現在是營業中。

1
Why is the woman visiting the place?
(A) To make a reservation
(B) **To attend a seminar**
(C) To buy some coffee
(D) To cancel a membership

女子為什麼拜訪這個地方？
(A) 預約
(B) **參加研討會**
(C) 買咖啡
(D) 取消會籍

解析 女子拜訪的原因很有可能來自於女子說的話。一開始女子說自己來參加研討會，因此正確答案是 (B)。後面雖然出現與咖啡相關的內容，但不是整體談論的主題，因此答案不是 (C)。

詞彙 attend 參加　technology 技術　not~until 直到~才~　reservation 預約　make a copy 影印　location 位置　visit 拜訪　beverage 飲料

2
When will the event begin?
(A) At 8 o'clock
(B) At 9 o'clock
(C) **At 10 o'clock**
(D) At 11 o'clock

活動何時開始？
(A) 8點
(B) 9點
(C) **10點**
(D) 11點

解析 貌似準備活動的男子很有可能會說出活動開始的時間。意思是「要到B（時間）才會進行A（事件）」，因此必須多加熟記。<Not A until B>是多益考試中經常出現的句型，因此必須多加熟記。<Not A until 10 o'clock> 才會進行A（事件）。由於活動10點才開始，因此正確答案是 (C)。

3
What is the woman looking for?
(A) A machine to make a copy
(B) A location to meet clients
(C) A restaurant for a party
(D) **A place to get a beverage**

女子在尋找什麼？
(A) 影印的機器
(B) 見客戶的地點
(C) 聚會的餐廳
(D) **買飲料的地方**

解析 女子要尋找的地方很有可能來自於女子說的話。女子最後詢問等候期間附近是否有地方可以喝咖啡，因此答案是 (D)。女子在對話中說 where I can get a cup of coffee，就像使用beverage代替coffee一樣，改寫時可以使用意義更廣的詞彙。

詞彙 place to get a beverage 買飲料的地方

Questions 4-6 refer to the following conversation. 美W 美M

W ❹ How was the consumer product testing for our new headphone sets? Did they like it?

M ❺ Well, customers were mostly happy with the design, but ❻ they were concerned about its durability.

W You know, ❻ you should talk to Tammie. She is an expert in plastics and should know some durable material that can be used in headphones.

M Good idea. I'll contact her right away.

女 顧客試戴我們新耳機的測試結果如何？他們滿意嗎？

男 顧客大部分對設計感到滿意，但對耐用性有些疑慮。

女 那你應該和泰咪談談。她是塑膠方面的專家，也清楚那些可以應用在耳機上的耐用材質。

男 好點子，我會馬上聯絡她。

詞彙 be concerned about 擔心~　durability 耐用性　expert 專家　durable 耐用的　material 材質　material 材料　contact 連絡　launch 發表　competitor 競爭對手　conduct 進行　hiking boots 登山靴　delay 延後　customer survey 顧客調查

4
What product are the speakers discussing?
(A) Sunglasses
(B) Hiking boots
(C) **Headphones**
(D) Blue jeans

說話者討論的產品是什麼？
(A) 太陽眼鏡
(B) 登山靴
(C) **耳機**
(D) 牛仔褲

5
According to the man, what are the customers worried about?
(A) **Durability**
(B) Price
(C) Ease of use
(D) Style

解析 GQ是詢問對話的主題，主要在前半部出現提示。第一句話詢問關於新耳機的產品測試結果，因此正確答案是 (C)。

6

(A) 耐用性
(B) 價格
(C) 使用便利性
(D) 設計

根據男子的說法，顧客們擔心什麼？

解析 先掌握題目的Key Word是worried about，再仔細聆聽對話。雖然說設計令人滿意，但顧客擔心耐用性，因此答案是 (A)。be worried about和be concerned about的意思相同，必須加以熟記。

What does the woman suggest?
(A) Testing a competitor's product
(B) Conducting a customer survey
(C) Delaying a product launch
(D) Talking to an expert

女子提議什麼？
(A) 測試競爭對手的產品
(B) 進行客戶調查
(C) 延後推出產品
(D) 與專家談談

解析 女子提議的事情100%的機率來自於女子說的話。女子第二句話提到素咪是專家，也許可以幫忙，因此答案是 (D)。

Questions 7-9 refer to the following conversation. 美W 澳M

W OK, Alex. Here's the problem. **7** For the last couple of months, we haven't had as many customers as we had last year. We need to do something to attract more people to our restaurant. Even though we lost of one of the chefs, I'd like to know if you have any suggestions.

M Well, **8** why don't we plan discounted lunch specials where all entrees are at a reduced price? In that way, we can promote the name of restaurant to local residents. I'll come up with some recipes for dishes that are not too expensive to make.

W That's a good idea. Go ahead and prepare those. But **9** I'd like to sample them before we decide to put them on the menu for our customers.

M Of course, Ms. Olvera.

女 好的，艾力克斯。有個問題是最近這幾個月，我們的來客數不如去年，我們必須想辦法吸引客人。雖然一位廚師離職了，我想知道你是否有任何建議。

男 何不推出商業午餐主菜降價的計畫呢？這樣可以向當地居民打開餐廳知名度。我會想一些成本不會太高的食譜。

女 真是好主意。去準備吧，但在決定放上菜單給客人品嘗前，我得先試吃。

男 當然，奧爾維亞小姐。

詞彙 attract 吸引　lunch special 商業午餐　reduced 折扣的　local 當地的　resident 居民　come up with 想出、提出　recipe 食譜　dish 菜色、盤子　expensive 昂貴的　sample 樣品、試吃　unusually 不尋常的　customer 顧客　complain 抱怨　ingredient 材料　suggest 提議　offer 提供　cater 供應似食　corporate 團體的、公司的　hire 雇用　prepare 準備　organize 組織、籌畫　inspection 審查

元老師的 REAL SOLUTION

在國高中的社會科目中是否聽過公司 (corporation/company) 的目的是創造利潤？現場最典型中關於業績 (performance) 的考量是。提升業績的計畫最常考的題材，內容包括吸引客戶 (attract customers)、提升業績收益 (sales/revenue) 並尋找能提供員工分紅、營業績下滑時、便縮減成本 (cut cost) 並夠維持獲利率的公司。多益考試中必須熟記公司主要部門和業務的常識，以順利解題。

7

What problem does the woman report?
(A) Business is unusually slow.
(B) Some of the customers complained.
(C) There are not enough employees.
(D) The price of some ingredients has increased.

女子報告的問題是什麼？
(A) 生意明顯下滑
(B) 一些客戶抱怨。
(C) 員工不夠。
(D) 一些材料成本上漲。

解析 女子第一句話提到過去幾個月來的來客數不如去年，可以得知生意下滑，因此答案是 (A)。

8

What does the man suggest?
(A) Offering outdoor dining
(B) Moving to another neighborhood
(C) Lowering some prices
(D) Catering corporate events

男子提議什麼？
(A) 提供戶外用餐
(B) 遷到另一個社區
(C) 降低一些價格
(D) 提供企業外燴

解析 男子提議的事情來自於男子說的話。男子提議推出商業午餐折扣並詢問意見，因此答案是 (C)。discounted在選項中被重新詮釋為lower the prices。

9

What does the woman ask the man to do?
(A) Hire a new chef
(B) Prepare some food samples
(C) Get ready for an inspection
(D) Organize a training

女子要求男子做什麼？
(A) 聘請新廚師
(B) 準備一些試吃樣本
(C) 準備好接受檢查
(D) 籌畫培訓課程

解析 女子要求男子做的事情100%的機率來自於女子說的話。女子最後提到在推出新菜單之前要先試吃樣品，因此答案是 (B)。

Questions 10-12 refer to the following conversation. 美W 美M

W Hi, Rodger. ⑩ Welcome back from China. I know you were visiting the companies to provide scarves for our new clothing line. Were you able to find us a new supplier?

M Yes, I think we should use the place called Ying-An Clothing Supplier. Their products are very high quality. The only problem is that their scarves cost almost twice ⑪ as much as other suppliers.

W If they're as well-made as you say, they might be worth the extra cost. ⑫ Why don't we place a small order to see how well they'll fit with our new line?

M Good idea. Let me check with Ying-An to find out the minimum order quantity.

嗨，羅傑。歡迎從中國回來。我知道你在拜訪為我們服飾系列提供圍巾的公司，你有找到新的供應商嗎？

有，我想我們可以和一間叫安怡衣的供應商合作。他們的產品品質很高，唯一的問題是他們的圍巾的成本是其他供應商的近兩倍。

如果他們的產品如同你說的製作精良，那外加的成本是值得的。要不要下個小批訂單來看看是否符合我們的新系列？

好主意。我來和怡安聯絡，看最低的訂貨數量是多少。

10　What did the man do in China?
(A) Bought some property
(B) Visited some suppliers
(C) Attended a professional conference
(D) Trained some personnel

解析 男子在中國做了什麼？
(A) 買了一些房產
(B) 拜訪了一些供應商
(C) 參加了一專業會議
(D) 培訓了一些人員
做過的事情通常出現在前半部。女子第一句話就知道男子拜訪了為服飾系列提供圍巾的供應商，因此答案是 (B)。

詞彙 clothing line 服飾系列　quality 品質　well-made 製作精良　worth 值得～　place an order 下訂單　fit 符合、適合　minimum 最少的　quantity 數量　property 房產　supplier 供應商　professional 專業的　personnel 人事、人員　item 物品　satisfied 滿意的　contract 合約、契約　renegotiate 重新協商　reimburse 補償　purchase 購買　sample 樣品

11　What problem does the man mention?
(A) Some items are expensive.
(B) Some clients are not satisfied.
(C) Some products had low quality.
(D) A contract has to be renegotiated.

男子提到了什麼問題？
(A) 有些物品很貴。
(B) 有些客戶不滿意。
(C) 有些產品的品質很低。
(D) 合約必須重新協商。

解析 男子提出的問題源來自於男子說的話。首先注意題目中的Key Word是problem之後聆聽對話。男子提到唯一的問題是該供應商的圍巾價格是其他廠商的近2倍，因此答案是 (A)。

12　What does the woman suggest?
(A) Renting storage space
(B) Advertising on the Internet
(C) Reimbursing a purchase
(D) Ordering a small sample

女子建議什麼？
(A) 租用儲存空間
(B) 在網路上打廣告
(C) 為購買退款
(D) 訂購少量樣品

解析 女子提議的事情來自於女子說的話。女子提議少量訂購以確定是否符合新系列，因此答案是 (D)。

Questions 13-15 refer to the following conversation with three speakers. 美W 澳M 英W

W1 Hi, Maria and Kevin. Has either of you seen Pablo today? The lights and computer were off in his office.

M No. But I have his mobile phone number. ⑬ Do you want me to call him, Ms. Haze?

W1 No, that's okay. ⑮ I know Pablo speaks Spanish, and I need him to translate this letter I got from a client in Spain.

M You know, Maria lived in Spain for about seven years. She used to work at a Spanish firm.

W2 That's right, and I have some free time this afternoon if you'd like me to work on it.

W1 Great. I'll give you the copy of the letter so that you can look at it. Thanks, Maria.

嗨，瑪麗亞和凱文。你們今天有誰見過巴勃羅嗎？他的辦公室的燈和電腦都關著。

沒有。但我有他的手機號碼。哈澤女士，你要我打給他嗎？

不，沒關係。我知道巴勃羅會說西班牙語，我需要他翻譯我從西班牙客戶那裡收到的這封信。

你知道，瑪麗亞在西班牙生活了大約七年。她曾經在一家西班牙公司工作。

沒錯，如果你們想讓我看看，我今天下午有一些空檔。

太好了。我會給你這封信的影本，以便你可以看一下。謝謝，瑪麗亞。

詞彙 either 兩者其一、任何一方　translate 翻譯　copy 影本　purchase 購買　colleague 同事　what for 為什麼、為了何事　contact 連絡　equipment 設備　overseas 海外的　recommend 推薦　promotion 升職　correct 修改　warn 警告　danger 危險

13　What does the man offer to do?
(A) Purchase tickets
(B) Make a reservation
(C) Check a calendar
(D) Call a colleague

男子提議什麼？
(A) 購買門票
(B) 預約
(C) 確認日程
(D) 打電話給同事

解析 男子提議的事情來自於男子說的話。男子向要找巴勃羅的女子詢問是否需要幫忙打電話，因此答案是 (D)。詢問提供 (offer) 內容的答案提示來自於以 "Do you want me to～", should I ~"開始的句子，需多加熟記。

14 What is Pablo needed for?

(A) Translating a document
(B) Contacting an agency
(C) Repairing some equipment
(D) Preparing a trip overseas

需要巴勃羅做什麼事？

(A) 翻譯文件
(B) 連絡代理商
(C) 修理一些設備
(D) 準備海外旅行

解析 需要理解找巴勃羅的原因。女子們中說似乎上司的女子就需要翻譯來自於西班牙客戶的信件，因此正確答案是 (A)。

15 Why does the man say, "Maria lived in Spain for about seven years"?

(A) To recommend Maria for a promotion
(B) To suggest that Maria help with a task
(C) To correct some mistakes
(D) To warn about some dangers

男子為什麼說「瑪麗亞在西班牙生活了大約七年」？

(A) 舉薦瑪莉亞升職
(B) 建議瑪莉亞幫忙工作
(C) 糾正一些錯誤
(D) 警告一些危險

解析 新多益題型的掌握意圖題型，必須理解引用句中在前後文的意思。聽到女子說在巴勃羅會說西班牙文，於是提到瑪麗亞也像巴勃羅一樣可以在西班牙生活了7年左右，意思是將瑪莉亞提到瑪麗亞可以幫忙翻譯，因此答案是 (B)。（B) 中的task指的是翻譯工作。

Questions 16-18 refer to the following conversation and list. (美W)

Melbourne Technology Conference Fees		
Day 1 Only	Member	$70
	Non-member	$80
Day 2 Only	**❶ Member**	**$95**
	Non-member	$105
Both Days	Member	$150
	Non-member	$170

W Hello, I'm Dr. Louise Reynolds. I'm calling about the Melbourne Technology Conference. I want to register but ❶ your Web site is down again.

M I'm sorry for the inconvenience, Dr. Reynolds. I can help you register over the phone. Will you be attending both days of our conference?

W Actually, no. ❶ I'm just interested in the second day. And I am a Melbourne Technology Institute member.

M Okay, fine. ❶ If you give me your member ID number, then I'll make sure you get the necessary discount.

W Of course, hold on for a minute while I get my ID card.

女 你好，我是露薏絲雷諾斯博士。我打來是關於墨爾本科技研討會，我想報名參加。可是你們的網站又當機。

男 抱歉造成不便，雷諾斯博士。我可以透過電話幫您登記。您是要參加兩天的研討會嗎？

女 事實上沒有，我只對第二天有興趣。我也是墨爾本科技學會的成員。

男 好的，給我您的會員身分號碼，確保您獲得必要的折扣。

女 沒問題，等我一下。我去拿會員證。

---

16 What problem does the woman mention?

(A) A Web site is not working.
(B) A bill is incorrect.
(C) Some staff members are unavailable.
(D) Some schedules have not been updated.

女子提到了什麼問題？

(A) 網站無法正常運作
(B) 帳單不正確
(C) 一些工作人員無法使用
(D) 一些日程尚未更新

解析 女子提到的事情來自於女子說的話。女子第一句話說想要報名研討會，但是網站當機，聽到這個部分能夠選出無法運作（not working）的答案。

17 Look at the graphic. How much will the woman most likely pay?

(A) $70
(B) $80
(C) $95
(D) $105

請看圖表，女子最有可能支付多少錢？

(A) 70美元
(B) 80美元
(C) 95美元
(D) 105美元

解析 表格/圖片相關題型必須先讀完題目，預測可能出現哪些和圖表相關的內容。女子並非參加完兩天（both days）的研討會，而只參加第二天，並表明自己是會員身分，由此可知需付95美元。

18 What does the man ask the woman to provide?

(A) A registration form
(B) A meal preference
(C) A company name
(D) An identification number

男子要求女子提供什麼？

(A) 登記表
(B) 餐點喜好
(C) 公司名稱
(D) ID號碼

解析 男子要求的內容100%機率來自於男子說的話。男子表示為了取得折扣，需要提供會員卡號，因此答案是 (D)。

詞彙 register 報名 be down 故障 inconvenience 不便 institute 學會
hold 等待 work 運作 incorrect 錯誤的 staff member 工作人員
unavailable 沒有時間的、無法見面的 update 更新、更換 provide
提供 preference 偏好

PART 4

Unit 12 主題 I - 公共介紹

Step 2 眼睛和耳朵完美搭配 Practice   P94

正解
1. (A)   2. (B)   3. (B)   4. (B)

Question 1 refers to the following announcement. 英W

Attention Hillman's Supermarket customers. While you're in the store today, be sure to check out our newly expanded bakery section located right next to the dairy products. Our bakers have been busy creating new cakes and bread for you.

希爾曼超市的顧客請注意，今日來店顧客，請參考本店在乳製品區旁邊新增的烘焙區，我們的麵包師為您精心製作新款蛋糕及麵包。

1 Where is the announcement being made?
公告在哪裡？
(A) In a grocery store   (B) In a cooking school
(A) 在食品雜貨店   (B) 在烹飪學校

2 What was the cause of the delay?
延誤的原因是什麼？
(A) There was bad weather in the area.
(B) An airplane needed more fuel.
(A) 該地區天氣惡劣。
(B) 飛機需要更多燃料。

Question 2 refers to the following announcement. 美M

Attention passengers of flight 1820 to Casablanca. We apologize for the delay while the aircraft was being refueled but we are now ready to begin boarding. It's going to a full flight tonight.

搭乘1820班機前往卡薩布蘭加的乘客請注意，我們深感抱歉。由於飛機補充燃油造成時間延誤，我們目前已準備開始登機，今晚班機將是客滿狀態。

3 Who probably is the speaker?
說話者可能是誰？
(A) A professional singer   (B) A theater manager
(A) 專業歌手   (B) 劇院經理

Question 3 refers to the following talk. 英W

Good evening and welcome to the Berkley Theater. Tonight's dramatic performance will last for approximately 2 hours. There will be a 15-minute intermission during which you can enjoy drinks and refreshments available in the lobby.

晚安，歡迎蒞臨柏克利劇院，今晚這場精彩感動人心的表演將歷時大約2小時，中途有15分鐘的中場休息，您可以享用在大廳準備提供的飲料及茶點。

4 What will the company offer at a discounted price?
該公司將以折扣價提供什麼？
(A) A sightseeing tour   (B) The evening meal
(A) 觀光旅遊   (B) 晚餐

Question 4 refers to the following announcement. 美M

There was some mix-up in our schedules and we will be staying at a different hotel. The new hotel is as pleasant as the one we reserved before. We're very sorry for the inconvenience. To make up for the confusion, there will be a special discount on tonight's dinner buffet.

由於行程被打亂的關係，因此我們住宿飯店有變動，新的飯店和原先預定的一樣舒適，造成不便敬請見諒。為了彌補這場混亂，今晚晚餐自助餐會有特別折扣。

Step 3 基本掌握   P95

正解
1. (B)   2. (B)   3. (A)   4. (B)   5. (B)
6. (A)   7. (A)   8. (B)   9. (B)   10. (B)
11. (B)   12. (A)

Questions 1-3 refer to the following talk. 美W

Good afternoon. ❶ ❷ We'll start the tour of the historic Wellington House in just a few minutes. First, I'd like to tell you a few rules to keep you safe and to protect the artworks. Please be careful of your footing because the floor is uneven in many places. Also when we go up the staircase, you will need to watch your step as it is very steep. And finally, ❸ no flash photography is permitted anywhere in the Wellington House. Thank you for your consideration. Now let's begin our tour in the main entryway.

午安，幾分鐘後我們將展開歷史悠久的威靈頓大宅之旅。首先，我要說明規則以確保各位的安全並且保護其中的藝術作品。由於多處地面不平的關係，請小心您的腳步。另外上樓時請留意，上樓時的階梯陡峭。最後，在威靈頓大宅內禁止使用閃光燈拍照。感謝您的關照。現在讓我們從主要的入口通道開始參觀吧。

詞彙   historic 歷史性的   artwork 藝術作品   footing 立足點   uneven 不平坦的   staircase 階梯   steep 陡峭   permit 允許   consideration 關照   considerable 相當大的   entryway 入口通道   photographer 攝影師   prohibit 禁止

1 Who is speaking?
誰在說話？
(A) A photographer
(B) A tour guide
(A) 攝影師
(B) 導遊

解析 GQ是詢問說話者是誰，主要提示出現在前半部。從一開始提到即將開始導覽雙的部分，可以得知說話者是導遊。

2 Where is the announcement being made?
公告在哪裡？
(A) At a photography studio
(B) At a historic building
(A) 在攝影工作室
(B) 在一座歷史建築

3

Questions 4-6 refer to the following announcement. 美M

Attention passengers, thank you so much for waiting here on the bus while I investigated the problem. Unfortunately, ❹ we have a flat tire. So I had to call a mechanic to come and help change it. We have called the closest mechanic who should be here any moment now. I'm sure we'll get the tire replaced and get back on the road soon. If everything goes according to plan, ❺ we should be able to leave here at 3:00 p.m. Until then, feel free to get off the bus to take a look around or visit the coffee shop at the corner. Right now is 1 o'clock, ❻ please make sure you're back by three. We'd like to depart as soon as the problem is fixed.

According to the speaker, what is prohibited?
(A) Taking flash photographs
(B) Using mobile phones

解析 GQ是前兩題發生的地點，提示出現在前半部。同一句話可能作為幾個題目的提示，重要的是先讀完題目之後再分析題型。前面提到地點是歷史性的建築，由此可知答案是 (B)。

解析 對照文中往前半部是公告內容，後半節是指示事項的注意事項。(A)。由於提到不可使用閃光燈拍攝，因此正確答案是 (A)。尤其歷史悠久的文物經常禁止攝影，需熟記此一常識。
(A) 使用閃光燈拍攝
(B) 使用手機

4 What is causing a delay?
(A) An engine problem
(B) A flat tire

解析 延誤是公告是交通公告中最常考的類型。原因或目的內容經常作為GQ主題，提示通常出現在前半部，調查結果發現輪胎爆胎，因此答案是 (B)。

什麼導致了延誤？
(A) 引擎問題
(B) 輪胎爆胎

5 According to the speaker, at what time is the bus expected to depart?
(A) At 1 P.M.
(B) At 3 P.M.

解析 這是典型的SQ需要從短文中出現的各種時間中掌握最正確的答案。公告提到如果按照計畫，3點可以離開這裡，因此正確答案是 (B)，而1點是目前的時間。

根據說話者，巴士預計在何時出發？
(A) 下午1點
(B) 下午3點

6 What does the speaker ask the listeners to do?
(A) Return on time
(B) Find their tickets

解析 說話者要求聽眾做什麼？說話者提醒輪胎一修好就要出發，務必在3點前返回，因此答案是 (A)。短文的be back by three往往在選項中被重新詮釋為 return on time。

說話者要求聽眾做什麼？
(A) 準時回來
(B) 找到他們的票

Questions 7-9 refer to the following announcement. 美M

May I have your attention please! ❼ We'll be arriving shortly at Heathrow International Airport. The current weather is 21 degrees Celsius, a little cloudy but warm for this time of the year. I hope you have a wonderful time in London. ❽ Now, in preparation for our landing, we ask you now bring your seats back to upright position and return your tray table to the locked position. Please fasten your seat belts and ❾ remain seated until we safely land on the ground and the captain turns off the seat belt sign.

7 For whom is this announcement intended?
(A) Airplane passengers
(B) Air traffic controllers

解析 GQ是前兩題出現在前半部，一開始提到即將進達機場，主要提示對象在前半段內容，因此答案是 (A)。

這個公告是對誰說的？
(A) 飛機乘客
(B) 航管員

8 What are the listeners asked to do?
(A) Turn off electronic devices
(B) Prepare for landing

解析 GQ是前兩題的內容以命令或要輸掇形式出現。為了準備降落，要求乘客回復座位餐盤，而最適合的解釋是為了降落做準備，因此答案是 (B)。

聽眾被要求做什麼？
(A) 關閉電子設備
(B) 為降落做準備

9
When can the listeners leave their seats?
(A) After the captain gets off the plane
(B) When they safely land on the ground

聽眾什麼時候可以離開座位?
(A) 模長下飛機後
(B) 當他們安全降落地面時

解析 如果對Part 4的各種具備基本常識的話，聽起來非常有利。為了安全降落，必須好好坐著帶好直到完全降落，因此可知答案是下飛機後的內容。
(B) 雖然出現captain (機長) 的單字，但並未提到機長需先下飛機的內容。

詞彙 perfect 完美的　historic 歷史性的　site 地點　scenery 風景　last 持續　grab a snack 吃點東西　bottled water 瓶裝水　opportunity 機會　departure 出發　weather forecaster 氣象播報員　travel agency 旅行社　provide 提供

10
Who probably is the speaker?
(A) A weather forecaster
(B) A travel agency employee

說話者可能是誰?
(A) 氣象播報員
(B) 旅行社員工

解析 GQ是詢問說話者是誰，提示出現在前半部。第一句的內容經常使用和答案近似的詞彙來表達。

Questions 10-12 refer to the following talk. 美W

Good morning, everyone. ⑩ My name is Melanie and I'll be your guide for the day. With this great weather, it will be a perfect day for our bus tour. We will visit all the major historic sites of the city and have plenty of time to relax and enjoy the beautiful weather and scenery, too. Our trip will last about 4 to 5 hours, so you might want to grab a snack before we go. ⑪ We will be providing bottled water for everyone. Also, get your cameras ready because there will be many opportunities to use them. We have about 30 minutes until our bus arrives ⑫ for our 10 o'clock departure.

大家早安。我叫梅蘭妮，我是您今天的導遊。有了這個好天氣，這將是我們搭造城市巴士旅遊的完美日子。我們將造訪城市所有主要的景點，也有充分的時間能夠放鬆並享受美好的天氣和景色。整趟旅程大約4到5小時，所以出發前您也許想要先吃點零食。我們會提供瓶裝水給各位。此外，相機準備好，會有許多用上的機會。距離巴士10點出發還有30分鐘左右。

11
What will be provided for listeners?
(A) Light snacks
(B) Drinking water

將為聽眾提供什麼?
(A) 輕食點心
(B) 飲用水

解析 內容提到將為大家準備瓶裝水，因此可知答案是飲用水。雖然提到零食 (snack)，但並沒有旅行社為觀光客們提供點心的內容。

12
What time are the listeners leaving?
(A) 10:00 A.M.
(B) 10:30 A.M.

聽眾什麼時候離開?
(A) 上午10點
(B) 上午10點30分

解析 這種典型的SQ須從各種時間點中選出題目間的正確時間。提到巴士在10點出發，目前還剩下30分鐘，因此出發時間是10點。注意避免將聽到的時間加總起來而誤選10點30分。

Step 4　實戰練習

正解
1. (A)	2. (D)	3. (B)	4. (B)	5. (C)
6. (A)	7. (A)	8. (B)	9. (D)	10. (B)
11. (B)	12. (A)	13. (A)	14. (B)	15. (C)
16. (C)	17. (D)	18. (D)		

Questions 1-3 refer to the following announcement. 澳M

① Attention all passengers. This is your captain speaking. You're on the 8:30 P.M. flight to Hamburg. ② We'll be taking off 15 minutes later than expected to allow some passengers from a connecting flight to board the airplane. Despite this delay, ③ we still anticipate an on-time arrival in Hamburg as weather conditions continue to be favorable. Thank you for your patience.

① 各位乘客請注意：這裡是機長廣播。本次為20點30分前往漢堡的班機。② 我們將比預計時間晚15分鐘起飛，讓一些乘客從另一班轉程航班登機。儘管延誤起飛，③ 由於天候良好有利於飛行，我們預計仍然能夠準時抵達漢堡。感謝您的耐心等候。

詞彙 captain 機長　connecting flight 轉程航班　delay 延誤　continue 持續、繼續　favorable 良好的　anticipate 預計　cause 原因　load 裝載　luggage 行李　patience 耐心　departure 出發　weather forecaster 氣象播報員　vehicle 汽車、車輛　refuel 加油　condition 情況　on time 準時　provide 提供

1
Where most likely are the listeners?
(A) In an airplane
(B) On a train
(C) On a bus
(D) In a waiting room

聽眾最有可能在哪裡?
(A) 在飛機上
(B) 在火車上
(C) 在公車上
(D) 在候機室

解析 GQ是詢問聽眾所在的地點，提示出現在前半部。提示可知最接近的選項是 (A)。

2
What is the cause of the delay?
(A) Some workers are loading the luggage.

(B) There is a stormy weather.
(C) A vehicle has to be refueled.
(D) Some passengers have not yet arrived.

延誤的原因是什麼？
(A) 一些工作人員正在裝載行李。
(B) 暴風雨的天氣。
(C) 車輛必須加油。
(D) **有些乘客還沒到達。**

解析 交通延誤的原因是與交通有關的考題中最常考的類型。上一個選項的答案不一定也是下一題的答案，必須完全理解短文和題目再作答。為了等待轉機的旅客搭機，需延後15分鐘起飛，因此答案是 (D)。雖然背景知識很重要，但必須正確掌握每個題目的Key Word以用於解題。

---

3 What does the speaker say he expects will happen?
(A) Weather conditions will get worse.
(B) A flight will arrive on time.
(C) Some seats will be available.
(D) Some food will be provided.

說話者預期會發生什麼？
(A) 天氣狀況會變得更糟。
(B) **航班將準時到達。**
(C) 將有一些空位。
(D) 將提供一些食物。

解析 說話者對未來預期的事情往往在後半部出現提示。後面提到雖然延誤出發，但預計將準時抵達漢堡，因此答案是 (B)。

Questions 4~6 refer to the following talk. [美M]

Welcome to Rock Point Caves. My name is Oliver and I'll be your tour guide this afternoon. ④ Our tour will last about 2 hours, and we will walk about 3 kilometers through the caves. ⑤ You're welcome to take pictures during the tour, but you must stay on the wooden walkway all the time. Due to the caves' natural moisture, the rock floor is wet and slippery. ⑥ So please watch your step and walk carefully. One final note — please leave any food or beverages on the tour bus because you are not allowed to bring them into the caves. Now, let's begin our tour.

詞彙 wooden 木頭的 walkway 走道 natural 天然的 moisture 濕氣 slippery 滑的 step 腳步 carefully 小心地 note 注意、筆記 beverage 飲料 be allowed to 允許～ describe 描述 award 獎勵 promote 推廣 take a break 休息片刻 in the middle 在中間 suggest 建議 safety glasses 護目鏡 wait in line 排隊等候

歡迎來到岩石角山洞。我是各位今天下午的嚮導奧利佛。我們的旅途將歷時大約2小時，並且穿越山洞共3公里左右。沿途歡迎自由拍照，但請保持走在木頭棧道上。由於山洞內的天然濕氣，岩石地面相當潮濕，因此請注意腳步。最後一點，請把所有食物和飲料留在巴士上，因為洞內禁止攜帶飲食。現在讓我們開始參觀吧。

---

4 What is the main purpose of the talk?
(A) To introduce a new employee
(B) To describe a nature tour
(C) To give an award
(D) To promote a product

談話的主要目的是什麼？
(A) 介紹一名新員工
(B) **描述自然之旅**
(C) 給予獎勵
(D) 推廣產品

解析 GQ是詢問目的，通常提示也出現在前半部。聽到介紹導遊身分之後，說明洞穴之旅的行程，由此可知答案是 (B)。注意避免看到introduce的詞彙就誤選 (A)。

---

5 What are the listeners invited to do during the tour?
(A) Take a break in the middle
(B) Come to a dinner party
(C) Take pictures
(D) Bring some food

推薦聽眾在旅程中做什麼？
(A) 中途在旅程中休息片刻
(B) 來參加晚宴
(C) **拍照**
(D) 帶些食物

解析 <be invited+to不定詞>具有「推薦～」的意思，是多益中經常出現的表達句型。在推薦別人做某件事時經常使用。參觀期間可以盡情拍照，可以得知答案就是推薦的內容。

---

6 What does the speaker suggest?
(A) Walking carefully
(B) Putting on safety glasses
(C) Asking questions
(D) Waiting in line

說話者建議什麼？
(A) **小心行走**
(B) 戴上護目鏡
(C) 提出問題
(D) 排隊等候

解析 題目是從選項中選出說話者建議的內容，必須待聽短文的同時，眼睛瀏覽選項來確認。以 'be sure to ～, don't forget to, please' 開始的句子經常使用在懇切的請求～。從小心腳步的內容可知正確答案是 (A)。

Questions 7-9 refer to the following announcement. 美W

Attention all shoppers! ⑦ Trader Joe's will be closing in 15 minutes at 10 P.M. ⑧ If you still haven't paid for what you wanted to purchase, please go to the nearest cash register. ⑨ Please go to the registers where they have green lights on. Do not go to the registers where they have already closed for the day. Trader Joe's will be closed tomorrow for a Jewish Holiday, but will reopen on Thursday at our regular time at 9:00 in the morning. Thank you for shopping at Trader Joe's and have a good evening.

詞彙 purchase 購買、購入 register 結帳台、收銀機 Jewish 猶太人的 reopen 重開 trading 交易 certain 特定的

7 What is being announced?
(A) The closing of a store
(B) The opening of a new business
(C) Special prices on some items
(D) Trading price for a certain product

公告什麼事?
(A) 關閉商店
(B) 開新商店
(C) 一些物品的特價
(D) 特定產品的交易價格

解析 注意題目中的Key Word是green signs(綠色標誌)再聽聽短文。由於沒有亮綠燈的是不開放的櫃檯，並要求顧客前往亮綠燈的結帳台。由此可知green lights/signs指示有開放的結帳台。

8 What are listeners invited to do?
(A) Close the register
(B) Pay for the purchase
(C) Shop at the new store
(D) Come back the next day

話可以得知最佳的地點是購物場所，而店將在15分鐘之後關門，因此答案是 (A)。

聽眾被要求做什麼?
(A) 關閉收銀機
(B) 支付購買費用
(C) 在新商店購物
(D) 隔天回來

解析 GQ是詢問公告的整體主題，通常在前半部出現提示。從第一句

9 What do green signs identify?
(A) The clothing department
(B) The emergency exit
(C) The direction to the manager's office
(D) The open registers

綠色標誌代表什麼?
(A) 服裝部門
(B) 緊急出口
(C) 經理辦公室的路線指引
(D) 開放的結帳台

解析 是員。因此答案不是 (A)。

要求想購買物品但尚未結帳的顧客就近至收銀台結帳。雖然出現register的詞彙，但能夠關閉收銀機的人只有店員。(B)，因此答案不是 (A)。

Questions 10-12 refer to the following talk. 澳M

⑩ Welcome to the Marshall Textile Factory tour. As most of you know, our factory provides high-quality fabrics to clothing manufacturers across the world. During the tour of the facility, you will see the care that goes into making each of our many types of fabrics. I am sorry to tell you about a change made to our schedule. Normally, we'd start by showing you how fabrics are made on our weaving machines. ⑪ However, another group is still in that area, so today we'll start in the final packaging room and do the tour in reverse, visiting the weaving machine at the end. Also, ⑫ we'd like to offer a 10 percent discount on fabric purchased today only.

詞彙 textile 紡織 manufacturer 製造廠商 weave 編織、編織 duration 期間 distance 距離 location 位置 discussion 討論、對話 provide 提供 care 照料、關心 final 最後的 leader 隊長、領導 quality 品質 packaging 包裝 outdoor 戶外 special 特別的 fabric 織品、布料 normally 通常、一般 in reverse 相反地、倒過來 trade fair 貿易博覽會

10 Where is the tour most likely taking place?
(A) At a fashion show
(B) At a fabric factory
(C) At a trade fair
(D) At an outdoor market

參觀最有可能發生在哪裡?
(A) 時裝秀
(B) 紡織工廠
(C) 貿易博覽會
(D) 戶外市場

解析 GQ是詢問參觀的地點。從第一句話提到紡織工廠的部分可以選出此出答案。尤其需熟記textile、fabric可表達相同的意思。雖然後半部也出現這個詞彙，但盡可能在第一個提示時就能選出正確答案。

11 What does the speaker say has changed about the tour?
(A) The duration
(B) The distance
(C) The starting location
(D) The tour leader

就話者提到參觀行程有什麼改變?
(A) 進行時間
(B) 距離
(C) 起始位置
(D) 領隊

解析 行程變更是活動相關主題中經常出現的題目選項。內容提到一般是從紡織機開始參觀，因這次反過來從最後開始，再參觀紡織機。因此答案是 (C)。需熟記各種同義詞，以利在高難度題目中作答。

12 What does the speaker offer the listeners?
(A) A special discount
(B) A longer tour
(C) Free samples
(D) Discussion time

就話者為聽眾提供什麼?
(A) 特價折扣
(B) 更長的參觀行程
(C) 免費樣品
(D) 討論時間

解析 提到只有今天提供布料打折的優惠，因此答案是 (A)。

Questions 13-15 refer to the following announcement. 美M

May I have everyone's attention please? ⑬ Thank you for coming to the Science Theater of the Delvin Museum and thank you all for waiting so patiently in line. Unfortunately, ⑭ we have just filled all the seats for the 11 o'clock showing of today's documentary film, *Into the Space*. However, ⑮ there will be another showing at 2 o'clock and we'll have fewer attendees at this time. We hope you'll return then. In the meantime, feel free to continue exploring the museum exhibits, cafeteria and gift shop.

詞彙 in line 排隊 patiently 有耐心地 unfortunately 不幸地 attendee 參加者 feel free to 隨意～ continue 持續、繼續 explore 探索 cafeteria 自助餐廳 exhibition 展示

13 Where is the announcement being made?
(A) At a museum
(B) At a university
(C) At a department store
(D) At a restaurant

公告在哪裡提出現？
(A) 博物館
(B) 大學
(C) 百貨公司
(D) 餐廳

解析 提示出現在前半部。從歡迎各位來到博物館劇院的內容可以得知，公告是出現在博物館內部的劇院。選項中各有答案，但這是出現在特定地點的題型，有時會出現現機場的停車場、百貨公司的餐廳等特定地點細分出的內部場所的情況。避免以先入為主的觀念作答，而是從選項中選擇最適合的答案。

14 What are the listeners waiting to attend?
(A) A lecture
(B) A documentary film
(C) A special exhibition
(D) A musical concert

聽眾等待參加什麼？
(A) 演講
(B) 紀錄片
(C) 特展
(D) 音樂會

解析 從排隊等待觀看紀錄片的內容可以得知答案是 (B)。

15 What does the speaker imply when he says, "there will be another showing at 2 o'clock"?
(A) He wants to get a deadline extension.
(B) A renovation will be completed.
(C) The listeners should return at a later time.
(D) The listeners should make a reservation.

男子說「2點還有另一場放映」的意思是什麼？
(A) 他希望延長期限
(B) 裝修即將完工
(C) 聽眾應該晚一點再過來
(D) 聽眾應該事先預約

解析 詢問說話者意圖的題目必須導守掌握前後文的一致性。就說話者提到2點會有另一場放映，而且參加者較少，希望聽眾到時回來，由此可知意思是晚一點再過來。

Questions 16-18 refer to the following announcement and timetable. 美W

Attention all passengers leaving on the 6:30 P.M. ferry to Nelson Island. ⑯ Due to a storm along the coast, this ferry has been cancelled. ⑰ However, the storm is moving quickly so that it should be out of the area before the last departure of the day. While you wait, you can explore the area on your own, but please be back in time for the last ferry of the day. Also, if you want to enjoy the scenery of the area, you can come to the upper deck of the boat later on, but ⑱ you might want to put on a sweater or jacket because it can be pretty chilly up there. Thanks for your patience and we apologize for the inconvenience.

Oceanfront Island Ferry	
Departures	Arrivals
9:30 A.M.	10:00 A.M.
10:30 A.M.	11:00 A.M.
6:30 P.M.	7:00 P.M.
⑰ 8:00 P.M.	8:30 P.M.

海濱島渡輪	
出發	抵達
上午 9:30	上午 10:00
上午 10:30	上午 11:00
下午 6:30	下午 7:00
下午 8:00	下午 8:30

16 What has caused the cancellation?
(A) Mechanical problems
(B) Security issues
(C) Bad weather
(D) A lack of passengers

是什麼導致了取消？
(A) 機械問題
(B) 安全問題
(C) 惡劣天氣
(D) 乘客不預

解析 交通公告中最常出現的是延誤，其次是取消/停運的內容。一開始提到因為海邊風暴的關係而取消渡輪，因此答案是 (C)。

17 Look at the graphic. What time will the ferry leave?
(A) 9:30 A.M.
(B) 10:30 A.M.
(C) 6:00 P.M.
(D) **8:00 P.M.**

請看圖表。渡輪何時會出發？
(A) 上午 9:30
(B) 上午 10:30
(C) 下午 6:00
(D) **下午 8:00**

詞彙 ferry 渡輪 departure 出發 scenery 風景 upper 上方的 deck 甲板 put on 穿上 chilly 冷的 patience 耐心 apologize 道歉 inconvenience 不便 mechanical 機械的 security 安全 lack 缺乏 souvenir 紀念品

解析 所有搭乘晚間6點30分前往尼爾森島渡輪的乘客請注意：由於海岸線的暴風，此班渡輪取消。然而暴風移動速度很快，預計在今日最後一班開船前會離開這個地區。在您等待的同時，可自行探索本地區，另外，您若想欣賞本地區的風景，稍後可於上方甲板，但因為本地區的風景，稍後時間內可您的耐心等候，不便之處向您致歉。

Step 2　眼睛和耳朵完美搭配 Practice　P100

正解

1. (B)	2. (A)	3. (B)	4. (B)

1

What business is the speaker calling?
(A) A doctor's office　(B) A transportation service

說話者打電話到什麼行業？
(A) 醫生的辦公室　(B) 交通運輸中心

Question 1 refers to the following telephone message. 美M

Hello, I'm calling about a problem I had with your bus service. I ride the 6 o'clock bus home from work. Yesterday evening, I waited for the bus for over an hour before giving up and taking a taxi home.

你好，我打來是因為你們公車服務出了問題。我搭6點的車下班回家，但昨天晚上我卻等了一小時以上卻沒來，只好放棄坐計程車回家。

2

What problem does the speaker report?
(A) A printer is not working properly.
(B) A finance report is not ready in time.

說話者呈報了什麼問題？
(A) 印表機無法正常運作。
(B) 財務報告沒有及時準備好。

Question 2 refers to the following telephone message. 英W

Hi, this message is for the technology department. This is Gena Williams from finance. I'm calling because our printer has jammed again and this is the third time this problem happened this week.

你好，這是給科技部門的留言。我是財務部的吉娜威廉斯，我打來是因為我們的印表機又卡紙，本週已經是第三次發生這種問題了。

3

What is wrong with the number that was dialed?
(A) Nobody is at home right now.
(B) It is the wrong number.

Question 3 refers to the following recorded message. 美W

I'm sorry. The number you have dialed is not in service any more. Please check the number and call again later.

撥打的號碼有什麼問題？
(A) 現在沒有人在家。
(B) 是錯誤的電話號碼。

很抱歉，您撥的電話已經停止服務，請查明號碼後再撥。

4

What number should you press for the arrival schedule?
(A) Number 1　(B) Number 2

你應該按什麼號碼以取得抵達時間表？
(A) 1號　(B) 2號

Question 4 refers to the following recorded message. 英W

You have reached Delta Airlines Automated Information Service. At any time during this message, press 0 to be connected to one of our service agents. For departure schedules, press 1. For arrival information, press 2.

這裡是達美航空客服系統，語言通話期間，您可以隨時按0連接客服人員，查詢航班出發時間請按1，航班抵達資訊請按2。

18

What does the speaker say listeners may want to do?
(A) Travel the next day
(B) Visit the souvenir shops
(C) Take a picture of the scenery
(D) Wear warm clothing

說話者提到聽眾可能想做什麼？
(A) 第二天去旅行
(B) 參觀紀念品商店
(C) 拍攝風景照
(D) 穿上保暖的衣服

解析

說話者推測聽眾可能想做的事情，就是建議聽眾的內容。說話者提到甲板上非常寒冷，可能會想穿上毛衣或夾克，因此答案是(D)。其他選項聽起來似乎有吻合，但說話者並沒有提到。

元老師的 REAL SOLUTION

Part 4是由某人無停頓地說完短文，因此必須在聽完題目之後，預測會提到圖表的什麼部分。題目問題渡輪出發的時間，因此必須先從圖表中確認。短文提到6點30分的渡輪出發，並在最後提醒不要忘記回來搭乘渡輪，因此可以得知出發時間是8點。

掌握Key Word並從聽力中找出相關的部分。說出的話和要求聽者 (Listeners) 做的事。尤其在後半部出現的動詞要求/指示聽者的內容幾乎在每次考試中都會出現在三個題目之一，因此短文中建議/提議的事情可以畫上底線做標記，特別加強練習。

正解

1. (B)	2. (A)	3. (B)	4. (B)	5. (B)
6. (A)	7. (A)	8. (B)	9. (A)	10. (A)
11. (B)	12. (B)			

Questions 1-3 refer to the following telephone message. 澳M

Hi, Kathy. ❶ This is Edward Peterson from Advertising. I wanted to let you know that ❷ tomorrow's meeting has been postponed because the marketing brochures aren't ready yet. We've rescheduled the meeting for Friday at 9 a.m. and the vice president of Marketing is flying down from company headquarters to join the meeting. ❸ Please call me to confirm this time as soon as you receive this message. Thank you.

1

Where does the speaker work?
(A) Marketing
(B) Advertising
說話者在哪裡工作？
(A) 行銷部門
(B) 廣告部門

解析 GQ是詢問說話工作的地點，尤其大多是在音檔短文的前半部出現。第一句話先介紹自己是廣告部的愛德華，因此答案是 (B)。須記得電話訊息中的自我介紹會使用「This is ~」取代「I am ~」。

2

Why has the meeting been rescheduled?
(A) Some materials were not prepared.
(B) A conference room was not available.
為什麼會議改期？
(A) 有些資料沒有準備好。
(B) 會議室無法使用。

解析 詢問會議舉行程變更的原因，從檔中找出說明的部分在於宣傳手冊尚未完成，因此答案是 (A)。短文中 marketing brochures 在選項中被改寫經變為 some materials，難度稍高，就常出現以同義詞作為答案的情況。

3

What does the speaker ask the listener to do?
(A) Reserve a flight
(B) Contact him
說話者要求聽者做什麼？
(A) 預訂航班
(B) 連絡他

解析 說話者要求聽者的內容主要出現在短文的後半部，最後提到聽到留言之後請立即連絡以確認（變更後）時間的部分，因此答案是 (B)。

詞彙 postpone 延期　brochure 宣傳手冊　vice president 副部長　headquarters 公司總部　confirm 確認　reserve 預約　contact 連絡　reschedule 重新安排、改期

Questions 4-6 refer to the following recorded message. 美M

❹ Thank you for calling the Customer Service Center for Jenny's Shopping Haven. If you want to order a product through our automatic ordering system, please press one. If you have a question about existing orders, press two. For payment options or change of address, please press three. At any time during this recording, ❺ if you want to talk to a customer service representative, please press the star key. ❻ For more details on a store location near you, please visit us at www.jennyshaven.com.

4

Who are the intended listeners for this message?
(A) Telephone operators
(B) Store customers
誰是此訊息的預期聽眾？
(A) 電話接線員
(B) 賣場顧客

解析 GQ是詢問聽眾是誰，必須從前半部找到提示。尤其在前面聽到公司名稱，精錄音（commercial recording）可以在前面聽到公司的營業描述、表達出購物天堂顧客服務中心，因此可推測是賣場顧客為對象的告知內容。

5

What should listeners do in order to speak with a representative?
(A) Press one
(B) Push the star button
聽眾如何與代表人員交談？
(A) 按1
(B) 按*字鍵

解析 這種題型是經常出現在SQ，詢問要做什麼以和職員通話，必須從音檔內容來確認。短文提到想要和職員交談的話須按*字鍵，因此答案是 (B)。

6

If listeners want to find the nearest store, what should they do?
(A) Go online
(B) Visit the store
如果聽眾想找到最近的商店，他們該怎麼做？
(A) 上網
(B) 前往賣場

解析 短文提到如果想找到最近的商店可以上網，因此答案是 (A)。注意聽到如同樣找到最近的商店visit的單字而誤選 (B)。

詞彙 order 訂購　automatic 自動的　exiting 現有的　payment options 付款方式　any time 隨時　representative 代表　detail 細節　telephone operator 電話接線員　location 位置

Questions 7-9 refer to the following telephone message. 美W

Good morning, this is a message for Mr. Sato. Mr. Sato, ❼❽ I'm calling from the Grand Hotel in Madison Square because you left your camera in your hotel room. I'd be happy to mail the camera back to you and I won't charge you the shipping cost but ❾ I do need to confirm your mailing address. Just give me a call back with this information and I can mail the camera back to you later today. Thanks, and have a nice day.

早安，這是給佐藤先生的訊息。佐藤先生，這是麥迪遜廣場的格蘭德飯店，您的相機遺落在飯店房間。我很樂將相機寄回給您並不會收取運費，但是我需要確認您的郵寄地址。請回電，我將於今天稍晚寄還相機。謝謝，並祝您有美好的一天。

詞彙 charge 要求、收取（費用）　shipping cost 運費　confirm 確認　electronics 電子產品　defective 有瑕疵的、不良的　description 描述、表達

7

Where does the speaker work?
(A) At a hotel
(B) At an electronics store

說話者在哪裡工作？
(A) 飯店
(B) 電子產品店

解析　GQ是詢問說話者工作的地點，提示出現在前半部。一開始提到「電話來自於格蘭德飯店」，因此答案是 (A)。主題雖然是相機，但須注意說話者並不是在電子產品店工作。

8

What is the phone call about?
(A) A defective product
(B) A forgotten item

致電的原因是什麼？
(A) 有瑕疵的商品
(B) 遺失的物品

解析　GQ是詢問打電話的原因，提示出現在前半部。第 7 題和第 8 題的答案分別能夠從文章裡組織而致電、聽到這個部之間的連結，因此和這個問題沒有關聯。

9

What information does the speaker need?
(A) A mailing address
(B) A description of an object

說話者需要什麼資訊？
(A) 郵寄地址
(B) 商品描述

解析　說話者需要的部分是提出要求的內容。從提到不會收取費用，但需要確認郵寄地址的部分可以得知答案。

Questions 10-12 refer to the following recorded message. (美M)

You have reached the voice mail of Patrick Darrel at the New Product Development. **⑩** I will be in Hong Kong attending a business conference from August 25th through August 30th. However, **⑪** I'll be checking my voice mail messages every evening while I'm away. **⑫** If you need immediate assistance, please press zero to be connected to my secretary. Otherwise, stay on the line to leave a message. I will return your call as soon as I can.

這是創新產品部派崔克達洛的語音信箱。8月25日到8月30日我去香港參加商務會議，離開期間，每天晚上我會檢視語音信箱留言，如果你需要立即的協助，請按0由我的秘書轉接。其他情況則直接留言，我會盡快回覆。

詞彙　reach 致電、到達　voice mail 語音信箱　attend 參加　immediate 緊急的、立刻的　assistance 協助　connect 連接　secretary 秘書　otherwise 否則　stay on the line 線上等候　be on another line 另一通電話　hang up 掛斷

10

Where is Patrick Darrel?
(A) He is at a conference.
(B) He is on another line.

派崔克達洛在哪裡？
(A) 他正在參加一個會議。
(B) 他正在接聽另一通電話。

解析　GQ是詢問說話者 (speaker) 或聽者 (listener) 工作的地點，但與特定時間有什麼地點無關。短文前面提到香港有商務會議的內容，因此答案是 (A)。

11

When will Mr. Darrel receive the message left on the machine?
(A) Before he goes to work every morning
(B) At the end of each day

達洛先生什麼時候收到語音信箱上留下的訊息？
(A) 每天早上上班之前
(B) 每天晚上

解析　先記下題目是詢問確認語音訊息的時間點，再聆聽短文。由於提到不在期間每天晚上會聽語音訊息，因此答案是 (B)。

12

What are listeners asked to do if they need immediate help?
(A) Hang up and call again later
(B) Talk to Mr. Darrel's secretary

如果需要立即協助，聽眾需要做些什麼？
(A) 掛上電話並稍後再打
(B) 和達洛先生的秘書通話

解析　當要找的人不在時，大多數的人會留下訊息留言，但離開者也會另外提供緊急的連絡方式，以便連絡代理職員，由此便可作答。短文中提到（如果有緊急事項可以按0和秘書通話，留下訊息 (leave a message) 是除了有急事的人之外，提供給其他人的方法。

Step 4　實戰練習

正解
1. (A)	2. (C)	3. (B)	4. (B)	5. (D)
6. (A)	7. (C)	8. (D)	9. (A)	10. (C)
11. (A)	12. (B)	13. (B)	14. (A)	15. (D)
16. (D)	17. (A)	18. (C)		

Questions 1-3 refer to the following telephone message. (美M)

Hello, this message is for Mr. Nelson. This is Jeremy calling from Mark's Furniture. We received your online order for ten bookcases. **❶** Unfortunately, the metal bookcases you ordered are currently out of stock. It will take another six weeks to get the model you wanted. However, if you prefer not to wait, **❷** I can suggest the same style of bookcases but in plastic. They cost about 10 dollars less each and I can send them to you right away. **❸** Please call me back at 555-3845 and let me know what you would like to do. I'll be waiting to hear from you.

你好，這是給奈爾遜先生的訊息。我是馬克家具的傑洛米。我們收到您線上訂購十組書架，不湊巧的是，您訂購的金屬書架目前缺貨。能拿到您想要的金屬款式，如果您不願等候，我可以推薦您同款書架是塑膠製的，每組便宜10美元，可以立刻出貨，請回電555-3845告知我您的決定，靜候您的來電。

詞彙　metal 金屬的　bookcase 書架　currently 目前　out of stock 缺貨　prefer 偏好　right away 立刻　explain 說明　apologize 道歉　defective 有瑕疵的、不良的　item 物品　announce 告知　increase 流通　refund 退款　express service 快遞服務　request 要求　price 價格　switch 更換　similar 類似的　supplier 供應商　return 退貨　partial 部分的

1 Why is the speaker calling?
(A) **To explain a problem with an order**
(B) To apologize for a defective item
(C) To change a delivery address
(D) To announce a price increase

說話者為什麼打電話？
(A) **解釋訂單的問題**
(B) 為物品瑕疵道歉
(C) 更改送貨地址
(D) 告知漲價

解析 通常打電話的目的會在一開始自我介紹完之後出現。短文中由於在訂購的書架缺貨，需等待很久的時間才能收到貨，合的答案是訂購商品有問題的 (A)。

2 What does the speaker recommend?
(A) Using an express service
(B) Requesting a partial refund
(C) **Switching to a similar product**
(D) Calling a different supplier

說話者推薦什麼？
(A) 使用快遞服務
(B) 要求部分退款
(C) **更換類似的產品**
(D) 致電其他供應商

解析 說話者推薦的事情可以視為解決上述問題的建議。短文提到如果不想等待太久，提議可以換成塑膠腰製的書架。因此答案是 (C)。短文中的the same style of bookcases but in plastic在選項中被重新詮釋為similar product（除此之外，substitute（替代品）、alternative（替換品）等也是可作為答案的詞彙。

3 What is the listener asked to do?
(A) Return an item
(B) **Call the speaker**
(C) Check a Web site
(D) Fax a receipt

要求聽者做什麼？
(A) 退貨
(B) **打電話給說話者**
(C) 查看網站
(D) 傳真收據

解析 說話者被聽者要求做的事情 (be asked to do) 主要出現在後半部。最後提到要對方回覆要等訂購商品到貨，還是換成其他商品。因此答案是 (B)。

Questions 4-6 refer to the following recorded message. 美W

④ Thank you for calling Park Village Pharmacy. If you'd like to have your prescription filled, please press one now and we'll give you details on how you can safely get your medication. If you'd like to check on the status of the prescription for your medication, please press 2. Our customer service policy guarantees that ⑤ all prescriptions will be filled within 24 hours after they're placed. ⑥ If you would like to speak to the pharmacist in person, please press 3, and we'll connect you to the pharmacist on duty. We appreciate your patronage, and have a good day.

謝謝您致電公園村藥局。若您要領取藥請按1，我們會告訴您安全用藥的細節。若您想查詢目前服藥情況請按2。我們的顧客服務政策保證收到處方後，所有的配藥將會在24小時之內完成。若您想和藥師親自問題請按3，我們將為您轉接到執勤的藥師。誠摯感謝您的支持與愛護，祝您有個美好的一天。

詞彙 pharmacy 藥局 prescription 處方箋 detail 詳細知識，詳細事項 safely 安全地 status 狀態 policy 政策 guarantee 保證 pharmacist 藥師 in person 親自 connect 連接 on duty 值勤中、當班 appreciate 感謝 patronage 光顧、支援 public 公共的 option 選項、方法 accept 接受 order 順序 double check 雙重檢查 safety 安全 instruct 指示 reservation 預約 business hours 營業時間

4 What type of business recorded the message?
(A) A hotel
(B) **A pharmacy**
(C) A public library
(D) A department store

什麼類型的行業留下該訊息？
(A) 飯店
(B) **藥局**
(C) 公共圖書館
(D) 百貨公司

解析 營業錄音 (Commercial Recording) 中介紹哪一種行業的題目提示永遠在前半部出現。第一句話提到藥局的名字，因此答案是 (B)。

5 What does the business guarantee?
(A) All payment options are accepted.
(B) All calls will be answered in the order received.
(C) Medicines are double-checked for safety.
(D) **Orders will be filled within a day.**

店家店保證什麼？
(A) 所有付款方式均可接受。
(B) 所有電話將依來電順序回答。
(C) 藥品經過雙檢查以確保安全。
(D) **配藥將在一天內準備好。**

解析 先記下題目的Key Word是guarantee再對應內容。由於提到即使在24小時內完成配藥，因此答案是 (D)。短文中的within 24 hours的選項中被重新詮釋為within a day。務必記得SQ需在正確掌握Key Word之後，再進行解題。

6 Why are the listeners instructed to press 3?
(A) **To speak with a pharmacist**
(B) To cancel the order
(C) To confirm a reservation
(D) To find out the business hours

聽眾為什麼要按3？
(A) **與藥劑師交談**
(B) 取消訂單
(C) 確認預約
(D) 得知營業時間

解析 兩店營業錄音中經常以不同媒介代表特定的服務內容，題目中所要求的部分須從短文中找出答案。按下3可以和藥劑師親自交談，由此便可作答。

Questions 7-9 refer to the following telephone message. 澳M

Hi, this is James. **⑦ There is a new office space that just came on the market that we haven't advertised yet.** I think you'd really like it. It's right in the downtown area close to public transportation, just like you wanted. The only problem may be that **⑧ the rent is higher than your initial range.** But the office space is larger than the ones I've already shown you. If you foresee expanding your business in the future, though, it might be something you'd be interested in. Now, **⑨ you need to let me know as soon as you get this message if you want this. I can wait to advertise the property until I hear back from you, but I can't hold it long.**

7 Who most likely is the speaker?
(A) An architect
(B) A financial advisor
(C) **A real estate agent**
(D) A maintenance worker

8 What does the speaker say is a problem?
(A) An office is far away from downtown.
(B) Some staff have not been trained.
(C) A deadline cannot be extended.
(D) **The rent is higher than expected.**

9 What does the speaker ask the listener to do?
(A) **Return the call promptly**
(B) Review a document carefully
(C) Recalculate the cost
(D) Submit a deposit

詞彙　cowntown 市中心　public transportation 大眾運輸　rent 租金　initial 最初的　range 範圍　foresee 預見、預料　expand 擴展　hold 等待　architect 建築師　financial 財務的　real estate 房地產　maintenance 維護　train 訓練　deadline 截止日期　extend 延長　prompty 及時地　review 回顧　cost 費用　submit 提交　deposit 押金

解析　說話者最有可能是誰？一開始提到的商務空間已經立現在市場上，從這部分可以推測說話者是提供出租借辦公室或買賣的人，因此答案是 (C) 房屋仲介。

說話者說有什麼問題？說話者提到市中心問題？辦公室至離市中心很遠。有些員工沒有接受過培訓。截止日期不能延長。租金高於預期。先記下題目的Key Word是problem之後再聆聽內容。由於提到租金比一開始的價格範圍更高，因此答案是 (D)。音檔中提higher than your initial range被重新詮釋為higher than expected。

說話者要求聽者做什麼？及時回電話　仔細閱讀文件　重新計算成本　支付押金

要求聽者在聽完後半部出現。由於出現要求對方回電，以確認是否對商務空間有興趣的內容，因此答案是 (A)。電話留言的最後部分經常是為了留住顧客而要求回電的內容。

Questions 10-12 refer to the following telephone message. 美W

Hello, this is Sonya Mendoza, head of the public relations at Historic Brinkley House. **⑩ I'm returning your call about scheduling a group tour on Monday, February 27.** Unfortunately, we don't have available time slots that day. **⑪ Please call me back at 555-2836 with another date that works for you and I'll try to make your reservation right away. ⑫ For safety reasons, we don't allow more than 15 people in your group because it's not a problem if you have more people in each group. But I just want you to be aware of that restriction.**

10 What is the message mainly about?
(A) Scheduling a safety inspection
(B) Ordering out-of-stock items
(C) **Arranging a tour of a building**
(D) Reserving a meeting place

11 What is the listener asked to do?
(A) **To provide an alternative date**
(B) To confirm a renovation schedule

詞彙　public relations 公關　tour 參觀　time slot 時段　divide 分開　be aware of 了解、意識到　safety inspection 安全檢查　out of stock 缺貨　item 物品　arrange 安排、規劃　reserve 預約　alternative 替換品　renovation 改造、整修　participant 參加者　submit 提交　beforehand 事先　increase 增加、提高　admission fee 入場費　ongoing 進行中的　facility 設施

你好，我是布林克利古蹟公關部主任的桑雅‧門多薩，想回覆您2月27日安排一日的團體參觀行程。很不幸地，當天我們沒有時段可以安排，請回覆555-2836告知其他方便的日期，我會立即處理您的預約。為了安全起見，每團不超過15人，人數如果超過，我們必須將您的成員分成小組，還望您理解這項限制。

電話訊息的目的通常在自我介紹之後隨即出現。第一句提到的Historic Brinkley House可以視為像居民俗村一樣的古老建築物。電話的目的是為了特定日期預約的參觀的行程，因此答案是 (C) 安排參觀建築。

(C) To give the names of participants

(D) To submit the payment beforehand

要求聽眾做什麼?

(A) 提供替代日期

(B) 確認整修時間表

(C) 提供參加者姓名

(D) 提前付款

解析 短文中提到的要求事項一同確認，就能得知答案是重新經釋成 alternative date (替代日期) 的 (A)。聽到另外安排參觀，日期並回電的內容之後，

According to the speaker, what should the listener be aware of?

(A) An increase in admission fees

(B) A restriction on group sizes

(C) Rules about taking photographs

(D) Ongoing facility maintenance

根據說話者，聽眾應該注意什麼?

(A) 入場費的增加

(B) 團體大小的限制

(C) 關於拍照的規定

(D) 正在進行的設施維護

解析 先記下題目的 Key Word be aware of (了解～) 之後再聆聽內容。內容提到團體人數不可超過15名，希望對方能了解這規定，由此可知答案是 (B)。

12

Questions 13-15 refer to the following telephone message. (美W)

Hello, Ben. It's your neighbor, Angie. ⑬ My return flight was scheduled to leave in an hour but they just announced it's been cancelled. I'm standing in line to talk to a ticket agent to arrange another flight reservation. ⑭ It looks like I won't make it home this evening. I'm just so tired of traveling. I think the next flight is in the morning. Anyway, I have a favor to ask you. ⑮ Could you stop by my house after work and see if a package arrived for me? It was supposed to arrive this afternoon, and I'd rather it didn't just sit in front of my door overnight. Thank you, Ben.

你好，班恩，我是鄰居安妮。我的班機預定在一小時後起飛，但剛剛宣布取消了。我正在排隊請票務人員安排其他班機，我受夠旅行了，看樣子我沒辦法今晚回到家。我想下一班飛機是早上起飛。可以麻煩你下班後繞路到我家，幫我收個包裹嗎?應該今天下午會收到，我不想讓包裹在門口過夜。謝謝你，班恩。

詞彙 stand in line 排隊等候　ticket agent 售票人員　make it 去、來　stop by 順道　be supposed to 應該～　rather not 不想～　sit 坐　overnight 過夜　package 包裹　annoyed 厭煩　confused 困惑　embarrassed 尷尬的　security 安全　colleague 同事　pick up 領取、撿起

---

13 Where most likely is the speaker?

(A) At a post office

(B) At an airport

(C) In a taxi

(D) On a train

就話者最有可能在哪裡?

(A) 郵局

(B) 機場

(C) 計程車

(D) 火車

解析 GQ是詢問說話者所在的地點，提示出現在前半部。一旦有要求事項出現時，必須取得提示，提示有可能並不明顯，前面先說自己是鄰居，目前因為班機取消而正在排隊等候安排搭下一班飛機，聽到這裡必須能夠推測地點是機場。

---

14 What does the speaker imply when she says, "Can you believe it?"

(A) She was annoyed.

(B) She was excited.

(C) She was confused.

(D) She was embarrassed.

說話者提到「你能相信嗎?」時是什麼意思?

(A) 她很生氣。

(B) 她很興奮。

(C) 她很困惑。

(D) 她很尷尬。

解析 掌握意圖的題目必須從句子中找與前後文一致的部分。因為要掌握短文內容對解題最有利。提到由於航班取消，疲倦又無法回到家的內容，可以得知女子對無法按預定計畫的情況感到不滿。因此選項中最適合的答案是 (A)。

---

15 What does the speaker ask the listener to do?

(A) Open the window

(B) Check the security system

(C) Meet with a colleague

(D) Pick up a package

說話者要求聽者做什麼?

(A) 開窗戶

(B) 檢查安全系統

(C) 與同事見面

(D) 領取包裹

解析 要求聽者的事情通常在後半部出現，必須能夠聽到最後作為答案。短文後半提到要求對方到自己的家裡，看看包裹是否送達，因此答案是 (D)。避免先預測答案，而是從選項中提選最適合的答案。聽到最後會知道要求對方收取包裹。

Questions 16-18 refer to the following telephone message and seating chart. (澳M)

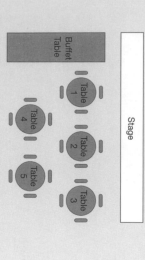

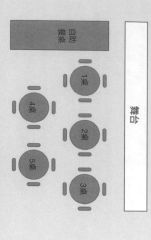

Hi, this is Mark. ⑯ I'm calling about tonight's International Photography Awards Ceremony at the Triton Hotel. Ms. Azawa, the event coordinator, emailed me a seating chart, so we know where our seats are. ⑰ We're in the first row from the stage closest to the buffet table. I'm really excited because I think we've got a great chance to win one of the prizes. ⑱ I'd like us to talk to other nominees before the dinner starts. So let's try to get to the event a little bit early. Hope to see you in a few hours then.

詞彙 ceremony 活動；典禮 coordinator 統籌者；協調員 seating chart 座位表 row 排 nominee 入圍者 retirement 退休 performance 表演 banquet 宴會 refer to 提到；涉及 a little bit 稍微 backstage 後台

---

16 What is the speaker calling about?
(A) A retirement party
(B) A musical performance
(C) A wedding banquet
(D) An awards banquet

解析 說話者為什麼打電話？
電話訊息通常在自我介紹之後就說出目的。自我介紹完後到了「今天晚上的頒獎典禮而禮貌致電」，聽到這裡應能夠選出答案是 (D)。須謹記提供飲食的活動可以稱做banquet (宴會)。應該先作答第16題再看圖片，視覺資料則有當看題目提到的再用來解題。

17 Look at the graphic. Which table does the speaker refer to?
(A) Table 1
(B) Table 2
(C) Table 3
(D) Table 4

請看圖表，幾號桌是說話者提到的桌子？
(A) 1號桌
(B) 2號桌
(C) 3號桌
(D) 4號桌

解析 看圖表，得將資料相關的題目最好先讀完題目和圖片之後，預測題目當中出現的桌子之外，還得事先提到哪些部分。短文中除了提到選項中出現的桌子之外，還得事先提到舞台 (stage)、自助餐桌 (buffet table)，可以預測座位是在這些的前、後或旁邊的位置。由於提到座位是離舞台第一排，就在自助餐桌旁邊，因此可以得知是1號桌。

18 Why does the man want to arrive early?
(A) To change into a uniform
(B) To prepare a speech
(C) To talk with other guests
(D) To visit backstage

解析 男子為什麼想要早到達？
(A) 換穿制服
(B) 準備演講
(C) 與其他客人交談
(D) 去後台參觀

題目是詢問想要提早到達的原因。做完第17題之後，先瀏覽第18題的選項再接著聽內容，是最好也最有效率的解題方法。因為想和其他人圍者交談，所以想要提早抵達，聽到這裡應該知道答案是 (C)。

Unit 14 主題III- 新聞/廣播

Step 2 眼睛和耳朵完美搭配 Practice

P106

正解
1. (B)　　2. (A)　　3. (A)　　4. (B)

1 Who probably is the speaker?
(A) An air traffic controller (B) A radio announcer
說話者可能是誰？
(A) 空中交通管制員　　(B) 電台播報員

Question 1 refers to the following news report. (美M)

Now let's check on the traffic situation. The evening rush hour is starting with tie-ups on major roads. Since tomorrow is the first day of the rather long holiday weekend, I'm afraid the situation will get worse. Allow extra time to get to your destination.

現在讓我們檢查一下交通狀況。晚上的高峰時段將始於主要道路的停滯。由於明天是假期週末的第一天，恐怕情況會變得更糟。須預留額外的時間以到達您的目的地。

2 Where is the speaker?
(A) At a car dealership (B) At a parking garage
說話者在哪裡？
(A) 汽車經銷商處　　(B) 停車場

Question 2 refers to the following broadcast. (英W)

Welcome to Business News on Channel 7. This is Tara Jenson, reporting to you from Martin's Car Dealership right here in our city. Now, I'm going to speak with the owner of Martin's Car Dealership.

歡迎來到第7頻道的商業新聞。我是塔拉詹森，我正位於我們城市的馬丁汽車經銷商處進行直播。現在，我要和馬丁汽車經銷商的老闆談談。

3 What does Bradford Industries make?
(A) Cleaning products (B) Gardening supplies
布拉德福企業製作什麼？
(A) 清潔用品　　(B) 園藝用品

Welcome to WNY radio's weekly small business report. Our first story is about recent development in Bradford Industries, the country's leading manufacturer of cleaning supplies.

歡迎收聽WNY每週商業速報。我們第一則新聞是布拉德福德企業最近的發展，該公司為本國主要清潔用品的龍頭。

4.
What are the listeners advised to do?
(A) Take the subway
(B) Use a different road
(A) 坐地鐵
(B) 使用其他的道路

Question 4 refers to the following news report. (美M)

The traffic is already slow on Washington Bridge. There has been an accident on Highway 95 near the exit to the International Airport. To avoid this, I suggest you take an alternate route such as Route 9 or local roads.

華盛頓大橋車速緩慢，靠近國際機場出口的95號公路有事故發生，為避開該路段，建議您改道行駛，如9號幹線或地方道路行駛。

Step 3 基本掌握 P107

正解
1.(B)	2.(A)	3.(B)	4.(A)	5.(B)
6.(B)	7.(A)	8.(A)	9.(B)	10.(B)
11.(B)	12.(A)			

Questions 1-3 refer to the following news report. (美M)

❶ And now today's weather report. Some rain is expected early this morning, but the skies should be clear by noon. This afternoon will be quite sunny. ❷ Remember to apply sunscreen or wear a hat if you plan to be outside today. Temperatures will drop in the evening, so if you are going to participate in outdoor events tonight, you may want to bring a jacket or sweater. ❸ We will be right back after these advertisements.

詞彙 report (新聞) 報導 expect 預期 apply 塗抹 sunscreen 防曬品 temperature 溫度 participate 參加 be back 回來 broadcast 廣播 condition 情況 local 地區的 recommend 推薦 protection 保護 review 評論 commercial 廣告

1
What is the radio broadcast mainly about?
(A) Traffic conditions
(B) Local weather
電台廣播主要是關於什麼？
(A) 交通狀況
(B) 當地天氣

解析 GQ是詢問整體主題，最主要的主題是出現在前半部。第一句提到播報今日天氣，可以得知主題是天氣預報。即使出現好幾個提示，盡可能從第一個提示找到正確答案。

2
What does the speaker recommend the listeners do this afternoon?
(A) Use sun protection
(B) Purchase new jackets
就話者建議聽眾今天下午做些什麼？
(A) 採取防曬措施
(B) 購買新夾克

解析 SQ是必須集中注意力聽出連接今天下午做什麼的內容。由於午後氣象晴朗，陽光普照，最好外出時塗防曬用品或戴帽子。聽到這裡應該可以知道答案是(A)。

3
What will the listeners hear next?
(A) Some movie review
(B) Some commercials
聽眾接下來會聽到什麼？
(A) 一些電影評論
(B) 一些廣告

解析 題目是詢問新聞一結束接下來會出現什麼內容的未來式題型。短文的最後提到廣告，一結束會回到新聞報導，由此可知接下來會聽到廣告。短文的advertisements在這裡換下來為some commercials。

Questions 4-6 refer to the following news report. (美W)

Good evening listeners. ❹ Here's the WXYN traffic report. For anyone traveling near the city center, there are 20- to 30-minute delays entering the city and the traffic is backed up on highways. As you know, ❺ our city is hosting the regional basketball tournament this week. It begins this afternoon in Reynolds Arena and the attendance is expected to reach around 20,000 people. So, if you have to commute into the city this week, ❻ we strongly encourage you take the bus or train to avoid unnecessary delays.

各位聽眾晚安。這裡是WXYN路況報導。前往市中心附近的民眾會注意，進入市區會延誤20到30分鐘，高速公路交通壅塞。今天下午開始將於雷諾茲體育館舉辦區域籃球賽，今天下午開始往返於市中心，進場近2萬名觀眾，因此，若您本週通勤往返於市中心，我們強烈建議您乘公車或電火車，以避免不必要的耽擱。

詞彙 delay 延誤；延遲 tournament 賽事 be backed up 交通壅塞 host 主辦 regional 地區的 stadium 體育館 expect 預料 commute 通勤 strongly 強烈地；強力地 encourage 鼓勵 update 更新；升級 maintenance 維修 public transportation 大眾交通

4 What is the main topic of the broadcast?
(A) The traffic update
(B) A new city project

廣播的主要話題是什麼？
(A) 交通動態更新
(B) 新的城市工程

解析 GQ是詢問主題，前半部提到現在正在播報交通新聞，由此可知第一個題目關於的題型，同樣準備解題。面對一次包含三個題目的題型，先正確理解解題目之後，從第一個題目開始解題。

5 According to the speaker, what will begin today?
(A) Highway maintenance
(B) A sports tournament

根據說話者，今天會開始什麼？
(A) 高速公路維修
(B) 體育賽事

解析 先記下題目的Key Word是begin, today再聽短文。中後半部提到由本市主辦籃球聯賽，今天下午開始舉行，因此答案是(B)。注意避免因為聽到交通堵塞就誤選(A)。

6 What does the speaker suggest that listeners do?
(A) Wait for the discounted tickets
(B) Take public transportation

對話者建議聽眾做什麼？
(A) 等待打折後的門票
(B) 乘坐大眾交通工具

解析 提醒聽者的資訊常常在後半段出現。為了避免交通堵塞，建議搭乘公車或火車。聽到這裡應該可以知道答案是利用大眾交通 (public transportation) 的 (B)。須謹記，隨著難度增加，會以重新改句的詞彙作為答案，為此需要不斷地練習。

Questions 7-9 refer to the following broadcast. 美M

7 This is Matt Watson with your weekly entertainment. **8** Actor Jacky Chang will be in town today. He's here to look for some possible places to film his next movie, The Double Dragon. City officials are meeting with him at 10 o'clock this morning to discuss the details. Then they are having lunch together at a famous Chinese restaurant in town. **9** At 3 o'clock, Chang will be leaving for the airport again. He's flying back west to finish his current project, a movie with Angelina Lewis.

詞彙 weekly 每週的、一週的 entertainment 娛樂 possible 可能的 film 拍片、電影 details 細節 leave for 離開前往~ current 目前的 station 廣播台 official 公務員 depart 出發

7 Where does the speaker work?
(A) At a radio station
(B) At a movie theater

說話者在哪裡工作？
(A) 廣播電台
(B) 電影院

解析 GQ是詢問說話者工作的地點。主題雖然是電影演員，但話者是傳達電影演員消息的電台主持人。必須留意題型再作答。

8 Who is Jacky Chang?
(A) A movie star
(B) A city official

誰是張傑奇？
(A) 電影演員
(B) 城市官員

解析 為了瞭解說話者 (speaker) 和聽者 (listener) 以外第3人稱的身分，必須注意名字前後提到的內容。由於是提到演員張傑奇前來尋找電影拍攝場地，因此答案是 (A)。

9 What will Jacky Chang do at 3 o'clock in the afternoon?
(A) Meet with Dianne Watson
(B) Depart for the airport

張傑奇將在下午3點做什麼？
(A) 與麥特森見面
(B) 出發前往機場

解析 先記下題目的Key Word是3 o'clock再聽短文。在說明行程時，通常會從今天上午開始介紹，因此當提到下午3點的時間點時，即將出現答案的提示。由於提到3點將前往機場，因此答案是 (B)。

Questions 10-12 refer to the following radio broadcast. 美M

10 Good morning and welcome to Morning 4 on national radio. I am your host, Russell Jones. It has been a hot summer and we are all looking for ways to stay cool. Today I will be interviewing Dr. Sanchez Patel, a medical doctor who is a specialist in helping people adapt to their local environment. He will offer our listeners some simple tips on how to deal with hot weather. For example, **11** drinking plenty of water and staying in the shade are the easiest ways to protect your health and staying in the shade during the summer. **12** Stay tuned. We'll be right back with Dr. Patel with these medical tips and more after the commercial break.

詞彙 host 主持人 specialist 專家 adapt 適應 local 當地的 environment 環境 offer 提供 shade 陰影 protect 保護 commercial break 廣告時間 climate 氣候 broadcaster 廣播員

10 Who is the speaker?
(A) A climate specialist
(B) A radio broadcaster

說話者是誰？
(A) 氣候專家
(B) 電台廣播員

解析 詢問職業、地點、主題的GQ包含各種資訊，但必須聰明題目中，避免聽到正在進行廣播節目，因此必須選擇目要求的部分再聽短文。這個題目中，第一句話就說話者提到正在進行廣播節目，因此必須選擇以廣播員 (A)。作為答案。

11 What does the speaker mention as a way of dealing with summer heat?

(A) Taking a shower
(B) Drinking water

解析 說話者提到應付炎熱天氣的方法是什麼？

說話者提到今天邀請會提供如何應付炎熱天氣的方法，需準備即將聽到的答案的提示。例如喝水和待在陰涼處是最簡單的方法，聽到這裡應該就能選擇 (B) 作為答案。

12 What will the listeners probably hear next?

(A) An advertisement
(B) An interview

解析 聽眾接下來會可能會聽到什麼？

聽完今天邀請的內容之後，必須選擇接下來會出現什麼。廣告之後桑柏托博士將分享醫學知識，由此可知聽眾接下來會聽到廣告。雖然廣告經常作為答案，但避免因此而誤選，必須根據給予的提示來解題。

正解

1. (D)	2. (A)	3. (B)	4. (D)	5. (A)
6. (C)	7. (A)	8. (A)	9. (D)	10. (C)
11. (D)	12. (B)	13. (C)	14. (B)	15. (C)
16. (A)	17. (B)	18. (D)		

Step 4 實戰練習 P108

Questions 1-3 refer to the following broadcast. 美W

This is KBN Radio. ❶ We've just heard "Once more, happiness," the latest song from Amy Shore. She is one of the most successful female Jazz singers, and she has been performing with some of the world's top musicians. ❷ If you're interested in learning more about Ms. Shore's musical history and her future plans, be sure to tune in this evening. She'll be the guest of our program, "Musical night." During the interview, ❸ Ms. Shore will tell us about her fascinating life. ❸ We'll be accepting questions from listeners at home so, you can email or text us here at the station.

詞彙 the latest 最新的　perform 表演　learn 得知　tune in 收聽　fascinating 有趣的、迷人的　author 作家　current events 時事　offer 提供　review 複習、檢視　request 要求　submit 提交　in person 親自

1 Who is Amy Shore?

(A) An author
(B) An actor
(C) A history teacher
(D) A singer

解析 誰是艾咪辭爾？

(A) 作家
(B) 演員
(C) 歷史老師
(D) 歌手

解析 除了說話者和聽者以外的第3人稱的職業/身分提示通常出現在人名的前後。由於提到艾咪辭爾的職業，便可知道正確答案。

2 According to the speaker, what will Amy Shore do this evening?

(A) Talk about her life
(B) Discuss current events
(C) Offer professional training
(D) Review a book

解析 根據說話者，艾咪辭爾今天晚上將做什麼？

(A) 談論她的生活
(B) 討論當前事件
(C) 提供專業培訓
(D) 複習一本書

解析 先記下題目中的Key Word是this evening再聆聽內容。提到將請大家關定今晚的節目之後，提到來賓艾咪辭爾暢談自己的精彩人生，因此答案是 (A)。須讓記錄間來賓的職業生涯起點或未來計畫是訪談中經常出現的內容。

3 What are the listeners invited to do?

(A) Request a song
(B) Submit questions
(C) Buy some tickets
(D) Visit the station in person

解析 說話者要求聽眾做什麼？

(A) 點歌
(B) 提問
(C) 買票
(D) 親自到電台

解析 廣播中要求聽眾的事情大多在最後出現，要求的內容也有限制。提到可以透過電子郵件或簡訊的方式提出，由此可知答案是重新改寫成Submit questions的 (B)。

Good afternoon. ❹ This is Liam Watson with your five o'clock traffic report. Most of the traffic is moving smoothly for a Friday evening. But expect delays on Highway 45. Traffic there has been reduced to a single lane because of a water pipe that was damaged during the construction project. Due to this flooding of water, people on Highway 45 are reporting delays of around 30 minutes. ❻ You may want to find an alternative way and take Route 5 instead. We hope everything gets back to normal soon. Now, here's Jim Stiller with the weather report.

午安，連恩華森為您帶來五點鐘交通報導。❹週五傍晚間交通大多行駛順暢，但45號公路預計將塞車。由於施工造成水管破裂之故，港水導致45號公路的車程縮減至僅存單線行駛。港水導致45號公路的車程縮減約30分鐘左右。您可以改走5號替代道路。❻希望一切很快就能恢復正常。接著，由吉姆史提勒為您帶來氣象報導。

詞彙 traffic report 交通報導　smoothly 順暢地　delay 延誤　reduce 減少　lane 車道　flood 港水　alternate route 替代道路　其他道路　get back to normal 恢復正常　intend 打算　crew 工作人員　commuter 通勤族　stalled 熄火的　recommend 推薦　update 新資訊

4. Who is this report intended for?
(A) Newspaper readers
(B) Road crews
(C) Police officers
(D) Commuters

這則報導的對象是誰？
(A) 報紙讀者
(B) 道路施工人員
(C) 警察
(D) 通勤族

解析 GQ是詢問聽眾的對象是誰，提示出現在前半部。一開始說話者自報是電台新聞的連恩華森，由此可知以用路人為對象，播報資訊。希望一切休能恢復正常。因此答案是 (D)。

6. What does the speaker recommend?
(A) Leaving early
(B) Traveling by bus
(C) Taking a different road
(D) Listening for news updates

說話者建議什麼？
(A) 提早出發
(B) 搭乘公車移動
(C) 選擇其他道路
(D) 聆聽最新報導

解析 說話者建議的內容通常出現在後半部，尤其交通新聞所議的大多是替代道路的利用與大眾交通工具，隨時聆聽最新報導等限定的範圍。即使是已經寫過的內容，仍需熟記頻繁出現的詞彙和表達方式。聽到利用其他道路如5號替線的部分，就能得知答案是 (C)。

Good morning, SKL Radio listeners and welcome to Weekly Business World. Today, ❼ I'll be speaking to professional career counselor Jackie Blumberg. Over the next two hours, Ms. Blumberg will outline strategies for finding a profession that matches your skills, interest, and personality. During the latter part of the program, ❽ she'd like to hear you in person so we encourage you to call in when we open up our lines. Well, let me start off by saying welcome Ms. Blumberg! From what I understand, ❾ you are publishing a book about this topic which will be in print next month. Is this right?

SKL電台的聽眾們早安，歡迎收聽商業世界週報。今天訪問到職業職涯諮詢師潔琪布倫伯格。兩小時的節目中，布倫伯格小姐將會簡介尋求職業策略，以符合您的技能、興趣和個性。在節目的後半段，開放電話連接之後，歡迎打電話撥來和布倫伯格小姐連繫。那麼，先和布倫伯格小姐打聲招呼吧，就我所知，你將下一本關於這個主題的書，下個月即將出版，對嗎？

詞彙 outline 概述、略述　strategy 策略　profession 職業　personality 個性　line 連接；線　publish 出版　in print 印刷中／付印　expertise 專業知識　finance 財務　career 事業／生涯　guidance 指引、指導　coordination 協調　update 更新　cost of living 生活開銷　attend 參加　professional 專業的　workshop 研討會／工作坊　promotion 宣傳　take place 發生　résumé 履歷

7. What is Ms. Blumberg's area of expertise?
(A) Personal finance
(B) Career guidance
(C) Event coordination
(D) Company management

布倫伯格小姐的專業領域是什麼？
(A) 個人財務
(B) 職業指導
(C) 活動協調
(D) 公司管理

解析 介紹第3人物布倫伯格的經歷或職業內容常出在人名前後出現。主持人介紹完自己的節目之後，提到將和專業職涯諮詢師潔琪布倫伯格小姐談話，從這部分可以得知答案是 (B)。

8. What are the listeners encouraged to do?
(A) Call in with their opinions
(B) Update their résumés
(C) Reduce the cost of living
(D) Attend a professional workshop

鼓勵聽眾做什麼？
(A) 打電話進來提供意見
(B) 更新他們的履歷
(C) 降低生活開銷
(D) 參加專業研討會

解析 這為詢問廣播中要求聽眾的典型題目。來賓會親自接聽電話；鼓勵聽眾來電，因此答案是 (A)。注意避免先入為主下定論，必須從含有邀請的選項中選擇適合的答案。

9. What does the speaker say will happen next month?
(A) A class will be offered.
(B) A discount promotion will take place.
(C) An interview will be conducted.
(D) A book will become available.

說話者提到下個月將發生什麼事？
(A) 將提供課程。
(B) 將進行促銷。
(C) 將進行面試。
(D) 將出版著作。

Questions 10-12 refer to the following news report. (美W)

In national news today, ⑩ the head of Horseman Appliance, President Tim Bauman, announced that the March launch of Horseman's new vacuum cleaner model has been postponed. ⑪ Horseman's vacuum cleaners such as RX2000 which was introduced 2 years ago have been very popular with customers because of their light weight. However, initial reaction from consumers who field-tested the new vacuum cleaner has been mixed. It turns out that some of the vacuum cleaners have faulty wiring and get overheated when used for a long time. Later today, ⑫ Mr. Bauman will hold a press conference to discuss how Horseman Appliance will address this issue.

閱中發表重大內容的人，通常是公司總經理 (executive) 或發言人 (spokesperson)。

今日國內新聞，霍斯曼家電的老闆，董事長提姆鮑曼宣佈三月份霍斯曼新款吸塵器將延遲上市。霍斯曼的吸塵器如RX2000是在兩年前問世，由於重量輕而深受消費者的歡迎。然而，消費者對於新款吸塵器的最初實測回應不一，有的吸塵器線路故障，並且使用長時間會產生過熱情形。今天稍後，鮑曼先生將召開記者會，說明霍斯曼家電會如何處理這個問題。

詞彙:
appliance 電子產品 launch 新產品上市 initial 初期的 reaction 反應 field-test 現場測試 mixed 混合的，錯雜的 turn out 發現~ faulty 有缺陷的、損壞的 wiring 配線，線路 overheated 過熱 address 應付、處理 issue 問題點、論點 press conference 記者會 counselor 諮商師、輔導員 reliable 可信任的、可靠的 inexpensive 低價的 merger 合併 solution 解決之道 technological 技術性的 staff 員工 manufacture 製造 cost 費用

10 Who is Tim Bauman?
(A) A software designer
(B) A financial counselor
(C) A company president
(D) A photo journalist

解析 說明第3人物提姆鮑曼的內容主要在人名前後出現，身為老闆的提姆鮑曼發表了某些談話，由此可知答案是 (C)。須謹記商業新...

提姆鮑曼是誰？
(A) 軟體設計師
(B) 財務諮商師
(C) 公司總裁
(D) 攝影記者

11 According to the speaker, why have the vacuum cleaners of Horseman Appliances been popular?
(A) They're reliable.
(B) They come in different colors.
(C) They are inexpensive.
(D) They're light.

根據談話者，霍斯曼家電的吸塵器為什麼深受歡迎？
(A) 它們很可靠。
(B) 它們有不同的顏色。
(C) 它們價格不貴。
(D) 它們很輕。

解析 先記下這個題目的關鍵字是popular，霍斯曼電器的吸塵器為什麼深受歡迎？霍斯曼家電的產品機體很輕，因此深受顧客歡迎，聽到這個部分，就可以知道答案是 (D)。

12 What will Tim Bauman discuss at a press conference?
(A) Plans for a company merger
(B) Solutions to a technological problem
(C) Changes in management staff
(D) Increases in manufacturing cost

提姆鮑曼在記者會上將發表什麼？
(A) 公司合併的計劃
(B) 解決技術問題
(C) 管理人員的變動
(D) 製造成本的增加

解析 先記下題目的Key Word。discuss, press conference再將聽短文，鮑曼先生將在記者會上針對吸塵器的過熱問題提出解決之道。因此答案是 (B)。隨著難度提昇，就更需要聽懂當中更多的單字和改寫後的詞彙，才能夠順利作答。因此在多多加強詞彙和句型會有助於解題。另外，Part 4需要更多關於嘗試表達部分的練習。

元老師的 REAL SOLUTION

多益中關於職場部門和業務常識的題目，有時是更容易掌握的題型。先來了解新產品開發程序 (new product development process)。相關知識吧！最基本的流程如下。

概念會議 (concept meeting) —關發雛型 (prototype) —市場調查 (marketing research) —修正模型 (updating the model) —廣告/發起活動 (ad/launching campaign) —一補充說明，市場調查的詳細階段包括實地測試 (field test) 和焦點小組測試 (focus group test)。

Questions 13-15 refer to the following news report. (澳M)

In local news, ⑬ Central Railway officials have revealed a plan for a new railway line to be installed between Gordon City and the popular tourism destination, Tampa National Park. According to the announcement, the project is scheduled to begin at the end of the year. ⑭ The new project will attract more attention to the city and the national park and boost the local economy in the end. The Travel and Tourism Association has already voiced strong support for the new railway line. ⑮ Jamal Townsend, spokesperson for the association, says tourism professionals are happy to learn about this much-needed upgrade. **This is what we've been waiting for.**

今日地區新聞，中央鐵路局官員透露一項計畫，將在高登市與觀光景點坦帕國家公園間設置一條新的鐵路線。根據這項聲明表示，這項計畫將於年底開始進行。這項新計畫將吸引更多人潮注意城市和國家公園，最後促進當地經濟發展。觀光旅遊協會已經表達強烈支持這條新的鐵路線的興建，協會發言人賈梅湯森德表示，觀光專業人員樂見此項急需的提升計畫。

詞彙:
local 地區的 reveal 透露、顯示 railway 鐵道鐵路線 install 設置 destination 目的地 attract 吸引 boost 促進、提升 in the end 最後 support 支持 spokesperson 發言人 professional 專業的 much needed 急需的 upgrade 升級，進步 renovation 改造、整修 merger 合併 take place 發生 association 協會 take off 起飛 inconvenience 不便 ranger 管理員，看守者 organization 組織，團體

13 What is the main topic of the news report?
(A) The renovation of a tourist resort
(B) An airline merger with Central Railway
(C) Construction of a new railway line
(D) A new president for the hotel association

新聞報導的主題是什麼？
(A) 旅遊勝地的重整
(B) 航空公司與中央鐵路的合併
(C) 建設新的鐵路線
(D) 飯店協會的新任總裁

解析 作為GQ的新聞主題顯示出現在前半部，內容提到鐵路相關計畫，因此答案是 (C)。為了不多花費時間理解全文，平常需要多加練習閱讀新聞和理解能力。

14 What does the speaker imply when he says, "This is what we've been waiting for"?

(A) He thinks it is taking too long.
(B) He is happy about the news.
(C) He is tired of working long hours.
(D) He is sorry for the inconvenience.

解析 說話者提到「我們引頸期盼」的意思是什麼？

(A) 他認為耗費太久時間。
(B) **他對這個消息感到高興。**
(C) 他厭倦了長時間的工作。
(D) 他很抱歉帶來不便。

說話者提到「我們引頸期盼」，就說話者聽到鐵路開通後的各種好處，畫面時說出「我們引頸期盼」之後也談到鐵路開通後的各種好處，因此可以得知說話者對於這個消息感到高興，因此答案是 (B)。

15 Who is Jamal Townsend?

(A) A ranger of a park
(B) A construction manager
(C) **A member of an organization**
(D) A famous travel writer

解析 買梅湯森德是誰？

(A) 公園管理員
(B) 施工經理
(C) **組織的成員**
(D) 知名的旅遊作家

介紹第3人時，必須注意其前人名的前後內容。買梅湯森德是協會的發言人，因此還須注意選項中最適合的答案是 (C)。尤其須謹記公司、協會、同好會等團體會使用organization來詮釋。

Questions 16-18 refer to the following broadcast and map. (美M)

詞彙 disappointed 失望的　snowstorm 暴風雪　ongoing 持續中、進行中　arena 競技場　removal 剷除、排除　sold out 售罄

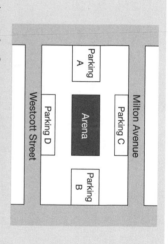

Milton Avenue

| Parking C | | Parking D |

Arena

| Parking A | | Parking B |

Westcott Street

And now for Greenwich City sports news. We were all disappointed that ⑩ the baseball championship game between our own Blueclaws and Indians was cancelled last Saturday night because of the big snowstorm. The game has been rescheduled for this Friday evening at 7 o'clock at Angel Arena. Tickets are going fast, but ⑰ don't worry if you don't get a ticket. You can watch the game on the local television channel. Snow removal is ongoing and all parking areas at the baseball stadium will be closed except one. ⑱ The area that will be open closest to Westcott Street. Go Blueclaws!

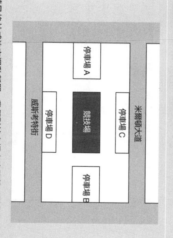

米爾頓大道

| 停車場 A | | 停車場 B |

競技場

| 停車場 C | | 停車場 D |

威斯考特街

16 Why is the baseball game rescheduled?

(A) **The weather has been bad.**
(B) Some players got sick before the game.
(C) Not enough tickets have been sold.
(D) The stadium is being repaired.

解析 為什麼重新安排棒球比賽？

(A) **天氣惡劣。**
(B) 有些球員在比賽前生病了。
(C) 門票售出不夠。
(D) 體育場正在整修。

根據說話者，為什麼重新安排棒球比賽？先記下Key Word是baseball game, rescheduled再將相關短文。提到比賽由於暴風雪而取消，因此答案是 (A)。

17 According to the speaker, why might a listener watch a game on television?

(A) If a snowstorm gets worse.
(B) **If tickets have been sold out.**
(C) If there is no available parking.
(D) If he or she cannot find time to watch it in person.

解析 根據說話者，為什麼聽眾可以從電視上看比賽？

(A) 如果暴風雪變得更糟。
(B) **如果門票已經售罄。**
(C) 如果沒有可用的停車位。
(D) 如果他或她無法抽出時間到場觀看。

先記下題目的Key Word是why, watch a game, on television，詢問從電視上觀看比賽的原因。雖然門票已售完，即使沒買到票，也能透過電視看轉播，因此答案是 (B)。雖然提到雪和停車場的內容，但與在電視上收看並沒有關聯，因此無法作為答案。

18 Look at the graphic. Which parking area will be closed?

(A) Parking A
(B) Parking B
(C) Parking C
(D) **Parking D**

解析 請看圖表。哪一個停車場將會關閉？

(A) 停車場 A
(B) 停車場 B
(C) 停車場 C
(D) **停車場 D**

先看圖表/視覺資料的題目在提醒短文之前，需先分析題目和圖表再聆聽。聽內容。地圖中位於中央的球場周圍有兩處道路名稱，需要先說明哪一個停車場將會關閉。聽內容，除了某處的停車場之外皆有開放，而關閉的停車場離威斯考特街很近，因此答案是 (D)。

Step 2　眼睛和耳朵完美搭配 Practice

1

Welcome to the annual Water Conservation Convention. All representatives attending today's program should go to the main entrance to receive their name tags and schedules. Please do not go to the reception area inside. 英M

歡迎蒞臨年度水資源保護大會。今天所有與會的代表請到大門口領取名牌及行程表，請勿進入裡面的接待處。

Question 1 refers to the following talk. 美M

1. How often is this convention held?
　(A) Once a month
　(B) Once a year

這個會議多久舉行一次？
　(A) 一個月一次
　(B) 一年一次

正解

1. (B)　2. (B)　3. (A)　4. (A)

2

Welcome to the annual staff meeting, first I would like to remind you that we are going to lay new carpets in all offices over the next two weeks. The maintenance supervisor has asked everyone to let him know when you want the work done in your office.

今天的員工會議我要先提醒各位，接下來的兩周我們要在所有的辦公室鋪設最新的地毯，維修主管要求大家告訴他你希望自己的辦公室何時完工。

Question 2 refers to the following announcement. 英W

2. What is the main purpose of this announcement?
　(A) To announce a schedule change
　(B) To announce a maintenance job

這個公告的主要目的是什麼？
　(A) 宣布行程變更
　(B) 宣布維修工作

3

Who are the instructions intended for?
　(A) Employees in a factory
　(B) Managers in a store

Every morning, as soon as you get in here, you should check the printed schedule to see which division you will be working in on the production line. After that, you can get your safety goggles and a hard hat for yourself.

每天早上，一到這裡後，請你立刻瞄紙本進度表，查看自己在生產線上的哪個部門工作。接下來，你可以去領取你的護目鏡及安全帽。

Question 3 refers to the following announcement. 美M

這項指示的發布對象是誰？
　(A) 工廠的員工們
　(B) 商店的經理們

4

What are the participants asked to do?
　(A) Complete the registration form
　(B) Send in their résumés

這些參加者被要求做什麼？
　(A) 填寫報名表
　(B) 發送履歷

參與者被要求做什麼？
　(A) 填寫報名表
　(B) 發送履歷

Question 4 refers to the following announcement. 英W

Welcome to the 10th Annual Job Fair for the New York Asian Community. I know you want to talk to your potential employers or prospective coworkers. But first, I'd like you to fill out all the forms in your registration packet.

歡迎光臨第十屆年度紐約亞裔社區就業博覽會。我知道您想趕快和準雇主及未來的同事談談，但首先要請您填寫報名文件袋中的所有表格。

Step 3　基本掌握

正解

1. (B)　2. (B)　3. (A)　4. (B)　5. (A)
6. (B)　7. (A)　8. (B)　9. (B)　10. (A)
11. (A)　12. (B)

Questions 1-3 refer to the following excerpt from a meeting. 美W

❶ Welcome to our annual dealers' meeting. I'm looking forward to showing you the exciting new line of winter products. I'm sure your customers will like them as much as we do. ❷ My part of the session, which starts with a video presentation, will take about 2 hours, but we will take a 15-minute coffee break in the middle. The lunch hour is from 12 to 1 p.m. In the afternoon, we will have a discussion with technical staff. Meanwhile, ❸ if you have any questions, please feel free to interrupt and ask me at any time.

歡迎蒞臨年度經銷商大會。我非常期待為您展示多套新的產品系列。我相信您的客戶和我們一樣喜歡。我會以影片簡報的方式開始我的部分，將會進行兩小時左右，到了下午，中間會有15分鐘的喝咖啡休息時間，午餐從12點到下午1點。到了下午，我們會與技術人員進行討論。同時，若您有任何疑問，歡迎隨時打斷我並提出問題。

詞彙 annual 年度的　dealer 經銷商　line 產品線　session 時段、課程　break 休息時間　discussion 討論　staff 工作人員　meanwhile 同時　feel free to 隨意～　interrupt 打擾、打斷　at any time 隨時

1. How often does this event take place?
　(A) Once a month
　(B) Once a year

活動多久舉行一次？
　(A) 一個月一次
　(B) 一年一次

解析 活動公告是經常出題的內容，但也是經常答錯的題型。通常會問活動的名稱和舉辦的頻率。從歡迎參加活動是一年度第一次。
　句話會同時提到活動的名稱，聽到annual時，就應該知道活動是一年舉辦一次。

2. How long is the speaker's presentation?
　(A) One hour
　(B) Two hours

說話者的簡報花了多長時間？

(A) 1小時
(B) 2小時

解析　活動中經常出現各個演講者和演講主題，時間等各種公告。說話者提到自己的簡報將進行2小時，因此答案是 (B)。

3

What should the listeners do if they have questions?

(A) Stop the speaker and ask
(B) Ask the speaker during lunch break

[A] **打斷說話者並提問**

解析　所有公告通常都是出現在半部公告的內容，後半部提到提醒或注意事項。從若有疑問，歡迎隨時打斷提問的內容來看，答案是 (A)。短文中的interrupt在選項中被重新詮釋為stop the speaker。

Questions 4-6 refer to the following excerpt from a meeting. 〔美M〕

Let me start off the meeting with an important reminder. **④ Our week-long winter sale begins tomorrow, and we're** almost ready for this special event. We've already changed the price tags on **⑤ winter jackets, hats, and scarves.** We've brought out all our winter stock from the warehouse. Now, the only thing left for us to do is to put up a large sign on the store window. **⑥ The sign has already arrived so I'd** like to get a few people to help me hang it.

4

What is the announcement mainly about?

(A) Opening a new location
(B) Preparing for a sales event

這則公告主要是關於什麼？

(A) 開設新據點
(B) 準備銷售活動

解析　公告先從這項重要提醒開始吧，明天開始是為期一週的冬季特賣，更改了冬季外套、帽子和圍巾上的標價，現在唯一要做完成的就是在店面標牌，招牌已經送到，所以我需要一些人幫忙掛起來。

詞彙　reminder 注意、提醒　almost 幾乎　price tag 價格標籤　bring out 拿出、取出　stock 庫存、物品　warehouse 倉庫　put up 貼上　location 地點、位置　prepare 準備　clothing 服飾　furnishing 家具、陳設　place an ad 放置廣告　hang up 掛上

5

What type of product does the store sell?

(A) Clothing
(B) Home furnishings

這家商店販售何種產品？

(A) **服飾**
(B) 家居擺飾

解析　選性的提示中找到，也就是從冬季的天、外套、帽子、圍巾等物品，可以得知是銷售服飾的店家，因此答案是 (A)。

6

What does the speaker ask for help with?

(A) Placing an advertisement in the paper
(B) Hanging up a sign

說話者尋求什麼協助？

(A) 在報紙上刊登廣告
(B) **掛上一個看板**

解析　說話者要求的事情可以視為為拜託的指示。最後提到順序看板已經送到，希望有人能幫忙掛上去，因此答案是 (B)。

Questions 7-9 refer to the following announcement. 〔美M〕

As you all know, **⑦ Aland Hardy is retiring at the end of the** month after 30 years at our company and we're planning a small party in his honor. **⑧ Mr. Hardy started as a sales** associate of our Fort Lee branch office and moved on to the general manager of our company for a long time been a valuable employee of our company. He has and we are going to miss him a lot. The party will be held at the company cafeteria next Friday, the 5th and everyone is invited. We have prepared a cake and a card for him and **⑨ I'd like everyone to stop by at the reception desk to sign** their names on the card. This will be a good gift for him. Thank you and see you at the party.

詞彙　retire 退休　honor 榮譽、尊敬　associate 助理　branch 分公司　head office 總公司　valuable 寶貴的、珍貴的　be held 舉辦　cafeteria 自助餐廳　reception desk 服務台

7

What is the speaker discussing?

(A) A party for a retiring employee
(B) A schedule change for the event

說話者在討論什麼？

(A) **退休員工的派對**
(B) 活動行程的變更

解析　GQ是詢問主題。提示出現在前半部，第一句話提到哈迪先生即將退休，為此將舉辦派對的內容，可以知道答案是 (A)。當然退休派對也可以稱為event，但並沒有行程變更的內容，因此答案不是 (B)。

8

What is Mr. Hardy's current position?

(A) A sales associate
(B) A general manager

哈迪先生目前的職位是什麼？

(A) 銷售助理
(B) **總經理**

解析　SQ是詢問與current時間點相關有的內容，必須仔細聆聽。前問目前職位所代表的意思是過去的職位也會被提及，因此須多加

9

What are the listeners asked to do?
(A) Buy a gift for Mr. Hardy
(B) Sign their names on a card

聽眾被要求做什麼?
(A) 買禮物給給迪先生
(B) **在卡片上簽名。**

解析 指示聽眾做的動作常在後半部以請求的句子出現。提到已經準備了卡片,希望大家在卡片上簽名,由此便可以得知答案。以 (A) 的情況來說,雖然出現gift的詞彙,但並沒有要求買禮物的內容。因此無法作為答案。

Questions 10-12 refer to the following announcement. 美W

May I have your attention, please? ⑩ Due to high sales and increased orders, we're far behind our schedule. ⑪ Our facility coordinator has decided to keep the assembly lines running for an extra three hours a day to meet the high demand. ⑫ Any line workers who are interested in working overtime and making more money should notify their supervisors by the end of the day. Remember, those who work less than full-time will have the priority in extra hours. Thank you for your cooperation.

請注意這裡。由於銷量很好、訂單增加,所以我們的進度落後。設備調度人員決定讓產線每天增加三小時運作,以應付這樣的高需求。任何想要加班及賺多點錢的有興趣的生產人員,請在今天以前告知主管。記得,工作時數比全職員工少的人可以優先加班。謝謝配合。

詞彙 behind schedule 進度落後 facility 設施 coordinator 調度人員 assembly line 組裝產線 run 經營、運作 extra 增加的 demand 需求 notify 告知 supervisor 主管、上司 priority 優先 cooperation 合作 put in extra hours 加班 volume 量 production 生產 benefit 利益、好處

10

Why are the workers asked to put in extra hours?
(A) Sales volume has increased.
(B) Staff size has decreased.

為什麼要求員工加班?
(A) **銷量增加。**
(B) 員工人數減少。

11

Where is this announcement being heard?
(A) In a production plant
(B) In a sales seminar

這個公告在哪裡被聽到?
(A) **生產工廠**
(B) 銷售研討會

解析 GQ是詢問談話發生的地點,提示經常是特定場所的詞彙。組裝產線 (assembly line) 應視為題目最大的提示。雖然提到銷售的(sales)增加而產量增加的內容,但避免因此誤選到銷售研討會的(B)。

12

What are the benefits of working overtime?
(A) Employees can sell more products.
(B) Employees can earn more money.

加班有什麼好處?
(A) 員工可以銷售更多產品。
(B) **員工可以賺更多錢。**

解析 一旦知道談話的重點是選項中的工廠之後,利用刪去法就能選出答。提到想要加班多賺點錢的人需告知主管,由此可知答案是(B)。

解析 詢問原因或目的項目也包含在GQ的範圍內。第一句話提到由於銷售和訂單增加,組裝產線需要增加運作時間,並要求想要加班的人提出申請,由此可知答案是(A)。

正解
1. (A)	2. (C)	3. (D)	4. (D)	5. (B)
6. (C)	7. (C)	8. (A)	9. (B)	10. (B)
11. (A)	12. (C)	13. (D)	14. (A)	15. (D)
16. (C)	17. (C)	18. (D)		

Questions 1-3 refer to the following excerpt from a meeting. 澳M

Before we start today's meeting, ① I want to update everyone about the office remodeling project beginning on Tuesday. We can't allow the construction to affect our work, so please follow these directions carefully. ② Tomorrow, you should begin packing your things into boxes. Packing boxes and other supplies will be in the main lobby. If you need more supplies, please contact the maintenance department. Now, during the construction period, you'll be using conference rooms as temporary work spaces. ③ I'll be sending out an e-mail later today to let you know which conference rooms you'll be working in.

在我們開始會議之前,我要告訴大家辦公室改建計畫在週二開始。為了不讓施工影響工作,請仔細遵守以下說明。明天開始請工具放在辦公大廳。如果工具不夠,請連絡維修部。施工期間,會議室會當作暫時的辦公空間。今天稍晚我會寄電子郵件告訴你們使用哪間會議室。

詞彙 update 提供最新資訊 remodel 改建 construction 施工 direction 指引、指示 pack 打包 收拾 supplies 用品 contact 連絡 maintenance 維修 period 期間 temporary 暫時的 renovation 整修 assembly 組裝 equipment 設備 preparation 準備 arrange 安排、整頓 extra 額外的 pay 工資 job offer 提 notification 通知

1

What is mainly being discussed?
(A) **Office renovation**
(B) Directions to a site
(C) Assembly of equipment
(D) Seminar preparation

主要討論什麼?
(A) 辦公室整修
(B) 到現場的路線

(C) 組裝設備
(B) 準備研討會

2

[解析] GQ是詢問整體主題，最主要的提示出現在前半部。提到關於辦公室的改建（改造、整修）內容，因此答案是 (A)。

What should the listeners do tomorrow?
(A) Arrange some meetings
(B) Begin interviews
(C) **Pack their things**
(D) Move some furniture

聽眾明天應該做什麼？
(A) 安排一些會議
(B) 開始面試
(C) **打包他們的東西**
(D) 搬一些家具

[解析] 聽眾未來必須做的事情來自於說話者的要求或拜託事項，需要仔細聆聽。由於對方要求大家將自己的東西打包裝箱，因此答案是 (C)。雖然出現物品裝箱的內容，但沒有搬動家具的部分，因此答案不是 (D)。必須整理包裝相關的主題和聽者必須做的詳細相關事項分開之後，一一確認。

3

What will the listeners receive later today?
(A) Extra pay
(B) A phone number
(C) A new job offer
(D) **An e-mail notification**

聽眾今天晚一點會收到什麼？
(A) 額外的工資
(B) 一個電話號碼
(C) 一個新的工作機會
(D) 電子郵件通知

[解析] 先記下題目的Key Word是receive, later, today再將聆聽內容。由於提到今天晚一點會寄電子郵件告知可以使用的會議室，因此答案是 (D)。

Questions 4-6 refer to the following announcement. [美M]

Good morning. I am Jeremy Harmon, head of the engineering department here at Southwestern University. I hope you are enjoying the conference so far. ❹ I have an announcement about a change in the program. Dr. Steve Cullen, who was scheduled to speak this morning, has been delayed and won't arrive here until late this afternoon. ❺❻ His talk on Innovative Designs in Production has been rescheduled for tomorrow morning at 10 o'clock. I hope this doesn't give you any confusion. If you have any questions, please visit our information desk located near the main entrance.

詞彙　head 首長、領導者　so far 至今　be delayed 被耽擱　innovative 創新的　production 生產　reschedule 重新安排　confusion 混淆　main entrance 大門　attendee 參加者　directions 路指引、指示　talk 談論　accounting 會計　regulation 規定　organization 組織

早安，我是傑瑞米哈蒙，西南大學工程系系主任。我希望會議目前為止大家都還滿意。❹ 跟大家宣布，議程有所變動。史帝夫卡倫博士原本預計今早要演講，但行程延誤了，要到下午才能抵達這裡。❺❻ 他的生產創新設計的演講重新安排在明早10點。希望不會造成大家的混淆。如果有其他疑問，請向大門處附近的服務台詢問。

4

Why is the announcement being made?
(A) To thank the attendees
(B) To give directions
(C) To cancel a reservation
(D) **To report a schedule change**

為什麼要發布公告？
(A) 感謝參與者
(B) 給予指引
(C) 取消預訂
(D) **報告行程變更**

[解析] 談話的原因或目的是GQ的內容，通常提示出現在前半部。一開始在自我介紹和簡短問候之後，通知計畫有所變動，因此答案是 (D)。

5

What is the subject of Dr. Cullen's talk?
(A) Marketing techniques
(B) **Design ideas**
(C) Accounting regulations
(D) Organization skills

卡倫博士的演講主題是什麼？
(A) 營銷技巧
(B) **設計理念**
(C) 會計法規
(D) 組織能力

[解析] 活動或人物介紹中經常出現特定人物進行的演講時間、主題、變動等。由於提到以〈生產部門的創新設計〉為題的演講改到明天早上10點，可知主題是有關於設計的創新理念，更好的做法是一邊確認完並記下整篇內容再答題，同時選擇答案，這也是最安全的方法。

6

When will Dr. Cullen give his talk?
(A) This morning
(B) This afternoon
(C) **Tomorrow morning**
(D) Tomorrow afternoon

卡倫博士什麼時候會演講？
(A) 今天早上
(B) 今天下午
(C) **明天早上**
(D) 明天下午

[解析] 提到卡倫博士的演講行程改變，有原本的時間和變動後的時間。根據題目來決定要回答的是哪個時間，但原本計畫今早上10點進行演講，但因為卡倫博士抵達的時間延遲，因此最後決定改到明天早上10點，可知整篇內容的答案是 (C)，即使掌握了整篇內容的情況還是對特定部分產生混淆而誤答的情況，因此務必確認題目的內容。

Questions 7-9 refer to the following excerpt from a meeting. 美W

I'm happy to announce that Pioneer Advertising will be getting a new printer. We'll now be able to offer our clients print materials of the best possible quality and ❽ our commitment to protect the environment. This printer is the latest model and ❽ uses special environmentally friendly soy-based ink and ❽ maintain our commitment to protect the environment. This printer will also use recycled paper to prevent deforestation. All employees will be given training on how to use and maintain the new printer on Friday. And ❾ to be sure that workers on all shifts will be able to attend, we're holding two training sessions, one in the morning and one in the afternoon, so please make sure you take one of them.

我很高興宣佈，先鋒廣告即將擁有新的印表機。我們現在能夠提供客戶最高品質的印刷材質，並且遵守保護環境的承諾。這台印表機是最新機型，使用對環境友善的大豆油墨，同時為了避免森林砍伐而使用回收紙張。所有的員工將在周五接受培訓，學習如何使用並維護新的印表機。請確認所有輪班人員都能參加，我們舉辦兩個課程，一個在早上另一個在下午，請務必參加其中一個。

7 What is the purpose of the announcement?
(A) To introduce a new employee
(B) To describe a new printer
(C) To report an upcoming project
(D) To warn about the danger of deforestation

這則公告的目的是什麼？
(A) 介紹一名新員工
(B) 描述新的印表機
(C) 報告即將展開的計畫
(D) 警告森林砍伐的危險性

解析 GQ是詢問公告目的。短文的第一句話提到很高興即將有新的印表機，聽到這個內容可以知道答案是 (B)。

8 What benefit does the speaker mention?
(A) Reduced harm to the environment
(B) Increased output capacity
(C) Greater publicity for the company
(D) Fewer maintenance problems

說話者提到什麼優點？
(A) 減少對環境的危害
(B) 增加產能
(C) 擴大公司的宣傳
(D) 減少維護問題

解析 由於提到新印表機的優點是提供顧客高品質的印刷材質，也能遵守環保的承諾，因此答案是 (A)。解題時並非以常識或既定的答案，而是根據每個題目選擇答案。

9 According to the speaker, why have two training sessions been scheduled?
(A) To lower the operating costs
(B) To accommodate employees on all shifts
(C) To switch to a larger room
(D) To hire qualified trainers

根據說話者，為什麼安排2個的培訓時段？
(A) 降低營運成本
(B) 順應所有輪班員工
(C) 要換到更大的房間
(D) 聘請合格的培訓師

解析 問題的核心是安排兩個培訓時間的原因。在不同時段讓所有輪班員工能夠一樣安排培訓，從這個部分可以得知答案是 (B)。請務必謹記，必須熟悉職場生活中經常出現的詞彙，在高難度題目中才能更得心應手。

詞彙 offer 提供　material 資料　quality 品質　commitment 承諾　protect 保護　the latest 最新的　recycle 回收　deforestation 森林砍伐　shift 輪班　describe 描述　danger 危險　benefit 利益　output 生產　capacity 能力、容量　publicity 宣傳　maintenance 維修　session 課程、活動　lower 降低　operate 運作、操作　accommodate 容納、遷就

Questions 10-12 refer to the following excerpt from a meeting. 美M

Before we end today's meeting, ❿ I'd like to call your attention to a change in the company's time-off policy. As you know, employees currently get one week of holiday during their first year here at the Alton Corporation. Many of our employees have expressed dissatisfaction with this policy, and then left after a few months. The company had to continuously train new employees for this reason. So, ⓫ in order to prevent the new hires from leaving the company, ⓫ we're offering two weeks off for new employees starting next year. ⓬ Please meet with your department employees and inform them of this policy change.

結束今天的會議之前，請注意接下來在公司休假政策的變更。大家都知道，目前員工第一年在歐頓有限公司可享有一星期的假期，許多員工表達不滿意這項政策，幾個月後便離職。為此公司必須一直訓練新進同仁。所以，為了避免新人離職，從明年開始我們為新進同仁提供兩星期的假期，請與貴部門的員工會面，並且告知這項政策的改變。

10 What is the main topic of the talk?
(A) Providing managers with training
(B) Giving new employees more time off
(C) Making work schedules more flexible
(D) Boosting sales with new campaigns

談話的主題是什麼？
(A) 為經理提供培訓
(B) 為新員工提供更多休假
(C) 使工作時間表有彈性
(D) 透過新廣告促銷進銷售

解析 GQ是詢問的主題，提示通常出現在前半部。如果知道一開始出現的 time off 的意思是「休假」的話，就可以知道答案是 (B)。隨著難度增加，選項的句子會愈長，詞彙也愈難，很難在短時間內讀懂。除了了解題之外，也需加強快速瀏覽內容的訓練。

詞彙 attention 注意　time off 休息時間、休假　policy 政策　dissatisfaction 不滿意　continuously 一直　prevent 防止、避免　new hire 新進員工　provide 提供　flexible 彈性的　boost 促進　current 維持、保持　improve 改進　safety 安全　retain　procedure 程序　regulation 規定　remind 提醒　update 更新　contact information 連絡資料　consult 諮詢　counselor 顧問　regularly 定期地

11 According to the speaker, why is a change being made?
(A) **To retain current employees**
(B) To improve employee communication
(C) To introduce better safety procedures
(D) To follow government regulations

根據說話者，為什麼要做出改變？
(A) **留住現有員工**
(B) 改善員工溝通
(C) 引進更好的安全程序
(D) 遵守政府規定

解析 員工會議 (staff meeting) 中宣布公司的決定事項是最常見的主題。不只業績等業務，也可能出現停車場維修，打鐵趁2周假期，品管等各種內容。為了避免新進員工離職，從明年起提高2周假期，從這個部分可以得知答案是 (A)。

12 What are the listeners reminded to do?
(A) Update the client contact information
(B) Consult with a professional counselor
(C) **Inform their employees of company policies**
(D) Change passwords regularly

聽眾被提醒要做什麼？
(A) 更新客戶連絡資料
(B) 諮詢專業顧問
(C) **告知員工公司政策**
(D) 定期更改密碼

解析 短文最後要求與各部門員工面談並告知政策的變更，由此可知答案是 (C)。補充說明，由最後內容可以知道，參加會議的人是部門主管 (department heads)。

Questions 13-15 refer to the following announcement. 美M

13 Welcome to this morning's seminar on Starting Your Own Business. Today, we'll be discussing strategies for financing your project and introducing your product into the market. **14** I know some people are still on their way, but another conference is scheduled to begin here at 3 o'clock. **15** So let's go over some administrative details to begin here, first. **15** The parking fee was included in your registration fee, so I made passes for everyone. I'll come around and hand those out now. Just show it to the attendant on you way out, and you won't be charged.

歡迎參加今早的創業研討會。今天，我們將要討論如何為您的專案籌措融資，以及如何讓您的產品進入市場。有些人還在來的路上，但這裡有另一場會議，我現在開始進行會議，所以我們先開始了解一些行政上的細節吧。停車費包含在報名費用中，因此我製作了每個人的通行證。我現在就拿過去發放給各位。離開時向服務人員出示即可，不會另外收費。

詞彙 strategy 策略 finance 融資 be on the way 去來的路上 go over 了解、檢視 administrative 行政的、管理的 details 細節 pass 許可證、通行證 charge 收取（費用）include 包含 banker 銀行家 entrepreneur 創業人、企業家 session 時間、課程 fee 費用 overcharge 超收 reorganize 整頓、重組 distribute 分發 sign up 登記 sheet 紙 material 資料 contract 契約、合約

13 Who most likely are the listeners?
(A) Bankers
(B) Lawyers
(C) Drivers
(D) **Entrepreneurs**

聽眾最有可能是誰？
(A) 銀行家
(B) 律師
(C) 司機
(D) **創業人**

解析 GQ是詢問聽眾是誰。內容前半部提到「創業」的研討會，可以推測聽眾是想要開始經營自己事業的創業人，因此答案是 (D)。

14 What does the speaker mean when he says, "another conference is scheduled to begin here at 3 o'clock"?
(A) **He wants to start the session now.**
(B) He needs to go somewhere now.
(C) The fee was overcharged.
(D) The room needs to be reorganized.

說話者提到「這裡下午三點安排了另一場會議」時，意思是什麼？
(A) **他想要現在開始進行會議。**
(B) 他現在需要去某個地方。
(C) 費用被收了。
(D) 房間需要改編。

解析 詢問說話者這句話引用的和前後文關係。說話者提到繼有些人還沒到，但3點這裡有另一場會議，意思是暗示馬上來就，必須現在開始進行會議，因此答案是 (A)。

15 What will the speaker distribute to the listeners?
(A) A sign-up sheet
(B) Training materials
(C) Employment contracts
(D) **Parking passes**

說話者要發放什麼給聽眾？
(A) 登記表
(B) 培訓資料
(C) 僱用合約
(D) **停車通行證**

解析 在培訓或研討會中最常提到的是資料 (material)，但不能因為過去經常作為答案而誤選。SQ必須正確掌握並記下Key Word，將聽內容同時尋找答案。提到已經做好停車證，將發放給大家，由此便可以知道答案。pass作為動詞是「通過」，名詞是「通行證」之意。

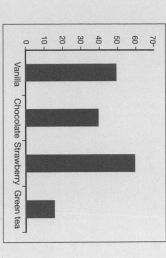

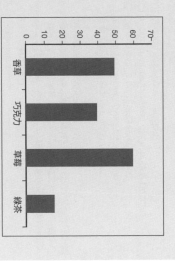

OK, everyone, just a quick meeting before we open the ice cream store today. ⑯ If you take a look at this chart, you'll see this week's winning ice cream flavor. As promised in our newsletter and in-store advertisement, we'll have a 30% discount on the flavor that has most votes. ⑰ I'd like to thank Bruce for his creative idea of holding this weekly contest. Our customers really loved this idea and sales have increased because of this promotion. ⑱ I know a lot of you have similar great ideas, too. Remember, you can share them with me at any time.

好的，各位，今天在我們的冰淇淋店開店之前，先很快地開個會。看一下這張圖表，可以看到本週冰淇淋口味冠軍。如我們的通訊期刊和店內廣告所示，票數最多的口味可以打七折。我要謝謝布魯斯創意發想舉行這項每週競賽活動，顧客很喜歡，也因為促銷關係，營業額提升。我知道你們很多人也有類似的好點子，別忘了，隨時都可以和我分享。

詞彙 chart 圖表　winning 優勝的　flavor 味道、香氣　newsletter 公司期刊　creative 創意的　hold 舉行　contest 比賽、競賽　similar 類似的　share 分享　in person 親自　propose 提議　work overtime 加班　remind 提醒、告知　sign up 申請、報名　count 計算　vote 投票　notify 通知　winner 優勝者　suggestion 提議

16 Look at the graphic. Which ice cream flavor will be discounted this week?
(A) Vanilla
(B) Chocolate
(C) **Strawberry**
(D) Green tea

請看圖表，哪一種口味的冰淇淋將在這週打折？
(A) 香草
(B) 巧克力
(C) 草莓
(D) 綠茶

解析 看看圖表/視覺資料最重要的是先讀完題目，再測圖表部分會如何問來。從柱狀圖的順序看來，銷售排行依序為草莓、香草、巧克力-綠茶，先記下此順序。內容提到這週的銷售冠軍是草莓口味，並針對該款冰淇淋推出折扣價，由此可知打折的是草莓口味。

17 Why does the speaker thank Bruce?
(A) He developed a new ice cream flavor.
(B) He talked with many customers in person.
(C) **He proposed a sales promotion.**
(D) He worked overtime for a week.

話者為什麼向布魯斯致謝？
(A) 他開發了一種新的冰淇淋口味。
(B) 他親自與多名客戶交談。
(C) **他提出了促銷活動。**
(D) 他加班了一星期。

解析 內容提到「投票結果最高票的冰淇淋將推出折扣價優惠」，並向發想這個創意點子的布魯斯致謝，由此可以得知布魯斯想出的點子是促銷活動的點子，因此答案是 (C)。

18 What does the speaker remind the listeners to do?
(A) Sign up for a task
(B) Count customers' votes
(C) Notify the winner by phone
(D) **Make some suggestions**

說話者提醒聽眾什麼事？

解析 談話者最後部分要求聽者將其中一項是點子、反饋、提議（idea, feedback, suggestion）。由於提到其他人應該也有很好的點子，隨時可以提出，因此答案是 (D)。短文的similar great ideas在這項中被稱為suggestions。

元老師的
REAL SOLUTION

多益中最常作為提高「業績」的方法有① 促銷 (promotion) 及② 開發新產品 (new product development)。無論商品再怎麼受歡迎、總會有銷售下滑的一天，為此進行促銷，或不斷開發新商品以維持銷售量，這些都是公司經常採取的方法。必須深入了解多益中經常出現的促銷/開發新產品等主題。

Unit 1 名詞與代名詞

Step 1 Practice　P120

P120

正解

1.(B)	2.(A)	3.(B)	4.(A)	5.(B)
6.(A)	7.(B)	8.(A)	9.(B)	10.(B)

1
解析：湯普森先生對股票的分析到目前為止都非常準確。
必須找出對應動詞片語 has been very accurately 的主語。所有格後面缺少名詞，因此正確答案是(B)。
詞彙　stock market 股票市場　accurate 正確的　analyze（動）　so far 至今　analysis 分析（名）

2
解析：我們部門為了獲得項目的批准，一直在努力工作。
動詞後面缺少了受詞，須後面接名詞，因此正確答案是(A)。-al 也常作為形容詞的詞尾，必須清楚分辨並記下容易混淆的詞彙。
詞彙　department 部門　project 企劃、工作業務　approval 批准、許可　applicable 適用的

3
解析：今天下午有暴風雨的可能性非常高。
定冠詞的後面缺少名詞，possibility 是「可能性」之意的名詞，因此正確答案是(B)。
詞彙　thunderstorm 暴風雨、雷雨　possible 可能的　possibility 可能性

4
解析：山田先生是一位在業界贏得許多獎項的有名建築師。
形容詞後面缺少名詞，architect 是「建築師」之意的名詞，因此正確答案是(A)。空格作為 be 動詞的補語位置，用來說明山田先生。
詞彙　architect 建築師　architecturally 建築學層面、建築樣項的

5
解析：申請人必須具有零售方面至少三年的經驗。
介係詞後面應該接名詞，但需要尋找能夠修飾 sales 的形容詞或名詞的名詞。retail sales 是「零售銷售」之意的複合名詞，因此正確答案是(B)。retailed 的形容詞並不存在。
詞彙　at least 至少　experience 經驗　retail 零售

6
解析：如果機器因任何原因停止的話，您可以聯繫我們。
須找出名詞 reason 前面的限定詞。您可以填入複數名詞前面作為 any 的限定詞，a few 後面可以加上單複數名詞。
詞彙　reason 原因　contact 聯絡　a few 少數的、幾個的

7
解析：當你簽署合約時，必須要仔細地閱讀它。
代名詞須署名合約，必須找出指稱前面的名詞。須找出指稱前面 the contract，同時作為受格代名詞的受格，因此正確答案是(B)。them 只能使用在複數名詞。
詞彙　sign 簽署　contract 合約、契約　review 檢視　carefully 仔細地、慎重地

8
解析：我們的客戶可以隨時透過他們的資訊進入網站。
名詞格代名詞在指稱前面適通性。所有格作為 their 是能夠承接 our customers 的所有格，因此正確答案是(A)。theirs 是所有代名詞。
詞彙　access 進入　through 透過　24 hours a day 隨時、一直

9
解析：彭普頓先生獨自一人撰寫了預算報告。
by oneself 是「獨自」之意的反身代名詞慣用法，因此正確答案是(B)。
詞彙　budget 預算　by oneself 獨自

10
解析：那些規律運動的人也傾向於均衡飲食。
<those+who～> 是「做～的人們」之意，因此正確答案是(B)。
詞彙　exercise 做運動、運動　tend to 傾向於～、有～習性　balanced diet 均衡的飲食

Step 2 基本掌握　P125

P125

正解

1.(A)	2.(B)	3.(B)	4.(A)	5.(B)
6.(B)	7.(A)	8.(B)	9.(A)	10.(B)
11.(A)	12.(B)	13.(B)	14.(A)	

1
解析：他寫了這封信。
動詞 wrote 前面適合加上主格代名詞 He，因此正確答案是(A)。
詞彙　write 撰寫

2
解析：我們重視您的意見。
動詞 value 和名詞 opinion 之間適合加上所有格 your，因此正確答案是(B)。
詞彙　value 重視　opinion 意見

3
解析：有些人當他們開會時會自言自語。
反身代名詞 value 和主語相同時使用。答案是第3人稱複數形，適合 themselves，因此正確答案是(B)。
詞彙　talk to oneself 自言自語　alone 單獨

4
解析：房間裡擺滿了許多家具。
限定詞 much 後不可數名詞，而 furniture 是不可數名詞，不加複數形，因此正確答案是(A)。some people 是加上複數形，因此正確答案是(B)。
詞彙　be filled with 填滿了～　furniture 家具

5
解析：員工要求延長截止期限。
冠詞 an 和介係詞 of 之間填入名詞，extension 是「延長」之意的名詞，因此正確答案是(B)。
詞彙　request 要求　deadline 截止期限　extended 延長的　extension 延長

6
解析：他透過電子郵件 express 的受詞位置是 appreciation，因此正確答案是 appreciation。
詞彙　express 表達　donation 捐獻　appreciate 感謝　appreciation 謝意

7
解析：該公司決定將其總部遷至亞洲。
題目中 head office 應該是 The company 所擁有，空格內適合填入所有格 its，因此正確答案是(A)。
詞彙　decide 決定　head office 總部

8
解析：在推出新產品之前，我們需要解決一些問題。
a few 後面加上複數名詞，因此正確答案是(B)。
詞彙　solve 解決　launch 推出

9

我們將全額退款。

解析 refund是可數名詞，與不定冠詞a一起使用，或後面加上複數形-s，因此正確答案是 (A)。

詞彙 refund 退款

10

星期五晚上，每個人都被邀請參加她退休的派對。

解析 retirement party是<名詞+名詞>的複合名詞，具有「退休派對」之意，因此正確答案是 (B)。

詞彙 invite 邀請 retire 退休 retirement 退休

11

如果您想與接線員交談，請立即按1。

解析 空格前面出現不定冠詞an，因此填入名詞，說話的對象必須是人，因此正確答案是 (A)。

詞彙 press 按下 operator 接線員 operation 運作、手術

12

該計畫由貝克先生監督。

解析 定冠詞the和介係詞of之間須加上名詞，由於是「在～監督下」之意，under the supervision of最為適合，因此正確答案是 (B)。

詞彙 under 在～之下 supervisor 督察、主管 supervision 監督

13

你有見過建築師對編新建築的設計打勾了嗎？

解析 作為met的受詞位置，「見面」的對象是「建築師」最為貼切，因此正確答案是 (B)。

詞彙 architecture 建築物 architect 建築師

14

這個地區的競爭非常激烈。

解析 定冠詞the和介係詞in之間加上名詞，因此正確答案是 (A)。

詞彙 area 地區 fierce 激烈的 competition 競爭 compete 進行競爭

Step 3 實戰練習 (Part 5) P126

正解

| 1.(B) | 2.(D) | 3.(C) | 4.(A) | 5.(C) |
| 6.(B) | 7.(C) | 8.(A) | 9.(A) | 10.(D) |

1

如果您想要折扣價，您必須在線上預訂。

解析 冠詞the之後面必須加上名詞。make a reservation是「預約」之意，因此正確答案是 (B)。

詞彙 discounted price 折扣價 reserve 做預約 reservation 預約

2

經理們希望他們在新系統上取得進展。

解析 即動詞前面主語的位置，取代前面出現過的these managers，適合使用第3人稱複數代名詞they，因此正確答案是 (D)。

詞彙 make progress 取得進展

3

我們為客戶提供各種服務，滿足不同需求。

解析 a variety of具有「各種的」之意，用來修飾名詞，因此正確答案是 (C)。

詞彙 offer 提供 need 需求 vary 變化、相異 various 各種的 variety 種類、多樣性

4

該公司被認為是客戶滿意度最好的航空公司之一。

解析 當名詞後面出現空格時，需考慮是否是複合名詞。customer satisfaction是「顧客滿意度」之意的複數名詞，因此正確答案是 (A)。

詞彙 consider 認為 in terms of 就～而言 satisfaction 滿意 satisfy 使滿意 satisfying 令人滿意的 satisfactory 滿意的

5

編輯邀請著名建築師寫下他最喜歡的飯店。

解析 favorite (最喜歡的) 通常會出現所有格，因此正確答案是 (C)。

詞彙 editor 編輯 invite 邀請 architect 建築師

6

懷特先生自己更新了公司的網站，因為其他程式設計師的密碼有問題。

解析 懷特先生在沒有別人幫忙的情況下，更新的by himself在一致性上最為恰當，因此正確答案是 (B)。

詞彙 update 更新 password 密碼

7

將發生許多變化。

解析 「許多、多數」之意的a number of後面會加上複數名詞，因此正確答案是 (C)。

詞彙 take place 發生 change 變化

8

預算委員會將於每位成員都公開這些訊息。

解析 限定冠詞every後面出現單數名詞，因此正確答案是 (A)。

詞彙 budget 預算 committee 委員會 disclose 公開 employers 僱主門 employment 僱用 employees 員工門

9

定期運動能讓人住往比沒有運動的人更健康、更長壽。

解析 以who開始的關係子句能夠修飾的是those，經常使用的是<those who ～>，必須記熟<those who ～>「做～的人們」之意。

詞彙 exercise 運動 regularly 定期地 tend to 傾向於～

10

你有要得到經理核准的文件才能進入本區域。

解析 所有格後面必須加上名詞，因此正確答案是 (D)。

詞彙 restricted area 管制的區域 approve 批准 approved 遭批准的、被許可的 approval 批准、許可

Step 4 實戰練習 (Part 6) P127

正解

| 11.(B) | 12.(C) | 13.(C) | 14.(B) |

[11-14]

嗨，瑪麗安。

我是大衛，我希望妳在這裡出差的時光愉快。想跟妳一提，我知道我的新工作，弗雷明漢本公司過得很好。那裡，妳是否願意在本公司做訪問嗎？⑩ 推薦該地區的旅遊勝地？這將是我第一次訪問國家的南部地區，我們對此區願非常興奮。⑪ 尤其我希望妳能夠那地區的海灘這件 意見。謝謝妳的幫助。

11

解析 空格是填入動詞的位置，因為Everyone是單數名詞，動詞須加上misses，因此正確答案是 (B)。(C)和(D)是動狀態動詞，因此不適合做為答案。

詞彙 enjoy 享受、度過愉快時光 travel destination 旅遊勝地 southern 南部的 area 地區 in particular 尤其 miss 想念 opinion 意見

12

解析 空格是填入動詞的位置，因為正確答案是 (B)。(C)和(D)使用使役動詞，通合做為答案。(A)佛羅里達州是美國人口最多的國家。(B)我想在貴公司找一份新工作。

(c) 我知道你以前住在那裡。
(D) 請不久之後去拜訪我們。

14. 解析　這封信是請求推薦安排成旅遊，推薦可以視為對方的「意見」，而 opinion 最為適合，因此正確答案是(B)。
詞彙　opinion 意見、看法

13. 解析　選擇句子的類型，判斷有關連。在閱讀短文時，選擇最符合前後文一致性的選項（必須在計畫進度（空格前句），和前後推薦不錯的地點（空格後句）之間的內容找出適合的內容；以一致性來說，這位人員有足以推薦 Florida, company 的詞彙，內容上完全不具連貫性。
詞彙　make a recommendation 所表達的意思是「推薦」，因此正確答案是(C)。

Unit 2　形容詞與副詞

Step 1　Practice　P128

正解

1.(B)	2.(B)	3.(B)	4.(A)	5.(A)
6.(A)	7.(B)	8.(B)	9.(A)	10.(A)

1 單和博士在研討會上發表了非常豐富的演說。
解析　空格前面有冠詞和副詞 very，後面有名詞 presentation，因此空格處需要既能修飾那名詞，又要被 very 所修飾的形容詞答案是(B)。「-ive」是構成典型形容詞的詞尾，「-tion/sion」是構成典型名詞的詞尾。
詞彙　give a presentation 演說、發表　informative 有用的、提供的　information 資訊

2 解析　作為修飾複數可數名詞用的 customers 的數量形容詞以 many 最合適。因此必須填入形容詞(A)。「much 是修飾不可數名詞。
詞彙　customer 顧客　complain 抱怨　service 服務

3 宮城先生為了與餐廳經理爭論等了很久。
解析　空格前後分別為冠詞和名詞，因此必須填入形容詞，所以答案是(B)。(A)是動詞，因此無法修飾名詞。
詞彙　wait for 等待　moment 瞬間、時間、時刻　extensively 廣泛地

4 重新整修後，這件老舊建築物變得寬敞。
解析　形容詞放在名詞前面來修飾名詞，或放在 be/become 之後作為表語。此空格是 spacious 的位置，即使名詞也能作為補語，「老建築」變成「空間寬敞。之意即顯格格不入。
詞彙　renovation 整修、改造　spacious 空間寬敞的　space 空間

5 文件被高度努力地推薦。
解析　high 是高度很高時可以使用的副詞，highly 則是「極度」的副詞，因此正確答案是(A)。
詞彙　paper 文件　high 高、高地　highly 極度

6 解析　空格是修飾前面 tried 的副詞的位置。一致性來看，具「努力地」之意的 hard 最適合，因此正確答案是(A)。
詞彙　try to 致力於～　position 位置、職位　hard 努力地　hardly 幾乎不～

7 費南迪斯女士正在南美洲旅遊。
解析　這句話是現在進行式(be-ing)，能夠放在 be 動詞和 traveling 之間修飾 traveling 的必須是副詞，因此空格要填入 present 加上 -ly 形成 presently 是形容詞 present 的副詞形式。
詞彙　travel 旅行、旅遊　present 目前的　presently 目前、當下

8 每位新職員在來上班前的必須讀熟他們的手冊。
解析　空格前面是完整的句子結構，空格後面是名詞片語，能夠填入 carefully。carefully 是可以修飾後面 read 的副詞，因此正確答案是(B)。
詞彙　handbook 手冊、指南　careful 小心的、注意的　carefully 慎重地、小心地

9 我的成績跟你的一樣好。
解析　原級比較 as A as 形容詞/副詞 as B。句型的意思是「A 和 B 一樣～」，as A as 之間必須填入原級詞，因此正確答案是(A)。
詞彙　score 分數

10 這家餐廳的食物品質比以前好很多。
解析　than 前面出現比比較級的很多，much 是強調比較級時使用，因此正確答案是(A)。
詞彙　quality 品質　used to 以前　than 比

Step 2　基本掌握　P133

正解

1.(A)	2.(B)	3.(B)	4.(A)	5.(A)
6.(B)	7.(B)	8.(A)	9.(A)	10.(A)
11.(B)	12.(A)	13.(B)	14.(A)	

1 董事會對員工政策做出了最終決定。
解析　不定冠詞 a 和名詞 decision 之間填入的是形容詞位置，因此正確答案是(B)。表示「最終決定」之意的 final decision 是經常使用的表達方式，必須熟練。
詞彙　board 董事會　policy 政策　finalist 決賽選手

2 這家代理商受到其他公司的高度推薦。
解析　be 動詞和過去分詞之間的位置是副詞，high 和 highly 都是副詞，但是表動詞 recommend 的單字是具有「非常」之意的 highly，因此正確答案是(B)。
詞彙　agency 代理商　recommend 推薦

3 我們目前進度落後。
解析　選擇因為看到 be 動詞而選擇形容詞 current。但 current（目前的）無法作為 Web 的補語，必須是能夠修飾後文整體的副詞，因此正確答案是(B)。
詞彙　behind schedule 進度落後　current 目前的　currently 目前

4 則這是個城市最好的餐廳。
解析　「中最棒的」適合是最高級的描述，因此正確答案是(A)。
詞彙　best 最好的　better 較好的

5 讓我們盡全力不要太晚完成報告。
解析　not too late（太晚地）這句子的意思是「不要太晚地」，因此正確答案是(A)。
詞彙　do one's best 盡全力　late 很晚　lately 最近

6 如果您還需要額外的員工資訊，請與我們的辦公室連絡。
解析　空格是修飾後面 information 的形容詞的位置。additional information 意思意思的形容詞意思是「額外的資訊」，因此正確答案是(B)。
詞彙　contact 連絡　additionally 另外、補充地　additional 額外的

7 公司試圖保持競爭力。
解析　remain 的後面必須填入主格補語，形容詞 competitively 可以做為主格補語，因此正確答案是(B)。
詞彙　remain 維持～　competitively 競爭地　competitive 具競爭力的

8 解析 比較級前面用以強調比較級的副詞有much, even, far, still, a lot 等,因此正確答案是 (A)。very則用來修飾原級。
這款新車比以前的快得多。

9 解析 as和as之間用以強調形容詞或副詞原級。以前後文一致性來看,空格所修飾的是一般副詞finish,適合填入副詞,因此正確答案是 (A)。
詞彙 hope 希望~ successfully 成功地
計畫將按照我們的希望成功完成。

10 解析 空格是 The orchestra's performance的補語填入位置,必須填入形容詞,因此正確答案是 (A)。
詞彙 performance 表演、表現 impressive 印象深刻的 impressively 印象深刻地
管弦樂隊的表演十分令人印象深刻。

11 解析 不定詞to和名詞revision之間可以填入的是形容詞,因此正確答案是 (B)。
詞彙 revision 修改 résumé 履歷表 apply 申請 carefully 仔細地
在申請之前,您必須仔細修改您的履歷。

12 解析 可以填出冠詞後、名詞前的詞類是形容詞,因此正確答案是 (A)。remark具有名詞(傳述、提及)、動詞(發言)之意,無論從文法上或語意上來看都不適合。
詞彙 product 產品 achieve 取得 success 成功 remarkable 驚人的 remark 提及、陳述
我們應該要加倍努力以獲得最好的結果。

13 解析 空格應該要當作主語 (We) 的補語、適合使用形容詞reliant。
詞彙 result 結果 reliance 依賴 reliant 值得信任的
他是我們團隊中經驗最豐富的員工。

14 解析 <最高級>, in +團體/地點名詞>具有「當中最~的」之意,因此正確答案是 (A)。
詞彙 employee 員工、雇員 experienced 有經驗的

Step 3 實戰練習 (Part 5) P134

正解

1.(B)	2.(D)	3.(C)	4.(D)	5.(C)
6.(D)	7.(A)	8.(A)	9.(C)	10.(D)

1 解析 能夠放在不定冠詞an後面並修飾名詞way的形容詞,因此正確答案是 (B)。
詞彙 come up with 想出~ increase 增加 profit 利潤 effect 效果 effective 有效的 effectively 有效地 effectiveness 效果
我們應該要想出一個增加利潤的有效方法。

2 解析 能夠修飾具有「出處」之意的名詞source,也能加上最高級the most的形容詞,因此正確答案是 (D)。
詞彙 source 出處 information 資訊 industry 產業 reliability 可靠性 reliable 可靠的 reliably 確實地 rely 依賴
〈金融時報〉是業界內最可靠的資訊來源。

3 解析 <the比較級+of the two>意思是「~兩者中比較~的」,因此正確答案是 (C)。
詞彙 qualified 具資格的
在這兩名員工中,唐娜女士更有資格能完成這項工作。

4 解析 造種新的溝通方式越來越受年輕一代的歡迎。
詞彙 communication 溝通 generation 世代 increase 增加 increasing 增加的

5 解析 be動詞後面應該填入形容詞,因此正確答案是 (C)。注意避免和「相當的」之意的considerable混淆。
詞彙 visitor 遊客 quietly 安靜地 consider 考慮 considerate 體諒的 consideration 考量 considerable 相當的
所有遊客都應該安靜地consider 考慮博物館裡最popular的(最受歡迎的)展覽品。

6 解析 所有格和名詞information之間可以填入的是形容詞,因此正確答案是 (D)。熟記具有「個人資料」之意的personal information個性化。
詞彙 customer 客戶 secure 安全的 personality 個性 personalize 個性化 personal information 個人資料
托倫公司將保護客戶的個人資料安全。

7 解析 as~as之間適合填入形容詞或副詞原級,所以答案是 (A)。
詞彙 score 分數 expect 預期
我很遺憾分數不如我們預期的那麼好。

Step 4 實戰練習 (Part 6) P135

正解

11.(A)	12.(C)	13.(B)	14.(D)

[11-14]

敬啟者,

我們的組織將於5月2日舉辦一次會議,(11) 估計的出席會議的人數為1,000人。我們的客戶之一——一般計畫會給我們留下了深刻的印象。但是,我將您的設施能否滿足我們的需求表示擔憂。(13) 尤其擔心主會議室的大小。您能否告訴我主會議室的確切 (12) 容納量以及您還有哪些其他可使用的房間?

感謝您的時間和關注。

木村安德森
明昆市場營銷

詞彙 organization 組織 host 舉辦 attendance 參加人數 individual 個人 recommend 推薦 client 顧客 frequently 經常 result 結果 reputation 聲譽 facility 設施 accommodate 容納 capacity 容量 available 可使用的 estimate 推測、估計 deposit 訂金 especially 尤其 especial 特別的

8 解析 比較級前面用以強調甚至比以前更好。
新版本的出版比原版前面用以強調甚至比以前更好。

9 詞彙 publishing 出版
新版本的出版比原版前用以強調much, even, still, far, a lot 等,因此正確答案是 (A)。

10 解析 放在最前面修飾整個句子的副詞,後面會加上逗號 (,),因此正確答案是 (D)。
詞彙 motivated 積極的 productivity 生產力
員工的積極度越高,就能輕鬆解釋。

11 解析 遺憾的是,我必須通知你,我們在本月底即將關閉設施。<the+比較級>句型,因此正確答案是 (D)。
詞彙 inform 通知 facility 設施 regret 後悔 regrettable 遺憾的 regretful 後悔的

12

(A) 我們不會向您收取額外費用。
(B) 如果有可能，你能給我們一些折扣嗎？
(C) 貴公司的良好聲譽給我留下了深刻的印象。
(D) 我們不會匯款給您。

解析 未確定的人數或價格等數值時，會使用「估計」之意的過去分詞 estimated，因此正確答案是 (A)。

13

解析 描人句題目在解題時必須根據前照標格短文，(同時找此密格前後內容具一貫性的句子。從公司舉辦活動的推薦地點來看，必須是能夠自然連貫前文，又能與後面However開頭的轉折內容連接的句子。由此可知應該選人選推薦公司的原因，因此正確答案是 (C)。) (A) 是站在提供服務的立場，(B) 應該放在文章的最後面，(D) 適合放在與顧客第一次在見面的電子郵件中，因此不適合作為答案。

14

解析 信件內容看來是顧問諮議者能夠答覆的「咨詢」，因此正確答案是 (D)。
放在be動詞和過去分詞worried之間修飾的必須是副詞，因此正確答案是 (B)。especially是具有「尤其」之意的副詞。

Unit 3　動詞1－形態、主語與動詞的一致性

Step 1　Practice　P136

正解
1. (B)	2. (A)	3. (A)	4. (B)	5. (A)
6. (B)	7. (B)	8. (A)	9. (B)	10. (A)

1 新的安全政策應該從下面一開始實施。
解析 助動詞後面必須加上動詞原型，因此正確答案是 (B)。
詞彙 safety 安全 policy 政策 take effect 生效、奏效 as of 截至～為止、從～起

2 報告的影本會在會議期間開始發放。
解析 <助動詞>＋be動詞之後的動詞形態必須是-ing或-ed。報告的影本「被發放」之意，所以以-ed形式最適合，因此正確答案是 (A)。
詞彙 copy 影本 distribute 發放

3 在您進去之前，請填寫包裹內的申請表格。
解析 以Please開頭的典型命令句後面必須加上動詞原型，因此正確答案是 (A)。
詞彙 fill out 填寫 registration 登記 form 表格 packet 包裹

4 工廠發生的問題就在事件發生後處理了。
解析 在可以使用<have been + -ing/p.p>的情況中，The problem是「已處理完畢」的對象，後面必須加上p.p.，須語記動詞deal的不規則變化(deal-dealt-dealt)，因此正確答案是 (B)。
詞彙 promptly 迅速、及時 incident 事故、事件 deal 處理

5 在銷售部門的員工每個月都會參加討論會。
解析 主語是複數形Employees，適合加上複數動詞attend，因此正確答案是 (A)。
詞彙 department 部門 seminar 演討會 attend 參加

6 從我們網站比訂購的顧客可獲得八折的優惠。
解析 主語是第3人稱單數形A customer，所以動詞必須加上一(e)s，因此正確答案是 (B)。
詞彙 order 訂購 receive 獲得

7 想要應徵這職位的申請者需繳交履歷。
解析 主格關係代名詞who的先行詞是複數形Applicants，所以適合複數動詞wish，因此正確答案是 (B)。
詞彙 applicant 申請人 apply for 應徵～ position 位置、職位 wish 希望 résumé 履歷

8 安全規範要求每個人戴上安全帽及護目鏡。
解析 安全規範(安全規則、辦公、進議、要求動詞後面的that子句可以省略should，使用動詞原型，因此正確答案是 (A)。
詞彙 safety rules 安全規範 require 要求 hard hat 安全帽 goggles 護目鏡 wear 配戴

9 銷售代表和經理都參加了會議。
解析 Both A and B (A和B兩者都) 被視為複數形，所以動詞必須是複數，因此正確答案是 (B)。
詞彙 department manager 部門經理 present 出席的

10 銷售人員的數量在過去兩年內迅速地增長。
解析 <the number of + 複數名詞>的句子的型態<the數量>因此正確答案是 (A)。相反地，<a number of + 複數名詞>是「許多的」之意，視為複數名詞。
詞彙 grow 成長 rapidly 迅速地 last 過去

Step 2　基本掌握　P141

正解
1. (B)	2. (B)	3. (A)	4. (B)	5. (B)
6. (B)	7. (A)	8. (B)	9. (A)	10. (B)
11. (A)	12. (A)	13. (A)	14. (B)	

1 請按時完成計劃。
解析 句子一開始出現please，可知是以動詞原型開頭的命令句，因此正確答案是 (B)。
詞彙 on time 按時

2 對新產品的需求正在快速成長。
解析 配合主語的需求狀況成長。
詞彙 demand 需求

3 其他部門負責人也同意這項議題。
解析 主語The other department heads是複數，所以必須加上複數動詞，因此正確答案是 (A)。
詞彙 department head 部門負責人 subject 主題、議題

4 秘書已經完成所有準備工作。
解析 has後面可以接連用的動詞形態pp.，因此正確答案是 (B)。
詞彙 secretary 秘書 preparation 準備

5
在研討會開始之前還有很多時間。
解析 <There be動詞～>句子中be動詞後面出現的名詞數量一致，time是不可數名詞，必須使用單數動詞，因此正確答案是 (A)。
詞彙 workshop 研討會

6
布拉德在人事部門工作。
解析 主語Brad是第3人稱單數，一般動詞必須加上動詞原型，因此正確答案是 (B)。
詞彙 personnel department 人事部門

7
山米為報告寫了資料。
解析 主語Sammie是第3人稱單數，所以要加上同樣的所態，因此正確答案是 (A)。如果想使用現在式，須為writes。
詞彙 material 資料 presentation 報告、簡報

8
我對廣告領域感興趣。
解析 須讓句be interested in是「對～有興趣」之意，因此正確答案是 (B)。
詞彙 advertising 廣告的 field 領域

9
每個人都必須準時參加會議。
解析 主語Everyone是單數，所以適合單數動詞has，因此正確答案是 (B)。
詞彙 have to 必須～

10
電腦技術相關的書籍在接面走道。
解析 about computer technology只是修飾語，所以修飾主語Books的修飾語Books一致的複數形are，因此正確答案是 (A)。
詞彙 aisle 走廊、走道

11
你明天之前可以發貨嗎？
解析 疑問句中使用助動詞can，有助動詞的句子必須配合動詞原型，因此正確答案是 (A)。
詞彙 merchandise 商品

12
請至少出發時間15分鐘前往出發。
解析 由於句子中沒有動詞，因此必須以動詞開頭的命令句。命令句使用原型開頭，因此正確答案是 (A)。
詞彙 at least 至少 departure 出發

13
坂田先生將擔任新員工研討會的領導的
詞彙 employee 員工、從業員 lead 指導、主導 leading 領先的、領導的

正解

1.(D)	2.(D)	3.(C)	4.(A)	5.(A)
6.(B)	7.(D)	8.(B)	9.(A)	10.(A)

1
我們必須盡最大努力與供應商保持友好關係。
解析 助動詞must後面須加上動詞原型，因此正確答案是 (D)。
詞彙 friendly 友好的 relationship 關係 supplier 供應商

2
去年露西為她的服裝系列開發了一種新口味。
解析 出現表達過去的last year，必須加上動詞過去式，因此正確答案是 (D)。
詞彙 flavor 味道

3
佐藤先生是他部門裡最好的銷售人員。
解析 主語Mr. Sato是第3人稱單數，所以須加上Lis，因此正確答案是 (C)。
(D)……避免只看主語Lucy而誤選 (C)。
詞彙 sales person 銷售人員

4
回答問題與答題時請
解析 這是以動名詞Answering questions作為主語的句子。動名詞作為主語時，動詞須加上單數形，因此正確答案是 (A)。
詞彙 responsibility 職責

5
技術人員建議每名用戶每年更改一次密碼。
解析 當出現像recommend一樣表達意識、要求、主張的動詞時，在that子句中使用省略的動詞should的動詞原型，因此正確答案是 (A)。
詞彙 technician 技術人員

6
您的文件有一些需要立即修正的錯誤。
解析 主語Your document是單數，添加上單數動詞是 (B)。be動詞的意思上並不適合。
詞彙 document 文件 error 錯誤 fix 修正

7
解析 主語是Many buildings，而around the city 或library是修飾主語的修飾語，所以動詞必須是配合Many buildings的複數動詞。由於有表達過去時間於200 years ago，需使用過去式複數動詞were，因此正確答案是 (D)。
詞彙 city library 市立圖書館

8
季節性變化會對某些產品的銷售成影響。
詞彙 seasonal 季節的 variation 變化 certain 特定的
～產生影響

9
線上銷售的成功關鍵是以合理的價格提供我們的商品。
解析 主格是Guests，所以須使用有複數動詞……中的先行詞Guests，所以須使用有複數動詞，因此正確答案是 (A)。
詞彙 offer 提供 affordable 負擔得起的

10
喜歡吃素食料理的客人應事先通知我們。
解析 除了修飾名詞之外，適句話中的主語是The key，所以動詞必須單數一致，因此正確答案是 (B)。
詞彙 vegetarian 素食 dish 料理 beforehand 事先

14
飯店可以容納更多客人。
解析 為了解開放問題，必須掌握句子的意思。飯店是更多客人以「容納」來表達最為適合，因此正確答案是 (B)。
詞彙 guest 客人 accompany 伴隨 accommodate 容納

正解

11.(C)	12.(B)	13.(A)	14.(C)

[11-14]

請所有二樓廚房使用者注意

為了保持我們的廚房區域舒適乾淨，在使用冰箱和所有其他廚房用具時，請為他人設想。⑪ 請丟棄在您某任何食物的並立即照料任何溢出物。每次使用後……造成某人不舒服的氣味。另外，請不要丟棄某本 ⑫ 將放在冰箱上方的小蘇打盒。這有助於保持冰箱無異味。⑬ ……感謝您的合作。

詞彙 attention 注意、留心 pleasant 舒適的、愉快的 considerate 為他人設想的 refrigerator 冰箱 kitchen appliance 廚房用具 spoiled 腐壞的 wipe up 擦拭 spill 溢出物 prevent 防止 unpleasant 不舒服的 throw away 丟棄 baking soda 蘇打粉 odor 臭味 free 沒有～的 cooperation 合作 surface 表面、外部 measure 措施 skill 技巧 filter 過濾裝置 element 要素 discard 丟棄 place 放置

11

解析 這是以Please開頭的典型的命令句，意思是「若集貨員食物」，因此正確答案是（C）。

12

(A) 魚排搭配今蒜麵上桌。
(B) 每次使用後，請保持廚房檯面清潔。
(C) 當您購買一個以上的電器時，您可以獲得特別折扣。
(D) 今晚的晚餐特色是燉菜的菜單。

解析 從您文最前面開始讀起，掌握文章的連貫性，並在空格前後找到最大的提示。在這段句子後面可以一同維持廚房整潔的內容，因此正確答案是（B）。

13

解析 清格變資食物或述出物是能夠的止異產生的「借施」，因此正確答案是（A）。

14

解析 that是主格關係代名詞，前面的the box of baking soda是先行詞，盒子是被放置在架上的對象，須加上被動語態的p.p.，因此正確答案是（C）。
其他選項和主體主題，也就是廚房要素沒有關聯。

Unit 4 動詞2—語態和時態

Step 1 Practice   P144

正解
1. (B)	2. (B)	3. (B)	4. (A)	5. (B)
6. (A)	7. (B)	8. (A)	9. (A)	10. (B)

1

解析 合約必須由雙方當事人簽署。
主語The contract是被簽署的對象而使用被動語態，因此正確答案是（B）。空格前面有助動詞should，因此被動語態須為be signed形式。

詞彙 contract 合約，契約 party 當事人，關係者 sign 簽署

2

解析 這是遊客們參觀這個地區來欣賞著名地點。
（B）。空格前面有名詞在主語位置時才能作為答案

詞彙 traveler 遊客 visit 參觀 area 地區 famous 著名的
landmark 有標誌性的建築物、地標

3

解析 作為主語的Our hotel guests是接受接駁車服務的對象，需使用被動語態，因此正確答案是（B）。這句是以Our hotel guests放在前面的被動語態形式。後面加上直接受詞free shuttle bus service。

詞彙 encourage 獎勵，鼓勵 technical 技術的 participate in 參加
~

4

解析 encourage作為目的補語，後面加上to不定詞，由於受詞employees成為主語位置，因此是被動語態的句子，目的補語不定詞使當作被動語態也維持同樣形式。

詞彙 encourage 獎勵，鼓勵 technical 技術的 participate in 參加
員工被鼓勵參加技術培訓課程。

5

解析 像usually一樣表達習慣性，反覆性事物的副詞會使用現在時態，因此正確答案是（A）。

我們的服務職員通常維修電腦需要二至三週工作天。

詞彙 representative 代表 usually 通常 fix 修理，修改 take 花費
（兩週）

6

解析 由於出現未來時態副詞片語next Friday，需使用未來時態，因此正確答案是（A）。

董事會即將在下週五聚集以討論新的行銷策略。

詞彙 board of directors 董事會 strategy 策略 gather 聚集

7

解析 當麥克來拜訪我們時，我正在和其中一個客戶說話。
此正確答案是（B）。

詞彙 client 客戶 visit 拜訪

8

解析 由於出現副詞currently，必須表達現在時間點正在進行式的我們，需使用現在進行式，因此正確答案是（A）。

我們現在正經歷巨大規模的變化。

詞彙 currently 目前，最近 undergo 經歷，遭受 change 變化
process 過程

9

解析 句子最後<for the last + 期間>主要與現在完成一起使用，因此正確答案是（B）。

田中先生過去的七年來一直為公司工作。

詞彙 last 過去的

10

解析 從過去到現在獲得無數獎項以現在完成式來描述，但這個副詞的主語不是高谷，而是多數料理（whose dishes），所以必須使用複數動詞，因此正確答案是（B）。

高谷先生是屢獲無數獎項的有名廚師。

詞彙 famous 知名的 dish 料理 receive 獲得 numerous 無數

Step 2 基本掌握   P149

正解
1. (B)	2. (A)	3. (B)	4. (A)	5. (A)
6. (B)	7. (A)	8. (B)	9. (B)	10. (B)
11. (A)	12. (A)	13. (B)	14. (A)	

1

解析 <be crowded with~>意思是「擠滿了~」，因此正確答案是(B)。

商店在假期期間擠滿了客人。

詞彙 holiday season 假期，度假旺季

2

解析 我下次旅行時將會拜訪你的家。
「」是拜訪行為的主體，空格後面會出現受詞，需使用主動語態，因此正確答案是（A）。

詞彙 place 地點、（個人的）家

3

解析 由於出現描述過去的three years ago，空格內需使用過去式動詞，因此正確答案是（B）。

加入先生3年前加入了我們公司。

4.
羅伯遜女士持續每個月拜訪總部。
解析 由副詞consistently和every month看來，可知是現在時態，適合的時態是現在時態，因此正確答案是(A)。
詞彙 consistently 持續地 head office 總部

5.
他一收到我們的信之後會立刻回覆我。
解析 表達時間的連接詞as soon as帶頭的子句以現在時態表達未來語意，必須加上現在式動詞，因此正確答案是(A)。
詞彙 as soon as 一……就 respond to 回覆～

6.
我明天在公園散步。
解析 描述過去的yesterday適合過去式動詞，因此正確答案是(B)。
詞彙 take a walk 散步

7.
告別派對將於下週一舉行。
解析 next Monday適合下週的未來，適合未來時態，因此正確答案是(B)。
詞彙 farewell party 告別派對 take place 舉行

8.
我被要求發電子郵件給下圖一先生。
解析 具有<ask+受詞+to不定詞>結構的句子由被動語態組成時，成為<be asked to不定詞>。目的補語為不定詞的句子即使在被動語態中仍維持不定詞的形式，因此正確答案是(B)。
詞彙 email 發電子郵件

9.
她昨天告訴我，他去年曾在韓國工作過。
解析 獨立子句的時態是「昨天」的過去式時間，從屬子句的時態是早於昨天的「去年」，所以空格需填入過去完成式 (had+過去分詞)，現在完成式使用在從過去到現在的事情，所以不適合(A)。

10.
新企劃由新任主管賴特先生主導。
解析 作為主語的The new project不是部份~to去，句中的to不定詞部份lead的實行主象，必須加上the現在式，意思是「大～而須法～」，因此正確答案是(A)。
詞彙 director 主管 lead 主導

11.
該產品的價格太高，我們無法接受。
解析 ……須加入被動語態，所以空格現在完成式使用從過去到現在的事情，因此正確答案是(B)。
詞彙 product 產品 acceptable 可接受的

12.
我們需要部門主管的簽名。
解析 所有格後面應該做出姓名名詞，因此正確答案是(A)。
詞彙 supervisor 主管 signature 簽名

13.
下一屆特別展覽定於5月1日開幕。
解析 exhibition和exhibit都是「展示會」之意，但空格後面的動詞是單數，所以主語也是單數，因此正確答案是(B)。
詞彙 be scheduled to 定於～ exhibit 展示會／展覽

14.
該公司致力於為下一代提供安全的環境。
解析 be committed to具有「致力於～」之意，是常考的表達句，必須熟記。正確答案是(A)。
詞彙 environment 環境 generation 世代

正解

1.(B)	2.(B)	3.(C)	4.(D)	5.(B)
6.(A)	7.(C)	8.(D)	9.(A)	10.(D)

1.
解析 我們的商店通常在早上7點開門。
usually用以表達反覆的習慣，是現在時態的代表性辭彙。主語Our store是第3人稱單數，所以(B)最符合。
詞彙 usually 通常

2.
解析 這張照片呈現一位著名設計師所拍攝的。作為主語的This picture是被拍攝的對象，所以必須使用被動語態，因此正確答案是(B)。

3.
解析 公司銷售額在上一季季大幅下滑。
last quarter(上一季)代表過去式，因此過去式動詞fell最符合，正確答案是(C)。
詞彙 sharply 大幅地 quarter 季 fall 下跌

4.
解析 如果金額超過200美元，所有款項可通過信用卡支付。
作為主語的款項(All payments),是以人作為實行主體，所以空格內需要加入被動語態，因此正確答案是(D)。
詞彙 payment 支付 amount 金額

5.
解析 自2010年以來，該公司一直聚焦於女性服飾。
從選項中來看，可以搭配用在完成式的介係詞是Since（自～以來），雖然before也可以和現在完成式一同使用，但必須具有「自2010年到現在」之意，因此before並不符合。
詞彙 focus on 聚焦於～ apparel 服飾

6.
解析 由表達時間的連接詞when帶頭的副詞子句中，現在時態取代了未

7.
新增的設備預期能提高員工生產力。
解析 新增的設備預期能提高生產力，所以必須使用被動語態。expect是使用現在式動詞和受詞補語的動詞，作為受詞補語的the additional equipment放在主語位置，成為被動態的句子，因此正確答案是(C)。
詞彙 additional 增加的 employee productivity 員工生產力

8.
公寓鄰近地鐵站，位置便利。
解析 動詞locate是具有「位於」意思的及物動詞，作為主語的The apartment成為動詞的對象，因此正確答案是被動語態的(D)。be located(位於)是常考的辭彙，必須牢記。
詞彙 conveniently (便利地) subway station 地鐵站

9.
麥克斯特汽車公司上個月推出了一款新車型。
解析 由於出現描述過去的two months ago，必須使用過去時態動詞，因此正確答案是(D)。happen是不及物動詞，所以被動語態形式均不符合。
詞彙 substantial 大量的 advertising 廣告

10.
由於線上廣告，兩個月前銷售額大幅增加。
解析 由於出現描述過去的last month，必須使用過去時態動詞，因此正確答案是(A)。
詞彙 introduce 介紹／推出

正解

11.(D)	12.(C)	13.(B)	14.(A)

[11-14]

我們鎮上發生了什麼事？

紐伯斯，9月1日—至9月19日，紐伯斯市立美術館的30件作品，希漢先生是一位居住在我們社區的著名藝術家，他……月裡，希漢先生也訪問了歐洲許多……著名景地提供了我們專屬的……他的最新作品近期在這些個……發現。除了常態的入場……遊這個特別展覽的門票費格為5美元，博物館能從上午11點開放到下午5點，週一至週六，而週日休息。

詞彙　happen 發生　well-known 著名的　reside 居住　neighborhood 鄰近地區　offer 提供　recent 最近的　work（作品、工作）village 村莊　available 可使用的　in addition to 除～之外　regular 常態的　admission 入場費　exhibit 展示、展覽　opportunity 機會　inspire 啟發靈感　bounce 反彈　recession 不景氣、衰退

14 解析　博物館開門和關門是持續進行的反覆行為，所以需使用現在時態的 open（得到）提示。
因此正確答案是 (A)。也可以從前面那刻的現在時態得到提示。

13 解析　整體主題是希漢的展覽，空格前面提到其他的歐洲之旅，後面接上
（B）。其他選項只單純提到歐洲或歐體的內容，和跨文並沒有連貫性。
「這次旅程為作品帶來靈感」的內容最為流暢，因此正確答案是

12 解析　藝術家向別人展示自己的作品，可以說是特別的「機會」，因此正確
答案是 (C)。（詞彙題目中，往往難以自己的母語來選擇，必須熟記。）
(C) 歐洲需從此從想要退中慎選。
(B) 我們長久以來都很遐邇他。

11 解析　美術館是展示的主題，未來將持續展出至9月19日，所
以未來進行時態選項中最適合的答案，因此正確答案是 (D)。
opportunity（提供機會）是常考的綜合答案選擇。

Unit 5　動狀詞

Step 1　Practice　P152

正解
| 1. (B) | 2. (B) | 3. (B) | 4. (B) | 5. (B) |
| 6. (A) | 7. (B) | 8. (B) | 9. (A) | 10. (B) |

1 解析　店家將會提早關門以便在建築物前安裝新看板。
由於空格前面是完整的句型結構，不需要另外的動詞，空格中適合
填入具有「為了」之意的不定詞，因此正確答案是 (B)。
詞彙　sign 看板、標誌　install 安裝

2 解析　我們建議使用線上資訊來取得基本數據。
動詞後面需要有動狀詞形式，「recommend 的受詞」也必須將the
information 當作受詞；recommend（使用）名詞的 to 不定詞作為受詞，因
正確答案是 (B)。請謹記包含動名詞在的動狀詞可以像動詞一樣
使用受詞。
詞彙　recommend 推薦　obtain 確保、獲得　data 數據、資料
製造商拒絕要更換瑕品。

3 解析　refuse是「拒絕」之意，使用to不定詞作為受詞，因此正確答案是
(B)。
詞彙　refuse 拒絕　manufacturer 製造商　defective 有瑕疵的

4 解析　所有員工透過填寫表格可以預約會議室。
<be able to>動詞原型是具有「能夠～」之意的慣用表達，必須記
以熟記。正確答案是 (B)。
詞彙　be able to 能夠～　fill out 填寫　reserve 預約

5 解析　推出一項新產品需要大範圍的規劃和研究。
空格必須填入能夠making a new product的動名詞，並具有主格作用的
(B)。
詞彙　require 需要　extensive 廣泛的、龐大的　launch 推出、上市

6 解析　他對我上班遲到很生氣。
當動名詞在意義上的主語和句子的主語不一致時，以所有格表示意
義上的主語，因此正確答案是 (A)。
詞彙　angry 生氣的　be late 遲到

7 解析　根據我的計算，這報告中的銷售數據不太準確。
由於data顯示在報告上是書中，所以適合加上被動語態意的過去分詞shown，
因此正確答案是 (B)。
詞彙　data 數據　accurate 準確的　based on 根據～　calculation 計算

8 解析　情緒性動詞由來表達人所感受到的情緒時會使用過去分詞，當作引
發情緒的原因時，則使用現在分詞形式，所以impressed使用受詞
為觀眾受情緒化的主題，因此正確答案是 (A)。
詞彙　result 結果　representative 員工、代表　satisfied 滿意的

9 解析　這份說明書含有如何設置密碼的資訊。
介係詞on後面出現名詞時，由於空格後面必為名詞，因此正確答
案是 (B)。
詞彙　audience 聽眾　ovation 鼓掌　impressed 印象深刻的

10 解析　經理的演講讓員工對未來的銷售更有信心。
聽眾們對於演講「深受感動」而熱烈鼓掌，因此正確答案是 (B)。當作為引
受他的滿滿麻讓、聽眾孩子也深感到的驚喜。
詞彙　manual 說明書　contain 包括　create 製作　password 密碼

Step 2　基本掌握　P157

正解
1. (B)	2. (B)	3. (A)	4. (B)	5. (A)
6. (B)	7. (A)	8. (A)	9. (B)	10. (A)
11. (B)	12. (B)	13. (A)	14. (A)	

1 解析　學習外語並不容易。
由於出現動詞，必須加上能夠作在主語作用的動狀詞，因此正確答
案是 (B)。
詞彙　foreign language 外語

2 解析　讓我們繼續討論這個問題。
動詞continue是將動名詞和to不定詞作為受詞的動詞，因此正確答
案是 (B)。
詞彙　continue 繼續　matter 問題　discuss 討論

3 解析　你不需要擔心。
空格必須填入to worry在意義上是個介係詞，所以空格內需填入名詞，因此正
確答案是 (B)。
詞彙　need 需要

4 解析　該公司致力於有利組織的非營利組織。
be dedicated to的to是介係詞，所以空格後需加入動名詞，因此正
確答案是 (B)。
詞彙　be dedicated to 致力於～　non-profit organization 非營利組織

5

這項特別優惠僅限於期限有效。

解析 這是選擇冠詞和之間適合的分詞形式。被修飾的time是受限的對象，所以須加上過去分詞，因此正確答案是 (A)。

詞彙 special offer 特別優惠

6

我們決定支持當地的一家慈善機構。

解析 動詞decide是將to不定詞作為受詞的動詞，因此正確答案是 (B)。

詞彙 local 當地的　charity 慈善團體　support 支持

7

請在兩週內寄回附表。

解析 這是選擇冠詞和名詞之間適合的分詞形式。form是受詞的對象，因此正確答案是 (A)。只要熟記具有「附件表格」意思的attached form就能輕鬆解題。

詞彙 return 回覆　within 在～內

8

我根據情報查布獲選者。

解析 情緒形容詞用來表達感受與情緒的人時適合使用過去分詞，因此正確答案是 (A)。需記熟「很高興能～」之意的be pleased to。

詞彙 award winner 獲選者

9

為了擁有健康的生活，你需要與其他人社交。

解析 作為修飾整體句子的副詞，使用具有「為了～」之意的to不定詞為順暢。因此正確答案是 (B)。

詞彙 healthy 健康的　socialize 社交

10

我喜歡早班。

解析 prefer使用to不定詞或動名詞當作受詞。由於空格前面出現to，因此正確答案是 (A)。

詞彙 prefer 喜歡　morning shift 早班

11

我們收到了許多符合資格申請人的履歷。

解析 many和名詞applicant之間可以填入適合修飾名詞的分詞形式，因此正確答案是 (B)。需記熟「符合資格申請人」之意的qualified applicant。

詞彙 quality 符合資格　receive 獲得　applicant 申請人

12

我希望能再多學一點英文。

詞彙 wish 希望

13

該公司進行了一項調查，以確定客戶的需求。

解析 以受詞為對象進行調查，目的是了解客戶需求，適合使用to不定詞，因此正確答案是 (A)。

詞彙 conduct a survey 進行調查　needs 需求　identify 確定

14

當造訪紐約約，你應該在那裡看一齣音樂劇。

解析 分詞構句是省略連接詞，將動詞改為-ing，為了表示明確意義，有時也會保留連接詞。正確答案是 (A)。

詞彙 musical 音樂劇

Step 3　實戰練習 (Part 5)　P158

正解

1.(C)	2.(A)	3.(A)	4.(D)	5.(B)
6.(C)	7.(C)	8.(A)	9.(D)	10.(B)

1

當你有空閒時間時，你喜歡獨自旅行嗎？

解析 enjoy是使用動名詞作為受詞的動詞，因此正確答案是 (C)。其他使用動名詞作為受詞的動詞還有mind, recommend, suggest等。

詞彙 by oneself 獨自　free time 空閒時間　travel 旅行

2

我們決定在歐洲國家銷售我們的產品。

解析 decide是使用to不定詞作為受詞的動詞，所以正確答案是 (A)。其他使用to不定詞作為受詞的動詞還有choose, wish, hope, would like, plan等。

詞彙 distribute 發布

3

客戶可能會對我們的新產品線反應良好。

解析 be likely to後面須加上動詞原型，favorably雖然置於中間但屬於副詞，文法上並不會因此改變，所以答案是 (A)。

詞彙 be likely to 可能會～　favorably 良好地　respond 反應

4

PAE渡假村正考慮在下一季之前具有設計新公司的網站。

詞彙 consider 考慮

5

為慶祝成立50週年，現代古典音樂劇將推出莫尼克李坦斯坦的新作品。

解析 動詞consider後面須添加上動詞原型或動名詞，但空格後面還有另一個屬於the company's Web site的受詞名詞，因此空格內必須是能夠形成新作品的不定詞，因此正確答案是 (D)。

詞彙 anniversary 紀念日　piece 作品　celebrate 慶祝

6

我們已為提高的生產成本做好準備。

解析 需選擇適合的分詞，放在介系詞和名詞之間的位置，作為修飾名詞的形容詞。rising cost具有「增加的費用」之意，因此正確答案是 (C)。

詞彙 prepare 準備　production cost 生產成本　rise 增加

7

你是否已檢視過建議設計的修訂版？

解析 需選擇適合過的動詞當以事物作為主詞時，整體屬過去分詞 (C)。

詞彙 review 檢視　revise 修訂

8

對所有有研有趣參加未來時，盡體經驗十分令人滿意。

解析 表達精確的動詞當以事物作為主詞時，使用過去分詞的形式。參加者作為主詞時，會使用「對～感到滿意」之意的be satisfied with。正確答案是 (A)。

詞彙 whole 全體的　experience 經驗　participant 參加者

9

今天當讀物目標為該地區的人增加時。

解析 針對動詞後面的目的地加上附加說明，也就是適合具有主格補語作用的to不定詞，因此正確答案是 (D)。

詞彙 goal 目標　provide 提供

10

寄送包裹時，您必須確保盒子用膠帶黏牢。

解析 連接詞when帶領的子句中，省略主語的you是寄送包裹的主體，動詞是作為主語的you，所以需使用現在分詞的分詞構句。「作為主語的子句中」省略主語you，動詞是作為主語的you，所以正確答案是 (B)。

詞彙 package 包裹　securely 牢固地

正解

11. (D)　12. (B)　13. (C)　14. (A)

[11~14]

恭喜您的貴公司遷好，伯明罕電力電子公司 ⑪ 已準備好將您現居地的服務轉移到未來路的新地點。但是，出於安全考慮，您的授權移轉對我們而言是必要的。為了保證住在 ⑩ 入住的第一天起滿足您的電力需求，⑫ 我們將於方便時請盡速在隨附的表格上簽字並傳真至215-555-3453。⑭ 我們致此。

羅珊沃爾特斯
客戶服務部

11. **解析** 以前後文一致性來看，「公司為了顧客做好準備」be ready to 最為合適，因此正確答案是 (D)。

詞彙 transfer 轉移、調動　current 目前的　residence 居住地　security 安全　purpose 目的　authorize 授權　guarantee 保證　electricity 電力　enclosed 附上的　convenience 方便　definite 確定的　possible 可能的　unable 無法的　occupant 居住者　occupied 使用中的　confirmation 確認　authorization 授權、認可　package 包裹　questionnaire 意見表　fill out 填寫

12. **解析** 這是選擇正確動詞形式的題目，需搭配前形容詞 necessary，所以 to 不定詞最為合適，因此正確答案是 (B)。

詞彙 last night 昨晚

13. **解析** 所有格後面可以加上名詞或動名詞，以具有「居住」之意的 (C) occupancy 最適。

14. **解析** 接在要求顧客填寫文件（問卷）回覆之後的句子，以寄出確認函的內容最為流暢，因此正確答案是 (A)。

詞彙 contact 連絡　about 對於~

Unit 6　介係詞與連接詞

Step 1　Practice　P160

正解

1. (A)　2. (B)　3. (A)　4. (B)　5. (B)
6. (B)　7. (A)　8. (B)　9. (A)　10. (B)

1. **解析** 由於此意思是營業時間之「過後」支付的金額，因此正確答案是 (A)。

詞彙 payment 支付　account 帳戶　show 顯示

您帳戶的支付金額在我們的營業時間過後不會顯示。

2. **解析** 這是區分表達時間的介係詞 for/during 題目。for 和特定數字時間一起使用，during 則和特定事件名稱一同出現時，「during 持續時間」的片語，因此正確答案是 (B)。

詞彙 update 更新　safety 安全　manual 手冊　include 包含　guideline 指南、指引　entire 全部的

昨晚我們花費了三小時的比賽。

3. **解析** 介係詞後面出現名詞或名詞片語（the entire factory），前面放入 for 具有「為整個工廠」之意，可以作為修飾 guideline 的形容詞片語，因此正確答案是 (B)。

詞彙 report 報告書、報告

更新的安全手冊包含了整個工廠的指南。

4. **解析** 「~之前」表達時間的期限，聚焦在行為完成的 by 最為合適，因此正確答案是 (B)。

詞彙 questionInquiryabouton]（詢問）之意／meanagainstA也會用來表示「與對抗~」的意思／against A 具有「對於、對抗~」的意思／until 表示持續待直到結束為止的時間點為止。

威爾遜先生告訴他的團隊要在星期四下午前前繳報告。

5. **解析** 若您的我們的產品有任何疑問，請致電我們辦公室。

詞彙 question[inquiry]和about[on]一起使用，具有「詢問~的問題」之意。

如果對我們的幫助，我很樂意幫助您。

6. **解析** 如果知道您有權利可以 be entitled to 具有「有權享有~」之意就能輕鬆解題，正確答案是 (B)。

詞彙 temporary worker 臨時工　paid leave 帶薪假

臨時工有福利享有新假。

---

7. **解析** 大部分的團隊成員都信任我們依賴相同的執行長。對等連接詞和 and 信任，以及後面必須使用現在形態。由於 and 前面出現 trust，and 後面接上相同的詞類或形態。

詞彙 trust 信任　depend 仰賴　dependent 依靠的

8. **解析** neither A nor B 必須和 B 保持動詞一致性，所以以單數名詞 management 以單數動詞 wants 最符合，因此正確答案是 (A)。

詞彙 go to work 上班　subway 地鐵

9. **解析** 由於出現該利女士被雇用的原因，使用 because 最為合適，因此正確答案是 (A)。unless 意思是「如果不~」

詞彙 shareholder 股東　management 管理階層　incident 事件　public 公開的、公共的

薩利女士被雇用，因為她是最具資格的候選人。

10. **解析** 空格後面出現名詞片語 (our discussions)，填入介係詞 during 最適合，因此正確答案是 (B)。while 作為連接詞，後面必須加上子句 (S +V)。

詞彙 hire 雇用　qualified 符合資格的　candidate 候選人

在我們討論的期間我提出了議題。

Step 2　基本掌握　P165

正解

1. (B)　2. (B)　3. (A)　4. (B)　5. (A)
6. (B)　7. (A)　8. (A)　9. (A)　10. (B)
11. (A)　12. (A)　13. (B)　14. (A)

1. **解析** either A or 一起使用，因此正確答案是 (B)。either A or B 是「A 或 B」的意思。

詞彙 bring up 提出　subject 議題

我們那不接受支票，也不接受信用卡。

2. **解析** nor 與 neither 一起使用，因此正確答案是 (B)。「neither A nor B」的意思是「既不是 A 也不是 B」的意思。

詞彙 check 支票

3. **解析** 以連接詞來看，「如果~的話」最為順暢，因此正確答案是 (B)。unless 意思是「如果不~」，等同「~ not」。

詞彙 be glad to 很樂意、很樂於~

正解

1. (D)	2. (C)	3. (D)	4. (C)	5. (A)
6. (B)	7. (B)	8. (C)	9. (A)	10. (C)

1.
解析：使用「位於~」因為我們無法獲得該樓的頂層，「be located in/at/on」介係詞後面的the top floor代表平面或需加on，因此正確答案是 (D)。
詞彙 locate 位於

2.
解析：我們取消了訂單，因為內容上來看，無法獲得資金是取消訂單的原因，適合加上on，因此正確答案是 (C)。
詞彙 cancel 取消 order 訂單 funding 資金 in spite of 儘管~ unless 除非~ although 雖然~ 少

3.
解析：如果我們設計公司在五月之前沒有送達您的商品，我們將給您退款。在某個時間點之前才會完成行為，所以適合加上介係詞by (到~前)，因此正確答案是 (D)。
詞彙 deliver 送貨 merchandise 物品 discount 折扣

4.
解析：我們必須熱情和積極地改善環境。中間加上對等連接詞and，前後必須是相同的詞彙，and後面出現副詞aggressively，所以空格也必須是副詞，因此正確答案是 (C)。
詞彙 aggressively 積極地 protect 保護 passionless 冷淡的 passionately 熱情地

5.
解析：最近的惡劣天氣導致了未來價格的上漲。account和介係詞for一同使用，意思是「說明了~是~的原因」，因此正確答案是 (A)。
詞彙 account 和介係詞for一同使用 recent 最近的

6.
解析：兩名候選人應做了該職位，但只有一名候選人會接受面試。內容上來看，有兩名候選人，但只有一名會接受面試，所以適合加上whereas 然而
詞彙 candidate 候選人

7.
解析：選項和句子中的neither A nor B是連接詞neither A nor B的題目，與其他電子設備一同使用~
詞彙 accept 接受 check 支票 in cash 以現金

8.
解析：該公司以其對客戶服務的奉獻精神而聞名。空格後面出現be famous for具有「以~聞名」的意思就能輕鬆解題，正確答案是 (A)。介係詞during以代表特定活動的名詞一同使用，表示期間
詞彙 dedication to 奉獻於~ performance 表演 electronic device 電子設備

9.
解析：在表演期間，請勿使用您的手機和其他電子設備。空格後面出現the performance，必須加上介係詞，因此正確答案是 (C)。
詞彙 performance 表演

10.
解析：招待會將於6:30開始，持續進行到晚上。特定時間前面出現介係詞at，因此正確答案是 (C)。
詞彙 reception 招待會 continue 持續

4.
解析：空格後面是片語和可連接入連接詞，因此正確答案是 (B)。是介係詞所以無法作為答案。
詞彙 during 在~期間

5.
解析：空格後面出現包括主語和動詞的子句，所以要先打電話給我的秘書。(B)。(A) 是介係詞所以無法作為答案。
當你抵達到我的辦公室時，請先打電話給我的秘書。

6.
解析：由於下雨，飛機晚點了。(B) 是接面包含主語和動詞的子句的連接詞。
詞彙 delay 延誤

7.
解析：到下週為止是持續的狀態，所以最符合，因此正確答案是 (A) 是過去式動詞，(B) 是~
我們可以待在這個辦公室到下週嗎？
詞彙 stay 停留

8.
解析：通貨膨脹對經濟產生不良的影響，have an effect on意思是「對~造成影響」，因此正確答案是 (B)。by是列舉某個時間點動作完成的意思。
對等連接詞and前後必須加上相同詞類或同樣結構，因此與and前面的動詞wait時態不一致，無法作為答案。
詞彙 inflation 通貨膨脹 economy 經濟
詞彙 happen 發生

9.
解析：帕特森先生自從2016年以來一直在這裡工作。since具有「自~以來」之意，適合加上表達過去時間點的詞彙，經常和現在完成式一同使用，因此加上表達過去時間點的詞彙，之意，後面加上表達期間的名詞。
詞彙 since

10.
解析：某件事做得很好，但他並不滿意。的連接詞，因此正確答案是 (B)。
雖然他做得很好，但他並不滿意。

11.
解析：我想在搬到另一個城市之前關閉我的銀行帳戶。兩個子句之間出現變格，所以是必須加入連接詞的位置，適合加上搬到另一個市「之前」，關閉銀行帳戶的語意最為順暢，因此正確答案是 (A)。
詞彙 bank account 銀行帳戶

12.
解析：合約的條款對我們來說絕對有利。「有利」在語意上最為順暢，因此正確答案是 (A)。
造份合約的條款對我們來說絕對有利。
詞彙 terms 條件 contract 合約 definitely 無疑地 favorite 最喜愛的

13.
解析：行業「有利可圖」的語意最具有連貫性，因此正確答案是 (B)。
我相信這種新型美甲服務可能是一項賺錢的行業。
詞彙 cleaning 清潔 refundable 可退款的

14.
解析：被要求登記的對象是參與者，所以必須加上代表人物的名詞，因此正確答案是 (A)。(B) 是「參與」意思的抽象名詞。
所有參加者都必須在線上登記。
詞彙 require 要求 register 登記 participant 參加者

6.
解析：兩名候選人應徵了該職位，但只有一名候選人會接受面試，所以了解這是一名候選人，有兩名應徵者，但只有一名會接受面試，因此顧客必須加上轉折連接詞neither A nor B的題目，因此正確答案是 (B)。
詞彙 candidate 候選人

7.
解析：選項和句子中的nor是不接受信用卡，也不接受其他電子設備。連接詞neither A nor B的題目，與其他電子設備一同使用，因此正確答案是 (B)。
詞彙 accept 接受 check 支票 in cash 以現金

8.
解析：如果知道be famous for具有「以~聞名」的意思就能輕鬆解題，正確答案是 (A)。介係詞during以代表特定活動的名詞一同使用，表示期間
詞彙 dedication to 奉獻於~ performance 表演 electronic device 電子設備 whereas 然而

9.
解析：空格後面出現be動詞的手機和其他電子設備。空格後面出現片語和介係詞at，因此正確答案是 (C)。介係詞during以代表特定活動的名詞一同使用，而
詞彙 performance 表演

10.
解析：特定時間前面出現介係詞at，因此正確答案是 (C)。
招待會將於6:30開始，持續進行到晚上。
詞彙 reception 招待會 continue 持續

正解
11. (D)　12. (B)　13. (B)　14. (A)

本章頭公寓大樓

親愛的住戶，

① 對於您決定在我們這頓宏偉大樓承租公寓，我們深表感謝。我們的建築位於賽城的中心地帶，您將居住在可步行到達一些最好的建築歷史地標之內。此外，我想提醒您，身為住戶的您將負責在您的遷入日期起安排啟用電力和電話。我們 ⑫ 期待為您服務。謝謝。

最美好的祝福，

威廉仕意門
設施管理員

詞彙　resident 住戶　rent 承租　walking distance 可步行到達的距離　historical landmark 歷史地標　in addition 此外　remind 提醒　responsible for 負責～　arrange 安排、準備　activation 啟動　move-in 遷入　look forward to 期待、盼望　maintenance 維護　coordinator 專員　concern 擔心、關心的事　rental contract 租賃契約　set up 設置、建立　facility 設施　rent 租

11. 解析　最適合與thank一起使用的介係詞是for，因此正確答案是 (D)。

12. 解析　(A)如果您有任何問題或疑慮，請隨時來電。(B)這封信是提醒認您的租賃合同已經收到並已簽署。(C)我們可以安排會面，以便您可以親自理顧慮呈現。(D)租金是每月2000美元，您可以直接寄支票給我。
這是寫給初次承租住戶的信，接在第一句問候語之後的內容最為適合，因此正確答案是 (B)。其他選項和局勢無關，因此無法作為答案。

13. 解析　作為「時間或距離」以內的，意思而使用介係詞within，因此正確答案是 (B)。

14. 解析　look forward to的to作為介係詞是 (A)。

Unit 7　關係詞和名詞子句

正解
1. (A)　2. (B)　3. (A)　4. (B)　5. (B)
6. (B)　7. (A)　8. (A)　9. (A)　10. (B)

1. 解析　先行詞是a friend，空格後面直接加上動詞，所以需要代表人的主格關係代名詞，因此正確答案是 (A)。
詞彙　government 政府
我有一個在政府工作的朋友。

2. 解析　出現表達地點的先行詞The office，空格後面的子句具有完整結構，必須加上關係副詞where，因此正確答案是 (B)。
詞彙　be held 舉行
正在舉行會議的是在辦公室三樓。

3. 解析　先行詞是The applicant是人物，空格後面的子句缺少代表人的主格關係代名詞who的受格whom，因此正確答案是 (B)。
(A) whose作為所有格，後面須加上被修飾的名詞。
詞彙　applicant 應徵者　select 選擇
我們選定的應徵者很快就會公布。

4. 解析　先行詞是The computer software，所以關係代名詞以that最符合，因此正確答案是 (B)。補充說明，that作為受格是purchased的受詞。
詞彙　purchase 購買
我們購買的電腦軟體才能地有用。

5. 解析　空格前面的先行詞是地點the place，空格後面是完整的子句，因此須加上關係副詞where，因此正確答案是 (B)。
詞彙　regularly 定期地
經理解釋了我們為何需要去其他地方的原因。

6. 解析　疑問詞where帶頭的名詞子句作為主語，後面連接單數動詞，因此正確答案是 (A)。
詞彙　explain 解釋　move 搬家、搬動　location 位置
目前還沒決定活動要在哪裡舉辦。

7. 解析　疑問詞先行詞的先行詞是原因句子作為主詞，後面連接的是關係副詞why，因此正確答案是 (A)。
詞彙　event 活動　be held 舉辦

8. 主管剛剛特爾女士正在從事什麼工作。
解析　ask需要受詞，而空格後面出現what，因此空格後面子句須帶頭的what，所以空格內容句子上來說，about是連接詞加上名詞子句。
詞彙　supervisor 主管、上司　work on 做～工作

9. 部門主管宣布史密斯獲得升職。
解析　題目是考適合的名詞子句連接詞，空格後面的內容適合加上表達去向的that，因此正確答案是 (A)。whether仍使用在尚未決定的事情。
詞彙　department 部門　director 主任、主管　get promoted 升職

10. 有些員工忘了會議開始的時間。
解析　題目是選出具有名詞作用的疑問詞，以when最符合，因此正確答案是 (B)。
詞彙　forget 忘記

正解
1. (B)　2. (A)　3. (B)　4. (A)　5. (B)
6. (B)　7. (A)　8. (B)　9. (B)　10. (A)
11. (A)　12. (A)　13. (B)　14. (B)

1. 解析　空格後面出現關係代詞collects，所以空格需要主格關係代名詞，因此正確答案是 (B)。(A)是受格關係代名詞。
詞彙　collect 收集
我有一個朋友收集來些。

2. 解析　出現作為先行詞的事物the watch，空格後面主語和及物動詞，所以應加上受格關係代名詞，因此正確答案是 (A)。(B)使用在先行詞是人物時。
詞彙　purchase 購買
這是我10年前購買的手錶。

3. 這是挑出形的城鎮。
詞彙　born 出生的
解析　由於出現代名詞的先行詞the town，應加上關係副詞where，因此正確答案是 (B)。同時關係副詞關係副詞where，無法加上主格關係代名詞who或及物動詞was。

4. 他正和一個我從未見過的人說話。
解析　關係代名詞that無論先行詞是人或事物皆可使用，因此正確答案是 (A)。(B) 使用在先行詞是事物時。

14. 解析　內容上來看「污染物，最為順暢」，因此正確答案是 (B)。
詞彙　eliminate 消除　environment 環境
應該消除各種污染物以拯救環境。

7. 解析　雖然空格後面出現了完整的子句，應加上連接詞that作為補充說明前面關係副詞的子句，因此正確答案是 (A)。但空格後面是現在～
詞彙　appealing 有吸引力的
調查顯示，客戶認為網站很容易引導。

8. 解析　空格後面現出子句是完整的子句，在那裡獲得了大學的學位。之後作為補充說明前面關係副詞是where，因此正確答案是 (A)。
詞彙　degree 學位
文素女士將從美國返回，在那裡她獲得了大學的學位。

9. 解析　從安格和safety都是說明王先生後的子句，應加上主格關係代名詞，因此正確答案是 (D)。
詞彙　responsible for 負責～的　present 呈交
負責飛機安全的王先生應向董事會提交報告。

10. 解析　由於及物動詞note後面現出完整的子句，應加上名詞子句連接詞that，因此正確答案是 (D)。
詞彙　note 注意
請注意，我們的公司名稱已更改。

---

1. 解析　由於先行詞accountants是代表人物的，應加上主格關係代名詞的who，因此空格後面出現動詞，而空格後面出現主格。
詞彙　accountant 會計師　newly 最近　graduate 畢業
KG容器公司僱用了3位剛畢業的新會計師。

2. 解析　先行詞A woman是代表人物的名詞，空格後面加上met的受詞，為及物動詞met的受詞，應使用受格關係代名詞的that，因此正確答案是 (C)。
詞彙　next door 隔壁
我在派對上遇到的女子住在我們隔壁。

3. 解析　這是考適合的關西詞題目，其後面是賓助亞洲的貧困兒童。動詞是is，所以無法使用受格關係代名詞，而需要連接先行詞和名詞mission的所有格關係代名詞，因此正確答案是 (D)。
詞彙　non-profit organization 非營利組織　mission 使命

4. 解析　空格是放在及物動詞decide後面，帶出受詞的名詞子句的連接詞，空格後面加上完整的子句，因此正確答案是 (A)。
詞彙　next door 隔壁
帕克先生必須決定是否提交預算報告。

5. 解析　珍特別喜歡那個產品的部分是它的設計。主語位置出現子句，可知是帶出名詞子句的連接詞，需要連接不完整句子的連接詞What，因此正確答案是 (B)。
詞彙　particularly 尤其

6. 解析　哈洛維女士提出的企劃管理階層採納。代表事物的先行詞the project和缺乏主語的the空格關係代名詞，因此正確答案是 (D)。what前面不加作代名詞。
詞彙　accept 接納　management 管理階層

[11-14]

回收用過的墨盒

高印公司致力於保護環境，我們鼓勵顧客 ⓫ 回收用過的墨盒，這有助於拯救地球。⓬ 銷售列印產品的辦公用品店也欲用過的墨盒送到任何一家回收箱。然後商店會將它們送回給我們進行處理。每次回收時，您都有資格在下次購買墨盒時享更多 ⓭ 詳情，請造訪我們的網站www.highprint.com。

詞彙　recycle 回收　office supply 辦公用品　discount 折扣　contact 連絡　view 觀點　made from 以～製成　environmentally friendly 環保的　issue 爭論、問題　details 細節、詳情
be committed to 致力於　bin 箱子　process 處理　matter 問題
preserve 保護　urge 敦促　entitled 有資格

---

5. 解析　由於現現連接兩個的先行詞the day，應加上關係副詞when，因此正確答案是 (B)。why主要適合搭配先行詞the reason。
這是我初次見到他的那一天。

6. 解析　空格後面接著無法理解的那，這是一個語意表達無法理解的問題。why主要適合搭配understand的受詞，缺少動詞understand的受詞，因此正確答案是 (B)。
詞彙　understand 理解
希望參加計畫的新員工與我連絡。

7. 解析　空格後面出現先行詞的問題，由於空格後面的子句使用動詞participate，應加上代表人物的主格關係代名詞，因此正確答案是 (A)。
詞彙　participate in 參加～　contact 連絡
新加坡是一個擁有多年歷史的城市。

8. 解析　這是分辨關係代名詞和關係副詞的題目。由於空格後面的連接詞位置，需要加上主格關係代名詞，因此空格後面的使用代名詞後面加上不完整的子句。
請讓我的秘書知道，您是否希望透過～

9. 解析　空格是名詞子句的連接詞放在受詞位置。內容來看，透過電子郵件收到通知是未定的事情，帶動及物動詞know，以內容來看，透過電子郵件收到通知是未定的事情，因此正確答案是 (B)。
詞彙　notify 通知
請讓我的秘書知道，您是否希望透過電子郵件收到通知。

10. 解析　由於先行詞代名詞出現在動詞purchase，空格後面出現動詞，因此正確答案是 (A)。
詞彙　purchase 購買　receive 收到　order 訂購商品
購買商品的顧客將在3天內收到訂購商品。

11. 解析　助詞前面have to在後面加上動詞原型，因此正確答案是 (A)。
詞彙　spending 支出　competitive 有競爭力的
我們必須控制我們的支出以保持市場競爭力。

12. 解析　be動詞後面的補語位置再加上必須「鄰近～」之意，因此正確答案是 (A)。
詞彙　major 主要的　highway 高速公路
市中心的飯店非主要的高速公路和地鐵站。

13. 解析　包括前任總裁在內的所有高階主管都將出席開幕式。
詞彙　executives 高階主管　former 前任的　show up 出席

11 解析 urge作為及物補項，是使用to不定詞的動詞，內容是敘動受詞our customers進行回收，因此正確答案是 (B)。

12 (A)回收盒蓋很容易。
(B)如需申請，請致電555-1212與我們的辦公室連絡。
(C)如果您購買超過兩箱紙，今天您將獲得85折的折扣。
(D)它們是由世界材料組成。
解析 第一段文章句以得知主題看回的墨盒，12號空格的後面隨即接上回收方法，所以應該是和回收有關的句子，因此正確答案是 (A)。尤其先就其他事情很容易 (easy) 之意再敘說出的連貫句型。

13 解析 這是選項連接先行詞any office supply store和後面句子的關係代名詞。由於空格後面直接出現動詞，應加上代表事物的主格關係代名詞，因此正確答案是 (C)。

14 解析 填選在公告文的空格裡，可以看出其主格空格關係，以保持性看，具有「細節詳情」之意的details最為適合，因此正確答案是 (D)。

Unit 8 假設語氣．特殊語法

Step 1 Practice P176

正解
| 1. (B) | 2. (B) | 3. (A) | 4. (B) | 5. (B) |
| 6. (B) | | | | |

1 解析 如果我發現有錢的話，我就可以付學費了。
詞彙 pay for 支付～ tuition 學費
解析 由於獨立子句的could pay來看，是假設語氣過去式句子，假設語氣過去式的形式，所以必須加上have的過去式had，形式的句子，因此正確答案是 (B)。

2 解析 如果你今天旦上準時上班的話，就可以參加會議了。
詞彙 be on time 準時到 attend 參加
解析 由獨立子句的would have attended的完成式來看，是假設語氣過去完成式的句子，假設語氣過去完成式的形式為if + 主語 + had + p.p.，助動詞過去式+have p.p.的形式，因此正確答案是 (B)。

3 解析 如果這提案書更加詳細描述的話，次倫工程將很可能成為我們城市的企劃合作夥樣。

4 解析 如果您的地址有變動，請連絡我們
詞彙 change 改變、更改 contact 連絡
解析 由於這個句子的動詞be changed看來，可以知道該句是被動形式的句子，由於獨立子句是命令句，適合加上根據助動詞should未來式的 should，因此正確答案是 (B)。
詞彙 proposal 規畫、提案 detailed 詳細的 construction 施工、工程

5 解析 附件是您所要求客戶的名單。
詞彙 include 包含 list 清單 client 顧客 request 要求
解析 空格在是動詞面，可能被說應該為是主語的位置，但是The list of clients that you requested is included中為了將長主語置於句子後面，而將補語included置前端倒裝，因此正確答案是 (B)。

6 解析 我從來沒有看過美麗的景色。
詞彙 such 如此 scenery 風景
解析 否定副詞出現在前面是倒裝句的形式，因此正確答案是 (B)。

Step 2 基本掌握 P179

正解
1. (B)	2. (A)	3. (B)	4. (B)	5. (B)
6. (B)	7. (B)	8. (A)	9. (A)	10. (B)
11. (A)	12. (B)	13. (A)	14. (B)	

1 解析 如果我們現在住在一個人造城市，我們的生活會變更容易。
詞彙 lab生活 人生
解析 由於假設語氣的獨立子句中出現<would+語氣過去式>句子，獨立子句的動詞需使用<would+動詞原型>，所以是假設語氣過去式。

2 解析 如果沒有她幫助我，我就會陷入困境。
詞彙 be in trouble 陷入困境
解析 因為if子句中出現有<had+過去分詞>，是假設語氣過去完成式子，獨立子句需要加上過去式，所以此句子需使用<would+have+過去分詞>的形式，因此正確答案是 (B)。

3 解析 如果他說實話，我們就不會誤認他。
詞彙 contract 合約
解析 獨立子句中出現<would+動詞原型>，很然假設語氣過去式中if子句的be動詞和主語無關，一律使用

4 解析 如果我發現我自身有錢，我就會借給你一些。
詞彙 were honest 誠實的
解析 由於現在式if子句中出現<were，if子句中必須使用假設語氣過去式，因此正確答案是 (B)。

5 解析 如果您有任何疑問，請打我的行動電話。
詞彙 lend 借出
解析 if...should關倒的句子，獨立子句以please開始。應加上命令句的動詞原型，因此正確答案是 (A)。

6 解析 如果我到在上接到這，我會帶到答案馬。
詞彙 cell phone 手機
解析 if子句中使用<had+過去分詞，可以得知是假設語氣過去完成，獨立子句中須使用<would+動詞原型>，因此正確答案是 (A)。

7 解析 會議開始沒有多久，就有人進出問題。
詞彙 find 尋找
解析 否定的副詞出現在句子的前面，是將主語和動詞倒裝的形式，<hardly~when~>意思的副詞<hardly~when~>一起使用時，意思是「才～就」。

8 解析 如果我們需要更多的知識，
詞彙 begin 開始
解析 空格需要填入連接<had + 過去分詞 和子句內容相互連接，從空格後面as是連接詞句，could+have+過去分詞 excellent?as是連接詞句，是 (A)。

9 解析 我的銷售知識非常出色，同樣地，我與人溝通的能力也很出色。
詞彙 laboratory 實驗室
解析 if子句中出現<had + 過去事實相同的內容，從空格後面子句容相同的內容，所以獨立子句需使用<had+過去分詞>的形式，因此正確答案是 (A)。

10 解析 如果你促成這了合約，就可以拿到獎金。
詞彙 knowledge 知識 ability 能力 communicate with 與～溝通
解析 從獨立子句的動詞would have received來看，可以知道是假設語氣過去完成式的句子，if子句中須使用<had+過去分詞>的形式，因此正確答案是 (B)。

11 解析 沒有許多外國投資者的幫助，很難以完成這個計劃。
詞彙 contract 合約
解析 能夠被放foreign前面的限定詞many修飾的是複數名詞，因此正確答案是 (A)。

詞彙 investor 投資人 investment 投資

12
當您抵達機場後，您需要領取所有行李。
解析 從語意上來看，「需要領取行李」的內容最為適切，空格內應加上 collect，因此正確答案是 (B)。
詞彙 once 一～就 luggage 行李 complain 抱怨

13
您可以要求特別的送貨服務。
解析 題目是選擇「送貨服務」的內容最為適切，因此正確答案是 (A)。
詞彙 request 要求 delivery 交貨 deliver 送貨

14
我們對工程沒什麼好擔心的。
解析 從語意上來看，「不需要擔心」的內容最為適切，因此正確答案是 (B)。
詞彙 construction 工程 lose 遺失 worry 擔心

Step 3　實戰練習 (Part 5)　P180

正解
| 1. (C) | 2. (D) | 3. (B) | 4. (C) | 5. (D) |
| 6. (A) | 7. (D) | 8. (B) | 9. (C) | 10. (D) |

1
如果我們現在在室內舉辦研討會，就不用擔心天氣。
解析 獨立子句中出現<would+動詞原型>，可以得知是假設語氣過去的句子。if子句中需要使用hold的過去式held，因此正確答案是 (C)。
詞彙 indoors 在室內

2
如果她有收到電子郵件，á金斯女士本可以將報告轉發給其他同事。
解析 由if子句<had+過去分詞>來看，可以得知是假設語氣過去式。獨立子句的動詞需使用<助動詞的過去式+have+p.p.>形式，因此正確答案是 (D)。
詞彙 forward 轉交 colleague 同事

3
如果這個時間安排您不方便，請告訴人力資源部門。
解析 從獨立子句是命令句，可以得知是現在式，因此正確答案是 (B)。
詞彙 convenient 方便的 HR department 人事部門

4
如果我們現在有錢，就可以翻新我們的建築。
解析 與現在事實相反的假設使用假設語氣過去式，獨立子句加上<could+動詞原型>。由於省略了if we were rich中的if作為倒裝句，因此正確答案是 (C)。

詞彙 renovate 翻新

5
這封電子郵件的附檔是我們公司的年度報告。
解析 空格內是倒裝的補語位置，主語是our company's annual report，但報告書必須具有「附加在電子郵件中」的被動意義，因此正確答案是 (D)。
詞彙 attach 附上 report 報告書

6
凱洛格建築只透過電子郵件傳送估價書。
解析 強調只透過電子郵件寄出，「only出現在句子前面，是將主語和動詞倒裝的句子。send是一般動詞，所以do放在主語前面，而主語是第3人稱單數使用does，因此正確答案是 (A)。
詞彙 via 透過～ estimate 估價

7
如果我們有更多時間，我們就會全面地完成報告。
解析 由if子句<had過去分詞>來看，我們就會全面地完成報告。分詞的形式，因此正確答案是 (D)。
詞彙 thoroughly 全面地

8
如果這公司獲得更高的利潤，我們就會在生產上投入更多資金。
解析 這是省略假設語氣過去的if，將had倒裝的句子，所以使用假設語氣過去完成式would have invested，因此正確答案是 (B)。
詞彙 profit 利潤 production 生產 invest 投資

9
如果您在使用我們的產品時遇到任何困難，請隨時致電我們。
解析 這是省略假設語氣過去式中的if，將should倒裝的句子，因此正確答案是 (C)。
詞彙 experience 經歷 difficulty 困難 feel free to 隨意地～ even 即使

10
他在巴黎時從未去過羅浮宮博物館。
解析 空格後面出現did的主語和句子，可以得知把主語和動詞倒裝的句子，將have有否定意思的副詞移到前面可以完成倒裝，因此正確答案是 (D)。
詞彙 hard 困難的；堅硬的 認真地

Step 4　實戰練習 (Part 6)　P181

正解
| 11. (A) | 12. (D) | 13. (A) | 14. (B) |

[11-14]
致尊敬的客戶：
我們的貴賓客戶，我們都將為您提供作為我們最優秀客戶的一些熱門產品的特別優惠。我們將給您的小用子包含 ❶ 許多當前產品的折扣券 給您。只需將您的優惠券帶到馬克西超市與連同馬克百貨商品的會員卡一同出示即可。❷ 您的會員卡也可以當場更新，電話是555-2843，請造訪您最近的連鎖店。
謝謝。

詞彙 preferred 優先的 special 特別的 offer 提供 hottest 熱門的；最受歡迎的 include 包含 current 目前的 present 出示 nearest 最近的 outlet 賣場、暢貨中心 be eligible for 獲得～資格 renew 續簽、更新 on spot 當場 apply 申請 responsible 有責任的 be located 位於 profit 利潤 chain 連鎖店

11
解析 這格內需要接以複數名詞products的詞彙。<many of+複數名詞>的意思是「許多～」。因此正確答案是 (A)。
詞彙 eligible for 是「具有～資格的」之意，因此正確答案是 (D)。

12
解析 空格後面出現did主語的句子，可以得知把主語和動詞倒裝的句子，將有否定意思的副詞移到前面即可完成倒裝，因此正確答案是 (D)。

13
(A) 您的舊會員卡也可以當場更新。
(B) 我們的商店位於553主街。
(C) 第一分季銷售額增長了12%。
(D) 梅克百貨北部地區最古老的連鎖超市。
解析 這格需要給客人折扣券一同寄出的信，為了獲得折扣，需要進同內出示會員卡，接在這個內容之後最適切的句子是 (A)。Part 6的空格題和Part 7的句子描入題需考量文章主題式類型，例如什麼人為什麼原因而寫信，愈快就愈能理解到解題就愈有利。

14
解析 這是省略假設語氣未來式中的if，將should移至前面的句子，所以正確答案是 (B)。

Unit 9 Part 6 集中分析

Step 2 基本掌握　P186

正解
1. (C)　　2. (B)

[1]
這封廣告是告知您的求職狀況。我們邀請了您的履歷，對於您的經歷相當印象深刻。您網路行銷的專業成為本公司行銷主管的最適當候選人。...想邀請您下周和我們幾位主管會面，請回電至555-3849，以安排面試。

詞彙 go over 審視、瀏覽　résumé 履歷　be impressed 印象深刻的　position 位置、職位　experience 經歷　suitable 適合的　candidate 候選人　director 主管、經理　executive 管理階層　in person 親自　inform 通知　opening 空缺、開放　set up 建立、安排　application 申請　enclose 附上　request 要求

1
解析 Part 6 是選擇正確句子的題型，和 Part 7 一樣，如果理解前後文結構，就會更有利。紹文前半部出現印象深刻時，經常是主題句，想安排面試時的內容等等內容，可以得知是人事部門通知的敘述，因此無法作答案。

(A) 我下週會造這個城市，所以我會親自面試。
(B) 我們很遺憾地通知您，空缺已滿。
(C) 這封信是告知您的求職狀況。
(D) 隨附的是您之前要求的文件。

[2]
您好，馬汀玆小姐：

感謝您向我們確認訂閱海音音樂服務的電子郵件。您註冊的熱情音樂套餐成為每個月50小時的音樂權益成為訂閱。這封信向您確認每個月最初收費6.99美元，包括每個月50小時的音樂權益。

若您要終止服務，請上我們的網站，並找到您的帳號設定，按下「關閉帳戶」即可。

詞彙 confirm 確認　sign up 登記、註冊　include 包含　playback 播放　terminate 終止　navigate 瀏覽　account 帳戶　process 處理　newsletter 通訊期刊　charge 收取　offer 提供　reasonable 合理的

Step 3 實戰練習　P187

正解
1. (C)　2. (D)　3. (A)　4. (C)
5. (A)　6. (D)　7. (D)　8. (B)
9. (A)　10. (B)　11. (D)　12. (B)

[1~4]
親愛的馬先生，

這封信是要通知您6月2日的訂單履行服務時有 ❶ 中斷，我們要開始把所有的設備和存貨搬至另一個新倉庫，❷ 在此期間，我們冷藏搬至海外倉庫。搬運需要花3到4天，❸ 請勿花3到4天。若您有其他緊張，請您隨時與我聯繫。繼免任何的延誤，請在5月20日以前下單。若您有其他緊張，請隨時聯繫 ❹ 為了我。

致此。
珍妮絲楊謹
客服部主任

詞彙 supplies 用品、物品　temporary 暫時的　fulfillment 履行、滿足　inventory 庫存、物品　ship 運送　place an order 下訂　hesitate 猶豫　contact 連絡　extension 延長　improvement 改善　disruption 干擾　solution 解決方法　limited 有限的　track 追蹤　status 狀態　facility 設施　industry 產業、業界　prevent A from B 防止A發生B　may as well 還是~好

1
解析 這是選出符合連貫性的名詞的詞彙。內容是公司基於以下原因，必須暫時中斷往服務並且致歉，因此正確答案是 (C)。

2
(A) 這些可以限時內改以特價供應。
(B) 您可以線上追蹤該地點訂單狀態。
(C) 這種設施已成為該地區的重要產業。
(D) 因此我們無法將放大量庫存。

解析 空格前面提到客戶的訂因是倉庫搬移而產生的問題和該倉庫搬移的內容，也和插入句自然的呼應，其他選項是與銷售和訂購有關的敘述，和填空處並不合適。

3
解析 這是選出合適介係詞的題目。在倉庫搬移的期間（為了~）須加上表示期間的during，因此正確答案是 (C)。

4
解析 這是選出合適的副詞形式的題目。空格內填入的不是主要動詞而是連接詞，以一致性來看，須加上to不定詞的副詞用法（為了~）因此正確答案是 (C)。

[5~8]
恭喜您購買了塔達電子的優質產品。在最嚴峻的環境下，本公司產品不才能使用，為了符合公司對於下才能使用。每項器材皆經過一連串嚴謹的測試。每項器材皆經過一連串嚴謹的測試，以及重複數小時從公尺高度落下進行測試中，我們隨機選擇數台產品均須經過 ❻ 可靠性的測試。員 ❼ 降落在相同的測試中，即使一台器材無法通往一公尺高止生產，進行這些相同的測試 ❽ 即使一台器材無法通往一。這就是為什麼我們塔達電子會對所有產品均須經過一連串嚴謹的測試。

品質是我們的首要任務
塔達電子有限公司

5
解析 這是選出合適的動詞詞彙的題目。這次購買的吸塵器暫中臨眠往服務並且致歉，因此正確答案是 (c)。讓顧客對產品長久「信任」之意，進行（訓練等）面臨中臨眠往服務並且致歉。

詞彙 electronics 電子產品　quality 品質　concern 關心、擔心　purchase 購入、購買　challenging 有難度的　strict 嚴格的　requirement 條件　undergo 經受　rigorous 嚴峻的　be exposed to 暴露在~　drop 落下、墜落　inspection 檢查　randomly 隨機地　quality control 品質管理　faithfully 忠實地　needlessly 不必要地　conditionally 有條件地　pricing 價格　reliability 可靠性　application 申請、應徵　make up 組成、構成　turn down 降低、拒絕　put through 進行

6

解析 這是找出合適的詞類和意義的題型。須找出能夠和後面 requirements（條件）一起使用的複合名詞，或者可以放在前面作為形容詞的詞的詞彙。reliability requirements意思是「使產品品質達到可靠性的條件」，因此正確答案是（C）。

7

解析 這是找出合適的片語動詞的題型。在吸塵器（vacuum cleaners）「被測試」的意思下，可以使用put through。

8

(A) 從這些結果來看，我們一向試圖削減成本。
(B) 即使一台器材無法通過任一測試，也會停止生產，進而調查出癥結點所在。
(C) 藉由此過程，一致性很重要的。後面通過公司產品的品質，並提到品質管理的過程，享受特別的VIP折扣。
(D) 可以購買額外的吸塵器，享受特別的VIP折扣。

解析 確認空格前後的一致性的過程是很重要的。強調成品的品質，並提到品質管理的過程，享受特別的VIP折扣，品運送的內容，並沒有連貫性。

[9~12]

西蒙斯國際併購麥氏科技

香港，3月10日—西蒙斯國際周一宣布併購麥氏科技。

西蒙斯發言人表示，公司預料今年底將獲利將翻倍，藉由在普遍通路來實現此目標。

多數亞洲市場廣大的銷售通路將成為實現目標點。

金融專家相信，收購麥氏將使西蒙斯成為電腦及電子業中的市場龍頭。「他們將會進進領先其他 ⑨ 競爭者。」金融時報首席分析師羅伯特印格說。

西蒙斯計畫保留目前全球的員工及全球250分之一的公司 ⑫ 在那之後，西蒙斯目前僱用或向西蒙斯國際提過需要額外的員工。

9

解析 這是選出合適代名詞的題目。公司名稱使用此指稱十分常見。由於需要代名詞來指稱前面提過的西蒙斯國際，因此正確答案是（A）。

10

(A) 其他公司的報價遭到拒絕。
(B) 麥氏科技近來光是在中國便增加了20間據點。
(C) 將於明年收購另一家公司。
(D) 員工也會對交易感到滿意。

解析 必須選擇與空格前後文語意一致的答案。空格前面提到麥氏科

11

解析 這是選出合適名詞的題目。公司透過併購而將成為市場龍頭的內容，後面接上領先其他「競爭對手（competitors）」最為順暢，因此正確答案是（D）。

12

解析 這是選出合適副詞的題目。必須選擇與前後文一致性的答案。先保留現有的員工，之後再考慮額外增聘人員的內容最為順暢，適合加上「在那之後」意思的After that time，因此正確答案是（B）。

技在亞洲銷售通路的內容，適合加上光是在中國就新增20個據點的內容，因此正確答案是（B）。

詞彙 spokesperson 發言人　double 使增加兩倍　profits 收益、利潤
accomplish 達成、實現　distribution channel 通路、頻道
expert 專家　acquisition 併購　electronics 電子產品　ahead
of 領先於～　analyst 分析師　workforce 勞動力　branch 分公司
evaluate 評估　additional 額外的　offer 提議　reject 拒絕
acquire 收購　transaction 交易　critic 評論家　supplier 供應商
investor 投資人　competitor 競爭對手

PART 7

Unit 10　題型1

Step 2　Paraphrasing 基礎訓練　　　　P196

正解
1. (A)　2. (B)　3. (B)　4. (A)　5. (B)
6. (A)　7. (A)　8. (B)　9. (A)　10. (B)

1 演唱會結束後我頻頻回憶到了我最喜歡的音樂家。
(A) 現實中　　　　　(B) 在夢中

2 他很確定顧客的想法。
(A) 告訴　　　　　　(B) 知道

3 百貨旅行社的客戶可享受大量的飯店折扣。
(A) 偉大的　　　　　(B) 大幅的
詞彙 travel agency 旅行社　discount 折扣

4 這將有助於您留住您的客戶
(A) 保留　　　　　　(B) 明白

5 不幸的是，這家商店去年倒產了。
(A) 很受歡迎　　　　(B) 沒錢了
詞彙 go bankrupt 破產

6 這本書能解釋了企業如何有效地執行其策略。
(A) 實現　　　　　　(B) 製作
詞彙 strategy 策略　effectively 有效地

7 你可以在自由國到各種樣的鮮托。
(A) 栽培的地方　　　(B) 治療的地方

8 此優惠券只能在今年12月底兌換。
(A) 恢復　　　　　　(B) 使用
詞彙 redeem 兌換　voucher 優惠券　by the end of 在～底

9
(A) 使用優惠券可以搭船。
優惠券可以享受別貼之旅。

(B) 使用傳單可以進入遊輪。

詞彙　entitle 賦予資格　excursion 旅程　ride 搭乘　permit 允許
entry 進入　cruise ship 郵輪

10 所有防護衣物都必須放在箱子裡以便之後清洗。
(A) 所有防護衣物必須放妥善存放。
(B) 所有防護衣物必須妥善存放。

詞彙　protective clothing 防護衣物　bin 箱子　throw away 丟棄
store 存放　properly 妥善地

Step 3　基本掌握　P197

正解
1. (D)　　2. (C)　　3. (C)

[1]

布瑞南貨店顧客意見調查

感謝您在布瑞南雜貨店購物，❶ 為了確保所有顧客的優質購物經
驗，請就最近的購物經驗回答以下幾個問題：

1 請描述布瑞南雜貨店的員工：（符合選項請打勾）
　□ 細心　　□ 專業　　□ 以上皆非
2 關於本店經常沒有買到需要的東西嗎？
　□ 每次　　□ 有時　　■ 很少　　□ 從來沒有

詞彙　appreciate 感謝　ensure 確保　quality 高品質的
attentive 細心的　knowledgeable 有知識的　describe 描
述　determine 確定

解析

1 為什麼進行意見調查？
(A) 與其他商店的價格作比較
(B) 了解員工是否有偷竊行為
(C) 確定食物的品質
(D) 了解客戶如何被對待

GQ 題目可以從短文前半部找到主要提示，尤其表格
通常一定會有標語，此內容是以主要提示以供顧客
的立場來敘述，因此正確答案是 (D)。

---

[2]

機場工程持續進行

法蘭克福，7月2日-法蘭克福國際機場的主要擴建工程正在進行中，此
項計畫預估花費29億元，新的航廈坐落在主要擬建的土地上，
然而，新的航廈坐在狹長的土地上，造對增加旅客約一年之內開幕。
大的挑戰。如果機場的保有目前的吞吐量，❷ 處理空中交通流量是極目
能力可能在三年之內達到期上限。

詞彙　expansion 擴建　underway 進行中　estimate 估計、預測
billion 10億　approximately 大約　confined 有限的、預測的
challenge 困難、挑戰　take off 起飛　landing 著陸　current 目
前的　capacity 容量　handle 處理、操作　maximum 最高、最大

2

在第2段第4行中，「handle」一詞意思最接近什麼？
(A) 觸碰
(B) 檢查
(C) 管理
(D) 釋放

解析　同義詞的題目是選出與語意一致性的詞彙，平時多熟記詞彙的各
種意思很有幫助，「handle」作為名詞的意思是「把手」，作
為動詞則有「處理（問題）、操作」，「處理」飛機交通流量
是最適合的敘述，因此正確答案是 (C)。

[3]

素木拿州中部法律扶助服務

為預算有限的當地居民引薦經驗豐富的律師

服務項目包括：
● 20分鐘免費的初步諮詢
● 提供家庭、移民、稅務及就業法領域的建議
❸ 以低廉價格成為失業者辦任法律代理

※注意：我們不提供刑事案件的諮詢
請造訪我們的網站，獲取法律諮詢會議的完整列表，以幫助您準備
早日達以完成文件工作，您也能在我們的網站上找到到完整的
律師商會議，如果您無法參加固定的會議，可以在線上提交問題，律
師會以文字回覆。

詞彙　legal aid 法律扶助　resident 居民　tight 少的　initial 初步
的　consultation 諮商　immigration 移民　employment 就業
legal representation 法律代理　unemployed 失業的　criminal
case 刑事案件　paperwork 表格、文件作業　instruction 指
南、說明　advisory 諮詢的　submit 提交　in writing 以書面方
式　guarantee 保證　applicant 申請人　low-income 低所得的
charge 起訴　robbery 搶劫

3

關於素木拿州中部的法律扶助服務提到了什麼？
(A) 他們保證作為所有申請人的代表。
(B) 他們只透過網站自會面來回答合法問題。
(C) 他們為低收入群提供服務。
(D) 他們可以幫助那些被控告的人。

解析　提及及內容應是不比較困難的，(A) 保證為所有
訪者，(D) 則是提到了負責解決法律辯護，也會提供線上
供低廉費用的法律辯護，因此正確答案為失業者提
供低廉費用的法律辯護，因此正確答案是 (C)。

Step 4　實戰練習　P199

正解
1. (C)　　2. (A)　　3. (D)　　4. (B)　　5. (B)
6. (D)

[1~3]

收件者：ann.longton@mail.com
寄信人：services@zzboutique.com
日期：2017年4月22日
主旨：感謝顧客大優惠

親愛的隆頓小姐您好
紀錄顯示近日於本店北部的乙精品退貨，❷ 您回饋的表
示，商品並未達到您的品質標準。為了表達感謝，我們提供了在五家分店
在Z精品，我們只提供您本店最優良的品質與及配件。❶ ❸ 我們誠摯的
使用的40美元折扣額度，使用額度時，請提供結帳員憑代碼「關懷」
感謝您的惠顧，
Z精品

詞彙　recently 最近　return 退貨　form 表單　complete 完成　quality
standard 品質標準　ensure 保證　appreciation 感謝　offer 提
供　credit 信用、額度　cashier 結帳員　upcoming 即將到來的
policy 政策、方針　hold on to 堅持～、抓住～不放　overcharge
超收費用　discourage 勸阻　refund 退款　replacement 取代

1

電子郵件的主要目的是什麼？
(A) 為即將來臨的折扣打廣告
(B) 說明精品店的政策
(C) 為了留住客戶
(D) 宣布新產品系列

解析　信件的目的雖然主要出現在前半部，但有時核心內容是在後半部。內容是為了不滿意而申請退貨的顧客提供商品券在商店使用。可以得知退貨是為了讓顧客繼續光臨自家商店，因此正確答案是（C）。注意避免因為是商店而誤選與折扣相關的選項。

2
她對這家精品店的產品很失望？
(A) 她對這家精品店的產品很失望。
(B) 這家精品店對她收了費用。
(C) 她買錯了尺寸。
(D) 她勸阻了其他的購物者。

解析　解題時須將選項和選項做比對。由於第一段最後提到，因為對商品員工不滿意而申請退貨，因此正確答案是（A）。

3
電子郵件中提供了什麼？
(A) 退款
(B) 推薦
(C) 替代品
(D) 商品券

解析　針對顧客抱怨的解決方法是提供等同現金40美元的額度，因此正確答案是（D）。

[4-6]

快樂園丁

🅱 派恩布拉福路1421號
22312 奧克拉荷馬州奧克拉荷馬
(412) 555-9633

🅱 傑佛森路45466號
22331 奧克拉荷馬卡爾文鎮
(422) 555-9935

如果你已準備好動手做自己的蔬菜園，要由正確的方法。要由正確的方法，要由正確的方法所需的所有材料和苗圃。🅵 知識豐富的人員，可提供你成功種植自己食物所需的所有材料和苗圃。🅵 知識豐富的人員，可提供你成功種植自己食物所需的所有材料和苗圃（🅱 派恩布拉福分店不提供）。

顧客可找到：
• 🅶 種類齊全的種籽，載有詳細圖解技巧及本土植物
• 🅶 當地天然的成熟土壤 — 沒有經驗化學土壤
• 🅶 適合所有技巧和經驗程度的園藝課程（🅱 派恩布拉福分店不提供）
• 🅶 提供多種本土植物和維護健康的資訊

順道走訪我們任何一家分店吧，容我們的植物專家為你解答，並協助你的植物園欣欣向榮。

― 營業時間 ―
週一：早上11點 - 下午4點
週二~週五：早上9點 - 晚上9點
週六：早上9點 - 晚上9點
週日：中午12 - 晚上6點

詞彙　gardener 園丁　nursery 苗圃　knowledgeable 知識豐富的、博學　material 材料　a wide selection of 種類齊全的　method 方法　detail 細節、詳情　native 本土　chemically 化學性地　variety 種類　stop by 順道走訪、路過　location 分店　expert 專家　imported 進口的　fertilizer 肥料

4
關於快樂園丁暗示了什麼？
(A) 水果和蔬菜作為食物出售。
(B) 員工們提供豐富的園丁。
(C) 進口植物可供購買。
(D) 本週化學肥料正在打折。

解析　解題時須將內容和選項進行比對。（A）這家店不是直接販賣新菜和水果，而是幫助顧客建立可以栽種它們的苗圃，所以內容不正確。（C）並沒有提到，（D）中的化學肥料也沒有提到，因此正確答案是（B）。

5
快樂園丁沒有提供什麼？
(A) 訓練課程
(B) 到府服務
(C) 健康的植土壤
(D) 園藝建議

解析　Not true題型在解題時，須將短文中列出的內容和選項比對之後，刪除錯誤的選項找到答案。為顧客提供建立可以種植本土植物和維護的方法是（A）。提供各種本土植物和維護的方法是（A）。提供當地生產的天然土壤是（C）。提供各種本土植物的方法是（A）。因為沒有提到到府服務，因此答案是（B）。

6
什麼只在傑佛森路分店提供？
(A) 園藝指南
(B) 本土植物
(C) 熟練的建議
(D) 訓練課程

解析　通常短文中的地址或電話號碼等連絡方式我們讀得有難度，因此當出現有關造址資訊的題目時會很得仔細閱讀，只在另一家傑佛森路分店提供，因此正確答案是（D）。

Step 2　Paraphrasing 基礎訓練

正確
1. (B)　2. (A)　3. (B)　4. (A)　5. (B)
6. (B)　7. (A)　8. (B)　9. (A)　10. (A)

1
他們在商店裡吃了一小杯冰淇淋的雕像。
詞彙　sample 試吃
(A) 說話　(B) 嘗味道

2
孩子們喜歡這個公園裡熱鬧的雕像。
詞彙　statue 雕像
(A) 火災　(B) 傷心的

3
人力資源部一直努力培訓著有前途的新成員。
詞彙　Human resources 人力資源部　promising 有前途的
(A) 受歡迎的　(B) 僱用

4
表演展現了音樂的真諦。
詞彙　performance 表演
(A) 有趣的　(B) 外表

5
每個人都描述那名新員工勤勞可靠。
詞彙　hardworking 勤勞　describe 描述
(A) 經驗豐富　(B) 值得信賴

6
誠摯地邀請所有學生和教職員參加。
詞彙　faculty 教職員　attend 參加
(A) 自動地　(B) 描繪地

7
這條街上有許多高檔的精品店。
詞彙　boutique 精品店
(A) 奢侈的　(B) 關達的

8
本研討會提供您如何振興事業的方法。
(A) 使失望　(B) 賦予活力

9
這些插圖為作者帶來更生動的故事。
(A) 描畫而讓書更好　(B) 藝術使圖畫更好
詞彙　illustration 描畫　bring~to life 使~更生動　artwork 描畫

10
(A) 律師在法庭上為他辯護。
(B) 律師不認識那個男人。
詞彙 representation 表現；代表　in court 在法庭上

Step 3　基本掌握　P205

正解
1. (C)　　2. (B)

[1]

柏娜特蓮恩 [上午 11:32]
我接到里吉華街2350號的電話，那裡的租客打算二月底遷出，但合約要到六月底才到期。

提姆蘇利文 [上午 11:38]
租約到期前應撤出租客需繳交罰金，但他許屋主不會收。① 妳打給屋主問看看，他是否會例外？

柏娜特蓮恩 [上午 11:40]
值得一試。況且里吉華街那間房子特別不錯，我很確定找到新租客不難。妳有華蕙那個區域已經很多人等著出租物件。

提姆蘇利文 [上午 11:45]
沒有。

1
上午11點40分，蓮恩小姐說「值得一試」，最有可能是什麼意思？
(A) 她想說服租客留下來。
(B) 她認為出租的房產要改善。
(C) **她願意聯繫屋主。**
(D) 她同意應該降低租金。

解析 說話者意圖題目必須找出引用句與前後文的連貫性。原本未到期約需支付違約金，但「值得一試」的意思是，可以問看看是否能免付罰金，因此正確答案是 (C)。

詞彙 tenant 租客　move out 搬走　lease 租約　expire 到期　fine 罰金　owner 屋主　waive 放棄　rental 出租的　property 房產　persuade 說服　contact 連絡　lower 降低　potential 潛在的

---

[2]

歐斯戴爾宣布參展計畫

閱普敦，6月22日—零售業巨擘歐斯戴爾服飾今天宣布，今年11月不會在閱普敦舉辦的博覽會中展示新的服裝系列。-[1]-

閱普敦博覽會通常被視為服飾業該年度最重要的活動之一，國內大型零售業者都會出席。董事長唐娜拉盧西安妮表示，「雖然沒有太大影響，」② 然而，近年來一般民眾的出席率明顯滑落。-[2]-

在公司總部舉行的記者會上，零售業者發言人並不代表缺席這次的博覽會。-[3]- 該公司發言人說，「但我們打算和經銷商及零售合作夥伴舉行小型商務會議。」-[4]-

詞彙 reveal 宣布；公布　retail 零售的　apparel 服飾　significant 重要的　elaborate 認真做、用心做　show off 炫耀　upcoming 即將來臨的　attendance 出席　decrease 減少、減退　press conference 記者會　headquarters 總部　forgo 放棄、停止　host 舉行、舉辦　distributor 經銷商；批發商　spokesperson 發言人

2
[1]、[2]、[3]、[4]位置中，哪一處最適合放入下列的句子？
「因此，業界人士對歐斯戴爾的宣布並不感到驚訝。」
(A) [1]
(B) [2]
(C) [3]
(D) [4]

解析 必須事先讀過一遍插入句，再從短文中找出符合語意的位置。尤其像插入句中「thus（因此）」的接續副詞有助於解題。宣布不參加博覽會是短文的主題，而插入句應放在說明不參加的原因之後，因此插入句那樣的答案是 (B)。

Step 4　實戰練習　P207

正解
1. (B)　　2. (A)　　3. (C)　　4. (A)　　5. (B)
6. (D)　　7. (C)

[1-3]

收信者：亞當・辛格 <asignh@google.com>
發信者：米娜哈米爾頓 <mmhamilton@tuboproducts.com>
日期：5月2日
主旨：TUBO 3000

親愛的辛格先生：

① 感謝您對TUBO 3000的使用經驗，而讓我們注意到這個問題。我們正立刻一步步解決您的難處。-[1]-自從您購買了配件運送到您的住址，TUBO 3000已版本能夠解決您之前所做購的問題。-[2]-

② 如果沒有的話，請撥1-800-555-1323到我們公司，並代表TUBO電子，為這次事件提誠摯地向您致歉，希望能很快再次為您服務。

若還有需要製的地方，不吝指教，請撥打所有的產線移往比較大的大廠。-[3]-

米娜哈米爾頓，客服經理
TUBO電子有限公司

1
電子郵件的目的通常是什麼？
(A) 提供有關文貨的細節
(B) **回應客戶的投訴**
(C) 解釋新的退款政策
(D) 宣傳新的產品系列

解析 信件的目的通常會出現在前面，第一句提到顧客指出公司產品的問題，可以得知目的是回應顧客的投訴，因此正確答案是 (B)。短文中雖然提到退款 (refund)，但並非說明新的退款政策，因此 (C) 不是答案。

詞彙 attention 關注；注意　issue 問題；議題　address the concern 解決疑慮　confident 確信的　version 版本　ship 運送　unit 件數　take steps 一步一步　transfer 轉移、移動　resolve 解決　procedure 程序　repayment 償還　cause 引起　complaint 抱怨　refine 改善、修整　improve 提高　quality control 品質管理　overlook 忽視　refund 退款

什麼是提供作為問題的解決方案？
(A) 修理購買的物品
(B) 退還購買費用
(C) 提供替代產品
(D) 改善製造工序
解析　必須根據短文中出現的資訊選擇答案，不可依據個人常識來回答。提到若送新產品以代替瑕疵品，如果退貨是有問題則會全額退費，並且會改善生產程序，因此答案是 (A)。

3
[1]、[2]、[3]、[4]位置當中，哪一處最適合放入下列的句子？「我們的品管經理將來訪，以確保沒有任何部分被遺漏。」
(A) [1]
(B) [2]
(C) [3]
(D) [4]
解析　插入句的意思是，工廠品管主管會採取措施以確保沒有任何問題。適合放在改善生產程序之後，因此正確答案是 (C)。

[4~7]

肯尼斯冠斯塔 [上午 9:40]
各位好，我剛進會議室，發現投影機有問題，它一直自動關機，有人知道原因嗎？

貝絲蘿斯齊 [上午 9:41]
我上次也發生過。試著按紅色重置鍵看看。

朴珍承 [上午 9:41]
不是應該在9:30之前為我們設置好一切嗎？我希望在新進員工托達前每件事都準備好。

肯尼斯冠斯塔 [上午 9:43]
本來是安妮瑪要設置的，但有另一場會議，結束時間拖得太晚，她沒辦法，所以她要來會議室來預備。

貝絲蘿斯齊 [上午 9:44]
⑥ 不，按鈕沒用。貝絲妳可以來幫我一下嗎？

朴珍承 [上午 9:45]
在路上了。

肯尼斯冠斯塔 [上午 9:48]
你們都在這樣下處理了嗎？

肯尼斯冠斯塔 [上午 9:50]
是的，簡報一切都準備就緒。我印了簡報的紙本和新進員工要填寫的所有表格。

朴珍承 [上午 9:54]
太好了。⑦ 我會在中午那裡新人去吃午餐，然後去警衛室領他們的識別證。1:30前帶他們回來進行下午的行程。

詞彙　shut off 中斷、關閉　new hire 新進員工　hard copy 影本

4
冠斯塔先生準備做什麼？
(A) 訓練新進員工
(B) 影印一些文件
(C) 關買新電器
(D) 與朴小姐見面
解析　登場人物有好幾名，必須掌握人物之間的關係和對話的連貫性。第一句話是冠斯塔先生在準備會議室，之後朴小姐提到應該在新進員工托達之前準備好，由此可知他們是進行員工訓練的人員，因此正確答案是 (A)。

5
為什麼會議要在上午9:30之前沒有準備好？
(A) 因為投影機放錯了地方。
(B) 因為一場會議沒有按時結束。
(C) 因為朴小姐不在公司。
(D) 因為新進員工遲到了。
解析

6
上午9點45分時，需斯齊小姐說「在路上了」是有可能是因為會議室的投影？
(A) 她打電話連絡維修部門。
(B) 她正在上班途中。
(C) 她將修改完成一些文件。
(D) 她會來幫助冠斯塔先生。
解析　be on the way 的意思是「在路上了」。冠斯塔先生在因會議室的投影機發生問題而要求幫忙，此時回答「正在路上」的意思是會前往協助，因此正確答案是 (D)。

7
中午會發生什麼？
(A) 員工將聽取簡報。
(B) 員工將吃完午餐回來。
(C) 朴小姐會帶新進員工去吃午餐。
(D) 冠斯塔先生會前往會議室。
解析　必須從短文內的各種相關詞句中，正確選出問題要求的部分，造是關於典型的SQ。朴小姐中午會到那裡（there）帶新進員工去吃午餐，而there是冠斯塔先生所在的會議室，因此正確答案是 (C)。

解析　SQ題型是最重要的掌握Key Word。從9點43分的訊息來看，另一場會議延誤與導致無法完成準備工作，因此正確答案是 (B)。雖然投影機發生問題，但並不是新進員工的集合準備未完成的直接原因，因此 (A) 不是答案。

Step 2　Paraphrasing 基礎訓練　P214

正解
| 1. (A) | 2. (A) | 3. (B) | 4. (B) | 5. (B) |
| 6. (A) | 7. (B) | 8. (A) | 9. (A) | 10. (B) |

1 書架和玩具散落在地板上。
(A)弄亂。　(B)安排

2 我們提供有競爭力的時薪。
詞彙 hourly wage 時薪
(A)相當多的　(B)攻擊性的

3 這是回答您疑問的信件。
詞彙 answer 回答
(A)要求　(B)問題

4 顧客受到店主的重視。
詞彙 store owner 店主
(A)忽視　(B)受到器重

5 這位監督在建築的翻新計劃。
詞彙 renovation 翻新
(A)審視　(B)幫忙～

6 這些化學原料也在待價拋售。
詞彙 chemical 化學 on sale 特價販售
(A)審理　(B)燃料

7 公司高層主管似乎對未來的擴展持樂觀態度。
詞彙 利潤
(A)利潤　(B)成長

8 人必須習慣於外國環境。
詞彙 company executive 公司高層主管 optimistic 樂觀的
(A)熟悉的　(B)訓練有素的

9 網站試圖呈現出最新的內容。
詞彙 foreign 外國的 environment 環境
(A)網站試圖呈現現有以前的數據。
詞彙 list 列出　latest 最新的　seek 試圖～　present 呈現
previous 以前的

Step 3　基本掌握　P215

正解　1. (B)　2. (A)

[1-2]

3月23日
親愛的洛佩茲先生，
① 我們已收到您對以下刊物的請求。
- ② 《巴黎和羅馬的徒步之旅》
- ② 《米其林亞洲指南》
① 您的訂單確認編號是M3483。與往常一樣，所有地區和城市的指南都是以特價提供給我們的客戶。您應該在三到五個工作日內收到您的刊物。如果您的計劃有變動，請致電212-555-5432聯繫我們的代理人員。
③ 前兩日的特別優惠。
感謝您讓我們有機會為您服務。
環球旅行社

詞彙 publication 刊物 confirmation 確認 price 定價 business day 營業日 significant 顯著的 discount 折扣 cruise 郵輪旅行 rental 租賃 opportunity 機會 request 請求 advertise 宣傳 shipping date 出貨日 mention 提到 currency exchange 貨幣兌換

10 下週之後，我們可以如常恢復運作。
(A)我們將面臨到下週才能繼續工作。
(B)我們要到下週才能繼續工作。
詞彙 resume 恢復 look for 尋找～ continue with 繼續～

解析 信中沒有的出現在前面，第一句提到顧客要求提供刊物，後面告知訂購編號，從這個部分可以得知為了確認訂單的信件，因此正確答案是 (B)。

2 信中沒有提到的部分是什麼？
(A)外幣匯率
(B)旅行刊物
(C)租車優惠
(D)聯絡電話
解析 選出沒有提到的選項再刪去，必須將短文中提到的選項刪去。(B)是信件前面提到的刊物，(C)在第二段提到租車優惠，但沒有提到匯率，因此答案是 (A)。

Step 4　實戰練習　P216

正解
| 1. (B) | 2. (A) | 3. (D) | 4. (A) | 5. (A) |
| 6. (C) | 7. (B) | | | |

[1-3]

收件者 customerservice@furnitureplus.com
寄件者 nwilliams443@mail.com
日期 11月27日
主旨 我近期的購入品
親愛的客戶服務部經理，

① 上個月，我訂購了家具加一的客廳家具。我的訂單包括沙發、椅子、咖啡桌和電視音響櫃。我總共花了1800美元。在商店購物時，店員很友好，回應迅速。
① 但是，我對送貨部門處理訂單的方式感到失望。11月1日到貨，但直到兩週過後才到貨。當我打電話詢問送貨的日期時，我被告知在沒有任何通知的情況下被延遲了。
② 桌面電話音響櫃。我總共花了1800美元。在電話上等待超過30分鐘才知道。
② 當家具送達時，我再次感到失望。沙發被撕破，咖啡桌有刮痕，電視音響櫃的架子掉了下來。
③ 我希望獲得全額退款和店主的道歉信。否則的話，我會勸我所認識的每個人去其他地方購物。
敬祝
納茲威廉森敬啟

詞彙 order 訂購、訂單 include 包括 respond 回應 handle 處理 in charge 負責的 shipment 送貨 delay 延遲 notice 通知 店知 damaged 損壞的 torn 撕破 scratched 刮痕的 refund 退款 otherwise 否則的話 complain 抱怨 missing 缺少的、消失的 purchase 購買(品) in poor condition 狀態不佳的 for free 免費 at no cost 免費 written 書面的

1 威廉姆斯先生為什麼寄這封信?

(A) 想要更改訂單
(B) 對服務提出客訴
(C) 告知缺少的購買商品
(D) 要求退件產品資訊

解析 電子郵件信件的目的可以從前面得知。購買家具的後面是對送貨部門感到失望的內容,由此可知是對他感到抱怨,因此正確答案是 (B)。注意避免對購買有關就選擇部門退回為信件內容與服務提出購買有關就選擇 (A)。

2 有提到什麼是威廉姆斯先生訂的家具?

(A) 狀態非常糟糕
(B) 花費低於他的預期。
(C) 所有的物品都包括在內。
(D) 那是別人的東西。

案是 (B)

解析 KeyWord是the furniture Mr.Williams received,也就是必須找出威廉姆斯先生收到家具之後發生的事。威廉姆斯先生訂當他換貨送達的家具終,商品已經購得了,因此正確答案是 (A)。

3 威廉姆斯先生向傢俱公司提出什麼要求?

(A) 免費維修家具
(B) 下次購買時的折扣
(C) 他下次購買時的折扣
(D) 金錢和書面回應

解析 信件的結構大多是＜主題 → 詳細事項 → 要求＞的形式。短文最後要求退款和道歉信,因此正確答案是 (D)。短文的a full refund和a letter of apology在選項中分別被重新詮釋為money和written response。

[4~7]

克萊兒轉恩 [上午 10:53]
早安,夥伴們。 ❹ 與奧克蘭公園的投標案有任何消息嗎?

大衛轉恩 [上午 10:54]
我週五和他們其中一位經理談過,他說,前會有決定,但目前什麼都還沒聽說。

克萊兒轉恩 [上午 10:55]
目前問題是即使我以前沒有下材料訂單的話,我們就無法在此計算重載止。期限前及時收到的材料。

克萊兒轉恩 [上午 10:56]
我已經下訂單了,就在昨天。

瑪麗亞門多薩 [上午 10:56]
但如果我們沒拿到合約,造這是個問題,還是得支付所有無法使用的東西。

瑪麗亞轉恩 [上午 10:58]
我猜想他們上次選擇了我們,這次應該也會。 ❺ ❼ 我剛接到奧克蘭的電話,他們說投標很接近,但他們的執行長決定這次造大和森基兄弟合作。

克萊兒轉恩 [上午 11:01]
不需要了。 ❻ ❼ 我剛接到奧克蘭的電話,他們說投標很接近,但他們 我確認一下。

大衛轉恩 [上午 11:02]
真令人失望。但別讓這次打擊我們,下次運氣會更好。

詞彙 bid 投標 supplies 用品、材料 meet the deadline 趕上截止期限 stuff 物品 cancel 取消 incur 招致 (損壞等) fee 費用 figure 認為、判斷 disappointing 失望的 let down 使~失望 penalty 罰金 offer 提議 position 位置、職位 revise 修正、修訂 reconsideration 重新考慮、重新審查

4 說話者在討論什麼?

(A) 投標案
(B) 新的職位
(C) 價格調降
(D) 修訂的時間表

解析 GQ是詢問主題,通常短文前面會出現提示。第一句詢問與奧克蘭公園...投標案是否有任何新消息,可知主題是與投標案相關的內容,因此正確答案是 (A)。

5 上午10點58分時,鮑曼先生說「我確認一下」最有可能是什麼意思?

(A) 他會詢問截止日期。
(B) 他將重新安排約定。
(C) 他將確認預約。
(D) 他將計算企劃的成本。

解析 就話者著意圖是屬於新多益的題型,先請完項目,將提到的訊息時間在話文中做標記,再從前面關句閱讀並確實連貫以及意思。以取消訂單而言生費用,鮑曼先生則接著會議接考看,詢問還有多少時間可以...是,鮑曼會詢問還有多少時間就將何時之前取消訂單可以不額外支付費用,因此正確答案是 (A)。

6 奧克蘭公園要做出什麼決定?

(A) 他們的供應商要退到哪裡
(B) 他們的物品要退到哪裡
(C) 誰將為他們的計畫施工
(D) 最終合約何時要準備好

解析 11點1分的訊息中提到「接到奧克蘭決定...其兄弟簽約」,因此正確答案是 (C)。

7 鮑曼先生接下來有可能做什麼?

(A) 去參加會議
(B) 取消訂單
(C) 建立工作計劃
(D) 致電奧克蘭以重新考慮

解析 先請完項目,從短文中尋找能夠預測鮑曼先生接下來行為的提示。原本在投標案還沒確定時,希望若取消訂單時能避免衍生費用,當最終聽到奧克蘭投標案失利的消息時,會採取的行動就是取消訂單,因此正確答案是 (B)。

Unit 13 短文類型

Step 2 Paraphrasing 基礎訓練　P222

1 這位歌手由她的樂隊陪同。
(A) 確定　　(B) 職業的
詞彙 experience 體驗

2 這有助於確保所有顧客的優質體驗。
(A) 擴大的

3 我有一些在文書工作的學習經驗。
(A) 消失的　　(B) 同行的

4 她們最近的成就和貢獻。
(A) 製造　　(B) 販賣

5 研討會有生動而內容豐富的講座。
(A) 令人興奮的
詞彙 informative 有用的

6 她從商店購買了一件有缺陷的產品。
(A) 創新的　　(B) 真實的

7 請來店享受的成就和貢獻。
(A) 升職　　(B) 下台

8 在這裡多年工作之後，布魯克斯先生將在下個月退休。
(A) 承認　　(B) 區分
詞彙 achievement 成就　contribution 貢獻

9 此優惠適用於退款或換貨。
(A) 優惠可用於退款或換貨
詞彙 offer 提供、提議、優惠　valid 有效的　refund 退款　exchange 換貨

正解
| 1. (B) | 2. (A) | 3. (B) | 4. (B) | 5. (A) |
| 6. (B) | 7. (A) | 8. (B) | 9. (A) | 10. (A) |

10 當我拜訪時，她高興地在門口迎接我。
(A) 她立刻對著我打招呼。
(B) 她阻止我進入。
詞彙 greet 迎接　enter 進去
解析 True/Not true題目必須比對短文選項的內容，刪去錯誤部分並找出答案，(A) 內容不正確，(B) 此優惠券是在一月份發放，但無法得知是否提供一整年，(C) 也是錯誤敘述，因此正確答案是 (D)。

Step 3 基本掌握　P223

正解
| 1. (C) | 2. (D) |

[1~2]

優惠兌換券

水花飛濺大冒險
發行日期：2017年1月1日

① 此張兌換券持有者，可享單人水花飛濺大冒險所提供的划船之旅。
* 可將兌換券換取現金的日期如下：3月1日至4月30日、8月20日至10月1日。
② 此張兌換券僅限部分乘坐設施，包含賞鯨之旅、浮潛以及深海潛水之旅。但是不包括賞鯊之旅。帆船航行及滑水冒險。
* 此張兌換券持有者及另一人必須年滿18歲以上。
* 兌換券到期日：2017年8月31日

1 優惠券可用於什麼？
(A) 賞鯨之旅　　(B) 區分
(B) 飛往墨西哥的換票
(C) 划船活動
(D) 兩人免費午餐
解析 短文前面提到優惠券可享單人划船之旅，因此正確答案是 (C)。

2 關於此張水花飛濺大冒險何者為真實？
(A) 它擁有很多員工。
(B) 提供一般歷史性的建築旅行。
(C) 僅在夏季開放營業。
(D) 提供各式各樣的旅程。

詞彙 voucher 兌換券、憑證　entitle 賦予～權利　bearer 持有者　excursion 遊覽　exchange 交換　valid 有效的　holder 持有者　mention 提到　monument 歷史性建築　run business 經營生意

Step 4 實戰練習　P224

正解
| 1. (A) | 2. (D) | 3. (B) | 4. (B) | 5. (D) |
| 6. (B) | 7. (A) |

[1~3]

收拾大師
協助您保持有條不紊，讓家煥然一新！

① 當生活逐漸繁忙，我們的家也帶一片凌亂。沒時間整理新的、髒衣服堆積在椅上、書籍、玩具丟在地板上。
② 就讓收拾大師來幫成一樣，我們將您所有房間一衣櫥、廚房、辦公室、甚至是車庫，處理所有雜務，幫忙收拾乾淨亦淨。
③ 為了慶祝大開幕，我們將會免費提供給前五名客戶到府服務，請記住，只有前五位客戶享這項免費服務，所以快撥打預約專線：555-2255。

1 廣告的對象最有可能是誰？
(A) 忙碌的雙薪夫妻
(B) 預算低的人
(C) 住在宿舍的學生
(D) 15歲以下的兒童
解析 從文中的「忙碌的雙薪夫妻」提示出現在短文前面，第一句提到太忙碌而沒時間整理和打掃家裡，也提到書籍和玩具，從這部分來看正確答案是 (A)。

2 關於收拾大師提到了什麼？
(A) 它擁有很多員工。
(B) 這間行業已有悠久年歷史。
(C) 某些地方無法提供服務。
(D) 免費的服務僅會是有限的
解析 必須從提到收拾大師公司的內容中則出正確的敘述，這種題目住在將短文的內容重新詮釋後放大還原出現在五名客戶將。

詞彙 organize 整頓　messy 雜亂的　throw out 丟棄～　pile up 堆積　litter 亂丟　container 容器　clutter 雜物　dorm 宿舍　numerous 為數眾多的　limited 有限的　reward 獎勵

PART 7　098・099

3
為什麼商家提供此項專到府的服務？
(A) 為了填寫日程安排
(B) **為了慶祝開幕**
(C) 為了獎勵客戶
(D) 為了幫助工作人員

解析 短文中同時出現第2和第3選項的提示。最後一段提到為了慶祝開幕而提供免費服務，因此正確答案是 (B)。

4
這份文件的目的是什麼？
(A) 呈現缺少的物品
(B) **為已售商品收費**
(C) 更改送貨地址
(D) 要退回損壞的物品

詞彙 client 顧客、委託人 billing 開票 shipping 運送 item description 物品明細表 quantity 數量 unit price 單價 sub total 小計 total 總金額 damaged 損壞的 merchandise 商品 amount due 應付金額

[4-7]

馬尼拉有限公司
馬尼拉市區
亞利桑那大道19號

④ **明細單據**

訂單日期：7月2日
訂單編號：39488
⑤ 付款人姓名：東岸銀行
⑦ 送貨日期：7月10日
國家：加拿大
城市：綠地市
街區：羅薩斯大道214號

客戶帳單及送貨地址
收件人姓名：丹尼爾記當斯
顧客編碼：8892

購買產品

項目編號	商品描述	數量	單價	總價
13553	書桌	1	180美元	180美元
13890	書桌椅	2	130美元	260美元
25530	桌燈	1	80美元	80美元

小計：520美元
⑥ 運費：100美元
⑦ 總金額：620美元

感謝您的購買
寄件人簽名：約翰李

5
誰會為這些商品付款？
(A) 馬尼拉公司
(B) 約翰李
(C) 亞利桑那公司
(D) 東岸銀行

解析 詢問寄件人和收件人也包含在GQ的範圍內。表格（圖示）中的主題/目的提示也出現在前半部。標題出現某公司名稱和明細單據（invoice），由此可知是請求支付物品款項的內容，因此正確答案是 (B)。

6
客戶需要支付多少運費？
(A) 80美元
(B) **100美元**
(C) 260美元
(D) 620美元

解析 這是典型的SQ，須從各種數據中找出運費。短文的shipping標示在短文中出現可以免運費的條件。100美元，因此正確答案是 (B)。補充說明，閱讀難度增加，有時會在短文中出現某一項客戶資訊Billing Name (付款人姓名)，由此可知正確答案是 (D)。

7
這份文件沒有提到什麼？
(A) 折扣價格
(B) 應付金額
(C) 配送日期
(D) 送貨地址

解析 必須比對短文的資訊和選項，刪去錯誤答案。由於沒有提到折扣部分，因此答案是 (A)。

Unit 14 短文類型3

Step 2 Paraphrasing 基礎訓練

P230

正解
1. (A)　2. (B)　3. (A)　4. (B)　5. (A)
6. (B)　7. (A)　8. (B)　9. (B)　10. (A)

1 他要求減少工作時間。
詞彙 work hours 工作時間
(A) **更少**　(B) 更多

2 公司改善了財政狀況。
詞彙 improve 改善 situation 狀況
(A) 策略的　(B) **財務的**

3 銷售員很注意客戶的話。
詞彙 salesman 銷售員
(A) **仔細聆聽**　(B) 關貼

4 她想和你討論募資活動。
詞彙 discuss 討論
(A) 投資者　(B) **慈善活動**

5 對於天然土壤，沒有任何化學處理。
詞彙 natural soil 天然土壤 chemically 化學性地
(A) **處理**　(B) 照顧

6 青少年可能在家裡或學校面對棘手的情況。
詞彙 face 面臨
(A) 大的　(B) **困難的**

7 這些物品由收銀員準確地計入。
詞彙 ring up 計入
(A) **精確地**　(B) 仔細地

8 公司試圖激勵員工能有最好的工作表現。
詞彙 perform 表現 optimally 最佳地
(A) 強迫　(B) **激發**

9 本次活動的參加需要穿著休閒裝。
(A) 人們應該在這次活動需要穿著較為正式。
(B) 人們在這次活動可以穿著較輕鬆的衣服。

10

詞彙　casual attire 休閒裝　attendee 參加者　formally 正式地　comfortable 舒服的　merchandise 商品　in high demand 需求量大

我們的商品需求量很大。
(A) 許多人想要我們的產品。
(B) 我們有很多產品。

Step 3　基本掌握　P231

正解

1. (D)　2. (A)

[1~2]

強納森 & 荷莉有限責任公司

親愛的顧客，

本公司盡可能列出最新產品及價格以保持目錄的最新狀態。然而，由於全球市場的價格波動之故，我們目錄裡的有些商品可能不再有供貨。❶ 此外，因全球市場的價格波動之同時，此商品目前無法供貨，我們的價格也會隨之調整。

因此建議您瀏覽本公司的網站www.jsholly.org，產品及價格會立即更新。

在您的森&荷莉我們盡全力滿足顧客團隊的一切需求，❷ 如果您願意推薦我們給您希望供應最優質的商品，我們會非常感激。您的惠顧使我們購買多元的產品種類。

謹此感謝您的持續惠顧！

詞彙　up-to-date 最新的　merchandise 商品　in high demand 需求量大　browse through 瀏覽～　fluctuation 變動　adjust 調整　constantly 持續地　strive 努力　appreciate 感謝　recommendation 推薦　expand 擴展　range 範圍　patronage 惠顧　suggestion 建議　purchase 購買　return policy 退貨政策　subscriber 訂閱者　current 目前的

1

關於目錄顯示了什麼？
(A) 它沒有列明退貨政策。
(B) 它有許多訂購者。
(C) 它是免費提供給客戶的。
(D) 它可能不會列出當前的價格。

解析　暗示題顯示了什麼？一段落提到的資訊會將短文中提到的資訊重新詮釋之後放在選項中，第一段最後提到由於價格波動，也許會需要價格變動，由此可知，目錄中顯示的價格可能不是最新資訊，因此正確答案是 (D)。

2

水星聯盟出售什麼產品？
(A) 雕像
(B) 兩傘
(C) 冰淇淋
(D) 工藝品

解析　第一段第二句提到，水星聯盟銷售的其中一項是工藝品 (crafts)，因此正確答案是 (D)。雕像並不是水星聯盟展示型展示物，所以無法作為答案。

2

客戶被要求傳達些什麼？
(A) 對新產品的建議
(B) 更改他址表單
(C) 他們的花園照片
(D) 未來購買物品的折扣優惠券

解析　顧客被要求的事項在短文中以勸誘、建議命令的形式出現，短文後半部提到，若能推薦販售的產品會十分感激，因此正確答案是 (A)。

3

瑞秋哈里森為水星聯盟做了什麼？
(A) 她招募了新成員。
(B) 她幫助成立了一個新的基金會。
(C) 她改善了財務狀況。
(D) 她為居民提供藝術課程。

解析　先記下特定人物瑞秋的名字，再從短文中找出她所採取的行動，(C) 她改善了財務狀況，作為短文內載的敘述。瑞秋在任期內改善了財務狀況，因此正確答案是 (D)。雖然並不是以語文展開販售的品項，而是公園裡的展示型展示物，所以無法作為答案。

Step 4　實戰練習　P232

正解

1. (A)　2. (D)　3. (C)　4. (C)　5. (B)
6. (D)　7. (A)

[1~3]

公園藝術品拍賣，成功非凡

6月19日，紐約─以擁有怪誕雕像聞名的 ❶ 派拉蒙展覽組公園，於上周六進行第三屆六星聯盟年度公園藝術品拍賣活動。 ❷ 拍賣的作品有水星聯盟的藝術家製作的照片及工藝品。經由週五的雷雨添加，❸ 許多民眾、眾人湧明無需的天氣吸引了數以百計的居民及遊客來到公園，許多民眾一邊吃冰淇淋，並試吃當地的咖啡廳和瑞其他的甜點。水星聯盟五年前瀕臨破產，❸ 但在瑞秋哈里森的帶領之下，扭轉了財務狀況。公園藝術品拍賣是哈里森計畫之一。另一項則是藝術家舞會，將於周日在市中心河畔舉行。

詞彙　whimsical 怪誕的　craft 工藝品　alliance 聯合　resident 居民　display 展示　sample 試吃　bankruptcy 破產　turn around 扭轉　fiscal 財務的　directorship 主管任期　upcoming 即將到來的　recruit 招募　establish 設立　foundation 基金會　financial standing 財務狀況

1

這篇文章主要討論什麼？
(A) 戶外活動
(B) 新公園的啟用
(C) 即將上映的音樂劇
(D) 新的企劃主管

解析　GQ是指前項主題，最大的提示出現在短文之前的半段。第一段短文上用六字標明了聯合藝術品展售活動，因此正確答案是 (A)。注意避免給文提到park而誤選 (B)。

2

水星聯盟出售什麼產品？
(A) 雕像
(B) 兩傘
(C) 冰淇淋
(D) 工藝品

安全規定

須隨時刻刻穿戴防護衣物（實驗室工作服、手套、面具及護目鏡。 ❺ 離開實驗室前，請先更衣至脫掉的護衣物，並放置在標示「防護衣物」的櫃子裡。 ❻ 將瓶子、管子及其他容器儲存在櫃存前或水洗前。 ❼ 為了避免打翻的溶量，所有容器必須放在防濺來或籃子裡再運送，請先確認這些容器都為了您的安全著想，❼ 如果員工未能遵守以上的預防措施，管理者將給予整告單。

詞彙　safety regulations 安全規定　observe 遵守（規定等）　remove 撤除　protective 保護的　laboratory 實驗室　bin 箱子　store 儲存　spill 濺出　transport 運送　securely 安全地　prevent 防止　leak 溢出　precaution 預防措施　lid 蓋子　complaint 抱怨　designated 特定的　issue 發出　supervisor 主管　surface 表面　divide 分成　workstation （辦公室裡的）工作站　penalty 處罰　discard 丟棄　notice 通知　entry 進入

4

公告的目的是什麼？
(A) 回應員工的投訴
(B) 宣傳新的服務項目
(C) 告知員工安全規則
(D) 說明新設備的使用方法

解析　詢問目的的GQ可以從標題或短文前段提示。這篇文章前段提示，要知道目的需要找出安全規定。因此正確答案是 (C)。隨著難易度提示，有時需要找出安全規定中較詳盡的細節內容。

5 員工應該把使用過後的防護衣物放在哪裡？
(A) 在衣架上
(B) 在指定的箱子裡
(C) 在儲物櫃裡
(D) 在他們的工作站

解析　這是詢問防護衣物應置於的題目。第二點安全規定提到，須放在寫有「防護衣物」的箱子內，因此正確答案是 (B)。

6 在存放實驗容器之前，員工應該怎麼做？
(A) 表面貼上標籤
(B) 按大小區分
(C) 丟棄舊的容器
(D) 正確清洗它們

解析　先記下題目的Key Word是laboratory containers，再從短文中尋找相關訊息。第三點的注意事項包含各種內容，其中提到容器在儲存之前必須先洗淨，因此正確答案是 (D)。

7 根據公告，不遵守規則則會受到什麼懲罰？
(A) 主管將發出書面通知
(B) 將僱用別人遞補該職位
(C) 將被限制進入實驗室
(D) 將被降薪

解析　短文經常會在最後部分提到注意事項或叮嚀事項。由於規定中提到未遵守這些規定的人會收到書面警告，因此正確答案是 (A)。

Unit 15　多重短文

Step 2　Paraphrasing 基礎訓練　P240

正解
| 1. (B) | 2. (B) | 3. (B) | 4. (B) | 5. (A) |
| 6. (A) | 7. (A) | 8. (A) | 9. (A) | 10. (B) |

1 該公司發布了位於斯普林菲爾德的新分公司的計劃。
(A) 反對的
(B) 公之於眾的

2 首先，請從包裝盒中取出所有部件。
(A) 組裝
(B) 置於一旁

3 我代表藝術研究公司的經理寫信。
(A) 代替
(B) 回應

4 這篇文章包含了一些事實上的錯誤。
(A) 錯別字
(B) 錯誤的訊息

5 超級電子是這個顧客專屬唯一的賣商。
(A) 唯一的
(B) 熱情的

6 這些物品目前缺貨。
(A) 不可購買
(B) 遺失

7 畫廊宣布了即將到來的查爾斯拉米需斯特的作品展。
(A) 接近的
(B) 成功的

8 請容我向您的負面體驗表達誠摯的歉意。
(A) 提供
(B) 接受

9 只有符合資格的申請人才會被要求填寫申請表。
(A) 只有符合資格的申請人會申請。
(B) 只有少數的申請人會申請。

10 這是所有成員的強制性活動。
(A) 所有成員都缺席活動。
(B) 所有成員都必須參加活動。

Step 3　基本掌握　P241

正解
| 1. (A) | 2. (C) | 3. (B) | 4. (D) | 5. (C) |

[1-5]

愛默森百貨公司

我們 ❷ 立即開放 ❶ 各種初階職位的兼職缺。

家居用品部：家居用品部收銀人員。協助顧客購買商品。時間為每週五、週六及週日，每週15至20小時。

男女鞋部：男女鞋部收銀人員。協助顧客購買商品、退換貨等，需求時間為每週一、週三及週五的正常營業時間，每週最高25小時。

櫥窗陳列助手：協助設計師擺放及即下櫥窗展示，協助布置樣品商品。時間為每週六及週日晚間，每週12小時。

我們 ❹ 需求提供具有競爭力的時薪及員工訓練。如需安排面試，請將您的電子郵件傳給manderson@emerson.com，或致電612-555-2855轉分機8367。

收件人：麥克安德森manderson@emerson.com
寄件人：蕾貝卡紐曼 <rebecca80@aol.com>
主旨：應徵職缺
日期：8月10日

親愛的安德森先生，

❸ ❹ ❺ 我目前是華莫瑞大學的學生，正在尋找周六及周日的兼職工作。我想每周工作10到20小時。前兩年夏天我在米蘭百貨是否有任何適合的職缺。我會非常感激。謝謝。

誠摯地，
蕾貝卡紐曼

詞彙　entry level 入門等級、初學　housewares 家居用品　register 收銀機　assist 協助　regular business hours 正常營業時間　setup 設置　takedown 撤下 (物品等)　arrange 整理　merchandise 商品　competitive 有競爭力的　hourly wage 時薪　contact 連絡　experience 經驗、經歷　reliable 可靠的　branch 分店　retail 零售　position 位置、職缺　respond to 回應～　suitable 適合的　publicize 宣傳　colleague 同事　request 要求　inquiry 疑問　contact information 連絡資訊　salesperson 銷售人員

1 這則廣告的目的是什麼?
(A) 提供兼職工作
(B) 宣布年度銷售額
(C) 宣布開幕信件
(D) 回覆詢問信件

解析 從廣告一開始可以得知,這是百貨公司想要徵求兼職人員的內容,因此正確答案是 (A)。注意要避免光看標題 Department Store 就誤選 (B)。

2 在廣告中,第1段第1行中的「immediate」最接近什麼意思?
(A) 直接
(B) 附近
(C) 目前
(D) 個人

解析 同義詞題目在掌握單字的位置後,必須再看前一點的內容。「立刻」有空缺,意思就是「目前」有空缺,因此正確答案是 (C)。

3 電子郵件的目的是什麼?
(A) 要求應徵者先告知他們的聯絡方式
(B) 詢問職位空缺
(C) 推薦銷售人員
(D) 要求減少工作時間

解析 信件的目的提示出現在前半部,第一句話自我介紹後,希望兼職工作10~20小時看來,可以得知想要應徵職位,因此正確答案是 (B)。

4 什麼連合組合適小姐的日程安排?
(A) 分店長
(B) 家用品銷售人員
(C) 鞋類銷售員
(D) 櫥窗陳列的助手

解析 這是連貫短文題目,連貫短文題目在解題時,必須找出其中一篇短文提供的線索,選出符合要求條件的敘述。第一則短文出現3個職缺,紐墨小姐的周末可以工作10~20小時,符合此條件的職缺是櫥窗陳列的助手,因此正確答案是 (D)。

5 關於紐墨小姐無法得知什麼?
(A) 她在郵局有時間
(B) 她是學生
(C) 她目前在一家店工作
(D) 她在尋找兼職工作

解析 Not true題目在解題時,必須將正確敘述一一刪去,選出沒有提到的選項。紐墨小姐的周末未可以有3個職缺,她在尋找兼職工作,或錯誤的選項是紐墨小姐有售貨經驗,但沒有說到自己目前正在工作,因此答案是 (C)。

Step 4　實戰練習　P243

正解

1.(A)　2.(D)　3.(B)　4.(D)　5.(C)

[1~5]

http://www.ipa.com

首頁 | 會議 | 課程 | 課用 | 會員

❶會議將在他先來飯店10月8日至10日的第十屆年度公共會計師大會

國際公共會計師(IPA)大會將是業界專家一個最好的機會。今年大會將在紐約曼哈頓舉行,❹導題主題會計領域最新趨勢與變化。❶雅傳菜家朴智洋博士。她將探討有關國際會計法的變化,❺其他主題講者有關。

主席。雅德利娜·巴羅斯博士。布萊爾·利維恩恩。麥可·山口以及蜜雪兒·帕里。所有講者於課程和主題講者的資訊可以在其負面的「課程」選項中找到。

會員。只要預約住宿時,提供會員號碼即可。報名將於8月1日開始,9月1日價格就很快很快額滿,部分課程將很快額滿,所以請從速。您可以於線上註冊「報名」選項中註冊。

收件人:❺ 麥可山口<myamaguchi@nieman.org>
寄件人:史黨拉韓菜<Hanson85@ipa.com>
日期:10月14日
主旨:資訊

親愛的麥可,

很高興見到您,感謝您光臨出席的時間來到紐約,我也要感謝我參加這次的IPA會議。❷❺ 您的非常欣賞和圓國際公司及政府打交道所要付出的努力。關於您程度,她的回答是相當典型的正面評價。

國際公共會計師大會參加者問卷調查

	非常滿意	有點滿意	有點失望	非常失望
報名過程			V	
主題內容	V			
舉辦地點	V			
食物&飲品	V			

其他建議:

報名申請過程不是很順利,即使早早在截止日期之前我就報名了,但我的會議報名卻非常麻煩,還必須得等一小時才能找到我的資料。❹而錯誤了我非常實務為題的會計師的課程,演講本身很精采,非常吸引人入勝,❺我尤其喜歡那位公共會計師主講人,獲益良多。

其他主題演講者都很好。

依據雅韓德拉

詞彙 accountant 會計師　professional 專家　trend 趨勢　take place 發生　key note speaker 主講人　featured 主要的　include 包括　rate 價格　accommodations 住宿設施、房間　participation 參加　fascinating 引人入勝的　attach 附加、附上　attendee 參加者　complimentary 稱讚的　survey 問卷調查　process 過程　satisfied 滿意的　smoothly 順利地　misplace 放錯地方　feedback 回饋、意見　layer 層

1 關於會議提到了什麼?
(A) 一些參加者可能在飯店獲得折扣。
(B) 為向紐約的居民開放。
(C) 每年在相同地同地舉行。
(D) 所有參加者必須在8月1日之前報名。

解析 詢問會議提及的內容必須與可提供網路的飯店住宿優惠,因此正確答案是 (A)。

2 電子郵件的目的是什麼?
(A) 為未來的會議提供建議
(B) 安排到紐約的旅行計劃
(C) 詢問有關會議的問卷調查
(D) 提供有關演講的意見

解析 信件的目的通常出現在短文前面,難提較高的讀及意見,但麥可山口先生在閱讀這封意見,前面先向演講者麥可山口先生致謝,並告知可提供回饋意見,因此正確答案是 (D)。(C) 在問卷調查內容中有針對山口先生的有提到,但並非針對問卷調查者的問卷調查,因此不是答案。

3 在電子郵件中，第1段第4行中的「level」意思最接近什麼？

(A) 層
(B) 量
(C) 姿勢
(D) 條件

解析　意思是對於和國際企業及政府交涉時付出努力的「量」感到讚賞，因此正確答案是 (B)。

---

4 關於錢德拉女士暗示了什麼？

(A) 她參加了去年的活動。
(B) 她認為有些課程太長了。
(C) 她對報名過程感到滿意。
(D) 她沒有參加尼爾森博士的演講。

解析　這是連貫實短文的題目，須將有關錢德拉女士的事實和選項中重新詮釋的內容比對之後作答。不僅如此，這也是必須參考多重短文才能回答的棘手題型。在第三則短文中錢德拉女士提到，因為報名程序延誤而錯過了專題演講，由此可知是尼爾森博士的演講，因此正確答案是 (D)。

---

5 錢德拉女士特別喜歡哪位演講者？

(A) 朴女士
(B) 楊恩先生
(C) 山口先生
(D) 帕曼女士

解析　這也是連貫實短文的題目。錢德拉女士在問卷調查中提到，她最喜歡「亞洲會計實務」為題的課程，而信件中主講「亞洲會計實務」的人是山口先生，因此正確答案是 (C)。

解題技巧＋多樣試題＋詳盡解析，提高作答準確率！

全攻略：培養聽力‧閱讀實戰能力！

新制多益完全自學 BASIC LC+RC NEW TOEIC

● 特級英語講師帶領多益團隊，掌握最關鍵出題趨勢

由多益滿分英語講師主編、知名多益團隊修訂，掌握每年考題趨向，精心介紹各種題型，指出新舊制差異，並分析各題型出題方式、解題關鍵，教你解題技巧以破解多益難關！

● 即時測驗配上超級詳盡解答，解題能力快速提高！

為了各種單元各搭配對應題型，並附上超詳細解析，讓你不再徬徨，快速熟悉各種類型題目，理解出題法則，實戰怎麼考也不怕!另附有兩週及四週進度表，準確快速地練習多益。

● 考題後方附上相近單字，增強考試詞彙量！

每題例題與解答下方皆附上多益常出現單字以及相近詞，讓考生在做題時不僅可以熟悉題目，更可以順便學習其他相近字彙，增加考試字彙量。

● 多種版本音檔，加上單題點選除聽方式，提升聽力能力

音檔採取單題點選聆聽方式，節省尋找音檔所花的時間，另探英、美、澳式真人對話，不僅能練習多益測驗，更能增強不時英文聽力能力。加上考場版本，白噪音模式模擬考場效果，讓你身歷其境！